南开英美文学精品教材

英 国 文 学 简 史

（英文版）

A Survey of English Literature

常耀信　著

南 开 大 学 出 版 社
天 津

图书在版编目(CIP)数据

英国文学简史 / 常耀信著.—天津：南开大学出版社，2006.1(2025.1 重印)
ISBN 978-7-310-02398-1

Ⅰ.英…　Ⅱ.常…　Ⅲ.文学史－英国－英文
Ⅳ.I561.09

中国版本图书馆 CIP 数据核字(2005)第 106907 号

英国文学简史
YINGGUO WENXUE JIANSHI

南开大学出版社出版发行
出版人：刘文华
地址：天津市南开区卫津路 94 号　　邮政编码：300071
营销部电话：(022)23508339　营销部传真：(022)23508542
https://nkup.nankai.edu.cn

天津泰宇印务有限公司印刷　全国各地新华书店经销
2006 年 1 月第 1 版　　2025 年 1 月第 21 次印刷
880×1230 毫米　32 开本　18.75 印张　534 千字
定价：49.00 元

如遇图书印装质量问题，请与本社营销部联系调换，电话：(022)23508339

Foreword

I

This book is a general survey of English literature. It is based on my decades of reading, teaching, and research experience in this literature and my acquaintance with the general tenor of the available literary criticism on it.

The general layout of the book roughly follows the critical notion that the major authors get the lion's share of the space while the lesser lights settle for less or nothing. The 26 chapters here offer a sketch of the major writers with some mention of those, though minor in stature, who have made a scratch on the rock of time in their way. Thus the survey discusses the Old English and Medieval English periods in two chapters, focusing on *Beowulf* and Chaucer; the Elizabethan period in another two, highlighting Christopher Marlowe and Shakespeare (as the great age is basically one of poetry and verse drama and the figure of Shakespeare towers so far above all the rest); the whole of the 17th century in one chapter, with Donne and Milton as the primary interests; the Classic 18th century in three, two on poetry and one on fiction, with Pope, Gray, Blake, and Burns in verse and Swift, Defoe, and Fielding in fiction taking up most of the coverage, and the Romantic period in two, centering on Wordsworth, Coleridge, and Keats. The Victorian period is a preeminent phase of English literary history, in which many writers distinguish themselves in many divisions of literature. They vie vehemently for attention, and none seems able to overshadow the others. So this period takes up eight chapters, with Dickens, George Eliot, and Hardy in fiction, Tennyson, Browning, and Arnold in poetry, and Shaw in drama making a greater claim on time in the discussions. The first decade of the 20th century is handled in one chapter, devoting more space to Conrad; the 1920s in two, touching more on Joyce, Woolf, Lawrence, and Yeats; the 1930s in two, discussing Auden, Thomas, Greene, and Orwell in greater detail; and the postwar period in three, in which Movement poetry with Larkin and Hughes, the "angry young man" fiction with Amis and Sillitoe, other famous novelists like Golding, Lessing, and Murdoch, the theater of the absurd with Beckett, Pinter and Stoppard, and the famous playwright Osborne and some others who have developed a distinct personal signature of their own—all these manage to share most of the space in between them. This is, then, the broad outline of the book.

II

The book is intended to cater to the needs of students, teachers, and the general reading public in their study, teaching, or research in English literature. The survey's basic features are as follows:

First, it is intended to do an all-purpose and heavy-duty job for its users. Despite its scholarly nature, the book is written in such a way that it serves all those interested in English literature. These include undergraduate students, graduate students, instructors of literature at all levels, and scholars and researchers. It enables undergraduate students to get a quick glimpse at this literature, and helps graduate students of English to study literary history and locate topics for term papers, MA theses, and doctoral dissertations. It also imbeds designs of literature courses for teachers of graduate and undergraduate students, and suggests possible subjects for further research and writing to budding scholars and other researchers in general.

Furthermore, it tries to be specific in its introductions and interpretations. In the introductions of the authors and their works, this survey endeavors to be particular and detailed instead of merely dealing out general statements and juggling with abstractions. Focusing on the analyses of the major works of the major authors, its sole purpose is to help the readers acquire and accumulate a series of concrete experiences of the major authors and their major works so as to help achieve a three-dimensional perspective of English literary history. It offers a variety of possible critical approaches for students and scholars at varying levels to have something to go by or react against at the beginning of their scholarly careers. This is done mainly in the detailed discussions in the text and also with the help of the comprehensive "Notes and References" at the end of the book. "The Notes and References" contains a bibliography of publications that sum up the cumulative outcomes of generations of careful criticism. The listings are mostly simple, but some are annotated.

Finally, this survey offers a wide leeway for choice for the readers. As it intends to make relevant material available for all around as a resource of reference as well as a textbook, the survey tries to include many authors and works, major or minor, famous or notorious, enjoying critical acclaim or lying in neglect and oblivion. Hopefully the readers may be happy to have a wide range of options in their reading and research. For classroom instruction, it is important for the instructor to choose some from the many sources available so as to fit them into the semester or annual teaching schedule. In the case of Shakespeare or Dickens or many others, for instance, the instructor is free to prioritize and discuss just one major work by these writers and leave the rest as extra-curriculum reading or simply as reference material for the students. The availability should prove, I should hope, to be an asset rather than a liability to classroom instruction.

III

Now I come to the huge amounts of debts I owe in the writing of the book. As English literature is the first major interest in my career, I feel indebted, in my process of immersion in the study and research, to many creditors, from whose indispensable help I have profited profusely. These include a long list of people such as Dr. Robert Cosbey, the late Professors Chen Jia, Wang Zuoliang, and Yang Zhouhan, whose critical spirit as well as writings have either inspired me in my reading or directly enriched the survey in the form of loaned information. I would also mention Hugh Kenner, Leslie Fiedler, and Alfred Kazin, whom I met and heard in person and felt inspired beyond measure by their provocative, seminal modes of perception and the sweep and depth of their critical acumen. In addition, their writings with their pioneering edge have been the sources of my courage in exploring the profundity of literature as a reflection of the human experience. It has been basically in keeping with the spirit more than armed with the knowledge of all these scholars that I began this project well over three years ago. The sky is the limit for my gratitude to them. My debt to all of these people and other people can never be fully discharged in the "Notes and References" that I attach at the end of the book. Any slight or offence on my part will be my unintentional oversight, and my apologies, when called for, will be ready and forthcoming.

There are, in addition, my Chinese colleagues working hard in the field of foreign literature all over the country. Those of my generation deserve exceptional commendation. Their diligence and perseverance have always been an uphill push to me in our concerted research endeavor. And never should I allow myself to forget my enduring debt to my students of successive generations, of whose responses and research I have taken a good deal of advantage in my writing.

Now I come to my wife, who has been always of help whenever there is need, and whose research and editing and proofreading efforts have been vital to the completion of the book.

IV

Special acknowledgments should be made to the preeminent scholars who have been kind enough to read portions of my manuscript and help improve its quality in conception and execution. These include Dr. Robert C. Cosbey, Professor of English at Regina University of Canada and Dr. Robert A. Burns, Professor of English at the University of Guam, USA. Their help has been essential for me to avoid or forestall unpardonable errors and gaffes of some kinds.

This is not to say, naturally, that the book is free of mistakes by any means. On the contrary, I believe in nothing like perfection and remain painfully awake and aware that there is always ample room for improvement. Here I humbly invite all scholars and readers to feel free to criticize and offer their invaluable advice on the book.

Yaoxin Chang, Ph.D.

Professor of English
Nankai, China/Guam, USA
April 2005

Table of Contents

Chapter 1 The Old English (Anglo-Saxon) Period • Beowulf • The Middle English Period

The Old English (Anglo-Saxon) Period

The British civilization is one of the oldest in the world. One of its extant signs, the Stonehenge, dates back to 1400-1800 BC, when mankind was still wrapped in the mist of time. This prehistoric monumental pile of stones indicates a fairly advanced level of engineering and astronomy. As such advanced engineering and astronomy could only be part of a whole fairly advanced culture, and an advanced culture, as human history shows, has to have an advanced literature as its offshoot, the ancient people of the land must have had a prehistoric literature of their own. But whatever might have existed, in oral form or otherwise, nothing is left now except for some scraps and fragments. It might have been destroyed by the Celts.

The Celts were probably the first inhabitants of the British Isles in recorded history. These powerfully built and fair-haired people were tenacious and loved war. One of their tribes, the Britons, came over in the 5th century BC, stayed for some five hundred years, and gave its name to the place: "Britain" means "the land of the Britons." The Celts left behind a rich oral tradition of myths and legends, of which the Arthurian legends are an important part. About 55 BC, the Roman soldiers of Julius Caesar came to stay for five centuries and transplanted their civilization to the land. The Romans built roads and bridges, erected sculptures, and built baths beside the warm springs of Bath with heating systems in them. Then the cultural heritage of the Celts and the Romans was destroyed by the invading Anglo-Saxons in the 5th century.

The Anglo-Saxons were a branch of the Germanic tribes who lived at the mouth of the Elbe and along the North Sea. They came over the sea, drove the

Celts to the north and west, and slowly developed their own language and culture. Anglo-Saxon became Old English, and the place became England, or the Angle-land, "the land of the Angles." The period was generally one of wars between the petty kingdoms in the land. In 597 AD the Anglo-Saxons began to be converted to Christianity. In the second half of the 7th century, the first English poet, Caedmon by name, began to sing. Another century passed and *Beowulf*, the first English poem still intact as a whole piece today, was composed in Old English. In the 9th century King Alfred the Great defeated a new wave of invasion from Scandinavia and brought peace, security, and prosperity to his kingdom. The king built schools, wrote annals, and encouraged cultural growth. It was King Alfred who decided that literature should be written in the vernacular, or Old English. In 1057 Macbeth, king of Scotland, died, only to be resurrected a few hundred years later in Shakespeare's famous tragedy. [1]

Now let's turn to the literature of the period under discussion. The Anglo-Saxon period was basically barren in literary creations. The reason for this was easily found: the fact that people wrote on animal skin and frequently scraped old things out to make room for the new, or the destruction by wars or simply through loss to time—all accounted for the scarcity of writings still extant from the period. What has been left through the ravages of time is mostly fragments. These include both pagan and religious poems. There are, for instance, the pagan poems such as *Widsith*, *Waldhere*, *The Fight at Finnisburg*, *The Complaint of Deor*, *The Seafarer*, *The Wanderer*, *The Wife's Lament*, and *The Battle of Maldon*. For nearly two centuries into the period, pagan poetry and pagan spirit remained dominant on the poetic scene. It was essentially a body of heroic poetry. Mostly the poems were songs about wars, sea-faring, and violence in a cruel world with little or no tenderness or joy (*The Seafarer*, *The Wanderer*, *Waldhere*, and *The Battle of Maldon*). Some tell about the lives of the minstrels, ancient poet-singers, who roamed around entertaining people with stories often of superhuman deeds and in oral traditions (*Widsith* and *The Complaint of Deor*). Some others reflect and record the fine emotional texture of the first English people well for posterity. *The Wife's Lament* and *Ruin* are good examples. The wife in the first of these laments her husband's absence not for her own sake. The man has left because he believes in some slanders about her, but she is not angry with him though she is innocent. She feels sad because of the pain the misunderstanding has caused her man. This alone defines her as an archetype of an ideal woman. *Ruin* illustrates a very refined and sophisticated feeling of loss for the ruined glory of the past. A wandering minstrel happens to visit the debris of a once grand building and writes a poem about it. Seeing the bleakness of the former prosperous scene, the man meditates upon the pride and joy of the builders and grieves over the fact that they are all no more, sadly devoured by time at the will of the gods. The poet's is a highly civilized, sophisticated mode of thinking and perception indeed.

With the arrival of St. Augustine in 597 AD and the subsequent spread of Christian influence and classical learning, heathen poetry was slowly and steadily maneuvered out of the scene. There was a time of intermingling of the pagan with the Christian components in poetry such as *Beowulf*, but then the pagan was superseded by the religious spirit, and minstrels gave way to learned men. The religious poetry that took over was chiefly based on Biblical stories. Among the religious poets of the period one stood out with his captivating story of growth. This was Caedmon (c. 670 AD-) from Northumbria (a center of Anglo-Saxon literature), a monastery herdsman without any education, who could not even sing to the harp at feasts. One night he had a dream in which someone, apparently an angel, told him to sing of creation, and Caedmon was happy and surprised to find himself singing well. When he awoke, he wrote down what he sang in his sleep. Then he became a monk, learned the Bible stories by heart, and tried to paraphrase and note them down in verse. Then the Danes invaded Britain again at the close of the 8th century, and a good deal of religious poetry was destroyed. Some of Caedmon's poems have survived in a Wessex dialect. These include the paraphrases of Genesis, Exodus, Daniel, and Judith, and also a poem about Christ and Satan. A poet in transition from the pagan to the religious way of writing, he was at his most exciting when writing about fighting, seafaring, and passions of strong men. Caedmon became the first known poet in English literary history.

A hundred years after Caedmon, Cynewulf of Northumbria came on the scene. This happened about the 8th century. He was the first English poet ever to sign his compositions. He was a scholar, knew Latin and religious literature, and wrote excellent poetry. The poems generally attributed to his authorship include, among others, *The Legend of St. Elena*, and *Christ*. *Christ*, happy in mood and alive with the poet's creative talent, consists of three parts: the Virgin Birth, the Ascension of Christ, and the Day of Judgment.

Regarding the prose of the period, two works of any historical interest merit attention here. One was *The Ecclesiastical History of England* by the venerable Bede (673-735) and the other was *Anglo-Saxon Chronicle*, founded by King Alfred the Great, the earliest of its kind in Europe, which was continued after his death up to the early twelfth century. Although most of these is dull reading, they are of great value to historians. [2]

Beowulf

The only organic whole poem to come out of the Anglo-Saxon period is *Beowulf*, an epic of well over 3,000 lines. It is important as the first major English poem and the greatest work of literature of the period. It is probably the greatest epic ever left by the ancient Germanic tribes, and the most ancient ever since the demise of the Greek and Roman literatures. The story takes place in Scandinavia, and there is no mention of England at all. The hero comes from Sweden, and performs his deeds in Denmark. The work was possibly brought over to England at the time of the Anglo-Saxon conquest, and was handed down by word of mouth from generation to generation until it was anonymously recorded in Anglo-Saxon, or Old English, in the 8th century. The existing manuscript of the poem is dated 10th century.[3]

The poem tells the story of a 6th-century hero, Beowulf. It is basically a two-part narrative—Beowulf's fight with the sea-monsters Grendel and his mother in the first part (ll. 1-1798), and his killing a fiery dragon and his death in the second (ll. 1799-3182). The first part begins with the rise of the Danish nation (ll. 1-85) and continues with the present King Hrothgar, who is having trouble. His palace has been for twelve years harassed by a sea-monster, Grendel, who comes to grab and devour the king's people as he pleases, and no one seems to be his match (ll. 186-188). The king of Sweden sends over his nephew, Beowulf, with some retainers to help out. King Hrothgar welcomes his hero and spreads a feast for him (ll. 189-661). At nightfall Beowulf waits in the hall for the monster to show up and fights him by hand as the demon is vulnerable to no weapons of steel.

Beowulf, who has the strength of 30 men in his grip, tears off one arm from his enemy, and sends him howling away to his death in his haunted pool (ll. 662-835). The overjoyed king celebrates the victory (ll. 836-1250), but little expects that a greater danger is to appear and play havoc with his peace. That very night Grendel's mother, furious over her son's death, storms in to avenge him and kills several of the king's retainers. Beowulf follows her to her lair, dives in, fights with the she-monster, almost loses to her, but manages to kill her in the end with the help of a magic sword. He returns to the palace with the heads of the two demons (ll. 1251-1650) and receives gifts from the grateful king, "the gift-giver," at another celebration (ll. 1651-1798). In the second part of the poem, Beowulf goes back to Sweden, and then succeeds his uncle and his cousin as king and rules the country well for half a century (ll. 1799-2199). The last adventure he has in his old age is his fight with a fiery dragon. One day the fire-spitting monster comes and threatens to devastate the country. Beowulf goes with a servant to kill it, which he does, but not before he is fatally wounded. He dies for his people as an ideal king (ll. 2200-2820). The poem ends with his funeral (ll. 2821-3182).

In theme, *Beowulf* has little new to offer as another adventure story about a hero killing monsters to make the world safe for people, but the story is unique as a hybrid of fact with legend. It also serves to add testimony to a universal tradition that the humans always manage to get a sense of control over life with the help of their imaginative powers. Similar stories, basically myths, occur in the mythologies of different cultures such as Greek and Chinese. The Greek Heracles' 12 Herculean labors and the Chinese mythic hero Yi's feat of shooting nine of the ten suns down from the sky are just two prominent examples of the heroic exploits out of an amazing multitude in ancient mythologies. In a serious way, mythologies may have been man's religious beliefs and as such a means by which man makes the universe comprehensible and amenable to his control.

There are a few things that merit attention in the reading of the poem. First, the basically pagan story has an evident Christian overlay. For example, "God" or "Lord" is frequently mentioned as the omnipotent supreme being along with such Christian concepts as the belief in "future life," and Grendel is said to be a descendant of the errant biblical figure, Cain. This indicates that the story was put down on paper after Britain embraced Christianity, or some of the scribes of the story must have been either Christianized or sensitive to Christian influence. Then, there is the use of "kennings." A kenning is a kind of metaphor chiefly designed to appeal to people thinking in images and pictures and facilitate a process of attaining knowledge by guesswork. Kennings embellish the whole of *Beowulf*. For example, the sea is often "swan's way" or "whale-path" or "whales' road" or "pathway of sails"; a soldier is often a "shield-holder" or "battle-hero" or "sword-hero" or "spear-fighter"; a battle is a "spear-play" or "edge-play" or "crash of standards"; blood is "war-sweat"; the king is frequently a "gift-giver"; eyes are "head-jewels"; and the body is "flesh-coat" or "bone-chamber." Such word combinations can easily call forth a physical response and effectively avoid juggling with abstract counters. Thirdly, there is the conspicuous occurrence of alliteration in versification. Almost every line in *Beowulf* is held by this pattern of sounds. Alliteration is by definition a succession of similar consonant sounds repeated at the beginning of successive words. It is good for rhythmic chanting effects, emphasis, and helping to memorize things, to name just a few of the purposes it can serve. Equally noticeable is the use of assonance, another popular sound pattern of repeating vowel sounds in successive words either initially or internally. Both alliteration and assonance serve the purpose of slowing down the reading and focusing attention. These Old English sound patterns have long been imbedded in English verse.

In addition, the narrator of the poem, the "I," is clearly a minstrel, or "scop" or "gleeman." The poem itself must have been brought over to Britain through the traveling minstrels in the form of an oral tradition. Another point of interest relates to the story's digressive manner of narration. Whereas the story proper is simple and even slim, its length is swelled up by the digressions and interpolations, some of which can be irritatingly protracted (ll. 1063-1159; ll. 1632-1784; ll. 2349-2509). These are mostly either sung by the gleeman or appear as reminiscences of the hero and some other characters. They are not superfluous, however, as they offer a backdrop of manners, customs and mores, moral teachings, as well as events of historic interest such as the terrible scenes of the Northern battle-fields, the clashing of swords, the howling of the wolf, and the screaming of the eagles and the ravens. The whole poem was written in an elevated tone meant to be chanted for effect.

Medieval Literature: A Brief Introduction [4]

The date that even a child of three in England is supposed to know is 1066, the year of the conquest of England by the French-speaking Normans. It was the year in which the Normans came under William the Conqueror, and the last Anglo-Saxon King Harold died with an arrow shot through his eye at the battle of Hastings. It was also the year that marked the beginning of the Middle English or Anglo-Norman period (1066-1400). The Norman line of kings sat on the throne for some 90 years and gave place to the Angevin kings (or the Plantangenets) in 1154. King Henry II and his descendants stayed in power for 245 years until they were superseded by the House of Lancaster in 1399 when the last of the Plantangenets, Richard II, was dethroned. This happened just one year before Chaucer died. Regarding this period there are a few occurrences of historic magnitude that should be kept in mind:

(1) The Establishment of the Feudal System: William the Conqueror did this effectively within a short space of time. He grabbed Anglo-Saxon land by force and gave it to his nobles and followers. These became lords of manors demanding allegiance from their Anglo-Saxon serfs and owed it to their immediate superiors. The hierarchy was a multi-tiered degradation with the king at the top keeping all the power in his hands. The relative peace that followed brought power and wealth and made the milieu congenial to the growth of art and literature.

(2) The 1381 Peasant Uprising: Within the system the nobles and the aristocrats had all the power and privileges while the serfs remained as wretched as ever. The widespread disaffection led eventually to the peasants' revolt in 1381 which was led by Wat Tyler of Kent and Jack Straw of Essex. 100,000 people marched on London, destroyed manor-houses, burnt court papers—records of their bondage, and demanded the abolition of serf slavery and a general pardon. Though it was eventually put down, serfdom died out gradually.

(3) The Completion of the *Domesday Book* (1086): Though undertaken as a tax-book or rent-roll to provide the king with an estimate of his resources, the *Domesday Book* serves also as a historical record of Anglo-Saxon institutions, customs, and way of life which would have otherwise been lost to time.

(4) The Launching of the Crusades: This was a series of wars between Christians and the Muslims that lasted for about 170 years (1096-1270). Richard the Lion Heart of England and Saladin from the Islamic side were about the most famous names to remember about the period.

(5) The Signing of the Magna Carter in 1215 by which King John was forced to recognize the rights of the powerful barons. This was an event of significance in the long drawn-out decline of the monarchy.

(6) The War with France or the Hundred Years' War (1337-1453): Britain first won at Crecy and Agincourt, but was in the end driven out. That was the point at which the Norman nobles began to see England as their only home, Norman and Anglo-Saxon elements began to coalesce into one nation, and the English language started to revive.

Sizing up the literary scene of the period, one can readily detect a few important points of interest to the student of literature:

(1) The Growth of the Arthurian Legends: The legends of King Arthur and his knights had existed as an oral tradition since the time of the Celts. It was not put down on paper until 1147 when Geoffrey of Monmouth (1100?-1154), a 12th-century Welsh priest came out with his Latin *Historia Regum Britanniae*. He claimed that the book was a translation of a Welsh history of King Arthur and his knights of the Round Table, but it proved to be a lie. In fact he wrote it himself, drawing as he did from sources such as Bede and British traditions. He might have been collecting the legends about the king, and he certainly had a very rich imagination. With Monmouth's effort, the Arthurian Legends, which has become in time one of the vitalizing sources of inspiration for English writers, came into being.

The legends were to be enriched by a good number of later writers. One of these was Wace of Jersey whose *Roman de Brut* (c. 1155) made the story a romance of chivalry. Then in 1205, Layamon, a priest, wrote his vast verse work of 32,000 lines *Brut* in English; this event has been seen ever since as the beginning of the revival of English as a literary medium. "Brut" means "chronicle," and the book is in the main an English rendition of a French version of King Arthur's legends. It was here that the Arthur story first appeared in English. The latter part of the twelfth century saw a sudden growth of the legend.

New additions emerged either in the form of the writers' inventions or incorporations from other sources. Such stories include those of the Holy Grail, Merlin, Sir Lancelot, Quest for the Holy Grail, and the death of the king. These romances were compiled by Robert de Borron and Walter Mapes. Then in the 13th and 14th centuries, the legend flourished first in verse and then in prose, and the Celtic King Arthur became a national hero for the English nation.

It is good to add that the legend had always been popular on the European continent. There had been French and German poets writing to enrich it. In 1470 Sir Thomas Malory, a Welsh Knight, compiled his *Morte d'Arthur* from certain French sources after a good deal of revision. This has become the source book of the Arthur Saga for later generations.

(2) *Sir Gawain and the Green Knight*: One important story in the Arthurian legend has been refined in detail in a famous medieval poem entitled *Sir Gawain and the Green Knight*. Little is known about its author except he was a contemporary of Chaucer and probably a Christian priest. The poem was composed towards the end of the 14th century (about 1375) as an evident effort to extol Sir Gawain and his knightly virtues of loyalty, valor, rectitude, and integrity. Sir Gawain is an upright knight, ever ready to uphold the ideals of King Arthur's court. One Christmas, as the story goes, a knight all in green appears at court and challenges the king to cut off his head on the condition that he comes to meet him in one year's time. Sir Gawain stands out for his lord and beheads the weird visitor. The Green Knight takes up his head and leaves. When the appointed time comes, Sir Gawain sets off to meet him. He comes to a castle and is well received by its lord and lady. The lord invites Sir Gawain to go hunting with him, but the knight prefers to stay at home. The two agree to share in the evening whatever they may have won during the day. This goes on for three days. On the first day the lord of the castle hunts for a deer, while Sir Gawain is under the lady's siege to kiss her. The lord is happy to give half of his trophy in the evening to Sir Gawain in return for his brief kiss on his cheek. The second day ends with the lord giving half a boar for another brief kiss. When the third evening comes, the lord gets three kisses for half of his fox's skin, Sir Gawain having withheld the girdle that the lady has forced on him for his safety. Then the day comes to meet the Green Knight, who turns out to be the lord of the castle. Sir Gawain shrinks a little but

soon recovers his valor to face the blow. But the Green Knight only cuts a scratch on his neck, saying that he would not even have done that to him had he shared the girdle with him in honesty. They become good friends. Sir Gawain goes back to the king's court.

Sir Gawain and the Green Knight is a 4-part work of 2,530 lines in 101 sections. Part one (ll.1-490) deals with the beheading; part two (ll. 491-1125) tells of the long and arduous trip Gawain makes to the castle; part three (ll. 1126-1996) relates the three days he spends in a bargain with the lord; and part four (ll. 1997-2530) wraps up his trip with his final encounter with the Green Knight and the anti-climatic revelation of the moral of the story. In structural terms the narrative is well conceived and neatly knit into an organic unity. The different parts and sections interlock and the threads are pulled together to offer a sense of finality. There is also a fine psychological element that enriches the plot and adds to the characterization. Sir Gawain is not presented as a rigid heroic type but as a human being with his worries and fears. The description of the change of seasons and the difficult terrain of his route with its waste land and wild animals, which appears in a long portion of the second part of the poem, serves in fact as a means of externalizing the complex inner world of the man going to his death. In addition, Sir Gawain's hiding of the girdle, which the lady says can protect him from harm, is a nice *tour de force* to throw the man's fear into relief. There is then the three days' bargaining, which reveals the nature of the temptations that put Sir Gawain's integrity to a strenuous test—the lady's progressive advances to him. To the intensity of the lady's offensive, the hunting serves as an apt foil—deer (timidity), the boar (the wild and aggressive), and the fox (the cunning).

The characterization of Sir Gawain is very interesting to note. His portrait is vivid and fully rounded. There is in him a strange medley of conflicting qualities that makes him perfectly human. Alongside the best of all human virtues, there is also an indication of traits not altogether admirable. He hesitates in face of possible danger as Roland in *Chanson de Roland* does not. He meditates as Roland does not. He is just a little short of an ideal hero. The effect of allowing readers to see all the aspects of his personality is achieved by a subtly imbedded irony, a good-natured satirical edge, against chivalry. Knighthood under the scrutiny of the Christian lens is found wanting. It is not totally without weakness. The knights are just fallible as common humanity, and their best example, Sir Gawain, has his ordinary human weaknesses. The point that the author makes here is amazingly modern if we consider the modern and contemporary tendency to debunk war and heroism. There is reason to see the poem as a thematically Christian composition.

Sir Gawain and the Green Knight shares quite a few basic features with Old English poems like *Beowulf*. In line structure and the use of devices such as alliteration, it is notably similar. As it was written in the north Midland dialect, it is less approachable than Chaucer's London dialect. Usually, a modern translation is indispensable.

(3) *Robin Hood*: This was a collection of 15th-century medieval ballads about Robin Hood, the hero of the poor, and the enemy of the rich and the powerful. The ballads reveal the cruel reality of medieval life with its gross injustice and its underlying discontent as well as the aspirations of the poor. As the ballads go, Robin Hood has been a well-to-do farmer, but he is evicted from his property when he kills some knights to save a poor serf. Thus outlawed, he takes to greenwood life. A group of people of a similar mindset gather around and they all vow with him to be just and harm no good people. They give to the poor what they take from the rich and win the love of the people. The ballads are many in number, complex and intriguing in plot interest, and each and all self-sustaining. They all possess the basic features of folk ballads such as repetition of words, uniform in mood, and dramatic in plot or character portrayal. All have gone through changes over time, but the major stories are still intact with their medieval theme. These include "Robin Hood and the Monk," "Robin Hood and Guy of Gisborne," "Robin Hood and the Porter," and the *Lytell Geste of Robin Hood*.

(4) John Wycliffe (1320-1384): Wycliffe was an Oxford scholar. He did one thing that has had far-reaching influence upon the evolution of the English language—the translation of the *Bible* from the sonorous Latin Vulgate Version into Middle English. This was the first attempt ever to translate the Holy Scripture into English. Although his version was not error-free, Wycliffe made an admirable literary rendering. The much better King James' or the Authorized Version was to appear over 300 years later (1611), but Wycliffe was the pioneer in the field. Another thing for which Wycliffe was noted in history was his stature as a precursor of Martin Luther's Reformation, or as "the Morning Star of the

Reformation." All his life Wycliffe kept speaking vehemently against the Pope and the whole religious hierarchy, against the abuses of the Church of Rome such as the sales of indulgences, and against the corruption of the religious orders. He saw no need for the corrupt Church; the *Bible* alone was enough for the people. His followers formed what later came to be known as the Lollard movement. Wycliffe was such a powerful preacher among the people that he was even said to have helped start the 1381 Uprising.

(5) William Langland (1332–end of 14th century): Langland was a reformer. He wrote *Vision of Piers the Plowman*, a dream allegory of 7,000 lines to attack evil in both Church and state. It was a great work of medieval preaching, a Christian poem dealing with salvation, and a very difficult one with its ambiguous language and imagery. As it is, the book exists in three versions known as the A-text (in 9 books), the B-text (in 21 books), and the C-text (in 28 books), of which the B-text is the best known. This text can be divided into two parts, with part one covering the first 7 books and part two the rest of the poem. The first part touches on the physical aspect of human life such as the procurement of necessities and the reform of society. The second part deals with the spiritual aspect of life, the winning of salvation. Basically, the book consists of a series of dreams of a vagrant with whom the poet identifies himself. Langland wrote in Middle English with a mastery not really inferior to Chaucer's though he was not as easily approachable.

(6) *Chanson de Roland*: Medieval literature is noted for its vast number of romances, which deal with heroes rather than common life. These include the four cycles of King Arthur and his Knights, Charlemagne and his peers, Alexander the Great, and the Trojan War. Of the Charlemagne cycle this much needs to be kept in mind, that King Charlemagne (or Charles the Great) was a famous king of 8th-century France. He was able to expand the French empire across a good part of Western Europe at the height of his reign. In 777 he led his army against the Arab forces (called the Saracens) then occupying Spain and lost out in the end at the famous battle of Roncesvalles on the Spanish border. This was the battle in which one of his able captains, Roland, met his heroic death. This constitutes the basic subject of the most famous work of the Charlemagne cycle—the *Chanson de Roland*. Roland dies, falling into his rival's traitorous trap and fighting

overwhelming numbers. In the end the furious Charlemagne burns the Spanish capital, hangs the scheming Spanish king, and quarters the body of the traitor. It is a story of valor, loyalty, honor, and treachery, heroic in tone and expression. It was said to have inspired William the Conqueror's Normans in their conquest of the Anglo-Saxons.

Chapter 2 Chaucer • The Pre-Elizabethan Period • More

Geoffrey Chaucer (1340-1400)

Chaucer was the first preeminent English poet in history and ranks with Shakespeare as the most popular and most widely read of all poets today. He has been one of the major influences on writers of later generations not only in England but also across the world.

Chaucer lived an eventful life. He was born into a prosperous London vintner's family and received a very solid education. He could speak most of the important languages of the day—French, Latin, and Italian, and was widely read and learned. When still a boy, he became a page to a prince's wife, and remained in the service of the royal household for quite a few years. Then he fought in France, was captured, but was ransomed by the king. His marriage with one of the queen's maids brought him money as well as more royal favor. He was also at different phases of his life a diplomat (to Spain, France, and Italy), and served as a controller of the customs, a justice of the peace, and knight of the shire for Kent. He lost and then regained favor with the change of kings, and was made by the new king Clerk of Works for royal castles and palaces. The last job he held was one as a civil servant. He died in 1400.

This colorful experience with life and people paved the way for his writing career. Although not a professional writer, Chaucer wrote profusely and won the admiration of his contemporaries. In addition to his *Canterbury Tales*, his works include *The Book of Duchess*, a dream allegory of 1,300 lines, *The House of Fame*, an incomplete work of a dream vision in three books, *The Parliament of Fowls*, another dream allegory of 699 lines in rhyme-royal (a seven-line stanzaic form), *Troilus and Criseyde,* an 8,000-line adaptation of the Italian Boccacio's story, one of the greatest poems in English, and a subtle and passionate psychological study of love, with the basic ingredients of a novel, and *The Legend of Good Women*, also a dream vision with a prologue and nine stories (the ninth being incomplete). Chaucer was the first most significant poet in English literary history to write in Middle English. The evolution of the English language would have been different had Chaucer not lived to help perfect it as a literary medium. [1] It is good to add, incidentally, that although he is easily accessible and highly enjoyable in the modern translations, it is necessary to read him in the ME original to appreciate his literary merits really well.

By far the most famous of all his works is *The Canterbury Tales*, a collection of 20-odd stories. The framing of the stories by means of a fictitious pilgrimage, as the *Tales* uses as a unifying device, was common in medieval times. Boccacio's *Decameron* works in a similar way in that ten narrators each tell a story a day for ten days. Chaucer's book sets out with an ambitious plan. There are altogether 30 travelers (including the inn-keeper as host) on the pilgrimage to Canterbury to pay homage to the religious martyr, Sir Thomas à Becket, who was murdered in his own Cathedral in 1170. Each of the pilgrims agrees to tell 4 stories on the way there and back, and that would bring the total up to 120. But the book actually contains only 20 complete stories and 4 fragments, which is already an amazing number. The stories in the *Tales* come from different sources. These include, among others, the French sources, the Italian, the biblical, the Asian, and folklore. For instance, the knight's tale is taken from the Italian Boccacio's *Teseida*, The Physician's tale is a Roman moral tale, the poet-narrator Chaucer's tale of Sir Topaz is a parody of some English popular romance, the monk's tale of "tragedies" comes from sources such as the *Bible* and Boccacio, and the Parson's tale is based on some Latin works on morals.

However, it should be noted that, whereas the substance is from others, the telling is always, ultimately, entirely Chaucer's own. The salient features of Chaucer's narration are its enormous sense of humor, its loyalty to reality, and its infinite sense of humanity. For one thing, Chaucer just can not resist the temptation of a good, good-natured laugh. No one can read the *Tales* without a chuckle or at least a hearty smile. Chaucer's moods do change, sometimes hilarious and occasionally wry, but he never ends his narrative without a happy face. Secondly, Chaucer sticks to his policy of honesty and stays true to life. It is a miracle how he transplants his various sources firmly to the 14th-century English setting and makes foreign faces look like those of his own people. The change is at times intangible, but the readers can feel it as it is built into the very texture of the telling. Then there is Chaucer's humanity to consider. He is one of the most magnanimous natures in human memory. His world is peopled with almost all the interesting types of humankind as is real life—vain, lewd, covetous, proud, and sinning, and therefore needs tolerance and forgiveness, of which Chaucer as a writer has an abundance as his works readily reveal. Incidentally, Chaucer is always smiling at people and life, sometimes with a touch of irony, and sometimes even with a smirk, but he remains always good-natured and generous and never allows himself even to frown upon some of the evil and vicious. The readers of the *Tales* tend to come away with the impression that Chaucer is speaking to his readers, as it were, so as to remind them that theirs is in fact basically the same kind of existence as that of the 14th-century England, that the humans are essentially the same despite their temporal and spatial discrepancies, and that human nature never changes much, with its time-honored weaknesses and vices that make people what they are—human. Chaucer is a first-rate story-teller. Reading him can be an immensely enlightening and educational experience.[2]

Chaucer's gallery of portraits of the people is ambitious: They come from virtually all walks of life, from the upper strata all the way down the ladder to the lower. The painting begins in the *General Prologue*, which is Chaucer's purely English work. It offers such a panorama of social life that the readers can instantly imagine themselves back into the time tunnel and relive the 14th-century as one of the travelers in the *Tales*. The variety of lifestyles, customs and traditions, the ways people walk in their peculiar gaits and talk in their peculiar language, the juxtaposition of the serious and the dignified alongside the jocular and the vulgar, the candid folk with the treacherous, the high with the low, and female with male—all these reveal Chaucer's thorough knowledge of his country and his rare gift for adequate expression. The character sketches of the *General Prologue* are so well done in such bold strokes that they provide the guidelines for the later tales with their separate prologues. In a sense the tales all serve to footnote the *General Prologue* and flesh out the skeletal structures well provided for them there. The

Knight's tale, for instance, relates a love romance, praising knightly virtues and the force of love stronger than that of the swords, and exploring the themes of determinism and freedom. The tale is told in a style, dignified and serious, befitting both the subject and the storyteller. The Miller's tale, however, sounds radically different in tone and mood. It is one about the life of the lower strata, noisy, frivolous, and exuberantly lewd and voluptuous. An aside here about Chaucer is that the 14th-century poet can be very modern in taste and allow himself to dip very low at times into the deeps of life just so as to be true to it. True to form, Chaucer is a master of realism. In addition, the *General Prologue*, famous especially for its description of a sunny fresh spring and a general happy and harmonious crowd of people, offers testimony to the basically moral nature of the Chaucerian world with the sense of certitude and assurance still intact, despite the prevailing ills of the Church and society in general that the *Tales* censures vehemently.

Nor is this all. Chaucer's portrayal of the people merits more attention in this, that it is amazingly selective as well as inclusive. Some of the people come from the nobility like the knight, quite a few from the holy orders, quite a good number from the trading and manufacturing segment, and some from the country. This is a microcosm of the society at large in itself. Chaucer might just as well have in mind to paint an authentic picture of the life of his time for posterity. In retrospective, it is quite safe to say that it is enough for people to read just the *Tales* to get to know about 14th-century English life. Especially noticeable is the coverage he gives to the prominence of two groups of people—the holy orders and the middle class. The first of these consists of a parson, some nuns, a monk, a friar, a summoner, and a pardoner. The description of the clergy group is done not without a touch of irony. This becomes noticeable the moment the readers get in contact with them in the *General Prologue*. Chaucer the writer and Chaucer the poet-narrator in the *Tales* do not always see eye to eye with one another about people and things. They have, for instance, quite different conceptions about the holy orders. It is interesting to note that, whereas Chaucer the writer is mild and tolerant, the Chaucer as narrator of the *Tales* just cannot withhold a stab at the corrupt condition of the Catholic Church and its members. His sketches of the characters of the Prioress, the Monk, the Friar, the Summoner and the Pardoner are all downright pejorative. The one possible denominator they share is that they do exactly what they should not as required. Thus the Nun is concerned with her appearances and manners and full of tender feelings for cats and dogs; the Monk, personable, well-dressed and well-fed, delights in nothing but hunting and inspecting farms; the Friar is wanton, merry, amorous, and greedy; the Summoner, a hot and lecherous bully, promises salvation in return for gifts of money; and the Pardoner, a honey-tongued braggart, sells pardons fresh from Rome with which his wallet bulges. There is only one person from this group, the Parson, who is holy and virtuous, denounces the world and the devil and the flesh, and devotes himself to the service of God and the spiritual welfare of his herd, but his abject aloneness tends to leave the readers sometimes with the question, "Is it worth it sticking it out and suffering the way he does?" and the question points fingers back at the clergy and the church. The ironic tone of the narration concerning these people is so evident, so unmistakable, that one tends to think that they may have been placed in the group of pilgrims as a butt for satire for their corruption and depravity. As to Chaucer the author, however, it is difficult to gauge his mindset; he may have introduced them as a mirror to reality, for he does not stereotype them in colors of pure white and black; he presents their bad as well as their good side at the same time.

The other large group—a merchant, the Wife of Bath, a haberdasher, a dyer, a carpenter, a weaver, a carpet maker as well as a skipper—are depicted in some detail as a reflection of the emergent middle class, beginning to taste the combination of power with wealth and aspiring to more of both down the road. Their very overwhelming numbers are already impressive enough to give people the idea that these must be the people dominating the scene there in society. In addition, the author devotes quite an amount of space and time to introduce them to his readers. Take the Wife of Bath for example. She is made out to look and sound like one of the most outstanding figures among the pilgrims. Her portrait in the *General Prologue* is one of the most impressive, and it is good to add that this is Chaucer's purely English work. This "gap-toothed" woman manufacturer from the city of Bath, an uninhibited chatterbox, can be seen as a symbol of a lot of things: she is an aggressive middle class person, for ever poised to bounce on the faintest opportunity of making a profit; she is an aggressive person with a vision about her future; and she may be viewed as a precursor of sorts to feminism who anticipates the women's lib movement by some five centuries. She has married five times and is just getting ready for her man number six. Her major feature is her huge sense of self-worth and her strenuous self-assertiveness in face of social disapproval. The way she dauntlessly contests the anti-women stances in some of the books she has read is ample indication of the potential of the female gender for growth. In addition, the tale that she is about to tell, one of an old hag turning into a beautiful young lady in a twinkling of an eye, serves as a kind of "objective correlative" for her desire—her wish-fulfillment—as a woman past her prime, and offers in turn a glance at her inner emotional fabric and a window to peer into womanhood in general. Chaucer's characterization of the Wife of Bath is one remarkable *tour de force* in literary history.

Now let's take a closer look at some of the tales in the book just to have a taste of Chaucer's storytelling. "The Wife of Bath's Tale," "The Pardoner's Tale," and "The Miller's Tale" are chosen here as specimens because they represent the different walks of life the storytellers come from more graphically. "The Wife of Bath's Tale" is exceptionally interesting as it raises a very challenging question for the readers. As the story goes, a young knight in King Arthur's time violates the knightly code and rapes a young woman. The furious king would have had him put to death instantly had the queen not intervened and asked for some reprieve for the knight. The queen gives the knight a year and a day's time to go and find the answer to her question, "What is it that women desire most?" The knight leaves and encounters many women on his way. The answers he receives from them vary vastly from wealth, honor, jollity, fine clothes, and fun in bed. Here the narrator drags in some ancient authority who says that women want to be thought of as trustworthy in keeping secrets, and goes on to tell about the tale of King Midas who at one time has two ass's ears growing on his head and tells his wife not to tell it to anyone. His wife manages to keep it for a while until she feels that she would die to have it bottled up inside her. So she ends up rushing to a reedy marsh where she whispers the secret to the reeds, and the reeds all whisper like her in their susurrus (and have been doing so ever since). Then the story of the knight picks itself up. Soon one year is out, and now there is only one day left. As he rides homeward dejected, the knight sees a group of pretty girls dancing on a meadow. At his approach, however, all vanish into the air, except only one poor ugly old woman who is crouching on the ground. Calling her "dear mother," the knight goes up and relates all his trouble, but is surprised to hear the old hag say that she could help if he would comply with her request whatever it may be. The young man, having no choice, agrees and goes together with her to see the queen. The queen is happy when she is told that a woman wants to be the mistress of her own house most. Before he has time to feel happy, the old woman says that she would like him to marry her. Now the knight finds himself in a real dilemma. He does not want to marry her, but he has given her his word of honor. So he goes ahead with the wedding very unhappily. On the wedding night, he finds to his great joy that the old witch has turned into the most beautiful young woman in the world.

In addition to the approach mentioned earlier on that the story is an apt illustration of the Wife of Bath's inner psychology, the tale has a surprising modern ring about it. The very question about what women want brings the female gender up from the bottom of society and places women on an equal footing with men. Women's desire has been of little or no interest to anyone at all before Chaucer asks the question, and even women do not know seriously and exactly about their needs as most of the answers to the question reveal. Chaucer seems to sense the inequality between the sexes and feels the lack of attention that womenfolk deserves. In addition, the story teaches the world, especially the male part of it, through the old woman's catechizing of the young man toward the end of the story. On seeing the reluctance of the knight to wed her, the old woman begins to read him a lecture in her torrential language. She says that wealth and gentle birth are not important, a gentleman is one who does a gentle deed, poverty teaches one what is holy, and an old and plain woman may just as well make a loyal and true wife. The knight, thus educated about life, is now willing to marry her, and it is just then that she asks him to cast up the curtain to reveal her beauty. The implication is that hers may not be a physical beauty, but one that resides in the soul and that a man should love a woman for her worth rather than her face. All these are still questions that people forever face and try to address.[3]

Of all the holy clerics in the *Tales*, the Pardoner alone has the honor of being singled out for unusual ironic treatment. The irony receives an exceptional intensity with the well-wrought correlation of the description of the Pardoner in the *General Prologue* and the "Prologue to the Pardoner's Tale." The two prologues deserve an in-depth discussion because it is as revealing of the Pardoner's personality as does the Tale if not more. The *General Prologue* makes it instantly clear that this Pardoner, coming from the medieval "fountainhead of sales" of indulgences—Roncival and just returning from Rome with a bag of new supplies of indulgences, is of an infamously shady breed. A closer scrutiny of his physical features reveals his surprising similarity to animals such as his hare-like eyes, his voice "as smal[l] as hath a goot [goat]," and his sexuality, which as the poet-narrator speculates, is compared to that of a mare. The mare image insinuates that he is not masculine. This is further evidenced by the strange fashion in which he wears his long hair and by his beardlessness, and his sex is probably the same as a eunuch's: "I trowe he were a gelding or a mare." The contempt in which the Pardoner is held cannot be mistaken. However, there is an intriguing twist in Chaucer's handling of the matter. All the three animals were seen in the medieval times as representing lechery. If one reads the Pardoner's Prologue carefully, one may find the Pardoner's confession that one of the benefits of his occupation is "a joy wenche in every town," which is another way of saying that the Pardoner is quite possibly guilty of promiscuous sex. Then the alert about his want of masculinity and sexuality in the *General Prologue* is thus undercut ruthlessly in effect by the "Prologue of the Pardoner's Tale," and shows the true colors of the guileful silver-tongued preacher. The man may be the most zealous of all the holy group for religion, but he is that for the wrong reason—his self-serving.

Nor is this all. The placement of the Pardoner in the *General Prologue* is conspicuously noticeable. Whereas the Knight is given the first place, the Pardoner comes the last on the list. This can be probably explained in two ways. One reason may be that these two represent the two extremes on the moral spectrum of the gallery. The Knight, who "loved chivalrye, [trouthe] and honour, freedom and courteisye," forms a distinct contrast to the spiritually much inferior Pardoner. And the poet-narrator adds another touch of sarcasm when he makes it explicit that his portraits in the *General Prologue* are not arranged according to social standing. Another reason may be the poet-narrator's effort to give the Pardoner the end-position emphasis for people to pay more attention to his notoriety. It turns out in the end that the Pardoner preaches against the sin which he bodies forth in the most glaring way. Whereas his creed claims that "greed is the root of all in evil," he knows very well that he is a living contradiction of the tenet itself as he feeds his own sin by attacking it. The best part of the irony lies in the fact that he may not know that he serves as an example and a warning to the people to whom he tries to sell his doctrine through his Tale. His attack on the greed that leads to the death of the three young drunkards, the central subject of his sermon in the first part of the Tale, boomerangs and causes the symbolic death of the Pardoner as he fails to cajole his fellow travelers into donating money for his promise of absolution.

Now his Tale is very intriguing as well. As it goes, three young people getting dead drunk all vow to find and kill Death between them because it is stalking the land and killing a lot of people including children. They meet, on their way, with a very ugly-looking old man and accuse him of having been an accomplice to Death. They tell him that, as he is so old and is still allowed to live, he must have been working hand in glove with Death in killing people around the country. The old man, in face of their threat of death, points to a tree some distance away and says that Death must be lurking somewhere behind it. The young drunkards rush to the tree and find, to their great surprise, a huge glittering pile of gold there under the tree, instead of Death. Instantly forgetting their search, the youths sober up and decide that they will wait for the cover of the night to divide the money between them. Then they feel hungry and draw lots so that one of them will go and fetch food and drink for the others. The one to whom the lot falls goes and the other two begin immediately to plot his death so that the two of them can have the money between themselves. When the one comes back with the food and drink, the two bounce upon him and kill him. But as soon as they settle down to have their lunch, they feel an excruciating pain in their stomachs. Before long, they both lie dead poisoned by the arsenic that the dead one has put in the food so as to have all of the gold to himself. [4]

The Miller's Tale is the most hilarious and indecent of all the tales in the book, and Chaucer knows this better than anybody else. As he knows that it may be objectionable to many people, he begins by alerting his "squeamish" audience with an apology for the theme of the tale and goes on to disclaim any personal responsibility for it. He calls the Miller in the *General Prologue* a "churl," while making the Miller confess in the prologue of his tale that, if he happens to tell any tale of distaste, people should blame it all on the undue amount of Southwark ale he has drunk. The tale is one of jealousy, infidelity, courtly love, and obscenity. John the old carpenter is a possessive, jealous husband and tries to "cage" his young wife Alisoun. The woman is a cunning seductress, taking special delight in cheating on her man for her voluptuous gratification. Their lodger, Nicholas, a college student, kicks in here and, one day when the carpenter is away, "privately... [catches] hire by the quiente." "Quiente," a Middle English word, is a pun or euphemism for a woman's genitalia. There is a young parish clerk, Absalom by name, who loves Alisoun, but does not feel loved as the woman is fond of Nicholas. One Saturday night, the scheming Nicholas devises a plan to move the carpenter out of the way so that he can sleep with Alisoun. He cheats the husband into believing that a huge flood will come to drown the world on Monday and that he needs to find three tubs to tie on the rafter of the house for the three of them to survive it. He tells the man to wait for his word "water" to cut the tying rope and set their tubs afloat in the deluge. The candid carpenter does as he is told and sleeps exhausted on the roof, while the lovers enjoy their night together. Absalom happens to come along at cockcrow to show his love for his woman and enrages the sleeping lovers so that Alisoun decides to play a trick on him and turn him away for good. She asks Absalom to come close for a kiss and gives him her naked "bearded rear." The humiliated clerk goes away and borrows a hot iron, and comes back to avenge himself. Nicholas feels it will be fun for him to repeat the game on the clerk but gets, instead, severe burning on his jetting buttocks. In racking pain he yells out "water" three times so that the old carpenter is waken up, cuts the rope, and falls from the roof. He suffers serious maiming, and becomes the butt for poplar derision. The Miller ends his tale by admonishing foolish men never to try and marry sly flirtatious young women.

The Miller's tale is told in the style of the medieval "fabliau" (a funny vulgar story). Chaucer takes this from the medieval French writers, and makes the best of it in telling some of the tales, the best specimen of which is the Miller's tale. A fabliau normally involves deceptions concerning sex or money and displays a good deal of coarse humor. In the Miller's tale, everything fits together to make it work out in an admirable way. The jealousy of the carpenter, the designing Nicholas, the love-sick but revengeful Absalom, and the tempting flirt of a young wife are all appropriate matter for treatment in this style. And sure enough the tale of the four different people almost asphyxiates the pilgrims with its bawdy humor. The success of the style has a lot to do with the plotting. The carpenter has to be a fool ignorant enough to believe in the "learned" prophecy of the Oxford student about the oncoming of another Noah-time-like flood. The parish clerk has to be a fool both sentimental enough to fall into the kiss trap and vicious and impetuous enough to avenge himself out of it. Nicholas is the most devious of all and gets the most of the hurt in the end. He plays in a petty clever way for a reward countless times less than the punishment that waylays him ahead. He is made to sleep in the bed he makes for others to begin with but eventually for himself. Here is another good example of the ways of the moral world that *The Canterbury Tales* tries to portray. [5]

The Pre-Elizabethan Period: A Brief Introduction

The 150 years between the death of Chaucer and the ascension of Queen Elizabeth I (1400-1557) was a very important period in history. Some events of great magnitude occurred that ultimately brought England and Europe out of the Middle Ages into the modern time. These included the Reformation, the Renaissance, and printing from movable type. [6]

The Reformation was, in historical retrospect, a natural corollary of the popular disaffection with the growing corrupt practices of the Catholic Church and the long pent-up anger and desire on the part of the more enlightened religious minds for reform and improvement. Any readers of Chaucer will find his portrayals of the holy orders in *The Canterbury Tales* highly dubious and ironic though subtle to a fault. The church and the holy clerics had been for long obsessed with the worldly concerns of amassing wealth and power through devious means such as selling indulgences, and had seriously deviated from the teachings of Jesus Christ and the Holy Scripture. They were in sore need of censure and correction. The first voice of revolt came from John Wycliffe (1320-1384), known now as the "Morning Star of the Reformation." He was dauntless when he took the religious orders and even the Papacy to task for their depravity and greed. In his opinion the church was not necessary, and the *Bible* alone would meet the popular need for faith. He was too much ahead of his time to effect the change he had in mind. It took about two centuries and a man by the name of Martin Luther to bring forth the wind of change.

The Reformation first started in Germany by Martin Luther (1483-1546), an Augustan friar. When he visited Rome and saw the widespread corruption from the grass roots to the very top of the hierarchy of the Catholic Church, he made up his mind that a change in the nature of things within the church was not just necessary but inevitable. In 1517 he took a spectacular action which set off the blazes of the Reformation across the Catholic world. He nailed his 95 theses on to the door of the castle church in Wittenberg, just to start a discussion of matters relevant to the faith and the church. The fire soon spread across the continent and echoes of positive responses were heard from prominent places such as France and Switzerland. Such preeminent theologians as Johannes Calvin (1509-1564) spoke out vehemently for the change, and Europe soon found itself in the tormenting throes of discord. The followers of the movement, distinct now from the Catholics, became known as the Protestants, and the Reformation has also been known in history as the Protestant Reformation.

The Protestants, such as the Lutherians and the Calvinists, would like to cleanse the church of its departures from the norm and restore it to the purity of the first-century church established by Jesus Christ. They believe in the doctrine of justification by faith, that man's justification or salvation depends on the grace of God which comes through faith alone. As long as there is faith, man stands directly under God and needs no mediation from church or priest. The *Bible* alone is the Word. Thus the Reformation made a great historic contribution in the intellectual history of humankind: it set the human mind free from the fetters of the tenets and dogmas of the Catholic Church and opened human eyes to the new and promising vistas of the new age. The Reformation indicated that man had made considerable progress in his epistemology. Whereas there was little more than submission and acceptance in face of the church and other forms of external power and control, there appeared individual expression and critical thinking. Of the former the medieval mind was basically incapable, and the latter broke the back of religious tyranny and fanaticism. Thus, with the Reformation, nothing, the church as well as the world at large, could never be the same again. The modern age was zoomed into sight.

This emancipation of the human mind offered an immediate fillip to a movement the historical impact of which on the human condition was no less powerful than the Reformation. This was the Renaissance, or the rebirth or revival of classical learning, which first began in 14th-century Italy. By classical learning was meant Greek and Roman learning, their literature and art, which had lain buried in oblivion for a long time. Then with the fall of Constantinople and the collapse of the Eastern Empire in 1453, Greek scholars fled in cohorts to Italy with their carefully preserved manuscripts. Upon publication, these classics immediately fascinated the sensitive thinking minds and won the love and admiration of all who read them. For the first time in history, the medieval minds saw the beauty of the human form and learned about the importance of human life and human values. A new view of life, a new outlook on the world and a new attitude toward living, first making its tentative appearance at the end of the Middle Ages, was now fast becoming a surety. Man began to live for his own sake more than for God and for the next world.

Humanism as a movement came into existence. In addition to its attempt to trace classical learning back to its origins and excavate the most significant facets of classical thought, the movement placed its primary emphasis on the world here and now, so that the proper study of mankind, at long last, became man. The humanists were acquisitive, dynamic, ambitious, and aggressive. They were well poised on the verge of attack and conquest in face of the mysteries of life and the universe. To them the world was up for grabs for those who had the courage and confidence as well as knowledge, and nothing was impossible to accomplish. It was "a world of profit and delight" and of "power, honor and omnipotence," one in which "All things that move between the quiet poles/ Shall be at my command" (to quote Christopher Marlowe [1564-1593]). This is an eloquent testimony to the tremendous energy and the huge sense of mission with which the generation in between the phases of history looked forward to high achievement. So the stage was set for individual assertion and growth in the blossoming of the human genius and the flowering of literature and art destined to happen in this and the next period—the Elizabethan age.

Both the Reformation and the Renaissance had an immense impact upon the England of Henry VIII. The aging king, who began as a humanist but had become a tyrant, did something good and important by sheer accident. He was divorcing his Queen Catherine, of which the Pope disapproved, and the long quarrel he had with Rome led to his decision to take church affairs into his own hands and make himself the head of the Church in England. This move paved the way for the influx of Protestant thought into the country and for humanism to play its major role in English social and cultural life. In addition to the efforts of such enlightened minds as Thomas More (1478-1535) and John Colet (1467-1519), Desiderius Erasmus (1466-1536), the famous Dutch scholar and theologian, then visiting England as a Divinity Professor at Cambridge, added an energetic impetus to the English humanist movement now just blooming. Erasmus did a lot toward breaking the Catholic hegemony. He was such a force scourging the Catholic Church for its ignorance and intolerance and he made such a contribution toward the success of the Reformation that a famous motto went around that said, "Erasmus laid the egg and Luther hatched it." The efforts of these men pointed forward to the singular accomplishments of the forthcoming Elizabethan age.

Now the third significant event in human intellectual history was printing from movable type. This technology helped a good deal to preserve Greek and Latin literature through reprinting in Italy. The first English printer, William Caxton (1422-1491), brought the technique back to England from Italy where he traveled as a merchant and helped save a good many English books from extinction. The new method made classical books accessible to the public and further piqued the interest for more and better reading matter. It is good to note here that the Elizabethan Age would probably not have been as great in achievement and permanent in human memory had there not been the help of printing from movable type to do the spadework for it.

Thomas More (1478-1535)

Despite the seminal nature of life in this long period, few great names appeared in the field of literature that merit attention. One that stands out is Sir

Thomas More who was regarded as the wisest and noblest person that lived then. He was precocious as a student and received his education in Greek scholarship at Oxford and in legal matters at Lincoln's Inn. As a young man, he stayed with Cardinal Morton, Chancellor to Henry VIII, and met famous Renaissance scholars Erasmus and Colet. He wrote and published his *Utopia* in 1516 (first in Latin, then translated into English 1551). A couple of years later he became privy councilor to the king and was made Chancellor in 1529. As he did not go along with the king's divorce, he was indicted of high treason and beheaded in 1535. This was one of the most outrageous and notorious things that Henry VIII ever did in his long reign. More was first and foremost a humanist at heart. He witnessed the evils of the world and sought to help mend things. His *Utopia* takes a look forward to the future of man and offers an ideal which has inspired generations of serious social thinkers, political scientists, writers as well as humankind as a whole ever since its publication. It is one of the best books ever to appear in human memory and will stay as such in history.[7]

Utopia consists of two books with emphasis on book II in which the Utopian weal republic is described in detail. As few people have access to the book, or care enough to read it, the synopsis of it offered here is lengthy enough to introduce the major points of interest to the readers. Book I is written in the form of a dialogue between More and a traveler by the name of Rapael Hythloday. It introduces the meeting between the two and their conversation, and hints at the notion that the whole work is not a manifesto but rather an endeavor to explore the potential of human life. Hythloday has been to Utopia, a kind of "Nowhere Land." He is a learned man, and has been to many unknown lands and seen strange peoples. In their conversation which involves the ills of the time, Hythloday mentions the Utopians and their wise laws, and is asked to give a full, first-hand account of this island. This leads to book II which contains nine sections. Section one, which begins with a lengthy title, "The Best State of a Commonwealth, the Discourse of Raphael Hythlodaeus as Reported by Thomas More, Citizen and Sheriff of London," describes the geographic contours of the country. It is an island that lies somewhere beyond the equator. About 200 miles in width and 500 miles in circumference, it looks like a new moon. King Utopus, who gave his name to the island he conquered, had the country well fortified by the sea. Being a natural haven, it needs only one garrison on top of a great rock. It has had a history of 1760 years behind it. There are 54 large and fair cities on the island with Amaurote as the head city. There are farms each of which has 40 people and two bondmen on it. The Utopians sow corn for bread and raise oxen for meat and farm work. Every 30 farms or families have one head ruler called phylarch or syphogrant. City and country folk change places every year so that everyone has a full experience of life.

Section two, "The Cities, Especially Amaurotum," relates city life with Amaurote as an example. The city is strong in defense, its streets are wide, and its houses fair, well-built, and solid with back gardens. The doors remain unbolted as there is nothing private. People change houses every tenth year. Section three, "The Officials," talks about the administration of the country. It is a tiered system, with the syphogrant at the bottom level, the tranibore in the middle, and the prince at the top. The job of the syphogrant is to see that no one sits idle. Each tranibore, whose term of office is one year, heads ten syphogrants. The prince, elected by a secret ballot of the syphogrants (200 in number), has the job for life and is forced to step down only when suspect of tyranny. Matters of great weight are discussed by the people in the council-houses, and care is taken that no hasty decision is made to the detriment of the commonwealth. Section four, "Occupations," introduces the Utopian lifestyle. Men and women all have to do farm work everyday. They are also encouraged to learn one or more crafts. They work six hours a day, three in the morning, and three in the afternoon, with two hours' nap after lunch. They go to bed at eight p.m., and sleep for eight hours. The rest of day they spend attending lectures or on healthy recreations. Overwork is abhorred. No one is allowed to be idle, or engage in vain and dishonest occupations. There are no idle priests, no idle rich or nobility, no bullies, and no deceitful beggars. Only the old and weak and the learned are exempt from labor. People are dressed in one fashion and one color, which never change, except that there is a distinction between men's garments and the women's, and between the unmarried and the married. No gorgeous clothing is honored. When there is little work to do, an open proclamation announces the shortened hours of work so that people will devote more to the free liberty of the mind.

Section five, "Social Relations," introduces the Utopian family structure, city planning, and eating custom. Every city consists of 6,000 families commonly made up of kindred. Each of these is governed by the eldest father. A family should have 10 to 16 children of 14 years of age at one time. When the population increases, the Utopians build foreign towns in some waste or unoccupied lands (by force if need be) and emigrate there. If the population dwindles for any reason like a plague, they fill up their cities with citizens from their foreign towns. The city is divided into four equal quarters, in the center of which there is a market-place. The householders bring whatever they have to offer and take back what they need without money, exchange or pledge. Abundance removes greed and covetousness. The people usually gather and eat in the hall of their syphogrant at the sound of a brazen trumpet. Dining at home is not encouraged though not prohibited. In the hall men sit on one side of the table next to the wall and women sit opposite them. Mothers with children under the age of five eat in a separate parlor. Unmarried boys and girls stand and serve, eating whatever is given them from the table. The syphogrant and his wife sit in the midst of the high table with two oldest men. The oldest get first served. Before eating something short is read concerning good manners and virtues. Dinner is short but supper is longer and enjoyed against a musical background. They have pleasant banquets once in a while. Country folk, who live apart, dine and sup at home. In the circuit of the city there are four spacious and clean hospitals. Great care is taken that the city is tidy and clean and kept free of any form of pollution. The magistrates, princes, bishops, and strangers are allowed to enjoy certain privileges.

Section six, "Utopian Travel, [Etc.]," says that travel is possible with the permission of the syphogrant and the prince's letter, without which, however, it is punishable with disgrace or bondage. Within the bounds of the city, everyone is free to walk around provided that he has finished his share of work. There are no taverns, ale-houses nor anything of the kind. No unlawful assembly is permitted; everyone has to be present under the eyes of all. The cities are mutually complementary in supplies and form one big family. They have no use for money except in cases of emergency such as war. They value iron more than gold and silver. Bondmen are made to wear gold. Criminals are fettered with instruments of gold, with gold rings on their fingers and gold chains about their necks. Their precious stones are used for children. The Utopians are devoted to learning music, logic, arithmetic, and philosophy, the principles of which are based on their religion: they include the immortality of the soul and the rewards and punishments of the next world. They condemn painful virtues and condemn grief without good reason. To the Utopians, happiness lies in good and honest pleasure, and virtue is life ordered according to nature. They enjoy life and help others to do so, for nature prescribes a joyful life for all. A good deed brings joy to the mind and is encouraged. The Utopians abhor the perverse and malicious. Fine gowns, noble birth, precious stones and superfluous wealth are seen as ridiculous and vain. Gambling, hunting and working as a butcher are all despicable. The Utopians embrace two kinds of pleasures: those of the body, and those of the mind. They enjoy food and drink as good to health and admire the beauty of mother nature. No true pleasure brings displeasure. It is madness to disrupt the pleasant motions of nature such as does fasting for a vain shadow of virtue. Asceticism is condemned there. The people love learning to explore the mysteries of nature, and are generally good at inventions. They are friendly and hospitable and curious about new lands.

Section seven, "Slavery, [Etc.]," states that there are bondmen alongside free citizens in Utopia. Bondmen come from three sources: miscreants from the island, criminals from other lands, and poor laborers willing to stay as slaves. The first of these is severely dealt with while the third is allowed to leave when they so wish. The Utpoian sick are well treated; the incurable are comforted and advised to end their suffering by voluntary death but are never forced to do so against their will. The Utopians marry at twenty for men and eighteen for women. Divorce is possible in case of infidelity or other intolerable behavior; the party found in the wrong is not allowed to remarry. Physical mishap or old age is no reason for divorce. But divorce is not encouraged. Breakers of wedlock are punishable by bondage or death on a second offense. The punishment of various offenders is decided by the council. Bondmen who rebel are put to death, but if they repent, they can hope to be better treated. It is bad taste to mock at fools and physical deformity. Virtue is rewarded with images of virtuous people set up in market-places as paragons of virtue to posterity. Excessive ambition is not encouraged. People live in harmony. The syphogrants behave like fathers. The prince is known by a little sheaf of corn carried before him and a bishop by a taper of wax. The magistrates are all incorruptible and impartial. The Utopian laws are simple and plain. Every Utopian is his own lawyer. The Utopians have no faith in leagues between nations, believing that the fellowship of nature knits people together with love and benevolence. Europe's holy and inviolable leagues administer no true justice at all.

Section eight, "Military Affairs," describes the Utopians' attitude toward war. They detest war. They have military drills just to defend their country or drive out tyrants. When in battle, they prefer victory by strategy to that with bloodshed. They wage war only to remove injustice to themselves or their friends. They usually hire mercenaries to fight for them. The Utopians all fight with courage and honor; women are encouraged to fight along with their men. They defend those cities which surrender and punish those trying to hold out. They make the conquered pay the cost of war as well as tribute to them. Section nine, "Utopian Religions," says that most Utopians worship Mithra, an everlasting godly power, father of all, maker and ruler of the world. Religious tolerance is a virtue; bigotry and fanaticism are condemned. There exist various kinds of religions such as the Christian faith. King Utopus conquered the island because of the religious strife there, and he made laws on free worship, gentle conversion, and punishment of intolerance and violence by exile or bondage. One Christian fanatic was banished. The Utopians believe that souls do not die with the body and that the world runs on governed by a divine power. They despise those who refuse to embrace these tenets and deprive those people of all honors. They also believe that the souls of beasts are immortal. They lament unwilling death but honor a willing one. The dead are present invisible among the living and deter them from dishonesty. The Utopians despise soothsayers but worship miracles as proof of the power of the divine God. There are two religious sects devoted to good works in *Utopia*, one the holier, advocating celibacy and vegetarianism, and the other the wiser, embracing matrimony and honest pleasures of life. There are in every city 13 priests and one bishop, all carefully chosen by a secret election. These are held in high esteem. The priests keep the first and last day of every month and year as holy days. The churches are gorgeous and spacious. All sects agree that Mithra represents divine majesty. On holy days wives kneel before their husbands and children before their parents for confession so that they attend church service with a clear conscience. They are dressed in white, offer no sacrifices and light up no candles. People fall on their knees before the priest. They pray together.

According to Hythloday, there is nothing private in Utopia, no one has anything, yet everyone is rich. With the Utopian commonwealth as a point of departure, he goes on to examine the justice of other nations, where the idle rich enjoy without having to work while the poor toil and sweat yet have little on the table. There is an evident conspiracy of the rich robbing the poor there. Money is the root of all evils. If the desire for money is banished from social life, poverty would decrease or disappear. More in his comment at the end of the Tale wishes that "our cities" would learn from the Utopian commonwealth.

Utopia offers the best ideal social system possible that could be offered at the time. It outlines the ideal set of basics governing human institutions and regulating human life. It is amazing how More figured out the nuts and bolts of the best government and lifestyle for man. Utopia is an imaginary country where democracy replaces tyranny, commonwealth replaces private property, the work ethic is valued and idleness frowned upon, there is no distinction between the rich and the poor, education is free for all, money is abolished and gold and silver depreciated, religious tolerance is enforced and bigotry outlawed, and there is peace and abundance for all. On the whole the Utopian system represents a substantial improvement over the existing system of England where, as Hytholday (the fictional character) comments in Book I, problems pile up and cry for attention such as the hanging of the thieves, the plague of the veterans and the unemployed serving men, the breeding of sheep that brought the country to ruin, the juxtaposition of poverty alongside luxury, the princes and their wars, their means of raising money and their false councilors, and private property which lies at the root of all evil.

Apart from its idealism, the picture of Utopia also shows up some problems in clear outline. One of these is its strict adherence to conformity, which would result in the curbing of individual rights and freedom and would in the long run encompass the collapse of the visionary system. The emphasis on uniformity in dress, behavior, and lifestyle would deprive life of its intrinsic diversity and complexity and reduce human existence to a simplicity and monotony totally incompatible with human nature. There is also the slave system, which allows some humans to be superior and rule over their fellow creatures. This is the obvious injustice which goes against individual dignity and self-worth. An offender can be punished by means such as a prison term or even banishment or even death and still keep their sense of self-respect, but should not be reduced to the indignity of slavery, which relegates them to utter nonentity. Furthermore, in the book's discussion of wars, there is a hint of possible superpower politics at work, however faint it may be. It is difficult to draw the line where self-defense ends and helping friends to remove injustice begins. The idea of helping friends leaves a wide leeway for maneuver for people of undue ambition. Then there is patriarchy to consider. The Utopian society is clearly male-dominated: there is no mention of gender equality, no equal opportunity for administrative and religious jobs, no clear recognition of the female sex and their rights, but a very clear indication that the women folk have to submit to their men folk as, for instance, they have to kneel before their men and confess on days of religious observance. All these "weaknesses" reveal the force of the temporal and spatial constraints out of which even a man of genius like More cannot break with complete success. Despite all these, however, Utopia is unique in more than one way and forms a direct, positive contrast to England and Europe of the time.

Chapter 3 The Elizabethan Age • Spenser • Sidney • Marlowe

The Elizabethan Age (1558-1625): A Brief Introduction

The Elizabethan period began with the ascension of Queen Elizabeth I in 1558, and its afterglow shone well beyond the 16th century. To see the new queen and her contribution in proper perspective, it is necessary to go back in history a little. After the Norman conquest, the Norman line of kings sat on the throne for some 90 years and gave place to the Angevin kings (or the Plantangenets) in 1154. King Henry II and his descendants stayed in power for 245 years until they were superseded by the House of Lancaster in 1399. Then the House of York took over but was short-lived, lasting only 24 years. Then the War of the Roses (1455-1483) broke out and ended with the reconciliation of the two rival houses of York and Lancaster. Henry VII of the Tudors became king in 1485, and was succeeded by his son Henry VIII (1509-1547). This terrible king began as a promising youth of learning and love for learned men, but the long reign turned him into a bloodthirsty tyrant. He is best remembered now for having had six wives, one after another, two of whom he beheaded, and two he divorced. His divorce with Queen Catherine led to his break with the Roman Catholic Church and inadvertently paved the way for the inroads of Protestantism. The country was thus split between the Catholic and the Protestant faith. Henry VIII is remembered also for heading Thomas More for dissenting with him on his divorce and other matters. After Henry VIII his son, a sickly boy, was king for a few years and then died so that his sister, "Bloody" Mary, a devout Catholic, became queen, and had the opportunity to persecute the Protestants as she pleased. Her five-year reign threw the nation into complete discord and chaos. She left no offspring behind.

Her successor, her half sister, Queen Elizabeth I, was a different individual altogether. She was shrewd and tactful to a fault. On the continent, she made friends with the opposing sides of the religious conflict—Catholic Spain and Protestant France, and at home she set about uniting the divided country. She made the Church of England steer strictly the middle of the road, leaning toward neither the Catholics nor the Protestants, and effectively practiced religious tolerance to the relief of the people. She was the head of the Church but she behaved as if she were not, and she was the master of the house in her relation to Parliament, but she acted as though she were not. In addition, she encouraged learning and adventures, and was a great patron of literature. As a result, she was able to secure a 30-year period of peace for the country so that England slowly but steadily crawled to the zenith of wealth and power during her reign. When Francis Drake defeated the Spanish Armada in 1588, England became the first sea power in the world. This was the point at which the expansion of the British Empire began. Queen Elizabeth I was able to say on her deathbed to her people, "You may have had queens and kings, good or bad, but you'll never have one who loves you better."

The Elizabethan age was one in which Renaissance transformed Chaucer's Medieval England into Shakespeare's modern one. The intellectual energy that gushed out of the Renaissance and Reformation was amazing and spectacular, and the spirit of adventure permeated all the fields of activity. When this energy was channeled into the creation of literature, it made the Elizabethan age one of the few greatest in the literary history of the world. Genius was unrestrained, and imagination ran wild. With no hard and fast literary standards to follow in literary creation, experiments were legion, everyone was out for a new form, and the thirst for the unique was unquenchable. Emotion received its most ample and adequate expression in the literary works of the period. It was also an age in which people felt little or no restraint in their behavior. All the three major departments of literature—poetry, drama, and prose—bloomed, and countless authors vied in offering their very best in a tremendous outburst of creative power. It is true that many "poor, poor, dumb names" (to quote William Hazlitt [1778-1830]) have sunk into an obscurity from which it would be hard to resurrect them, but many others have stood the test of time for the admiration of posterity. All in all, the age furnished a fertile soil, as it were, on which a plethora of fresh flowers and plants grew to survive.

The Elizabethan age can be divided into three sub-periods. The first of these stretches over two decades (1557-1579), beginning with the printing of *Tottel's Miscellany* and concluding with the publication of Edmund Spenser's *The Shepheardes Calendar*. The main contributors to *Tottel's Miscellany* were Thomas Wyatt (1503-1542), who introduced the sonnet into the country, and Henry Howard, Earl of Surrey (1517-1547), who brought the blank verse into English poetry (blank verse being rhyme-less iambic pentameter or a line of ten syllables in five iambs, a rhythmic unit of two syllables with the unstressed followed by the stressed syllable). Both forms became perfect poetic media in the hands of Shakespeare and Milton. *The Shepheardes Calendar*, Spenser's first known work, immediately placed its author at the head of the English poets of his day. In addition, over one hundred playwrights rose to meet the fast growing public demand for more literature.

The second phase covers some two decades from 1580 through 1599, the year of Spenser's death. This was a period of intense literary activity in which the greatest Elizabethan writers made their presence felt. The literary outcomes of these twenty years were seldom if ever equaled in originality and force in literary history. In poetry Spenser came out with his *The Faerie Queene*, and Philip Sidney (1554-1586) wrote some of his best sonnets in *Astrophel and Stella* (1591). In prose Sidney's *Apologie for Poetrie* (1595), his pastoral Romance, *Arcadia* (1590), and John Lyly's (1554-1606) *Eupheus* are all among the best attempts to come out of the period. Lyly's *Eupheus* is slim in plot interest. Its two parts tell a story of love with ample discussions and letters on love. The book is remembered today for its quaint style with its extravagant, conceited, and florid language and its excessive antitheses and similes. It was an attempt on the part of Renaissance England to make its language as grand as the classical languages of Latin and Greek. Incidentally, "euphemism," the word that John Lyly contributed to the English language, is a term often derogatory in meaning.

In drama the exuberance showed itself well in the great number of great plays that were written and staged at the time. First, there were the "University Wits," each and every one of whom was a man of genius, out with their brilliant creations, and would have all taken up a lot more space in literary history had there not towered above them the all-time Shakespeare. These "Wits" include Christopher

Marlowe (1564-1593), Robert Greene (1560-1592), George Peele (1558-1597), Thomas Lodge (1558-1625), Thomas Nash (1567-1601), and Thomas Kyd (1557-1595). All were graduates either from Oxford or Cambridge or both, had a short but brilliant literary career that placed them among the ancestors of modern English writers, and most left the scene as soon as they came mainly as a result of their reckless and dissolute Bohemian lifestyle for which the Elizabethan age was famous or notorious. Marlowe's career was short but stormy. Greene wrote remarkable prose pamphlets, a good number of plays, and some songs of poetic merit. Peele showed his skill at blank verse and wrote, among other things, *Old Wives Tale*, which helped to inspire Milton in his *Comus*. Kyd is known for his terrible tragedies of blood, thunder, and horrors, *Jeronimo* and *Cornelia*, both products of the vogue of blood, massacre, treachery, and intrigue of the time. His *Spanish Tragedy* (1592) shares quite a few thematic and formal features with Shakespeare's *Hamlet*—the avenging of a dear one's murder, a ghost revealing the truth, the major character feigning madness, and the mechanism of the play within the play. And he might have written some play, entitled *Ur-Hamlet*, on the subject of Hamlet, but it is well lost now. Nash was an effective prose writer and not much of a dramatist. Lodge's *Rosalynde* gave the storyline for Shakespeare's *As You Like It*. The work of the University Wits paved the way for the rise of Shakespeare, who had come out of his "dark period" and begun writing.

In this period Shakespeare wrote sonnets and some 20 of his 37 plays and alarmed the University Wits so that Robert Greene warned his fellow wits of "the only Shakescene," "the upstart crow beautified with our feathers." In addition, a group of writers appeared on the horizon with their impressive literary activity. These included Ben Jonson (1573-1637), Thomas Dekker (1570-1641), John Webster (1580-1625), Thomas Middleton (1570-1627), George Chapman (1559-1634), and a host of other writers that rose to varying degrees of prominence. Special mention should be made of Thomas North (1535-1601) and his renowned translation of Plutarch's *Parallel Lives of Famous Greeks and Romans* (known often as *Plutarch's Lives*). Plutarch (46-120 AD) was a Greek essayist, biographer and philosopher; his *Parallel Lives* was one of the best books to come out of the ancient world. Thomas North's translation of the book was a healthy influence on the literary outburst of the time, especially on Shakespeare who borrowed plots and incidents from North for at least three of his Roman plays. There was also Francis Bacon (1561-1626), publishing some of his first essays. It is good to note that, for the first time in history, writers began to make a living by writing for the theater or the publishers.

The third phase spans over some three decades (1599-1625). This was the period in which Shakespeare finished all his later plays, and Ben Jonson did almost the whole of his work. The two collaborators, Francis Beaumont (1584-1616) and John Fletcher (1579-1625), wrote good plays such as *The Maid's Tragedy* and *Philaster*, and John Fletcher's *The Two Noble Kinsmen* has been seen as one of the distinguished dramas from the period, though it is good to note that their effort to cater to the vulgar taste of the audience helped sow the seeds of immorality and evil in the theater. John Webster wrote his best works *The White Devil* (or *Vittoria Corombona*), one of the most glorious of the time, and *The Duchess of Malfi*. Webster was a serious and hard-working writer with his high poetic gift. He portrayed a world of violence, almost amoral, where love, truth, honor, loyalty, and meaningful relationship no longer exist, and people engage in violence and brutality. In the meantime, Thomas Middleton continued his career as a versatile playwright, writing high tragedy with true-to-life characters and well-woven plots. His memorable works included *The Changeling* and *Women Beware Women*. Then there was George Chapman's translation of the Homeric classics, *Iliad* and *Odyssey*, which won him the title "a translator of the prince of poets." *Chapman's Homer*, as his translation has been popularly known, remained for two hundred years the one source of information on Homer for all those who were unable to read the ancient poet in the original. An apt example that comes to mind is, of course, John Keats (1795-1821), who immortalized Chapman's work in one of his well-known sonnets, "On First Looking into Chapman's Homer" (1816). Chapman was a poet and a playwright. On one occasion (1605) he wrote *Eastward Ho* in collaboration with Ben Jonson and Christopher Marlowe and was thrown in prison on account of its criticism of the King. His literary powers were such that he was identified as the "rival poet" of Shakespeare. With regard to Bacon, he did his best work in the period, dominated English prose literature for decades, and won for himself a singular place in English literary history. Last but not least was the stupendous undertaking of the translation of the *Bible* from Greek to English

(1604-1611), the outcome of which was the grand, almost impeccable *The Authorized Version of the Bible*, or *King James' Bible*, still the best of its kind today, unequaled in precision, beauty, and power.

The Elizabethan age is famous in every possible sense of the word, in volume, quality, variety, originality, and permanence. The first sub-period was basically a preparation for the coming of Shakespeare, while the third and the half century after it continue the momentum for the rise of the next greatest landmark in poetry—John Milton (1608-1674). After that the cooling process began, in which Dryden (1631-1700), Pope (1688-1744) and Johnson (1709-1784) were to play their parts in history. The pattern of rise and fall will thus continue as it has always done. [1]

Edmund Spenser (1552-1599)

Spenser was educated at Cambridge and served under some men of prominence such as the Earl of Leicester, Queen Elizabeth's favorite, and Lord Grey of Wilton, Lord Deputy of Ireland. In the household of the former, he met Philip Sidney and dedicated his *The Shepheardes Calendar* to him. Later he went to live in Ireland where the queen gave him a gift of a castle and some land. The first three books of his masterpiece, *The Faerie Queene*, came out in 1590 and made him the best of poets of his time. Then he published another three books in 1596 and became the "most poetical" of all poets. When his house was burned in the Irish rebellion of 1598, he fled to London and died there the next year. He was buried near Chaucer in the Poet's Corner of Westminster Abbey. Spenser's major works include *The Shepheardes Calendar* (1579), *The Faerie Queene* (1590, 1596), *Colin Clouts Come Home Againe* (1595), two odes to Marriage—*Epithalamium* (1595) and *Prothalamium* (1596), and *Amoretti* (1595), a collection of sonnets.

Spenser was the greatest non-dramatic poet of the period under discussion. He read and loved Chaucer and saw him as his pattern in literary creation. He was determined to revive Chaucer's poetic legacy and reinvent English poetry. His first known major work, *The Shepheardes Calendar,* consists of 12 pastoral eclogues, one for each month of the year. It was modeled mainly upon two classical pastoral works—the *Idylls* of the Greek poet Theocritus (3rd century BC) and the *Eclogues* of the Roman poet Virgil's (70-19 BC). The classical eclogue is a form of pastoral poetry which generally depicts, often in the form of dialogues between shepherds or of soliloquies, the everyday life of country people, their feelings and attitudes, and their simple life of harmony with nature. It often serves as a means of making critical comments upon contemporary life. Spenser's *Calendar* abounds with such observations on the religious strife and political turbulence of his day. [2]

A fact to note about the text of the *Calendar* is that it is full of archaic or "Chaucerian" words, which Spenser meant as an echo to Chaucer and also an attempt to bring into relief a rustic effect. The difficulty of comprehension that this can bring about is addressed in the text by a commentator, "E.K." by name, who appends a "Glosse" to each eclogue to explain such words as well as any difficult concepts that may appear in the eclogues. The identity of E.K., who also wrote a general introduction to the *Calendar* and praised Spenser as a new poet, has been a point of interest for inquiry: he may be a close friend to the poet or simply the poet himself. The eclogues in the *Calendar* fall into three groups—plaintive, recreative, and moral (E.K.'s classification), dealing with different themes such as love, religion, and poetry. One eclogue that offers a good illustration is the *October Aegloga Decima*, or the tenth eclogue, which discusses the contempt in which poetry is held and the author's defense of the art as work of a divine gift and celestial inspiration. The dialogue occurs between Cuddie, a poet figure, and Piers, his fellow shepherd. The woodcut prefacing the eclogue shows the pastoral setting against the background of a palace.

The Faerie Queene is a grand epic poem. Fusing adroitly the strands of legend, fable, and praise of Elizabeth I's England in itself, its ambitious plan was to include twelve books of twelve cantos each, featuring one knight in one canto as the embodiment of one of the twelve Aristotelian virtues and the knight's enemy as that of one of the twelve vices. The Faerie Queene, Gloriana, would eventually marry King Arthur—the paragon of supreme virtue. Spenser had time to finish only six books and a fragment of the seventh book, and the epic broke off suddenly. But it is already a work of magnitude with its many varied excellences. The six books tell respectively about the Red Cross Knight of Holiness, the Knight of Temperance, the legend of chastity, that of friendship, the Knight of Justice, and the Knight of Courtesy. The poem was intended to be a paean of the "glorious" reign of Queen Elizabeth in the person of the Faerie Queen Gloriana. The epic is so long that one critic sees it as "the only long poem that a lover of poetry can sincerely wish longer." The work is now read mostly for the enjoyment of Spenser's creative virtuosity and appreciation of his literary importance.[3]

Spenser's effort to write a new poetry is best illustrated by his courageous experimentation with the meters. In the *Calendar*, he used 13 different kinds of meters: three kinds of couplets, three kinds of 4-line stanzas, and three kinds of 6-line stanzas in addition to stanzas of eight, nine and ten lines and a sestina. Some of these he invented, some he adapted, but most were new. Further innovations appeared in the special rhyme scheme of the Spenserian sonnets, and in the Spenserian stanza in his *The Faerie Queene*. The Spenserian stanza, which has continued to be a popular stanzaic form for dreamy and meditative works, is a nine-line stanza of 8 lines in iambic pentameter plus an iambic hexameter (6-foot line). The rhyme scheme is abab bcbc c. Spenser has been the model for many poets of different generations. Shakespeare's plays reveal traces of acquaintance with Spenser's poems. Milton calls him his "poetical father." Dryden and Pope were both indebted to him. And so were James Thomson (1700-1748), Wordsworth, Byron, Shelley, Keats, Tennyson, and hundreds more. Spenser is one of the most important of English poets.[4]

Philip Sidney (1554-1586)

Sidney was a very popular poet in his own time. He was educated at Oxford and was widely read. His missions took him across the English Channel and put him in contact with European excellence to which he was hypersensitive. The experimental French poets and the classic beauties of such poets as Petrarch and the overriding Renaissance freshness all proved conducive to his imagination. Sidney was devoted to helping create a lovely, "brazen" world of poetry for people (as he states in his *Apologie for Poetrie*). His experimental daring was amazing. He drew on classical traditions, imbibed the Renaissance spirit, tried with different rhymes, meters, and stanzas, and strove untiringly for excellence in versification. He was never ready to settle for the second best, and took enormous delight in tackling problems that challenged his intellect. And nothing was a better reward for him than the discovery of something new. Impatient with courtly verses and conventional expressions, he set out in quest of a new and better poetry. There was nothing in verse that he did not regard as his legitimate province of experiment: rhyme, meter, line, stanza, and overall form, and his tireless effort proved immensely rewarding to him and to the readers as he came up with a variety of new rhyme schemes, lines with a varying number of syllables, and different stanza forms and meters. His verse reveals his stunning accomplishments in poetic techniques, the variety and diversity of which alone are enough to dazzle the readers. Sidney left behind a good number of sonnets, lyrics and pastoral poems all notable for their formal virtuosity. He was, along with Edmund Spenser, one of the two most important poets to break through the dullness of English poetry of the time and pave the way for the success of other subsequent literary careers that made the Elizabethan age flourish into one of the most distinguished periods in literary history. [5]

A good number of Sidney's poems appear in *Arcadia* (1593), his pastoral prose romance, which these verses punctuate either as eclogues between the five books of the romance, or in the form of speeches or songs for its characters. These compositions showcase the astounding sweep of his poetic gift. Both the lyrics and the eclogues are a good demonstration of his consummate techniques and the intensity of his experimental enthusiasm. The song, "Ye Godherd Gods," is for instance written in double sestina. In addition, Sidney's subjects in the poems correlate to the thematic features of the romance well—the love laments, elegies, an epithalamion, comic pieces, and reflections. Some of the songs such as those of Philisides' (said to represent the poet himself) can touch serious ground like meditating on the human condition. The country of Arcadia has become, ever since, a symbol for pastoral life with the blue sky, the rising sun, the nightingales, the sheltering trees, the wooded hills, the valleys with their refreshing rivers, meadows, flowers, thickets, birds, the serene pastures, the pretty lambs, the singing shepherds and shepherdesses, and all that help make for its civil wildness. The story is one in which the lover is entangled in an emotional tug of war between the two poles on the emotional spectrum: passion and reason, pain and bliss, hope and despair. The plot is well knit, enriched with its disguises and melodrama.

Sidney's sonnet cycle *Astrophel and Stella* (1591) contains his best poetic compositions of 108 sonnets and 11 songs. As a sonnet sequence, this was probably the first of its kind ever to appear in English literary history. It tells a love story between Astrpophel (the Starlover) and Stella (the Star), supposedly referring to the poet's real or fictional love for Penelope Devereux, wife of Lord Robert Rich. The sonnets do not offer a sequential plot; they reveal Astrophel's mind. Astrophel falls in love with Stella, secretly admires her, feels happy at intimations of her returning his love, but also torn between passion and reason. Nothing happens in the end, and the lovers part company. Most of time it is Astrophel talking, living through the stages of his love odyssey, and Stella does not show up though she is heard in the dialogues of some of the songs. The sonnets come, as Sidney claims in sonnet 1, straight from his heart: he sees the "feet" of others (in the sense of a beaten path or written work) as a road block in his way (of invention [ll. 11]), and decides to "look into [my own] heart and write" (l. 14). This is another way of saying that he does not like to follow others' footsteps and that he would like to take the road not yet taken. The outcome of his endeavor is of course the beautiful works of art in the sonnet cycle. There are the visible traces of Petrarchan conventions, it is true, but Sidney manages to put a personal stamp on his work with his dexterous use of the English rhyming couplets and his own simple language. These poems function differently within the frame of the story: some touching on Stella's beauty, others on Astrophel's self-searching and analysis, and still others on the writing of love poetry. The songs dotting *Astrophel and Stella* here and there are also fresh and charming lyrics both in theme and in form.

Sidney's *Apologie for Poetrie* (1595) defends the noble nature of poetry and its moral value against Puritan criticism and elevates poetry as the supreme form of art that helps enrich and make nature. He touches on the nature of the poet and poetry, compares poetry with both philosophy and history and finds the latter wanting. He dwells on the variety of poetry like the pastoral, elegiac, satiric, comic, tragic, lyric, and heroic, answers the charges against poetry, and discusses both ancient and modern versification. It is at once graceful and cogent as an effective defense.

English Drama: A Sketchy Account [6]

As the Elizabethan age is in the main the age for drama, here is perhaps a place as good as any to offer a sketch of the history of English drama. The drama had gone through a number of phases over the centuries including those of the mysteries, the miracles, the morality, the interlude, and the true drama. The mysteries were religious or sacred dramas that the church found one most effective way to instill Christian teachings in the hearts of the people. These dramatized the biblical mysteries, both from the Old and the New Testaments, such as the stories of the patriarchs (like Noah and Abraham), the gospel stories like the virgin birth, the crucifixion, and the resurrection. The plays were staged on religious holidays (such as Easter and Christmas) with the holy clerics acting out the parts. The phase of miracle plays that followed has often been indistinguishable from that of the mysteries; indeed the two terms and the two phases they represent denote often one concept to many people. Maybe there is some hair-splitting here. If we treat these as two separate entities, it is more for the sake of clear exposition. The phase of the miracles began when the lives and the legends of the saints were acted out along with the mysteries, which introduced a change significant but at first imperceptible. The change, substantial in nature as the human element was represented along with the divine, became more and more noticeable and the stage productions grew more secular and less religious. The most famous miracle play was probably *The Harrowing of the Hell.* The mysteries and the miracles were first brought in by the Normans at the beginning of the 12th century, flourished in the 13th, became a huge business in the 14th, and reached their full potential in the 15th and the 16th before they gave way to newer kinds of productions. The extant miracle plays are classified by the towns where they were put on. These include the Chester Cycle, the York Cycle, the Conventry Cycle, and the Wakefield or Towneley Cycle. Altogether about 150 such plays have survived the ravages of time.

Then new dramas came on stage and became more popular. One of these was known as the interlude and the other the morality play. These two were not always clearly distinguishable, the difference probably being only this, that the interludes came earlier in time, were generally shorter in length, simpler in plot, and requiring fewer characters. They were performed at court or for nobles or in colleges. The most famous interlude is *The Four P's* in which all the names of the four characters begin with a P—Palmer, Pardoner, Pothecary, and Peddler. Shakespeare's *A Midsummer Night's Dream* contains an interlude entitled *Pyramus and Thisbe*. Generally the interludes and the morality plays were allegorical, dealing with moral subjects relating to the real facts of life like virtues and vices, and concerned with teaching people to be good and virtuous. These were peopled with one-dimensional characters personifying human qualities, with characters as abstractions bearing quaint names like Good Deeds, Knowledge, Beauty, and Death. The most famous morality play was the 15th-century *Everyman*. Probably a Buddhist work in origin, the play presents a parable about one aspect of life, i.e. the judgment day that all have to face. The major character, Everyman by name, lives happily in the company of his people until one day he meets Death for the last reckoning. Now he asks in turn the people around him—Fellowship, Kindred, Cousin, Goods, Beauty, Strength, Discretion, and Five-Wits—to go together with him on his journey down there, and finds no one, except Good Deeds, willing and ready for the undertaking. The basic theme is well expressed in a line Good Deeds utters, "All earthly things is [sic] but vanity," and the only life worthwhile striving for is life in heaven. Another good example of the morality play was *Magnyfycence* by John Skelton (1460?-1529). Skelton was one distinguished poet of his time, wedged between the medieval and the Elizabethan ages. He was noted for the style known as the "Skeltonical verse," a headlong voluble kind of doggerel with its quick recurring rhymes, and full of fascinating, baffling, bawdy verbal games. He is occasionally mentioned as an influence in modern and contemporary poetry.

The true drama that appeared next in the Elizabethan age had its deep roots in the miracle and morality plays. It swept all the other categories off the stage with its representation of real life as lived by real people. Here were real people with real names with no abstract personifications, involved in real events that were culled from reality, and replicating human behavior in their daily existence. Plots evolved around intriguing true-to-life stories in some conceivable order, which were normally sequential at first in well-arranged acts and scenes. The first true drama was probably Nicholas Udall's comedy, *Ralph Royster Doyster* (1567), an adaptation of some classic—Roman—work, and the first wholly English comedy was a domestic drama entitled *Gammer Gurton's Needle* (1553/1575), which is famous still for its old drinking-song with its interesting refrain about the belley's insatiable desire for "the good ale" despite its effect upon the body as a whole. Then tragedies followed such as the one by Thomas Sackville (1536-1608) in collaboration with Thomas Norton—*Gorboduc* (1561). Then the Elizabethan age arrived with its robust and profuse dramatic productions by the University Wits and by Shakespeare among a host of other minor lights.

Christopher Marlowe (1564-1593)

The most preeminent figure among the University Wits was Christopher Marlowe, who was the greatest playwright before the rise of Shakespeare. Marlowe's advent and demise are both archetypal in history. A genius of a rare kind with a huge amount of potential crying for an outlet, Marlowe represents the creative exuberance and explosive energy in which his age excelled. Within the space of some six years after he left Cambridge University, he published three great tragedies in quick succession—*Tamburlaine the Great* at the age of 23, *The Jew of Malta* at 25, and *The Tragical History of Doctor Faustus* at 28 in addition to a lot of remarkable poems such as *Hero and Leander* and *The Passionate Shepherd*, and left the scene in a sudden death at 29.

Young as he was, he lived at the right point of history to taste the full gamut of human experience of his time with its conspiracies, chaos and upheavals, and matured enough to see the age's actual need for people of a superman character. Hence the magnificent gallery of overreaching tragic heroes in his plays. *Tamburlaine*, the play which pushed the young playwright instantly to prominence, is a dream vision in blank verse (rhyme-less iambic pentameter). It is about the life of Tamburlaine or Timur the Lame, the terrible 14th-century Mongol conqueror (said to be a descendant of Genghis Khan [1162-1227]), whose irresistible troops played havoc with vast areas of the world from Turkestan to Siberia to Persia and India. Marlowe based his work on a translation of the biography by a Spanish scholar. The play is divided into two parts. The first of these traces the legendary conqueror's rise from humble origins and his conquest of the Turkish Empire, and the second deals with his continued victories in Babylon where he made the defeated kings draw his chariot. There is also a love interest in the form of Zenocrate, an Egyptian princess, whom Tamburlaine captures and spares out of love. The tragedy ends with the death of the both of them. Tamburlaine is portrayed as a man of superman ambition and energy with his exuberant aggressive spirit and high sense of accomplishment. His tragic flaw is his insatiability that drives him to his never-ending endeavor for acquisition.

The same can be said of the Jew in Marlowe's *The Jew of Malta*. Barabas, the rich Jew of Malta, refuses to pay as the Governor demands and is stripped of all his wealth as well as his house. He avenges himself by scheming to poison the Governor's daughter and her lover. He becomes a traitor when Malta is under Turkish siege and is made Governor in return for his service. Now he begins to plot the destruction of the Turkish troops by means of a collapsible floor, beneath which he places a boiling cauldron for the victims. He is betrayed and thrown into the cauldron himself. His tragic flaw is his superman-ness—his lust and greed and his capacity for anger, foul play, and evil when he deems it necessary to achieve his ends.[7]

Now let's take a closer look at the play for which Marlowe is chiefly remembered today, *The Tragical History of Doctor Faustus* (1592-1593). It was based on a German book *Faustbuch* or *The History of Doctor Faustus* (1587). Faust was a real person, a 16th-century German magician (1488-1541). Marlowe wrote the 13-scene tragedy in collaboration with others. The play was staged in Germany and led to the popularity of the Faust legend and Faust drama, and also to the interest of Goethe (1749-1832) two centuries later, whose drama, *Faust*, came out in two parts in 1808 and 1832 respectively. Marlowe's tragedy places emphasis on the cosmic nature of Faustus' quest for knowledge and power. The first part of the play tells of Faustus' dissatisfaction with earthly knowledge and of his pact with the devil, Mephistophilis, the bond that he signs in blood, for selling his soul in return for 24 years of supreme power and joy. The second part tells of Faustus' satisfaction with his newly acquired knowledge and power with which, among other things, he plays tricks on the Pope, conjures up, from the dead, Alexander the Great and his beautiful paramour at a palace feast, causes a pair of horns to grow on the head of an irritating knight, and offers a duchess ripe southern grapes in the middle of winter. The third section concludes with Faustus' soul being dragged down to Hell as the pact requires. When the last hour comes, Faustus tries to repent and pray to God to save him from eternal damnation. In despair he asks the devil to let him have Helen of Troy as his lover. He has his last desire and is hauled down to Hell.

The play is famous both for its thematic and formal features. Thematically, the image of Faustus is historically significant as a "photo" record of the new man, the modern man, the Renaissance humanist, who steps into modern light with all the glitter of Reformation and Renaissance. Faustus, the medieval man, has already had about everything including knowledge and power to make him happy, but he is not happy. Insatiability is his name. He sees the world as one of infinite power and profit and regards all that moves between the two poles as at his beck and call. He wants to be a superman, a virtual god figure, and he becomes one, though he has to pay an exorbitant price. Thus Faustus represents the archetypal Renaissance humanist of the 16th century, and a supreme specimen of Everyman for all time. Marlowe's tragedy marks a new phase in human epistemology, the one in which man emerges from his initial total submission to external forces and awakens to his own importance and power and begins to assert himself. As he is human, his potential is circumscribed and he often ends up overreaching himself, but the striving endows his life with meaning and purpose and makes it worth living. Formally, the play uses some dramatic devices like the choruses and the accompanying quarrels between the good angels and the evil ones. The three choruses in the play all serve to help guide the readers to keep track of the whereabouts of the man and his thought process. The constant verbal fights between the opposing angels serve at least two purposes, one of which is the indication they furnish for the readers, that Faustus lives still in part in the traditional religious shadow. The other purpose is more subtle and technically more attractive: that they help externalize the continual inner struggle that goes on in Faustus' mind, or his incessant interior dialogue. It is obvious that Faustus debates within himself all the while whether it is worthwhile doing what he is doing.

Marlowe loves the impossible. All the three tragic heroes in his dramas are cosmic in appetite and behavior. They defy all limitations and crave for the best of all in the universe. This is all a reflection of the daring Renaissance humanist in Marlowe himself. Marlowe strove for perfection and settled for nothing short of the best. As a result, he put some popular material in the classic form and gave the drama a new form of verse, the blank verse, which became a powerful instrument in his hands. And his "mighty line" (as Ben Jonson says of his poetry) has been well known through the ages. He was the only dramatist of the time who ever touched Shakespeare in power and beauty so that, at one point in time, some critics even went as far as to suggest that, had there not been Marlowe, there would not have been explainable Shakespeare.

Chapter 4 Shakespeare • Bacon • Jonson • King James' Bible

William Shakespeare is the most popular and most widely respected writer in all English literature. To show his popularity, more of the popular sayings we have come from Shakespeare than from any other source except from the Bible. His plays are still performed after all these years, and his poems are still read, despite the fact that the language has changed since his days, which makes problems for his readers.

Shakespeare was born on April 26, 1564 in Stratford-on-Avon. He attended grammar school and had some education ("small Latin and less Greek" as Ben Jonson says of him). But he did not finish as his father, once a respectful town official and businessman, was involved in financial difficulties, and he had to drop out to help support the family. He tried to make up for the deficiency in his education through wide reading, and was keen and quick to pick up things new. At 18 he married Anne Hathaway, and three years later, he went to London and stayed there for a period of five years (1587-1592), known now as "the dark period" of his life. All that is known about him in those years is that he may have worked with a theater, moved up the ladder from the bottom, and managed to emerge as a well-known actor-playwright. He became the "upstart crow beautified with our feathers," as one university wit, Robert Greene, called him when warning his fellow wits of Shakespeare's sudden rise in his malicious 1592 pamphlet. In 1594 Shakespeare joined a theater company, the Lord Chamberlain's Men, and later became its playwright and part owner. In 1597, when he was 33, he went back home and bought a house called New Place, and retired at 49. He died on April 23, 1616 and was buried at Stratford. [1]

Shakespeare has been said to have the "Midas' touch." Whatever he happened to do turned out to be a great success. He excelled in the literary field characteristic of the age of English Renaissance—poetry and drama. All his works have weathered well through time and resisted the threat of neglect and oblivion. First, there are his four poems, *Venus and Adonis*, *The Rape of Lucrece*, *The Lover's Complaint*, and *The Passionate Pilgrim*, all works of his early youth, and unequalled in their sweet enthusiasm, luscious sensuality, and unique humanity. These exquisite compositions draw from sources such as Greek and Roman mythology and some semi-historical and semi-legendary events of Roman history, and are all colored by the poet's own experience with simple and passionate life. Shakespeare has been known as a "physical" poet, and his poetry is alive with its sounds, colors, odors, and fine textures. The art of Shakespeare envelopes these poems with a halo of permanent fascination.

Shakespeare's sonnets, 154 in total, were first published as a collection in 1609. The dates of composition of the individual poems are impossible to determine, and so is the identity of the people to whom the poems are addressed: a young man, for instance, that appears in a good number of these poems, and a dark-skinned woman in some others. The sonnets fall essentially into three groupings: over 100 of these seem to be addressed to a young man, some 20 seem to be concerned with a young woman, and of these two (153-154) read like free translations of a Greek poem of about the fifth century AD. Upon publication, the sonnets drew instant attention for their grace in form, depth in thought, and vivacity in tone. They are peerless in freshness, poetical beauty, and human interest. The little love songs, which love, passion, and sparks of wisdom combine to illuminate, reveal a clear vision of life and people that few with less insight could hope to possess. They are in essence the Renaissance paean of man, his spirit, and his values, and as such they are a faithful record of the mood and tenor of the times. For example, sonnets 18 and 65 both assert the power of literature to combat the ravages of time and declare the greatness of man and his immortality (as literature is man's creation). By the same token, sonnets 29 and 30 both exalt the power of love which effectively offsets the negativity of low self-esteem, anger and jealousy, and sad memories of the past. A good many of the sonnets are inspired by love. Sonnet 147 is a good example, writing as it does about love that amounts to infatuation and obsession. At the same time the poems are personal and can serve as a mirror in which the readers can see Shakespeare's reflection as an individual. Although the reflection is basically our conjecture, we have reason to believe that there is truth in our surmise. He has his mood swings, for instance. He is "oppressed with melancholy," unhappy with his humble origins and depressed with old woes and new (sonnet 45), he is restless, thirsty for love and good fortune, and he is hopeful despite everything as "Love's fire heats water, water cools not love" (154).[2]

But the bulk of Shakespeare's work is his plays, 37 in number, each one of which is still able to captivate modern audiences. Shakespeare's universe is a veritable microcosm of the human world, where almost all types of people exist and all kinds of events occur. His dramatic work is amazing in its variety: the histories and comedies of his early period (before 1600), the tragedies of the middle or "tragic" period (1600-1608), and the late period of romances or the period of serenity (1608-1612). The progression from one phase to the next indicates, in historical retrospect, the stages of growth in the playwright's awareness of life and the world of man.

The works of the first period are generally happy and cheerful. The plays such as *Henry IV* (1590-91), *Love's Labor's Lost* (1590), *Richard III* (1593), *Romeo and Juliet* (1595), *A Midsummer Night's Dream* (1595), *The Merchant of Venice* (1596), *The Merry Wives of Windsor* (1597), and *As You Like It* (1599)—all these dramas end happily (though *Romeo and Juliet* is essentially a tragedy and *The Merchant of Venice* is tragic for Shylock). As the playwright experienced life at closer quarters, and tasted personal tragedy, including the death of his only son, a note of frustration sets in in the works of the second, or the tragic period. All his major tragedies were written within the space of a few years: *Julius Caesar* (1599?), *Hamlet* (1601), *Othello* (1604), *King Lear* (1605), *Macbeth* (1606), *Antony and Cleopatra* (1607), and *Timon of Athens* (1607). Even the comedies written in the period, *All's Well That Ends Well* (1603) and *Measure for Measure* (1603), reveal a Shakespeare wearing a wry smile. The last period of his life was one of emotional tranquility when he must have won through pain and possibly a nervous breakdown to acceptance of the inevitability of life. The plays of the period include *Cymbeline* (1609), *Winter's Tale* (1610-11), and *The Tempest* (1611).

Shakespeare did not seem to have as much faith in his plays as he had in his poetry. His sonnet 18, entitled "Shall I Compare Thee to a Summer's Day," offers good testimony, ending as it does with "As long as men can breathe or eyes can see,/ So long lives this...," "this" here meaning this sonnet. In addition, when he left London on retirement, he made no attempt to collect and publish his plays, leaving the manuscripts to his theater. It was actually two fellow players who collected them for publication. The First Folio Edition came out in 1623 with Ben Jonson's famous memorial poem, and was followed by repeated later attempts to bring all the plays together. These included, among others, the first critical edition of Shakespeare (1709), Alexander Pope's edition (1725), Samuel Johnson's edition (1765), the third Variorum edition (1821), the Variorum edition of 1871, the Globe edition (1874), and the Oxford Old-spelling edition of the early 20th century.

Over the years there have been people who question the very existence of Shakespeare as a person. That doubt has been put to rest now, and so has the skepticism as to whether Marlowe or Bacon or Chapman wrote the plays. There have also been attempts to question Shakespeare's stature, but Shakespeare has become too much an impregnable monument in literary history for such feeble queries.

Shakespeare's cosmos is highly moral, the salient attributes of which are its sense of certitude and justice. It is one in which God sees to it that evil be punished and good rewarded. Shakespeare praises virtue and censures vice, and never allows vice to have its way for long. The light of wisdom and profound philosophy, which keeps flashing through his works to touch the readers' souls, comes from his keen observation of and careful rumination over the human condition. Because of his supreme understanding of human nature, he avoids being rigidly judgmental. He is tolerant of human foibles and faults and seldom if ever allows himself to condemn his characters. In painting these, he avoids the use of just one color—pure black or white, but always brings in some shades in between. With the exception of Iago in *Othello*, there is virtually no one who is a total villain in the whole of his works. Shakespeare sees the reflection of life as the legitimate job for a playwright ("to hold...the mirror up to nature" as Hamlet puts it [III, ii, l.23]) and views mankind as a confusing yet natural medley of good and evil. He believes in the goodness of human nature and man's potential for self-improvement.

Naturally, this dictates his manner of characterization. Almost all his characters are more than one-dimensional. Claudius in *Hamlet* is not pure evil; he experiences conscience-stricken moments. Macbeth is ambitious but not quite fiendish. Ophelia, though she is an innocent victim, has serious weaknesses. And Othello's uprightness and greatness are questioned when his credulity and jealousy conspire to poison his honest mind and make it foolish. Very often, even a character with a few words to speak and making just one brief appearance in the whole performance of a play can leave an imprint upon the audience because he reveals in his small way some truth about human nature. Shakespeare creates no superhuman heroes. He has the common life of the common run of mankind in mind in his literary creations. This is the reason why people of all times and places can easily relate to his characters as their own contemporaries. Shakespeare is inexhaustible as a mine of experience and wisdom. His plays are capable of offering ever new messages each time one reads or watches them.

One dramatic device that Shakespeare uses in all his works involves the juxtaposition of the comic element alongside the serious. Even the most tragic situations are not always enveloped in gloom. The appearance of the absurd and the grotesque in the midst of a solemn scenario was not in keeping with literary traditions and may disconcert the fastidious critic, but the audience takes immense delight in the mix. The pretentious and obsequious Polonius in *Hamlet*, the three witches in *Macbeth*, Shylock in *The Merchant of Venice*, the subplot of Gloucester and his two sons, and Sir Falstaff in a few of his plays are good examples. The humor and the laugh may not be always stress-relievers; in fact they can often be a kind of black comedy; but they serve well to avoid monotony and glue the audience to the performance.

Shakespeare, as a child of English Renaissance, best exemplifies the *zeitgeist* of his time. All the best features of the age find adequate expression in his works. These include the sense of individual worth, the feeling of freedom in thought and action, the ambition and the dynamic aggressiveness, the plentitude of talent and the excesses of energy, the pioneering spirit of adventure and the desire for accomplishment, the daring to conquer and the exuberance to invent and innovate, the self-assurance, the vision, the insight, the perspicacity and, on top of these all, the emotional abandon with which Renaissance inspires all its writers. The temper and tempo of the Elizabethan age is well demonstrated in the works of its greatest literary figure.

An important point to make about Shakespeare concerns his method of creation. Although intensely unique and original, Shakespeare's originality does not lie exactly in inventing new plots. He borrows from existing works but revises and makes them substantially new and superior. *Hamlet* is a good example. Before Shakespeare's text there had been quite a few versions of *Hamlet*. Thomas Kid might have written one which is lost, and Thomas Lodge and Thomas Dekker both alluded to Hamlet in their works. Today three texts of Hamlet still exist beside Shakespeare's. But Shakespeare's version alone has made the story of Hamlet an enduring attraction to the world. The same can be said of *King Lear*. The Lear story goes far back to ancient British mythology, where Lear is a sea-god, and the story of the three daughters was added in the twelfth century. The myth had been dealt with by Raphael Holinshed and Spenser and some others before Shakespeare reinvented it. When his *King Lear* came out with its tragic ending and thematic ambiguities, Shakespeare made it so definitely his own (the original story ends happily) that no other version could ever hope to compete with it for power and permanence. Shakespeare did a lot of revision and amplification. He added the subplot of Gloucester and his two sons to echo and reinforce the main plot, and put in huge blocks of knowledge about man and his condition. In formal terms, it represents about the farthest point of perfection to which any one could take poetry and drama.

As to Macbeth, Shakespeare took his story from Holinshed's *Chronicles of Scotland* and made it into a lucid statement about man and his problems. Shakespeare's Macbeth is a complex multi-dimensional person. His ambition renders him vulnerable to the allurement of evil while his innate goodness keeps pricking his conscience. And his dignity in face of death never fails to impress the audience favorably. Equally graphic illustrations can be found in *Julius Caesar*, *Antony and Cleopatra*, *Mark Antony*, and a good number of other dramas. Here Plato's comment on the Greeks comes to mind. Plato once said that the Greeks were exceptionally good at making whatever they inherited from other races inevitably better. This can apply to Shakespeare without qualification.

It is necessary to note here that copyright, the personal ownership of writings, is a modern idea. It began in the 19th century. Before that, as the ancient Greeks illustrate, anyone was free to use any previous writer's stories, much as the case is still in folklore. That explains Shakespeare's free use of whatever he wanted of other writers' stories.

A sketch of some of Shakespeare's plays is in order here. We begin with *King Lear*, which is a well constructed story of an old king's relationship with his daughters—Goneril, Regan, and Cordelia. Now in his old age, Lear divides his kingdom and gives the shares away according to the protestations of love the girls cook up for him. Goneril and Regan end up getting the whole of it between them as the youngest princess only says that she loves her father according to her duty. The father is livid with rage, gives her nothing, and marries her off to the King of France. But when they have got what they wanted, the two elder daughters mistreat their father and finally turn him out in a storm. He goes insane. The King of France comes with an army to his rescue but suffers defeat, Cordelia is hanged, and Lear dies in agony. A parallel subplot runs on the loyalty of Kent, Gloucester, and Gloucester's estranged son Edgar, reinforcing the theme of the major plot.

Thematically, the play can be divided into three parts. Part one deals with a King Lear sinning, his "unnaturalness" in demanding professions of love from his daughters and his "aged tyranny" (1.1). Part two describes a Lear sinned against as he goes through the three ordeals, the end of which brings him close to spiritual rebirth: (a) maltreatment at the hands of Goneril and Regan, his manhood shaken, and his initial recognition of his wrongdoing to Cordelia (1.4-1.5); (b) reduced to choosing between the two evils of Goneril and Regan but still too proud to contemplate living with Cordelia (2.2-2.4); and (c) driven out in a storm, achieving initial self-revelation, moving toward resignation with fate, and about to accept the workings of the world, thus moving toward the last stage of his regeneration (3.1-4.6). The last part tells of a Lear learning his lesson the hard way, purified of his wrong notion of love and thoroughly humbled, and attaining to spiritual sublimity in his reconciliation with Cordelia and his death.

Now a few words about *The Tempest*, which is probably the most popular of Shakespeare's last plays. It has been seen as one of the finest representations of his dramatic talents. As the story goes, Prospero, the Duke of Milan, a powerful wizard, is maneuvered out of power by his brother, Antonio and is cast upon an island with his daughter Miranda. Then he conjures up a tempest and causes a shipwreck when he learns that his brother and the king of Naples and the king's son Ferdinand and their company are voyaging by. The accident lands everyone on board alive but bogged down on the island. In time Ferdinand meets Miranda and falls in love with her at first sight, and Prospero acts so that he gets his dukedom back and is reconciled with the king of Naples. *The Tempest* is a many-faceted creation which both defies and entices classification. The play may be seen as a pastoral romance, the evidence of which includes, among other things, Naplese councilor Gonzalo's vision of the Golden Age (Act 2), but scholars have been at variance on the point. The fact of the matter is that the play expresses the complexity of human existence so well that it is capable of more than one interpretation. As to characterization, the central figure in the play is Prospero whose stature as a dramatic hero is conspicuous. He is not just another theurgist; he is a new kind of hero guided by his wisdom rather than by his force of passion or greatness of soul. A testimony to the permanence of the play lies in this, that people have continued to respond to it warmly over the centuries. It always has some new questions for readers and critics alike each time they see it, and the answers people manage to find have not always been good enough. The search is forever ongoing.

The most famous and most profusely commented upon of all his works is *The Tragical History of Hamlet, Prince of Denmark*, generally known as *Hamlet*. [3] It is good to note here just as a simple proof of its popularity that over a 60-year period, doctoral dissertations on the play have appeared at the frequency of one in every 12 days.

The basic story of *Hamlet, the Prince of Denmark*, was first recorded by Saxo Grammaticus, a Danish historian. The story as it appears in the drama is fairly simple in outline. Hamlet, the young prince of Denmark, learns through his father's ghost the truth about his uncle Claudius' fratricide and usurpation of the throne, and feels furious over this and his mother's hasty marriage to the new king. In order to make sure if the spirit is really the ghost of his father, rather than an evil spirit posing as his father, he stages in the palace a play, the plot of which resembles his uncle's act of murder. When watching it, Claudius is shaken, and Hamlet knows instantly that the man is the culprit. Then he kills Polonius, mistaking him for Claudius. He is sent to England to be executed there, but manages to escape and return home. In a duel with Laertes, Polonius' son, arranged by Claudius, he is fatally wounded but does not die before he kills his rival and his uncle. Altogether six lives are lost in the confusion. An interesting subplot concerns the love between Hamlet and Ophelia, Polonius' daughter. Because of the tension Hamlet feels against her father, the girl gets caught in between the two important men of her life, loses her mind and dies in misery.

The secret of Shakespeare's success with *Hamlet* lies in this that, whereas revenge and violence receive most of the emphasis in previous versions, Shakespeare injects the thrilling Renaissance spirit into the story. He turns a one-dimensional stereotyped plot into one in which Hamlet is transfigured into a multifaceted Renaissance idealist, made to face a world of debilitating evil and having to learn to deal with it before he is ready. All of his "antic-disposition," his feigning insanity and his momentary but true madness, and his impulsive action—these all stem from the thinking mind of a Renaissance humanist as he picks up wisdom and fast matures to act properly. The other characters are similarly deftly transformed from the stock characters of the other versions of the story into complex individuals of this play, so that they all serve to rivet attention on Hamlet and enrich his personality. As a result, Shakespeare's Hamlet is no longer the mere agent of revenge and violence. Although his first priority is to avenge his father's death, this Hamlet has now a much larger and more worthy ideal, i.e. the Renaissance humanist ideal, which he knows sadly is lost to him, probably never again to be retrieved. He would still assert man's power—his noble reason and infinite faculties; he would still help mend the social ills, and save a society that is "out of joint"; but he knows that he is fighting a losing battle. He keenly feels that he is not born at the right time, and that reality is so sinister and overwhelming that it is probably not worthwhile fighting it out any more. Viewed in this way, the theme of the story assumes a much graver magnitude than one of mere blood and violence. The corrupt and criminal ancient Danish court versus Prince Hamlet becomes, in the hands of Shakespeare, a metaphor for—or a mirror reflection of—the real world of Shakespeare's England in confrontation with Renaissance humanism.

The question that has attracted Shakespearean scholars has been Hamlet's procrastination. People have found it hard to understand why the young man does not take immediate action and get the job of revenge done once and for all and proceed to put the country back in order. One obvious reason is that Hamlet has doubts about the ghost and his "truth." He has to prove it for himself before he acts. Actually, Hamlet seems to think that the ghost may be the devil that "abuses me to damn me" (II. ii). Another reason for his procrastination is the social and religious education that he has received, which explains why he does not kill Claudius when the man kneels and prays and makes himself a vulnerable prey; Hamlet hates to kill a man in his moments of repentance and help send his soul to heaven (III. i). Then there is Hamlet's intense mental battle throughout the play, which indicates that his conscience may secretly feel that the revenge may serve no useful purpose as it cannot bring his dead father back to life nor save his mother's honor. As to the appearance of the ghost, although the watchman and Horatio confirm that it is not a figment of their imagination, it mystifies Hamlet as he is the only one to hear it speak and his mother can neither see nor hear it. Hamlet's repeated questioning of his mother as to whether she sees or hears the spirit suggests somehow to the audience that he is not quite sure of his senses and that he might be hallucinating and having a killer's "hidden voice" in him. He is very much afraid that he might do the wrong thing. More interesting is perhaps the Freudian approach to the "hesitation" question though it may sound a bit far-fetched and way off the mark. Psychoanalytical criticism seems to suggest that the young prince suffers from the Oedipus complex. But he could not kill his father as this would violate the moral principle on patricide and entail disaster for him. Yet if someone else kills the father, he should feel more than happy. But the son would have to avenge his father on the criminal, which is another way of saying that he would be denouncing and hunting himself to the kill. That is why, as the psychoanalytic critic says, Hamlet puts off his fatal strike at his uncle. The point sounds absurd but it opens one more window to look into the inner world of the fascinating youth.

The most famous speech in *Hamlet* is the prince's soliloquy, "To be, or not to be." Said to be the most famous soliloquy in the history of the theater, it discusses the attitude of a Renaissance humanist toward life and death. The speech comes at a critical juncture in the drama when the truth about Claudius' murder is about to be confirmed with the staging of a play within the play. While waiting for the moment to come, his sense of anxiety drives Hamlet to think seriously about the existentialist condition of man. Is it worth it dying in the fight with evil? Or is it better to settle for the passive acceptance of the second best, i.e. to ignore evil and endure the pain and live on (III. i. ll. 56-61)? He may die in his effort to remove evil and avenge the blood of his father. Death may be the way out of all the suffering of life (III. i. ll. 64-65), but is death the end of all? Isn't there more anguish and sorrow in the next world (III. i. ll. 79-82)? Hamlet realizes that, though thought guides action, excessive thinking makes people cowardly and jeopardizes the chances of success of great undertakings (III. i. ll. 83-88). This self-warning portrays the Renaissance humanists as both men of thought and action. Instead of talking about suicide and evading commitment as some critics think, Hamlet is in fact spurring himself to action. This speech is also a vehement criticism of the ills of the time—its oppression and its various other forms of injustice (III. i. ll. 58-59; ll. 70-78). What strikes the audience most is the density of thought and the poetry of the language. The substance of the soliloquy serves to indicate within the limited space of its few lines the whole process of growth of Hamlet's character, which is in a way an indication of the history of human thinking from the Renaissance through modern existentialism. As to the language, it is simply beautiful, with its blank verse, its impressive rhythm (smooth alternating with rugged) and pace (fast alternating with slow), and each of its lines presenting some wonder of its own kind.

Macbeth[4], or *The Tragedy of Macbeth* (1606), another famous tragedy, has also received a good deal of critical attention over the centuries. It is based on the story of regicide that is said to have occurred in ancient Scottish history. Shakespeare got the subject from his reading of Holinshed's *Chronicles of England, Scotland, and Ireland* (1577). As Shakespeare tells the story, Macbeth, having vanquished a rebellion and a foreign invasion, becomes ambitious enough to replace the weak King Duncan, his cousin. Encouraged by his wife Lady Macbeth, he murders the visiting monarch, and puts himself on the throne. He kills his fellow general Banquo in order to forestall a prophecy that Banquo's descendants may become future kings, and he removes many others to consolidate his power, thus alienating himself from his courtiers and people. Macbeth is now so anxious and high-strung that he cannot sleep well any more. Neither can his wife who, harassed by her guilt, sleepwalks, fast loses her sanity, and finally takes her own life. In the meantime, the English forces are invited in to help remove Macbeth and restore rule and order. Macbeth fights bravely, but dies.

The characterization of Macbeth and his wife merits special analysis. Macbeth begins as a man of integrity, a pillar of his country, enjoying admiration and popularity. In view of a weakling king on the throne, he may have harbored an ambition of his own, but he would not have descended so low as to achieve his ends by killing his king, had he not had Lady Macbeth to persuade him into doing it. He submits to her coercion, and oversteps the line between good and evil. That is when endless self-torment begins to prick his conscience so that he experiences sleepless nights and begins to admire the dead Duncan in his grave. The witches may be seen as an externalization of the complexity of his inner world. The first time the witches appear is when Macbeth is returning to a triumphant hero's welcome after his victories. The three women predict that he will be king, but add that his companion's children will also be kings. This is in fact an objectification of Macbeth's hidden ambition and fear, that he wants to be king but feels the threat from his fellow general—Banquo. The other occasion on which the witches surface is when they are sought by Macbeth. Their advice to him can again be construed as a mirror for Macbeth's inner soul: his fear lest Banquo's son should invite English intervention but at the same time he feels a dubious, qualified self-confidence. Macbeth represents the effect of sin and guilt upon the moral fiber of man: he ends with the tragic vision of human existence ("[life] is a tale/ Told by an idiot, full of sound and fury,/ Signifying nothing" (5.5. 26-28). The implication is that evil and sin and greed, all part of human nature, conspire to bring about man's inevitable helplessness and downfall. There is ample indication of his awareness of the odds overwhelming man. It is good to note here that William Faulkner derived from the quotation above the title for his famous novel, *The Sound and the Fury*.

Lady Macbeth has been seen as one of Shakespeare's greatest women. Her distinctive personality is marked by her amorality. Wanting absolutely in moral scruples, this dominant and heartless woman manipulates her husband so as to push him to murder. She calls upon the evil spirits to unsex her, pump direct cruelty into her being, and veil her evil plan from heaven. She overcomes her husband's upright nature ("full o' the milk of human kindness" [I. v. 31]), shames him into action by questioning his manhood, soothes him ("a little water clears [his hands] of this deed" [II. ii. 57]), and refuses to feel guilty until the last moment when her strength deserts her and her defenses crumble in face of Macbeth's deterioration and the dismal prospect that their day is lost. She turns insane, always walking with a candle, always washing an imaginable stain on her hands, and sleepwalking and wishing to be cleansed of her wrongdoing. Finally, when the guilt proves too much for her to handle, she kills herself in hopes of attaining inner peace.

The Merchant of Venice is another of Shakespeare's popular plays. As the story goes, young Bassanio, who needs money to win the hand of the rich young heiress—Portia, comes to Antonio, a merchant of Venice, for help. Antonio, as he has no ready cash, goes to Shylock, the Jewish usurer, who has been at odds with Antonio because of the competition and racial discrimination he has suffered at his hands. The Jew decides to loan the money but asks him to sign a bond which demands a pound of flesh from him in case he fails to pay in time. With the money Bassanio wins Portia, but Antonio is in trouble. His ships wreck and leave him in a quandary: he is unable to meet the deadline for the payment. Now Shylock insists on having his pound of flesh to have his revenge on Antonio and his friends. At a critical moment at court when the Jew is about to have his way, Portia arrives in disguise as a young lawyer and points out that, as the bond mentions nothing of blood, the flesh should be exactly one pound cut without bloodshed, and that any blood or difference in weight will be an offense to the law for which Shylock will receive severe punishment. Shylock's scheme is thus foiled. Nor is this all for him. He is then accused of conspiring against a Venetian, and loses all his wealth, half to the state and half to Antonio. Antonio gives up his share on condition that Shylock embraces the Christian faith and gives the money to Jessica, his runaway daughter. Jessica becomes a Christian and her husband inherits half of Shylock's property.

The characterization of Shylock presents an intriguing ambiguity. *The Merchant of Venice* was staged at a time when a high anti-semitic mood prevailed in England, so its happy ending of triumph of the Christian over the Jewish faith pleased the Elizabethans in general. Shylock portrays an archetype of vice, created as he is to body forth the sum total of social and human evil and is eventually brought to justice. His ending functions well as the effective proof of the moral nature of the universe. The audiences of successive generations have tended to come away with the impression of the Jew's vengeance, his cruelty, and his malice, along with the sense of gratification of the good guys winning over the bad.

But Shakespeare's mind was not so simple; neither was his portrait of the Jew. With a supreme sense of justice, he always took the side of the wronged. Although his play presents Shylock as the usurer, it does not point fingers at Shylock the Jew. In racial terms the play is not anti-semitic; in fact, it champions the Jew's protest against the racial discrimination to which he has been subjected. Shylock, now all alone at court and in face of a devastating defeat, behaves not as a coward and loser. He fights back though he knows his doom is sealed. His loud lamentation at court (I. Iii. ll. 108-130; III. i.) is a moving show of his "undefeated" mindset. Here stands upright this human being: grotesque, malicious, unflinching, and valorous in face of adversity, and subtle and complex in emotional make-up. Shylock's protest can also be seen, in a way, as Shakespeare's statement of support for the wronged Jew. The play is thus a kind of tragicomedy, tragic if we take Shylock's losses into consideration.

Francis Bacon (1561-1626)

Bacon did his best work, in the last phase of his life, for which he now claims a significant place in literary history. It was when he lost his Lord Chancellorship following Parliament's impeachment of him for corruption (1621) and lived in disgrace and solitude. These years he spent on writing works of immense literary and philosophical interest. His writings are remembered for two things: his contribution to modern empirical science of which he has been regarded as a progenitor, and his achievement in the art of prose writing.[5]

First, his inductive method of reasoning and learning proved to be seminal and critically important to the development of modern science and the progress of humankind. When still young, Bacon was ambitious enough to take all knowledge as his province and was determined to search for truth. In the field of philosophy, he wanted to come up with a new system of philosophy to replace that of Aristotle.

He valued experience and actual observation, and placed emphasis on the continuous adventure and investigation of facts on which alone man could base his conclusions. As long as facts remained to be explored, nothing could be seen as final. This was a great spur to the growth of modern science. His thought system represented the beginnings of materialism in English philosophy. His well-known philosophical works include *Advancement of Learning* (1605), *Novum Organum* (1620), and *New Atlantis* (1627).

Now with regards to his prose, it is fresh, vigorous, powerful, and aphoristic so that he was able to dominate English prose for decades from the last years of Queen Elizabeth I's reign to the end of that of James I. Bacon's *Essays* is the most cogent testimony to his wisdom and his unique style. The essay form was traceable to the work of the French essayist, Montaigne (1533-1592), but Bacon's *Essays* was the first of its kind to appear in English literature. Bacon drew chiefly on the various phenomena of nature and his careful observations and analyses. The *Essays* came out first in 1597 with a few short writings, but was revised and expanded in 1612 and 1625 so that the number finally rose to 58. The book touches upon a wide variety of subjects of permanent, universal interest. It is philosophy, experience, and perspicacity all well fused and aptly expressed in a succinct, lucid, precise, and occasionally poetic language. Adages and quotable sayings are legion, and wisdom and insight alone serve to hook and hold attention. The light of genius shines forth its frequent flashes of grandeur, so that reading becomes a joy that no one can sensibly dispense with.

Bacon's *Essays* are essentially his deliberations on man and his life. It deals with subjects such as truth, love, envy, high position, good nature, riches, ambition, beauty, vainglory, learning, and politics and economy. First and foremost, it reveals his intimate knowledge of human nature. He knows that human nature does not change easily when he says in the essay "Of Nature and Man": "Nature is often hidden, sometimes overcome, seldom extinguished," and again in the same essay, "Nature will be buried a great time, and yet revive upon occasion, or temptation." He knows that friendship is often colored by selfish motives when he says in "Of Friendship," "More men adored the sun rising than the sun setting." In his opinion love changes with fortune, human feeling is fluid, and utility and advantage often dominate human souls. In other words, there is little gratitude, less integrity, and selfish interest constitutes the basic nature of moral philosophy. Bacon also reveals his political concerns in essays such as "of Counsel," "Of Nobility," and "Of Seditions and Troubles," and his socio-economic ideas in such essays as "Of Riches," "Of Usury," and "Of Building." Some of the best readings include "Of Truth," "Of Great Place," and "Of Studies."

Ben Jonson (1573-1637)

Ben Jonson was the last great Elizabethan and probably the first poet laureate (1616) and the first literary dictator in English history. His reputation as a playwright was established by the success of his first comedy, *Every Man in His Humour* (1598). Shakespeare was said to have acted a part in it, which might be the beginning of the friendship between the two men. In his early years Jonson cultivated friendly ties with Donne, Bacon, as well as Shakespeare. This was also the period in which his best works appeared. In 1616 he published his *Works*, the complete collection of his poetry, which was an event of unusual significance as the first of its kind in English literary chronology. The same year he stopped writing for the stage. His plays may not approach those by Shakespeare and Marlowe in the depth of thought and the poetic quality of language, but they are the best as leverages of satire on reality. Jonson was never rich and died in poverty. He was buried in Westminster Abbey with the inscription: "O rare Ben Jonson." His death was mourned as the end of one era—the Elizabethan Age. He was a man of great learning, and his influence over the literary world of London was simply overwhelming, so that a group of young admirers—almost all the remarkable poets in the first years of the 17th century (except Milton)—gathered around him as "the Tribe of Jonson" or "the Sons of Jonson." For well over two decades he was the one to whom people looked up as a point of reference in literary values and tastes. He remained well in evidence right until the study of Shakespeare began in early 18th century when he seemed to begin phasing out of critical favor. [6]

Jonson was an honest and upright playwright and scholar. He tried through his writings to do two things, neither of which achieved spectacular success. One of these was to bring the classic form of the three unities—unity of action, unity of time, and unity of place—back to the stage. The theory of the Aristotelian unities stipulates that a good play should weave together interrelated incidents (unity of action) within one day (unity of time) in one place (unity of place). Some of Jonson's plays observe the rule well enough to move the audience by means of their focus on the dramatic intensity. Their plots unfold often within a few hours of a single day. The other undertaking was his effort to stop the theater from going downhill to immorality and evil. Commendable as it was, the endeavor also failed miserably so that, five years after his death, the theater was closed by the Puritan Parliament on account of its unwholesome impact on life.

Jonson was a realistic writer. His experience with the life, people, and places of his day could not be fuller. His was rather an eventful life. He was bricklayer, soldier, prisoner on the death row because of killing his rival in a duel, prisoner on account of his irreverent comments on the Scots (King James I was a Scot), suspect in the Guy Fawkes plot of 1605, prisoner for writing with Marston and Chapman a play (*Eastward Ho* [1605]) critical of the King and narrowly escaping death but with one ear cut off, writing to the taste of the court and receiving honor and pension in later years, and ending as a leader figure for admiring young writers. In addition, he had traveled widely. All these became the "mineral ore" from which poured out in time the "gold" of his literary creations. The colorful life was so well coupled with his erudition and scholarship that he seemed the only one living then singularly equipped for a realistic portrait of his country and people. The outcome of this was that his works have been taken as authentic records of Elizabethan life. They touch on almost all the possible aspects of the life of the age—the distinction of classes, the religious squabble, the technicalities of law, science, alchemy, morality, manners of speech, fashions and fads, Bohemianism, and the cant of all trades, and they reflect almost all the moods, tastes, and the mindset that, all put together, made up the *zeitgeist* of the period. Although his voluminous writings possessed a degree of dignity and grace seldom surpassed in his time, his importance as a playwright suffered not a little from the overshadowing of Shakespeare. Jonson needs some serious rehabilitation.

Jonson is remembered today chiefly as a playwright. Of his 18 plays, the best include *Every Man in His Humour* (1598), *Volpone or the Fox* (1606), and *The Sad Shepherd or A Tale of Robin Hood* (1641). The first of these, *Every Man in His Humour*, was a comedy: "humour" was used here in the sense of "essential temperament" to denote that everyone has a basic character trait in his personality. In the play, for instance, many human foibles are satirized: jealousy, undue worry, credulity, and boasting. As the story goes, the main character, Kitely, is a jealous merchant. He becomes suspicious when a group of young people frequent his house that their visit may have to do with the pretty face of his young wife, Dame Kitely. One of these, Edward Knowell, is not indifferent to young Bridget, Kitely's sister. The other is Bodadill, Knowell's friend, and a braggart of a cowardly soldier with an immense capacity for mischief. Knowell's father worries excessively about his son's moral behavior. Dame Kitely, when put on the spot, can be vigilant and credulous. The villain is Knowell's servant, the cunning Brainworm, who plans, through the devices and disguises in which Babodill gets involved, for the Kitelys to meet at a house where, when face to face, they each suspect the other of having some ulterior designs of their own. Eventually, Babodill is exposed and beaten, Knowell marries Bridget, and Justice Clement clears up the tangle for all. The play was basically an effort to amuse and entertain.

Volpone or The Fox is a scathing castigation against human greed. Volpone is an avaricious Venetian merchant. He schemes to cheat other people out of their pockets with his villainous servant Mosca. As he is childless, he feigns to be dying and is looking for an heir. The people around him lean backward and forward to worm themselves into his graces so as to become his heir. One of these disowns his own son to make Volpone his heir. Another, Corvino, offers his wife to Volpone just to please him. Then word is out that Volpone is already dead and has left his property to Mosca in his will, and the sycophants all feel bad and helpless. Little has Volpone ever expected that he will be outwitted by Mosca, who is clever and greedy enough to take advantage of the will and claim himself to be the real owner of all Volpone's wealth. Volpone's lawyer, Voltore, interferes, however, and reveals Mosca's blackmail to the Senate, because he does not like to lose his ludicrous legal fee in the operation. Both Volpone, Mosca, and Corvino are duly punished. The satirical edge of the play is obvious: Jonson can be a ruthless satirist as he sets out to help people recognize their faults and improve their nature. The names of the play are highly suggestive of the predatory nature of human life: Volpone means "fox," Mosca "fly," Voltore "vulture," and Corvino "raven," all out to harm others for selfish ends. In formal terms the play observes the theory of the unities, with a single plot occurring in one day in the same place—Venice.

Jonson's memorial poem, "To the Memory of My Beloved, the Author, Mr. William Shakespeare: and What He Has Left us," or simply "To Shakespeare," deserves special mention here. It first appeared on the complimentary page of *The First Folio*, the first collection of Shakespeare's plays (1623). The poem was Jonson's praise, warm, sincere, objective, and generous, of a fellow writer—Shakespeare's power and permanence. It also showcased Jonson's own good nature as a person and his moral and critical integrity as a commentator. Much more than a mere occasional composition, the poem has served well as a critical commentary of historic importance. Jonson reveals his critical acumen and perceptive powers when he says it all for all time as a final and definitive statement about Shakespeare. He calls Shakespeare "the Soul of the Age," and "Not of an age but for all time." In addition, it is also a good place to add here that Jonson reveals his keen insight when he detects the element of the eternal in "Marlowe's mighty line." And this is not all. The heroic couplet that he used in the poem was to become a tyrannical vogue in the next century, and his emphasis on "Nature" the basic principle in 18th-century literary criticism.

King James' Bible

First, a brief sketch of the evolution of the *Bible* is in order. The *Bible* consists of two parts—the Old Testament and the New Testament. It is said that its composition took over one thousand years, stretching from around the 9th century BC right through the 2nd century AD and enlisting the contribution of numerous writers. The Old Testament became the Holy Scripture for the Jews at the end of the first century AD, and a century later both the Old and the New Testaments were accepted by the Christians as their holy book. The whole *Bible* took final shape around the beginning of the 3rd century.

The Old Testament tells of the history and religious beliefs of the Jews while the New Testament relates the life of Jesus Christ and the birth and the growth of the Christian faith. The word "testament" means "contract," referring here to the one between God and the Jews, His first chosen people, that God promises the land of Canaan (today's Palestine) for the Jews in return for their faith in Him. Later when the Jews degenerated, God punished them and then promised a "Messiah" or Savior for them, which led to the coming of Jesus Christ. This is the reason why the Old Testament was included in the Christian *Bible* as well. Jesus came on the scene around the first century to challenge the Jewish faith, was crucified, and his followers suffered persecution for a long time until the 4th century when the Roman Empire finally declared it its state religion. From then on Christianity spread across Europe and then to the rest of the world.

The writing of the *Bible* went through different stages. The Old Testament was written in Hebrew, while the New Testament was done in Greek. In 270 AD seventy-two Jewish scholars spent seventy-two days translating the Old Testament into Greek, and brought out the version known as *The Septuagint*, which influenced the writing of the New Testament and is still in evidence today, especially with regard to the chapter titles and their sequential arrangement it offers. Toward the end of the 4th century, St. Jerome (340-420) translated the *Septuagint* version of the *Bible* into Latin. This version, known as the *Vulgate*, was the only one in popular use in the medieval times and widely accepted among the Catholics. It contains numerous errors as it went through endless copying over one thousand years. John Wycliffe (1320-1384) was the first Englishman to render the whole *Bible* into English, and William Tyndale (1494-1583) came up with his English translation of the New Testament in 1524 and the first five books of the Old Testament in 1530. Five years later *The Coverdale Bible* was out in Zurich, which was followed another five years later by *The Great Bible*, when the Catholic Queen Mary was on the throne. The protestant *Geneva Bible* was published in Geneva in 1560, the biases of which the Anglican Church in the reign of Queen Elizabeth tried to remove with their *Bishops' Bible* (1568).

In 1604 King James I ordered scholars to retranslate the holy book, which took seven years to finish. Thus the most enduring *King James'* or *the Authorized Bible* came into being in 1611. The version has been seen as the authoritative text because it is accurate in sense and beautiful and dignified in language. It has influenced generations of writers in their literary endeavors over the centuries.

There have been other attempts since then at improving the English rendering of the holy scripture, with their various merits and weaknesses, but none seems to have been able to touch *King James' Bible* in authority or popularity. This version is about the best that the West has going now.

Chapter 5 The 17th Century • Donne • Milton • Dryden • Bunyan • The Restoration Theater

The 17th Century: A Brief Introduction

The 17th century began with an ominous indication of discord within the nation. King James I of the Stuarts came to the throne in 1603 and began to impose his will upon religious matters as well as on parliament, his financier. The religious strife, well under control during Queen Elizabeth I's reign, was beginning to surface once more. A group of people with high morality and principles, an extreme Protestant sect, would like to see the church more free of the control of the state and restored to the purity of the first-century church of Jesus Christ. These Puritans, or the "Roundheads" (as they cut their hair short), failed to influence the new king, found it hard to face the mounting persecution, and began to emigrate, out of despair, first to Holland and then some of them to America. The majority remained and resented the centralized religious hierarchy. This was the religious aspect of the chaos that was about to reign supreme in the country.

In the meantime, the tension between parliament and the monarch kept skyrocketing. The king saw Parliament as his servant, but Parliament refused to take his orders without good reason. The king then decided to dissolve it and ruled the country on his own for seven years (1614-1621). When his successor Charles I came on the scene, the crisis soon came to a head. The king claimed his rule as a divine right, but Parliament saw him as a human being. This led to the dissolution of the first three parliaments and also the fourth, the Short Parliament, lasting for three weeks only. The fifth one, the Long Parliament, the most obdurate, remained in evidence for 20 years (1640-1660). The deadlock was not to be addressed except through war. This was, by and large, the political aspect of the chaos in the time of the Stuarts. Sure enough, the Civil War broke out. For a few years (1642-1648) it raged between Parliament with its army of the "Roundheads" on one side and the King with his Cavaliers on the other, and ended with the capture and the beheading of Charles I and the founding of the commonwealth in 1649. Then to deal with the disorder that ensued, Oliver Cromwell (1599-1658) and his Ironsides moved in, and England became a Protectorate with Cromwell as its Protector.

With the death of Cromwell in 1658, the country fell once more into anarchy. There was a popular mood swing to the monarchy, and Charles I's son was welcomed back as Charles II. This occurred in 1660 as the Restoration. Charles II was an exceptionally evil king. He brought back from France the most decadent and corrupt court in English history, which contaminated national life with the utmost immorality and debauchery for a whole generation. As he was clever enough, however, to agree to act as a figurehead and not to enrage Parliament, his reign was uneventful. But not that of his brother, James II, who tried once more to rule absolutely and restore the Roman Catholic religion. Parliament felt insecure and invited his son-in-law, William of Orange, in 1688 to come with an army to protect the English people. James II saw his day was lost and fled to France. The new king and his wife Mary (James II's daughter) became the joint ruler of the country. This was known as "the Glorious Revolution," glorious because bloodless. The Bill of Rights which the new king signed with Parliament endowed Parliament as the *de facto* ruler of the nation and the king became a titular head. The long power struggle between Parliament and the Monarch was thus brought to a rough finish, and no king or queen has ever again thought of competing with Parliament (except for the dramatic show of an attempt of Edward VIII which ended with the his abdication in 1936).

The period under discussion was one of transition, chaos, and great perplexity. The old value system was on its way out, new values were taking shape, and the conflict generated an acute sense of loss, which was felt on all conceivable levels of life in terms of certitude, faith, and honor. This led to the attempt to seek certainty and intellectual harmony on the one hand, and to address the question of values through violence and sexuality. These incidentally constituted the basic features of the literature of the period. The prevalent mood that enveloped literary works was one of gloom, pessimism, decadence, and frivolity. The theater was somehow interesting to talk about. It was closed since1642 as sinful by the Puritan Parliament, and was reopened in 1660. The Restoration theater was the most depraved of its kind, and the Restoration plays, such as those by William Congreve (1670-1729), William Wycherley (1640-1716), John Vanbrugh (1664-1726), and George Farquhar (1678-1707), were basically frivolous, decadent, and trivial, representing the immoral lifestyle of Charles II's court in a naked realistic manner with its sex and violence and diverse forms of depravity. Although they showed improvement in their later works, these writers did a lot of polluting to the moral and intellectual milieu of the time. Even John Dryden (1631-1700), one of the major figures of the period, was not exempt from this accusation in his earlier dramas. The literary scene of period was by no means prolific, but a few names stood out to be remembered. These include John Donne, John Milton, John Dryden, and John Bunyan. Although John Locke (1632-1704) lived and wrote in this time, his philosophy pointed to the next century, and therefore will be discussed there.

John Donne (1571-1631)

Donne's life was colorful. He was born into a rich London merchant's family and educated at Cambridge and Oxford Universities without taking degrees as he was a Catholic. He studied law at Lincoln's Inn in the early 1590s when he led a life of dissipation. He was then under the influence of Renaissance secularism. Then he became a soldier and took part in the sea battles of Cadiz and Azores (1596, 1597). In 1598 he became secretary to the Lord Keeper but was dismissed when he married the Lord's niece in secret. He was thrown in prison for a short while and experienced poverty. Donne's religious life was unique in its own way. Although of a Catholic background (he was said to be related to Sir Thomas More through his mother), he renounced all denominations and was contented with being simply a Christian. Later in life he had to switch to the Church of England, became chaplain to the king, and then the dean of St. Paul's Cathedral. Gifted and ambitious, Donne wrote love, satirical, and religious poetry and a good deal of sermons, and made his presence felt and visible. His holy sonnets, which dwell on the themes of humility before God and the horror of the last judgment, made him a St. Augustine figure of his time, as both led a depraved lifestyle early in life but embraced religion later. Donne's love poetry appeals by virtue of its dexterous interweaving of passion with reason. His famous works include such poems as "The Flea," "A Valediction: Forbidden Morning," "Song," "The Canonization," "Death be not proud," and "Batter my heart, three-personed God, for You," and his prose work, the 23-section *Devotions*, which contains his *Meditations*. Of his *Meditations*, suffice it here to say that one of these, no. XVII, in which Donne says, "All mankind is of one author and is one volume," and "Any man's death diminishes me because I am involved in mankind, and therefore never send to know for whom the bell tolls; it tolls for thee[,]" offers the American novelist Ernest Hemingway (1899 1961) the title for one of his famous novels, *For Whom the Bell Tolls* (1940).

As a poet, Donne was original and great. His poetry possessed a highly idiosyncratic quality that reveals a peculiar, brilliant imagination at work, with an unconventional mode of perception and thinking, and the power of a mind, at once voluptuous and meditative, and capable of leaving an enduring imprint on his readers. His type of poetry has been known as Metaphysical Poetry and the group of poets, sharing some of his poetic features, has been called "Metaphysical Poets." But there was no school of poetry by the name of the Metaphysical school; the major features of "Metaphysical" poetry in fact characterize mostly Donne's works.

The "Metaphysical Poets" as a group included George Herbert (1593-1633), Henry Vaughan (1622-1695), Richard Crashaw (1613-1649), Robert Herrick (1591-1674), Thomas Carew (1595-1640), Abrham Cowley (1618-1667), and Andrew Marvell (1621-1678). Herbert's one book of verse, *Temple*, indicates his intention to reclaim poetry for God. Vaughan is remembered for his collection of religious poems entitled *Silex Scintillans*, the most famous of which is "They are all gone into the world of light." Crashaw, while sharing Herbert's desire, was noted for his use of the baroque style, the major features of which are its sensual, florid, and rhetorical exuberance. Herrick wrote, among other things, a number of love poems on the *carpe diem* theme of "mak[ing] much of time" to make love as time flies. The most notable of these is his "To the Virgins, to Make Much of Time" (the third stanza of the 4-stanza poem runs, "That age is the best which is the first,/ When youth and blood are warmer,/ But being spent, the worse, and worst/ Time still succeed the former"). Carew was a favorite of Charles I and a disciple of Ben Jonson who wrote graceful lyric and some licentious poems and a court masque which implied some criticism of the court then. Cowley wrote with a good many "conceits" in his poems and called for a definition of "wit" as a comprehensive idea. His essay on the writing of a religious epic drew Milton's attention as the latter was working on his *Paradise Lost*.

The term "Metaphysical" comes first from 17th-century poet-critic John Dryden (1631-1700) who, commenting on Donne, feels that Donne loves to play with metaphysics both in his satirical and love poetry, so that his love poems reveal the subtleties of metaphysics instead of focusing on love. Samuel Johnson (1709-1784), the literary dictator of the second half of the 18th century, elaborated Dryden's concept when he criticized Donne and his group for showing off their knowledge rather than describing natural human sentiment in their love poetry. Johnson did admit that these poets would not have been able to write this kind of poetry had they not read much and thought hard. His views later found echoes from such 19th-century critic as William Hazlitt (1778-1830). Thus "Metaphysical" became derogatory, and Metaphysical poetry lay in silence and obscurity for the long period of the 18th and 19th centuries. It managed to recover from this eclipse only in the early years of the 20th century, first anthologized by a well-known scholar, Herbert J. C. Grierson and then especially when T. S. Eliot, another literary dictator so to speak, took interest in it and brought it back to light. Today the school is so well known that no one can ignore it without good reason. Now the nomenclature "Metaphysical" has long lost its pejorative denotation and come to mean simply the poems by Donne and his group.

The basic features of Metaphysical poetry are its "wit" or "conceit." "Wit" here means being clever at "yok[ing]" the most heterogeneous ideas together by violence so as to impress people (to paraphrase Samuel Johnson's statement on the subject), and "conceit" denotes a fantastic fancy or way of thinking in the form of peculiar, ingenious, knotty, many-sided metaphors. These are employed along with far-fetched, difficult imagery in the works of Donne and his fellow poets. There is good reason to believe that these people tried to conquer by sheer unconventionality rather than follow the normal channel of communication. They went out of their way to find a way of expression which demanded the readers to stretch their perceptive and imaginative powers to the farthest limit possible to make sense of it. Hence the prophecy of Ben Jonson (1572-1637) that this kind of poetry is too difficult for people to catch on in history. So it has remained unprecedented with virtually no successful followers, and it is often an exacting exercise of the mental powers for those who read it. The reward, however, hard-won often after a battle of wit and intellect, is often a combination of grateful pleasure, gratification, and fun. [1]

Donne's love poems are good examples of Metaphysical poetry. His conceits touch upon diverse fields of knowledge, and his comparisons tend to be amazingly grotesque. These manage to fuse lively thought and strong passion well in the white heat of the metaphysical imagination, and exhibit their impact not so much by virtue of their depiction of physical beauty and tender feelings, as by the compelling force of their "strong lines," masculine, dramatic, and colloquial.[2] One of his most famous poems, "The Flea" (1633), is disconcertingly fantastic in equating "the flea" with "love." This is a three-stanza work, the scenario of which is a lover proposing to his beloved. The man first draws the lady's attention to the fact that the flea has bitten him and is now sucking her and that their two bloods are mingled in it. So he feels (according to a prevailing conception of marriage in the 17th century), that the two of them are already married (stanza I). Then he tells the woman, now apparently bringing her hand down upon the flea, to stop and desist from killing it because she would have committed murder, self-murder, and sacrilege (by attacking a marriage temple [l. 13]): "three sins in killing three" (stanza II/ l. 18). The last stanza shows that the lover feels angry, sad, and sorry that the woman has killed the flea, and calls her cruel and false for her rejection of him. The poem gives people a clear sense of how ridiculous, outrageous, and impossible Metaphysical conceits can be. The flea is the most sordid, disgusting, and hateful parasite in the world, while love is the sweetest, noblest, and purest human emotion in life. No one else would have ever thought of the flea as the "marriage bed" and "marriage temple" (l. 13) and as embodying the consummation of love. Donne's uniqueness lies in this sudden jump from the conventional to the unconventional and metaphysical, and making it appear rational and acceptable. Thus when the one is used to represent the other, the sense of unpleasant yet funny incongruity becomes so strong and revolting that it has better chances of engraving itself upon the mind than does a stereotyped expression. And so it has. Anyone who ever reads the poem will surely find it hard to brush its impression off his memory. Here lies its permanent and immortal power.

Another illustrating example is easily found in his "Valediction: Forbidden Mourning" (1611), which Donne wrote for his wife as a gift upon leaving for France. The poem consists of nine quatrain-stanzas. The first and second quatrains express the deep love that he feels for his wife but deems it "profane" to profess in public. He tells her, and himself, not to cry over the separation: There should be no tears in parting (l. 6) though the trip is a huge movement to them (ll. 11-12), which is a hyperbole for the vast dimension of their love. Though ours is a higher kind of love than that of ordinary lovers, he says, as we are "[i]nter-assured of the mind" and care little about its sensual aspect (stanzas 4, 5), we cannot endure separation and can only accept it as an expansion of our love (stanza 6). The last three stanzas, on which the meaning of the poem depends, reveal Donne's Metaphysical imagination at work which, true to form, chooses an odd and idiosyncratic image—in an abrupt, dramatic manner—as its medium of expression. The novelty consists in the comparison of two separate lovers to the legs of a compass. The choice is strangely apt if the readers take into account the fact that the compass is a symbol of both firmness (its legs) and perfection (the circle it draws) and therefore one of their firm and perfect love. The legs of the compass move together as the two souls in love do (stanza 7), and part and unite as one of these "roam[s]" to draw but always "comes home" on finishing its job, the same way in which one of the two souls leaves on business but invariably returns to join the other (stanza 8). The last stanza compares his wife as standing and leaning firm in the center and himself as the roaming leg eager to get back to the end of the circle. The comparison has been considered to be the most famous conceit in English verse. In tone and mood the poem is steady, serious, serene, and even transcendent; but it is also muted and somewhat depressing so that, while the genuine love is thrown in relief, the readers tend to detect an ominous undercurrent of worry and anxiety. The idea behind this may be that love and care always go together.

The theme of another poem, "Song," represents a different kind of love poetry Donne wrote. Love here is portrayed as radically different from that in "Valediction: Forbidden Mourning." It is negative in nature as it harps on the notion that there is nothing like single-minded love on earth and so represents a cynical attitude to life. The poem is made up of three stanzas. The first of these lists the impossibilities in life such as catching a falling star (l. 1), insinuating that true love is likewise impossible to find. The second stanza states that one may travel far and wide for ages but may never find a true and fair woman, implying that true love does not exist. The last stanza portrays the speaker as one doubtful about anyone who says he has found one true woman. "Song" is a popular poem that has been set to music.

Whereas Donne's best work can rank with those of the greatest poets of the world, it has its obvious defects as well. It is uneven in quality: some are of the highest order with noble themes, but some are mere doggerel expressions of trivialities. Its imagery and thoughts can be licentious, and its form rugged and lacking in smoothness. However, Donne's poetic gifts and graces are such that he is here to stay as one of the major English poets. In his own time he exerted a measure of influence that none of his contemporaries ever dreamed of having, and established a stature that none of his time ever attempted to approach. He was, to Ben Jonson, "the first poet of the world in some things." Thomas Carew (1598-1639) saw him as "A king who ruled as he thought fit/ The Universal monarchy of wit." Today Donne has become a must in the curricula of colleges and universities across the world.

Andrew Marvell (1621-1678)

Marvell was born into a Calvinist family and stood on the Republican side in the Civil War. He was assistant to John Milton as Cromwell's Latin secretary (1657-1659) and was elected into parliament in 1659. After the Restoration he continued to be elected Member of Parliament. He became well known in early 20th century along with the revival of "Metaphysical Poetry." Although his work reveals some "Metaphysical" features, he has his own unique style, which is a subtle amalgam of "Metaphysical" with Elizabethan features—he was sensitive to the influences of Edmund Spenser and Philip Sidney. And the couplet, which he was fond of using, helped pave the way for its perfection in the hands of John Dryden (1631-1700) and Alexander Pope (1688-1744). That is why his place in literary history is not altogether negligible. Some of his works belong among the best and most permanent of English poetry. For instance, his "To His Coy Mistress" is the most famous of the *carpe diem* poems to come out of the 17th century, and his "Garden," containing lines such as "Annihilating all that's made/To a green thought in a green shade," exhibits the profundity which the poet's thought is capable of touching as he tries to explore the dichotomous nature of the world.

It is good to take a look at "To His Coy Mistress," which is probably Marvell's best poem and is certainly his most oft-anthologized. The speaker is a young man who tries to coax his beloved to stop tarrying and accept his love so as to avoid any further waste of her prime youth. The poem consists of three sections, all of which are composed in couplets. In the first of these the young man says in earnest that, if we had enough time and space, your shyness and the procrastination it causes are justifiable and not criminally wrong (ll. 1-2). Then follow a series of hyperboles that elaborate the possible leisure that infinite time and space would produce to the young in love. They would have virtually the whole world to loiter around and the vast expanse of all time at their finger-tips. The tone here hovers between all seriousness and jocularity. The brusque "But" at the beginning of the second section (ll. 21-32), however, marks an abrupt tonal transition. The images that follow in quick succession leave one with the impression of breathlessness: with Time's chariot hurrying near, the young man says, desert will appear, your beauty will vanish along with my love and admiration, your virginity and honor will turn to dust along with my passion, and we face death against our will. Therefore, as the third section (ll. 33-46) runs, the young man invites his love to make the best of their youth and passion and play now before time catches up with them. We may not be able to stop the sun, he says with a great sense of urgency, but we can join hands and make it run to bring our time of joy and pleasure sooner for us. The poem is written in couplets of iambic tetrameter with run-on lines signifying mobile continuity and acceleration of speed. It is famous for its diverse, apt, and effective imagery.

John Milton (1608-1674)

Milton is regarded as the third greatest English poet after Chaucer and

Shakespeare, and the greatest to come out of the 17th century. His life can be roughly divided into three phases: the early phase of reading and lyric writing (1620-1638), the middle phase of service in the Puritan Revolution (also known as the Civil War) and pamphleteering for it (1640-1660), and the last—the greatest—phase of epic writing (1660-1674).

Born into a pious wealthy Puritan family, he had a supportive father and a cultured mother and enjoyed the sweetest and the most sheltered period of adolescence of all. As a child he was an exceptionally avid reader and began at 12 his life-long endeavor at scholarship. As he refused to work for the state-controlled Anglican Church, he stayed at home after graduating from Cambridge University and subjected himself to a rigorous reading plan which covered such as Hebraic, Greek, Latin, and Italian classics, and Christian mythology. With the firm belief that he was born to be a great poet, he kept himself in solitude, immersed totally for six years (1632-1638) in the world of knowledge. When he emerged from his study and traveled in Europe at 20, he was revered as one of the greatest scholars across the English Channel. He met in his tour with some of the most preeminent figures on the continent. These included the Italian physician and astrologist Galileo (1564-1642), a father figure for modern sciences, whose observation of the space through the telescope and anti-traditional world view impacted the thinking of the future poet in a very profound way. Some scholars have speculated that, without the meeting and the experience with the telescope, Milton might not have been able to visualize heaven, earth, and hell as well as he does in his *Paradise Lost* (1667).

Then the Civil War broke out and hastened Milton's return to England. He took an active part in the parliamentary confrontation with the monarchy and became eventually Cromwell's Latin secretary. He wrote a good deal in vehement justification of the people's fight against the king and for freedom. Among these were the two influential writings in Latin—*Pro Populo Anglicano Defensio* (or *In Defense of the British People*, 1651) and *Defensio Secunda* (or *More in Defense of the British People*, 1654). King Charles I was beheaded and the country became a commonwealth. In the meantime, Milton was losing his eyesight and turned totally blind in 1652. After Cromwell's death, chaos set in, Charles II came back, and the period of restoration began. Milton was thrown in prison but was released. Alone, poor, and blind, Milton's early ambition revived. He began to write, dictating, and having many a sleepless night figuring out the best poetic expressions. When *Paradise Lost* came out in print in 1667, he became known as the greatest poet of his time in all Europe. Then he finished another epic *Paradise Regained* (1671) and a verse tragedy, *Samson Agonistes* (1671), in quick succession and felt finally contented that he had accomplished his mission in life. He died in perfect serenity at 66 and was buried in St. Giles, Cripplegate, London. [3]

Let's take a look at some of Milton's major works, *Paradise Lost*, *Samson Agonistes*, and *Lycidas*.

Paradise Lost, the epic that has successfully made its author the greatest modern epic poet in English literary history, draws its subject matter from the biblical story of creation. [4] Coming at the beginning of the Holy Scripture, *Genesis* or *Creation* relates the classic Christian story, that God created the world in six days, put Adam and Eve in the Garden of Eden (Paradise), Satan, who had led a rebellion in heaven against God and had been cast into hell along with his fellow recalcitrant angels, crept back into the Garden, tempted Eve and Adam to eat of the tree of knowledge that God had told them not to, and enraged God so that Adam and Eve were driven out into the wide human world to shift for themselves. This was what the title of the epic intended to mean.

The epic contains altogether 12 books. Book I records the downfall of Lucifer, now Satan, into the burning lake of Hell. There he and his fellow rebels lie for nine days before they recover and decide to foil God's plan by guile. In book II the evil cohorts discuss about the best course of action for them. Moloch, Belial, and Mammon, among others, speak their minds, but Beelzebub, Satan's second-in-command, gives the crowd his information about Earth which God has created and peopled with humans. The devils decide to take over the control of Earth and turn the human beings against their creator. Book III tells about Satan flying over to Earth to get some first-hand information for himself, and book IV shows God knowing everything, and observing Satan on earth trying to learn about Adam and Eve and the Tree of Knowledge. The angels, Uriel and Gabriel, try to protect the abode of Adam and Eve, but Satan acts more promptly. Assuming the form of a toad, he has already influenced Eve's dreams. Book V relates how Eve tells Adam about her dream in which she tastes the fruit of the Tree. Raphael is sent to warn the couple against disobeying God, tells them about Satan's rebellion and the creation of the world, and alerts Adam against becoming too curious about God's scheme. He readily answers some of the questions that Adam asks. In Book VI Raphael tells about how the Son of Heaven crushes Satan's hosts and sends them all down to Hell, where they writhe in pain and suffering. Book VII tells how God decides to create a new world and a new species soon after Satan's revolt. The Son of God is then sent to do the work in six days, and creates man and woman on the sixth day in the image of God and makes them lord of all. In Book VIII Adam asks about the heavenly bodies and receives an ambiguous answer from Raphael. Then Adam tells about his own experience after his creation, and how he asks God for a companion. Before he leaves Raphael tells Adam to obey God and warns him that the fate of his descendants will depend all upon his behavior. In Book IX Satan appears in the form of a serpent before Eve and coaxes her to eat the fruit. Adam eats it too. In Book X God sends His Son to pass judgment on the sinners. Satan is to become a snake, for ever the hated enemy of mankind; Eve is to bear children and suffer pain; and Adam is to toil and sweat for his bread. God begins to bring about changes to earth. Seasons are established instead of the eternal spring, and all manners of violence and suffering are introduced. The humans are to suffer the violence of the elements. Book XI notes how God expels Adam and Eve from Eden, how His angel Michael tells the future history of mankind, and of Christ as their redeemer. The last book relates Adam and Eve going down hand in hand to the plains below.

The poem's style is supremely unique. Written in highly regular blank verse (rhyme-less iambic pentameter), its very richness comes from an amalgam of diverse complex, well-interwoven stylistic features such as the power of the utterances, the exquisite aptness of diction, the countless run-on lines, the words, phrases, and clauses piling up in a well-wrought suspense, the variety of structural devices that dispel possible tedium, the vivid images and figures of speech, and the sonorous sound and the pictorial canvas. The poetic voice is dignified and effective.

One notable feature of the epic is its evident ambiguity in the poet's attitude toward God, the Devil, and man. Milton was a model Puritan. There was no doubt about his faith in God. His purpose in writing was to serve God by "... assert[ing] Eternal Providence,/ And justify[ing] the ways of God to men" (ll. 26-27). If we read his other writings such as his sonnet, "When I Consider My Light Is Spent" (1655), we will readily see his emotional piety. God's power over evil (Books I, V, VI), His prophecy of Satan's victory on earth and Christ's offer of self-sacrifice for man's redemption (Book II), God's warning to Adam (Books V, VI), God's creation of the world (Books VII), Adam's memory of his own creation and bliss with Eve (VIII), and God's gracious treatment of Adam and Eve after their fall (Book X), by showing them a vision of life on earth and giving them the hope of redemption and the courage to brave a new world (Books XI, XII)—all these well showcase the poet's faith in God. But there tends to be, after reading the work, the impression, however faint, that God can be ruthless and tyrannical, such as decreeing the inevitable success of Sin and Death and Satan and the suffering and pain of the humankind. He seems to represent control and power in life.

With Satan, there has been a continual controversy in literary and theological discussions in regard to the poet's attitude toward the Devil. Readers tend to feel after reading the work that Satan is not thoroughly condemned. The view was first well expressed by the Romantics such as Byron and Shelley. They detected the undercurrent of Milton's sympathy for Satan and his hosts. Although Satan is denounced in quite an obvious manner for his anti-God effort, there is nonetheless in between the lines an almost impalpable subtlety embedded in the texture of the very sections on Satan. In fact the epic devotes a good deal of space to the rebellious actions against God and His scheme. In Book I, Satan, awakening from his stupor to the horrors of Hell where he is cast down along with his angels, feels still proud and ambitious and not the least subdued in spirit. He holds a meeting of the rebels, calls upon the fallen cohorts to redouble their fight against the tyranny of God (Book I), and builds Pandemonium as his headquarters. Dismissing his friends' pessimistic, ineffectual or defeatist proposals, Satan takes action, bribes his way out of Hell (Book II), flies to Earth (Book III), locates the Garden of Eden (Book IV), and appears in the disguise of a snake to tempt first Eve and, then through her, Adam to disregard God's warning and eats of the Tree of Knowledge (Book IX), thus achieving his goal of destroying God's scheme of things. Satan returns to a hero's welcome in Hell and urges his friends to follow him to earth and continue the fight there. Readers tend to see in the image of Satan both the indomitable side of the poet's fighting spirit and its externalization and final assertion. Satan seems to be symbolic of the fight for freedom and against control in life. Milton's portrayal of God and Satan may be an index to the built-in ambiguity and dichotomy in the sensitive complexities of the poet's own inner soul.

As to man, the fall from Paradise has always been a point of heated discussion. Many, especially from the religious group, regard it as unfortunate as Adam's fall has led all to sin, evil, and death. But some have come to see it differently. These feel that, had there not been the fall, man would never have experienced life, attained to maturity and acquired identity and knowledge, and would never have grown up. The world would have remained one of childhood innocence, and life would have been downright tedious. Besides, the fall and evil and sin may all have been part of God's grand design. Milton's poem suggests that God knows everything before it happens. For instance, when Satan has had his way, God tells the returning angels that the sin has been inevitable. That is interesting because God is supposed to be omnipresent and omnipotent and He should have kept the Garden intact from His enemy's encroachment. He does not stop it for His own reasons. It was, after all, He who planted the tree of knowledge in the Garden of Eden and then forbade people to taste the mortal taste of its fruit. The whole plan of His hid in it an anticipation of the forthcoming fall. Then there is the question, why does He God allow Satan and evil to exist at all? This can be easily addressed if we follow Milton's clue and see life in its totality as God may have envisioned it: He may have meant it to be both good and evil for man's education and growth. Today people are still wrestling with the nature of the fall and have, with time, learned to live with the opposing views and agreed to disagree on the point.

In a similar manner, the verse drama, *Samson Agonistes* (or the Athlete, the powerful), can also be seen as objectifying the poet's own unflinching spirit. [5] The tragedy draws from a different section of the *Bible*, *The Book of Judges*. A story of praise for the undefeated, it relates the fall and rise of the seventh of the 16 "judges," as the great military leaders of Israel were called in the Old Testament. These people led the Israelites in their fight against the oppressive rule of the foreign nations that invaded Israel during the two hundred-odd years after the death of Moses and Joshua. The seventh oppression came from the Philistines, which proved to be the heaviest, longest, and most wide-spread. Samson, a man of exceptional physical power, whose strength lay in his long and thick hair, rose to the occasion and effectively checked the invasion of the Philistines. His enemies finally thought out a plan to break him. For Samson had a weakness for women, and often found it hard to resist the temptation of a pretty face. The Philistines took advantage of this and schemed for one of their beautiful women, Delilah by name, to lure him into the trap of marriage. And it worked. One day Delilah managed to cut his hair when he was asleep in her lap. Samson lost his strength, became a prisoner, and was blinded and humiliated. While in prison he prayed and renewed his pledge to God so that his hair grew again. When he was led to a Philistine Temple one day for the amusement of the Philistine lords, he placed his arms around two pillars of the mansion and brought the roof down. All died including himself, which offered an opportunity for his people to drive the foreigners out.

The drama, *Samson Agonistes*, begins at the point at which Samson is in prison. It was patterned on Greek tragedies, with its unity of time and space. There are a good number of references to the *Bible* about Samson's past glory, but the incidents of the play are all creations out of Milton's poetic imagination. At the beginning of the drama, Samson is allowed to have a day off from his prison labors, sits in front of the prison, wonders why God has chosen him as the Hebrew leader, and blames himself for his tragedy. When he hears some Jewish elders talk about his brilliant past and lament over the current Philistine occupation, Samson becomes angry and criticizes his people for being slave-minded and not doing their best when he was strong and frequently put their enemy to rout. When he hears from his sad father about the forthcoming Philistine celebration of their victory over both the Jews and Samson, he feels ashamed to have abused God's faith and prays for quick death. Then his Philistine wife, Delilah, comes to repent and offer her help, but Samson refuses to trust her again. She is followed by Harapha, the Philistine giant, who comes along to mock at the fallen Samson but is coward enough to leave at Samson's challenge for a fight. Samson's hair grows long again, and his strength, both spiritual and physical, has returned. Now the Philistine feast begins and Samson is summoned to appear before the Philistine crowd. At first he refuses to go as he feels it would bring dishonor upon his people and upon himself, but on second thought he goes. Whereas his father has almost succeeded in ransoming him, Samson does his last great deed: he pulls the temple down upon the thousands of his enemies. He dies but regains his dignity in death.

The character of Samson offers an obvious outlet of self-expression for the poet who resembled the biblical hero in more than one way. For one thing, the poet was blind. Then he married a woman from a Catholic family, with whom he was never on good terms. The most important of all, however, was the fact that he fought as did Samson for a cause of freedom, and was thrown in prison, deprived and humiliated. Although in defeat, neither Samson nor Milton was defeatist in spirit, and both of them found their ways of self-assertion and even revenge. Samson was said to have killed more Philistines at the Temple than he had ever done in his life, and Milton wrote his mighty works to immortalize the courage and perseverance of his own and his fellow-fighters in the Puritan Revolution. There is good reason to believe that Milton tries to paint his own portrait in his adumbration of Samson. And his success has been well registered in literary history.

In formal terms, the play seems to focus more on the emotional states of mind of the protagonist rather than on action. Milton himself made it clear that it was not meant for the stage. The three major episodes, involving the three visits—those of his father, his wife, and the Philistine giant, are probably meant to reveal the intense agony that the hero experiences, his growing faith in God and wisdom in handling Delilah, and his determination to avenge himself and his people and make himself worthy of God's trust through his last act of tact and valor. When viewed in this way, Samuel Johnson's criticism, that the play is inferior as it has no middle, may be beside the point though it has been seminal and influential over the centuries. [6]

Now a few words about *Lycidas* (1637) are in order here. It is a pastoral elegy of 193 lines in memory of Edward King, a young poet and one of Milton's fellow students at Cambridge University, who was drowned after a shipwreck on the Irish Seas in 1637. An elegy is in English poetry a lament or meditation often written on the occasion of the death of a loved one. "Lycidas" in the title of the poem is in classical mythology the name of a common shepherd, but is used here for Edward King. Milton is telling his readers evidently that he is writing a pastoral elegy, the conventions of which require that all the characters and even places be given classical names, that the characters live out their lives in a rural setting of the shepherds, and that the simple and honest life of the country folk in the poem acts as a foil against the sophisticated and corrupt life of the city. The pastoral elegy, as exemplified by *Lycidas*, thematically follows the conventional stages of the bereaved's emotional progression from the initial bewilderment and confusion at the death, through gradual, though painful and reluctant, resignation with and acceptance of the irrevocable fact of life, to pure peace and joy from hard-won affirmation, and to the sense of triumph of love over anguish, mortality, and time. It is impersonal in that the poet does not get involved himself as he speaks through the medium of a persona. The speaker in *Lycidas* is a "rustic swain" (l.186), who serves as the poet's surrogate. Milton's elegy was spearheaded against the Roman Catholic clergy who tried at the time to enforce uniformity and impose on Scotland the prayer book of William Laud (1573-1645), Archbishop of Canterbury and a staunch supporter of King Charles I in the Puritan Revolution.

Lycidas begins with a fellow shepherd's sad appeal to nature to join him in mourning the death of his friend, Lycidas. He appeals to the Muses for help (2nd stanza) and takes it upon himself to write this (first stanza) so that Lycidas' demise will be wept over and sung about (ll. 11-14). The first three stanzas also set the poem in a rich pastoral background and introduce the speaker as a "rustic swain" (l.186). The next stanza (ll. 37-49) depicts the devastating effect of the shepherd's death on nature, which accurately externalizes the shepherd-poet's agony. The complaint and the wishful dream in stanza 5 (ll. 50-63) further denotes the pain and the sense of helplessness on the part of the poet. Stanzas 6 (ll. 64-84) and 7 (ll. 85-102) tell about the shepherd-poet's awakening to the fact that a laborious life is a thankless affair not even to be remembered and that life itself is a haphazard thing subject only to chance and fate. The pessimism here indicates the fury and the depth of despair to which the shepherd-poet sinks. The 8th stanza (ll. 103-130) begins with Cambridge University's query about the killer and introduces the Roman Catholic clergy who tolerate no dissent. In the next stanza (ll.131-164), the shepherd-poet says on returning to lamenting the death of Lycidas, "Return, Alpheus, the dread voice is past" (l. 131), which signifies the end of the quest for the cause of death and the change in mood from anguish and anger to resignation.

He calls upon nature to sing for his friend and decorate his hearse, so as to make it easier for him to accept the fact of death and dally with the hope that the dead body might be recovered from the sea, where he sees his friend visiting or sleeping under the protection of the archangels (ll. 156-164). He asks the dolphins to help carry his friend's spirit to the Blessed Isles. This leads naturally to the epiphany that the shepherd-poet experiences in the next stanza (ll. 165-185), when he sees the vision of his friend being well received and happy in Heaven as the guardian spirit of the shore and feels strengthened with the faith in immortality. Immensely happy to win through grief and suffering to the recognition of the power of love and faith over time and death, the shepherd-poet is ready and eager to sing and looks forward to a new beginning (ll. 186-190).

Though it is not the first of its kind in English literature, *Lycidas* has certainly proved to be a frame of reference for the writing of the genre of pastoral elegies. Subsequent works of the category are very often, if not always, measured against its manner of composition for evaluation and comment. Such works that come to mind instantly include, among others, Gray's *Elegy Written in a Country Churchyard*, Shelley's *Adonais*, and Tennyson's *In Memoriam*. Some recent examples would be the American poets—Gwendolyn Brooks' "The Rites for Cousin Vit" and Theodore Roethke's "Elegy for Jane."

John Dryden (1631-1700)

Dryden came from a well-to-do country family, received his education from Cambridge University, and was regarded as the most learned person of his time. He was notorious for his frequent face-about in face of the changing political climate of his day. He was supportive of Cromwell when he wrote his famous "Heroic Stanzas" (1659) on the Protector's death, switched over to Charles II with his "Astaea Redux" (1660), and jumped ship again from the Church of England to Roman Catholicism to show his loyalty to the Catholic King James II with his "The Hind and the Panther" (1687). He had become very famous and popular by 1667 and was made Poet Laureate the next year. But when the Glorious Revolution occurred in 1688, he refused to pledge allegiance to the new ruler, King William of Orange, and was deprived of all his offices and pensions. From a literary point of view, this adversity came to him actually as a blessing in disguise. Had he continued to write his licentious dramas to cater to the depraved taste of his restoration royal audience as he did from 1664 through1687, he would have sunk into total oblivion as his 27 plays have by now. He was never a great playwright. His plots were often impossible, his dialogues absurd, and his themes infused with court ideas and sentiments. Of the number of dramas he wrote for the restoration theater, only one, *All for Love*, an adaptation of Shakespeare's *Antony and Cleopatra* written in blank verse, is anything worth mention at all. He wasted his genius well over two decades writing trash, but the last decade of his life, poor and in disgrace, proved to be the best phase of his literary career.

In historical retrospect, Dryden is remembered for two things he did admirably well for his country's literature. One of these was his successful effort to prune the Elizabethan language of its formless exuberance and turn it into a cool, lucid, plain, and natural medium for English writing. Musical, precise, and dignified, Dryden's language received reinforcements from Alexander Pope and neoclassic writers and stretched its impact well into the 19th century. Even the Romantic movement of the early 19th century, which was in fact a strenuous reaction to the excesses of Popian classicism, showed decent respect for Dryden's legacy. The fact was that the enthusiasm, which had characterized the romantic outburst of the Elizabethan age, had brought forth at once a colorful variety in theme and diction, and an obvious lack of form and discipline with it. It was like a sprawling botanical garden that needed proper trimming. Dryden saw the need for rectification and introduced the classic elements and heralded the beginning of Neoclassicism that was to become a tyrannical vogue in the next century. He was, in this sense, the first Neoclassic writer in English literary history. It was he who made the heroic couplet (rhyming couplets in iambic pentameter) almost the one poetic medium acceptable for poetry and thus paved the way for the rise of Alexander Pope. No wonder that Pope took Dryden as his model. Samuel Johnson (1709-1784) says it all when commenting on Dryden's contribution to the refining of the English language: "... he found it brick, and he left it marble." [7]

Another thing, more significant in nature, is his contribution to English literary criticism. Dryden was basically good at literary criticism. His insight and perspicacity of observation are well demonstrated in his critical works such as *An*

Essay of Dramatic Poesy (1668) and the number of prefaces he wrote for his various works, the most famous of which is the one for his book of translations from Homer, Virgil, Ovid, Boccaccio (1313-1375), and Chaucer, *Fables Ancient and Modern* (1700). He was a highly influential literary dictator of his time as Ben Jonson before him. His critical writings helped establish the canons of taste and principles of English literary criticism. These include, among other things, a catholic taste and a balanced approach, the critical emphasis on textual analysis rather than on juggling with theoretical abstractions, emphasis on erudition, deep thought, and comparative analysis, the critical focus on the major points of interest rather than on a comprehensive evaluation, the emphasis on asserting personal ideas rather than attempting a systematic exposition, and the use of a succinct yet lucid essay form. These Drydenian features have been visible in English literary criticism ever since. Some of Dryden's comments on certain authors like Chaucer and Shakespeare are still held in high esteem today. Thus Dryden has been seen as "the father of English criticism." [8]

Dryden's verse satire, *Absalom and Achitophel* (1681), is still well read today not so much because of its thematic concern as for its striking formal features. The poem is based on a biblical story concerning the power struggle between King David and his son Absalom (Old Testament: 2 *Samuel*). Absalom harbors the ambition to replace his father as king of Israel and starts a rebellion with the support of one of the king's advisers, Achitophel. When the conspiracy fails, Absalom meets his doom. Dryden's poem was written as a spearhead against the ambitions of Charles II's bastard son (Duke of Monmouth) and his fellow conspirator, Earl of Shaftsbury who, out of the interest of his political group, supported the Duke's bid for succession. The 17th-century scenario was amazingly similar to that in the *Bible*. The poet, taking the side of Charles II, felt obligated to write this to show his support for the throne. The historic significance of the work has to do with its stylistic aspect. Dryden, making the best of the heroic couplet as a satirical instrument and exhibiting its potential power, molded a style at once effective and pungent, revealed himself as a master of satire and a dexterous manipulator of language, and won a place of preeminence which few have ever touched.

John Bunyan (1628-1688)

Bunyan was born into a poor tinker's family, one of the meanest and most despised in English society then. He had little education. Honest, sincere, and endowed with a sensitive imagination, he was fired with an irresistible earnestness to teach people to be good and virtuous. He read the *Bible*, reformed himself, and wrote and preached among the common people. He became a man of the people, and the kindest man of all. He was so pious and faithful that he said once, "No one in England could please God more than I do." As his popularity and dissenting voice seemed a threat to the monarchy and the Anglican Church, he was arrested and stayed in prison for 12 years (1660-1672), and was again imprisoned for six months in 1675. But he never succumbed to the authorities' request to stop preaching as a condition for his release, and continued to write and also make laces to support his family when in prison. He wrote over 60 books and pamphlets, all in the service of God and his fellow men. He said that he could write in a much higher style, but he wanted to talk to the common people. In addition to his masterpiece, *The Pilgrim's Progress*, which is the most popular (said to be second only to the *Bible*), some of his other writings are still read with a good deal of interest. These include *Grace Abounding to the Chief of Sinners* (1666), *The Life and Death of Mr. Badman* (1680), a satire against the evil practices of the upper classes, and *Holy War* (1682), an allegorical censure of the sociopolitical ills of the day as well as an outcry for justice for the wrongly persecuted. Bunyan died working for his parish in 1688. He was known as "Bishop Bunyan" among the people.

The Pilgrim's Progress is an allegory. It consists of two parts, the first of which was out in print in 1678, and the second in 1684. It reads like a medieval miracle play with vivid and lively personifications of virtues and vices and all the human qualities in between. It became immediately popular on publication and went through over ten printings. The first part is generally considered the better of the two, containing as it does the ten stages of the pilgrim's progress. Part two relates a similar pilgrimage that his wife, Christiana, and his children undertake, which is rather a weak echo of the first. The book was intended to teach people to be faithful to God and win salvation by constantly purging one's heart of worldly evil.

Now let's take a look at the narrative of the first part.

It takes the form of a dream vision on the part of the narrator-author: the whole book, in fact, is the description of the visions of a dozen dreams. In stage one, the narrator begins by saying that he dreams of a man with a book in his hand and a great burden on his back, who keeps crying out, "What shall I do?" This man is the main character of the story—Christian. The story is about his effort to find faith and salvation by making his pilgrimage to the Celestial Kingdom. Coming from the City of Destruction, Christian would like to find a way of escape from death and judgment. Here the Evangelist comes along to his help and guides him on his way to the Celestial City. Christian takes leave of his family and sets out on his way. He overcomes resistance from his neighbors—Obstinate and Pliable, falls into the Slough of Despond and is dragged out by Help, meets a gentleman by the name of Worldly Wiseman, repudiates his advice with the help of the Evangelist, and goes on with his pilgrimage. In stage two Christian meets Goodwill who shows him a narrow way to the House of the Interpreter (i.e. Holy Spirit). From the Interpreter Christian learns about salvation and judgment. Stage three records a Christian, freed of his burden, with sin forgiven, clothed in a new garment and given a roll to read, feeling happy and ready to help his fellow humans. Christian keeps on going up a hill, experiences some doubt and recovers his faith, and continues on to reach a stately palace where he stays for a few days. The fourth stage is one in which Christian kills the monster Apollyon in the Valley of Humiliation and labors through the two parts of the Valley of the Shadow of Death. In stage five Christian and Faithful meet, get rid of the irritable company of Talkative, and go on their way together.

The sixth stage comes when the Evangelist joins them for a moment and warns them of the dangers and trials lying in store before them. Then the two come to the Town of Vanity in which Vanity Fair is located. As their presence causes a commotion, they are thrown in prison and then tried. Faithful is found guilty and put to a cruel death, and his body is carried to the Celestial City gate. Christian manages to escape with the help of the Lord and resumes his journey to Mt. Zion. In stage seven Christian, joined by Hopeful, resists the temptation of the silver mine—Lucre, reaches the river of God, and rests to refresh himself for a few days. As they avoid the rough right way and take an easy detour, they come to the Doubting Castle of Giant Despair who throws them into its dungeon. They finally escape with the help of the key Promise and get once more on the King's high way. The next stage, the eighth, witnesses the two of them meeting the shepherds—Knowledge, Experience, Watchful, and Sincere—on the Delectable Mountains, who take them to the Hill of Error and the Hill of Caution, give them more instructions, and warn them to beware of Flatterer and the Enchanted Ground. These and Atheist they meet in the ninth stage and reach the borders of heaven in the last stage, the tenth. Here they wade through a deep river as another trial of their faith, leave their mortal garments behind, and go uphill. Then they come within sight of Mt. Zion. The dreaming narrator sees a city of gold into which Christian and Hopeful are welcomed and transfigured. He wishes himself among the people there who enjoy eternal bliss. Presently he awakes.

Pilgrim's Progress abounds in acute social criticism. The section on Vanity Fair is one of the best. The Town of Vanity was first built by Beelzebub (Satan's friend in Hell). Here are found all kinds of human vanities on sale for a price (property, status, nations, husbands and wives, souls, honors, lusts and delights), and all kinds of people and sins (such as theft, murder, adultery, perjury). The different rows into which the city is divided, such the British Row and the French Row, are meant to denote the different countries and their religious denominations and factions, and the city stands as a metaphor for a microcosm of the sinning and corrupt human world and the sum total of its evil. It is a vivid satire against the corrupt and depraved England of the restoration, where the princes and nobles lived a reckless life of debauchery. It is also an authentic reflection of the popular mood, among the lower social strata, of disaffection at the compromise between parliament and the monarchy. Needless to say, the book is highly religious with its earnest appeal to the human soul to have faith and hope for the bliss of the Kingdom of God. It is good to know that the notion of Vanity Fair was to offer a title for one great Victorian novel, *Vanity Fair*, by William Makepeace Thackeray (1811-1863).

The book is also noted for its prose style. It is a nice amalgam of the basic features of the language of the *Bible* and popular speech. Simple, lucid, and forceful, Bunyan's prose has a striking modern ring. It has helped upgrade English prose and paved the way for the rise of the modern English novel in the next century. In addition, the book is of infinite value as a good source of the household words, familiar phrases, and picturesque similes with which it has enriched the English language. Bunyan became a great force in the history of English prose without ever desiring it. His art was great but unconscious.

The Restoration Theater [10]

For some 20 years (1642-1660) English theater remained closed and totally inactive. It was reopened when Charles II came back in 1660. Every bit the opposite of what the Puritans stood for, the king and his corrupt court lived without moral principles and went as far as to embrace promiscuity and sexual freedom. The plays written and staged in the restoration period were mostly comedies of manners representing the "manners" of the king and his court and the nobles. This mode of writing attained to maturity in the works of the three eminent dramatists of the period—George Etherege (1635-1691), William Wycherley (1640-1716), and William Congreve (1670-1728). Their works were accused in their time of immorality and indecency and have been known ever since for those stigmatic trademarks. The brand is not very just as some of the works did satirize the depravities and sexual laxities that they represented. George Etherege started the fashion of writing about the lifestyles and tastes of the nobles and the upper class in his *The Man of Mode*, which caught on with his contemporaries and later writers. A better craftsman with a clearer vision was William Wycherley who made himself famous with such famous works as *Love in a Wood* (1671), *The Gentleman Dancing-Master* (1672), *The Country Wife* (1672-73), and *The Plain Dealer* (1674), in which he gives full play to his satiric powers. He at once presents the corrupt people and their lives and loses no time to reveal his contempt for these. Wycherley was indebted to both Ben Jonson and Moliere in his dramatic career.

The best dramatist of the restoration comedy of manners was probably William Congreve. Always with a high moral purpose topmost in his mind, Congreve wrote a number of brilliant comedies such as *The Old Bachelor* (1693),

The Double Dealer (1693), *Love for Love* (1695), and *The Way of the World* (1700). He wrote also a tragedy, *The Mourning Bride* (1697). He is well noted for his comic genius and his witty and exquisite dialogues. *The Way of the World* has been seen as his best work. Whereas it is about the moral concerns regarding the relationship between the two sexes, the play reveals the author's stance clearly, i.e. exalting true love and fidelity between man and wife and censuring anything immoral and selfish in marriage. The genuine love and marriage of Mirabell with Millamant is made to contrast with the lecherous, prudish old widow Lady Wishfort and the greedy and hypocritical dandy Mr. Fainall. The bargaining scene (IV. 5) and the scene in which Lady Wishfort falls into a trap (IV.12) prove to be among the most entertaining of the whole performance.

Chapter 6 The Classic Age • Pope • Johnson • Gray • Goldsmith • Sheridan

The Classic Age: An Introduction [1]

The 18th century can be neatly subdivided into two halves, each with their notable social, economic, and literary features. The first half of the century was essentially centripetal, with all the forces coming together. The British Empire had become one on which the sun never set. It ruled over about ¼ of the world's population, dominated the sea, and had plundered and brought in a tremendous amount of wealth from its colonies. Inside the British Isles, things appeared basically all right. On the economic scene, the country became increasingly affluent, the factory system began to develop, trade flourished, and there was an outburst of productivity. A mercantile system came into being to meet the needs of trade and production, though it was still under tight government control. Things had changed for the better. The standards of living rose. People's diet was improving markedly along with their clothes and methods of transportation, which all made for a superficial kind of optimism. A feeling of prosperity was up in the air, of life getting better, a feeling of righteousness, that they must be doing things basically right. The change was slow, but no serious dislocation had yet occurred. These all received due representation in 18th-century literature.

On the political scene, a fragile kind of balance exited. On the one hand, the king's power was essentially broken after the Glorious Revolution of 1688, and the middle class-dominated parliament could decide who was to be king. But on the other, for a long time after that event, neither the monarch nor parliament was sufficiently aware of the shift in power, so that the monarch could still block the passing of laws, and the middle class still felt they did not have enough power to have things done their way. No matter how precarious the balance might be, however, it was still kept in place. This was by and large the situation with the first half of the century. Incidentally, the 18th century valued balance, middle things, the middle class, moderation, reason, common sense, traditional forms, and deism. The good words for the 18th century were "we," "submit," and "reasonableness."

But troubles began to appear in the second half of the century. The middle class continued its push for more freedom to do business as it pleased. Technology and science jumped, and inventions and the protection for patents faciliated change and growth. In addition, the discovery of the steam power, the advent of the steam engine, the adoption of the steam-driven machines in factories, the steam ships, the subsequent expansion of the merchant fleet, the use of chemicals, the mechanization of farming, and the further pillaging of the colonies—all these brought about huge changes in the basic eco-social scene of the country. The Industrial Revolution was now in full swing. This part of the century was a period of growing fortune for the middle class, but one of intensified debasement for the working class. With the factory towns making life ever more dirty, ugly, and unhealthy, the workers suffered nondescript degradation. Hence the occurrence of widespread social upheavals. If the first half of the 18th century remained good enough to ignore these problems, it was now no longer possible for the second half to do so.

Toward the latter part of the century and at the beginning of the 19th, serious upheavals and dislocations began to beset the country. The farmers went bankrupt and swarmed to the cities where, along with the city poor, they struggled for survival. The proletariat came into being and, with it, the long drawn-out conflict between capital and labor. With the growing discontent and disaffection among the poor, cries of rebellion began to rumble. The French Revolution was in the making, and so was the American Independence War. Sensing imminent danger from these quarters, the British ruling class lost no time intensifying their repressive rule. This was then roughly the backdrop against which the age of reason began to take a backseat, and the romantic spirit was getting ready for its outburst.

Regarding religion, there was a significant change as well. In the 17th century, religion was a serious matter enough to help start a war—the Civil War. The Puritans believed devoutly in their hard creed and painful virtues. John Milton was adamant that his religion had placed on him the obligation to do God's will and put his work and poetry at the service of society. The 18th century turned out to be radically different. Formal religion died down. The century believed in God, but it did not believe in formal religion with its tenets of revelation and supernatural elements. The nature of the universe changed as well according to the mechanical improvements for which the century is noted. It became a kind of mechanical universe as it was likened to a clock which God made but left ticking away on its own laws. The world owed its existence to God and the best way to worship God was to worship His creation—man, nature, and the world as a whole. This new doctrine has been known in history as Deism. There was no doubt that people were good believers. Pope was devoutly Catholic, Samuel Johnson published a book of prayers, and Joseph Addison called in his nephew at the time of his death just to witness his peaceful death as a good Christian. But religion was now considered private and personal, and it was bad taste to bring it out in public and let it interfere with public affairs. Franklin and Voltaire were both generous supporters of the church although neither ever set foot in it. Swift was the dean of a cathedral despite the fact that he did not believe in Christianity. When asked the question, "What could a priest do if he did not believe?" he replied with "Keep your mouth shut and do God's work." The prevailing notion seemed to be that God did not object to people not believing in Him, and that the best way to serve God was to do good to man.

Amidst such a scenario, new ideas appeared to make their presence felt. John Locke (1632-1704) became the theoretician of the 18th century, and Adam Smith (1623-1790) the champion of capitalism in the economic field. Locke's *Concerning Human Understanding* (1690) was the most important psychological work for his century, and his two treatises on civil government the most important political science work of its time. He was to the rising middle class what Karl Marks represented to the proletariat, offering a kind of understanding of the world that that class wanted. What he says in *Concerning Human Understanding* is this, that people have to learn through their senses and that the things they really know are the things they can check with their senses. People learn through their experience of feeling, seeing, touching, measuring and weighing, and reason is of the primary importance in learning to understand the world. This could, and did, lead away from religion and call in question the whole concept of God and Trinity, and inspire people to believe that they can deduce the nature of God by looking around His creation, that religion is based on reason, not revelation, and that God works through general laws and not the tablets He gave to Moses. That was, the background for Deism, the worship of God's creation as mentioned earlier on. Deism became the trend in the 18th century, and found an echo in such important authors as Pope and Jonathan Swift. This, together with the Locken idea that men come into this world innocent like a blank page, contradicted the notion of original sin and outraged the Puritans in particular.

Locke's political science concept on civil government was seminal and inspiring in human history. As he states in his *Two Treatises of Government* (1690), men are born with no innate prejudices and capable of reason; they are born good, their natural state being peaceful, tolerant, free and equal; all the people have the right to pursue their happiness; reason leads to cooperation and general welfare; people come together in a civil contract for mutual defense of their rights, property, and labor; and the pursuit of one's self-interest is a way to serve society. These ideas constituted a direct attack on the feudal system and the divine rights of kings and contributed a good deal toward breaking up feudal power and control. In addition, these promoted human rights and justified the growth of capitalism and middle class control in parliament. Locke would like to see a system of checks and balances in place to prevent tyranny and encourage political tolerance. These Locken concepts were not only to leave their imprint on the 18th century, but to produce a far-reaching global impact for all time. Both the French Revolution and the American War of Independence, which Locke had in mind to justify, owed obviously to his precepts.

Adam Smith was no less influential in his own way. His *The Wealth of Nations* (1776), proposing as it does the theory of *laissez-faire*, did a good deal of theoretical spade work to help bring down government control on industry and trade, boost the middle-class morale, and pave the way for immense further growth of capitalism. With his rationalization, the middle class felt more secure and freer than ever.

In the field of literature there existed also a balance between respect for the old and the emergence of new forms, and between reason and emotion. This was best expressed by the literary dictator of the first half of the century, Alexander

Pope, when he advised writers to "copy nature and read Homer." In the meantime, new forms like the novel appeared. The major features of the literature of the period are as follows:

(1) It was a literature of reason, common sense, and repudiation of enthusiasm and sentiment. This was in fact a reaction to the outburst of Romantic feeling in the previous periods (Elizabethan and 17th century). The romantic bloom continued in Milton and began to cool down with John Dryden, who took it upon himself to "prune and trim" the natural botanical garden of Romantic England. It came to a full stop with Alexander Pope when things experienced an about-face, the "natural" changed to its complete opposite, "artificial," and classic rules were prized and enforced. Hence the nomenclature of the century as "the classic age." This swing to Popian neoclassicism was further reinforced by Joseph Edison, Richard Steele, and Samuel Johnson. Edison and Steele did their best to help both "civilize" the still crude tastes and habits of their countrymen with their image of the English gentleman, and turn the English language into one akin to the classic languages in dignity, grandeur, and expressiveness. As to Samuel Johnson, his power as an absolute literary dictator of the latter half of the century made it difficult, if not entirely impossible, for writers to deviate from the classic manner of composition. The basic features of neoclassicism include, among other things, frequent allusions and references to Greek and Roman mythology and to ancient writers and historians; predilection for abstractions and excessive use of personifications; respect for and promotion of order and reason with emphasis on clarity of thought and orderly structure; focus on formal perfection like metric regularity, aversion to verbosity, and love of graceful language; and a conspicuous want of feeling and sentiment. The dominant neoclassic form was the heroic couplet, i.e. two rhyming lines in iambic pentameter. Neoclassic poetry tends to produce the effect of an artificially trimmed beauty, beautiful but often lifeless.

(2) Although the neoclassic tastes and values of Pope and Samuel Johnson dominated the better part of the 18th century, reason was not strong enough to totally stamp out the sparks of emotion. Thus there was, almost from the very outset, an undercurrent that moved in a different direction, i.e. the current that would eventually lead to a fresh outburst of romantic feeling. James Thomson's *Seasons*, Oliver Goldsmith's *The Vicar of Wakefield*, Percy's collection of popular

ballads, and James McPherson's *The Poems of Ossian,* are all obvious examples of the works that would point forward to the advent of Robert Burns and William Blake. If one reads Edward Young's *Complaint or Night Thoughts on Life, Death, and Immortality*, Thomas Gray's *Elegy Written in a Country Churchyard*, William Cowper's *The Task*, George Crabbe's *The Village*, and Goldsmith's *The Deserted Village*, one would detect the stubborn romantic sentiment that runs beneath a hard neoclassic surface and would then have a better sense of the inevitable emotional outpour that finally occurred in the *Lyrical Ballads* and the subsequent rise of the short but rich and brilliant reputations of the Romantic period. In the latter half of the century, poetry moved toward a closer contact with nature and society.

(3) At the same time, there were also writers who took a closer look at the social problems and undertook to help put things to rights by criticizing the society in which they lived. Remarkable in acumen and eloquent in saying the right things in the most effectively right way, they were worshipped and paid by society to tell it how bad it was. Jonathan Swift was one of the most forceful critics of the time. All of his writings were biting satires on the social ills of his time. George Crabbe, Richard Brinsley Sheridan, Joseph Addison and Richard Steele, Henry Fielding, Laurence Sterne, and Tobias Smollett all helped locate and address social problems in their different ways.

(4) As a result of the improvement of literacy and with leisure now available in life, the demand for literature increased. New forms of literary writings in the broad sense of the word came into being to meet the need. Newspapers, magazines, encyclopedias, dictionaries, and grammar—all were established as acceptable forms. On top of it all, the novel appeared. The new genre was basically a book telling a story about ordinary life as was lived then, a practice in sharp contrast with the romances of the previous periods which dealt with fantasy and far-away things. The novel proved to be exactly what the middle class wanted badly. The novels of Defoe, Richardson, Fielding, Smollett, and Sterne were out in print to the great gratification of the people in general.

Alexander Pope (1688-1744)

In more than one sense Pope was the most important English poet to come out of the 18th century. For one thing, he was the best known and the most influential not only in England but in the Europe of his time, and his heroic couplet, in rhymed iambic pentameter, took the stage and became the dominant vogue in poetic creation on both sides of the English Channel. Then he was the absolute literary dictator on the literary scene of his time, so much so that any departure from his theories would be considered downright "heathenish." The first part of the 18th century was altogether his time to shine over all. Over the centuries, however, Pope's reputation has gone through phases of ebbs and flows. When the Romantic spirit reasserted itself again at the turn of the 19th century, he was discredited by all except Byron (1788-1824), but he made a comeback in the 1920s when he received fresh critical recognition. Pope has been seen as one of the most important English poets ever since.

Pope was an unusual individual in more than one way. In terms of personal life he was very unfortunate. As he came from a Catholic background, he was denied a formal education and the prospect of a political career. Moreover, the disease that tormented him all his life, a form of tuberculosis of the spine, stunted his growth and deformed his body so that he was only about four feet in height. He suffered a lifelong stomach trouble, and could never marry and live normally. But Pope was not a person to give in easily to the odds. Though a dwarf in physical stature, he was to make himself a giant in poetry and in the literary history of his country. He taught himself how to read and write, picked up a good knowledge of some classic languages such as Latin and Greek with the help of dictionaries and grammar books, and became a classic poet in his own language. He enjoyed a highly successful poetic career.

He did one thing only all his life, but did it perfectly: The heroic couplet became a perfect poetic medium in his hands, so powerful and fascinating in his time that the rest of the world could not but write in the same manner, and no one has so far ever achieved as much as he did with this verse form. This form of writing had been used in fact by such previous masters as Chaucer, Spenser, and Marlowe, but had been for some time superseded by blank verse (rhymeless iambic pentameter). It resurfaced in the 17th century, became better especially in the works of John Dryden, but attained to perfection only in the 18th century as a result of Pope's painstaking effort. That is the why Pope is always closely linked with it. But Pope also did another thing every bit as well as this: he weeded feeling and emotion successfully out of poetry and so has been accused by some people of having almost killed poetry. Pope's poetic craft is impeccable. It is always an enjoyable experience to read him if only for knowledge, and for his rhythms, rhymes, and the musical ring of his words. He represents the typical 18th-century poet who was primarily a craftsman, a versifier, whose hallmark was that he could do his best work regardless of whether he felt it or not. And Pope was a good craftsman (but not a poet as some say). One of the major functions of the poet, as his poetry well illustrates, was to help people remember things. [2]

A sketchy introduction of some of Pope's works is in order here. Pope's well-known works include his translation of Homer, *Essay on Criticism* (1711), *The Rape of the Lock* (1712), *Essay on Man* (1733), *An Epistle to Dr. Arbuthnot* (1735), and *The Dunciad* (1743). First, his translation of Homer, which made him immensely famous and popular, and financially independent, was in fact a paraphrase of the original as his knowledge of Greek was not proficient enough for a more faithful rendition. The work was not even faithful in spirit. There was little Greek feeling in it; Pope infused the spirit and values of his own time into it, instead. But as things often have an uncanny way of turning out in an unexpected fashion, his translation catered inadvertently to the self-complacent taste of the English people of the 18th century. It possesses one redeeming grace to the readers of today, however: The beauty of his heroic couplet with its pleasant rhythms and rhymes proves to be irresistibly exquisite and charming.

Then there is *The Rape of the Lock*, the mock epic of five cantos about "a Homeric struggle of the teacups." It was based on an actual episode of little or no significance, which led to the discord of two noble families. Lord Petre, a fop of court, playfully cut a lock of hair from the head of Arabella Fermor, a lady he adored, and there ensued a bitter quarrel between the Fermors and the Petres. Pope was requested to write a poem so as to reveal the trivial nature of the row and help pacify the two houses, and the result was the humorous poem in 334 lines. It came out a great success in 1712. Pope reveals, in a mild satirical tone, the idle and silly high-society life of cards, parties, tea, lap dogs, lovers, toilets, the vanity of women, and the foolishness of fawning men. He also touches, though only in a tangential manner, on the position of women in a man-oriented social setting.

When he began to expand the first version in 1713, he brought in the mythological and supernatural elements and their epic behaviors. The effort added a good deal of humor to the poem but little substance to the satire. In addition to his perfect heroic couplets, Pope shows his poetic virtuosity in his adroit use of detail, his eloquent mastery of the epic conventions, and his ingenuity to turn a trifle into one of the most popular, the finest, satiric poems in his country's history.

As to *The Dunciad*, a work of four books, this was first composed as part of a controversy on Pope's edition of Shakespeare and a comment on the literary climate of the time. But as the poet proceeded with the writing, it became a leverage of revenge for his long pent-up bitterness against some of his literary rivals. The truth was that some of Pope's works might have suffered some slight, and that he might have had quarrels with some literary men and have been subject to humiliation on account of his deformity. Thus in his ruthless blows at his enemies, Pope occasionally descended very low so that his effort boomeranged somehow as it showed him to be narrow-minded and lacking in catholic taste. The good part about the work is, however, its revelation of the dreadful widespread dullness of his age and its brilliant satire on the vices of the literary world then. Though it is couched in humorous mock-epic form, Pope is dead serious with his warning to his country of the real danger coming from ignorance and the triumph of dullness.

Finally, there is *An Epistle to Dr. Arbuthnot*, which is one of Pope's best poems. Queen Anne's physician, Dr. John Arbuthnot (1667-1735), was a friend of such literary celebrities as Pope and Jonathan Swift and a celebrity of the time in his own way. He wrote on his sick bed a letter to Pope, advising him to be kind when writing satires. Pope wrote the poem in response, trying to convince the doctor that his satires had been all self-defenses and never meant to be vituperous. Thus the work was intended to be his "apologia" justifying his life, work, and personality. It is necessary to read it to get to know about the man and his mentality. As he says in the epistle, he is not happy, and he bitterly complains about a joyless existence (ll. 272-274). He is dutiful and loving to his parents (ll. 388-413), willing to learn and write (ll. 125-146), and proud of his independence (ll. 249-270/ ll. 334-359). He hates people picking on his deformity (ll. 115-124), and detests sleights of hand against him. His enemies include cohorts of people ranging from the friends and confidants of the queen to powerful politician-men of letters such as Joseph Addison (ll. 197-214). Pope could be cruel and mean in his satire, but he exercised tact as well. For Addison, for instance, he left room for making friends with the man in the future. [3]

Now let's take a look at some of Pope's major works.

Essay on Man is probably the most important of all Pope's works, and certainly the best known and most often quoted. As an authentic record of the views and values of the 18th century, this "ethic work" (as Pope calls it), his philosophical poem, is significant in the cultural and intellectual history of his country as well. As his survey of man and society, the essay presents a lucid synthesis of Pope's deliberations on the cosmos, the theology, and the ethics of his time following his conversations with his philosopher friend, Lord Bolingbroke. In addition, the poet had also picked up many clues for his ideas from Plato, Aristotle, and some Enlightenment philosophers like the German philosopher G. W. Leibnitz (1646-1716). The essay of four epistles intends, in the tone of Milton's *Paradise Lost*, "to vindicate the ways of God to man." All through the work, Pope keeps praising God as the source of goodness, telling people not to judge Him and His creation but accept and obey His plan for universal good and happiness. The essay is a cogent justification of the gradation or multi-tier hierarchy of God's creation and also of the 18th-century emphasis on order and harmony.

Now epistle I is a brilliant summary of the basic concepts of wide currency in England and Europe at the time. It offers the optimistic 18th-century view of the world created by God. God is the ultimate source of all creation in His carefully ordered system of gradation. In God's grand scheme of things, man who has reason stands in the middle, between the lower creatures at one end and angels and God at the other. Thus placed in the "Vast Chain of Being," man's knowledge and perceptive powers are limited, his judgment of the cosmos (seeing it as imperfect) is faulty, and his errors such as his pride and aspirations tend to disrupt God's plan. Man can be happy if he is ignorant and knows only to hope for a better future. Evil exists to make for good ("All partial Evil, Universal good"). Pope affirms the goodness of all that exists ("WHATEVER IS, IS RIGHT") and proves himself to be a supporter of the existing system. Pope was not a social critic as was Jonathan Swift. He was very conservative in his opinions.

Epistle II discusses human nature and the human condition. In his middle position between God and beast, man possesses both virtue and vice. His self-love motivates him to action, and his reason controls it so as to do good. When the two work together, nothing can go wrong. Passions are modes of self-love. The ruling passion in man determines his basic personality. Human weaknesses contribute to mutual dependence. Man should know his place and stay content with it. Epistle III talks about man's role in society. All is interrelated in the chain of being; all is allotted his share of happiness and should love itself and others. With regard to the species below him, man is given power as well as responsibility. In society there exist self-love and social love, the two linking with one another to work toward harmony and happiness for all. True religion and government are united in love; superstition and tyranny disrupt nature's order. Epistle IV relates to man's happiness. God intends all in His chain to be equally happy. Man's happiness depends on health, peace, and competence. Virtue's reward is not earthly and external. It is not his possessions and gifts of fortune, but his virtuous personality that matters to man. Virtue and love of God and man lead to the happiness of one and all. Self-love is a blessing when it transcends its limits and devotes itself to social and divine love. [4]

Regarding *Essay on Criticism*, the work has been regarded as one of the important works in English literary criticism. Here Pope is famous chiefly not for what he says, but for the way he says it. He wrote to introduce the accepted canons of tastes in memorable, beautiful language and help people remember them. Some of the critical theories that he discussed so well in his own words and style were actually gleaned from previous works such as Aristotle's *Poetics*, Roman poet Horace's *Ars Poetica*, Renaissance Italian poet Vida's *Poetica*, and 17th-century French poet Boileau's *L' Art poetitique*. In addition, he also drew from the works of Roman rhetorician Quitinlian, Ben Jonson's *Timber, or Discoveries*, and the prefaces of John Dryden.

Pope's essay consists of three parts. Part one (ll. 1-200) talks about the vital importance of literary criticism and the growth of a good critic. A good critic should have sound judgment or "true taste" and wit, which can be improved through good education. He should, to begin with, know his limitations and possible prejudices. Then he should learn to know about "Unerring nature," which is his standard and ideal. The best rules of criticism exist in the ancient works that have stood the test of time. The criticism today tends to overshadow the works of art that it is supposed to help people to appreciate. A true critic must copy Homer and Virgil and "the great men of the past." Part two (ll. 201-559) locates the causes of poor judgments, and traces the major reasons for deficient criticism. These include, among other things, pride that causes blindness; inadequate learning that impairs a balanced comprehension of a poem ("A little learning is a dangerous thing"); deviation from nature in preference for parts to whole; praising of style and language and over-fondness for metrics or imagery to the neglect of content; indulgence in intolerance and extremes of fashion and personal tastes; subjectivity, personal motives, self-love, jealousy, and personal spleen that conspire to distort evaluation. Part three (ll. 560-744) discusses the ideal character of a critic and the principles of literary criticism, and offers a sketchy history of European literary criticism and a summary of the character of the best critics. The good qualities of an ideal critic include such as integrity, modesty, tact, and courage. In addition, such a critic should have a good knowledge of books and humankind and should not rush in, like a learned fool, "where angels fear to tread." Among the most famous good critics of ancient Greece and Rome, Pope lists Aristotle, Horace, Dionysius, Quintilian, and Longinus as the best. For the modern times, Pope mentions Erasmus and Boileau, but feels that England has not much to offer in terms of good criticism.

Samuel Johnson (1709-1784)

Johnson's personal life is interesting to talk about. He was a poor but kind man. He came from humble beginnings, managed to receive his education at Oxford, and became a schoolmaster in his early twenties. He married at 26 a woman twenty years his senior in what he called "a love match," and was kind to her all his life. Though basically a poet, he did a variety of other writings. He wrote a novel in one week, spent seven years compiling a dictionary all by himself, edited Shakespeare's plays, edited magazines such as *Rambler* and *Idler*, and wrote a critical book on poets. After he received a pension from King George III, he began to take in people like a blind woman and a poor physician. Around the late 1860s, he started a famous club of important writers and thinkers of which he was unquestionably the center. It has become known in history as Dr. Johnson's Club. People with different ideas could sit and dine and talk, which reflected the notion of balance that the 18th century managed to sustain. Johnson was a paradox in literary history. He was a great man of literature who never wrote great literature. And although powerful as a king, he was poor all his life. Overall he was a conservative person: a Tory in politics, embracing the Church of England in religion, and emphasizing form and style in literature. He was a severe critic of his time, denouncing the slave trade and slavery and calling it indefensible, and censuring all manifestations of injustice. Johnson is eventually idealized and immortalized in James Boswell's famous book, *The Life of Samuel Johnson, LL.D* (1791), which is a faithful record of his strengths and weaknesses, and his problems and struggles.

Johnson was a great conversationalist, and a very witty and perspicacious person. He was famous for his sayings, which often assumed an epigrammic stature. Indeed, his mind seemed to work in an epigrammic manner. People in his time often approached him just to know what he thought about things. He said things off-hand frequently in a very interesting, provocative, often memorable way. For instance, he said of madness, "Madness is socially defined. If you do things with the majority, you are sane; but if you don't you are in danger of being called mad." On death he said to the effect that the important thing is how you live and not how you die. On another occasion, one lady came up to him and asked what he thought of the nearby naked stature of Venus when she said, "Sir, don't you think it is vulgar?" and the man replied in all seriousness, "No ma'am. Your mind is." [5]

As a writer, however, Johnson was not really remarkable. Though the period in which he was dominant on the literary scene has been called by some people as "The Age of Johnson," he did probably the least amount of memorable work of merit in it. His prose work, *Rasselas*, which he claimed took him one week to finish in a rush to get money to cover the expenses of his mother's funeral, is commonplace, and his best known poems, *London* (1738) and *The Vanity of Human Wishes*, are not particularly interesting from a literary point of view. As to his *Lives of the Poets*, it is not half as enduring as *A Fable for Critics* by the American poet, James Russell Lowell (1819-1891), in insight. But he was the most important literary figure of the 18th century, second only to Pope. As much as Pope if not more, he was for the second half of the century a literary dictator, one to whom the rest of the literary world looked up for tastes and values. His influence was such that the major literary figures of his time gathered around him to listen to him talk, and he kept on talking right up to the end of his time.

As a critic, Johnson kept strictly to classic rules and was ever on the alert with a hawk's eye on any deviation from these. One of the things neoclassic poets were expected to do was to imitate a classic work, substituting contemporary ideas and incidents for those in the ancient work and adapting the original as he moves along. Pope did this well with his Horatian epistles. Johnson modeled himself on the Roman moralist Juvenal (55?-120? AD). *London* is for instance based on Juvenal's third satire on the corruption of Rome. Johnson spearheads his satire against the abuses and vices of London of his day, such as government corruption, greed and flattery, and the wretchedness of the poor. In addition, Johnson goes back to ransack his country's past for ideal behavior: Elizabeth I, Edward III, and Henry V are put on the pedestal as a contrast to the ills of the present time. *The Vanity of Human Wishes* (1749) deals with a more universally applicable theme, the vain human aspirations for wealth, power, military exploits, and general approbation. It is based on Juvenal's tenth satire. Here Johnson lists the rise and fall of the fortunes of a cardinal, a scholar, and a king to illustrate his point. Even beauty can be destructive such as that of a king's mistress. The poet offers trust in God as salvation. Love, patience, and faith are the qualities he lauds that make life possible. Johnson uses the heroic couplet faithfully. If there is little emotion in his verse, there is plentitude of wisdom, taste, and decorum as well as classic grandeur.

The History of Rasslelas, Prince of Abyssinia (1759) is a heavily edifying book. It was very popular in Johnson's time. There is little plot movement, but a lot of digressions. Some of the chapters can be easily taken out as separate writing efforts. Structurally, it is loosely knit, though there is a visible framework of three sections of 16 chapters each and a concluding coda: section one focusing on the Happy Valley, section two on the prince's experience of life, section three on the group's involvement in life, and the conclusion, "A Conclusion in Which Nothing Is Concluded." What it deals with is basically a highly philosophical question:

What is happiness, and how it can be achieved. The four people—Prince Rasselas and his companions, set off from the Happy Valley where there is no want of anything except happiness, go through life as a learning experience, fail in the end to find happiness and any happy human being in the world, and decide to go back whence they come. The four people are no longer the same. They have seen life and people and have learned about the world so that it will not be possible for them to return to square one. They will move on, wherever it may be. The book is a satire on the prevailing sense of optimism of Johnson's time. Johnson persistently wrote to tell the truth about life and the world.

Closely connected with Johnson was a Scottish young man of some literary merit, James Boswell (1740-1795) by name, who came to London in 1762 to seek some employment in the Guards. There he experienced London life in its variety and jotted down in a journal his impressions as well as his encounters with the people; the journal is now known as *Boswell's London Journal: 1762-1763*. It might have been a casual and fun thing for him to do then, and he kept sending his notes back to his friend in Scotland. But the journal entries were discovered two centuries later and have now been prized as one of the most accurate and vivid records of 18th-century English life. The best thing that Boswell felt happened to him that year was his meeting with Johnson and his circle, and the young man devoted a lot of his energy and attention to recording Johnson's views on life and literature and the man's conversations with his fellow men of letters. Boswell was a friend of Johnson's for twenty years, and all that time he knew that he was to write a biography of Johnson. Johnson gave him all his papers and told him about his early life. Boswell's effort resulted in the publication of *The Life of Samuel Johnson, LL.D*, the book vitally interesting for the study of Johnson and the literary world of his time. [6]

The best part of the story was not merely Boswell's dedication, but his effort to include everything about Johnson that he could possibly manage. He made a point of being present at Johnson's conversations and listening to him intently and then going away and staying up late at night to jot down all that he could recall. In this way he trained his memory, and he also showed what he wrote sometimes to Johnson just to check on the accuracy of his information. As he was very persistent, and not always smart and not very pleasant to get along with, he could do things that would enrage the great man. For instance, he did silly things occasionally just to get Johnson to talk. On one occasion, Boswell said, "Sir, what would you do if you were locked in a tower with a baby?" Johnson said, "I would feed him." And he would say, "Go on, sir." Then Johnson would say, "Sir, no more of it, no more." On another occasion, Boswell said, "Sir, which leg should a man put his trousers on first?" And Jonson was angry and said, "Sir, when you deicide which leg to put your trousers on, your bottom is bare and cold." The good thing about all this is that Johnson was shown in this book in all his aspects, his pettiness as well as his greatness. Boswell defied all opposition and threw all the details in, believing that greatness would come through in the end. So it has. Never did Boswell expect that his endeavor was to represent a whole new concept of writing a biography, furnishing in his book the whole spirit of modern biography—to tell the truth, and the naked truth instead of just showing up the noble side of the subject. In addition, by placing emphasis on one individual, the book may be seen, in spirit at least, as a kind of anticipation of the Romantic period, one feature of which was the importance it attached to individualism.

Thomas Gray (1716-1771)

Gray graduated from Eton and Cambridge, and spent his quiet adult life as a professor of history and modern languages at Cambridge. Self-possessed and reserved to a fault, he was happy to live in a self-imposed kind of obscurity. A couple of things influenced his career as a poet. One was the "mood-swing" that the latter part of the century began to experience: the neoclassic milieu was giving way to something new now slowly but steadily bursting into life—the outburst of Romantic feeling. Sensitive minds began to feel its impact. Samuel Johnson exclaimed that popular interest in classic stories was waning fast. Gray sensed the wind of change in the same way. But the two responded differently. Johnson stood his ground, adamant with his neoclassic principles and ever ready to pounce on and put out any dissent (as he would with James MacPherson's *Ossian's Poetry*). But Gray took a different course as he did in his famous *Elegy Written in a Country Churchyard*. In addition, he traveled widely, and proved himself to be an interested, responsive observer, feeling genuine delight and amusement at whatever sights and sounds came his way. The colors and images of nature, the simple language that he used so often, and the intense emotional charge that filled portions of his poetry may most probably have to do with his intense experience with life and people. All these helped him with his writing. It was no accident that Gray turned out to be a poet of transition from the neoclassic to the Romantic period. In fact, he has been seen as a minor forerunner of the Romantic movement both in subjects and simple language.

Brought up in the neoclassic milieu as he was, Gray was naturally inclined to compose in keeping with the Popian principles. Most of his works still retain the obvious stamp of neoclassicism such as the elevated, figurative diction, the use of abstractions, and the excessive personifications popular in his time, all being the obvious neoclassic qualities to be admired by the readers and critics of his time. For good illustrations of the point, there are Gray's early odes, "The Bard" and "The Progress of Poesy," which eulogize respectively the Welsh struggle against aggression and the achievements of ancient poets, and in which the classic form proves congenial to the content. And Gray was meticulous, as was Pope, with formal perfection. His *Elegy* took him eight years to finish (1742 through 1750), making as he did endless, repeated revisions until he felt it was ready for publication.

However, Gray was also different from Pope and Johnson. He deviated from neoclassicism in a gradual yet tangible manner. One obvious change was the decrease in the number of allusions in his poetry to classic mythology and literature. Whereas classic traditions abounded in Pope and Johnson, Gray weeded these from his *Elegy* altogether. Furthermore, he was capable of more than one tone and one mood while Johnson kept to his one abstract and moralizing mode right to the end. Gray was amenable to reflective moods and sentiments, and could compromise his neoclassic grandeur for the expression of sympathy for the poor and obscure. His language could be charmingly simple at times. The small body of verse that he wrote displays a wide variety of interest and expresses the temper of his time adequately.

Gray is famous for his letter-writing. His letters are collected in three volumes, all written in the finest English that the resources of the language could offer. Later in life, he showed interest in Icelandic and Celtic poetry and wrote a couple of lays in its spirit. He was buried in Stoke Pogis, Buckinghamshire, a village which might be the setting for his *Elegy*. His best poems include "Ode on a Distant Prospect of Eton College," "Hymns to Adversity," and the *Elegy*. Some of his lines have gained a proverbial status. These include, among others, "... where ignorance is bliss,/ 'Tis folly to be wise" (the "Eton" ode) and "The paths of glory lead but to the grave" (*Elegy*). [6]

Now let's take a look at his masterwork, *Elegy Written in a Country Churchyard*, a poem of 128 lines in 32 iambic pentametric quatrains.[7] The immediate success of the *Elegy* established Gray as about the best poet of his day and made him a desirable candidate for the position of the poet laureate in 1757, but he declined the offer. The poem has always enjoyed wide acclaim as the best work to come out of the 18th century and has been even viewed by some as the best English poem. It started the tradition of graveyard poetry in English and American literature. The general mode is melancholy and meditative. The poem can be roughly subdivided into seven broad sections. Section one (ll. 1-12) sets the scene for the poet's visit to the churchyard. It is enveloped in gloom and grief, which is archetypal of graveyard poets' fascination with night, graves, and death. The tone is echoed by the last part of the poem (ll. 93-116). Section two (ll. 13-28) tells about the people entombed there and recalls their life experiences. When the "rude forefathers of the hamlet" lived, they got up early at the twittering of swallows, or a rooster's wake-up call or a hunter's horn, enjoyed family bliss with wife and kids in the evening, or were happily busy with farm work in the fields, but now that they lie in their "narrow cell[s]," their "useful toil" and "homely joys" happen no more. The tone is one of melancholy and regret for the dead.

Section three (ll. 29-44) warns the rich and powerful not to despise the poor since all are equal in face of death and the grave levels off all distinction. All nobility, power, and wealth "[await] alike" the inevitable end and "The paths of glory lead but to the grave." Nothing could ever bring anything back to life. Section four (ll. 45-72) expresses, on the one hand, the poet's regret that their life had not been congenial to the growth and full play of the poor farmers' native gifts and talents and, on the other, his feeling of "a blessing in disguise" for them in the sense that, because they did not take up positions of power and get the opportunity to do evil, they did not commit any crimes to humankind nor have to play the obsequious social climber against one's integrity. Section five (ll. 73-92) asserts the notion that, even though they lived a less eventful life, there is no reason to forget these farmers.

Section six (ll. 93-116) portrays the scenario that the poet envisions would happen after his own death. A villager would say of him: he got up early to go uphill to the lawn and lay there meditating under the tree until noon. He would wander in the wood, smiling at one moment, muttering to himself at the next, sad and pale, like one "in hopeless love." Then for a couple of days he did not show up, and on the third day he was buried in the churchyard. This is where the graveyard school of poetry exhibits its salient thematic feature: the indulgence in meditation on and obsession with death and solitude. Section seven (ll. 117-128), "THE EPIGRAPH," that picks up where the last section leaves off, is engraved on the poet's own tombstone. There he calls himself a youth (Gray was 28 when he first began writing the poem), learned and melancholy, with a generous, loving soul, and equally loved by Heaven. As he shows sympathy for the poor, he gains the friendship of man and God. He asks the passers-by not to get to know any more about his merits and weaknesses as he waits in his grave for God's judgment. The poem touches the readers to the quick with its notable sadness.

Formally, the poem is famous for its clarity in thought and its neatness in structure. Its style is graceful, effortless, spontaneous, and with no trace of laboring. Its diction is at once succinct and loaded, fluent and tight-knit, and lucid with room for imagination. The work is also renowned for its regularity in meter and rhyme. Its sound, harmonious yet not monotonous, helps achieve its theme wonderfully well. With the use of long vowels in most lines, the mood of grief and lamentation stands out in bold relief. But there is evident variety that forestalls tedium. Alternating with the long vowels, the poem deftly employs short vowels in some lines and quatrains either to express a mood of utter helplessness (e.g. ll. 41-44), or irritation (e.g. ll. 57-60), or some dramatic effect (e.g. l. 109). Even within the same line, long and short vowels intertwine at intervals for various effects. In addition, the colors, light and shade, flora and fauna, scenes culled from life, and symbols and figures that combine to make up the woof and warp of the poem—all these are well chosen, juxtaposed or superimposed so that the poem has become a tour de force unique in history.

Oliver Goldsmith (1730-1774)

Goldsmith was a versatile genius. He wrote in the three genres of poetry, drama and the novel, and managed to leave behind at least one work of some significance in each for posterity. His poem, *The Deserted Village*, his play, *She Stoops to Conquer*, and his novel, *The Vicar of Wakefield* are all still read today. His was a moral vision of the world and life. Man is good, life is good, and God still smiles upon the world below. Here crime and punishment go together, and good gets its due reward. It may not be the best possible of all worlds, but it is basically good and tolerable. Of tragic awareness there is little or none in his works. Goldsmith is prone to a kind of idealizing and sentimentality that is not always easy for modern people to comprehend. [8]

Take his *The Deserted Village* for example. Here the poet visits a village, Auburn, and feels disturbed at its desertion and desolation. The modernization of agriculture has increased wealth for a few but has driven most of the former independent yeoman farmers to shiftlessness and poverty. The good old pastoral way of life vanishes never to return. The first 34 lines of the poem offer the most charming picture of village life that was ever lived on earth: a sweet, lovely village nestling itself in the broad plain, with its health and God's plenty, its "dear lovely bowers of innocence and ease," green and happy, the sheltered cottage, the well-tilled farm, the ever gurgling brook, the busy mill, the church on the hill, the bush and the seats in its shade, the various village sports, the dancing pair, the bashful virgin with sidelong glances of love and her mother's reproving look—charm, charm, and charm everywhere. But all is lost now. The "tyrant's hand" is seen, all the pastoral sights and sounds are gone, the people have left, with the result that "wealth accumulates but men decay" (ll. 35-50). Trade dispossesses the farmers and destroys all rural mirth and manners. With the denunciation of the destructive forces then alternating with a painful nostalgia for the golden past in the rest of the work, the poem ends with the wish that man learns from their errors and "Trade's empire hastes to swift decay" (ll. 424-427), and the pastoral way stays alive for ever.

Whereas the attack on the encroaching forces is genuine and forceful, the idealizing of the village life is no less apparent. The fact of the matter was, however, that rural life was never that happy and beautiful and country people had always suffered, though differently, in the old days. When the poem came out in 1770, it enraged at least one of the poet's contemporaries who knew rural poverty and its degrading effects from personal experience and observations at close quarters. This was George Crabbe whose *The Village* is said to be a reply to Goldsmith's and, for that matter, all similar efforts to idealize village life. Goldsmith's poem was written in the fashionable heroic couplet of the time. The author's sentiments of grief and nostalgia are genuine and convincing.

She Stoops to Conquer (1773) is a classic in world theater. It is a funny boisterous comedy of melodramatic misunderstandings. Mr. Hardcastle would like to marry his daughter Kate to Marlow, son of his old friend, Sir Charles, and Mrs. Hardcastle is busy arranging a match between Tony, her son from her previous marriage, and Constance, her ward. Tony, who does not like Constance, plays a trick on the two visitors to his stepfather's house—Marlow and his friend Hastings, the latter being in love with Constance. He directs Marlow and Hastings to the house but tells them that it is an inn and that they have to stop there as they are lost. The two young men mistake Mr. Hardcastle as the inn keeper and Marlow takes Kate for a serving girl. Marlow really loves the "serving girl" and Kate finds him a fine gentleman. Her father is convinced of her truth when he hears the still hoodwinked Marlow confessing his love to her "as the serving girl" before she reveals her identity. The story ends well for all—the two pairs of young people get married, and Tony is able to wrestle himself free from his mother's control.

The play has been regarded as one of the most beloved comedies of all time. The humor and humanity of the characters, especially Kate and Tony, adds a touch of immortal power to it. As a satire on the artificial and pretentious behavior of the day, the play exalts the quality of truth and honest feeling. Kate is not dressed in her Sunday best when she wins her man's love, and Marlow loves her for what she is and not as a respectable young lady of standing and expectations. The drama also brings out in full relief the notion of individual choice and right to choose one's own happiness. Tony can be scheming, but he is good-natured essentially, not self-serving and inflicting hurt on others. Goldsmith is generous and tolerant of human foibles and follies, he does not censure or punish any of his characters, but takes pains to see to it that everyone get fair treatment in the end. The way in which the characters interact in their cultured and well-intentioned manner makes for geniality and interpersonal cordiality, helps civilize public behavior, and decrease its violent and crude elements. The salutary influence the play exercised on the 18th century is said to be considerable. In addition, Goldsmith's dialogues are vivacious and immensely humorous, and the whole performance impresses the audience with its vitality and joyful mood.

The Vicar of Wakefield (1766) is a romantic novel that tells a romantic story. Dr. Primrose, the Vicar of Wakefield, lives happily with his wife, Deborah and five children. His son George is to marry Arabella, a neighbor's daughter, but the change in the family fortune makes it impossible: Primrose's broker runs away with all his money. With the neighbor canceling the wedding, George goes off to London. In the meantime the Primroses move house to the estate of Thornhill. A fellow traveler, Mr. Burchell, happens to save one of the Primrose daughters, Sophia, from a fall into a stream, and wins the welcome of the family. The young squire of Thornhill comes to visit to the distaste of Sophia who likes Mr. Burchell better. The father does not favor Burchell who has lost his fortune. Later the young ladies are thrilled at the prospect of going to the city as companions to two noble ladies, but fail to go because Burchell writes slanderous letters about them to the ladies. The angry father orders him to leave the house. Then Olivia, another daughter, believes that the squire of Thornhill is in love with her, but is convinced by her father to marry a young farmer. She disappears, however, a few days before the wedding. Informed by the squire that it is Burchell's doing, the father sets out to find her. He meets Arabella who asks about the whereabouts of George, but he has nothing to tell her about him. Then George comes back, as poor as ever, and receives the squire's help to join the army. Arabella, whom the young squire is courting, vows to wait for George to return. The vicar finally finds Olivia in an inn and learns that the villain has been the squire, who has ravished and deserted her. Father and daughter come home only to find that their house has been burned down. The young squire, while he intends to marry Arabella, is also trying to find a husband for Olivia so as to keep her close to him. The vicar feels furious, and drives the squire from his house. But the villain asks him to pay the rent and sends him to a debtor's prison when he fails to do so. There the father meets his son

George who, having attacked the squire for his villainy, is waiting to be hanged. Then, to add to his despair, the vicar hears of the kidnapping of Sophia. But a sudden turn of events brings a change in fortune. Mr. Burchell rescues Sophia, exposes the squire's evil plans, and restores the Primroses to their happiness. Burchell, who turns out to be the squire's uncle, marries Sophia, George marries Arabella, Olivia's disgrace is cleared, and the vicar eventually gets back the money that his broker has stolen from him.

The Vicar of Wakefield is a sentimental work based on the moral vision of man as innocent and kind. There is goodness, nobility, and fidelity in life, and old values and verities still function well. This may appear incredible and even ridiculous to modern people, but it was a work of an age when the world was still considered a moral one. In addition, there is such to consider as Godlsmith's wit, humor, his craft of planting ballads and tales within tales, and his philosophical depth, which all make for the fascination it holds for its readers, modern as well as ancient.

Richard Brinsley Sheridan (1751-1816)

Sheridan's dramatic career was short but amazingly brilliant. It occurred at the time when English drama stagnated at its lowest ebb and called for reinvigoration. What Sheridan did proved to be vitally important for the resuscitation of the declining genre: he injected fresh energy into it and helped keep it as a viable link in the continuity of the nation's dramatic tradition. Sheridan had the reputation that whatever he did was the best of its kind. His plays, especially *The Rivals* and *The School for Scandal* were the best in his time and have since become famous world classics. His speeches in parliament, notably the one against English interference with the French Revolution and the one calling for freedom of speech, proved to be the best in tune with the growing middle class influence then. Sheridan wrote his plays before he was thirty and left for politics after that. *The Rivals* and *The School for Scandal* are in historical perspective two of the three best comedies to come out of the 18th century, the other being Goldsmith's *She Stoops to Conquer*. *The School for Scandal* made him famous and rich, and ultimately entitled him to a place in the Poets' Corner of Westminster

Abbey.[9]

The School for Scandal (1777) is a five-act comedy of manners noted for its brilliant wit and satire. Here two plotlines run parallel: Lady Teazle's loss of innocence and growth and Sir Oliver Surface's selection of an heir. As the story goes, Lady Sneerwell sets out to slander other people for her own good, and pays Snake to do the dirty work for her. Sir Peter is not sure about his marriage with his young wife, Lady Teazle, and Sir Oliver Surface, away for 15 years, is not sure which of his two nephews—Joseph and Charles—is good as his heir. At one of Lady Sneerwell's parties—the "school for scandal," people are talking behind people, and there Lady Teazle sees Joseph proposing to Maria, who loves really Charles. When approached by Sir Oliver, Sir Peter wagers his life on Joseph's goodness. Charles, who frequently needs money, now plans to borrow money from a Jew. Sir Oliver goes to him in the disguise of a moneylender, and Charles sells to him his ancestors' portraits, but keeps his uncle's. Then Charles sends some of the money instantly to one poor relation, an act which impresses Sir Oliver favorably.

Joseph has designs on young Lady Teazle. One day—here comes the famous scene of the play—when he is talking with Lady Teazle in his study, Sir Peter walks in, and Lady Teazle hides behind the screen, only to hear her husband tell Joseph about her having an affair with Charles, and about Joseph's possible marriage with Maria. Lady Teazle now comes to see the true Joseph. Then Charles breaks in, Sir Peter hides himself in a closet, and Charles tells Joseph that Lady Teazle loves the latter better. Sir Peter walks out to tell Charles that Joseph has an affair with a French Milliner who is now standing behind the screen. The screen is then removed, Lady Teazle comes out to accuse Joseph of his ill intentions, and Sir Peter leaves the two brothers to thrash it out between them. When Sir Oliver poses as Mr. Stanley and comes to Joseph as a poor relation, however, not only does he not get a penny from his nephew, but he hears also the young man's complaint about his miserly uncle. That makes up the elderly man's mind once and for all. Snake comes out in the open, and Lady Sneerwell and Joseph are both stripped to their evil nakedness. Charles promises his uncle to reform, inherits his fortune, and marries Maria. Lady Teazle graduates from Sneerwell's school of scandal.

The satiric spearhead of the play is obvious enough—the vices of English upper class life and its influence on life and people in general. Sheridan was perceptive and courageous enough to lift the lid off the can of worms that was the polite life in London and by extension in English society, and bring them under the close scrutiny of his minute analysis. The negative side of human nature in its variegated manifestations is examined and castigated, and the upper class suddenly finds itself somewhat stripped naked before the eyes of the world. The audience tend to split their sides in full appreciation of the humor and the laughter at the expense of others' weaknesses and foibles, but often come away with a better awareness of their own behavior as humans. This is where the universal applicability of the work lies.

As the play exhibits, self-serving and the human inclination to suspicion are the major root causes of all evil—the hypocrisy, depravity, and corruption. These stay at the core of the parasitic existence of the upper class, which Sheridan sees as their breeding ground. One of their member, Lady Sneerwell, sneers well enough to cause aggravation to others mainly out of her greed for a prospective inheritance. Her school of scandal muddies the waters and scandalizes both Lady Teazle and Charles in order for her to rehabilite her own already notorious name. Joseph works hand in glove with her out of his own vicious motives: his lecherous and covetous eyes are well fixed upon the innocent Lady Teazle's sexiness and Maria's wealth. The two schemers both meet with their ulitimate undoing when their shady plans are brought to light and boomerang. Lady Teazle is an interesting character for analysis. Coming from the country, the simple girl submits willingly to the temptations of polite life and readily picks up its evil ways such as flirting and wasteful spending. Her change is archetypal of the serious, irresistible evil influence that the city can have upon the innocence of the country. Sheridan may not be fully aware of the subject that he chances to touch upon, but it was a topic the magnitude of which will draw the full attention of the next generation of writers, i.e. the Romantics.

Sheridan's character portrayal can be an intriguing feature for discussion. It begins with the names of the characters. There are Teazle, Surface, and Snake, along with the names referred to in the play like Flirt, Prim, Tattel, Candour, and more. Some names are concocted by yoking words together such as Sneerwell, Boastall, and Backbite. The names say a lot about the personalities of the people so named. This seems to be a borrowing of some medieval morality trick, but Sheridan goes well beyond moralities in his dramatic endeavor. He fleshes out his main characters well with cogent details so that they are no mere skeletons for moral abstractions. Furthermore, Sheridan shows his consummate craftsman in leaving loose threads here and there but never failing to pull them together in some climatic scene, where the two plotlines nicely intersect with one another and converge and run to their final resolution. This scene occurs when all the major people come together and square things out in Joseph's study. The ensuing hide and seek and the suspense it causes along with the fun—this alone could have ensured the all-time success of the work as a comedy. In addition, Sheridan's language is lucid and humorous and presents little or no paradoxes. His theatrical performances have always been famous for the boisterous laughter they bring to their audiences.

Chapter 7 Movement toward Romanticism • Thomson • Young • Cowper • Crabbe • Blake • Burns

Extremes tend to provoke a reaction. With Pope and then Samuel Johnson at the helm, the 18th century raged forward with the heroic couplet and almost outlawed all other forms. However, from the very outset, some dissenting voices existed and tried to make themselves heard. The two obvious good examples from the first part of the 18th century were James Thomson's *The Seasons* (1740) and Edward Young's *Night Thoughts* (1742), both written in the then unpopular blank verse. There was also the sly but steady assertion of emotion in this age of reason. This often took the form of undercurrents of thought flowing beneath a classic surface. The poem that comes immediately to mind is Thomas Gray's *Elegy Written in a Country Churchyard* (1750). Although open rebellion did not become a major trend until the death of Johnson in 1784, something the nature of which Johnson did not approve had begun to surface. First in the form of James MacPherson's *Poems of Ossian*, then in the sudden outburst of feeling in the Rowley poems of Thomas Chatterson (1752-1770), and in the publication of Percy's ballads. Toward the end of the century, varying dissent also appeared in the works of the writers who had been mostly writing in the neoclassic form. Goldsmith came up with his *The Deserted Village* (1770), Crabbe with his *The Village* (1783) and Cowper with his *The Task* (1785), all adding considerably to the gust of change. With Robert Burns (1759-1796) and William Blake (1757-1827) coming forth eventfully on the scene, the stage was well set for a new generation of poets, the Romantics.

Now James McPherson (1736-1796), a Scot, published in 1760-1763 some poems that he claimed to have translated from the Gaelic of an ancient Scottish poet, Ossian (c 3rd century). That this was literary forgery has been well proven now; he actually edited some traditional Gaelic poems and inserted in them some of his own writings. The poems, lyrical in tone and emotional and vivacious in spirit, brought a fresh breeze of change in the otherwise ambient kill-feeling neoclassic milieu, and enraged Johnson so much that the dictator challenged him to produce the original manuscripts. MacPherson refused to budge in the quarrel though he was bluffing. The matter ended unresolved with ruffled tempers on both sides. McPherson must have been a gifted poet as his *Poems of Ossian* became immediately popular and went well beyond England. It was to influence a whole generation of Romantic poets both in England and across the English Channel. Not so fortunate was young Chatterson, however, whose precocity led to his early fame, but eventually to his instant downfall. Chatterson wrote, among other things, some lyrics which he claimed to be translated from the original of a 15th-century Bristol poet, Thomas Rowley. The freshness in spirit and the originality of the author as revealed in these poems caught immediate critical attention. The boy then came to London, but did not do as well as he had hoped he would. He suffered dire poverty, and took his own life at the age of 17. Chatterson added to the fire for change fast spreading across the literary field of the country.

Then in 1765 appeared *Reliques of Ancient English Poetry*, popularly known as *Percy's Reliques*. It was a collection of ballads and songs that Bishop Thomas Percy (1729-1811) edited and published. Touching on matters of the heart like love, death, and loyalty, and fresh and emotional in tone and mood, these melodies contributed a good deal toward reviving interest in and restoring feeling to poetry. *Percy's Reliques* set the model for such Romantic geniuses as William Wordsworth, Samuel Taylor Coleridge, and Sir Walter Scott, who were soon to follow with their *Lyrical Ballads* (1898) and *Minstrelsy of the Scottish Border* (1802-1803) respectively. [1]

James Thomson (1700-1748)

Thomson was son of a clergyman and received his education at Edinburgh University. He wrote a miscellany of plays and poems, but he is remembered now mostly for his *The Seasons* (1740). His last work, *The Castle of Indolence* (1748), with its medieval allegorical kind of story, is read occasionally as well. Thomson is important in literary history for more than one reason. For instance, he did not go with the flow of his day and write in the tyrannical heroic couplet; his *The*

Seasons was composed in blank verse, and his *The Castle of Indolence* in the Spenserian stanza. Then there is Thomson's choice of subjects, which decides the texture of his works. *The Seasons* represents nature in its totality. The "rural song" as he calls it himself inevitably touches upon pastoral beauties and joys and country life in general, and as inevitably involves the outburst of feeling. Although there is a good deal of metaphysical speculations and reflections, the major substance of the poem is about rustic sights and sounds that call naturally for emotional echoes from the human bosom. The preface to one of the sections, "Winter," is a graphic illustration. Thomson feels, as he states there, that nature, "a great and serious" subject for his time, can "at once amuse the fancy, enlighten the head, and warm the heart," which clearly indicates the author's emphasis on imagination and emotion at a time when reason alone was prized and extolled. *The Seasons* juxtaposes its discussions nicely with its descriptions. [2]

A long poem of over 5,500 lines, *The Seasons* consists of the four seasons and a "Hymn." Each of the four seasons begins with a prose preface introducing the verse that follows, and the preface to "Winter," first to appear in 1726, can be read as a general introduction to the whole poem. Following "Winter" comes "Summer" in 1727, with "Spring" out in 1728, and "Autumn" in 1730. The whole work first came out in print in 1730, and the revised and final edition in 1746. The poem offers a pictured life of nature. Spring with the plowing, the north winds and the rain, the passions of the animals, and the joys of pastoral life; Summer with the delightful morning labor of the farmers, the waterfall and the noontime meditations on the sun, the afternoon thunderstorms, the lightning that kills a young life in love, and the youth spying on his beloved swimming nude; and the evening walk with discussions of the British achievements; the "sober Autumn fading into age,/ And the pale concluding winter," that tells the transient nature of life of this world with the dreams of greatness, hopes of happiness, the aspirations for fame, the worries and cares, the rush and bustle, the festive nights, the veering thoughts, and the wavering between good and evil; and "Winter" with storms of rain on land and at sea, the trembling boat, the robin redbreast, and the snow scenes, which is the best-known vignette in the work, the poet's imaginary visits to Lapland and Siberia. The "Hymn" that concludes the poem is a hymn to the God of Seasons, who is present in all the "mysterious round" of nature, though man fails to see the "mighty hand" at work, and nature with all its elements should help increase man's awareness with their praises of the Creator. The hymn ends with reference to the poet's death and his singing of the beauties of Heaven, the "infinite progression" of this and other worlds, and the contemplation of "the mighty chain of being." All through the work the poet advises people to keep in sight the larger eternal scheme of God omnipresent in "the rolling year," and the eternal Spring around them all.

Edward Young (1683-1765)

Young, son of a clergyman, was educated at Oxford University, and became first chaplain to the king and then a rector later on in life. He wrote some dramas and prose work, but he is now known solely for his long poem of some ten thousand lines, *Complaint, or Night Thoughts on Life, Death, and Immortality* (1742), popularly known as *Night Thoughts*. It contains in its nine books the poet's thoughts on nine sleepless nights and his meditations on man and his life in this world and the next. To Young man is a creature both wormlike and godlike, a worm miserable in this world, subject as he is to the plaguing of so many hazards and disasters, but not entirely hopeless with the hope of death and immortality in the next world, Heaven. Young's "man" in the poem is the infidel Lorenzo, who may not be sure about his immortality, but the poet hopes to convince him of it and see him embrace Christianity. The mood of the poem is gloom, and the tone is definitely morbid, as the poet finds happiness in the constant thought of death and hails midnight as signaling the light of eternity. Today the poem is of value chiefly as a brilliant example of the graveyard poetry to which it belongs.

The work is of some historic significance: it helped, in its small way, to move poetry forward toward the age of Romanticism. It did this well in its radical deviation from the neoclassic vogue of its time. For one thing, it was written in blank verse, not in the fashionable heroic couplet, blank verse being a verse form more amenable to the expression of feelings. Then the poem is an adequate expression of emotions, a restoring of the legitimate thematic concern to poetry at a time when Pope and Johnson had between them successfully banished feeling from poetic expression. Poetry devoid of feeling is not generically poetry. Young was one of the poets of his age to infuse his work with human responses. He shows his genuine feeling when he allows his mind to run wild with its exuberance, which results in the discursive, sprawling structure of the poem. With its repetitious though essentially static condition, the poem can touch the mind with its vivacious ruminations. It is a kind of weird, macabre response to life that it tries to record. *Night Thoughts* is noted for its psychological probings and its mixing of personal sentiments with religious deliberations. It sees man and his life in a negative manner, and finds solace only in faith and religion. The poem enjoyed fame in its own time and remained so for a century before its excessive sentimentalism and morbidity began to alienate modern sympathies.

William Cowper (1731-1800)

Cowper was a very interesting person to talk about. His personal life was turbulent and depressing. He was high-strung and suicidal, so that he had to move to the country as a recluse, where he led a generally quiet and contemplative life. A gifted person without any ambitions and aspirations, he excelled in the areas of poetry and criticism quite in spite of himself. His blank verse proved to be the best of his time; and his criticism, disapproving of the neoclassic form and urging a return to nature and God, happened to signal the change of values and taste in anticipation of the coming of the Romantic outburst early next century. He was instrumental in a way in the transition to a more natural and simple style, and contributed in his way to the movement away from Pope and Johnson's classic influence. His subjects are basically personal, with an intense interest in rural and domestic settings, and his primary mood is lyrical and melancholy, expressing the sense of human limitations. He is satirical of social ills and compassionate to the lower strata of society. His major work includes the *Onley Hymns* (1779, in collaboration with John Newton), and *The Task*, for which he is known and read today. The latter was such a critical success that he was to become the most popular poet of his time. [3]

The Task actually has no definite subject as it was written under a very interesting circumstance. "The Advertisement" of the poem tells about it: "A lady, fond of blank verse, demanded a poem of that kind from the author, and gave him the SOFA for a subject. He obeyed; and, having much leisure, connected another subject with it; and, pursuing the train of thought to which his situation and turn of mind led him, brought forth at length, instead of the trifle he at first intended, a serious affair—a Volume." What happened was that the poet was complaining about having no subject to write about when Lady Austen, an intimate friend, came along to suggest that he describe the sofa in the parlor. Thus beginning with the sofa, the poem rambled along and eventually grew into a long meditative work of 5,000 lines, covering a wide range of topics such as country sights and sounds, village life, garden, parlor, occasional condemnation of cities and worldliness, war and slavery, luxury and corruption, and freedom and tyranny. Its tone is muted, its language is lucid and simple, and its discussions alternate with descriptions. It was the first time Cowper ever wrote in blank verse instead of the heroic couplet.

The poem consists of six parts: "The Sofa," "The Time-Piece," "The Garden," "The Winter Evening," "The Winter Morning Walk," and "The Winter Walk at Noon." The first of these, "The Sofa," talks about the vanity of man's indulgence in comforts and the poem's intention to justify God's ways to man. "The Time-Piece" is a satire on the political institutions of the day. "The Garden" brings the poet to subjects such as nature, family life, compassion, condemnation of wars, praise of simple rural life, and renunciation of the city—all point forward to the coming of William Wordsworth. "The Winter Evening" is a continuation of the dichotomy between country and city. "The Winter Morning Walk" sees in winter a hope for immortality and attacks tyrants and slavery. The last section, "The Winter Walk at Noon," elevates rural harmony and anticipates spring. Here the poet also takes a look at his meditative life in the service of God.

George Crabbe (1754-1832)

Crabbe is said to be the last great neoclassic poet. Living through two ages—the neoclassic and the Romantic, there is a visible movement in his works toward concern with social life. His poetry is often neoclassic in form (he used the heroic couplet) but emotional in theme. His humanity breaks through the hard crust of the surface and makes its voice well heard. In his small way Crabbe helped with the neoclassic transition to the next phase of literary evolution. [4]

The poem which keeps a niche for him in literary history is his *The Village*, written in response to Goldsmith's poetic reflection of country life in his *The Deserted Village*. The Crabbe poem describes the suffering of the peasants who toil from sunrise to sundown for their bread. The pastoral ideal of country life vanishes (ll. 93-101, 304-317) and the reality of pain and anguish comes in its stead. The country here presents a sorrowful sight. The land is barren, the weeds are rampant, and the scene is bleak and gloomy (ll. 63-88). Here live the people, who suffer nondescript poverty and pain. The minute description of a poorhouse in the country indicates the tenor of the poem well with word-pictures such as "walls of mud," "putrid vapors," the dolefully humming "dull wheel," "heart-broken maidens," "joyless bed," "forsaken wives," "dejected windows," "unheeded tears," "crippled age," "childhood fears," "the lame," "the blind," "the moping idiot," and "the madman gay" (ll. 228-239). In addition, there is the unfeeling doctor, "whose most tender mercy is neglect" because the quack can insult and murder his victims (ll. 274-295); there is the priest, who is too busy hunting and playing whist to come to the dying or say the funeral service in time, having no scruples about leaving the dead unblessed (ll. 343-346), and there are smugglers and drunkards. Death saves and levels off all (l. 323: "the happy dead, from trouble free"). The human spirit manages to assert itself through the poem.

William Blake (1757-1827)

Blake was an important landmark in between two literary periods, pointing directly to that of Romanticism. He was poor and little known in his time. There were two factors in his life that helped to orient his thematic thrust. One was his native sensitivity that enabled him to see visions and develop a kind of mysticism. The other was his contact with such radical people as Mary Wollstonecraft and Thomas Paine, through which he developed his own views about religion, mysticism, and the major events of his time—the American and French revolutions. The two major thematic strands that make up the basic fabric of his poetry include his concern with social events and his mysticism. His major works, in addition to his famous volumes—*Songs of Innocence* (1789) and *Songs of Experience* (1794), are his voluminous prophetic and mystical writings, the themes of which have inspired different interpretations as they are often painfully obscure. These include *The Book of Thel*, *Tiriel* (1789), both being allegorical; *Visions of Daughters of Albion* (1793), *America, A Prophecy* (1793), *Europe, A Prophecy* (1794), all of which stress man's revolt against common moral standards for regeneration; *The First Book of Urizen* (1794), *The Songs of Los* (1795), *The Book of Ahania* (1795), introducing a myth; *Vala*, an early form of *The Four Zoas*, the poet's story of the origins of the universe; and *The Four Zoas* (1797), *Milton* (1804-1820), and *The Ghost of Abel* (1822), all indicating a shift to a belief in a beneficent God. The works show the poet's mysticism and his effort to connect it with art. Blake kept his attack on traditional theology and moral codes. Although he tried to create his own system of mythology, he left no fully coherent myth behind. He is noted for his originality both in theme and form. Though he has been frequently classified as a pre-Romantic, the emotional pitch and the amazingly variegated styles of his writings clearly place him among the Romantics.

By far the most powerful and the most permanent of Blake's works are his *Songs of Innocence* and *Songs of Experience*. "Innocence" and "Experience" here denote two different phases of human life with the different states of the human soul as the title of the edition combining the two sequences indicates. The two volumes contrast with one another in such a way that the poems in these illustrate the distinct stages of human existence graphically. They make a clear statement about the author's acutely conscious responses to life and society. Generally *Songs of Innocence* reveals a pair of innocent eyes, those of a child, looking at life and the world, while the later sequence shows clearly a different mode of perception, that of the adult, as a result of the cumulative experience through which the poet lived in the intervening years. Those were the years of change, as marked by the French Revolution. The poet, sensitive both to the influence of the revolution and the change in his personal outlook on life, seems to feel an acute sense of urgency to get his vision across to his readers. Hence the change and difference in the tone and tenor of the two collections. It is enlightening to see the way the poems in the volumes are well paired off and throw the contrast of their subjects in bold relief. Blake did this on the strength of his growing belief in the notion of contraries. Without contrast and contraries, he says in one context, there is no progression. For instance, poems from *Songs of Innocence* such as "Infant

Joy," "The Blossom," "The Lamb," and "The Divine Image" stand in direct opposition to the poems in *Songs of Experience*—"Infant Sorrow," "The Sick Rose," "The Tiger," and "The Human Abstract." There are in addition the two poems both entitled "The Chimney Sweeper," the two both entitled "A Little Lost Boy," and other similar instances in which the mood and the tone change from happy to gloomy.

Let's take a look at some of the poems in contrasting pairs. "The Chimney Sweeper" is a good starting point. The poems both offer an adequate expression of the suffering of the child sweepers, of the anger at the adults who make their lives miserable, and of the wish that the sweepers be allowed to enjoy a happy childhood rather than face the threat of the "coffin" of the chimney. However, there is a visible tonal difference between them. In the *Innocence* poem, there is compassion for the children's total naked immersion in soot and darkness, the anger is somehow played down, and Tom Dacre the child has faith in God and accepts his lot with the warm hope that his dream of naked white cleanliness will come true. The child in *Experience*, however, learns about the causes of his wretchedness, loses all faith and hope, lives in an enveloping gloom, and ends up in utter bitterness and despair.

"The Lamb" and "The Tiger" form a natural contrast in every possible sense of the term. The images stand as self-evident opposites, and everything else changes accordingly. The blissful, confident tone of "The Lamb," not colored with any shadow of doubt or pain, with the pervasive pastoral setting and the comforting wooly tender assurance of God's blessing—all these find a direct foil in the world of "The Tiger." Here instead of the delightful bright day, there is "the forest of the night," a reminder of a labyrinth wrapped up in total darkness. Then there is the description, both outright and implied, of the terribleness of the Tiger, and the harrowing question, rather rhetorical, "Who had the art and the courage to make the Tiger?" The "he" throughout the poem refers in a progressively clearer way to the Being or God who made the Lamb. The riddle or the labyrinth left to the imagination after reading the poem remains yet to be addressed. It seems to relate to the fact that life is not all rosy and bright, and that there is a downside to it as well. But the ultimate enigma may lie in the question, much deeper and more philosophical, which has not been adequately, unequivocally resolved even today, that is, Why does He place evil alongside good? Or in the more stereotyped phrasing, Why does God allow evil to exist?

Social criticism becomes more apparent in the poems such as "The Sick Rose" and "London." In the former work two images stand out one against the other—the rose and its bed of crimson joy, and the invisible worm flying over in the storm to destroy it with his "dark secret love." Rape is apparent, but the identity of the rapist needs the power of the imagination to figure out. The criminal is powerful and irresistible, probably supernatural ("night" and "storm") in its destructive force. The metaphor here may stand for Time (as the villain with a T) imposing upon the mortal humanity. It may stand for a repressive society versus the people, in which case social satire is at work here evidently.

"London" is a poem more profound in its thematic concern. Here is a Blake walking around his native city and looking intensely, through the city's exterior of pallor, woe, and prohibitions, and beyond it, at the root cause of all the wretchedness. The first two lines seem to level his attack on the visible rich strata of society, but the implied butt of satire may well be the invisible society which the wealthy, the privileged, dominates. Here Blake is attributing all the social ills to society as the chief culprit and is feeling for all people—man, infant, chimney sweeper, soldier, the prostitute and the related outcomes of moral depravity—the unfortunate new-born with prenatal blindness and blighted marriages. Blake knows London—the place of his whole life—inside out, and his intimate portrait of it reveals the bitter truth of life of his time. The poem thus moves from a plane of personal wrath and sympathy to one that includes all humanity. The call for change is hidden in the lines, but it is an intrinsic part of the poet's prophetic vision here. This is the reason why it possesses the rare power and permanence.

"Jerusalem" is a later work. It appeared first untitled in *Milton* (1804-1810) and was titled so in 1916 when the poem was set to music. Here Blake speaks more vehemently against the evil society of his time and with a determination to bring about a change. The dominant image in the poem, Jerusalem, the holy city, stands for the ideal order of God and in opposition to the industrial progress which means to the poet more destruction than creation. The first two stanzas paint an ideal picture of ancient or pre-industrial England where God created a paradise of green mountains and pleasant pastures, and built Jerusalem in the country. The second stanza, which has already begun pointing fingers at the clouds and the dark mills, all stemming from industrialization, tides over naturally to the last two stanzas when the poet arms himself up for a fight, involving his whole being, to bring the lost Jerusalem back to the land. Blake was basically a visionary. His fight was a "mental" fight, one that he hoped would restore England to spiritual and social health.

Robert Burns (1759-1796)

Burns was born into a poor Scottish farmer's family. He experienced dire poverty and had close contact with common life and common people. His education was not formal, but he managed to make up for the deficiency somehow with a combination of the good instruction from his father and his tutor and with his own reading of such writers as the Scottish poets Ramsay and Fergusson and his intimate acquaintance with ballads and folklore. One practice typical of his manner of composition was that he put his own words into existing tunes or stanza forms and channeled his own enthusiasm and vigor into his verse. Burns was a warm individual with a variety of experiences as his source of inspiration and as his subjects. He was a romantic both by temperament and in behavior. Keats says it all when he states to the effect that people can see in Burns' poems his whole life and his sincere love of freedom, people, and life itself.

Burns lived in a period of transition from 18th-century neoclassicism to Romanticism. True to form, his works exhibit affinity to both modes of expression in style and emotional intensity. They show the strengths of both but adroitly avoid their weaknesses like extremes and excesses. His poetry reveals a great virtuosity and competence in handling diverse stanza forms and styles. Burns is supremely human. He knows human nature well and knows how to express it well in ways appealing to his fellow creatures. Human life and human feelings always remain topmost in his mind when he writes poetry. Thus even his nature poetry offers not so much an aid to enjoying nature as a natural backdrop against which life is enacted. His heart is full with love, compassion, and warmth. When he writes about love, he quotes from his own experience with the women who inspired some of his writings like "Highland Mary," "Mary Morison," and "Sweet

Afton."

Burns' convictions are well expressed in his poetry. He is critical of Calvinism and its hypocrisy and rigid morality (in such poems as "The Holy Fair," "Holy Willie's Prayer"). He values human freedom and equality and is eloquent in defending the lower social strata ("A Man's Man for A' That" and "The Jolly Beggars"). He extols love and genuine feeling as in his love lyrics and finds value in human fellowship and friendship as in his famous "Auld Lang Syne" (a song set to music and still sung all over the world today). His democratic ideas are evident in the poems like "Scots Wha Hae," a famous work of his rich in Scottish patriotism. And he is a good superbly entertaining storyteller as well shown in "Tam O'Shanter."

Burns wrote in the Scottish dialect, English, and a medley of the two. "Tam O'Shanter," composed in the Scottish dialect that tells of an old legend of the supernatural, reveals the poet at his best. The poems he wrote in English with the help of the Scottish dialect are often highly enjoyable and rewarding. His famous, immortal love lyric, "A Red, Red Rose," is a good example. It is the most beautiful, adequate expression of the noblest and sweetest human sentiment that ever gets recorded on paper.

"Tam O'Shanter," a later work of 224 lines, is probably the poet's masterwork. The narrative poem retells a legendary story of a man, Tam O'Shanter by name, and his experience of a frightful disaster. It is morally healthy and formally entertaining. As the story goes, Tam loves to drink and refuses to take any advice to remove the habit. His sorely disappointed wife foresees the calamity befalling him and alerts him to the dangers of being snatched away by wizards and devils on a dark night (l. 29-32). Tam "despises" her "sage advices" (ll. 35-36) and cannot resist any temptation of a bottle of beer. Sure enough, the thoroughly drunken man comes back from his market drinking and runs into a carousal of the devils one night by the side of the Kirk-Alloway (ll. 105-142), and the "bewitched" Tam roars out in the middle of the carnival at one witch—the wildly dancing Nannie, "Weel done, Cutty sark!" ("Well done, Nannie!" ll. 183-189). At this the hellish legion all sallied out to fly at Tam's heels. Tam is eventually able to struggle clear of the witches with the help of his lovely horse, Maggie, but the horse loses its tail which Nannie wrings away from it (ll. 192-218). The poem ends with admonishing people to think of Tam and the danger of "buy[ing] the joys o'er dear" (ll. 219-214) whenever they drink excessively or feel entranced with a pretty face. The poem still fascinates the readers not only because of the nature of the legend on which it is based, but also because of the way the author handles the material. The vitality and vivacity which Burns manages to breathe into the folk story, the suspense, the inherent drama, the sense of urgency that the poem successfully generates, and the huge capacity for humor and laughter that both the tale and the cream of the Scottish dialect conspire to create—all these indicate the consummate craftsmanship of the poet in the composition of this masterpiece.

"For A' That an' A' That" (1795) is another famous work for which Burns is remembered today. The poem is very rich in its multi-tier significance both as a work of its period and in terms of its universal applicability. From a historical perspective, it is good to note that it was written in the most repressive period of English history when the British formed the Holy Alliance with the continental monarchies against France and intensified its repression at home. Although Burns sensed the stress personally and with his friends, he kept his faith in and sympathy with the French Revolution. The poem had existed in different versions before Burns worked at it to change it into a medium for the expression of new, revolutionary ideas. What is brought into relief is a number of ideas stemming from the French Revolution such as liberty, equality, and fraternity, and the relentless, forceful jibes at the behavior of the cowards, the rich, the gentility, the nobles, the courtiers, and the king. The poem ends with a prophetic proclamation that the day will come when people all over the world will become brothers.

In addition, the poem is loaded with a universality embedded in its lines and stanzas. When read out of its temporal and spatial constraints, the poem exhibits an archetypal awareness of human worth, with the sense of pride, optimism, and perseverance for truth. As the poem states, we are proud of our honest poverty and obscurity: the rank is superficial, and personality is what really counts (stanza 1). An honest person may eat simple and be dressed simple, fools may wear silk, and knaves may drink choice wine, but it is the honest poor who prove to be "king of men" (stanza 2). A lord with his show of rank and arrogance as a master is a fool all the same and deserves the derision of the man of the independent mind (stanza 3). Although the king can create rank and nobility and the honest person possesses no such power, his wisdom and noble person are in fact higher (stanza 4). The last stanza expresses a wish, a faith, and a certitude, that with the sense of innate worth spread all over the world, all the people on earth will become brothers one day.

Chapter 8 18th-Century Fiction • Swift • Defoe • Richardson • Fielding • Sterne • Smollett

The 18th century was one in which the novel as a genre prospered not only in the practice, but also in the theory of the craft. The writers developed the realistic method of presentation and brought story-telling infinitely closer to the real life as lived by the real people. The novelists of the period were trailblazers of a kind, departing from the portrayal of the heroic, the extraordinary and the distant and breaking the back of the previous tradition of the medieval romances. In characterization, they tried to approximate the behavior of the people of flesh and blood, and in language, they tried to borrow from the common speech of the people. They had nothing but the real world to replicate in their writings. These people worked hard, wrote profusely, and won respect and popularity. At the same time, they drew diligently from their experience of writing and tried to offer their views as to how the novel should be well written. Defoe, Richardson, and Fielding were among the most conscious literary artists of the time, doing the job and theorizing about it so as to do it better. Fielding's theory proved to be the most far-reaching and seminal in its influence on the evolution of the genre. Richardson's exploration of the inner world of his characters pointed forward to the birth of the psychological novel in the latter part of the 19th century. All of them, especially Fielding, Sterne, and Smollett, were to leave some imprint on later generation of writers. Whereas all were satirists in their unique ways, Swift and Sterne deserve special mention here as idealists, aware of the difference between reality they experienced and the ideal they envisioned, and trying to contribute toward improvement. [1]

Jonathan Swift (1667-1745)

Swift was born into an old but poor family in Dublin, Ireland, and was educated in Trinity College, Dublin. Then he went to stay under one distant relative, Sir William Temple, whose arrogance hurt his pride in an intolerable way. But he swallowed his anger and devoted his energies to reading and writing. After he broke with Temple, he settled down as a clergyman in a little Irish church, and gradually discovered his satiric talent. Through his pamphlets and as senior editor of the journal *The Examiner*, he made himself a frightening power to reckon with in politics for quite a few years (1710-1713). In the field of literature he became a dictator from whom even Alexander Pope had to take his cue at times as to what to write and who to attack. Swift helped the struggling young in his most typical manner. Instead of waiting for them to come to him for help, he took the initiative and offered them succor of all kinds. Then the change in politics made it different for him, and he became the Dean of St. Patrick's Cathedral in Dublin, where he stayed with the Irish in their fight for improving their lot, and died as a hero for the people there.

Swift has been seen by some people as the literary king of his day. He wrote a lot of powerful satirical essays and books, relentless and biting when dealing with the injustice and corruption of the rich and the upper classes. His major works include his scathing satire, *The Battle of the Books*, aiming a sidekick at one of Sir Temple's writings; *Tale of a Tub* (1704), one of his greatest satires, equally keen and powerful as an attack on the church; pamphlets like *The Irish Drapier's Letters* (1724), which helped foil the Irish government's smug plan to mint 100,000 pounds of coins out of 60,000 pounds' worth of copper; *A Modest Proposal* (1729), in which the intensity of the attack on the English oppressors enraged the English government beyond measure, and the great book, *Gulliver's Travels* (1726). *A Modest Proposal* merits special mention here because it is one of the most caustic satires ever written in literary history. It was written in face of the utmost wretchedness of the Irish people suffering from the ruthless rule of both the British and the Irish governments. In order to address the problem of overpopulation in Ireland that was discussed then, Swift made a "modest" proposal, that Irish babies should be reared and cut and sold as food for the British rich to help earn money and alleviate the misery of their poor parents. The author wrote it in such a grave manner that the readers tend to think that the man is serious all the way until they suddenly realize that he is proposing in fact that the

English eat Irish babies and relish their food, while the Irish get their money, and the problem of overpopulation will be happily resolved for all. The explosive power of the essay is self-evident.

In addition to the thematic thrust of his works, there is the quality of his prose to consider. Swift finds value in the use of language and insists on choosing the right word for the right place to make it do its utmost work. His lucid and terse prose, noted for its simplicity, grace, and forcefulness, has contributed not a little toward the development of the best English prose tradition. His is a very significant place in the history of English prose.

Let's take a look at his most enduring work, *Gulliver's Travels*. This is a savage satire in the form of a fabulous travelogue. It appears as the personal narrative of a Captain Lemuel Gulliver, who is said to have traveled for some eleven years to distant places unknown to his contemporaries. The book was able to pass as a real travelogue of a real person (while both were fictional) because the people of the 18th century knew that there existed some parts of the world they had not been to, and the editor's note concerning the book helped a good deal to make it sound like a true story.

The book consists of four parts, each recording one voyage to one outlandish "remote" place. The first part, made up of eight chapters, "A Voyage to Lilliput," proves to be the most imaginative and entertaining, especially to kids. Lilliput is a nation of dwarfs, despicably small in stature, their adults being as tall as some six inches, but every bit as evil in behavior as men of the normal size. The Lilliputians treat the ship-wrecked Captain Gulliver cruelly as if he were their enemy and prisoner. What impresses the captain most is their manner of choosing their high-ranking officials. People are evaluated and employed for government offices according to the results of a competition in a slender rope dance. The one who jumps the highest will be qualified to serve His Majesty the Emperor (chapter 3 of part I). Another thing that the captain finds fascinating is the way the political parties align themselves. The two struggling parties, Tramecksan and Slamecksan, distinguish one another by the high or low heels they wear on their shoes. The latter, Slamecksan or the low-heelers, is in power at the time of Gulliver's captivity, but the other side has the crown prince with them, as the future emperor wears at least one heel higher than the other. Nor is this all to amuse the captain.

The Empire of Lilliput is currently at war with a neighboring empire because the latter prefers to break their eggs at the larger end and infuriates the Small-Endian Lilliputians. How to break the egg has become such an enduring dispute of religion for these people that hundreds of volumes have been written about it and some Big-Endian Lilliputians have opted to flee their country to avoid religious persecution (chapter 4 of part I). Captain Guliver stays in Lilliput for 9 months and 13 days before he escapes from it (chapters 7 and 8, part I).

Part II, also eight chapters in all, "A Voyage to Brobdingnag," recaptures Gulliver's visit to a land of giants, or Brobdingnag, another "remote nation" that lies somewhere near Alaska. A storm on May 3rd, 1703 pushes his ship to within the view of a great island, which he learns to be Brobdingnag. A sharp contrast to the country of Lilliput, here everything is of a humongous size inconceivable for his imagination. A footpath in the field is as wide as a highway, the people walk over ten yards at one stride, and a cat is three times the size of an ox. The giants are, however, the kindest race of all on earth. During his stay there, Captain Gulliver is taken good care of first by a farmer's family and then in the household of the royal family. The most interesting experience that he has had in his sojourn there is the series of six conversations between him and the king regarding the government of England (chapter 6, part II). Gulliver does his best to place his country's virtues and beauties in the best light possible, its parliament, its justice, religion, and sports and pastimes, just so as to impress the king. In the six audiences, the king asks him a series of questions, expressing his doubts, queries, and objections on everything Gulliver has said about England, and pointing out the ills and evil that inhere in English life. The king ends with the conclusion that the bulk of the English people are the most pernicious race of little odious vermin that nature has ever suffered to crawl upon the surface of the earth. Then Gulliver begins to learn about the nation of the giants and finds it the best of all in the world (chapter 7, part II). After a two-year stay there, he leaves the good people (chapter 8, part II).

Part III, of 10 chapters, "A Voyage to Laputa, Balnibari, Glubbdubdrib, Luggnagg, and Japan," is a narrative about his third voyage that he takes on August 5, 1706. The trip takes him to several places. One of these is Laputa, a flying island, a vast opaque body flying in the sky, on which a curious-looking race of philosophers and mathematicians live. They are so engrossed in their speculations that they constantly need their servants' flapping with a gentle bladder on their mouths and ears for those organs and senses to function and wake them up from their absent-mindedness (chapter 2, part III). The land of Balnibari that follows next in his itinerary is a place where scientists try to make sunshine out of cucumbers. There Gulliver is appalled at the fact that the wives of the scientists run away with their servants because the women feel neglected and not well loved. Then there is Glubbdubdrib, a nation of magicians, who can summon the dead from the past. As to Luggnagg, there live a group of immortals, the Struldbruggs by name, keeping their longevity but not youth and health and wisdom (chapter 10, part III). From there he goes to Japan and then returns home after an absence of over three years.

Part IV, of 10 chapters, "A Voyage to the Country of the Houyhnhnms," draws the readers to a strange nation in which the masters are the horses while the servants are the human-like creatures—the Yahoos. The Yahoos look every bit human but behave exactly like animals. They have all the beastly qualities that the beastly humans of Gulliver's own countrymen have—violent, evil, and despicable, but the horses possess all the virtues that the best of the captain's own race have—reason, wisdom, knowledge, manners, and self control. Gulliver lives well and happy on oaten cake and milk in a stable for quite some time. In his conversations with the horses, Gulliver introduces his country in a candid way, touching on the poor sailors, the unjustified wars and the murderous weapons, the unjust legal system and the self-seeking lawyers, the greed, the abuse of labor, the corrupt rich, a devious first minister, and the depravity of the nobility. Then he says good-bye to the wise horses and leaves for home, only to find that he has become a recluse and a misanthrope, feeling disgusted even with his wife's kiss. The horses have become his only friends on earth.

When it first appeared in print, *Gulliver's Travels* instantly became a popular success. For his contemporaries, Swift offered them an opportunity of self-scrutiny. The Lilliputians and their institutions were all about people and their institutions, especially those of England. The Brobdingnagians were incredible Utopians. The scientists and the philosophers represented the extremes of futile theorizing and speculations in all areas of activity such as science, politics, and economics with their instinct-killing tendencies, while the picture of the Yahoos made a clear statement about man and his nature. The book has remained on top of the popularity list across time. It is a fantasy but people of all time with any amount of imagination could feel the reality of human life in it. Children enjoy it as another book of Aesop fables or the Disney world kind of fabrication; adults read it to learn about humanity as well as to sense the fun and humor however grim these may be. It is a common reading experience that, in the middle of enjoying the lives of the dwarfs or Yahoos, people become aware, all of a sudden, that they are looking at their own reflections in a mirror at close quarters, and turn grave and serious about the book's salutary educational effect.

A point of interest merits notice here. Many readers and critics have, over the centuries, tended to confuse Gulliver with the author and see the narrator as Swift's surrogate. This critical position is on the whole untenable. It is true that the book is misanthropic in nature. The Lilliputians are petty as the humans are petty in their petty hair-splitting quarrels over the institutions of church and state, and they are vicious just as are the humans. The giants are good but gross and represent those qualities that are inconceivably good. The scientists are so lost in their rational thinking that they stop being human in their behavior with no contact and no family life, which is an acrimonious portrayal of the 18th century as an age of vain discoveries and of human efforts as futile as exacting sunbeams from cucumbers. The Yahoos, all veritable replicas of the human race, are inferior to the horses who rule over them, which is another way of saying that the humans are not even as good as beasts. All these point to the idea that Swift was a misanthrope at the end of his career as Gulliver becomes at the end of his travels. However, this is all open to discussion.

For the Swiftian book is a vast construct of delicate yet strenuous irony, which stems from the implied discrepancy between Gulliver and the author. Gulliver is fitted out as an archetypal man of the enlightenment, both at the beginning of the book and all through it. He is a scientist, a doctor, observant to a fault, and believing in progress and the goodness of human nature and all the 18th-century values. Swift was, on the other hand, a man intensely critical of his time, its rational thinking, its corrupt institutions, and its social evil and injustice in general. This difference in values results in an intense sense of irony with which the book is suffused. Since readers tend to see the world through the narrator's eyes and think through his mind, it is probable that the author would like them to be on the alert when they judge along with Gulliver. The embedded hint here is that some of the things Gulliver disapproves of may be those that the author would like people to think twice about before they decide on their own stance.

Gulliver is not a perfect specimen of the human race and as such he is part of the author's satire as well. The captain is prejudiced temporally and spatially as a child of his country and his age. For instance, he is too rational to see that the humans including himself can be irrational. While the wives of the scientists running away with the servants seems to him a repellent behavior (part III), Gulliver the scientist never for a single moment stops to be self-critical and think how little he cares for his own wife in his over ten-year stay away from home. Then there is the nation of the Houyhnhnms as another graphic illustration. Whereas Gulliver takes it as his Utopia, Swift finds its rationality totally intolerable. The horses mate solely for the sake of continuing the race and they do so without passion and love. These "noble" creatures come out of their sexual "business" and merge instantly into their common crowd without any sense of emotional attachment and family connection. Reason alone rules here with no room for human sentiments. As Gulliver finds his own race one of the detestable Yahoos, he becomes a hater of man, his own family included. Swift did not think the same way. A kind man at heart, Swift loved his fellow creatures as individuals though not as a group. It is true that he did not like the Lockean notion of human nature being good and improvable, but he was not a misanthrope. His vehement satires on the human institutions and social ills were all well meant to help improve the lot of man.

Daniel Defoe (1660-1731)

Defoe was born into a Protestant background and detested the repressive rule of the Anglican Church and the Roman Catholic Church. He became a firm supporter of the Glorious Revolution, but was imprisoned for his writings attacking the government's religious repression. He was a loquacious dissenter. He hated the efforts of the royalist Tories to stall the middle class from its growth in power and wrote vehemently against their policies. In addition to his satires and pamphlets, he ran an influential newspaper, *Review*, and was thrown in prison quite a few times. He was in a sense also a political chameleon, changing sides as he saw fit. As a businessman, he was no success; his business efforts all ended with failure and bankruptcy. He began novel writing later in life, and his first novel, *Robinson Crusoe* (1719) made him famous. Then he wrote some other novels such as *Moll Flanders* and *Roxana*, but none touched his first attempt in popularity and power. [3]

As the first major novelist in English literary history, Defoe was a highly conscious writer. He knew what he was doing and tried to do it well with his heightened awareness of the novel as an art form. His views on the novel, mostly explained in the prefaces to his novels, focus on two things of significance to the emerging genre: its realism and its moral aesthetic. Defoe makes it clear that his novels are a true record of facts, based on true events as part of history, or as a historical narrative of a living person's life experience, and that any story failing to deal with the human experience is pure fiction and a lie. He focuses his narratives on the representation of life as being lived. Thus his protagonists are common people with real common names and speak as "I," telling their own stories in the first-person narrative, addressing the readers directly without any mediation, just so as to increase the realistic effect of immediacy and involvement. Although this has to do with the theory of "literature imitating nature," Defoe's "nature" is not the neoclassic kind of human nature in general; it is the portrayal of the individual character that catches his attention. All these are the initial efforts in the history of the English novel to leave the traditional notions of romances, fables, legends, and myths behind and blaze a new trail for the genre. Defoe as a moralist wrote with the conviction that his works would be educational and help people behave. He extols reason, love, liberty, and equality, and infuses these into his narratives to enrich them in a manner unobtrusive to the realism and artistic nature of the works. Realism and moral aesthetic are the salient features of his fiction.

Robinson Crusoe is the work for which he is remembered by all. Defoe was nearly sixty when he brought it out in print. The story was based on the adventures of one real sailor, Alexander Selkirk, who ran away from home and was left on an uninhabited island for five years (1704-1709). The novel's hero, Robinson Crusoe, goes out to sea, experiences a shipwreck, and is left alone on a wild island (the first part). Then he goes back to colonize it and engage in trade with distant countries (the second part), and has some further adventures and musings and moralizations on his experiences (the third part). The popular Robinson Crusoe story as people normally know it is in fact the narrative focus of the first part (1719); the second part (1719) was never as popular and is no longer read, and the third part has never gone beyond its first printing in 1720.

As the story goes, Robinson Crusoe, a strong individual, does not feel happy with the easy comforts that his father has provided him with. He heads out to sea and becomes a planter in South America, but he is insatiable. He ventures further out, experiences a shipwreck, and is left all by himself on an island without any trace of civilized life. He soon overcomes his despair, and sets about building a life for himself. With the things he salvages from the ship, he builds a shelter, and then a house, finds food, raises goats, plants crops, makes clothing, makes boats, beats back savages from other islands, saves one, Friday as he names him, and makes him his servant. Later on he saves Friday's father and a Spaniard and becomes the master on the island. He begins to enjoy some comfort little by little and stays there for some 28 years. When an English ship goes by later, he saves its captain from mutiny, and returns to England on it. This is about the end of the first part of the book. The second part picks up from here and tells about Robinson going back to the island and his success to colonize it and become its moral guide as well as its magistrate. From there he travels further to the Persian Gulf, China, and Siberia to do trade. Our discussion here will focus on the first part and touch on the second only when it is necessary.

Robinson Crusoe is essentially a work of the time in which it was composed, but it possesses a permanence that classifies it as one classic for all time. It is first and foremost a middle class book, offering justifications for the class' forthcoming rise to pre-dominance in national life. The middle class had been growing in wealth and influence and engaged in a power struggle with the monarchy and aristocracy, the historic magnitude of which it might not have comprehended yet. Middle class values were steadily becoming dominant in social life, such as its emphasis on moderation, temperance, self-reliance, and the work ethic, and would soon prevail in national life. At the beginning of the novel, Robinson's father tells him that the happiest state is the middle state, the state that well characterizes the middle class, and Robinson comes to see eventually that "mine is the middle state." The 18th-century emphasis on society, a middle class value, is well illustrated in Robinson's effort to build a "community" on the island. He forms a group with Friday and his father and the Europeans under his protection and serves as its head, so that something resembling a human society, faintly at first but precisely later on, starts functioning.

The book is a typical Puritan tale. First, Robinson is eager for self-discovery, detests comforts, opts for adventure in becoming a sailor, and rebels in youth against his father's beliefs. This is a typical show of Puritan individualism. Then, he never gives up on life but always feels confident about creating a life for himself—this is an illustration of the Puritan spirit of self-reliance and self-sustaining. Next, Robinson is a veritable picture of the self-made, hardworking Puritan, believing in diligence and the work ethic, laboring from sunrise to sundown, and resourceful and creative with a thinking mind and a skillful pair of hands. Furthermore, initial failure to adapt on the island and reinvent life brings a fresh bout of despair and urges him to think about the basic questions like the creation of the world and self-identity. He discovers God for himself, and affirms his faith with which he now begins anew his effort to civilize the island on the cultural and moral pattern that he has inherited but has left behind. Thus he goes back to his father's middle class tenets—simplicity, moderation, and comfort. The novel raises an important identity question, "Whence are we?" and furnishes a good answer for it, thus justifying the whole spirit of the middle class—adventure, self-directing, and colonizing. In the end Robinson becomes a new man, well poised on the verge of building a middle class democracy at home and looking forward to establishing an empire abroad. He is in a very serious sense the prototype of the aggressive British beginning to envision the blueprint for the British Empire. In fact, the colonizing has already begun on his island, and he has already had the first taste of success.

On the other hand, *Robinson Crusoe* is also a book for all time. Its permanent appeal to readers of all generations stems from the fact that it is in essence a success story. A self-made success such as Benjamin Franklin's or Robinson Crusoe's can always touch the human heart and engrave itself upon the human mind. Robinson's dilemma when he is bogged down on the uninhabited island is archetypal of a recurrent human condition in which people seem to see in overwhelming gloom no glimmer of hope ahead. The human interest of a scenario like this never fails to fascinate when the trapped person tries to struggle out of the mire of despond and bring sunlight into his world. There is this perennial pattern of human behavior involved here that never stops delighting through suspense and to which people can always relate: initial suffering and despair, plucking up the courage to face adversity, and taking sane, effective steps to address the problem. The twists and turns of fate, so real and intimate and immediate to all, go a long way toward hooking and holding attention. Thus Robinson, when taken out of his temporal and spatial context, free from his middle class background, his religion, his sense of mission as a colonizer, and the zeitgeist of his age, is frequently seen simply as a true-to-life, no more and no less, specimen of the ordinary humankind, bodying forth the sum total of the perseverance and indomitableness of the human spirit. It is this quality in the character that remains eternally charming and great.

Samuel Richardson (1689-1751)

Richardson began as a printer's apprentice and then became a printer. He had little education, and chanced to begin his writing career as a novelist when he was over fifty years old. His first novel, *Pamela, Or Virtue Rewarded*, was an immediate popular success so that he became famous almost overnight next to Defoe. Encouraged and inspired, he went on to write another two novels in the same epistolary style. These are *Clarissa Howe* (1748) and *Sir Charles Grandison* (1754). Of the three works the second one is generally considered as his major work, though *Pamela* has been the object of much critical attention over the centuries. He won the admiration of famous writers such as Henry Fielding, Diderot, Balzac, and George Sand. Although a moralist, Richardson was not indifferent to the concerns of his art. *Pamela* was undertaken with a clear moral purpose topmost in the author's mind though the character somehow struggles free of the author's control, *Clarissa* proves to be a book in which the intended moralizing gives place to the artistic representation, while the third book is overloaded with morality. *Clarissa* is not popular now because its length, among other things, tends to try the patience of the modern readers.

Richardson was a pioneer in the history of the novel. He was one of the few who, responding to the taste of the audience of his time, began the tradition of writing about real common people and helped break the back of the hitherto dominant form of heroic or mythic romances. Their psychological depth has proved to be another powerful influence that Richardson's novels have been able to exert on later novelists.[4]

Richardson's literary theory, mostly documented in the prefaces of his novels and his letters, is not systematic, yet it contains elements significant enough to impact later literary criticism. He is well conscious of the essential concerns relating to the novel as an art form. In a radical departure from the prevailing theory of "art imitating nature (life)," he claims that he is a creator of fiction rather than an imitator of life and that art differs from life. In characterization he consciously avoids one-dimensional portrayal, and tries to endow individuals with their multi-faceted nature. Thus Pamela, Clarissa, and Grandison are all people natural and probable with their weaknesses as well as virtues. Richardson places emphasis on the harmony between structure and theme and between the different aspects of the novel, and endeavors to offer a sense of coherence and totality in the narrative effect. He avoids authorial intrusion in the narrative and dramatizes the life of the moment. In so doing, the characters show up and speak for themselves and reveal their inner world to the readers in a direct way. These all exhibit a degree of modernity in Richardson's artistic awareness, original and rare for his time.

Although the author's first creative attempt, the novel *Pamela, Or Virtue Rewarded* (1740-1741) possesses enough fascination to warrant some analysis here. Written in the epistolary form, the book marks the beginning of this controversial manner of narration. The novel became immediately popular and was translated into foreign languages.

It tells a love story between a maid and her master. Pamela Andrews, a servant girl, often writes long letters home to tell her folks about her life at her mistress' household. After the mistress' death, her son Mr. B. asks Pamela to stay on, but harasses her, kissing her one day by surprise, intercepting her letters, and hiding himself in her closet at night. When the virtuous girl's responses annoy the man, he tells her to go home. She decides to leave, but the coachman drives her to Mr. B.'s country estate and leaves her there a prisoner. In her confinement, Pamela continues to send letters home with the help of Mr. Williams, the village minister. The young minister proposes to her and, though rejected, tries to help her to escape but fails. The insistent Pamela drops herself from one window to get away from Mr. B.'s cluches, but is again found out. Mr. B. arrives from London and tries to ravish her, but she conveniently suffers seizures of fits. Mr. B. repents and offers her an honorable marriage. She accepts his proposal and is married to him in the presence of her father. Now Mr. B.'s relatives behave rudely toward her, but Pamela's virtue wins over both the man's sister and his uncle. Mr. B. confesses about having had a previous affair with a woman who gave birth to a little girl, but Pamela forgives him and asks to bring up the girl. Then Mr. B. has another affair with a countess. Pamela, giving birth to a son, controls her anger, and Mr. B. repents and stays faithful to her.

Richardson helped address some important problems in the beginning phase of the novel as a new genre. *Pamela or Virtue Rewarded* is interesting today largely for this reason. One of these problems relates to plot. The book manages to focus on one episode—love—rather than on many as was the case with the episodic novels of his contemporaries like Henry Fielding's *Tom Jones*. It is good to note here that the one-episode narrative has since caught on with later novelists as a tradition. Furthermore, *Pamela* is realistic in its descriptions of the vicissitudes of the love process, including, among other things, the complex emotional responses, the clever tricks of hiding pens and ink and letters in the probable places on the human body, and the efforts to ward off harmful attention. Next, there is palpable growth in Pamela's character from an ideal—almost allegorical—to a real human figure. Her virtue is put to test and proved to be no mere myth. The impeccable perfection of Pamela as a woman is punctured by a couple of things she is revealed to be capable of—for example, her womanly feelings of jealousy and pain and anger, and her redeeming self-awareness and self-censure of such foibles as her long-windedness and her weakness for praises and flattery. Finally, and this is exceptionally significant, there are the psychological excavations into the human inner world where the events are frequently digested and ruminated upon. Pamela's person is thus shown inside out and placed under the scrutiny of the readers so that she assumes a depth and a dimensionality that no other fictional characters could claim to possess before her. This is the reason why Richardson has been seen as the beginning point for psychological realism in the history of the English novel.

Pamela has its apparent deficiencies. Its sentimental idealism is one of these that tend to put off the sophisticated modern readers. Richardson in drawing a picture of virtue evidently prefers to see people as they should be rather than for what they actually are. Although basically real and believable, Pamela is too good and Mr. B. is too willing to change for the readers. In addition, it challenges the readers' imagination to see a servant from the lower social stratum write so long and so well and have the time for this leisurely intellectual exercise amid the rush and bustle of her harassed life. The other weakness that relates to the letter-writing is the slow prose movement and want of tension. Yet another thing that can bug the readers is the placement of the climax in the middle of the book, with endless pages of anticlimactic narrative before the conclusion.

Henry Fielding (1707-1754)

Fielding came from an aristocratic family and was well educated. In his early years he wrote plays of generally a comic and satirical nature. But he is known mainly for his novels, which include such major works as *Joseph Andrews* (1742), *Jonathan Wild the Great* (1743), *Tom Jones* (1749), and *Amelia* (1751). As a novelist as well as a playwright, Fielding was a keen, critical observer of life and an eloquent, outspoken satirist. He followed his own moral esthetic, wrote to censure evil and reward virtue, and became a great moralizing force in the social life of his time. (Honest and kind and courageous, he was known as a ruthless government official in his suppression of evil within the area of his jurisdiction). His *Joseph Andrews* offers a pugnacious castigation of the upper strata of society and the evil in the human heart as well as in life, and a sincere compassion for the wretched poor. *Jonathan Wild the Great* is an impeccable portrait of evil drawn to alert the world against such behavior both in life and in oneself. And *Amelia* extols the virtue of the heroine against the vice of the world with its evil designs on her. These along with *Tom Jones* established him as a major writer in literary history.

No less is Fielding remembered for his contribution to the perfection of the craft of fiction. In a time when the novel was emerging as a new genre, Fielding took it upon himself to make something clearly definable about the novel out of the pervasive nebula then, and achieved an astounding degree of success through his voluminous commentaries on the art of fiction.

Fielding was an innovator in the craft of fiction and a conscious literary artist. He was well aware of the nature of his lengthy literary discussions in his prefaces and the beginning chapters of his novels, that he was making ground rules for a new genre of writing for which nothing of the kind had ever existed before. He studied the classic literary criticism of such classic authors as Aristotle and Horace, and theorized a good deal about novel-writing at the same time he wrote novels. His contribution to the craft of English fiction was such that Sir Walter Scott called him the father of English fiction. He was certainly the one to usher English fiction into its modern phase. His literary theory is well integrated and expostulated in his novels like *Joseph Andrews* (with its critical preface) and *Tom Jones*, both of which begin with a chapter of discussion on fiction. [5]

Fielding's ideas cover a wide range of subjects relating to fiction. These include the definition of the novel as a genre, the truthfulness of its descriptions of life, its formal features, and the qualifications of a novelist. His was the first attempt ever to define the novel as a prose epic ("Prosai-comic-epic Writing" as he calls it) that is not inferior to an epic poem. A novel is comic but not grotesque with its lively and funny plot, its vulgar and crude common characters, and its humorous mood. It is a representation of real life. Concerning the fictional nature of the novel, Fielding sees the novel as a vehicle for moral inculcation, a mirror and an imitation of nature and life. All the characters and events should come from the author's observations and experience. Truthfulness includes probability and invariability in representing the reality of human nature and the inner world of man. Fielding's emphasis on psychic reality has contributed well to the growth of psychological realism. Within the frame of probability, Fielding encourages the depiction of the extraordinary and disapproves of total copying, thus making a distinction between artistic reality and real life. Though imitating life, art is, to him, not life.

With regard to the formal features of the novel, Fielding emphasizes sequential movement, priority, and probability. The author-narrator is like a God figure, planning, creating, and manipulating as he pleases, and the story as an organic whole moves sequentially from the beginning to the middle to the end. Priority should be given to important scenes and events, and plots must be made probable by the coherent actions and personalities of the characters. Regarding characterization, Fielding sees it as important for portraying real people and true human nature which is a mixture of good and evil, and for describing types or archetypes to reveal universal human characteristics. He touches upon the possible differences that exist between individuals and insists on their individuality. In addition, he attaches importance to the use of contrasts between good and evil, between plots, characters, and settings, which would add to the exquisite symmetry of the story and bring the types into relief.

On the qualification of a novelist, Fielding deems it necessary for a writer to have four basic qualities—native gift, adequate learning, rich experience with life, and a kind heart. Native gift or endowment refers to the capacity to observe and judge, which learning activates and increases. Social experience makes it possible for authors to represent people and life authentically, while sympathy and compassion endows a work with the power to touch the readers. Fielding finds value in constantly communicating with his readers both in his prefaces and the beginning chapters of his books and through plot development and various insinuations in the stories. In his critical commentaries, he explains the objectives of his stories, guides the readers through their reading, advises them to observe and judge well, and tells them about the educational value of the novel. Within the stories, he leaves room for the imagination of the readers by means of suspense, foreshadowing, and omission, and helps them conjecture about the plot, the formal devices, and the author's structural considerations. Fielding's theories impacted novel-writing not only of his own age but of all time.

Now let's take a look at Fielding's major works.

The History of the Adventures of Joseph Andrews, and of His Friend, Abraham Adams (1742), popularly known as *Joseph Andrews*, has been seen as the first realistic novel in English fiction. It was first begun as a parody of Richardson's *Pamela* which Fielding did not think much of and had written *Shamula* (1741) to mock at. In *Joseph Andrews* Joseph features as Pamela's younger brother. But after the initial attempt of parody, Fielding brought the story on its own track and wrote the novel in keeping with his own theory. The novel is loose in structure, but it is no longer episodic and sentimental. Its focus is on the presentation of English life as being lived then, so that it ends up as a novel of manners. The story is convoluted in a way. Joseph Andrews in his early twenties begins his life as a servant for Sir Booby, uncle of his sister Pamela's husband. After the old man dies, Lady Booby has her designs on the young servant and fires him when he rejects her attention. Joseph sets out for Somersetshire to look for his sweetheart Fanny. On his way, he is robbed, beaten, and left naked and half dead in a ditch, where he is picked up and dropped at an inn close by. There he meets the kind Parson Adams, who then goes with him to Somersetshire. They fall in with Mrs. Slipslop, Lady Booby's maid, and stop at an inn. As the innkeeper is snobbish enough to insult the shabbily dressed Joseph, a fight breaks out in which all the three battle with the innkeeper and his wife. Parson Adams emerges bloody-looking as the hostess has rinsed him thoroughly with a pail of hog's blood. The three leave and continue the trip. The Parson walks far ahead of his companions and walks into another fight with a man attacking a young woman. The Parson finds to his surprise that the girl is Fanny on her way to look for Joseph. The two go on and stop at an inn where Mrs. Slipslop and Joseph are staying. The young people are happy to see one another. The next stop is at the Wilsons, where the host is most hospitable and tells the Parson of his early life of vanity in London. His own sorrow now is that his third son with a strawberry birthmark on his shoulder has been stolen by the gypsies. From there the travelers plunge into a struggle for survival in which the Parson is mistaken by the hunting dogs for the hare. They fight with the squire, the hunter, who invites them over to his house, however, when he sees the loveliness of Fanny. The supper turns out to be a trying experience for the Parson who is made fun of. They leave to stop at inn, where the squire's men come to kidnap Fanny, but fail when Fanny's old acquaintance appears to her rescue. Arriving at home, the young people proceed to get married. Lady Booby comes to intervene and have the two arrested, but Pamela and her husband appear to save them. Pamela, now snobbish herself, tries to turn her brother away from the poor girl Fanny. Then it is discovered that Fanny is Pamela's sister and Joseph is Mr. Wilson's lost son. The two lovers marry and live happily ever after.

The moral nature of the story is self-evident. The world, despite its various forms of evil and imperfection, is still one which God presides over and regulates. The eventful career of the two major characters—Joseph and Parson Adams—through life, with all its misery and agony, concludes happily for the good and the kind. Joseph and Parson Adams are paragons of innocence and virtue and as such they are a touchstone to reveal evil and vice. Joseph takes most of the focus as the hero of the book. It is chiefly about his odyssey through life. Virtue is made to face vice and tries to shift for itself. The first ordeal is a test of his chastity and honor. Here he is portrayed as a parody of Richardson's Pamela. With Richardson the female is pursued by a male and tries to put up her defenses for her virtue, but here in Fielding's work, the male suffers the sexual onslaughts of a female in the form of the much older yet still sexually aggressive Lady Booby and wards off her clutches successfully. This serves as a vindication of male sexuality. When he is left naked and almost dead, he epitomizes the most naked vulnerability of a human to external forces that manipulate him. He is to suffer all forms of human hypocrisy including snobbishness and pretensions and all kinds of evil that get him into trouble and misery, but he survives whole and happy. Parson Adams is his companion and a guide in his initiation to life. The kind Parson represents all the Christian virtues—faith, compassion, justice, and courage to hold up virtue. He appears to be comic and didactic: he is absent-minded enough to forget to bring his sermons with him and to leave his horse behind at the inn of the snobbish innkeeper, and he talks and, of course, behaves like a holy man. He may be temporarily empowered by evil, but his goodness cannot stay overshadowed for long. Fielding's is always a moral world.

The novel's satiric edge is sharp and cutting. Although the story lauds the triumph of good over evil and showcases the goodness of human nature, it can be relentless to expose human foibles, one obvious manifestation of which is human hypocrisy, vanity and affectation. Parson Adams is, for instance, a very rare specimen of the holy clerics. His integrity is put to test and proven. But not that of his fellow parsons. Parson Trulliber is an obvious hypocrite. He is every bit what Parson Adams is not. When the good but penniless parson comes to ask for help to pay his and Joseph's bill at an inn, Trulliber refuses his request flatly. Although this can be taken as a mild satire on the good parson's naiveté, it is more a negative reflection upon his superficial counterpart, who cannot accept a shabbily dressed person as a servant of God.

The novel's eternal fascination also stems from its good number of deftly placed farces and events of a melodramatic nature. The Parson is a highly comic figure, itself a fact that he is a butt of the author's satire. A serious figure that he should be and in fact is, he is frequently thrown into impossible scenarios such as the one in which he falls in mud with the pigs, or the one where in trying to rescue Fanny from the rapist, he falls in with Mrs. Slipslop and touches her breasts and then ends up lying beside Fanny. The melodramatic note is sounded in many instances, the most glaring being the almost inconceivable hidden identities. Joseph's personal history is a good case in point. He begins not aware of his identity, stumbles through life with a good nature, and ends up with a surprising self-discovery and self-awareness. It seems to be that God is playing a trick upon him; only the God figure here is Henry Fielding. Another apt example is Fanny's birth secret. Think of the poor but kind girl finding herself Pamela's sister! Such coincidences can occur only in Fielding's universe.

Tom Jones, the Foundling (1749), popularly known as *Tom Jones*, is his masterpiece. This is a long story of 18 books in three sections of six chapters each. The structure of the novel is well balanced and symmetrical: the first six are set in the Allworthy estate, books VII-XII relate events on the road to London, and the last six, the climax, is set in London. Each book begins with a long chapter of detailed discussions of the character's motives, so that the chapters, if culled and put together, would make a good volume on the art of fiction.

As the story goes, Squire Allworthy finds, on coming back from London, a baby lying in his bed. People suspect Jenny Jones, a former maid in Schoolmaster Partridge's house, of being the mother, and Partridge being the father. Partridge has to leave the country as a result of the scandal. The foundling is named Jones after his supposed mother Jenny Jones. Later Allworthy's sister—Bridget marries Captain Blifil and gives birth to a son, Master Blifil, who becomes the squire's heir. As the squire is kind to Tom, Blifil feels jealous and tries to slander him. Tom is a naughty and deceptive boy, and his teachers along with Master Blifil dislike him intensely. Bridget seems to like the boy better than her own son. The credulous Allworthy is alienated from Tom. The boy has been close to the Westerns: Mr. Western likes the lad for his hunting skills, and his daughter, Sophia, is in love with him. Once rescuing Sophia from danger when her horse runs away, he is wounded, and is taken care of in the Western house. One day the two young people confess mutual love.

When Allworthy is very ill, he disposes of his fortune, giving Tom a generous share. Tom is the only one feeling happy and grateful. On her way home to see the squire, Bridget dies. Tom gets drunk as he happily celebrates the squire's recovery, and quarrels with Master Blifil. Now Mr. Western forces Sophia to marry Master Blifil, whom the girl does not love. She meets Tom and the two pledge constancy. Tom and Sophia exchange love letters with the help of their friends. Blifil slanders Tom before Allworthy for getting drunk on the day he is very ill, and the furious squire drives Tom out.

Tom is now involved in an inn brawl and gets wounded. The man who treats him turns out to be Mr. Partridge. The two become good friends and travel together. Sophia also runs away from home with her maid. Tom rescues a Mrs. Waters from a rape, who invites him to dine with her. Sophia comes to the same inn with her maid and learns that Tom and Mrs. Waters have been sleeping together. Disappointed, she leaves a muff of hers on his bed and goes to London. Tom follows her there and meets her and assures her of his attachment. Then Sophia's father comes and finds her. Allworthy is coming with Blifil to marry Sophia. Desperate and penniless, Tom gets in a fight and is sent to jail for murder. Partridge meets Mrs. Waters who is in fact Jenny Jones married now. Mrs. Waters then reveals the real identity of Tom as the son of Bridget who slept with a student. Bridget paid Jenny for her to play the scapegoat. Bridget also wrote a letter before her death telling the truth to her brother, but Blifil stole and destroyed it. So Tom turns out to be Blifil's half brother and Allworthy's nephew. Now Tom is cleared of the murder charge, and survives Blifil's plan to have him hanged. Allworthy disowns Blifil and makes Tom his heir. Tom marries Sophia and moves to the Western house.

The moral theme of the book is self-evident. Fielding sees the novel as a vehicle for moral teachings. His is a typical 18th-century universe in which the moral verities still function well. The good gets rewarded while the evil receives its due punishment, and the characters all act out their lives within God's grand scheme of things. The unity of the novel's structure correlates to its moral design. This is the reason why contemporary authors like John Barth have felt the temptation to parody Fielding: the modern age differs from Fielding's in nature and the modern novel finds it impossible to write in Fielding's smugly complacent manner.

Formally, Fielding embraces realism. His book is a truthful portrayal of the life and manners of the 18th century; the author's own experience with life and people ensures the effect of verisimilitude that his novel produces. In a sense Fielding can be seen as a social historian of his time as he tries his best to reflect the tenor and temper of his period. For instance, Tom Jones is portrayed as one from real life with his foibles as well as his innate goodness. He is as real as a person of blood and flesh whose behavior is basically good yet not flawless. So is Squire Allworthy, basically kind yet irritatingly credulous and gullible. Fielding's negative character, Master Blifil, is all hopelessly evil. The author's attitude almost tilts toward determinism: Blifil grows up in the same environment as does Tom but turns out to be a different human type altogether.

In addition, the book is well planned on Fielding's own literary theory. Its plot moves in a sequential order, from Tom's childhood vantage to his fall from his benefactor's favor to his worming his way back into the old man's graces. Tom stays in the center of the narrative, receiving most of the attention while his opposing forces are given enough coverage to form a sizeable contrast just so that he stands out in strong relief. In addition, the novel appears to be such a good replica of life that it is hard to find people and occurrences of an improbable nature. The lengthy digressions in which the author often appears in person may seem to be out of place or superfluous, but that ties in well with his notion of the author-narrator as a God figure. He is the wirepuller, the juggler, the manipulator, and he tells his readers so, creating a kind of esthetic distance and increasing objectivity and detachment in appreciation and judgment. This can be viewed as a step forward over the purely first-person narrative with which the modern novel as a genre first began. The wide sweep of life, the different walks of society, and the understanding of man, his nature, and his world—all these reveal Fielding as a master of the realistic novel. Together with Defoe and Richardson, he put a stop to sentimental romances and pushed the art of story-telling to a new phase—the modern novel.

Laurence Sterne (1713-1768)

Sterne was educated in Cambridge, and became a priest. He was not well suited to the job though he wrote good sermons. His literary passions were, among others, Cervantes (1547-1616) and Francois Rabelais (1494-1553). As a novelist, he was conscious and original, and contributed a good deal toward perfecting the art of the genre in its early phase. He was an iconoclast, an innovator, a trail-blazer, and an eternal presence in literary history. One of the 18th-century writers whom Charles Dickens admired and learned from, Sterne managed to leave an enduring imprint on later writers. Dickens felt deeply impressed by his fictions' major features such as their themes of grotesque goodness, sweet humility, sensitive humanity, their boisterous humor, and idiosyncratic discursiveness. Sterne's major works include *The Life and Opinions of Tristram Shandy, Gentleman* (1760-1767), and *A Sentimental Journey through France and Italy by Mr. Yorick* (1768). The latter book is not so much a travelogue as an outlet for the author's self-expression. It best illustrates Sterne as a moralist. The emotions permeating its pages are basically love, compassion, and tender sentiments. The author would like to help bring warmth and sentiments of love into life so that people would love their world and their fellow creatures more. [6]

Now let's take a look at his best known work, *The Life and Opinions of Tristram Shandy, Gentleman*.

Tristram Shandy, the narrator, begins with the interesting narration of some events of importance to his life. These include, among others, the interruption of the moment of his conception when his mother asked his father about winding the clock; the place of his birth that, according to a settlement between his parents, he had to be born at the ancestral Shandy Hall rather in London; his delivery by a midwife with the help of a quack doctor, Dr. Slop, whose forceps flattened his nose, while his father and Uncle Toby drank in the parlor; the fall of a window sash when he as a boy pissed through the window that caused his geniture problem, and his misnaming by the parson. He has a confused boyhood living with his father and uncle.

Tristram's father is a funny father figure. He is a longwinded chatter, good at discussions of a learned but always irrelevant nature. These include his discourses on the nature of women while he is waiting for the midwife and the doctor to arrive; his telling a long story of a man with a very long nose on hearing of his son's birth with a flattened nose; his responses to his older son's death by quoting and discussing all the philosophic ideas on death; his doubts about getting a tutor for Tristram or putting him into long trousers, and his endless discussions of war, medicine, business, and ancient fashions.

No less eccentric is Uncle Toby. Toby is an old soldier, wounded and retired, neurotically obsessed with playing soldier in his miniature battlefield with his former corporal Trim, another roguish grotesque in the novel. Toby is his brother's audience in the latter's perpetual discussions of something painfully obscure and irrelevant. He keeps whistling a favorite song of his brother's when he has to listen to his lengthy talk. His history in war and love is immensely humorous and amusing.

Then there are the maid and Widow Wadham. Both reveal their peculiar traits of grotesquery. The maid forgets to tell the parson the name his father would like Tristram to have. She wishes to show grief over Tristram's brother's death, but could think of nothing more than the dresses she would inherit when her mistress goes into mourning. Widow Wadman wants to know about Uncle Toby's wound, and Toby is totally embarrassed and stops thinking of marrying her altogether. One character comments on the book at the end of it that it is a cock-and-bull kind of book which leads the readers into "a mad but merry chase through the author's satirical and witty mind."

The novel is a book of its own kind in literary history. It came out in print over a period of years on an on-and-off basis from 1760 right up to 1767. There are altogether nine volumes, of which the first two (1760) made Sterne an instant celebrity. It caught attention on publication for a number of reasons. First, it is not really about Tristram Shandy, but about his father, his uncle Toby, Dr. Slop, and Widow Wadham. Tristram acts basically as the teller of the story about these grotesques, each with their singular ridiculous oddities: the father irrelevant with his erudition, the uncle with his immersion in his soldiery, the doctor a sloppy and clumsy quack, and the widow still sexually active in an inordinate way. As to Tristram himself, he does not get born until volume four and does not learn to wear trousers until volume six in which the description of the boy's change of pants has become one of the funniest artistic rarities in English literature. Sterne does not appeal so much by means of his plot as by his subtle and accurate choice of the best moments to catch his readers with the best surprises he could cook up. He does this admirably well with the help of his thematic and formal idiosyncrasies. The result of this endeavor is amazing. He makes a deep impression on his readers, and ends up with more than compensating for any deficiency in story interest.

Then, the book appears formless and out of focus as there is no sequential order of events, with a good deal of discursive and desultory rambling, a seemingly irrelevant jumble of digressions in which the author indulges in his verbal virtuosity as he pleases, or simply a blank page, white or black, or tables or diagrams, just room enough for the readers' imagination. It is not exactly a story per se, devoting as it does over half of its space to discourses on philosophy and morals or simply to wild flights of the mind or free associations of thoughts. However, it possesses a power to hook and hold attention and provoke laughter and tears. The magic lies in the fact that there is intrinsic coherence and unity which the author's pervasive sensibility assures. Sterne is capricious and, to a degree, willful and self-centered in his narrative. He is the one who dictates the direction of his prose movement. But he is well aware of his whims and knows well how to cash in on these to generate the best effect of his art. In addition, there is his psychological depth to consider. *Tristram Shandy*, with its subtle and sensible dips into the deeps of memory, has been seen by some as the first true psychological novel in English literary history. In a very real sense Stern wrote a good deal of his inner self into his works. He insists on representing human emotion and pathos more than anything else, which is an indication of his disaffection with the prevalent control of reason in his time.

Furthermore, there is the unique artistic effect that stems from the dexterous amalgam of a huge amount of humor, comedy, and laughter with occurrences that touch and move the human heart. Sterne possesses a comic vision encompassing everything. He finds life itself funny and laughable, and manages to extend his comic self into all the people and events in the book. His characters are particularly impressive with their eccentricities. Uncle Toby and Corporal Trim are among those who tend to linger in the readers' minds, funny and even absurd in exterior but really kind, gentle, and humble inside. That is why Sterne calls the book a picture of himself. Although he may not have any "Victorian children" as do Fielding and Smollett, his comedy and grotesquery definitely influenced such masters of the craft as Dickens.

One thing that may provoke distaste in more conservative readers (like William Makepeace Thackeray) is the plethora of obscenities with which Sterne's novel is strewn. Obscene language and scenes, vulgarities and profanities, and excessive sexual descriptions—all these may be the reason why some people have relegated it to the category of the low and lewd. However, even this, along with its aforementioned salient features, has helped to push the boundaries back for fiction and contributed toward the discovery of new freedoms and new possibilities for the art of the novel. Sterne is remembered for his originality and his daring to break new ground.

Tobias Smollett (1721-1771)

Smollett was born in Scotland and worked as an apprentice to a surgeon. In his early youth he came to London but failed to receive attention as a playwright. Then he served as a surgeon in the navy for a while before he began serious novel-writing. His first work, *The Adventures of Roderick Random* (1748), was an immediate success, and his next, *The Adventures of Peregrine Pickle* (1751), contains some of his best character portrayals. Among his other works, *The Expedition of Humphrey Clinker* (1771), his last novel, was the best, endearing in tenderness and geniality in which Smollett has been found wanting in his previous literary efforts.

Smollett was one of the most original writers of his time. His influence on later writers is not negligible. Charles Dickens for instance worshipped him. Of the eight novels that the Victorian novelist loved most in his youth as he said in his autobiography, three were by Smollett: *The Adventures of Roderick Random*, *The Adventures of Peregrine Pickle*, and *The Expedition of Humphrey Clinker*. Dickens learned from him a good number of things such as his manner of linking adventures in a loose way, putting a hero through a series of archetypal contemporary scenes, his comic devices with his comic breadth and buoyancy, his fearless censure of social evil, and his caricaturist manner of characterization. Smollett is now read chiefly for his wit and his satire. [7]

Now let's take a look at his first work, *The Adventures of Roderick Random* (1748), the book that made him immediately famous. Roderick is, as the story goes, a reckless and restless young man. His father has to leave England because he married a poor relation and a domestic—Roderick's mother, who dies at his birth. The boy suffers in school as well as at home as the son of a disinherited father and gets nothing when his grandfather dies. His maternal uncle Tom Bowling sends him to a university, but the man has to leave the country as the result of a duel. Roderick drops out of school, becomes an apprentice to a surgeon in London, and takes good care of Miss Williams, a prostitute, whom he loves. Later as a surgeon's mate on a man-of-war, he is abused by his superiors there. Still later he is robbed and wounded but is taken care of by a good woman. Then he becomes footman to a rich spinster and falls in love with her niece Narcissa. One day he is carried off by smugglers to France where he meets his uncle. Then on his way to Paris, Roderick is robbed by a friar and meets his boyhood friend Strap. The two scheme for Roderick to marry a rich heiress. They end up in London, where Tom meets and makes advances to rich Melinda but is rejected. Then he sets his eyes on crippled Miss Snapper but deserts her when he sees Narcissa again. Melinda slanders him and turns Narcissa's brother against him. But Miss Williams tries to help him out of gratitude. Back to London, Roderick leaves with his uncle on a slave trade ship to Guinea Coast and meets his father there, now a rich man, in Brazil. Back to England, Roderick goes to Narcissa, drives her suitors away, and wins her hand. The happily married couple goes to live on their ancestral Scotland estate that his father has bought back for him.

The Adventures of Roderick Random is a typical 18th-century picaresque novel. It is about a picaresque hero of both virtue and vice, being forced to face a world of vice and making shift for survival. Roderick is basically a good person with a kind nature. A boy thrown upon himself in adversity, he has no choice but brave the world of evil and learn to live on. On quite a few occasions he is on the verge of losing his virtues such as the time when he turns his back ungraciously on his faithful friend Strap whose job is to save him from death or disaster, or when he becomes sinister and cruel in his schemes for revenge, or when he easily befriends unpleasant, even evil characters. He is in a word capable of acting selfish and ill-intentioned to others. But he picks up wisdom, learns to improve himself, and remains essentially good. So he earns his reward—his financial rehabilitation and emotional gratification. He is best rewarded with Narcissa, his beloved.

The fictional universe of *Roderick Random* is a stage on which all types of people live and act out their dramas. The book deliberately reveals human nature in its variegated forms. There are the rich and the poor, the ill-natured relatives and the faithful friends, the effete lords, the kind-hearted whore, and the lecherous and greedy priests. It is a stage on which good and evil are entrenched in battle, good nature faces the challenge of sinful behavior, and wins out in the end. In the final analysis, Smollett's is a moral world, where good gets its reward. In addition to the experience of Roderick, Hugh Strap's life is a telling example as well. He comes to the rescue of Roderick and is well assured of a good life in return. Roderick's story serves to disseminate the values of the age—temperance, virtue, fortitude and honesty, and urge people to love virtue and hate vice. Smollett is committed to his world as a satirist.

In formal terms the book has little structure, but it enriches and endears itself to the readers with a series of engaging descriptions of the incidents. These occurrences seem disconnected but skillfully integrate themselves into a coherent whole, and are rendered enormously entertaining with a variety of humorous devices. The novel is episodic, and full of disguises. With Roderick venturing out, the author sees the opportunity to observe, record with minute detail, and satirize ruthlessly the ills of his crude and violent age. His frankness in his depictions of the seamy side of life such as the want of humaneness and kind sentiments in his English fellow creatures (as indeed showcased in the London scenes for example) without any show of redeeming grace—this is a feature of his writings that often bothers delicate readers.

Chapter 9 The Romantic Period • Wordsworth • Coleridge • Scott • Austen

The Romantic Period: An Introduction [1]

The Romantic Movement was international in the 19th century. It happened differently in different countries. In France it occurred after the Napoleonic wars were over, with such notable figures as Hugo, Lamartine, and George Sand on the scene. In Germany there were Geothe and Schiller, and in Russia Pushkin and Lemontov. American Romanticism came some 30 years later than its European counterpart. Irving, Cooper, Poe, Hawthorne, Melville, Emerson, Thoreau, Whitman, and Dickinson were among the most familiar American Romantic writers. The outburst of Romantic feeling in England was sudden. It was triggered off by certain specific events of historic significance. These included the two revolutions, the American and the French, especially the latter, and also what was happening in the country itself around the time.

The Romantic period was a very troubled phase in the social and political history of England and Europe. A few years before its advent, the United States broke away from Britain and was formed on the basis of the natural rights of men: "all men are created equal," an outcry that caught on and began to ring all over the world. Then in 1789 the French Revolution exploded on the other side of the English Channel. What happened was that France was going bankrupt and the moneyed classes, the aristocratic classes, refused to do anything about it. The three estates, the clergy, the aristocracy, and the commoners, were in a head-on clash, and the commoners took matters into their own hands and insisted on meeting as an assembly. This was an act of insurrection, but the king had to go along with it. On July 14 that year, the people stormed the prison Bastille and released all the political prisoners there, and the National Assembly approved the Declaration of the Rights of Man. There was a widespread feeling that there was going to be a revolution in France, and that the people were to have a better life and much more say about the affairs of the state. It brought out all the discontentment that had been built up in the bosoms of the people. The ideals of equality, liberty and fraternity instantly became the catchwords and inspired a vision of a better future, a new world of hope. What had happened was already scary enough for the British ruling class, but this was not the end of it all. In 1793 King Louis XVI was executed, and the Reign of Terror with the Jacobines in control began. A lot of blood was shed. The French army offered to help make revolutions in other countries, which incurred the wrath and hatred of the rulers of Europe. Then, the middle of the roaders, the middle class, took over with the Robespierres in the lead, overthrew the Jacobines, and started what has come to be known as the "White Terror." Then Napoleon made himself the dictator of the country, which signaled the end of the revolution. Napoleon first fought for the left wing of the French revolution, but he took more and more control and became an emperor in the end. When he was defeated at Waterloo in 1814, a long period of repressive rule began in the whole of Europe.

All this had a tremendous impact on the situation in Britain. The government became more conservative and repressive. At the beginning of the period it was already clear that the balance of the previous century was broken and that things were not all right any more. There were political upheavals, and the ideas of revolution were up in the air. In addition, London ceased to be the only center for social and economic activities. An intense labor warfare had developed in the country. On the one hand, trading and manufacturing flourished, and the factory system triumphed. Factory towns sprawled all over the country. Cities like Manchester, Edinburgh and Liverpool all began to spread out. The United Kingdom ruled over about one fourth of humanity, maintained its control over the seas, and became the empire on which the sun never set. It plundered and brought tremendous wealth into the country. On the other hand, all this enriched only the still existing aristocracy and the rising middle class. In the meantime social problems became serious and urgent. The working class became worse off with no protection and no power whatever. There was a good deal of poverty and starvation. People were becoming poorer and a large urban proletariat was struggling for survival in incredible misery. The government's laissez-faire policy worked to the detriment of the workers. The factory owners and managers tried to get as much as possible out of the workers but paid them as little as possible. The workers worked long hours, as long as 16 hours a day, yet their wages kept going down. Women workers were paid less, and many were forced into prostitution. The coal miners (the colliers) were the hardest hit. They worked to death in unspeakable conditions. On the whole there appeared a continual downward spiral. The working class lived in a slum environment.

The government became more and more repressive. All the laws were made in the interest of the middle class. The Combination Act of 1800 outlawed any combination of workers. The suspension of the *Habeas Corpus* endowed the government with the power of arresting anyone as it pleased. However, the forces working for change were gathering. The workers began to come together, and think and act in group terms. Societies of all kinds appeared; trade associations, illegal at first, were formed. The mills in Lancashire were mechanized, and seven or eight out of ten weavers were thrown out of job there. People blamed their misfortune on the machines and began breaking them, and a riot occurred. The government insisted that anyone who broke machines were to be executed or transported to Australia. Lord Byron made an influential speech in the House of Lords in defense of the workers, and that made him famous and a darling of England.

With the battle of Waterloo, the first modern depression in England began. The prices of wheat dropped. Oppressive laws like the Corn Laws were passed, forbidding the importation of corn. Byron's career as a darling of England was soon over. He had to leave the country in 1816, driven out partly by scandal, but mainly because he was championing the cause of the oppressed people. His friend Shelley did not fare any better. He talked about atheism, was basically a socialist at heart, and ultimately in 1818 had to leave England, too. The next year what has come to be known as the Massacre of Peterloo happened. It was a dreadful event in English history. About 60,000 poor people came together in a field called St. Peter's, and petitioned for relief. The government panicked. Police was let out to arrest the speaker. A riot followed in which many people were killed and wounded. In one of his poems Shelley mocked at the British army having won another victory, that of Peterloo, after they won it at Waterloo.

In the meantime there was an obvious sense of change and newness, and with it a tremendous energy for changing things. Some efforts to address the problems of the time were being made. For example, there was Robert Owen who came up with a very interesting alternative. As a factory owner, this smart man of humanitarian ideals, in face of the rapacity and greed of the capitalist class, ran his factory in Scotland in a different way on a different idea, that if the workers were taken good care of, they would work better. He tried to make it possible for his workers to work for decent hours, earn decent wages, and live good and dignified lives in decent houses. As a result, Owen made money! People from all over Europe came to see that factory. Owen told about it to the British Parliament which, however, did not believe it. Young Coleridge was planning to go to the U.S. to found a utopia there with Robert Southey, but did not go because the latter changed his mind. Writers on the whole responded well to the situation. William Blake, a supporter of both the American and French revolutions, wrote his *Songs of Innocence*. William Godwin came up with his *Inquiry Concerning Political Justice*, advocating the socialist theory. His wife, Mary Wollstonecraft, wrote about the rights of women, her writings marking the beginning of the Western feminist movement. Byron and Shelley did their best to show sympathy to the poor. And Wordsworth was very sympathetic to the French Revolution. These were but a few examples. Ultimately, the reaction of the English government to the French Revolution solidified the government's reactionary rule and killed any possible humanitarian initiative. 25 years of repressive rule followed.

One of the things to notice about the period is its difference from the 18th century. The 18th century was centripetal, with all the forces coming together. It valued balance, the middle things, the middle class, reason, reasonableness, common sense, traditional forms and values, deism, and moderation. The commonly used words were "we," "submit," and "reasonableness." There existed a balance of things, the base of which was essentially economic. There was increasing affluence, a sense of stability prevailed in general, and people felt that things were basically all right then. The *zeitgeist* of the time was reflected in the literature of the century. However, the Romantic period was centrifugal, with all the forces falling apart and flying out from the center. It was one of exploration in many directions, a little like the Elizabethan period. The commonly accepted concepts of the period had to do with words such as "enthusiasm," "intuition," "admire," "inspiration," and the pronoun "I," all concepts that Alexander Pope might find odd and difficult to accept. All the upheavals of the time testified to the fact that the British and European reliance on what Edmund Wilson terms "Divine Authority" was weakened and that a new value system based on the personal and individual values was coming in as a replacement. The emphasis on the individual became a dominant feature of the new, or Romantic era.

Representing the highest achievement in English poetry, the English Romantic period has been considered the second great period in English literature, second only to the Elizabethan period. A huge amount of energy was exhibited in the poets of this troubled period. The Romantics all revealed their singular talents and achieved a remarkable degree of success in their literary endeavors. Some of them like Wordsworth and Coleridge developed a nature mysticism. Others such as Shelley and Keats embraced a sensual kind of aestheticism, while Byron bodied forth the new concept in action, the Byronic heroism. The few Romantic poets that we discuss in the following pages, William Wordsworth, Samuel Taylor Coleridge, Lord Byron, Percy Bysshe Shelley, and John Keats were all part of the overall emotional and intellectual response to the sense of newness that came in the aftermath of the French Revolution. The former two turned out to be more conservative, while the latter three, "the Satanic School" (as Robert Southey called them), were more rebellious and aggressive. As the poet laureate Robert Southey wrote too much and with glib facility, and some say he wrote often for money (as he had to support his own family and that of his brother-in-law Coleridge's), he is not read very much now. But he is capable of brilliant pieces such as "After Blenheim," and probably deserves more attention. During their day Wordsworth was the most respectable, and Byron the most famous. Now with the mists of history clearing away, people seem to agree that the early Wordsworth, Coleridge, and Keats have stood the ravages of time better. But all of these Romantics, with perhaps the exception of Southey, are major poets in the annals of English poetry.

It is probably a good place here to mention briefly the names of the three famous prose writers who lived and wrote in this period to enrich the tradition of English prose in their unique way. These are Charles Lamb (1775-1834), William

Hazlitt (1778-1830), and Thomas De Quincey (1785-1859). All three were the contemporaries of Wordsworth and Coleridge, some were eyewitness to the brilliance of Coleridge's lectures in London like Lamb, and some befriended Coleridge like De Quincey. Lamb's essays on Shakespeare are still a must on the reading list of Shakespearean scholars; his Shakespearean tales did a lot toward increasing Shakespeare's popularity. Hazlitt's portrait of Wordsworth and Coleridge in his essay, "My First Acquaintance with Poets," remains the most authentic of its kind to which repeated subsequent references have been made in the appreciation of the two poets. His comment upon Wordsworth in his essay, "The Spirit of the Age" ("Mr. Wordswoth's genius is a pure animation of the spirit of the age. Had he lived in any other period of the world, he would never have been heard of"), sets the tone for later evaluation of the great poet and reveals his unusual perspicacity and remarkable critical acumen. And De Quincey, by expanding the boundaries of literary expression to touch upon the dark side of the human psyche and through his technical experiments, was able to impact the future writers such as James Joyce and T. S. Eliot. All of these have managed to leave their scratch upon the rock of eternity.

William Wordsworth (1770-1850)

Wordsworth was born and brought up in Cockermouth, Cumberland, on the northern fringes of the Lake District near the river Derment in northern England. This fact of his life proved to be immensely significant to his career as a Romantic poet. As a boy he loved nature and its sights and sounds, and got to know the peasants, shepherds, and wanderers well. The first natural beauty that fascinated young Wordsworth was probably the river's melodious flow, similar to his nurse's song. He came to appreciate the serenity and its sedating power on the human soul and made to the realization that nature cleanses and invigorates the human spirit. Nature began to assume the role of a nurturer and a guide in his mind. There the idea took root and blossomed into an important Romantic doctrine in history. [2]

Wordsworth was eager to experience nature. When he was attending Cambridge University, he undertook two walking tours during the summer time with one friend on foot, one through France and the Alps, and one through Wales.

During 1891-1892 he was in France and became a warm supporter of the French Revolution. He fell in love with a French girl, had a daughter born to him, but was forced to return to England out of financial constraint. Unable to go back when the war between England and France broke out, he suffered very much from his sense of guilt, the pain of his divided allegiances to the French Revolution as well as to his own country, and his disillusionment with the course of the French Revolution. He was at one time on the brink of a nervous breakdown. Eventually he met Samuel Taylor Coleridge and settled down with his sister, Dorothy, near where Coleridge stayed. The two men became very close and discussed and wrote poetry together. Wordsworth recovered, and at the age of 27 his poetic career began. So far Wordsworth had not been financially comfortable. He was now able to focus on poetry because a friend of his had left a sum of money to him at death. In 1798 he and Coleridge anonymously published a volume of verse, *Lyrical Ballads*, to which Coleridge contributed the supernatural poems such as *The Rime of the Ancient Mariner* and Wordsworth the poems of common life and poems like the famous *Lines Composed a Few Miles Above the Tintern Abbey*. After this initial success, Wordsworth continued to write and published *Poems in Two Volumes* in 1807. Then "the great decade" for him (1798-1807) came to an end. Later his friendship with Coleridge cooled down for a long time but they managed to patch up in the end. Wordsworth became more famous and prosperous as he was recognized as a poet of a national stature, and gradually turned conservative. In 1843 he became the poet laureate. At his death in 1850 his *Prelude* came out in print. As they lived close to the lake area in Northern England, these poets have been called "the Lakers." [3]

The *Lyrical Ballads* is a monumental work in the history of English poetry. It came out in print to the immense delight of the people and brought with it a fresh breath of wind of change to English poetry. Containing poems "materially different" from those currently written, it signaled the beginning of the Romantic period in English poetry. "The Preface" to *Lyrical Ballads* did not come first in the form in which we generally read it now. The 1798 volume contains an "Advertisement" in which Wordsworth states that most of the poems are experimental, testing the limits of adapting common speech for writing good poetry. The 2nd two-volume edition of the book (1800) came out with a preface which is an expansion of the "Advertisement." This preface claims that the poems in the volume were written not as experiments but to exemplify the principles of all good poetry. The preface was revised further for the 3rd edition of the book that came out in 1802. This is the version of it that we normally read now. In this preface, William Wordsworth explains his theory of valid language for poetry, new and revolutionary in nature, one that impacted the poetry writing of the time tremendously. It was a manifesto for Romantic poetry. It should be noted that Coleridge also contributed to the theory in no negligible way.

Regarding language, Wordsworth emphasizes, in the preface, the fact that his language and diction is "very different." Poetic language must be a selection of the language really used by the people. Such a language is free of the influence of social vanity, and is therefore more permanent and philosophical. He also insists that poetic language should not be essentially different from prose language. It need not be gaudy, inane, arbitrary and capricious, and elevated over common speech; it need not be contrived or deliberately artful. His theory of language was intended for the language of poetry to reach the common people.

Wordsworth had also a theory about the sources of poetry quite different from that of the 18th century. The 18th-century poet was primarily a craftsman, who could write well without feeling like it. According to Wordsworth, poetry comes from emotions, not from reason; it deals with feelings, attitudes, emotions—"the heart," not understanding, not common sense, as Alexander Pope thought it did. To Wordsworth poetry is "the spontaneous overflow of powerful emotion" "recollected in tranquility" by men of deep feeling and much thought. The key words here are "emotion," "feeling," and "deep thought" which is another way of saying "meditation." A real poet is one who thinks a good deal, knows and learns about humanity and his times, has very deep feelings, and is able to recollect these powerful emotions and writes. Wordsworth's poetry was mostly written in this mode. The obvious examples that come to mind may include "I wandered lonely as a cloud," and "The Solitary Reaper," but many other poems fit well into this definition.

Another of Wordsworth's basic beliefs is that the subject of poetry should be different from that of the previous age. The subject should come from the "incidents and situations from common life"; poetic diction and the coloring of the imagination should enable people to see the incidents in a new light, enable them to see the primary laws of human nature, and show them how to see, understand and enjoy their lives and judge them. Low and rustic life may be used to better represent the essential passions of the heart and the elemental feelings of men. People who come from the middle or lower classes of society, like peasants, children, outcasts, criminals and idiot boys, can be used as serious subjects of poetic or even tragic concern. The function of poetry is different from entertainment or from writing poetry to help people remember things. The readers will see his point readily with reference to poems like "Simon Lee" or "We Are Seven." [4] Wordsworth views the poet in a new light as well. He feels that the poet should understand life better than other people do, and he elevates the status of the poet. He does not go as far as Emerson or Whitman, probably, but he sees the poet as a "seer" of a kind as well.

Wordsworth was not a deep thinker, and his subject was limited. But he was trying to bring poetry down to the level of the people so that the people could understand their lives. In a certain sense he was not a great poet. Some of his works are among the greatest, but he wrote also a lot of uninspired, unimaginative poetry. Writing for him after 1807 became a routine, a need, something almost mechanical. It is just possible that his subjects might have been exhausted at a certain point in time when everything that needed to be recollected had been recalled in tranquility and written about. In a way he was a shallow person. His friend, Coleridge, whom he tended to look down upon as a little brother, was a lot deeper and more intelligent as is revealed by his *Biographia Literaria*. But right there in his time and place, Wordsworth proved to be a genius, a leader figure, presenting as he did a theory of poetry that worked as something like a fire. That was why he was remembered by Shelley and Browning as the great leader.

But when poetry and politics were entwined, the involved poet tended to fall from his height. And one thing that all Romantic poets were scornful about was that any of them would accept the job of a Poet Laureate, a hired poet by the king, writing to order. Officially, it was a great honor, but it meant a betrayal of what Romantic poetry stood for. In his *A Defense of Poetry*, Shelley is talking about the things that had been said against poets in the past: "Let us assume that Homer was a drunkard, that Virgil was a flatterer, that Horace was a coward, that Tasso was a madman, that Lord Bacon was a peculator, that Raphael was a libertine, that Spenser was a poet laureate." It is interesting that Shelley put the job of a poet laureate on the same level as the other notorious, dreadful things. And of course Wordsworth became a poet laureate. To Shelley and his group of young poets, Wordsworth went over to the enemy and became their spokesman. As such he earned the epithet of "the lost leader," very much in the way T. S. Eliot became one to his generation of writers like Hemingway about one century later. But history records only things of a permanent nature, and Wordsworth's "betrayal" has long been forgotten and forgiven. He is now remembered as one of the seminal figures in English poetry.

Let's take a look at some of the poet's major works. [5]

Wordsworth has been known as a famous nature poet. His is almost a Nature faith. Indeed, some critics have gone as far as to call him a High Priest of Nature. All his life he worships nature and tries to help people understand its significance. His idea of nature and its importance to human life is well demonstrated in his famous *Lines Composed a Few Miles Above the Tintern Abbey* (1798). The poem is written in the style of description and meditation that he picked up from Coleridge's *Frost at Midnight*. As it best exemplifies the basic elements of the poet's theory of nature and, by extension, of poetry, it functions to Wordsworth's notion of nature poetry like a wire-puller to loose threads. The poem and the meditation it contains were prompted by the poet's revisiting the Wye valley that he had passed five years earlier during his tour of the country in 1793. It is a scene to which the poetic mind returns with its recollection. Thus it illustrates the poet's idea of poetry as "the powerful overflow of emotion" "recollected in tranquility." The 1st stanza (ll. 1-22) describes the quiet pastoral beauty of the valley with its murmuring mountain springs, its "steep and high cliffs," the dark sycamore tree, the cottage-ground, the orchard tuffs, the unripe fruits in uniform green, the groves and copses, the hedge-rows, and the farmsteads, quiet and in green, sending up "wreaths of smoke," and its solitude with some vagrant dwellers in the houseless woods, or a hermit sitting alone by the fire in his cave. Now deep in nature, the poetic mind begins to meditate.

The 2nd stanza (ll. 23-48) focuses on the importance of nature in "[t]hese beauteous forms" when remembered at this moment of tranquility. These forms generate a feeling of love, kindness, and gentle affections, "sweet sensations," a "serene and blessed mood," which make life possible and tolerable for people living lonely amidst the din of the human world with its "burthen of mystery" and "heavy and weary weight." Like Rousseau, Wordsworth praises rustic people and simple country life as a contrast to the corrupt influence of city life. The lines here (23-42) bring instantly to mind the poet's other works such as "The world is too much with us" (1807), where people waste their lives in their frenzy of getting and spending and have no time nor eyes for the natural beauty around. The city and country antithesis embedded here reminds the readers also of his poems like "Lines Written in Early Spring" (ll. 1-8); "Resolution and Independence" (1807), "Michael" (1800), "London, 1802" (1807), and *Ode: Intimations of Immortality* (1807). The lines 43-48 body forth an essential Wordsworthian idea, that of transcendentalism, that human beings, when in total harmony with nature, transcend the limits of individuality and become able to "see into the life of things." The notion behind this is that nature is alive with spirit and God's presence. There is also an indication of Worsworth's mysticism here that corporal beings possess a spiritual nature of their own. The readers tend to recall in this connection the poet's other works such as "Lucy Gray" (1800), "The Two April Mornings" (1800), "It is a beauteous evening" (1807), "Nutting" (1800), the poem where nature is animated by one consciousness, and "I wandered lonely as a cloud" (1807), the poem in which the fixed gaze of the poet induces a mystic mood and turns the physical world into a fairy one.

The third stanza (ll.49-57) reiterates the notion that nature offers a counterpoint against the world, with its joyless daylight, its unprofitable activity and its fever, all weighing heavily on the mind (a reminder of Emerson and Thoreau and Whitman). The stanza ends with the realization that nature is the care-giver (for human spiritual welfare), the nurse, and the comforter (ll. 56-57). The 4th stanza (ll. 58-111) emphasizes the three stages of progression of the poet's mind slowly learning about nature. At first, when he was a boy with his "coarser pleasures," he ran into nature as if by accident. He was running away from something dreadful; he ended up in nature because there was nowhere else to turn (ll. 66-75). Then, when he was visiting the place five years earlier, he was a grown-up young man with a passion and craze for nature but he was still gross and physical in his taste (ll. 75-85). The lines that follow in this stanza (ll. 85-111) explain the third stage of the growth of the poet's awareness, the one which the mind reaches in the poet's present revisit to the scene. If the poet as a boy and as a young man has loved nature instinctively and blindly, the poet as he stands before the spot now has acquired a deeper understanding of nature and a deeper love of it. He sees nature now as a cosmic power that chastens and subdues our grosser persons, and elevates our thought so that we become aware of the cosmos, of which we are part and parcel. He also becomes conscious of the creative sensibility of the mind perceiving and half creating the world (a pointing forward to Wallace Stevens). He concludes the stanza with a quintessential Romantic thesis that nature and the language of the sense are the anchor of thought, the nurse, the guide, the guardian of the human heart, and the soul of all human moral being. The readers may see the point clearly with reference to his poems like "Expostulation and Reply" (1798, ll. 1-8; 13-24) and "The Table Turned" (1798, ll. 1-4; 9-16) in which the poet even says that books are no good and that we should learn from nature since the world is an expression of the thoughts, the feeling, the heart of God. Thus *Tintern Abbey* records the process of the poet's spiritual sublimation from lower instinctive love to a higher awareness and appreciation of nature as an influence over people.

The last, the 5th, stanza (ll. 112-59) is the poet's advice to his sister, and for that matter, to people like her or all his readers, as to what to do with nature. On his second visit to the place with his sister beside him, he sees, in her spontaneous, rapturous response to the beauty of nature, the reflection of his own as a boy (ll. 115-21). He reiterates the salutary effect of nature on man (ll. 121-34) and expresses the hope that his sister will sink in nature, mature in her response to it, and survive well as a result (ll. 134-46). He asks her to remember, when he is no longer around, their visit to the scene, remember him as a warm and holy lover of nature, and remember the great joy he felt on the second visit.

One thing that merits notice is Wordsworth's view on the "evil" aspect of nature. Wordsworth was a poet of his time. He never made to the realization that nature may be capable of something not good and benevolent. He did, for instance, mention his boyhood experience of nature turning grave and even threatening in works such as his *Prelude* where, once on the Salisbury plain, he sensed nature's anger or disapproval when he did something that was no good, like killing a bird or stealing a boat; but even in that context, he sees nature as his parent surrogate catechizing him for misbehavior, or in other words, nature shows its displeasure in order to edify and teach rather than doing anything evil. The fact that nature is capable of evil, the Tennysonian notion of nature "red with tooth and claw with raven," the Dickinsonian description of a cruel universe with an indifferent God as represented in her poem "Apparently with no surprise," or Frost's frightening "Directive"—all these were yet to appear in the future.

Another famous poem that merits careful analysis is his 11-stanza *Ode: Intimations of Immortality*. Its epigraph is taken from the poet's own work, "My heart leaps up" (1807), which contains the well known line, "The Child is father of the Man" (l. 7). The ode is an expression of the poet's idea of the human soul's progress through its earthly experience. The first four stanzas (ll. 1-57) present the poet's joyful childhood experience of nature with its celestial light, its glory, its beauty, and the blessed creatures, but all of these stanzas contain an element of grief over the fact that his childhood vision and dream have vanished not to return. This sets the poetic mind thinking and searching for the cause. Stanza 5 through stanza 9 (ll. 58-167) present the result of his ruminations and discovery. He finds that the human birth is the result of reincarnation, which is another way of saying that humans came to this earthly life from their previous existences. Having come from the glory of God, their childhood still retains the memory of the radiance and the vision of the past and is the nearest to God. Children are innocent, see wonders in nature, and understand life intuitively. The readers may remember the little maid of "We Are Seven" here. Boyhood is farther away from the light, but still sees it joyfully. Youth moves the human still farther away from his source though he is still Nature's Priest. And manhood experiences total darkness as the light dies away in this stage of human life (stanza 5). Stanza 6 presents Mother Earth as a dubious blessing. She tries, with good intentions to make her foster child—man—feel happy in his new home but forget his former one. Stanza 7 further discusses earthly human growth in direct proportion to their gradual loss of their memory of the past glory. It records man's growth from the phase of "his new-born blisses" to that of his experiences with weddings and deaths, of "business, love, or strife," maturity, and old age, ending up repeating what others have done before him. The first lines of stanza 8 (ll. 109-123) are famous for their accurate expression of the romantic notion of the child knowing life and its truth intuitively. The child is to Wordsworth everything that the adult is not and aspires to be. The latter part of the stanza (ll. 124-128) raises the provocative question, why are humans so eager to grow up and give up their blessedness and burden their soul with the crushing weight of earthly life? Stanza 9 is a follow-up on the themes of the previous four stanzas (5, 6, 7, and 8) with the famous references to "those [of a new born's] first affections" and "[t]hose shadowy recollections." The "affections" and "recollections" serve as "the fountain light of all our day" and "a master light of our seeing" that make "[o]ur noisy years seem moments in the being," and as the reminder of human immortality that the poet sees in his mystic vision (ll. 155-167). Stanzas 10 and 11 are apostrophes to nature as a mediating force between the "fallen" man and his prospect of immortality. To Wordsworth, nature brings the best out of the human heart—the primal sympathy, the soothing thoughts that come from suffering, and the faith in the future so that there is no reason to grieve or despair.

Now regarding *The Prelude*, this 14-book work was first envisioned as one part of the poet's long philosophical work—*The Recluse*, but it was published as an independent work in the end. In more than one sense, *The Prelude* repeats the basic ideas as exhibited in his more popular and effective poems such as *Lines Composed a Few Miles Above the Tintern Abbey*. It is his spiritual biography, in a way, recording as it does his early contact with nature, his interest in human life and the loss of contact with nature and the loss of his sense of mission to become a poet, and the recovery of his intimacy with nature and his sense of destiny. It is a record of his involvement with the French Revolution and the spiritual odyssey he goes through in connection with it. The long poem is beautifully written, meant to be comparable somehow to epics such as *Paradise Lost*. But it is ponderously massive and repetitive and, despite its importance in the Wordsworthian canon, it has been often neglected in favor of his shorter works.

Here is a sketch of the gist of the 14 books, and the highlights they contain that may merit attention. Books 1 and 2 describe the poet's life up to the age of 17. These are generally considered the best and the most poetic and the most expressive of Wordsworth's views on and worship of nature. Here is the child, in intimate contact with nature—its river, woods, fields, its occurrences, its mysterious calm, the fear that it can inspire, its cleansing of the human soul and purging it of its vulgar joys, its pastoral charm, and its fabric's glory. Here is a boy whose soul is totally immersed in nature, socializing with it, and getting completely naturalized (ll. 420-452). There is then a mild but clear indication that some kind of crisis is brooding, one probably stemming from possible dissociation from nature. Book 3, telling of the poet's life at Cambridge, basically repeats the thematic concerns of the first two books, especially in its first 200-odd lines. Book 4 talks about the poet becoming aware of himself both as a man and as a poet. It returns to the theme of greater love of nature after his vacation (ll. 131-159), experiencing the joy of rebirth (ll. 323-332), feeling a freeing and an expansion of the mind, feeling intensely the sense of destiny as a poet, describing his encounter with the soldier (ll. 387-469), and his subsequent awareness of the mind's power without divorcing nature.

Book 5, the book that originally concluded the first version of the long poem, contains three episodes—the dream (ll. 50-141), the boy of Winander (ll. 366-427), and the drowned man (ll. 428-459). One possible interpretation of the dream seems to be that it is sent by Imagination to lead the poet to the recognition of his powers, but what the dreamer desires or fears is its direct encounter with Imagination. The episode relating to the boy of Winander is autobiographical in a way, telling how nature attracts the child. The episode of the drowned man is in fact the poet's memory of "the dead Man" "with his ghastly face" that he as a boy of nine once saw bolting up from a beauteous scene of nature. It is true that the dead man looks grotesque, but the way the poet wirtes about it, death is no longer absolutely terrible in the midst of beautifull nature. It is an indication of the poet's pantheistic sentiment. Books 6 to 10 talk about the progress of the poet's awareness from love of nature to love of man. Book 6 tells about the naturalization of imagination and the poet's possible turning to social life. Book 7 records the poet's contact with earthly London and his fall from and loss of paradise as the social scenes balance off his feelings nursed by nature. The famous episode of his encounter with the beggar (ll. 635-649) teaches him the importance of faith and innocence. Book 8 notes down his change from love of nature to love of man (ll. 340-349).

Books 9 to 11 relate his experiences in France during the French Revolution. Book 9 depicts the contrast between a decaying world and one of revolution, and the poet's fear to face the contrast, which leads to a crisis. Book 10 begins with a description of beautiful nature as a counterpoint versus social ills (ll. 1-3), proceeds with the poet thinking about the massacres (ll. 66-77), and ends with England declaring war on France, which is a shock to the poet (ll. 264-283). Book 11 tells of the poet experiencing a crisis, of his sister and nature coming to his salvation, and book 12 records the process of his recovery and restoration, rediscovering himself and his original faith and sense of mission as a poet, and retrieving his love for nature, with nature helping him restore his love and faith. Book 13 is a recollection of his childhood experience with nature (see book 1) when he does something wrong and fears the catechizing of nature. The book also talks about Coleridge reminding him of his mission as a poet. The last book, book 14, describes his experience of climbing Mount Snowden, his vision there, and the maturity of his powers as a poet (ll. 302-311).

Samuel Taylor Coleridge (1772-1834)

Coleridge was a rare genius in the history of English literature. Not only was he a great poet, but he was also a philosopher and a seminal critic. He blazed the new trail together with Wordsworth and helped usher in the Romantic endeavor. At one time in his youth Coleridge was a radical. Out of their enthusiasm to help improve the lot of humankind, he and his Cambridge classmate Robert Southey came up with the idea of setting up a commune, Pantisocrasy as they called it, somewhere in North America, in which they hoped to show that mankind could live the way they should. The plan did not come through mainly for financial reasons, but Coleridge ended up marrying Southey's wife's sister anyway as their utopian scheme called on its members to get married first. His married life failed to be congenial to the life of his mind: for Coleridge the thing that mattered most was his creative imagination. In addition, he was an improvident person, never practical, and never quite able to make ends meet for his family as well as for himself. On top of all these, he was made to take an opium-based medication prescribed to alleviate the physical pain that had always been with him all his life.

As a result he was dependent on his friends most of the time: Southey had to write furiously to make enough money to support both of their families, and Coleridge eventually had to stay with a friendly couple. This was the personal backdrop against which Coleridge struggled to write his poems. This personal truth that he had to express, as it just happened, coincided with the public truth then, especially with that of the intellectually sensitive segment in face of the growing sense of the crisis of faith. In his later years Coleridge felt that he was not doing justice to his native talent and that he was losing his creative powers. His "Dejection: An Ode" is a good illustration of the abject dejection into which he had sunk. Even Wordsworth had been always condescending, seeing him as a little brother trailing behind him.

However, Coleridge did a lot, the magnitude of which he might not have been fully aware of himself. For instance, his was a highly innovative mind. He created, in his *Chritabel*, a kind of accentual meter with four stresses to a line, two on either side of a caesura, plus the alliteration of the three of the four stressed syllables. He developed the descriptive-reflective mode of poetic writing in such poems as his "Dejection: An Ode." These new poetic devices were immediately picked up by his contemporaries such as Wordsworth and Byron and caught on with later generations of poets. Also, there was his fascination with the supernatural, which indicated his interest in the exploration of the human unconscious and subconscious in addition to his attempt to add to idealism. Thus, time and history have proved to be on Coleridge's side. Wordsworth did not become aware that Coleridge was a lot deeper both as a poet and a thinker than he was himself. Posterity has come to appreciate both poets well enough, though rather for different reasons. [6]

For, whereas Wordsworth was strictly of his own age, Coleridge spoke ahead of his time on more than one subject. This was what John Stuart Mill probably meant when he called Coleridge one of the "two great seminal minds of England." "Kubla Khan," "Dejection: an Ode," and "The Rime of the Ancient Mariner" are all good illustrations of the point. [7] First, take "Kubla Khan" for example. The poet says when he explains about the genesis of the poem that, after taking a dose of anodyne (a medication containing opiate) one day, he fell in a deep sleep in which he composed some two or three hundred lines. Upon waking up, he tried to note these down from memory. He managed to write over 50 lines before he was called away on business for a while and, when he came back, he forgot the rest of it all. These 50-odd lines constitute the precious fragment that we have today. Hence the subtitle of the poem, "Or, A Vision in a Dream. A Fragment." The whole poem is entitled "Kubla Khan," because Coleridge was reading, at the moment of falling asleep, the part of *Purchas' Pilgrimage* which mentions, as he tells us in his note, "Here the Khan Kubla commanded a palace to be built, and a stately garden thereunto. And thus ten miles of fertile ground were inclosed with a wall." Actually, the poem is not about the Mongolian Khan at all. It is really about the mystery of poetic creation. The king that Coleridge has in mind is not the Khan but the perfect poet, and the beautiful garden, the grand palace, that the Khan decrees to build, is in fact the poet's idea of a perfect poem.

The poem consists of three sections of varying lengths. The first section, of 11 lines, touches upon a few things which are essential to the understanding of the poem. In addition to the physical description of the Khan's garden, there is mention of "Alph, the sacred river" and "caverns measureless to man/ Down to a sunless sea." The former could indicate the Muse, or poetic inspiration, and the latter possibly the importance of the unconscious to poetic composition. The reference to "many an incense-bearing tree;/ And here were forests ancient as the hills" endows the poem with a holy, religious, and mythic intensity. All these point forward to section two of the poem which illustrates the theme of the poem further.

The second section, of 19 lines, is probably the most difficult of all for the readers. It puts together a lot of images that do not seem to connect with one another well. Images such as "that deep romantic chasm," "cedarn cover," "A savage place," "a waning moon," "woman wailing for her demon-lover," "ceaseless turmoil," "a mighty fountain," the huge fragments, the chaffy grain, the dancing rocks, the river, the wood, and the cavern measureless to man and running into the ocean, etc.—all these do not seem to make much sense. They read like a person raving incoherently in his dream. But the section contains the major symbolism of the poem that makes the most important point of the work. Coleridge's notebooks can be of enormous help with the reading of the poem.

The fact of the matter is that the major images and symbols mentioned above all have to do with the Orphic rites which Coleridge wrote much about in his notebooks. The Orphic rites are related to the ritual that Orpheus and his sect of the followers of Dionysus observe. As the Greek myth goes, Orpheus is the poet and singer, the devotee of Dionysus (the wine-god and the symbol of freedom of the mind). Orpheus is able to become a great poet-singer because he goes down and experiences the underworld. He is able to sink down because he worships Dionysus, who helps him to visit the world below with his lyre, and come back again. The rites dictate that the initiate has to drink from "the River of Lethe" (the river of forgetfulness) before he is led down to a chasm in a grove, makes sacrifices there to the god of the tumultuous underworld, and comes back to drink from "the River of Mnemosyne" (the river of memory) to remember his underworld experience. A follower can be mad enough to have "flashing eyes" and "floating hair" (l. 50); he goes through a ritual of "the waving of the circle thrice around the head" (l. 51). The "milk and honey" (l. 54) may indicate the sacrifices to the underworld. Thus the second section tries to make it clear that, in order to write a perfect poem, the poet has to be a Dionysian, and has to go down to hell, which is another way of saying "dipping into the subconscious."

The third section, of 24 lines, begins with the poet's vision of the perfect poem, the symbol of which is the Khan's dome (ll. 31-36). It connects well with section two because the vision is possible only after the poet tastes of the chaos of the unconscious. Research has found that the pleasure dome is not the Khan's palace. It is actually envisioned on the basis of the poet's reading of some Oriental palaces such as some Islamic architectural feats. Then the poet dreams of the freedom and joy that a perfect celestial poet would enjoy (ll. 37-45). The Abyssinian maid with a dulcimer is Coleridge's vision of an ideal poet. She reminds us of Edgar Allan Poe's "Israfel," the poet singing in heaven that Coleridge aspires very much to become. The end of the poem (ll. 46-54) offers a clear statement of the poet's ambition to write a perfect poem. It connotes a kind of madness, almost divine, of which a follower of Dionysus and, by extension, an ideal poet should be capable of experiencing before he can hope to compose anything great. The implication of all these seems to suggest further that a great poet has to touch hell and the unconscious in order to "see into the life of things" and compose great poetry. And of course Coleridge dipped into his unconscious as the genesis of the poem suggests: the opium that he took became for him instrumental in his sinking into his unconscious. Upon waking he remembered some of the details, having drunk from the Lake of Mnemosyne, but forgot some others, which is a hint of the River of Lethe at work. This is the reason why there remained only a fragment.

A question to ask in this connection may be this, "Why did Coleridge entitle his poem 'Kubla Khan'?" We mentioned the fact earlier on that he was reading about Kubla Khan when he fell asleep. This can be one reason, but there is a deeper cause here. It may have more to do with Coleridge's fascination with the wine-god Dionysus. Now the mystic origin of Dionysus was both Greek and Indian. "Indian" means broadly "East" to the poet. There is evidence in his notebooks that Coleridge wanted to compose a poem with Robert Southey about Mohammad, the prophet of the Islamic faith, a subject also suggestive of the East. Thus Kubla Khan and his Tartars who conquered India smell strongly of the East and offer an immense charm to the poet. It was also natural that the Orphic rites in which the poet took an enormous interest became the structural symbolism of the poem.

A point to note here is that Coleridge anticipated Freud by well over half a century in drawing attention to the importance of the subconscious. He spoke even well ahead of modern criticism concerning the concept of Dionysus as the emblem of the unconscious in modern poetry. When all is said, "Kubla Khan" is a highly symbolic poem, and Coleridge is a highly symbolic poet.

"Dejection: An Ode" is the work of a lonely, and meditative mind. Its subject is the poet's sad awareness that he was losing his creative powers. The 8-stanza poem is thematically more significant in more than one way. In the first stanza the moaning of the wind mirrors the moaning of the poet's agonizing soul. The dreadful description of a relief-less grief in the first part of the 2nd stanza expresses not only the pain the poet feels alone, but also proves to be an authentic picture of the kind of spiritual poverty which the intellectually sensitive minds of the time had already begun to feel. Moreover, this acute sense of grief would soon assail the masses in a few decades after Darwin's theory of evolution shook the Christian faith. If Matthew Arnold's "Dover Beach" is a faithful record of how people felt in mid-19th century, Coleridge anticipated him by a whole period of 50 years.

And this is not all. The 2nd stanza of the poem talks about nature in a way drastically different from Wordsworth's. For Wordsworth nature is all good and, even if it occasionally exhibits any threat of any kind, it is meant for man's good. Coleridge, in his dull pain, feels no comfort and no inspiration from his observation of beautiful nature. He does not sound totally negative about nature, but the notion he expresses in his "The Rime of the Ancient Mariner," that nature may not be kind and may be apathetic and capable of evil, is subtly hinted here.

"Dejection: An Ode" is famous for another thing it does for poetry. After the loaded stanza three in which the poet laments over the alienation of man's consciousness from the universe and the failure of nature to energize and vitalize his imagination, stanza four puts forward a well-known Romantic notion that has caught on ever since. Here Coleridge assigns a very seminal role to the human mind: the imagination helps give life to the external world. To Coleridge nature is alive because the human mind sees it that way or endows it with life. The imagination is a shaping force. Thus if the world is faithless, loveless, and joyless, it is the job of the poetic imagination to create all those things that make life tolerable. This is Coleridge's notion of the function of the poet and poetry. This stress on the role of the imagination has inspired later poets such as Wallace Stevens whose well-renowned statement, "The world we inhabit is the one we half create," is a veritable replica of Coleridge's idea here in this poem. Then what follows in stanza five is naturally the poet's thirst for that sense of joy and harmony which stems from overcoming the alienation between the soul and nature. Stanza six is the poet's woeful way of saying goodbye to health and happiness, with the sad awareness that his physical afflictions are "suspending" the shaping spirit of his imagination and "stealing" all the natural man from his nature and that he has to put up with his drug addiction in order to survive.

Stanza seven begins with a sorrowful self-analysis and a description of the howling wind and the desolate scene outside, which is an externalization of the poet's total inner bleakness. The stanza ends with a scenario which reminds the readers of that of Wordsworth's "Lucy Gray," with this difference that Coleridge's picture is one of an existentialist nature: a person is all alone on a lonesome wilderness, his soul weeping and craving for help that is not forthcoming from any quarters. The awareness of the existential sense of crisis is further enhanced in his "The Rime of the Ancient Mariner." The last stanza is a wish for Sara Hutchinson, the "Lady" of the poem, for whom the poet had cherished deep love and to whom the poem was addressed. The poet wishes all the best for her, good sleep, good spirits, divine guidance and protection, and harmony between her and nature. These also indicate the depth of despair that the poet feels for himself. In retrospect, it has been recognized that the poet's personal dejection was emblematic of the spirit of his own time and the decades to come, a happy coincidence which ensures his greatness and permanence.

The prophetic greatness of Coleridge is best illustrated also in his "The Rime of the Ancient Mariner." The seven-part narrative poem tells a rather spooky story. The old sailor goes out to sea, kills an albatross for no apparent reason, brings doom to all his fellow crew, and lives on alone only to endure a perpetual spiritual suffering. Now on his voyage out, the old man kills the bird, then his ship meets a ghost ship on which sit Death and his woman companion. They play dice, kill all the crew except the old man, and leave his ship to be tossed about near the Antarctic. Eventually he repents, blesses the sea snakes and other creatures, and is returned home, not before he has become a ghost-like person himself. Despite his repeated repentance, the curse for his wanton killing returns at intervals, and he has to retell his tale of woe over and over in order to expiate his sin and feel better. He is like a wandering Jew or Cain, for ever on the move, roaming the wide world and catechizing people with his story of sin and confession. So the poem begins with him grabbing and stopping a wedding guest and forcing him to listen to his story, and ends with turning the listener into a different person, one like a prophet. The poem is beautifully written, in the four-line ballad stanza form, with the striking musical rhythms and the sounds of the words used, and the salient images not the least of which relates to the vivid description of the colors. It is an artistic rarity in world poetry.

The story is simple enough, but possesses a wealth of meanings worth exploring. For one thing, it is basically a Christian story, but also plants doubts in the readers' mind as to whether faith serves any purpose in life at all. It can be read as a Christian poem as repentance and love bring redemption. Once he begins to love his fellow creatures, the stigma of his sin—the albatross—falls from his neck, and he has to repent to feel better. The overall framework is Christian with all its allusions to the Holy Mother and Jesus Christ on quite a few occasions. There is, however, a kind of skepticism imbedded in the texture of the poem. The fact of the matter is that, according to the Christian faith, after one sins, one confesses and repents once for it, and it should be enough to receive the absolution. But the old man in the poem has to repent over and again and there seems to be no end of repentance. The implication could be that God does not hear his confession and prayers. This strain of skepticism that Coleridge felt and put in the poem was prophetic of the impending crisis of faith in his century.

Then there is nature to consider. To the Romantics, and Coleridge along with them to some extent, nature is all good, restorative, wholesome, a refuge, a guide, a teacher, a nurse, and most of them, notably Wordsworth, being of their own time, failed to see the other aspect of nature, or the evil aspect of it. For nature is capable of indifference and evil, too. Here Coleridge speaks ahead of his time again. He sees nature differently from Wordsworth and his contemporaries. Nature in the poem behaves in a way which is at best apathetic. The old sailor's world is an amoral world, indifferent, naturalistic, and basically Godless, in which man is utterly thrown upon himself for survival. As we all know, this concept of the amoral universe did not take clear shape until the latter part of the 19th century. Then, the ancient mariner is seen all alone on a wide, wide sea, presenting a vivid, pathetic picture of an existentialist, trying to make sense of his world over which he has not the slightest control, and generating a frame of reference for himself. Here again, Coleridge sees ahead of his time: Sartre's existentialism became definable as a philosophy only in the 1940s.

The poem also demonstrates Coleridge's belief in the existence of the supernatural and an invisible higher plane of life. The poet places an obvious emphasis on the authentic description of the physicality of the old man's circumstances, deliberately employs the wedding ceremony as the framework of the old sailor's story-telling, and takes meticulous care to see that all the details relate to the voyage (such as the behavior of the sea at different times of the day, the natural elements like the moon, the sun, and the wind and also the creatures in the sea). All these are meant to anchor the story in the solid physical setting of the phenomenal human world. However, that is not all to it in the opinion of the poet. There is an extra dimension of existence that men need to learn about: the supernatural. Thus the tale here is not meant to be a Gothic horror story; it is a poetic expression of the poet's idealism. The glosses that Coleridge offers serve to make the point beyond doubt. His belief in the supernatural reveals one dimension of Coleridge's idealism.

Coleridge is also famous for his prose work, *Biographia Literaria* (1817). Now a classic source to which modern criticism is directly traceable, the work is a collection of his writings in two parts, one about his own growth as a poet and his critical opinions in general and the other on his analysis of Wordsworth's poetic diction. In addition to the brilliant statements and remarks in which the book abounds, one thing for which it has been famous is as a record of Coleridge's critical acumen. His notion of the importance of the imagination as a synthetic and magical shaping power is for instance well expounded in the book (and faithfully followed by latter-day Romantics). Another thing for which Coleridge is noted as a seminal influence is his notion that a literary work can have more than one level of meaning and that it is important to read the text of a work carefully. This idea was taken up by I. A. Richards in the 1920s as support for his New Critical thesis that a poem can be rationally analyzed, its textural structure is more important than its "period" background or the author's biographical information, and critical focus should be placed on the text of the work. As a result, Coleridge was looked up to as an authority for the New Critics, and his *Biographia Literaria* was reprinted and exercised a far-reaching influence on the literary criticism of the time and a long time afterward.

Walter Scott (1771-1832)

Walter Scott and Jane Austen are placed here alongside Wordsworth and Coleridge chiefly because they wrote within the same time frame. It is good to note that Walter Scott and Jane Austen differ vastly in their modes of representation. Scott's imagination is essentially romantic whereas Austen's is realistic. In fact it was Austen who reasserted the tradition of realism.

Sir Walter Scott was the one spectacular literary genius in English literary history who was engaged in two departments of literature and achieved great success in both. In the early phase of his career, Scott wrote poetry and became the most widely read poet of his day. Then in the last two decades he turned his attention to novel writing and fathered the historical novel proper in England and Europe. Scott loved living in an extravagant style, and his was almost an open house. What drove him to his early grave was the slump of 1826 which left him up to his chin in debt. Instead of running away from his liabilities by declaring himself bankrupt, Scott faced his adversity squarely in the face. He worked hard and paid off all his debts before he died. He proved himself to be a sound "piece of British manhood" worthy of his ancestors.

Scott was born in Edinburgh. When small he suffered from an illness that left him lame for life. During the few months of recuperating at his grandfather's farm at the Scottish Border area, he heard with intense interest a number of tales about the distant, unhappy, but heroic Scottish past. That accounted for his enduring singular love for folk ballads. His interest went way beyond his own country. Not only did he collect the ballads and lays in the mountainous regions of Scotland; he collected and translated the folk ballads of European countries as well. His first verse work, *The Minstrelsy of the Scottish Border*, made his presence felt. Scott was a great poet. He was not happy with just collecting and translating; he composed poems such as *The Lay of the Last Minstrelsy*, *Marmion*, *the Lady of the Lake*, *The Lord of the Isles*, and *Rokeby*, which brought ancient times back to life in a rich Romantic style. Most of these are narrative verse, telling immensely fascinating stories to the readers. *The Lay of the Last Minstrelsy* is particularly interesting for its medieval and supernatural features. Scott's poetry was the most welcome verse works in the first ten years of the 19th century. It is said that he turned away from poetry probably because Byron's reputation as a rising star over England and Europe dimmed the glitter of everyone else and Scott felt that he might be no peer for the young poet. However, it should be noted that Scott's contribution to English poetry cannot be overrated: he was instrumental in bringing in the influence of folklore in poetic composition.

Scott's chief achievement was, however, the 20-odd fictions he wrote, which have given him a unique place in literary history. They marked the advent of the genre of the historical novel. Scott finds value in the past, and uses the best of the past to contrast with the present. The historical sense that these works express is truly amazing. Scott's novels are essentially romantic in spirit, excavating as they do the buried heroic tradition of the past. That had to do with his intense interest in ancient books, documents, and papers, his frequenting museums wherever possible, and his love for the stories that came down from generation to generation by word of mouth. The images of the ancient scenes of life, the people interacting, their clothes, houses, food, their customs and mores—everything that ancient records and stories could conjure up in his imagination would enliven and enrich it so that he could draw vivid pictures in his books for his readers to appreciate. Reading his novels, people could feel that sense of immediacy and involvement that could be inspired only by a highly absorbing subject or plot.

Scott's historical novels cover a wide range of subjects. He gleaned some of these from the history of the ancient Scottish highlands, such as is the case with "the Waverley" novels, a series of works describing the vicissitudes of the rise and fall of the upper classes, the uprisings of the suffering people, the ceaseless border wars, and the life of the Puritan period. Some of his novels deal with the history of England such as *Ivanhoe* and *The Woodstock*, some relate to the Crusades like *The Talisman* and *Count Robert of Paris*, and still some others derive their themes from the past of continental Europe like *Quentin Durward*. The past stops being an abstraction with Scott, and history becomes so many picturesque scenarios in which people of blood and flesh interact with each other. It is good to note that Scott's focus in presentation is not merely on the famous historical figures; he also brings the lower strata of society on to the stage of history. His characterization is facilitated by his skilled manipulation of the Scottish dialects which he knew very well. His characters flesh out admirably well when placed in their own linguistic settings. In the field of the novel, Scott touched Byron in the latter's far-reaching influence in European and American poetry. His "Waverley" novels influenced such famous world authors as Victor Hugo, George Eliot, Tolstoy, and James Fenimore Cooper. And American Romantic literature would have looked totally different if Scott had not played his part in its creative endeavors.

The most famous of his fictions have come to be known as his "Waverley" novels. These are all Scottish novels which represent Scott at his best as a novelist. His first novel, the three-volume *Waverley* (1814), remained on the best-seller list for over a decade. It has become the best known of his work as it lends its title to a series of novels that would come after it. Although it is not necessarily the best of all his works, it contains the major ingredients with which his later works would swell out in further detail. *Waverley* tells a romantic story set sixty years back from the author's day. It occurs during Pretender Prince Charlie's rebellion of 1745. It is a time of change. The Stuarts are challenging the reigning Hanoverians. The major character, Edward Waverley, is a person of mixed allegiances as his name indicates. He wavers between the reigning King George and the ambitious Prince Charlie of the Stuarts. As his father serves in a ministry, Waverley gets a job in George II's dragoons stationed in Scotland. There he goes and gets in touch with Fergus Mac Ivor, a local clan chieftain loyal to the cause of the Stuarts. He is encouraged by the latter to court his sister, Flora Mac Ivor, a firm woman supporter even stauncher than her brother is to the Stuarts. Waverley goes to Edinburgh, is arrested on the way by the suspicious government, is rescued by a Scottish rebel, and meets the Pretender. He becomes the Pretender's guest and swears allegiance to the Stuarts. The Pretender's bid for the throne fails at the battle of Culloden. Fergus is captured and later executed. He faces death as does a true hero. Waverley is pardoned with the help of an English Colonel whom he had saved before. He eventually regains the favor of the king, inherits his father's family wealth, and marries Rose Bradwardine. [8]

The characterization of the major figures of the novel merits attention. Waverley is the protagonist, but he is not so much a hero as is Fergus. Waverley is vain, Romantic, passive and ordinary, and self-centered in a way. He is silly with little or no acumen to decide which side in the scramble for power is to emerge the winner. That is the main reason why he oscillates between the two forces bidding for the throne. But he is a fully drawn character, with every phase of his growth well detailed. His growing resentment against the Hanoverians, his belated recognition of his love for Rose, the change of his attitudes toward Fergus (respect—contempt—respect regained), his occasional show of courage and generosity—all these are well adumbrated. Still his stature is not "heroic" enough for the novel. That is why Fergus and a host of other characters cut in to flesh it out. Fergus is the true hero in the real sense of the word. He is selfish, it is true, but he is capable of nobility, allegiance, and heroism. In non-critical times, he could use his sister Flora as a bait to allure Waverley to the Pretender's side, and he could ask Prince

Charlie to help him win the hand of a rich baron's daughter. But when the Prince faces possible failure, he stands firm and fights for him, and dies a true generous hero. Scott portrays the man with such meticulous care that Fergus comes out a full-blooded figure vibrant with life. Some of the scenes in which Scott places people like Evan Dhu Maccombich for them to act themselves out are truly touching. Evan offering the life of five of his men as well as his own in exchange for that of Fergus reveals the heroic spirit against which Waverley pales not a little. There are also Flora, the single-minded girl, Baron Bradwardine and his comic loyalty and heroic resignation to fate and acceptance of the failure of the rebellion, Colonel Talbot who saves Waverley, and more—these contrast interestingly with Waverley, either to highlight his flaws or help sort out his thoughts. The most blaring contrast is offered by Fergus: Waverley survives because of his wavering, and Fergus has no part to play in the post-rebellion period because he is too committed and loyal. This means that Waverley represents the focus of the novel, not Fergus, in the confrontation between the two sides trying to grab at each other's throat.

Jane Austen (1775-1817)

Austen came from a well-cultured country family. She wrote her novels for her own family circle. As she published her works anonymously, she was not famous in her lifetime. Scott admired her talent for portraying ordinary life in a wonderful way. Her vision of real life as lived in a particular segment of society has placed her as part of the "Great Tradition" of the English novel, i.e. realism. Among her numerous strengths are her exquisite, compact prose, her moral judgment, her wit, and her vivid character portrayal. She was not married.

Austen wrote six novels: *Sense and Sensibility* (1811), *Pride and Prejudice* (1813), *Mansfield Park* (1814), *Emma* (1815), *Northanger Abby* (1818), and *Persuasion* (1818). One thing to note about her fiction is its limited subject. Her novels cover just that section of society to which she belonged: the country gentry such as the Dashwoods (*Sense and Sensibility*) and the Bennets (*Pride and Prejudice*) and their lives in the rural village setting. There is hardly any aristocrat like a lord of the manor, or a poor peasant to feature as her major characters. She was so acquainted with the life of the country and its gentry that she had at her fingertips every detail that she might need for her plot interest. It was not that she did not know about other strata. Her brothers had seen the wide world, and one of her cousins had been to France at the time of the French Revolution, and her sensitive mind might have picked up any information that might have happened to be available to her. But she desisted from venturing into areas little known to her. Her "limitation" reveals a principle in literary creation that one can show one's best when one makes the best of one's best knowledge. There is good reason to believe that it was her own choice to write just about her circle.

Austen was not anxious to get her works published. *Pride and Prejudice* lay in silence for a decade after its first rebuff by a publisher, and *Northanger Abbey* was accepted by another who was, however, in no hurry to put it out in print. Nonetheless, she won for herself, already in her lifetime, a reputation not at all negligible, and her popularity has been ever on the increase with readers all over the world. The secret of her fascination lies in the fact that her understanding of human nature is so accurate that it is forever capable of awakening warm echoes in human bosoms. Her fictional world, small, narrow, and confined as it may be, is not parochial, however. It is portrayed as a world of humans of flesh and blood with feelings and responses and foibles and weaknesses that characterize the human species. It is a microcosm of the world at large with virtues and vices and archetypes of human behavior to which all humanity of all time can relate. This is the ultimate source of Jane Austen's permanence and power. [9]

Now let's take a look at her masterpiece, *Pride and Prejudice*.

The book has been on top of the reading list for scholars as well as common readers. Its story is at once simple and complex, simple because it deals with just one thing—love and marriage, and complex in the sense that there are so many narrative threads loose at the same time, and so many characters of widely diverse personalities with exhibitions of such a rich spectrum of human emotions. The opening line of the book has been so oft-quoted that it has become almost an epigram: "It is a truth, universally acknowledged, that a single man in possession of a good fortune, must be in want of a wife." It introduces the readers right away to a world where marriage features as the topmost concern.

As the story goes, Mr. Bennet of the Longbourn estate has five daughters and no son. That means by law that the estate will change hands after his death. The heir is Mr. Collins, Mr. Bennet's distant cousin. Mrs. Bennet has only one concern in life: to marry her five daughters off to eligible men. When she hears about a rich bachelor Bingley moving into the country, she sees him as one of her prey. Bingley appears at a ball with his two sisters and a friend Darcy. Bingley meets Jane Bennet, the oldest daughter of the Bennet household, and is favorably impressed, but Darcy tries to cool him down. In addition, Darcy behaves in a way that enrages Elizabeth, the second oldest of the Bennet daughters: he says something rude in her hearing and refuses to dance with her, and she is furious over his arrogance. Jane and Bingley become closer. The Bingley sisters poke fun at the Bennets. One day Jane rides in the rain to Bingley's lodging and falls sick. Elizabeth comes to nurse her and meets Darcy, who now keenly feels her attraction. In the meantime Mr. Collins proposes to Elizabeth and is rejected. He turns to the homely Charlotte Lucas and is accepted immediately. A young officer, Mr. Wickham, befriends the Bennet sisters, and tells Elizabeth that he has been cheated out of an inheritance that his Godfather, Mr. Darcy's father, has left him. Elizabeth's dislike of Darcy intensifies. Then the Bingleys leave the area for London, Jane receives a note from one of the Bingley sisters that Bingley is to marry Darcy's sister, but Elizabeth firmly believes that the Bingley sisters and Darcy are working hand in glove against Jane and that Mr. Bingley still loves Jane. At the invitation of her aunt, Jane goes to London. On her way to see Charlotte, Elizabeth stops in London to visit her aunt. She learns that Jane has not received any call from Mr. Bingley and feels convinced that Darcy is behind all this foul play. At a party at Darcy's aunt—Lady Catherine's house, Elizabeth treats the old aristocratic woman coldly. Darcy comes and proposes in a haughty tone to Elizabeth, who promptly rejects him, accusing him of separating her sister and Bingley and of mistreating Mr. Wickham. Darcy leaves in anger but brings a letter the next day to answer her charges. He admits to the first one but clears himself with regard to Wickham. Though she begins to see him in a different light, Elizabeth leaves without meeting him. She accepts her insistent aunt's invitation to go on a tour to Darcy's home county and his estate when the Darcys are not at home. But she meets Darcy there anyway, and the two become closer. Then word comes that Lydia has eloped with Mr. Wickham. Soon Darcy helps the runaways to get married, and brings Bingley to the Bennets. Mr. Bingley and Jane are engaged. Lady Catherine comes to order Elizabeth not to accept Darcy's proposal, but meets with the girl's forthright refusal. Darcy and Elizabeth are engaged.

The major plot evolves around the love story of Elizabeth and Darcy. The young man, coming from an aristocratic background, behaves arrogantly toward those below him in social rank. He despises the Bennets as vulgar and beneath him. For the same reason he alienates his friend Mr. Bingley from Jane Bennet. So Elizabeth harbors a suspicion of Darcy's class and does not think much of him at first. Her prejudice deepens when she hears Wickham viciously slander Darcy, claiming that the aristocrat has mistreated him. Later Elizabeth visits Darcy's estate and learns about the genial side of the man. Her prejudice is disarmed when Wickham elopes with Elizabeth's kid sister Lydia, and Darcy intervenes to put things to rights. As Wickham has been brought up by his family, Darcy feels involved in the event. He seeks Wickham out and pays his debts on condition that he marry Lydia, which the villain does. The warm, caring side of Darcy's that the whole incident reveals changes Elizabeth's mind about the man. The other plots that interweave with the major one include the hurtful but eventually happy love and marriage of Bingley and Jane, the humdrum, probably dreary prospect of the married life of the Collins, the eloped Wickham and Lydia destined to lifelong wretchedness and a probable unhappy resolution, and the often ignored miserable marriage of the older Bennets.

The portrayal of the characters is amazingly varied and colorful. The gallery of women here is simply glittering. Jane Bennet is a serene, reticent beauty, Elizabeth the spirited, vocal beauty, one of the most endearing girls in English literature, Lydia a spoiled brat, innocent and hopelessly silly and romantic, Charlotte Lucas, plain, practical, and mistress of her own life, Mrs. Bennet, silly but devoted to her daughters and determined to marry them off to happiness, the worldly Bingley sisters, the haughty Lady Catherine de Bourgh, and her listless daughter, Anne de Bourgh. It is the panoramic view of the female gender in the world of men, the inside-track examination of its motives and behavior so true of the womankind, that keeps attracting eternal attention. In addition, the portraits of the men are no less noteworthy. These include the complexities of Darcy's personality, the eccentric Mr. Bennet, the good-natured, impressionable Mr. Bingley, the mediocre Mr. Collins—a mixture of pomposity and humility, and of course Mr. Wickham, the rake and the villain of the novel. It is not so much the artistic virtuosity of the portrayals that impresses as the very humanity that the gallery represents.

Chapter 10 Byron • Shelley • Keats

The younger romantics formed a separate group from the older ones, or the Lakers. They have been called by some people "the Satanic School." The label is good for the rebellious Byron and Shelley who looked as if they were setting out to upset the system. It is, however, not quite appropriate for the quiet Keats who did not constitute a threat to the existing order but simply sought the muse in the ancient world of myths. Keats, a boy of humble parentage and little formal learning, may have irritated the conservatives such as the *Blackwood* reviewers as too ambitious and too cultivated for them. The three young poets, however, shared a lot in common. They were all young, brilliant, endowed with an unusual gift, and wrote to leave a rich legacy behind and left the scene almost as soon as they came. They between them represented an outburst of creative energy not repeated in history ever since. They constituted a contrast with Wordsworth and hated and saw the older poet as "a lost leader," who "sold his birthright for a mess of pottage." They did their best to carry the new spirit of the new era to its utmost limit.

So they were treated differently by the conservative Tory society of England then. Whereas the older group were accepted and rewarded as in the case of Wordsworth and Southey, the younger ones were dealt with very harshly. Two of these, Byron and Shelley, were subject to ruthless slander and were socially ostracized, so that they had to leave the country for good. As for Keats, he fared no better though in a different way. He became the butt of merciless, devastating criticism and mockery, which hurt the young poet emotionally as well as physically and, in a sense, drove him to his early grave. Associated with the group was a young woman author, Mary Wollstonecraft Shelley (1797-1851), daughter of the socialist thinker William Godwin and Mary Wollstonecraft—the vociferous first-generation feminist in English history. Mary Shelley deserves mention for her work, *Frankenstein, or the Modern Prometheus* (1818), a horror story, becoming a minor classic now as it has given birth to a good number of similar tales of terror in modern and contemporary literary history. [1]

George Gordon Byron (1788-1824)

Byron was born, clubfooted and handsome, into an aristocratic family. He inherited the title of the baron from his great granduncle. As a boy he was moody, impetuous, and vain. As a young MP in the House of Lords, he was the most vocal about the injustice done to the machine-breakers. He was also a flamboyant society figure and a sex rebel, always attractive, proud, and idiosyncratic but always the idol for the London drawing rooms. In his mid-twenties, he became an internationally known poet, and a notorious sexual veteran. He was said to have had a passionate love affair with his half sister Augusta Leigh. The scandal was mainly instrumental in his social exile. He left for Italy, lived first with a countess and then with his friend Percy Bysshe Shelley. Then he organized an expedition at his own expense to help free the Greeks from the Turkish rule. There he caught a fever and died soon after his 36th birthday. He is still remembered today among the Greeks as their national hero. Byron fought all his life for the liberty of the individual as well as the nation. He was easily hurt because highly sensitive and high strung. All his life he was harassed by conservative public opinion of which he never thought much. He was clear about his mission as a committed artist, and never swerved from his responsibility. His was truly a rebellious revolutionary spirit.

Reputations wax and wane. In the mid-19th century, Byron surpassed all his romantic contemporaries as the leading poet not only in his own country but also in Europe. Today, however, he tends to be ignored by critics and readers alike. The main reason for this neglect, as T. S. Eliot seems to suggest, lies in the fact that he makes a lot of noise but has little substance. Another possible reason offered is the fact that he was so closely tied up with his period that the concerns of his works are not immediately relevant to other times any more. Yet another reason is that he is lacking in depth, and although he locates the ills of his age, he fails to prescribe cures. There is truth in all these and other explanations, but it is not the whole truth as an analysis of his works may readily illustrate. The fact will remain in the annals of English poetry that Byron's contribution is great in the overall achievement of English romanticism. [2]

One famous thing to remember about Byron is that he created a hero of his own type, the Byronic hero, handsome, chivalrous, energetic, pathetic, lonely, remorseful over a sin, gloomy and misanthropic, sexually free, and capable of generous acts and magnanimity. This figure is not simply the poet's self projection; it is also his aspiration for what he would like to become. The protagonists in his major works such as his two famous long poems, *Childe Harold* and *Don Juan*, are all the archetypes of the Byronic hero. The significance of this heroic figure goes way beyond the poet's time. It reflects a mindset that aspires for the ideal—the best possible life—that the world can offer. It also symbolizes the human will to justice, freedom, and happiness. There is also a possible downside in the personality of this hero, however, which may be seen in his individualistic spirit, aloofness, arrogance, and occasional contempt for the common people.

Byron is a highly inspired poet. He has a direct, forthright, and forceful voice. His poetry is noted for its spontaneity, exuberance, and humor. He says what he feels in a charming manner. He may not possess much profundity, and may offend people of a conservative taste, but no one can ignore the enchanting beauty, the bewitching power, and the sweeping fascination that radiate from his works. As an artist, he is mainly descriptive rather than prescriptive, but the vision and insight in his descriptions can only be the work of a genius of the first intellectual order. Byron's influence has been felt all over the globe. His theme of quest for freedom and against tyranny and his romantic spirit have made their imprint upon the life and the literature of the world. His major works include *Childe Harold's Pilgrimage* (1812-1818)—his first important work, *The Giaour* (1813), *The Corsair* (1814), and *Lara* (1814)—all long narrative poems of exotic beauty describing rebellious characters, *Manfred* (1817) and *Cain* (1821)—verse dramas exploring the misery of life and lauding the struggle against overwhelming odds, *The Vision of Judgment* (1822)—a scathing political satire against the British monarchy and the men of letters in its service, *The Age of Bronze* (1822)—a satirical attack on the "Holy Alliance" of conservative European monarchies against Napoleon, and a number of lyrics as well as his *English Bards and Scotch Reviewers* (1809), a bitter refutation of the poets and critics who had been harsh in their judgment of his first volume of verses, *Hours of Idleness*. [3]

Let's take a look at some of his major poems.

Childe Harold's Pilgrimage (1812-1818) was the poem that made the poet immediately famous on both sides of the English Channel: "I woke up one morning and found myself famous," to quote the poet himself. The poem was popular chiefly because it was a travelogue about some European countries like Spain and Portugal in which the English people took an enormous interest then. In addition, its hero, Childe Harold, proved fascinating as a type, which has since come to be known as the Byronic hero, dark and melancholy, proud, dissipated, and life-weary. The poem contains four cantos of 156 Spenserian stanzas, the stanza form that appealed to the poet because it was accommodating to all variations. The poem was first begun in 1809 when the first two cantos were composed, and the fourth was not written until eight years later. Byron specifically denied that the hero was himself in disguise. But the fact that the name of the hero in the first two cantos is Childe Burun ("Burun" being the old form of the poet's family name) and that the poet announced that he would speak out himself in the last canto—this did a lot to encourage the autobiographical approach.

In Cantos I and II Childe Harold, tired of the dissipated life he is leading with evil company and dissolute women and sick at heart, sails away from his home and country for Europe. Portugal is his first stop, where he enjoys the beauty of nature, meditates upon his sins and repents a little. Spain that comes next fascinates him with its romantic atmosphere, its proud past and liberty. Greece and Albania revive in him memories of the classical past, with Penelope and Ulysses and all, and he meditates further on liberty. Canto III portrays the hero driven and adrift as a wandering outlaw and growing old in the miserable world. It also tells about his almost Wordsworthian love for nature and his associations with historical events and people like Waterloo and Napoleon. Some consider this canto the best of the poem in further fleshing out the features of the Byronic hero and in emotional substance and intensity. The last canto is the longest of all the cantos. Byron makes it clear to the effect that he will have to speak out in his own voice in order to do justice to the topics such as Italian literature on which he intends to comment. Here he sees a Venice without Tasso, the village of Arqua that has buried Petrarch, a Florence far from which sleeps Dante, and a Rome haunted by the spirits of her great men. Again he expresses his appreciation of the beauty of nature, the woods, shore, sea, and the universe. The poem ends where it started, with the Byronic hero feeling weary, exhausted, and wasted. The power of *Childe Harold* is everlasting for a few reasons. One of these is its description of the Byronic hero in his full-fledged form, of the mind behind the panorama it unfolds, gifted, capricious, human, anti-conventional, and misunderstood and hurt. The poem will go down in history as one of the most romantic works that ever came out of 19th-century England.

Don Juan (1819-1826) is Byron's masterpiece. It is a mock-epic, possibly the only great long epic poem in English. It is a fragment of 16,000 lines, broken off at canto 16 as a result of the poet's untimely death. The satire has the whole of Europe as its backdrop, revealing as it does the poet's keen observation of life and his satirical depth and sweep. The "Don Juan" in the title of the poem is the name of a Spanish legendary figure with an almost superhuman sexual energy. In Byron's poem Don Juan comes from Serville, Spain. This libertine has a very protective mother, who tries to keep him from the facts of life, allowing him to read only expurgated classics and to associate only with old or ugly women. Don Juan is handsome and mischievous. He falls in love at 16 with a married woman of 23, Donna Julia. The affair is discovered, Julia is sent to a convent, and Don Juan is forced to go to Cadiz, where he sets out by ship for a trip abroad. The ship sinks in a storm, the survivors are adrift on a longboat, and are driven to cannibalism by starvation. Don Juan swims and reaches a tiny Greek island, unconscious, and is picked up by the tall and lovely island beauty, Haidee, with whom he has a sweet but short-lived romance. The girl's pirate father comes back, Don Juan fights with his men, and is wounded and sent on to a slave ship. Haidee dies of illness and grief with his child in her. At the slave market of Constantinople, Don Juan is bought by the Sultana and, disguised as a woman, sleeps with her. The Sultan sends him to the palace harem. There Dudu, a lovely girl, takes him to bed, and the enraged Sultana orders them both to be executed. Don Juan manages to escape with another Englishman, John Johnson, to somewhere outside Ishmael. As John has fought for the Russians, he is welcomed by the Russian General who is about to lead his troops to attack the Turkish town. During the capture of Ishmael, Don Juan fights for the Russians and saves a ten-year-old Muslim girl. He is sent as a messenger to the Russian court with the news of the victory at Ishmael and becomes Empress Catherine's favorite. Then he falls ill and is sent back to England on a diplomatic mission. The last six cantos record in detail his observations of English life and reveal the hypocrisy and cruelty of the English polite society. In England Don Juan attracts the attention of the amorous duchess of Fitz-Fulke, who disguises herself as a ghost and wins his love. Don Juan has considered marrying a young Englishwoman, Miss Aurora Raby who, however, does not seem to respond with enthusiasm.

A fairly common approach to the poem is to identify its first-person narrator with Byron. The autobiographical position can be misleading because some of the events the poem describes were not direct quotations from the author's life.

Byron insisted on the authentic—and moral—nature of his work. When it first came out, its moral value was questioned as it narrated scenes and encounters that appeared "immoral" to his contemporaries. One way of interpretation is to see the poem as the author's effort to tell the truth, nothing but the truth about the life of his time. It vehemently exposes the depravity, corruption, the moral hypocrisy, and the absurdity of existence that characterize Victorian England and Europe. For instance, the picture of the Turkish court and the Russian court offers an obvious allusion to their counterparts in England. It is true that the poem offers no solution to the problems and no suggestion of the best course of action, but its vivid description does enhance human awareness of the disease that besets their age. In addition there is the "hero" of the poem to consider. The long poem opens with the famous line, "I want a hero," but Don Juan is evidently not the Don Juan of the Spanish legend. He is moved around, acted upon rather acting, and always at the mercies of the forces ready to manipulate him. His inaction speaks volumes about the life then. It illustrates the fact that his age provides no congenial milieu for heroes and heroism. That explains why Byron chose the traditional Don Juan who, when placed in the 19th-century setting, becomes watered down however, so that he emerges in his new identity of Byron's Don Juan.

Also, what the poem tries to show is "the Don Juan Question" (George Bernard Shaw's phrase) that this handsome and amenable young man has been subject to the "preying" of the women he happens to stumble into. Shaw made a big case of the Don Juan question, or the Life Force in his masterpiece *Man and*

Superman (1891).

The poem is structurally loose. The countless digressions are baffling to people who look for consistency and cohesion. The different episodes appear to be separate beads, but they are well strung together. Although Byron claimed that he had no plan when writing this work, the episodes somehow coalesce into an organic whole. That has a good deal to do with the narrator who has the author's dominant theme in mind all through the poetic narrative. Byron's poem was composed in the stanza form of ottava rima (an 8-line stanza ending with a couplet). Don Juan doubles as a comic traveler and as an avenue for its creator to vent his satirical comments on the social ills of his time. Hence the verse form of a medley of descriptions with discussions that Byron took from Coleridge's "Dejection: An Ode."

It is interesting to note the comic effect of the poem. It is the way seriousness is undercut that deserves attention. The protagonist has a rather complex personality, or at least a show of it. He can be innocent and morally inhibited at times, but he can also, at other moments, be the opposite of all these, and behave as an imprudent worldly cynic. Any possible serious intention can be turned into a comic cynicism when he reveals these traits at moments inappropriate to the scenarios in which he is involved, and he does this pretty often. Another way of deflating seriousness is through the appearance of various speakers. These sometimes take over from the narrator and pop in with some comments so inapt to the situation that they would turn any serious potential into a comic water-down. The moving scene of Don Juan's encounter with Haidee may be one of the many instances that come instantly to mind. [4]

Percy Bysshe Shelley (1792-1822)

Shelley was one of the famous Romantic poets in English literary history. He came from a family of nobility, read widely, and cultivated a passion for influential philosophers of the time such as Jean Jacques Rousseau (1712-1778), Thomas Paine (1737-1809), and William Godwin (1756-1836) whose socialist thought left a deep imprint upon his mind and whose daughter Mary Godwin Shelley (1797-1851) he married. Young Shelley seemed to have an inveterate revulsion to established values and a strong affinity to exploration and discovery. He went to Oxford University but was expelled because of his anti-Christian essay, "The Necessity of Atheism," which he sent to the heads of the colleges. His impulsive nature led to his elopement with his first wife Harriet Westbrook, both in their mid-teens, which caused immense suffering to Harriet and her ultimate suicide. For a while Shelley was in Northern Ireland to support the national independence struggle there, but eventually he left England and roamed Europe with his second wife Mary Godwin before they settled down in Italy. It was there that he and Byron spent some of their happiest moments of life together. It was there, also, that Mary Shelley wrote her famous and historically important novel, *Frankenstein* (1817). In 1822 Shelley went boating out in the sea and was drowned in a storm in the Gulf of Spezia.

Shelley is an idealistic and prophetic Romantic. He does not seem to live in this world: he has been seen as immaterial and ethereal, and not much in touch with this earth earthy that he dreams of reshaping. Here lie at once his strength and his weakness. He sees life on the horizon and gives the vision a tangible form in his poetry, but his idea is sometimes not taken seriously enough. It is considered "ineffectual" (Matthew Arnold's word) because far removed from here and now. All his life Shelley keeps ruminating and formulating his thought into a message that he hopes will make a change in the life of man. He refuses to accept life as it is and tries to envision life as devoid of oppression, injustice, tyranny, and corruption current in the social life of his day. He visualizes the birth of an ideal social order based on the regeneration of man and the virtue of love. This is then the gist of his message put in a nutshell. He tries to enunciate it in his verse dramas *Queen Mab* (1813) and *The Revolt of Islam* (1818), but does not quite succeed in getting it across to his readers until he finishes his most famous lyrical drama, *Prometheus Unbound* (1820). Here he paints with his heart and soul the picture of the ideal man despising authority and fighting tyranny with his indomitable spirit. Shelley sees this spirit as the most valuable human asset with which man can build a new, ideal life. In social and philosophical terms, Shelley's influence on the course of human life has been considerable. He made himself a kind of precursor to the socialist movement soon to sweep across Europe and England. [5]

Shelley is one of the best English lyrical poets. His genius reveals its versatility and virtuosity in his works. In addition to his themes of protest against tyranny and quest for freedom and an ideal social order, he writes a good number of lyrics, the most impressive of which are his love poems. He is noted for the wild flights of his imagination, his dextrous use of colors, sounds, images, and the touching beauty of his rhymes and music. His works include also *The Cenci* (1819), one of his best received in his time, *The Mask of Anarchy* (1819), and such well-known and oft-quoted lyrics as "Ode to the West Wind" (1819), the still widely read "To a Sky Lark" (1820) which is not really unique to his spirit and style, and the famous sonnet "Ozymandias." His legacy in literary theory is his prose work, *A Defense of Poetry* (1821). Shelley has weathered through time well. He did suffer along with other romantics in the mid-20th century, but he has remained well above water. His presence is stubbornly felt still today though some may choose to get around him somehow.

Let's take a look at some of Shelley's major works. [6]

"Ode to the West Wind," with its well-renowned ending, has been an absolute must on the reading list of Shelley's readers. It can be seen as his signature poem. It is his representative work both in theme and form, forcefully prophetic in its fighting spirit and singular in its lyrical beauty. Talking about the poem, Shelley says that it was his emotional response to a strong hailstorm in which he happened to be swallowed one autumn evening in 1819 on the Arno near Florence. Shelley sees, in the storm of the natural world, an apt metaphor for the storm of revolution in the human world. The poet had been feeling depressed at the triumph of the reactionary Holy Alliance over Napoleon and the French Revolution and was emphatic in his forecast that the storm of revolution would make a powerful comeback yet. The poem, composed in iambic pentameter, consists of five stanzas of 14 lines each, or four 3-line sub-stanzas plus one 2-line couplet sub-stanza. There are many run-on lines and sub-stanzas, which suit well the depiction of the unruly wind and the onrush of emotion. The emotional turmoil, long pent-up in the bosom of the poet, bursts out with its utmost force. It is reinforced with the use of appropriate imagery and impeccable rhyme and rhythm, though colored at times with a sentimentality that may detract a little (but never much) from the power of the eruption. It is one of the best, endearing English lyrics to come out of literary history.

The first stanza (ll. 1-14) is in fact one sentence broken into different lines with the verb "hear" appearing in the last line of the stanza. It describes the power of the west wind and its double role as both destroyer (ll. 2-5) and preserver (ll.6-12). Line 14 sums up the wind's two basic characteristics, which also constitute the thematic focus of the poem. The second stanza (ll. 15-28) is made up of two sentences, one long from line 15 through line 23, and one short from line 24 through line 28. The whole stanza focuses on the adumbration of the wind's power driving clouds before it and bringing storms with it (ll. 15-23) with lightning, rain, fire and hail (ll.23-28); it also describes its destructive aspect of "closing night" enveloping all under its dome of a vast tomb (ll. 24-25). The third stanza (ll. 29-42) talks about the wind's impact upon the sea, its first touching on the calm of the Mediterranean (ll. 29-36), and then on the turbulence of the Atlantic (ll. 36-42). The Mediterranean sleeps in serenity in the summer but is waken up by the wind to see the quivering of the shadows of ancient palaces and towers (ll. 29-35) and the Atlantic cleaving asunder into gigantic chasms (ll. 35-38). Even the vegetation at the bottom of the sea "grow[s] gray with fear,/ tremble[s] and despoil[s] themselves" (ll. 41-42).

The next, the fourth, stanza (ll. 43-56) expresses the poet's emotional response to the west wind. The poet says to the wind (ll. 43-47) that he wishes to be spirited away like the leaves, to dance like the clouds, to breathe like the waves, and enjoy a share of the wind's strength like the storm though with a lesser degree of freedom of movement. The poet takes a nostalgic backward glance at his free, uncontrollable boyhood when he could fly like a swift cloud like the wind, and even outstrip it in speed (ll. 47-51), and wishes for the wind to lift him up like a leaf or wave or a cloud (l. 54). But it is only a figment of his imagination, and he has to face "the thorns of life" that he has fallen upon, chained and weighed down, and no longer "tameless, swift, and proud" like the wind (ll. 54-56). The last stanza (ll. 57-70) expresses both the poet's request for the wind to help spread the words of his poem "among mankind" and wake it up from its deep stupor (ll. 66-69) and his prophecy that spring will come in the wake of winter (ll. 69-70). The poem ends upon a note of confidence and hope.

Prometheus Unbound (1820) is Shelley's famous lyric drama. [7] The poet drew his subject from Greek mythology—the conflict between Prometheus and Jupiter. In the original of the myth which is detailed in the classic tragedy of Aeschylus (525-456 BC)—*Prometheus Bound*, Prometheus brings fire down to man and enrages Jupiter so that the god of gods chains him to the Caucasian Cliff for him to repent. Prometheus suffers long and hard but refuses to give in. The Greek tragedy ends tragically with the unswerving Prometheus hurled down into the abyss of the earth.

Shelley's drama follows the outline of the original well through most of the story. As it goes, Prometheus is firmly chained to a cliff, exposed to the elements as well as the eagle pecking at his liver every day. Then one day when the apparition of Jupiter appears to repeat the Titan's curse to him, the suffering Titan withdraws it, but still refuses to disclose his prophecy about Jupiter's future, in return for which Jupiter will set him free. He says just this much, that Jupiter will fall some time, and he would like to get his freedom back then. Despite the threats of further afflictions, Prometheus refuses to succumb to the tyrant's will. He is shown visions of the misery of the earth, Jesus' death, and human disregard of His love message. Then some spirits appear to foretell that love will be the medication for human evil and that Prometheus is to bring love to men. Prometheus embraces the idea of love as his own love of his wife, Asia, has sustained him well through his ordeal. In the meantime, Panthea, one Oceanide, and Asia are called upon to see the supreme being of all, Demogorgon, who tells them that God created the world, no evil person can be master, and only Eternal Love will rule all. There the Spirit of the Hour leads them through visions of the phases of human life and the sight of a paradise. Then Demogorgon comes to Jupiter and puts an end to his reign, Hercules sets Prometheus free, and the man kisses the earth and infuses love through all its sectors—animal, vegetable, and mineral. Changes occur in human nature as well as in the social and political life. Man, now king over himself, is free from pain and guilt, but still subject to chance and mutability that serve to keep his right place on earth. A vision appears to the Oceanides that all evil is dead, all ills like hate, fear, and pain vanish, love pervades the earth and the moon, and man becomes master of his fate.

Shelley's work departs from its classic counterpart basically in its ethos as well as its substance. In subject, the later work differs not much in the bulk of the story, but significantly with the ending. Prometheus is set free, and the vision of a better world for man concludes the play. In terms of its thematic ethos, Shelley's drama throws the notion of universal love in relief, and proffers it as the cure for the ills of human life. Whereas confrontation and hate dominate the emotions of the two sides in the classic work, the note of love is heard almost from the outset in Shelley's drama. The suffering Prometheus withdraws even his curse upon Jupiter because the Titan has learned positively from his ordeal and wishes no pain to any living being including Jupiter. This represents the poet's response to the troubled life of his time. The drama is a good exposition of Shelley's philosophy.

In technical terms, the work is remarkable. Shelley impresses by the sheer force of his vital, fresh, and varied lyric energy. Here he reveals his lyric genius by the amazing variety of lyric forms he employs in the work. Not only does he create and perfect his own lyric patterns, he also successfully adapts other forms like the Pindaric ode, the Spenserian stanza, and the couplets, to serve his own lyrical outburst. The result is God's lyric plenty, a "lyrical flowering" as one critic aptly puts it, so that some critics even claim that, had Shelley not written anything else, his lyric passages alone here would have earned him a distinct place as one of the greatest English poets.

John Keats (1795-1821)

Keats' life was one of downright misery. He came from a poor background, son of a stable-keeper, lost his parents early in life, and was apprenticed at 15 to a doctor, a job that was galling to his sensitive soul. He had no formal education and no one to help him with either education or literary training. But he was a highly sensitive spirit. He made up for the deficiency with voracious reading. He read well in Greek and Elizabethan literature, and had Homer, Spenser, Shakespeare and Milton among his literary passions. He spotted gorgeous beauty in these and classical dictionaries and reference books. It is good to note that his former teacher Charles Clarke (1787-1877) introduced him to the ancient world of *Chapman's Homer* in 1816 and widened his vistas of beauty and poetry. Chapman's translation brought him a sudden sense of discovery and hastened his artistic maturity. "On First Looking into Chapman's Homer" (1816), the sonnet that he wrote after reading and discussing the book together with Clarke one whole night in 1816, was the first work marking a life-long quest for eternal beauty in art, the result of which was that the poet managed to revive the importance of Greek myth in English poetry. Keats had also a deep interest in paintings. Misfortunes befell him ruthlessly. His brother died, and he contracted the then terminal disease—tuberculosis. He loved a young girl, Fanny Browne, but had to cut off ties with her because of his illness and experienced the worst emotional torment for a human being. Later in life he went to Italy to improve his health, but in vain. Born in the same year as was Thomas Carlyle, he died 60 years earlier. He was slightly over twenty-five years old then.

Keats was a person of singular determination. His imagination was sensual as he lived more in sensation than in thought. He seemed to believe that he was born for the pursuit of beauty, and made it the major business of his short life. He would like to be an Apollo, the god of poetry. If his contemporaries Wordsworth and Shelley were enthusiastic pursuers of beauty, Keats was many times more devoted to his quest. He eventually left "the shop…the plasters, pills and ointment boxes" (to quote his previous job description by a vicious critic) and began to devote his energy to poetry. Keats befriended Leigh Hunt (1784-1859), a radical man of letters of the time, who discovered and appreciated his genius and was the first to publish his works. He participated in the literary activities Hunt organized, and became the butt of virulent attack from conservative writers and critics. Amid this agonizingly ugly milieu of social as well as personal life, no one else would ever think of doing what Keats was to do. Keats was not to give in to the odds overwhelming his young fragile existence, and he was not to give up on himself as well as his quest for a better life. For he loved "the principle of beauty in all things" and was singularly adamant in his belief that there existed a world of eternal beauty somewhere more real than the life being lived here and it was his job to search for and help create it. He believed in the life of the imagination and the validity of the moments of beauty occasionally perceived. But he also came to see as a mature artist that the life of change is as important as is art and its eternal beauty. [8]

The miracle of life was that this self-taught young man was singularly equipped with the powers for the poetic endeavor he was to undertake. He had a sharp eye for colors and a keen ear for rhythms and sounds, and a rare capacity to bring out the magic of words. For some five years out of his short life, he wrote tirelessly, did his best work mainly in the year of 1819, and managed to leave behind a legacy, the richness of which will take eternity to excavate. He has been well known for the exquisite texture of his poetry, with its beautiful imagery, sound, and diction. His sole object in life was to look for beauty, and he was a pure poet, but he was never an aesthete as some have made him out to be and was never bothered much by theories and dogmas. He was serious about life, and never strove for art only for art's sake. His major poems include *Endymion* (1818), a long romance with such flaws as its emotional excesses and elaborate plotting, but capable of offering individual sections of unmistakable beauty, the fragment *Hyperion*, his poems "Lamia" (1820), "Isabella" (1820), "The Eve of St. Agnes" (1820), his sonnets like "On First Looking into Chapman's Homer" (1816)—representative of Keats' early work, "On the Grasshopper and Cricket" (1816), "When I Have Fears" (1818)—a poem of the early maturity of his poetic talent, "Bright Star" (1819), and his odes like "Ode to Psyche," "Ode to a Nightingale," "Ode on a Grecian Urn," "Ode on Indolence," "To Autumn," and "Ode on Melancholy." His recognition was well overdue in mid-19th century when the first book-length of introduction appeared with a collection of his poems and letters. Keats' letters were duly collected and published and contributed not a little to the growth of his reputation. Now people need only to read his poems and letters to appreciate his achievement as a poet.

Keats is also an influential literary theorist. His letters contain his major ideas on poetry. These include, among other things, his notions of "negative capability," poetic identity, and emphasis on the oneness of truth and beauty. The "negative capability" is to him the major quality of a man of achievement: "that is [as he writes in a letter to his brothers] when man is capable of being in uncertainties, mysteries, doubts, without any irritable reaching after fact and reason." In other words, it is the ability to be content with "half knowledge" or ambiguity or refusal to impose one's own judgment in the representation of varied human experience. So it leads to the annulment of the self and one's imperfect interpretation. And to annul self requires that one has to have a firm sense of self or identity. Keats sees the achievement of identity as the highest goal of human development. His idea on identity, or "identical soul," places stress on the importance of the world of pains and troubles in the process of schooling one's intelligence so as to make it a soul. Intelligence has to feel and suffer in many different ways and learn to accept one's identity as essential to one's being. This is what he calls "spirit-creation" or "soul-making." Keats went through this the hard way himself and emerged with a firm sense of self. Although he wavered at different moments of his life, he had faith in himself leaving some immortal work behind and winning fame. Of the things that mattered most to him, "Verse, Fame, and Beauty," the first he wrote a good deal of, the second he won, and the third he found in his intense experience with art and life. This leads to his concept of "Truth is beauty, beauty is truth" as he expresses it compactly in his "Ode on a Grecian Urn," a hard-won belief that real life is as beautiful and necessary as the eternal beauty in art (as the analysis of the ode that follows will attest).[9]

Let's take a look at some of his major works.

"Ode to a Nightingale" is one of Keats' masterworks. It was composed at a time when the poet was suffering an emotional upheaval of the utmost intensity. It was written in May, 1819 when he was staying with a friend in London. A nightingale had made its nest close by, and its singing fascinated the sick and sad young poet. One morning he sat under a tree for some two or three hours and wrote down the lines that became immediately well known. The poet was then going through a phase of agony, with his brother Tom dead a few months earlier, another brother having already emigrated to America with his family, and himself in love with his beloved and about to leave for Italy on account of his worsening tuberculosis condition. All these factors contributed to the rich and varied emotional fabric of the poem, expressing as it does the understanding of and sympathy for human misery and the desire to escape from reality into poetry and wine, and an ideal world for man. The ode is one of his best in diction, imagery and sound and rhythm.

The ode consists of eight stanzas of 10 lines each. The first stanza expresses the mixed feelings of weal and woe on hearing the nightingale. The poet's heart is aching, and a drowsy numbness is paining his senses, but the bird's song and its happy lot brings joy to the sad poet and enables him to forget his troubles. The 2nd stanza expresses the poet's desire to lose himself in his cups and escape into "the forest dim" (l. 20) with the bird. The idea of escape is continued into the 3rd stanza, in which the poet feels infinite sorrow at a world "Where youth grows pale, and spectre-thin, and dies" (l. 26). It is an obvious reference to his brother's death, his own imminent demise and, by extension, that of all youth in similar circumstances. But as wine is inadequate to sustain the escape, the poet resorts to poetry and hopes to get lost in the vision that poetry inspires. Line 35 contains the famous "tender is the night" which was to become the title of a famous American novel by Scott Fitzgerald in the next century. In the next, the 5th stanza, the poet visualizes himself enjoying the music of the nightingale and the fragrance, "the soft incense" (l. 42), of the vegetation in the bewitching night-enveloped forest. In stanza 6, his mirth reaches a point where he thinks of "easeful death" (l. 52) as an avenue to avoid the harassing human misery, and envisions the sod that will bury him so that he will become deaf to the everlasting song of the nightingale. The 7th stanza places the pain of life in contrast to the eternal joyful music of the nightingale. It contains the famous lines, "The same that oft-times hath/ Charm'd magic casement, opening on the foam/ Of perilous seas, in faery lands forlorn" (ll. 68-70). This is a reference to the ancient and medieval European romantic legendary tradition that a princess, imprisoned in a magic-controlled castle, waits for the rescue of a pious brave knight. The last stanza depicts the fading of the bird-song and the coming back of the poet to face reality, and his feeling of loss and frustration that imagination can offer reprieve for a moment but not for good.

The same desire for escape and transcendence is expressed in another famous poem, "Ode on a Grecian Urn" (1820). This ode is the work, along with some other odes such as "Ode to Psyche," "On Indolence," "On Melancholy," and "To a Nightingale," that indicates that the poet has achieved maturity and self-confidence, and is ready to speak with a voice for all humanity as well as himself. "Ode on a Grecian Urn" has been always one of Keats' most popular odes as its suggestive profundity appeals for ever to the imagination of the sensitive minds of all generations. The ode suggests that the poet's imagination takes wild flights when looking at a Grecian urn. He thinks of the urn as a symbol for the joy of eternal life and for the immortalizing power of art and imagination and their useful function, but he also realizes that the urn's carved beauty comes to life only with the help of the imagination and that real life is beautiful, too.

The ode consists of five stanzas of ten lines each. The first stanza tells of an urn with a legend and figures painted on it. The pictures of scenes and people there depict a life that might have been lived long ago in a Greek valley. Conspicuous to the attention of the poet is a youth in mad pursuit of a virgin maiden who is struggling to get away from him. And all the romance occurs amidst the unheard music of pipes and timbrels. The girl, who might be noisy and fleet of foot in actual ancient life, is now quiet, silent, and static on the urn. The second stanza begins with the poet's ecstasy on hearing the "unheard melodies," and goes on to express his joy at the fact that the trees under which the youth stands are forever covered with luxuriant foliage, the lover can never catch up with his "goal" and kiss her, but the girl is for ever in sight and the pair is for ever in love. The third stanza reinforces on the notion of the evergreen branches, the ever new song of the unwearied melodist, the ever panting and ever young lovers, and the eternal human passion—all that leaves the poet with a sense of frustration (ll. 4, 11-27) and sorrow in comparison (ll. 29-30). The first three stanzas thus reveal the power of art immortalizing life and joy.

The 4th stanza seems to introduce a different vein of thought on art. Here is seen on the urn a religious procession, with the priest and the sacrificial heifer, all heading to a green altar of sacrifices. The mind's eye of the poet also sees a little town or a mountain citadel that the crowd has left behind, for ever deserted in silence and emptiness. The poet seems to be musing over the idea that art also immortalizes desolation and prevents fulfillment: there is never consummation of the love between the youth and the girl, the altar can never be reached, the sacrificial ceremony can never be held, and the town or citadel will never be full of people again. Thus the poet sees the limitations and mystery of art. The last stanza records the poet's epiphany, his sudden awareness of art in relation to life, that artistic beauty is a picture of "cold pastoral"; it is always beautiful but lifeless, which can be complemented by real yet transient life; and so "Truth," or real life, is every bit as beautiful as is "Beauty," or art (the urn). Thus the two worlds of art and life are shown to be mutually dependent to reveal their value. The permanence of the world of art is reconciled with the ephemerality of the contingent world of fulfilled life. We will need nothing else to feel happy on earth if we can comprehend this nature of things with the help of such art works as the urn. Hence art as "a friend to man" (l. 48).

"To Autumn" (1819) has been considered to be one of Keats' best odes, if not the best. It is in fact his last greatest ode. It was composed after the poet's walk across the warm fields after autumn harvest. Keats was deeply impressed by the beauty of the season, the fresh air, the temperate weather, the dark blue sky, and the warm hue of autumn as compared with the icy green of spring. He saw a picture of warmth and had it painted in words of variegated colors, sounds and images for which the poem is noted. Incidentally, the theme of the poem is the warm plentitude of autumn. Instead of telling his responses and feelings, Keats contrives to show these by means of what T. S. Eliot would call "the objective correlative," i.e. with clusters of well-chosen images properly juxtaposed or superimposed or dexterously merging into one another. Thus the poem appeals to the senses and is meant to be seen, heard, felt, and tasted. In addition, there is a subtly imbedded motif of movement from morning to evening, which implies the transition through the different phases of life—growth, maturity, and death. In terms of tone and mood, the poem reflects the poet's spontaneous reaction to the season: first recognition, then enjoyment, and finally contemplation. It indicates Keats' appreciation of life in change.

The first of the three stanzas of the poem depicts the scene of autumn. Its opening line brings out forthright the thematic focus of the poem—autumn as the "Season of mists and mellow fruitfulness," with the sun as the source of all life and the season as its "close friend" (l. 2). The images that follow are all visual, auditory, and tangible, and conspire to throw into relief the heart-warming scene of abundance. The mist reminds readers of an autumn morning, and the vines, the apples, the swelling gourd, the hazel shells, the budding flowers and the bees with their clammy cells—all these images emphasize growth and vibrant life that autumn exhibits. The 2nd stanza describes the people on the autumn scene, i.e. the laborers, sitting care-free on the granary floor or napping in between work in the fields, or gleaning the left-over grains of wheat to carry over a brook, or waiting patiently for the cider-press to finish its work. The gallery of working people reveals the joyful plenty of the season. The sitting or napping reminds the readers of the middle of the autumn working day and the harvesting that follows the arrival of the stage of maturity. The last stanza moves from the description of the autumn scene and people to autumn sounds. It begins with an advice not to feel sorry for the vanishing songs of spring. For autumn has its own peculiar music with the choir of the gnats over the harvested fields, the bleat of the lambs, the singing of the hedge cricket, the treble soft whistling of the red-breast and the twittering of home-coming swallows. All that the readers hear are the sounds of an autumn evening, conveying effectively an acute sense of the beginning of the end coming, with words such as "dying," "wailful," "mourn," "sinking" and "dies," and the sad symphony of the lamb, cricket, red-breast, and swallows. It is sad that beauty is short-lived and "nothing gold can stay," but by no means gloomy as exuberance keeps breaking out of the texture of the poem all the way through. Particularly impressive are the whistling of the red-breast and the swallows afloat yet about to alight, suggesting an attitude of resignation and a quiet assertion of dignity in face of the inevitable (a mild reminder of the ending of American poet Wallace Stevens' "Sunday Morning").

The poem exudes both a joyful appreciation of and an insatiable thirst for fulfilled life, and a sad yet calm acceptance of death. The poet is facing the life cycle with a moving serenity. The emotional pitch with which the work is suffused indicates that the poet was probably subconsciously writing a good deal of his psychic self into the warp and woof of the ode, although it is presumptuous to assume that the poet, still ambitious with plans and projects, was thinking of saying goodbye to this rich contingent world he was so ardently eulogizing. The ode differs from his sonnet, "Bright Star! Would I Were Steadfast as Thou Art" (1819), noticeably in that the sonnet expresses the poet's keen awareness of his impending death.

Keats' most beautiful work should be "The Eve of St. Agnes." It is based on a medieval legend that says that, if a maiden follows St. Agnes' ceremonies carefully on the eve of St. Agnes and goes without supper to bed, she may meet her lover in a dream. Now on this cold St. Agnes' Eve, beautiful Madeline is getting ready for such a dream. A party is going on in her father—the Baron's house, but she is oblivious to the revelry around. A Beadsman is going to church, saying his prayers all the time. Now a young man comes and hides himself from the crowd. He is Porphyro, an enemy of the maiden's family. The aged kind Angela comes along to offer to hide the young man in safety, but Porphyro asks in dead earnest her permission to have a glimpse at Madeline. Angela succumbs to his pathetic request and hides him in Madeline's closet. The young man almost swoons at the sight of the stunning beauty of the girl. Meanwhile, Madeline goes through her prayer and falls asleep. Porphyro comes out and begins to play on a flute. Madeline opens her eyes and the scared Porphyro falls on his knees. Madeline begs him not to leave her or she would die. It is late, the moon is down, and a slit storm is thrashing at the house. Porphyro and Madeline decide to run away at this wintry dawn. Angela dies in her sleep, the Beadsman sleeps cold among the ashes, and the Baron and his guests dream of nightmares.

The poem paints an idealized picture of the perfect world for human beings. It exalts the emotion of the moment and the role of the poetic imagination. Spontaneity of feeling is what the poet tries to capture. The poem reflects the whole spectrum of human emotions from joy to grief and all the shades of color in between. As it is set in medieval times, the poem sounds quaint, new, and full of wonder. Whereas the work is entitled for a virgin martyr, the lovers in the story it tells abandon tradition and elope. The contrast reveals the juxtaposition of the two complementary human traits: reason and passion. The two are mutually dependent, and between them they make life real and viable. The Beadsman is all piety without passion; he ignores the sensual aspect of life altogether. But the lovers behave differently. To Porphyro Madeline is heavenly beauty and awes him so that he is breathless in face of it, but Madeline is both pious and sensual and hypersensitive to the things of this world. The ideal world is one, as the poem illustrates, in which such human feelings enjoy full license. It is to this world, a sanctuary, that the lovers run to live ever happily after, but the misery that the rest of the household suffers testifies that life is not all rosy and that probably the poet is thinking of his own forthcoming tragic end. Formally, it is written in the Spenserian stanza. The language, though at times archaic, sounds like ordinary speech. [10]

Chapter 11 The Victorian Period • Victorian Prose • Carlyle • Mill • Newman

The Victorian Period: An Introduction

The Victorian period spans well over half a century (1837-1901). For one hundred years after the Napoleonic Wars came to an end in 1814, England began enjoying affluence as a result of relative peace and the advances in science and technology. The country changed from an agricultural to an industrialized nation. It became more urbanized, cities grew in size, and villages declined. Roads developed, canals were built, and so were railroads and steamships. National economy picked up at a high speed, education became more general, popular literacy increased, and health and hygiene improved. Despite the gaping extremes of wealth and poverty, life became visibly easier.

In socio-political terms the period can be roughly subdivided into two phases. The first of these, beginning from 1832 through mid-century, was one of development. Though there were upheavals such as the passing of the first Reform Bill in 1832 and the Chartist Movement when the workers demanded better chances of survival, the country's steady growth was basically undisturbed by large questionings. Change was, however, ever waiting to come around the corner. In 1859 Charles Darwin appeared on the scene with his theory of evolution, which kicked off the whole never-ending argument between science and religion and about the basic nature of man and society and all the related institutions. These questions shook the second half of the period tremendously, and things became radically different.

To read the literature of the period, the following features of its social, cultural and political life, which constitute what has come to be known pejoratively as "Victorianism," should be duly noted as they all, in their varying degrees, rubbed off on Victorian culture and literature:

(1) The growth of the middle class (chiefly the capitalists): In addition to the material gains from the further industrialization of the country, the middle class grabbed a huge amount of political power from the landed aristocracy. This was done through the Reform Bill of 1832 which changed the way people were elected to Parliament. It helped, on the one hand, remove the rotten boroughs, i.e. rural areas with few or no people (who died either of cholera or as a result of the depression)—which used to "vote" for the aristocracy and, on the other, extended the right of vote to the towns where the middle class had the control. The highly controversial bill caused bitter dispute but eventually got through the two Houses of Parliament. While the middle class was immensely better off, the working class was as wretched as ever. Poverty, overcrowding, and crime—all these made life impossible for the millions. The country branched off into what politician-novelist Benjamin Disraeli (1804-1881) called "two nations." Then the Chartist Movement began with over one million people signing the People's Charter, asking for universal male suffrage, voting by ballot, no property qualifications for candidates, annual parliament instead of parliaments called by the monarch, and payment for the members of Parliament. The request was summarily rejected, which led to the Second People's Charter of 1842 with over three million signatures. Again the workers failed miserably, and their 450 leaders were arrested and deported to Australia. The next 30 years witnessed increasing middle-class prosperity. Now dominating the nation's life, the middle class enforced its own values and tastes so that what Matthew Arnold (1822-1888) called cultural philistinism began to intensify its control and made the life of the mind difficult if not entirely impossible. Thus Victorian literature is essentially middle-class, urban literature.

(2) The development of a very conservative kind of morality: People became prudish and squeamish about life in general and about sex and love in particular. Clothes were made to hide the female body, respectable women never wore trousers and showed their legs in public, and it was bad taste to use words like "legs," "breasts," and even "swimming." Women were put on the pedestal for men to worship, which is another way of saying "to condescend to." Middle class women came to be called "lady," a title that had for long been reserved for aristocratic women, and were expected to be gentle, pale, sweet and submissive.

The implication of this was that the female gender was unlike men, unable to run things and ever dependent on the male sex. Read the novel *Susan Lennox, Her Fall and Rise* (1917), and one will understand how ignorant and helpless a Victorian girl could be, and what disastrous impact that could have on her life. At the opening of the story, Susan Lennox is taken out by a rich young man one evening and comes home late to answer the severe question of the anxiously waiting parents and clergyman, "Did he make love to you?" Susan, too innocent to understand what "making love" means, says "yes" because the man kissed her, and she becomes a ruined woman as no good man would marry her. Men, on the other hand, were dominant in life. Although the beginnings of feminism became visible—some women like Mary Wollstonecraft (1759-1797) had long begun to assert women's right, and the Victorian feminist thought was also very strong, middle-class men could lead a secretive depraved life, every bit depraved as any other age if not more. The contemporary novel, *The French Lieutenant's Woman* (1969) reveals that a Victorian man paid an average of two daily visits to a brothel. This feature of Victorian life has been furiously censured in modern times as part of Victorianism.

(3) The predominance of the moral aesthetic that proved binding to most Victorian writers: This literary aesthetic required that all write first to moralize and edify. The duty of a writer is to spread and confirm established values and help people behave accordingly. Incidentally, writers were looked up to as prophets or heroes of some kind, and most of them felt the weight of their mission and took it seriously. For instance, people learned about love and the home and hearth from Alfred Lord Tennyson (1809-1892), about God's immanent will and the work ethic from Thomas Carlyle (1795-1881), about compassion and benevolent action from Charles Dickens, about courage and striving from Robert Browning (1812-1889), and about morality from George Eliot (1819-1880) who was seen as a great moral force then. The presence of these great figures ensured the people somehow that God's prophets still roamed around, a sure sign that society was essentially doing good.

This aesthetic hurt those who found value in the life of the imagination. Tennyson himself exhibited "two voices" in his poetry—one public and one private, but he kept his private one in check. With time life became intolerant, beauty began to vanish, and people and things grew ugly to look at. The world seemed to be one of universal gray without a spot of color, and literature began to lose its legitimate autonomy. When the trend became general and extreme, a reaction set in. The result of all these was a movement, the aesthetic movement in the latter part of the century, the object of which was to fight for beauty, beginning with John Ruskin (1819-1900), involving a number of important authors such as Dante Gabriel Rossetti (1828-1882), William Morris (1834-1896), Algernon Charles Swinburne (1837-1909), and Walter Pater (1839-1894), and ending with Oscar Wilde.

(4) The wide currency of utilitarianism: This was a hedonistic kind of philosophy, embracing Utility, or "the greatest happiness for the greatest number" as the sanction of morality, and spreading the belief that everyone was the best judge of his own interest. Jeremy Bentham (1748-1832) and James Mill (1773-1836) set the tone, and John Stuart Mill (1806-1873) humanized it sufficiently to ensure its dissemination in the country. As a practical movement of philosophy, it advocated a few things which met the need of the age. One of these was its emphasis on the importance of representative government, universal education, trade unions, and philanthropy. It encouraged individual growth and social reform, and supported democratic politics and material progress. Thus it made its positive contribution to Victorian life. Almost all the legislative reforms including the 1832 Reform Bill and the 1870 Act of Education bore its tangible imprint on them. However, its call for laissez-faire in industry and trade and commerce encouraged selfishness, excessive individual freedom, middle-class material expansion, and the growth of capitalism. Its idea of Utility placed so much value on the machine and the usefulness of all the branches of the sciences that it virtually dismissed everything else as of little or no importance. For instance, Bentham saw poetry as a trifling game. Utilitarianism was on the whole the reflection of the spirit of Victorian middle class liberalism, or philistinism as Matthew Arnold called it. This was the main reason why it met with a good deal of hostility from the intellectual segment of the country. As it became the spirit of the age and dominated popular thinking, it provoked a reaction from the major authors of the period such as Carlyle, Tennyson, and Dickens, to name just a prominent few. Carlyle caricatures it as "Pig Philosophy" in his *Latter-Day Pamphlets*, and

Dickens' *Hard Times* is another good example of anti-utilitarianism.

(5) The advent of the theory of evolution: This brought about huge changes in the nation's social and religious life and in Victorian thinking in general. Charles Darwin (1809-1882) published his epochal work, *The Origin of Species*, in 1859, and nothing could be the same again. Darwin's book is about natural selection, the evolution of the species from lower forms of being to higher through an incessant natural process of "the survival of the fittest." In 1871 he published his *The Descent of Man* to extend the scope of his argument. These caused sensation. Then there was Thomas Huxley (1825-1895) who stated in his 1868 lecture "On the Physical Basis of Life" that man has no soul or spirit independent of his body. This apparently added fuel to the fire. The effect of the theory of evolution on the 19th century was electrifying. The whole nation was amazed to know that the world was not specially created by God and that it would remain basically the same as it kept evolving onward. This was a serious attack on the Christian faith, and put the church immediately on the defensive. The long-drawn-out struggle between outworn faith and modern thought had begun. There was also another dimension of thinking involved. People felt that, if evolution was true, then they were here not because they were good but because they adapted better. The idea caused quite a bit moral anxiety.

It was only natural that a heated controversy followed, which has never really stopped even today. Now the Victorians had to choose between science and faith; in the 19th century there was no middle ground. Darwinism threw some very sensitive minds such as Arthur Hugh Clough (1819-1861) into a state of nondescript ennui and agony. It affected literary writing in a profound way. Most of the major writers of the age exhibited some response to it; all found it impossible to evade it. Tennyson was first dismayed but then managed to reconcile it with faith. Carlyle fought against it. Arnold was alarmed, Charlotte Bronte (1816-1855) felt horrified, George Eliot (1819-1880) found herself oscillating but eventually absorbed it, and Charles Kingsley (1819-1875) felt as if standing on a cliff, falling into a dark sea. Samuel Butler (1835-1902) wrote a novel, *The Way of All Flesh* (1903), to explore it.

(6) Faith in progress and a sense of earnestness: The Victorians had a very deep faith in progress. The outburst of prosperity brought with it a great sense of

optimism that human nature and society were both perfectible. The people were self-confident and saw themselves working toward some promised end. Society looked forward to continual progress for all. People seriously believed at first that, when standards of living kept rising, they could ignore their problems. Then with time when things did not turn out the way they had expected they would, disillusion and despair set in. Read, among others, Tennyson's poetry of his different phases, and people will readily notice his obvious changes in mood.

Along with the hopefulness came a huge sense of moral earnestness, especially in the thinking people. There was a high feeling of responsibility among them to help solve the world's problems. Robert Owen (1771-1858) developed a way of running a factory with respect for working people and good housing and good wages for them. His idea was that, if people gave people a decent life, people would work hard. Owen did not succeed because of the deep-seated anti-labor antipathy among the industrialists. Charles Darwin devoted his whole life to a work which he had no way of knowing would lead anywhere, which certainly did not give him any money results, and for which he did not know that he would receive any recognition as a scientist. And there were such as Matthew Arnold, Thomas Carlyle, John Ruskin, Cardinal John Henry Newman (1801-1890), Thomas Huxley and the Huxley family, who all felt dedicated to doing something to help people live nobler and better lives. One thing these people shared was that they were not radical, seeking to improving things within the system, and some of them bitterly opposed to any idea of revolution. They were often scathing critics of society, but were also proud of it.

The Victorian period was on the whole one of transition from the past to the modern times, and one of radical change in values, institutions, and doctrines. Old medieval or even feudal ones were outmoded while new modern ones had yet to be established. People growing up in the early part of the nineteenth century keenly felt that something totally different was taking shape. It was an age of confusion and intellectual anarchy. Philosophies and ethical theories competed; different prophets offered their doctrines and advice. Issues such as God or hell, free choice or determinism were being thrashed out. Hope exited alongside dismay, and optimism was colored by anxiety. When Queen Victoria was out of the picture in 1901, the country was set for a future which the Victorians could not envision probably even with a stretch of their imagination. [1]

Victorian Prose

Victorian prose was rich and varied. In no other period were so many great writers writing so much such powerful and exquisite prose at the same time. These included, among others, scientists like Charles Darwin and Thomas Huxley, philosophers such as Jeremy Bentham, James Mill and John Stuart Mill, historians such as Thomas Macaulay (1800-1859) and Thomas Carlyle, and a whole group of religious people associated with the Oxford Movement. As some of these (Matthew Arnold and John Ruskin, for example) are discussed in connection with the issues to which they were immediately relevant, space constraint allows only a brief introduction here of the following three authors whose writings exerted their utmost influence upon the currents of thought of the time.

Thomas Carlyle (1795-1881)

In his lifetime Carlyle was a dominant force in Victorian poetry and prose. His influence extended well through Britain and America. By virtue of his honest and persistent efforts and of his consistent and prophetic vision, he was able to impact the spiritual make-up of his nation. His works were so powerful that they affected a whole generation of writers such as Tennyson, Dickens, Ruskin, and George Eliot. [2]

Carlyle helped form the moral aesthetic of his age and reinforce the feeling that writers should write to instill ideas first. Tennyson, his friend, responded and wore the mantle of prophet of the age. Dickens, who said to Carlyle, "No one knows your books better than I," proved himself to be a different prophet (of sympathy and charitable spirit). And Thackeray assumed the role of "a week-day preacher," "lift[ing] his voice and [crying] his sermon."

Carlyle was an angry man. All his life he fretted, fumed, lamented, and self-tortured. He was not happy with his countrymen for being so smugly complacent. He scorned the outlook expressed in the works of the economists and expressed doubt about the truth of their forecasts.

He had doubts about the idea of progress and the direction which the country was taking with utilitarian materialism dominating social life. He was indignant over the corruption of society and censured his generation as altogether given over to evil. He was furious over the higher classes' mistreatment of the lower and was compassionate toward the poor and the under-trodden.

Carlyle had a sense of mission. He would like to help make his country a morally and spiritually higher and nobler place for man to live. To him the present, with its optimism, its faith in progress, its democracy, and its advances in science and mechanical civilization, was all surface and appearance and was nothing of importance to human existence. The frenzy of worldly exertion convinced him that the people had gone astray, falling into a spiritual stupor or dearth. So he looked to the past for an idea with which to awaken his country from its slumber and bring it back on track with faith and the grace of God. Carlyle found great value in the past, especially the Middle Ages. His most famous works, *Sarter Resartus: The Life and Opinions of Herr Teufelsdrockh* (1833-34) and *Past and Present* (1843) were his obvious attempts to move the nation in the direction he would like it to follow. In the first of these, "Sarter Resartus" means "tailor retailored," and Herr Teufelsdrockh is an imaginary professor. The book was written in two parts: The first is a discussion of clothes which ends with the notion that the external world with its institutions and conventions is basically clothes. The implication is that all visible things are symbols of ideas, the whole universe is mere clothing, and nature is the clothing of God who is present in man's heart though invisible. Man is overwhelmed by the material expansion and the utilitarian monster; true life begins with renunciation. The second part is Professor Teufelsdrockh's autobiography (a veiled one of the author's own), relating his spiritual odyssey from the phase of his crisis "The Everlasting No" to that of his affirmation, "The Everlasting Yea" (these being also the titles of two major chapters of the book). Carlyle's way of addressing the problems of his day was by offering a moral and imaginative understanding. It was basically transcendentalism that he tries to teach. Carlyle's source of ideas came from some philosophers of the German romantic school and the Middle Ages. The book contains plenty of mysteries of Time and Eternity. The doctrines he presents here concern such as the transcendental values of reverence and obedience, the spiritual unity of society, the need for heroes (the true vs. the quack leaders), and the sacredness of labor.

His *Past and Present* is essentially a repetition of the ideas in *Sarter Resartus*. The book was written when England was going through a severe economic depression. Bad harvests, exorbitant prices of bread, starvation wages, unemployment, general poverty, and the outbursts of labor disturbances—all these threatened the nation's wellbeing, and Carlyle saw clearly the handwriting on the wall. In all his works including the ones under discussion here, Carlyle exhibited a warm sense of sympathy toward the poor. His vision was prophetic. Something had to be done, and nemesis was impending. (The idea is basically the one that underpins his *The French Revolution* [1837]). The "past" in the title of *Past and Present* is represented by a medieval monastery and its able leader Abbot Samson of St. Bury Edmunds. In the image and action of the abbot, Carlyle sees the recipe for the ills of the present. The values of Abbot Samson's time, faith and spiritual unity, are the only salvation. The basic ideas here include the author's critical stance on utilitarianism, the supply-and-demand practice, the "profit-and-loss philosophy," the "cash-payment nexus," and the decline of faith as a cohesive force. The book also raises the question of the need for heroes: Abbot Samson was a leader not by election but by virtue of his noble behavior and competence. (Carlyle's consistent call for strong just men or heroes is fully expounded and rationalized in his *On Hero and Hero-Worship* [1841]). Biblical quotations permeate *Past and Present*, all meant to give a spiritual lift to a nation engrossed in its blind worldly endeavor of getting ahead. In the final analysis, Carlyle's cure for the modern age was born out of his own conception, getting inspiration from the past, even the feudal heritage. *Past and Present* influenced a lot of writers such as Dickens (in his *Bleak House* and *Hard Times* for instance), Disraeli (his *Sybil*), Ruskin (his *The Stones of Venice*), and Charles Kingsley (his *Alton Locke*).

Carlyle's prose style is unique in its own way. He never speaks but to amaze his readers and audience. Words roll out as if out of a sense of urgency. His attempt to handle the language so as to make it do the most effective work is both deliberate and successful. His symbols, his use of personae, and his self-projections are among the best qualities of his prose that have caught on. In addition, there is his sense of humor and his irony that help make his writing attractive and charming.

John Stuart Mill (1806-1873) [3]

Mill was a well-known utilitarian philosopher. He has his own special place in the history of English utilitarianism. Although his father, James Mill, a leader of utilitarianism, prepared him carefully for the job, Mill did not quite follow the kind of doctrine that Bentham and his father handed down to him. He saw the fatal weakness of their philosophical position: Bentham did not know human nature well as he denied the validity of feelings and sympathy as sanctions of morality. As a result, Benthamite doctrine revealed a conspicuous lack of feeling and understanding. Mill, independent in idea and action, set out to make the utilitarian philosophy more human and better. As he had a receptive and sympathetic mind, he took some of the views from the school's critics seriously and tried to understand and integrate these into his own philosophical system. The outcome of the effort was a revised philosophy, well humanized to be better able to make its contribution to national life. Mill pushed utilitarianism to its new phase. The world owes the new form of the philosophy to no other but Mill. Mill's revision of utilitarianism is mainly recorded in one of his most significant works, *Utilitarianism* (1861-63)

Mill's emphasis on individual freedom constituted an important part of 19th-century English liberalism. This aspect of his thinking is expounded in another of his important work, "On Liberty" (1859). The essay explains the relations between society and the individual. What Mill tries to say here is this, that society would do well to leave the individual alone rather than compelling everyone to conform to the opinion of the majority. Enforced conformity subjugates the individual who is in fact more important than social institutions. In connection with the issue is the subjugation of women, which Mill personally witnessed and experienced in his love and marriage and felt most keenly about. He explains his unequivocal position on the question in his famous essay *On Women* (1869) and has been seen as a champion of women's liberation.

Although his main area of focus was philosophy, political economy, and political science, Mill had close connection with the literary world of his day and exerted quite a measure of influence on Victorian writing. His thought has offered one approach to understanding the literature of the period.

Cardinal John Henry Newman (1801-1890)

There was, on the Victorian scene, another man who felt that the 19th century was no good and, not unlike Carlyle, would like to lead the age back to a "better" past. John Henry Newman was sure that something had to be done about the directionless-ness of the time. Ultimately he became one of the important leaders of the Oxford Movement (1833-1845) of the Victorian period. Along with his group of Oxford fellows and historians, Newman saw that the Church was in danger. In his and his associates' opinion, the Church was not part of the State nor was it a convenience for the salvation of the individual. It was a divine institution, the Body of Christ. The Movement produced a series of religious tracts, trying to explain the nature of the Church, its historical and theological basis, its fundamental article of faith, its authority, and its independence from the State. They were known as the Tractarians. Newman's contribution was considerable. The tracts were effective enough to win a good number of converts, mainly Protestants, and the movement dominated the Church for a time. But eventually in attacking the Reformation, insulting Protestant martyrs, and emphasizing Roman Catholic ritualism, the movement overreached itself so that it fell into dispute and disrepute. Newman was so disgusted that he went over to Rome to become a cardinal. That happened in 1845, the year that saw the Movement tapering off into history.

The Movement reflected the desire of the perplexed Victorians to cling to the old faith in face of doubt and emotional stress. It was a part of the general and widespread revival of the "corporate" as against the prevailing "individual" spirit of the period. It sought salvation from the spirit and teachings of the Church of the 4th or 5th centuries, and tried to find authority in an age when all authorities were being questioned.

As a propelling force of the Movement, Newman was opposed to liberalism and enjoyed support and approbation. He wrote forcefully and eloquently and made his voice heard. It was impossible to ignore his presence and his impact on his contemporaries. As a religious thinker always in the nick of things, he managed to add to the rich variety and diversity of the Victorian intellectual scene. His major works that concern our discussion here include *Apologia pro Vita sue* (1864) and "Lead, Kindly Light" (1833), and "The Idea of a University" (1852). Newman's prose is simple, sincere, and beautiful.

Chapter 12 Victorian Fiction • Dickens • Thackeray

The Victorian Fiction: An Introduction

In more than one sense the Victorian period was an age of the novel. As literacy improved, more people became readers, and the Victorians proved to be voracious readers. They read both to learn about life and to seek entertainment, and a family often read together in their spare time. The novel became naturally the most popular form of all the literary art. The demand for books was always so huge that novels were often written in three installments, became normally drawn out as a result, and indeed had to be so just so as to meet the readers' urgent needs.

The Victorian novel went through three major phases of growth. The early phase stretched from the 1830s to the middle of the century when English society began to feel the impact of change but still managed to keep the old values intact. Industrialization and capitalism had begun to bring wretchedness into the country, but life had not become totally impossible. Writers who wrote then such as Charles Dickens (1812-1870) were basically optimistic. They were aware of modern ills which they lost no time to castigate, but still wrote with the notion that the world was basically good and could become better. In the mid or High Victorian phase of the 1870s, the country had changed from an agricultural to an industrial nation. Life improved, problems appeared with the progress of civilization, minds became confused as a result of Darwinism, and crises of different dimensions were right down the road. This was a period of dichotomy and high complexity. Writers such as George Eliot (1819-1800) dealt with it with subtle dexterity. She was sensitive enough to portray a moral world in which good and evil co-existed and each received with time what was its due. In her world people felt the manipulation of the forces out of their control, but they still had room for free choice. Although there were evil deeds and evil people, George Eliot seldom if ever drew the portrait of a total villain. Her censure could be ruthless, but her heart was big enough to tolerate. She still had faith in human nature and the goodness of a moral society. However, in the later phase of the period (from the late 1880s onward), dramatic changes had occurred. What had appeared in Dickens and George Eliot as a silhouette of the impending crisis became dazzlingly sharp in the vision of later novelists such as Thomas Hardy (1840-1928). Man became insignificant in a world cold and indifferent and probably Godless. He was impotent in face of the overwhelming odds of fate and struggled in vain for survival. What was in store for him was nothing but frustration and despair if not always exactly death. The age of naturalism had arrived. Although Hardy was not a naturalist *per se*, he stood very close to being one, while George Gissing (1857-1903) wrote essentially in the Zolanesque spirit.

Victorian novels have some salient features in common. They all try to teach as well as to entertain. They are essentially urban, reflecting the values of the middle class. In addition they have the pattern of spiritual conversion built into their textual fabric, exhibit a strong sense of history, and see home and marriage as sacred. All great Victorian novels follow the moral standard: Good triumphs over evil, good is praised, and bad castigated (though *Wuthering Heights* is not exactly in keeping with this pattern). Formally, the city metaphor recurs through them, and so does symbolic baptism. And despite departures such as Dickens' occasional romantic and half-surrealist methods, social realism remains the Victorian novelists' predominant mode of representation of life. The main point of view employed in Victorian novels is the third-person omniscient, the unlimited vision of which helps to paint the broad canvas of life.

The achievement of Victorian fiction was conspicuous and unique as a result of the concerted efforts of the cohorts of great writers working at the same time. In addition to the ones mentioned above, the list is still too long to include everyone. Space will allow room for discussion, in varying detail, of such authors as William Makepeace Thackeray, the Bronte sisters, George Meredith, Anthony Trollope, Samuel Butler, George Gissing, Oscar Wilde, Louis Stevenson, and George Moore. As to the rest of the glistening constellation of Victorian writers, all great in their own way though minor figures in history, space constraint does not allow much more than a brief mention here. One of these was Wilkie Collins (1824-1889), the first detective story writer in English history, and author of the famous *The Moonstone* (1868) and *The Woman in White* (1860). His secret of success, "Let'em wait, let'em laugh, and let'em cry," assuming epigrammatic status, has inspired later writers such as Thomas Hardy (1840-1928). Then there was Benjamin Disraeli (1804-1871), the novelist-Prime Minister, famous for his authentic representation of English life then, lashing out vehemently at industrialism as the culprit for prevailing poverty and wretchedness, and leaving behind his famous "two nations" observation about the existing extremes of wealth and poverty. Charles Kingsley (1819-1875) crusaded for social amelioration all his life and wrote, among other books, the historically significant novel, *Westward Ho!* (1855), which is imbued with rich Elizabethan spirit. Elizabeth Gaskell (1810-1865) came to literary preeminence with her touching, much-dissected novel, *Mary Barton* (1848), left her scratch on history with her vivid portrayals of the social ills of her time, and ended up with her best work, *Wives and Daughters* (1866). Lewis Carroll (pseudonym for Charles Lutwidge Dodgson, 1832-1898) is remembered mostly for his *Alice's Adventures in Wonderland* (1865) and *Through the Looking-Glass* (1872), singularly impressive for their eternal power that stems from an ingenious and powerful imagination. As to Conan Doyle (1859-1930) and his bewitching Sherlock Holmes cycle of detective stories, the people all over the world as well as literary history will forever offer a niche for him. And there was Lytton Strachey (1880-1932), not exclusively Victorian, one famous member of Virginia Woolf's Bloomsbury Group, and renowned in history as author of the epochal iconoclastic *Eminent Victorians* (1918), causing an uproar in its time but offering a paradigm for honest biographical writing. [1]

Now let's take a closer look at some of the major figures on the literary scene of the time.

Charles Dickens (1812-1870)

Dickens came from a poor background. When he was young, his father was imprisoned for debt, and he had to leave school and work in a nightmarish blacking shoe factory. Thus he had little formal education, but managed to make up for the deficiency through avid and extensive reading on his own. Still later he learned the shorthand and became a reporter on parliamentary proceedings. Then he wrote for a pictorial book, *The Pickwick Papers* (1837), which became immediately popular and started him off on his lifelong writing career. Dickens was a prolific writer. He wrote 20-odd novels, not to say the host of his other writings that came out in print. Reading him is always an enjoyable experience. His effect on the readers can be such that they feel instantly that they are in the presence of greatness.

Dickens' career can be roughly split into two broad sub-periods. The first of these runs from the beginning through 1850 when he published *Dombey and Son*. Here is seen a Dickens smiling through his pages. Not that there are no evil, cruelty and suffering, and tension; his novels reveal plenty of these. Think of the debtors' prison in *Little Dorrit*, *David Copperfield* and *The Pickwick Papers*, the poor little boy Oliver asking for more in a workhouse, the starvation of the pupils in a boarding school in *Nicholas Nickleby*, the death of the grandfather and granddaughter in *The Old Curiosity Shop*, the suffering of the little mistreated boy in *David Copperfield* (1850), and the terror of the Gordon riots in *Barnaby Rudge* (1841)—all these offer sufficient evidence that there is a good deal of pain and cruelty in English society then. Though change is just around the corner, the system is to Dickens still good and capable of becoming better. From the end of the first period to the end of his life, however, the readers tend to detect a Dickens pulling a long face and frowning profusely. He becomes more and more gloomy. His mood change has to do with the "progress" of the country toward the barbaric phase of capitalist development. The utilitarian disregard for human feelings and for the value of imagination as represented in *Hard Times*, the ruthlessness of the French aristocrats in *A Tale of Two Cities*, the gross injustice of the English legal system in *Bleak House*, and the ambient gloom that hangs over the prison of the "Marshalsea" (an apt metaphor for England as a whole) in *Little Dorrit*—these are so repulsive and repugnant that the readers have reason to believe that Dickens is sorely frustrated and even despairs toward the latter part of his life to see the country he has loved so much heading toward some ominous direction. What makes him feel very bad is man's cruelty to his fellow creatures. He thinks of his generation as a wicked one. In the first part of his career he seems to have faith in the charitable spirit of human beings, and portrays benevolent characters with warmth and enthusiasm. But as the country moves into the middle and latter part of the century, life becomes worse and Dickens feels depressed. The later phase of his career sees him painting a social picture disconcertingly dismal and agonizing. Works like *Dombey and Son*, *Bleak House*, *Hard Times*, *Little Dorrit*, *Great Expectations*, *Our Mutual Friend*, *Martin Chuzzlewit*, and the half-done *Edwin Drood* are all good illustrations. [2]

The Dickensian world is almost Shakespearean. Dickens' province is the whole of English society of his time, with its debtors' prisons, its law-courts, the new police force, parliamentary elections, government offices, the poorhouses, an assortment of social abuses, and child labor. It is a world thronged with the diverse specimens of humanity: characters that come from all walks of life—the disinherited orphans and street boys, children chimney sweepers, swindlers and thieves, cold-hearted employers, hypocritical philanthropists and evangelists, people as hard-hearted as Gradgrind (*Hard Times*), people as benevolent as Pickwick, people in the process of self-discovery and change like Scrooge (*A Christmas Carol* [1843]), very evil people without any conscience, very good people with no character flaws, and very funny people like Mr. Bumble (*Oliver Twist*) and the Micawbers. It is a world where the readers can get a bird's-eye view of the panorama of English life then: the London traffic, the fog, stage coaches, muddy roads, circuses, waxworks, inns, grocery stores, the steamboats on the Thames, the railroads, factories, slums, the Chartist Movement, and religious agitation. All the different decades overarching the whole historical period of his creative life get their share of description and offer a historical backdrop for his writings. The mood of *Hard Times* covers all the Victorian age. *A Tale of Two Cities* is set in the time of the French Revolution. *The Pickwick Papers* is clearly of early Victorian life. The imprint of the 1820s is visible in *Little Dorrit*, that of the 1840s in *Dombey and Son*, the 1850s in *Edwin Drood*, and the 1860s in *Our Mutual Friend*, to quote just a few.

To gauge the mood swings of this world, the readers in fact need only to observe the way Dickens pictures London. It is his beloved city, one that he can never stay away for too long, and one that is his best source of inspiration for his creative endeavors. If London's cityscape is upbeat and bright such as is found in

The Pickwick Papers, then England is doing good, and the mood of the Dickensian world is happy and hopeful. This is the case with Dickens' early phase of creativity. A gloomy London, with muddy streets and enveloped in fog and soot and gloom such as is found in his later novels, means England is sick and needs diagnosis and medication. That accounts for the increasing severity of his attack on the ills of a worsening society in those writings. So London is the locale for many of Dickens' works. Think of *Bleak House*, *David Copperfield*, *Great Expectations*, *Little Dorrit*, *Nicholas Nickleby*, *Oliver Twist*, *Our Mutual Friend*, *Martin Chuzzlewit*, and *Dombey and Son*, which are all set in this city, and the reader will readily understand why Dickens has so insistently used it as his metaphor for his themes of social amelioration with compassionate feelings and benevolent action. All in all, Dickens offers his readers a world of cheer and evil, a world of melodrama and pathos. To say that Dickens is a social historian is not in fact saying much. As a matter of fact there have been many historians to quote him for support. [3]

The archetypal Dickensian hero or heroine is often an orphan or a child whose parents, though still alive, are as well as dead to them. There is in these protagonists a visible silhouette of young Dickens suffering in a blacking shoe factory or visiting his father in a debtors' prison. They find themselves alone in a heartless world, without family love and any sense of security, ignored by society, and struggling against malignant odds for survival. They go through all the phases of painful growing up, experience repeated defeats, humiliation and frustration, but survive the trials and tribulations of human existence by sheer resilience and the will never to bow to external forces. Dickens' protagonists come close in type to the modern existentialist hero except for their happy ending. They go through the phase of despair, the downward movement to Hell, but manage to come back up. There seems to be always a light at the end of the tunnel. Even though his archetypal themes include dehumanization, alienation, and quest for self-identity—all modern in nature, Dickens was essentially Victorian, and his optimism did not allow him to go beyond the limitations of his age, after all.

Dickens was essentially an intuitive artist. Spontaneity was his trade mark. Even when he became more conscious in his structural planning, he never lost this primal quality of his creative genius. Generally, his early works were more spontaneous than his later ones. Such early works as *Sketches by Boz* (1836) and *The Pickwick Papers* portray a loosely linked series of incidents and adventures without much of a plot *per se* but conquer by their exuberance and vivacity of spirit and plentitude of humor. These novels read as if the author went wherever his pen carried him. Then, with time, probably because his themes became more serious and probably as a result of his improved craft, his writing shows more and more signs of conscious designing in conception, his plot interest thickens even more, and his talent at creating events and situations reveals itself at its best. The plots of Dickens' mature works are always complex and complicated, crisscross with surprises and abundant in grotesquery and melodrama. Dickens is never dull.

Dickens' genius is basically comic. His humor has to do with his happy nature and his optimistic outlook on life and society. One notable feature of his comic narratives is his adroitness at creating the grotesque effect. The grotesque is by definition something odd and fantastic that attracts and amazes by virtue of its out-of-ordinariness. This is produced mainly through incongruous, disproportionate descriptions or odd juxtapositions of things or people or scenarios which challenge accepted perceptions and concepts. Very often literary grotesque portrayals blow things out of dimension so as to provoke laughter at the quaintness of things or people and help the readers see better the true nature of man, life, and the world. Some of Dickens' characters are grotesque. His skill of exaggeration plays a valuable part so that many of his characters appear like caricatures; in such cases the evil is all evil while the good is all good. Such a grotesque person is Uriah Heep, the villain of *David Copperfield*, who looks subhuman with his uneasy hand and wringing body and his underhand scheming. Silas Wegg, the one-legged villain of *Our Mutual Friend*, is also a veritable grotesque. His reaction to the things around him defines him clearly as such: the little dead bird lying on the counter, with its head drooping to one side, or a Hindoo baby in a bottle—all these indicating his evil designs upon the good-natured Boffins. It is good to note, however, that grotesques may not include just the evil ones; the Boffins, for instance, are in appearance and action lovable grotesques. It is also good to note that some of Dickens' places can be grotesque, too, like Miss Havisham's house (*Great Expectations*), dim, smelly, damp, dusty, rotten, in which the center-piece on the wedding feast table offers space for the permanent home of a speckle-legged spider; it is so weird, evil, and deathly. And the dust-pile in *Our Mutual Friend*, which looms behind and above everything, portrays a grotesque image for the England of Dickens' later period.

Associated sometimes (though not always) with the grotesque is the melodramatic, another notable feature of Dickens' humorous narratives. The melodrama is a dramatic form of happy and boisterous farce, normally employed to produce laughter and relieve the heaviness of the main plot. Dickens is skilled in the use of melodrama. His unique manipulation of plot, masking, and disguised identities all conspire to give his works an exceptionally charming melodramatic effect. The incoherence, the medley of characters, the jumbling of situations, and the juxtaposition of diverse classes and backgrounds all serve well to contribute toward the effect. Dickens' works abound in melodramas. The two narratives in *Bleak House*, parallel in plotting, and the spontaneous combustion of Krook, to mention just two out of many in the novel, constitute a good melodramatic construct. So do John Harmon's disguise and the Boffins vs. the Wegg plot in *Our Mutual Friend*, Mr. Wemmick and his pastoral-paradisean castle in *Great Expectations*, the whole story of the Father of Marshalsea in *Little Dorrit*, the Micawbers with their pomposity and enormous good nature in *David Copperfield*, and Fagan and little Oliver thieving in a house in *Oliver Twist*. Dickensian comedy and melodrama never fail to provoke laughter, but the pathos hidden beneath the amusing surface is such that tears often gush out in between laughter. Dickens picked up a good number of these narrative devices from his 18th-century predecessors such as Tobias Smollett (1721-1771), Laurence Sterne (1713-1768), and Oliver Goldsmith (1730-1774).

Dickens is highly critical of his age.[4] Social criticism is a hallmark of all his works. He is supremely human and keenly sensitive to the problems of his age and the plight of his people. As mentioned earlier on, he spearheads his biting attacks toward English law and the prison system. Read any of such novels as *David Copperfield*, *The Old Curiosity Shop*, *The Pickwick Papers*, *Great Expectations*, *Oliver Twist*, *Our Mutual Friend*, *Little Dorrit*, *Bleak House* and *Hard Times*, and one will understand the fury that the author feels and the emotional intensity with which he deals with these subjects. The Court of Chancery, topical for the 1850s, is the object of his acrid satire in such works as his *Bleak House*. The evil of middle class philistinism, of which utilitarianism constituted an integral part, is thoroughly exposed in *Hard Times*. For the ills of the British parliamentary system and the elections and representative government, Dickens has nothing but contempt. Nor does he have any faith and trust in philanthropy and evangelical religion or in any organized social reform. The best testimony of all these is the extensive coverage he gives in his works to the number of social abuses and the misery of the poor; his descriptions are ever consistent throughout his writings. On the other hand, he stands forever on the side of the poor and feels adamant about the just and righteous nature of their struggles for survival. His descriptions of the Chartist Movement and the French Revolution are both good illustrations here.

However extensive, penetrating and scathing his criticism might be, Dickens does not mean to change the system. He cries out within the system like a prophet because he wants to help make it work better and believes that it is capable of improvement. In the final analysis he is not a radical, neither is he a revolutionary. He is a novelist with abundant faith in the goodness of human nature which he thinks is the basis of good life. When things fail to turn out the way he has expected they will, he feels helpless and melancholy. That is predominantly the mood in which he lived and wrote some time before he died.

Now let's take a closer look at some of his major works. As with Shakespeare, there are too many from his canon demanding attention, although we can only in this context discuss no more than a couple of them.

Great Expectations has been seen by some people to be Dickens' masterpiece.[5] The story is fairly simple. Pip, a poor little country orphan, saves a convict, Magwitch by name, and continues to run errands for a wealthy woman, Miss Havisham, to help support the household of his sister and her husband Joe. He falls in love with Miss Havisham's foster daughter, Estella. A few years later, he receives a visitor from London, a lawyer who offers to take him to London for education out of some money the source of which he refuses to disclose. Pip goes and begins to live like a gentleman. When the kind old Joe comes to visit, he feels uncomfortable with the village blacksmith's crude demeanor. Time passes. Then he has a secretive visitor and discovers to his bewilderment that he is Magwitch, banished to Australia where he has made money. When he finds that the former convict is his benefactor, Pip feels frustrated and his great expectations fall away.

Then he has to help Magwitch to run as the man is forbidden to return home on pain of death. In the fight that ensues on the Thames, the police shoot Magwitch, who dies in Pip's arms, gratified to see that the young man has grown into a gentleman with great expectations. The impoverished Pip comes back, recovers his ties with Joe, and unites with an Estella who has been well chastened by her marriage and life in general.

This is a *bildungsroman*, or a novel of growth or development. It tells a story about a young person growing from innocence to experience and from immaturity to maturity. The basic thematic pattern is surprisingly Romantic in nature, i.e. country vs. city, and innocence vs. experience. Like Michael's son Luke in Wordsworth's pathetic poem, "Michael," Pip leaves the country for the city and loses his innocence. His spiritual odyssey begins in the form of a quest for self-identity and for his true father. Eventually he learns humility, accepts guilt, retrieves lost values, and grows up. Pip's experience reveals the spiritual poverty of the time and the terrible moral decline, the cause of which is directly traceable to the 19th-century mechanical civilization. The novel has been regarded as a 19th-century fable, i.e. a young man goes from the country to the city to rise from rags to riches. But it is more than that. What it reveals is so human and so universally applicable that it transcends its time and space and becomes a fable for all humanity for all time.

The novel is carefully conceived. It falls roughly into three sections. The first section (chapters 1-17) opens the story, beginning with Pip inadvertently saving Magwitch and ending with the recapture of the prisoner. Here Pip is all innocent in the country, living with another innocent, Joe, the village blacksmith, and enjoying each other's company in their common plight. The second section (chapters 18-56) continues the storyline, with Pip getting an unexpected offer and going away to become a gentleman in London. He acquires great expectations, refines his manners and tastes, and feels ashamed of Joe's company. The section ends with the appearance of his true benefactor, Magwitch. After an awkward, snobbish beginning of their acquaintance, Pip gets to know the man's genuine love for him. With time Pip responds and learns to love him and fear for his safety. In the night escape that he plans for the man, Pip gets thoroughly wet, which is a symbolic baptism, signifying his regeneration. The second section is set in London, which offers Dickens an opportunity to satirize Victorian institutions and the lifestyles of Pip and his leisure-class friends. The last section (chapters 57-58) begins with his sudden brain fever, falling into a long coma, a symbolic kind of death of "the gentleman" in him, and surviving to face the new phase of his life. He comes back to Joe, recognizes his own roots in the country, sees Joe as the father-figure in his life, and is reunited with Estella who proves to be Magwitch's lost daughter. The ending of the novel is interesting to note. There are two endings: one unhappy, and one happy. Dickens took the advice of Bulwer-Lytton (1803-1873) and made the change from the unhappy to the happy ending. If Dickens had kept to the original unhappy resolution, it would have shown his firm tragic vision of Victorian life in his later phase. That tragic vision, though a bit blurred now, is still visible: the happy conclusion is not really happy. The moral rise is accompanied by a social fall; the last scene looks like Adam and Eve in the lost Garden. As the story of the novel is basically tragic, Dickens' original unhappy ending fits its narrative scheme better.

The novel is typically Victorian. It showcases some of the basic issues that beset the age. First, there is dehumanization that follows in the wake of industrialization. As people vie to get ahead in the world, human nature gets distorted and retrogresses. With few exceptions such as Joe, Biddy, Wemmick, and probably Herbert Pocket, all the rest of the cast display various levels of twisted growth and behavior with little or no compassion but plenty of self-seeking. The social gallery Dickens takes such pains to paint here turns out to be one that defeats his own perception of life. His dream of a better social order built on human sympathy and benevolent action is not happening as he sees his generation turned into a "wicked" one. Then, there is the sense of spiritual devastation that most people in the novel feel. This is well represented by little Pip, brought up "by hand" by his unkind older sister, now standing all alone in front of his parents' grave, "the small bundle of shivers growing afraid of it all and beginning to cry." His is a cold and indifferent cosmos, a stone's throw from the naturalist world of George Gissing and Thomas Hardy. There Pip cries for help, but none is forthcoming from anywhere. The acute sense of alienation, the supreme want of security in face of an unpredictable life, is in fact what affects most characters of the book. It must have been a universal feeling for the Victorians. Next is the quest for identity. People lose it and try to retrieve it. This is a theme not only popular for Victorian writers, but for all modern and contemporary writers as well. Pip undertakes the search for selfhood, and so do quite a few other thinking minds in the book like Wemmick, and in a sense Magwitch and Miss Havisham. As the motives of the searches vary, they end up with different results for different people. Last but not least is the Victorian emphasis on the home and the hearth. The home is the safe harbor for the weathered Victorians; they come back at the end of the day for security, love and happiness. Pip comes back to old Joe's forge, which has been for long his own home. So do so many other Dickensian heroes and heroines.

What merits special attention about the novel is its opening chapter. There Magwitch holds little Pip upside down so that the boy sees the quaint picture of a world just as well inverted. This event is important because it hints to the readers that everything they see in the book should be taken with a grain of salt as it may be just the opposite of the truth. Thus Joe, the village "idiot" in the eyes of the sophisticated London lawyer Jaggars, turns out to be the perfect pattern of the human species; Magwitch the convict is a much better person than all the Jaggars, Havishams, Pemblechooks, and Drummles put together; the "gentleman" that Magwitch would like Pip to become is in fact a snobbish, heartless, vain individual; the "education" Pip receives is what he tries in the rest of his life to vomit out; Miss Havisham, with all her social graces and personal vanity, ends up as the crudest of all womanhood, dying as if "in a ball of fire," an ill omen of going down to hell; and the "great expectations," which everybody, Pip included, struggles to realize, represent nothing but a moral deterioration characteristic of that age. The country village, which Pip has been so eager to leave behind, turns out to be infinitely superior in values to the city as the cradle of a material society. And as to Pip, the boy is not what he appears to be, and is what he is not. His secret self yearns to get ahead in the world whereas Joe is happy where he is. Pip's frequent visits to Miss Havisham's Satis House are ample evidence of his "great expectations" and offers a footnote to the joy he feels at Jaggars' "God-send" offer. Here Dickens shows clearly his disaffection with the direction that England was taking. *Great Expectations* is Dickens' most coherent work. There is no rambling, no discursion, with its first chapter fully loaded with an amount of information that might require the first 100 pages of *David Copperfield* to cover.

The novel is unique in characterization. Joe, Miss Havisham, and Magwitch are all good illustrations. All three affect Pip's life deeply: Joe is an emblem of life, trying to help Pip live a decent human life, and Miss Havisham is a symbol of death, trying to push the young man toward hopelessness and despair. Joe is the archetypal "natural man." His moral integrity, his generous and magnanimous heart, and his devotion and innocence are all the best qualities that make humans human and render life worth living. It is no wonder that he is the measure, the frame of reference, for Pip's "progress" through life. When he alienates himself from Joe, Pip loses his sense of direction and, returning to the forge, he retrieves what he has lost. Clumsy and humble, Joe is the best "gentleman" of all the *Great Expectations*' society. As to Miss Havisham, the most graceful of all in the novel, the rich woman has a heart of stone. All her life she wastes on contriving to avenge herself on her fellow creatures, the male gender in particular, because one of them stood her at the altar at the beginning of her life. Time stops ticking for her from that very moment; nothing in her bridal room has changed ever since. She allows herself as well as her house to decay and rot and hopes to do nothing but spread devastation around. Her hate devours all her life and threatens to destroy innocent lives like Pip and Estella. She adopted Estella when the girl was little and uses her as her instrument of revenge upon anyone of the opposite sex the young lady can attract. Havisham's way of getting back at society is not justified as hers is an isolated case of being jilted. It is devious and cruel as it works havoc with at least two young lives. Although she relents and asks Pip for forgiveness before she dies, the damage has been done, and there is no saving her from eternal damnation. There is also Magwitch, whose personality is painfully ambivalent. The positive thing about him is his sense of gratitude to Pip and his kindness and generosity to the boy as his "adopted son." But he can be seen in another, different, light. He is badly treated by an unjust society and resolves to fight back. He does it through Pip. By making a "gentleman" out of the under-trodden Pip, he manages to savor the sweet taste of a vicarious "getting even" with his oppressors. It is a devious way, in a sense, exacting the innocence of a good person as its price.

Dickens' another important novel is *Bleak House*. It is a great work of art. Two notable plotlines stand out: one concerns the narrator Esther Summerson's identity, and the other relates to her birth mother Lady Dedlock's tragic life. It is really one story in two threads, both of which are slim. Esther, a young woman, lives as Mr. John Jarndyce's ward in his Bleak House. She has been abused in her childhood by her aunt-godmother who is now dead. One of Mr. Jardice's lawyers in the Jarndyce vs. Jarndyce case, Tulkington, catches scent about Esther's mother and traces it eventually to Lady Dedlock, who fell in love when young with Mr. Hawdon and gave birth to Esther out of wedlock. Many people get involved in locating the truth, and one of them, a young surgeon, Woodcourt, falls in love with Esther. Esther falls ill and suffers facial distortion. When the elderly Jarndice proposes to her, she accepts him, mainly out of gratitude. Tulkington ends up murdered, and the famous Inspector Bucket solves the case promptly. Lady Dedlock tells Esther the truth herself and is found dead at the churchyard where Hawdon lies buried. When John Jardyce finds her true love is Woodcourt, he releases Esther. The two young people unite and live happily ever after. The case of Jarndyce vs. Jarndyce ends with the family fortune already all eaten up in the litigation process.

The narrative is complicated, with multiple interlocking threads of plot interest, events that occur in London, Lincolnshire, and Hertfordshire either separately or at the same time, people who live in odd relations to one another, and mysteries that await addressing. The narrative evolves around the stories of the Dedlocks, the Snagsbys, the Chadbands, the Smallweeds, and individuals such as Mrs. Pardiggle, Mrs. Jellyby, Detective Bucket, and the brick maker and his family, with a number of deaths and marriages, in addition to the activity of the Chancery courts and its countless numbers of people. On the whole, *Bleak House* focuses on the adumbration of the alienated interpersonal relationships. If people had the wish to live and let live in one inter-related community, nothing like the mysteries would have ever occurred. With more understanding and commitment, a number of the deaths and tragedies would have been easily averted. But rejection and alienation among the people prevail so that life inevitably becomes mysterious and tragic.

As to the novel's center of interest, it is not always easy to decide. It may be Esther's search for identity, but her doubt is put to rest about the middle of the book when Lady Dedlock tells the truth to her. It is probably, then, the unraveling of the riddles relating to Esther's birth mystery as well as to the murders. When seen in this light, the tangle of events fall in good order, with one leading to the next, which leads still to the next, and so on and so forth, until the puzzle is solved. Truth is let out bit by bit; knowledge increases step by step. One important document in the case of Jarndyce and Jarndyce, for instance, would not have been discovered if Krook had not died of spontaneous combustion, and neither would the complexity of the relations among the Smallweeds, the Snagsbys, and the Chadbands. Lady Dedlock would have lived if Tulkinghorn had not been murdered for poking his nose into a burning secret, and so would Jo, the crossing sweeper, if he had known better than blurt about things he should not have.

Bleak House is Dickens' strong protest not merely against the British legal system, but also through it, as a symbol, against the unhealthy mood of the whole English society.[6] It does attack the Chancery, the inertia of which results in cases lasting for decades and costs the fortunes the lawsuits are fought for as is the case of Jarndyce and Jarndyce, and it does attack the Oxford Movement in its caustic satire on the philanthropists like Mrs. Pardiggle and Mrs. Jellyby. But the novel does not locate the cause of evil in one person or institution as Dickens used to do in his early works. Social evil is to later Dickens no longer isolated, but has become the general atmosphere engulfing the nation. The Court of Chancery should have been the immediate cause of all the troubles and calamities that people in the novel experience and, as such, it is severely censured, it is true, but it is portrayed in a way that suggests that the root cause of evil lies elsewhere. The readers come to realize that the author is pointing fingers at the unwholesome society and its institutions that have poisoned life and the mentality of the people. The novel demonstrates an increasing awareness on the part of the author that the country is traversing a wrong, perverse road.

The salient feature of the book that has caught special critical attention is the way the story is told. As the story is both emotionally charged and extensive in scope, one point of view would have been insufficient to meet the narrative needs. The first-person perspective reproduces the emotional intensity and the sense of immediacy, while the omniscient third-person point of view would allow its consciousness to roam freely through space and time to see and tell all that happens and offer relentless comments. That must have been the reason why

Dickens took this inventive step and used both points of view in the narration of the story. It is true that Emily Bronte's *Wuthering Heights* employs a similar narrative strategy, but there it is mainly Mrs. Dean speaking. Here in *Bleak House*, Esther as a first-person narrator tells only about half of the whole story, and the rest is taken up by a third-person narrator. The two points of view alternate, and echo and correct one another. Although the novel seems to have no apparent center, Esther mostly represents its moral frame of reference for the web of relationships she is privy to. *Bleak House* is one of Dickens' most mature books.

William Makepeace Thackeray (1811-1863)

Although he suffers some form of neglect in modern times, Thackeray was one of the two outstanding early Victorian novelists, second only as he was to Dickens. While Dickens had on him most of the spotlight of his day, Thackeray received considerable recognition as well. He won due respect from many an admirer, and impacted quite a few distinguished writers in his lifetime. He wrote mainly about the upper and upper middle society, but he touched upon the life of the poor in some of his writings as well. He worked hard all through his career and drove himself to an untimely death in the same way as did Dickens. Thackeray's major works include *The Book of Snobs* (1847), *Pendennis* (1848), *Vanity Fair* (1847-48), *Henry Esmond* (1852), and *The Newcomes* (1853-55).[7]

Thackeray has been valued as a great social realist, moralist, and satirist. He differs from Dickens in many aspects, especially in narrative craft, where the two stay wide apart. Whereas Dickens often employs the grotesque and the melodramatic and appears sentimental, Thackeray firmly keeps to social realism and takes it upon himself to paint the immense panorama of real life. He decides that his pen and pencil would do nothing else. "This person writing," he states in the preface to his novel *Pendennis* (1848-1850), "strives to tell the truth. If there is not that, there is nothing." The concern of the novel is to Thackeray solely with real life and real people. "A coat is a coat to my ethics, not an embroidered tunic, nor a great red-hot instrument like the Pantomime weapon," he says in obvious disapproval of Dickens' narrative tricks like exaggeration.

Thackeray was a great moralist. He made morality the topmost of his concerns. As his age was squeamish about certain subjects, he endeavored to conform to social convention and avoid offending the prevailing tastes. He was sensitive enough to know that his century was different from the previous one when authors like Fielding and Sterne enjoyed more license in the representation of life in its all aspects and that his society had little or zero tolerance for anything like obvious references to sexual love in art. Incidentally, he inherited Fielding's social realism but rejected his "immorality," and tried to "defferentially submit to the fashion at present prevailing, and only to hint at the existence of wickedness, in a light, easy, and agreeable manner," as he puts it somewhere in his *Vanity Fair*. Although Thackeray was ambivalent about Victorian inhibitions as he complained about the restraints and limitations in one context, he retained his moral emphasis and desisted from writing what would "call blushes on women." He became a prude himself. And he regarded himself as a preacher crying out sermons for the world. This attitude won him admiration from his readers. One of the preeminent of these was Charlotte Bronte who dedicated the second edition of her *Jane Eyre* to Thackeray, calling him a prophet, "the first social regenerator of the day" to try and put to rights "the warped system of things." Anthony Trollope also had wonderful things to say about him, feeling that Thackeray's portrayal of life was real and offered "good teaching," and referring definitely to Thackeray's notion of a novelist as a "weekday preacher" when he said, "He will be the greatest teacher who spreads truth the widest."

Thackeray's satire is subtle and delicate but effective. He wishes to offer chances for his readers to tell the true from the sham. He keeps his characters under scrutiny so that any deviation from accepted moral values or any antics of theirs will not escape his ironic, critical censure. In fact Thackeray seems to suggest that life is vain because ironic and that, however hard one strives, one may get nowhere and may do better to live a virtuous life. Thus although *Vanity Fair* delineates a successful Becky Sharp, the author insinuates at how much she has lost in the meantime and how much of her true life has been wasted so that the readers may reconsider whether that amount of scheming and self-seeking as Becky's is really worthwhile. The author seems to be suggesting that the woman actually ends up where she would have been if she had gone as a governess after school: she would have made some money, settled in a provincial town, and made herself an eminent public figure.

Now let's take a look at this classic, *Vanity Fair*. The story has roughly two major characters and two parallel storylines loosely related to one another. One of these two women is Rebecca (Becky) Sharp, who is in personality everything that the other one, Amelia Sedley, is not. Becky comes from a humble background whereas Amelia's father is a wealthy merchant. Becky has to make the best of what life has to offer for her whereas Amelia is well taken care of. As a result, Becky is forward, aggressive, and scheming, but Amelia takes it easy and lives at the tender mercies of circumstances. Incidentally, the two major stories about their lives differ from one another in nature. Becky's dexterous designs ensure her steady, successful climb up the social ladder. She flirts with Jos, Amelia's brother, then ingratiates herself into the graces of Sir. Pitt and his sister, manages to get Sir. Pitt's son Rawdon to marry her, flirts with Lord Steyne and George Osborne, becomes the center of attention of all the military society at Brussels, achieves spectacular social success in Paris and a gorgeous presentation at court in London—all these highlight Becky's story of social arriving. Amelia, on the other hand, becomes a plaything in the hands of fate. Her father's bankruptcy, her fiancé George Osborne's divided allegiances, her total oversight of Captain Dobbin's lifelong devotion to her, George's death, her forced separation from her son and, on top of it all, the eventual revelation of George's infidelity—all these and more delineate her tortuous trials and tribulations through a hard life. The two people end up differently. Becky, deserted by Rawdon and despised by her son, manages to set a trap for Jos and realize a large sum of insurance money from his death, and becomes a virtuous and benevolent widow in some provincial town. Amelia finally unites with Dobbin and her son. The novel throngs with minor lights around the two stars. In addition to Sir Pitt, her eccentric sister, Lord Steyne, Captain Dobbin and George Osborne, there are such impressive figures as Duchess Richmond, Major O'Dowa, his sister, Lady Southdown, and a host of others from the aristocrat to the housemaid.

Thackeray wrote the novel with a clear moral purpose in mind. "I am quite aware of the dismal roguery... [which] goes all through the Vanity Fair story—and God forbid that the world should be like it altogether: though I fear it is more like it than we like to own." In the Preface to his 1848 edition of the book, which is entitled "Before the Curtain," he promises his readers that he would ensure that, after wandering with him through the fair, they would go home in a sober, contemplative, charitable frame of mind and apply themselves to their books or business. He would do his best to keep the readers so detached that they would not get involved in violent actions or shed sentimental tears. But he knew well that his world did not have enough patience for him to do anything like real satire. He knew that the same evil and vice existed in his time, probably more than it did in the previous centuries, but people just remained reticent about it. The same evil was done but society refused to call it by its real name. He made to the painful realization that his world had no particular objection to evil, but felt a repugnance to hearing it called by its proper name. The purpose and the awareness of the prudish nature of life in general then would invariably impact the way the novel was written.

First, Thackeray kept afloat before him a larger narrative design than his story apparently warrants. For instance, although it seems to be concerned with the lives of the two major characters, *Vanity Fair* does not deal just with their or anyone's individual lives. In fact the two plotlines tell really separate stories touching on each other only tangentially. People can read one of the two stories by skipping the chapters pertinent to the other, and will not suffer from any sense of serious dislocation in following either sequence. This will not be seen as a structural flaw if people understand that Thackeray's emphasis lies somewhere else rather than on different personalities. It is the broad sweep of life, with all the dynamics and logistics associated with life, especially that around London, that the novel sees as its narrative focus. All individual experiences, however distinguished they are from the rest of the cast, all individual events, however significant in history or otherwise, all people who appear as major or minor figures—all details receive coverage not as isolated and particularized but as indispensable parts of a panoramic canvas that is the Vanity Fair of notorious 19th-century London. Rebecca (Becky) Sharp, Amelia Sedley, the Crawleys, Lord Steyne, the battle of Waterloo, the devotion of Captain Dobbin, the infidelity of George Osborne, Becky's masterful machinations, Amelia's helpless gullibility and gentility, the scheming and chicanery that go on around these people and occurrences—all these and more serve to add to the colorfulness of the author's social picture and spread his sermon to the world that vanity is the nature of life as it is lived and that evil would get its due in the end. *Vanity Fair* censures the philistine hypocrisy and sham of the Victorian society, its snobbishness and vanity, and its ruthless social climbing. Thackeray is relentless on his castigation of the dominance of Victorian middle-class values and tastes, and hopes to help make the world a better one for all. This larger design has its obvious weakness: some characters are not drawn fully and human life is merely based on types.

Then there is the author's silence on a number of occasions of critical narrative interest from which he makes a point of keeping himself detached. He knows when to be long-winded and when to keep his mouth shut. He has his way of withholding information to the anxious readers, and deftly avoids saying the most attractive things in a highly sophisticated and cultural way. No matter how exasperating to the readers such deliberate concealment may prove to be, Thackeray will never budge an inch on his principle. The novel teems with such irritating instances. One of these occurs in chapter 15 in which Becky is secretly married to young Rawdon Crawley. The burning question on the part of the readers is how and when, but the narrator manages to get over it with a statement as tasteless as "How they were married is not of the slightest consequence to anybody." The readers can only conjecture that the marriage is one of convenience for Becky and the result of her own contriving. Another of these is offered in chapter 53, when Becky is found by her husband to be together with Lord Steyne. The question of what happened and whether she was guilty remains forever anybody's guess because the storyteller refuses to divulge anything more than is offered in the text about the "discovery." Whenever occasions of a subtle nature occurs, Thackeray always has something up his sleeves to keep off the inquiring readers. He would say, "Words refuse to tell it," or "[Here] I intend to throw a veil," or it is something "which it would do no good to repeat." Thackeray kept his silence on these morally delicate occasions and matters because he was aware of the squeamishness of his reading public, and he would not compromise himself as a moralist to inflame desires and provoke impropriety.

In terms of narrative strategies, *Vanity Fair* is well conceived and executed. Its basic features include the omniscient third-person point of view, the authorial comments, and the smooth prose of a retrospective soliloquy. First, the third-person narrator as the author's identical surrogate acts like a God-Creator, omniscient and omnipresent, privy to the most hidden part of his characters' soul, and standing on top of it all, surveying all his creation around and keeping everything well under control. Nowhere else in the English novel does the third-person narrative achieve such a superb effect ever since Henry Fielding first theorized about it. Then there is the authorial presence to consider. Thackeray, the wire-puller with his characters as his "puppets" (as he calls them), keeps popping up in the middle of the storytelling process to offer comments on the happenings of the moment. He comes in either as "I" or as "we": "Good God!" he would exclaim somewhere in chapter 29, "how pure she was..." or "we are authorized to state..." in the middle of chapter 47, or simply blurting out, "How is this? Some carping reader exclaims" as in chapter 12. Sometimes he would talk directly with the reader, addressing him as "you" often as if he was familiar with his audience, and betraying to him some confidential information on a character, a group, a scenario, or some gossip or popular opinion going around the social circles of London of the time. His mood swings cover the whole emotional spectrum except for hatred which his generous nature refuses to harbor toward even the meanest specimen of humanity. Thirdly, Thackeray is an eloquent discursive chatter. His novels like *Vanity Fair* read like a long soliloquy, with the author looking around and recollecting, enveloping and submerging all people and incidents in an atmosphere of his choosing. It is in this way that Thackeray's art becomes pictorial rather than anything else.

Thackeray was very much a child of his age. It might have affected his permanence and his reputation. But Victorian fiction and, for that matter, even English literary history would not be the same without his contribution. If people choose to ignore his other works, which is not just to him from any point of view, his *Vanity Fair* has become a world classic and is here to stay: this much we can be sure of.

Chapter 13 Charlotte and Emily Bronte • Meredith

Charlotte Bronte (1816-1855)

One thing to note about the Victorian period is that quite a few women writers made their voices well heard. The Bronte Sisters, George Eliot, and Mrs. Elizabeth Gaskell are some of the most prominent ones. Before these writers there had been Mary Wollstonecraft and Jane Austen, among others, who did a lot of commendable spadework both for the outburst of women's literary creativity and the increase of women's self-consciousness. Some of the Victorian women writers used male names as their pseudonyms. Charlotte Bronte's *Jane Eyre* was first published in the name of "Currer Bell," and George Eliot's actual name was Mary Anne Evans. This may have to do with the skeptical attitude that Victorian men took toward the creative power of the women and their tendency to call an emerging woman writer "another silly woman novelist." For George Eliot, some suggest that she might have been inspired by the French woman writer, George Sand (1804-1876) or may have taken the name from her "husband" George Henry Lewes, the man with whom she set up house keeping in 1855 without a marriage ceremony. [1]

Charlotte Bronte was an impressive presence on the literary scene of her time. She came from a poor clergyman's family of five daughters and a son. These sensitive and intelligent people lived in a house on the northern moors and suffered from the general polluted environment of moor gas so that they were all delicate in health and died ultimately before their time. The children were all gifted artistically and two of them, Charlotte and Emily, managed to leave an imprint on literary history.

Charlotte Bronte wrote four impressive novels of which *Jane Eyre* proves to be the most enduring. Her other works include *Villette* (1853), *Shirley* (1849) and *The Professor* (1857). Charlotte differs vastly from her sister Emily in inspiration and imagination. Whereas she is close to her age in values and technique, Emily goes ahead of her time and transcends it in her concerns. Charlotte quotes her own experience faithfully as her novels all more or less walk directly out of her life, but Emily allows her mind to take wild flights wherever its muses take it. Some say that the autobiographical genius is one of a lower intellectual order, but this is an ambiguous critical hypothesis. If Dickens, Mark Twain, and D. H. Lawrence are all great personal writers, and *Jane Eyre* is still well on top of the best-selling list all over the world, the notion is almost akin to a fallacy. Charlotte Bronte has her own way of ensuring her permanence. *Jane Eyre* offers ample evidence to her power as a novelist.

Jane Eyre tells a fascinating story of suffering, love, and growth. The major character, Jane Eyre, an orphan who stays with her aunt, suffers immensely from neglect and malice of her aunt's family. She experiences a nervous breakdown and an emotional outburst and is sent to a mental institution, where she becomes a teacher eventually. Then taking a job offer as a governess, she goes and falls in love with Rochester, the owner of the Thornfield manor. Their marriage is interrupted by Rochester's insane wife's brother. The sorely disappointed Jane leaves in disgust and despair, almost dies, and is picked up by the pious St. John Rivers and his sisters. Jane finds herself in an emotional tug of war: torn between her love for Rochester and St. John. Then just as she is about to accept St. John's proposal and gets ready to go with him to India, she seems to hear a call coming across space from Rochester and goes back to Thornfield, only to find Rochester's manor all devastated in a fire his mad wife has set on it and Rochester blinded in his attempt to save his wife from death. Jane and Rochester reunite, and begin a new chapter in their lives.

The novel is basically autobiographical. Although she denied that Jane Eyre was like her, Charlotte Bronte did write a good deal of herself into the story. The school at Lowood is some kind of a replica of the school the author attended when she was little where she saw two of her sisters die of consumption. The author's career as a teacher is reproduced in Jane's experience as a governess. Jane, like her creator, never succumbs to the forces trying to manipulate and hold her in leash. The sense of immediacy, the veiled success story of a self-made individual, the regenerating, ennobling power that lies hidden in the deepest recesses of both personalities—all these have endowed the story with eternal charm. In addition, *Jane Eyre* is unique in its gradual revelation of the rich and complex inner world of its heroine. Every incident, centering on Jane's response and subsequent action, is colored heavily by the subjectivity of the forward-looking young woman. She is the author's means of recapping and reliving her own life in a vicarious manner. Hence the emotional involvement that the novel coerces the reader to experience. No wonder that *Jane Eyre* has remained one of the most captivating stories across the world ever since its publication.

The power of the story stems also from its basic features: its characterization, and its description of the intensity of the human passion. First, the portrayal of Jane Eyre possesses an eternal appeal. The resilience of the human spirit and its indomitable nature as Jane exhibits break through the pages and keep its incredible hold on the imagination of the readers for all time. It is capable of awakening a warm echo from general humanity who finds it easy to relate to the book's basic tenets. Jane is neither good-looking nor rich. Hers is in fact the first image of an ugly duckling become heroine in English literary history. She braves life with courage and hope and refuses to submit to the overwhelming odds of negative circumstances. Both practical and realistic, she has, nonetheless, that human zeal and exuberance in her bosom that shines forth the grandeur of the persistent human quest for light through an otherwise ambient gloom until she finds it at the end of the tunnel. Her success story of rising from her poor social status fascinates the readers immensely. Secondly, Jane's warm and genuine passion touches the human heart in a peculiar way. The mutual attraction she and Rochester feel for one another is not so much romantic as it is based on the unique strength of character that they share. Jane leaves St. John Rivers and goes back to Rochester because her love for him never dies; it is a love firmly built on her morality and integrity. It is by the sheer force of her passionate character that she conquers her readers as well as Rochester and St. John Rivers. Just in passing, it is good to mention Rochester's personality, especially when it is viewed along with that of Jane's. He tends to put people off when he first appears, cynical, arrogant, and swashbuckling. There are hints that he may have been a dissolute rake. But to the curiosity of the readers, Jane begins to love him, and the two get close and unite in the end. The readers find to their joy that passion burns under a cool rational surface at the bottom of their souls, and that both exhibit the will to life and happiness and the readiness to meet life squarely in the face. It is the emotional intensity of the relationship that holds them together and enthralls the readers.

The book's formal features merit attention as well. First, the first-person narrative, exhibiting the Victorian intimacy between the writer and the reader, endears the story to the readers. The narrator tells the story in a tone expecting agreement every step of the way. The story, told chronologically, reads like an enchanting five-act play with the different phases of Jane's life well represented in Gateshead, Loowood, Thornfield, Norton, and Ferndean. Each of these chains up with and leads naturally to the next, the links being forged by a subtle amalgam of Jane's passion and reason. Each and every one of these phases constitutes some test of her personality and all work toward painting her full portrait in some helpful way. Gateshead testifies to her undefeatable spirit, Loowood proves her will to success, Thornfield witnesses her capacity for passion and self-assertion, Norton puts her through the ordeal of an emotional upheaval, and Ferndean wraps up the picture, revealing the reenergizing power of her character and spirit. There is a continual atmosphere of suspense keeping the readers riveted on the anxious look-out for what may lie down the road. And all through the diverse periods of Jane's life, there is the single presiding consciousness, that of Jane's, that ensures the unity of the narrative and the totality of its vision and effect. Then, the nature of Jane's emotional dilemma is always unfailingly charming. She is pulled apart between two extremes of the human emotional spectrum: the explosive physical and sexual energy of Rochester and the gentle but equally coercive spiritual sublimity of St. John Rivers. Both offer irresistible attraction, but meet with her rejection. Though St. John's spiritual and rational appeal eventually loses out to the prodigious physicality and the vibrant earthliness that Thornfield and Rochester represent, it is in fact a changed, more balanced, spiritually regenerated Rochester that draws Jane back to the fallen garden of an ancient manor-house. For Jane, reason is in harmony with passion. In the final analysis, this spiritualized earth earthy is for Jane the right place for love. Thirdly, there is the symbolism of the novel to consider. The whole story reads like a fairy-tale. One may call it another Cinderella tale, or another Bunyan allegory. The story is immensely enriched by its apt use of symbols. For instance, the sun and the moon, representing the male and female principles respectively, associate closely with Rochester and Jane, and the two planets meet at Ferndean as the two people do. In addition, the Gothic atmosphere (as pervades Thornfield), the melodramatic elements, the juxtaposing of the prudent with the unscrupulous, and of virtue with sin, and the extremes of religious devotion and secularism—all these serve to help achieve the artistic effect of the novel admirably well.

Jane Eyre is a typical Victorian book. The virtues and qualities that it tries to exemplify and disseminate are all of its age. These include society, family, morality, love, and responsibility. The world of *Jane Eyre* is still a moral universe where God is in heaven and all is well below. There are abuses and manifestations of evil, but man is still spiritually strong enough to challenge and overcome these and comes out winner. Individuals still possess the will to victory, and personal efforts still make a difference in one's life. Family and the hearth are still valued and love and devotion of a romantic nature still exist to enrich and revitalize the human existence. It is a world radically different from that of her sister's *Wuthering Heights*.

Emily Bronte (1818-1848)

When *Wuthering Heights* came out in print, Emily Bronte became the object of mockery and misunderstanding. Even her sister Charlotte Bronte complained about the younger sister's gallery of lost and depraved souls and her inability to put her gifts to better use. In retrospective, all that occurred then was a matter of course. Emily Bronte's book "violated" Victorian values and tastes and spoke ahead of its time. [2]

The novel tells a story of tragic love. Wuthering Heights is the name of a grange in a mountainous area. One day, its old owner Mr. Earnshaw brings home a gipsy foundling to meet his surprised family. Mr. Earnshaw treats the child, Heathcliff, as his son, his daughter Catherine changes her initial attitude of ridicule and befriends the "brother," but his son Hindley makes a point of seeing the intruder as one of the servants of the house. Nelly the nurse is not happy but feels kindly toward the poor boy. Years pass, the old Earnshaws die, Catherine falls in love with Heathcliff, but agrees eventually to marry young Edgar Linton of another farm, Thorncross Grange. Heathcliff suddenly disappears. A few years later, he resurfaces, goes to see Catherine, and revives her old flame for him but torments her ruthlessly, taking advantage of Edgar's sister Isabella's innocent love for him, eloping with her and eventually deserting her. In the meantime, he stays with Hindley at Wuthering Heights, tricks his "brother" into gambling, and encourages him to slide to alcoholism. Soon Hindley loses his farm out to Heathcliff and dies miserably, leaving his son, young Hareton, behind. The emotional upheaval that Catherine is put through proves too much for her weak nerves. It causes the immature birth of her daughter, Cathy, and sends her to her early grave. Isabella ends up giving birth to a weakling son, Linton, sends him back to her brother, and dies. Heathcliff sends his man over to claim his son, Little Linton, and take him back to Wuthering Heights. Over ten years pass, and the younger generation grows up. Heathcliff then lures young Cathy over and forces her to marry his invalid son. Her father Edgar dies in misery, then Linton dies, and Heathcliff now owns the two properties. He brutalizes the little ones, Hareton and Cathy. But he suffers from his psychic wound immensely. He often cries out at night for his long dead Catherine, has visions of Catherine clutching at his windows, and one windy rainy night he decides that it is time to give up and die. Young Cathy and Hareton unite in the end.

The power of the novel comes first and foremost from the psychic complexities of the two major characters, Catherine and Heathcliff. The first impression the readers tend to come away with is that it is a story of revenge, that the maltreated poor Heathcliff struggles and schemes to get even with his wealthy oppressors, and succeeds. The revengeful fire of his love would devour in its flames whoever stands between him and his beloved. He brings Hindley to his knees and enslaves his son. He hastens Edgar to his grave by a series of ruses: upsetting and "killing" Catherine, eloping with Isabella and treating her like dirt, grabbing his nephew Linton away and maltreating him to death, and enticing little Cathy over and cheating her out of her inheritance. Revenge looks as if it was all that the novel is about. The notion has its point, but it is essentially a conventional mode of addressing a mystery, and not tenable enough to explain the tragic end of the man. As *Wuthering Heights* does not tell a conventional story, the solution of the enigma that it presents must lie elsewhere. A host of riddles await unraveling. For instance, Heathcliff never feels happy all his life except those few years when he was a young underdog, and as such enjoyed Catherine's protection and love, and managed to forget his troubles. He never feels any gratification at the defeat of his enemies and never gloats over his trophies. All worldly gains seem to be beside the point to him. He seems to be a perpetual loser. And a perpetual loser he is.

For his is a loss that turns out to be never retrievable. It is his lost love, Catherine. Heathcliff loves her with all his heart and soul. Even when Catherine is confused at first as to who to marry—she loves the "dirty," unkempt Heathcliff dearly at the bottom of her soul, but feels drawn to the gentle, cultured life of the Lintons, Heathcliff shows his utmost patience and waits for her to define her emotions. When she becomes the young mistress of Thorncross Grange, he vanishes suddenly in a fashion very much like Fitzgerald's Great Gatsby, and makes himself rich and hopeful enough to return to reclaim his lost Catherine. When he is not around, Catherine awakens to the fact that she can never live and be happy without Heathcliff. She never feels happy in the warmth and comfort of the Lintons' love and devotion. It is clear that there is room only for one man in her heart, i.e. Heathcliff. The two suffer immensely in their separation. It is only natural that, when they meet again, the intense mutual love begins the long torture that finally kills off the both of them and destroys along the way all those involved in their intense relationship. The novel tries to show that love as a natural force can never do harm except when unduly interfered with. Had Catherine married Heathcliff at the beginning, the evil, violence, and devastation that follow Heathcliff's revenge would never have occurred. People would not have died, life would have been different, and would have moved on for all. The repressive forces on the two granges prove to be both destructive and self-destroying.

The love of the two souls for each other is of a special kind. In fact, people may feel justified in seeing *Wuthering Heights* as a modified, morbid version of the Romeo and Juliet story. Here is a tragedy with two tragic figures, their tragic flaw being the same: One is a one-woman's man, and the other a one-man's woman. Their single-minded love, heroic, elemental, and archetypal, does not allow them to look around. Anyone else would have lived except for these two and people of a similar mindset like Romeo and Juliet. After Catherine dies, Heathcliff is inconsolable: "Life after losing her will be hell!" All the time, and in his last days especially, Heathcliff fervently expects the spirit of Catherine to come and visit him at night. He raves with a gush of grief, "Do come in, my heart's darling!" "Haunt me!" "I can't live without my soul!" "Oh, Cathy, my life!" And he torments himself to a "queer" end. As for Catherine, she identifies herself with Heathcliff. When he reappears after a long absence, she confesses, "The last seven years are a blank." More than once she exclaims, "Heathcliff is in my soul," and life without him is hell to her. Theirs is an innocent, noble, pure love of the highest order, but it is tragic, and that alone explains their tragic ending. For Heathcliff it is finally a matter of "what is the use" avenging oneself on life? And for Catherine, it is sheer helplessness and despair that her love has driven her to. It may be a good idea here to bring in a footnote to this love, i.e. Emily Bronte's poem, "Remembrance," in which the living laments thus for the dead before the grave: "No later light has lightened up my heaven,/No second morn has ever shone for me;/All my life's bliss from thy dear life was given,/All my life's bliss is in the grave with thee." Emily Bronte's notion of love lies behind the poem as well as the novel.

The depth of the psychic world of the major characters leads to the next closely related point of interest about the novel: its exploration of the characters' emotional complexities. Here Emily Bronte's psychological excavations are both deep and extensive. She manages to dive into the innermost recesses of the human soul, find the most clandestine of all human psychic secrets, locate it as a confused bundle of psychic energy, or what Sigmund Freud (1856-1939) discovered at a much later date and defined as "instinctive impulses" or id. Emily Bronte recognizes this as the fountain of all human physical and spiritual vitality, and succeeds in giving it form in the description of the irrational, mysterious, and hidden features of the two major characters. Heathcliff and Catherine's craziness cannot be explained in any other, conventional, way. The intensity of their emotional responses to people and situations would have remained a puzzle. Their capacity for love, hate, and suffering, which often assume superhuman and supernatural proportions, would have been sealed off ever as a closed book to all.

As it is, they appear often as if stripped naked and revealing their native essence to a bewildered world. Heathcliff possesses, for example, that intensity of anger that is almost cosmic, and he is indeed a cosmic figure as his whole being does not show the faintest trace of any knowledge of human values. He hates concepts like "duty," "humanity," "pity" or "charity" and is absolutely disgusted with tradition and morality. He quarrels with God for letting his beloved leave him, and needs no Christian burial after he dies. As for Catherine, she may be a little more human as her education and background may have prepared her for a "normal" life. She exhibits some vague degree of acquaintance with human values and tastes like decency, compassion, vanity, snobbishness, and occasional conformity with accepted morality. But these are by no means deep-rooted and can be—and are often—ignored. When she is her right self, she is every bit as wild and wayward as her surroundings, and goes way beyond the pale of the established norm. Both Heathcliff and Catherine are children of nature, and the novel's frequent and consistent portrayal of the locale with its weather perpetually cold, cruel, dismal, tumultuous, stormy, tempestuous, and mischievous, offers the most apt "objective correlative" for their violent and ever whimsical personalities. They represent, in the final analysis, the archetypal, elemental forces of existence, and body forth emotional abstractions, not the images of ordinary human beings. They are not to be judged in common terms; neither are they meant to be. They are their own measures. With these two dominating the lives of the people on the granges, everybody else is torn between the natural and the supernatural and distorted so that they appear to be perverts and grotesques.

One slightly different way of looking at the story can reveal another achievement for its author. It concerns the nature of the world of *Wuthering Heights*. Here is painted a veritable portrait of an amoral universe. It is a world of man, not of God. Although religion and worship are touched upon such as in the case of Joseph, the ghost of a Methodist minister, these appear to be distorted and even discredited. Nature here is no longer quite as Wordsworth sees it. It appears to be indifferent, self-sustaining, roughly resembling the one that Coleridge first delineated in *The Rime of the Ancient Mariner*. In the meantime, it is the scramble and squabble between human beings that take the center stage of the narrative. Money, class, and love, all these otherwise very Victorian virtues, are presented in a non-Victorian, highly idiosyncratic way. God seems to have forgotten this nook of His world, and there is nothing that can be seen as *the* frame of reference. Thus the readers' own discretion is advised when they pass judgments. Most of the reading public would go along with Nelly Dean, the God-fearing housekeeper, and hate Heathcliff's interference with cosmic justice. But a careful reading will show up a palpable tug of war on standards between Heathcliff and Nelly Dean, and despite the strong wish of the readers to hope for a resolution from which any victory for the devilish Heathcliff would be excluded, the scale of judgment may not tilt toward Nelly altogether. For, after all, it is not about who is right and who is wrong that the author conceived her novel. Matters pertinent to right or wrong belong to a world upon which God still smiles, that of Dickens, Thackeray, and Charlotte Bronte, to quote just a few. Emily Bronte's cast of mind works differently from the Victorian temper. She sees into the nebulous future. She speaks ahead of her time. The Zolan naturalist idea of the amoral universe would not appear yet for another few decades.

In formal terms the novel proves to be immensely interesting, too. The story stretches over a period of thirty years: roughly from some time prior to 1778 when Heathcliff was 16 through 1802, the time for Lockwood's last visit, three months after Heathcliff's death. The narrative itself, however, covers only about the events of the last year of Heathcliff's life, 1801-1802, and fleshes out the details of the previous years' life at the grange through Nelly's flashbacks. Lockwood as a visitor comes to stay in Wuthering Heights and meets Heathcliff. In the first four chapters of the book, he operates as a third-person-narrator and gives the readers some kind of objective description of the country "completely removed" from the stir of society, thus paving way for the later narrative focus on the presentation of the inner world of man. Then he listens as an observer, to Nelly Dean, who takes over from that point on and, except for some interruptions, continues the story with her recollections. Lockwood cuts in once in a while and distracts and diverts her a little, offering some Victorian common-sense comments or asking some questions, but Nelly loses no time to move back to the original thread of the narrative. This kind of narrative strategy proves to be immensely intriguing because of the advantages it offers. For the readers there is the double perspectives of Nelly's and Lockwood's, mutually complimenting, and providing an additional avenue of reading and looking at the story. It also proffers a good deal of leeway for the author to maneuver and manipulate so as to achieve the superb effect of juxtaposing the past with the present and footnoting the behaviors which might have been difficult to understand. Thus things come to light little by little, and people get defined steadily against their backdrop. Another possible advantage the author might be able to enjoy is to increase the alertness of the readers. *Wuthering Heights* tends to create confusion among the readers as to the sequence of events, the ages of the people, and the effect these may have upon the plot movement and the understanding of the story. For instance, a second reading or even a third of the text may be desirable in order to figure out how Catherine dies at her mid or late twenties (27?), Hindley at slightly over thirty, Edgar in the neighborhood of late thirties (39?), and Heathcliff at about 40. The young ones come a generation later, and Nelly is 49 at the time she tells the story. Heathcliff stays away from Wuthering Heights for three years (chapter 9) or seven years (chapter 12), and his death occurs about 12 years after Catherine's (chapter 18). It is often hard to piece these loose threads together and work out a reasonably authentic timeline. But it needs to be done, as these basic facts, gleaned from the non-sequential narrative, are of value to the readers in gauging the extent of the tragedy.

Wuthering Heights has become a world classic. It never ceases to offer something new for its readers. Every reading brings out a new dimension of human self-awareness and adds to the understanding of man and his life. Incidentally, there are many ways of reading the book, and there is not such a thing as *the* interpretation. All agree, however, it is a mine of knowledge, the riches of which demand continual unearthing.

George Meredith (1828-1909)

Meredith was an impressive presence on the Victorian literary scene. He was a prolific writer both as a novelist and as a poet. All his life he kept writing. He wrote mainly about the life of the polite society with some interest in the portrayal of the inner world of man. He was not quite a psychological novelist *per se*, but he edged gingerly in the direction. Like most of his contemporaries, Meredith was a moralist of a kind. He portrayed a world of moral choice, in which man is at least partly in control, and life is still changeable by will. That shows the optimistic spirit he felt about his time. To him effort and exertion are honorable and body forth the highest of moral duties. Courage is virtue and weakness sin. People should take care of their own lives. Three of his novels deserve mention: *The Ordeal of Richard Feveral* (1859), *The Shaving of Shagpat* (1856), and *The Egoist* (1879). The last of these, as critical consensus agrees, is his greatest work. [3]

Meredith's reputation has been through a radical change. When he lived, he was the President of the British Society of Authors, and was respected by all. But now he has fallen. He is not much read and seems to be sliding into oblivion. But he will not. His name as one of the great Victorian writers pops up whenever Victorian fiction is discussed. He is still taught occasionally in college and receives an amount of critical attention however meager it may be. Readers and critics avoid dealing with him because they do not enjoy reading him; people cannot work up enough enthusiasm and sympathy for his stories and characters.

There are some reasons for the popular neglect and indifference. For one thing Meredith is not very easy to read. This is especially true of his later works when his financial security allowed him to ignore public tastes and write as he pleased. Then his vocabulary became more fastidious, his syntax more sophisticated, and his symbolism more deliberate and idiosyncratic. Words used out of context, images and metaphors hard to decipher, the amount of verbal pathos, the obscurity that results from all these and, in addition, the fact that he is not well communicative, as he seems enjoying talking to himself more than he does to his readers—all these can irritate the readers and leave them "cold." Then Meredith lived in a world different from the modern times. Whereas he believed that there was still sunlight, modern life has proved him to be less than convincing. Modern people often feel deprived of their free will and individuality and feel lost at the mercy of the forces out of their control. As Meredith's optimism fails to account for the tragic nature of modern life, people find his message irrelevant to their order of experience. The third reason may have to do with his characterization. The readers do not often see dynamic, vivacious, and endearing characters in his works.

Let's take a brief look at *The Egoist*. It is a story chiefly about Baronet Willoughby Patterne and his wife Clara Middleton. Sir Willoughby is egocentric.

He ignores the devotion of Laetitia Dale and proposes to Constantia Durham. The latter soon finds out his true colors and jilts him. Thus humiliated, Willoughby tries to win and marry Clara Middleton. Soon Clara begins to chafe under the bondage and becomes intractable in due time. Willoughby feels the threat and proposes to Laetitia, who rejects him out of pride. Clara marries a scholar. With this additional humiliation, however, Willoughby persists and eventually wins the hand of Laetitia.

Here Meredith's major theme, the will, is achieved through the delineation of the two major characters. Willoughby possesses a strong self-will. He must be in control. Manipulating others as he wishes and holding them in leash, he imposes his will wherever possible, and believes that he will get what he desires. He feels hurt by Constantia's rejection but picks up no wisdom from the setback. He rages on to bring Clara in his crushing embrace, but fails to vanquish her spirit. Then he pushes on to conquer Laetitia and refuses to give up until his will becomes effective in its scheme. His is a will that enslaves and ensnares and makes life difficult for others. Clara has her own will, too. It seems fragile, but it knows what it wants. It finally asserts and frees itself from its fetters. Like Clara, other people in Willoughby's world do not submit to his or anybody's will willingly. They struggle to extricate themselves from control and achieve self-growth. Thus there is still such a thing like will and choice in Meredith's fictional world.

In terms of the craft of fiction, Meredith tends to talk and tell instead of letting his characters reveal themselves. For instance, he makes frequent speeches in *The Egoist* about Willoughby's thought and action, but fails to place him on stage for him to act out his own drama. As a result, Willoughby becomes a flat character and a one-dimensional image and as such leaves little or no impression after his story is closed. This can be one of the weaknesses that have affected Meredith's permanence.

Chapter 14 George Eliot • Trollope • Butler

George Eliot (1819-1880)

Of the host of Victorian novelists, three stand out as the most eminent, representing the three phases of the period: Dickens for the early phase, George Eliot for the middle, and Thomas Hardy (1840-1928) the late and the third. All three were concerned with life in this world, and all subscribed to the Victorian moral aesthetic, wishing to do good to society. Dickens lived in a period when the world was slowly changing for the better. Though there were problems of various kinds, he believed that human effort could make life better. Basically an urban novelist, he championed the poor and the wretched, and called for benevolent action and compassion. He was basically optimistic though he appeared gloomy in his later works. Assent was there for him. George Eliot lived and wrote in the High Victorian period. Darwin, Mill, Thomas Huxley, Herbert Spencer (1820-1903), and the French positivist Auguste Comte (1798-1857) had been working so that unquestioning belief in God became difficult, and George Eliot became an agnostic. In her time, individual growth became crucial to social regeneration, but no serious dislocation had appeared. People still lived in a moral universe, and they still had a measure of control over their lives. "Life is faced with the labor of choice," George Eliot says somewhere in *The Mill on the Floss*. She placed social classes and individual interaction under scrutiny, and made in-depth philosophical, intellectual deliberations. If one can be carried away by Charles Dickens, it is difficult for a reader to get emotionally very deeply involved with, say, *Middlemarch*, one of the few novels for grown-up people as Virginia Woolf calls it. George Eliot, essentially a pastoral novelist, represents the more sober and contemplative mode of perception of the High Victorian period. One thing that makes her so prominent is the fact that she incorporates most of the 19th-century ideas in her works. She became a great moralist, a great moral force for her time, and a philosophical novelist. Now when Thomas Hardy appeared on the scene after the 1870s, society was going through drastic changes. Life was crisis-laden; people became helpless and insignificant in face of an overwhelming universe. The stance became fascinating to sensitive minds that man is impotent and lives at the beck and call of a malignant cosmos. He tries to assert his will, but meets inevitably with frustration and doom. Tragedy awaits him at the next corner, yet he has no freedom of choice. Hardy tried to find a way to accommodate man in this cold world and make life a little easier for him. Although he was not a naturalist, Hardy did agree, on some points, with Emile Zola and his naturalist aesthetics very much in vogue then. Hardy never gave Christianity his intellectual assent.

George Eliot's major thematic concern relates to individual choices. All her novels are full of making choices, and her plots develop with choices. Exploring the idea of the moral processes which man and his society go through in their development, she studies the classes and individuals in relation to their environment and the effect that their interaction has on each other. It is her belief that the individual has some limited freedom of will and that their choices define their personalities and their relationship to the controlling organic society. There are redemption, salvation, and reward and punishment for good or bad choices. Good choices do good to society and get rewarded, while bad ones do evil and get their due in the end. As she believes that society must function, choices must be measured against a moral standard to see whether they contribute to the greatest good for the greatest number. There is pain involved in making the right choice. People live by the consequences of their actions; the responsibility for a person's life and fate rests solidly with the individual. Individual growth should facilitate social evolution, and morality depends on the regulation of human feelings. Her emphasis on the individual has to do with her agnosticism: she does not know for sure whether there is a supreme being and where the reward or punishment comes from. It is important to notice that there is a strong hint of a broad determinism in George Eliot. For instance, she has faith in causality, "... the seed brings forth a crop after its kind," as she puts it somewhere in *Silas Marner* (1861), and sees heredity as one factor affecting a person's life. All of her major works such as

Silas Marner, *The Mill on the Floss* (1860), and *Middlemarch* (1871-72) keep making the point unequivocally. It is not far wrong to see her as a philosophical determinist. [1]

George Eliot has a big heart. She can be ruthless in her criticism of human foibles and flaws, but she exhibits a high degree of tolerance and understanding. She feels that people are basically not bad, they are just weak, and she has a large-souled sympathy for the weak. She tries not to be judgmental in black and white terms, and manages to leave areas of gray between the poles of the spectrum to accommodate the variety and diversity of humanity. No character of hers is a total villain without any virtue, there is really no grotesque in her works, and it is difficult to find a fussy scene in her writings. Her prose is rich and flowing. As she was fond of painting, her style frequently shows the tableau effect. Her major works include, in addition to those mentioned above, *Adam Bede* (1859), *Romola* (1862-63), *Felix Holt* (1866), and *Daniel Deronda* (1874-1876).

George Eliot has been regarded as a social historian. She sees the presentation of society in all its aspects and with all its segments as a novelist's legitimate province. In contrast to the emphasis that most previous writers put on the description of the lives of the gentlemen and gentle ladies and the middle class as a whole, she writes about the rural scenes of English life as in *Silas Marner* and *The Mill on the Floss*, touching on the lives of ordinary people like farmers, weavers, and other handicraftsmen. Her later works expand their social scope to include the lives of the upper strata as well. The major events of the time and the major ideas of the period all find their way into her works. Evolution, religious revival such as the rise of evangelism, utilitarianism, positivism, and agnosticism—all these and more get their share of space in her fictions. In addition, she writes in earnest to record change. The early Victorian period was so different in everything that the middle and late phases looked as if they were of another age. For people like George Eliot who still remembered the 1830s and the 1840s passionately in their middle age, a kind of nostalgia called them back to the past to contrast it with the present. They often felt strangely inspired by the recollections in their literary endeavors, and found these highly expedient to help highlight the present. Thus many of her works are set in the past instead of being contemporaneous.

George Eliot was serious with her research on society and history. All her novels are propelled by some historical impetus and rich in their levels of presentation as a socio-historical record of life being lived then: forces, classes, mores, habits, and what it means by being a Miss Dodson in 1810 for instance—she takes an immense delight in grappling with minute details like these. Basically, hers is a world where modern life was beginning but still encumbered by vestiges from the past. One way her friend Herbert Spencer (1820-1901), father of modern sociology, influenced her was to move her away from the ties of the past and bring her fiction to face the present. As a result, George Eliot took the novel as social history a step further so that her works edge steadily toward contemporary life. With her effort, the novel won respectability as serious literature rather than a mere medium of entertainment.

George Eliot is noted for her masterly psychological descriptions. In fact she has been seen as the precursor of "the psychological novel." In her intellectual meditations, she looks deep into the nature of social life and man's relationship to his localized conditions. To her the human milieu helps define human motivations and sheds light on the inner consciousness. She enjoys detecting and explicating why people behave the way they do and do what they do. A Maggie Tulliver (*The Mill on the Floss*) must live in her way, stumble through life, and pay for her mistakes. A Bulstrode (*Middlemarch*) must strive to achieve a balance between the two poles of spiritual pretensions and material greed. George Eliot's meticulous, profound psychoanalysis of her characters such as Lydgate and Dorothea (*Middlemarch*) and Hetty Sorrel (*Adam Bede*) is downright impressive. These characters, placed under the microscope, help the readers live through a vicarious experience, pick up wisdom, and become better able to cope and behave. That is an added reason why George Eliot was looked up to in her time as a significant moral force. She was basically a psychological realist. Her achievement in this aspect has won the most sincere admiration from many people. Thackeray, among others, called her the greatest philosophical novelist of all time, bringing as she did ideals, intellect, and philosophy to the novel. Henry James, on whom her influence was considerable, learned from her both thematically and in technical terms.

George Eliot was sensitive to the influence of some major forces affecting

19th-century English thought: utilitarianism, evangelism, and the theory of evolution. As is noted earlier on, utilitarianism was pervasive not only among the intellectuals of the time, but also with the working class. Because of its anti-intellectual position, assigning importance merely to the "usefulness" of material things and actions but seeing literature and the life of the mind as not "useful," it provoked a strong reaction from people such as Carlyle and Dickens. George Eliot's association with the journal, *Westminster Review* (founded by John Stuart Mill), first as contributor and then as assistant editor for some two or three years, helped her embrace the quintessential utilitarian principle of "the greatest happiness for the greatest number." Her kind of moral choice was in fact judged in keeping with the utilitarian tenet. As to evangelism, George Eliot was educated in an evangelical school. Evangelism advocated good works, charity, proselyzing, and building hospitals, orphanages, and working men's colleges. It was also instrumental in making the age prudish with its sexual inhibitions and hypocrisy. In presenting evangelism as an intrinsic element of life in her fictional world, she is ambivalent in her attitude: she juxtaposes its religious conviction alongside its shows of hypocrisy of which she loses in no time criticizing. In addition, George Eliot was not indifferent to Darwinism and the philosophy of Spencer's social Darwinism, the belief of "the survival of the fittest." Neither was she to agnosticism which says that nothing is known and can be known about the existence of God. Herbert Spencer might have influenced her heavily in that she became an agnostic (Spencer being a great agnostic). George Eliot was sensitive to Wordsworth's influence, too, especially in regard to the pastoral nature of her works, her views on nature, and childhood.

George Eliot was not very happy with her personal life. She was homely, though with plenty of will and brains, and no one seemed to want her. Her friendship with Herbert Spencer did not develop into a meaningful relationship. Her life with George Henry Lewes was the happiest of all her life and career but he died ahead of her. She did not see her life as a tragedy, but as one out of her control. She said on one occasion that the best a woman can do is to be a wife and mother, and this explains the happy ending for her women characters, who mostly either marry or become dependent on men. The way she handles women's dilemma is exquisite and has won respect and admiration from the feminists. It may be interesting though irrelevant to mention that George Eliot is not always kind and just to pretty women: they appear to be silly and frequently get into trouble. Her heroines are not exactly ugly, but provocatively intriguing. Maggie is a case in point, and so is Dorothea who, though pretty, is often thought of as odd. In formal terms George Eliot was a conscious literary artist. Her works show superb conception and execution. She is considered to be the most pre-eminent novelist in the mid-Victorian period. [2]

Let's take a look at some of her major works.

The Mill on the Floss tells the tragic story of a brother and a sister. The Tullivers have two children, Tom and Maggie. The family owns a mill but loses it out to the Wakens. There is bad blood between the families, but Wakem allows the Tullivers to continue to operate their business for him. He has a son, Philip Waken, studious and artistically gifted, but physically disabled. He is a dwarf with a stunted body. Maggie, an ugly duckling when little, grows up into a shapely young woman. She falls in love with Philip, but Tom firmly disapproves of the relationship as he sees it as degrading to the family. The two siblings become alienated. Maggie meets Stephen Guest, her cousin Lucy Dean's fiancé and agrees to spend a day together with him. Boating down the river with him, Maggie ends up compromising herself in the eyes of others. Tom is furious and drives her out while the rest of the community shuns her company. Over the years Tom has been working hard to regain the family business, which he eventually does. Then a flood occurs and submerges the mill with Tom stranded in it. Maggie rows frantically over to save him. The two meet, patch up happily, and die together in each other's arms. [3]

The Mill on the Floss is autobiographical in a sense. Maggie attending an evangelical school and her alienation from her brother are both direct quotations from the author's own life. George Eliot attended one such school at 13 and infuriated her brother later in life when she started keeping house with George Henry Lewes without a formal marriage ceremony. She may have written the novel to please her brother and offer reconciliation with her apology.

The characterization of Maggie and Tom reveals George Eliot's mature craftswomanship as a conscious literary artist. Maggie is a token of George Eliot's success in creating one of the full-scale heroines in the English novel. The girl is described to be more like her father, proud and obstinate, "that pitiable, furious bull entangled in the mesh of a net." Life seems to her to be always a suffocating straitjacket. As a child she is dusky, obdurate, and often offensive. She is not well liked, and is intensely unhappy for it. George Eliot devotes generous space and care to excavate the complexities of her inner world. She cuts short her hair and makes a freak of herself out of spite, thrusts pins in her doll, forgets to feed the rabbits, and experiences the impulse to push Lucy into the mud. But she grows up, lovely, spirited and vibrant with a dusky kind of vigor. She is emotional, high-strung, and artistic and poetic in tastes, hungers for admiration, but fears ridicule. She is susceptible to music, bonds with Philip who knows it is more out of sympathy than love (chapter 36), and always loves and adores her brother. But Tom forbids her to see Philip and makes life impossible for her (chapter 37). Always feeling the constraints, she looks like a lovely wild animal, a confined white bear, a pony, emotional and impulsive, a sheep with a long tail (which is a symbol of her Tulliver keenness being useless), a spider suffering the pain of exclusion, and a young lioness, spirited and untamed. Maggie is natural in her responses, but with the restrictive influence of St. Ogg's society, she is losing her native endowments. Life is so dreary and humdrum that there is not much that Maggie can do but dream and romanticize herself out of it (chapters 32, 52). She desires to live a larger life with music, books, and beauty, within a system spiritually nobler and higher. There is a faint hint, as is offered at the beginning of chapter 30, that Maggie may not be one of the fittest to survive in the back-moving society of St. Ogg's. The current of the time is philistine and worldly, and she is obviously out of tune with it.

Tom is different. He is said to be more like his mother. His mind is conventional and works with numbers rather than with imagination and feelings. He honors respectability and fits in with the Victorian system of values. His life is an emotional vacuum: there are no women in his life. Eager for success and social arrival, he conforms, craves for approval, and works hard. Rigid, insensitive, and capable of cruel behavior, he regards Maggie as weak and perverted, and treats her ruthlessly. Exercising a repressive pull over his sister, he is relentless enough to drive her out of the house after her boating incident with Stephen. He shows little or no sign of warmth and understanding for Maggie, and indeed he has none in him. His heart seems hardened, either as a hereditary trait, or as a result of seasoning by the cold reality of life.

The contrast between the two siblings inspires dramatic interest. They represent the antithesis between two important faculties of the human mind: the imaginative and the rational. Maggie is all passion, imaginative and instinctive, but Tom is all common sense, rational, and practical to a fault. Maggie is impulsive and spontaneous in her thought and action; Tom plans and schemes and calculates every step of the way. Maggie lives in her mind; Tom flows with the world. Maggie follows her own measure; Tom follows society's. Maggie lives for herself; Tom lives for others. Maggie brings "dishonor" to the family; Tom brightens its blackened image. Maggie is the object of ridicule since childhood; Tom always wins the admiration of all around him. The comparison can go on and on. The contrast may serve to make a statement about Victorian life, that society encourages conformity and censures dissent, that it values social arriving and despises uniqueness and difference, and that the life of the imagination is useless, outrages public taste, and "brutalizes" social taste in general.

This contrast may also reveal the author's ambivalence. On the one hand, George Eliot admires Maggie for what she is, her whims, her daydreams and fantasies, and her asceticism and self-renunciation. The author's sympathies here cannot be mistaken. She may seem not to like Maggie's choices for which Maggie pays dearly, and may not approve of Maggie's neglect of duty, which is a very Victorian virtue; but she believes Maggie is equipped morally to put things to rights. After all, Maggie is the center of her attention, and the novel tells more about her than about Tom or anybody else. The one image that the readers tend to come away with after reading is essentially that of Maggie's. However, the common readers of all time, less to say the Victorians, seem to be more interested in Tom's success story. They watch Tom more closely just to check out how far he has succeeded in getting the family business back. They tend to identify with Tom more than they do with Maggie. Tom's values are more in agreement with his time. As to Maggie, she is her own point of departure in life. She loves Philip because they both share the same interest and attach importance to the life of the mind. But Philip is presented as a dwarf, less than whole in the ordinary minds of the people, with something missing, something that would make life worth living. The common response to a blossoming comely Maggie falling in love with a deformed Philip is generally negative as Tom sees it. In addition to the fact that Maggie is in love with her family's "enemy," most readers would sigh heavily with "What a waste!" All this negativity stems from the narrative itself. But the end of the story is death-rebirth for both brother and sister. The scene has been seen as one of redemption through baptism. The implication is that both have sinned and both have been saved and reborn. The question would be, who has sinned against what, and in what way? George Eliot may have had the Victorian disapproval of art and imagination in mind in her painting of the two portraits. Her novel may have been an indication of her divided allegiances to her moral aesthetic and her private vision as a writer, as indeed was the case with most Victorian writers.

The contrast between country and town is also loaded with meaning. The mill on the river as a symbol offers food for thought. The country in which it is located, the mill itself, and the Tullivers, with the smells, sounds, the colors, the landscape, and the fauna and flora—all these receive adequate, detailed descriptions. The opening chapter of the book is famous for its painting of the setting, all nature, all harmony, with no human trace, the Floss flowing peacefully by, fertilizing and life-giving. The care, with which the author chooses the mill and the Tullivers, illustrates her backward glance at the past and her longing for a way of life that has been but is no more. It is a pastoral, emotional life of the good old days that the author still cherishes in memory and yearns for but knows that it is on its way out never to return. The flood of industrialization, the progress of materialism, is raging forward, with its irresistible tide ready to wash out all in its way and dump it into history. On the other hand, as a counterfoil to the country, there is the town of St. Ogg's, complacent and domineering as delineated in the opening of Book IV. Its middle class is invincible. The Dodsons, the Gleggs, and the Pullets are taking over the control of the world. They embrace the work ethic, have faith in diligence and struggle, worship money, and see the world as theirs for the conquering. And they lose no time doing it. St. Ogg's with its dominion is a well-organized society with its rigid self-righteous values, always ready to jump at any deviations from their norm and lash out against dissent. Dull in mind and spirit, and utilitarian and anti-intellectual, St. Ogg's offers no room for the life of the imagination, and readily smothers any tendency toward natural, emotional responses to life. The

Tullivers, including Tom, clinging to the mill and the rural tradition it represents and moving against the flow, are fighting a hopeless battle. Tom is confused and can not catch up with the age; Maggie is too fragile for it. They are a bunch of losers, out of step with a world in which they are found unfit to survive. They must go, and go they did. George Eliot's attitude is clear. She shows little or no feeling for the Dodsons and their like-minded victors and survivors. But she has an abundance of love and compassion for the Tullivers. *The Mill on the Floss* is a tragic book about the tragic lives of people made tragic by their time. Historically it is inevitable. The novel manages to keep the tragedy on record for posterity.

Now *Middlemarch* has been seen by some people as George Eliot's masterpiece, and rightly.[4] It represents the Victorian realistic rather than emotional response to life. The story is set in an early 19th-century fictional English provincial town—Middlemarch. The main plotline concerns Dorothea Brooke's life, especially her marriage to the middle-aged scholar Mr. Casaubon. She marries him out of respect and love, but her exuberance is thwarted by Casaubon's "devotion" to his research and singular want of emotion. Casaubon's young cousin Will Ladislaw befriends Dorothea and the two fall in love. Casaubon adds a codicil to his will before he dies that his wife will lose her fortune on marrying Will Ladislaw. But the two manage to get united in the end. In addition to the major plot, there are four other complimentary storylines developing in a loosely interlocking manner. These include the stories of young doctor Tertius Lydgate whose aspirations for scientific progress fail to materialize as a result of his marriage with the materialistic-minded Rosamond Vincy; the tale of old Mr. Featherstone, leaving nothing at death to his impatient expectant relatives; that of Fred Vincy in love with Mary Garth; and that of a banker, Bulstrode by name, who is torn between his immoral business ethics and his religious spirit. The keywords for the novel are in a sense "egoism" and "frustration."

Middlemarch offers a panorama of social life. Although subtitled "A Study in Provincial Life," it is meant to be a miniature of 19th-century English life. Here the town booms, bustling with activity, and going onward toward a hopeful future. Its spectrum of life is complete with all shades of feeling, all kinds of people, and all patterns of behavior. There is the aristocratic stock from which Dorothea springs, a family where no one has been lower than an admiral. There are the

Vincys, the world of manufacturers, with chemical dyes and other products. The Calebs toil with hands; lawyers, doctors, and bankers work with their brains. Virtue coexists with vice. Anachronistic pseudoscience lingers alongside the cutting-edge research of the day. All the segments of society interact; all the people mix and juxtapose. There are people who talk, and there are those who act. Some are innocent and anxious to do good, and others set their minds on scheming for self interest. Warm feelings and generous public spirit contrast with mean aggressive social climbing. Mayor Vincy and his middle class are in firm control, the professionals like Lydgate are rising in prestige and status, and philanthropists such as Bulstrode are experiencing the pricks of conscience. Marriages are contracted and dissolve like the Casaubons. Women are on the watch for a suitable husband like Rosamond Vincy. Countless constellations revolve around the shining stars. Life is vividly lived and characters of blood and flesh walk out of the pages to face the readers and audience. The novel is altogether a superb demonstration of George Eliot's solid realism.

The main plotline centers on the marriage of Dorothea to Casaubon. The general impression of the union of the two is repugnant because they are so different and incompatible. Dorothea is a blooming young lady, vivacious and vibrant, and expectantly standing at the threshold of life. She is warm-hearted and anxious to make herself useful to society (chapter 7). Keeping social duties topmost in her mind (chapter 10), she is in essence an idealist with great and noble plans destined to fail because of their defects and her short-sightedness. Casaubon, the middle-aged bookworm, cold, deplete of energy, physically repulsive, essentially selfish, working on something anachronistic and good for nothing, does not deserve her in any conceivable way. In the eyes of common readers, Dorothea's admiration for his research is girlish and ignorant, and her acceptance of his proposal is ridiculous and revealing of her immaturity in judgment. All these responses can be understood, but George Eliot offers a reason for everything that happens in her fictional world. Dorothea sees in Casaubon's research something important for society and fancies that she can help the man do it well. As she is an intellectually-thinking person, she enjoys the company of intellect and like minds. She feels such awe and wonder for Casaubon as if she was in the presence of greatness. For her, work always comes first, and she is ready and willing to do academic errands for Casaubon even during their honeymoon in Rome. But Casaubon has no use for her; his work on mythologies or mythography, which sounds grandiose, is in fact an attempt to hide his feeling of personal failure in life (chapter 21). It is rational to conjecture (as George Eliot is conveniently silent on the subject) that Casaubon is impotent and has no virility. Dorothea despairs. Theirs may have well been an asexual marriage, which is hard for the healthy and sexually sensitive girl. Thus she experiences a sexual and emotional crisis even in her honeymoon in Rome and feels relieved and happy to see Will Ladislaw. Her marriage with Casaubon slides toward an inevitable miserable disintegration. Her union with Will will not happen for some years to come yet, as Casaubon dictates in his will that Dorothea will lose her inheritance the moment she marries him. But it will eventually.

Lydgate and his wife Rosamond are further specimens of people worth careful analysis. Lydgate is a promising professional, devoted to his medical research. He sees social good and intellectual conquest as one, and represents the advance of science of his age (chapter 15). His hypothesis on cells fails for a couple of reasons. First, it has to do with his wife's manipulations in which she apparently overreaches herself. It is also because the research is too soon for his time; his microscope is not good enough yet for his experiments. The failure is not personal, but rather a result of the historical limitations. His setback is therefore not a real one as far as the future is concerned. Lydgate and Rosamond make an interesting pair, so different in personality and intentions. Lydgate aims high in life. He is an idealist and possesses some endearing kind of grandeur like Dorothea. He thinks he can make a difference, and is a typical Victorian example of earnestness and hard work. He is human and naturally has some spots of commonness about him. Rosamond, on the other hand, has only her self interest to consider. She is shallow, without depth, but somehow a remarkable presence in the town, not really negative or evil in any way. She is the archetype of the middle class.

Then there is Bulstrode to consider. Here is a psychic complexity which any easy answer may fail to explain well. The man leads two distinct lives, and every detail of his story vibrates with two distinct notes. On the one hand, he is the pious, evangelical wealthy banker of the town, respectable and influential, while on the other, his personal history is shady and sleazy and vulnerable to exposure. Bulstrode is encumbered by his past. Along with his fellow sinner John Raffles, he deviously robbed his boss—Ladislaw's grandfather's fortune by marrying the man's widow and thus stealing the money from its more legitimate heiress—Ladislaw's mother. As to this fortune, Ladislaw's grandfather made it by foul means, which was an act of evil Bulstrode helped to execute. Now that he is in a position of power, Bulstrode does some good, but cannot reveal his notorious past. Now John Raffles resurfaces and threatens to expose him if his blackmail of Bulstrode fails. Bulstrode pays him to stay silent. Thus Bulstrode is a religious hypocrite. His reflections on his past are worded in such a way that there is obvious self-pity, fear, and repentance, which inspire mixed responses from the readers: There is, always in close proximity, contempt alongside commiseration for him. Raffles' death is a mystery, which is designed to leave the readers in doubt as no one would have any means of getting to know whether Bulstrode is ever complicated in it. The readers' ambivalence to him is actually the effect that George Eliot would like to produce by her portrayal of the man. Bulstrode is a typical George Eliot character in this, that he does the devil's work, but is not exactly a devil; he is by no means "an eminent Christian," but is not quite a religious hypocrite, either. He excites contempt, but arouses compassion. At once an egoist and an idealist, he represents human unpredictability in a fashion comparable to Shakespeare's Claudius and Macbeth. The creation of Bulstrode is well in line with George Eliot's aesthetics, which places emphasis on increasing understanding of and enlarging sympathies for the struggling erring humanity.

Anthony Trollope (1815-1882)

Trollope came from a lawyer's family. His mother was the famous feminist Frances Trollope (1780-1863) who went to America, made tons of money and lost it and went broke. She came back to London to write a book, *Domestic Manners of the Americans* (1832), which became a smash, made lots of money, and launched her as a writer. She wrote for money and became notorious so that Thackeray refused to meet her at parties and her son Trollope wished her to stay at home. She died a rich woman in Florence. The son emulated the mother. [5]

Trollope was one of the three preeminent mid-Victorian novelists, the other two being George Eliot and Meredith. He wrote 65 novels, of fairly constant quality, some of which form the well-known Barset series. The series is a number of interlocked novels relating to the life of one particular region, such as *The Warden* (1855), *The Barchester Towers* (1857), and *The Last Chronicle of Barset* (1867). The interesting thing to note about Trollope is that there is little relation between his own life and his works. This means that the man had a very rich imagination good at making plots and drawing portraits. He wrote mainly about the life of the middle or upper middle class.

Trollope's reputation suffered not a little even in his own day. This was in fact very much his own doing. For one thing, he was over-prolific so that critics tended to take him for granted and assumed that his books could not be all great. Secondly, he was over-modest, with little or no pretences at intellectuality, conceding to Thackeray as the greatest novelist, and content to take the back seat and thus seen as a second-rate writer. The third cause for his slight was probably that he overreached himself in writing his *Autobiography* (1883), in which he discloses, rather to the dismay of his admirers, that he considers writing a business. He gets up at dawn and writes for three hours at the speed of 250 words a quarter of an hour and, then calling it a day, spends the rest of his time traveling or doing whatever catches his fancy. Moreover, he says frankly that he writes for money, brags that he has made over 70,000 pounds by 1879, and attaches a list of detailed accounts of his expenses. In addition, he could write anywhere he went. He always carried with him a portable desk, and was ever ready to write. Henry James was deeply impressed when he traveled once across the Atlantic together with Trollope and saw the latter sit and write intently on the violently rocking deck against the backdrop of a roaring ocean. On another occasion, Trollope was staying in a hotel where, amid the din of the boisterous hotel guests, he sat down beside the fire and wrote and eavesdropped at the same time. It is recorded that once one of those guests accused Trollope of allowing one character (Mrs. Proudie) in and out of his books and, on hearing this, Trollope moved closer and said in all seriousness to the man that that person would die next week. And sure enough he arranged for the character to die in his next week's installment of his serialized novel. Thus he left behind him, for decades after he was gone, the wrong impression to his contemporaries as well as critics that he had no muse and little art in him and his writing was mechanical and uninspired.

But the impression may have been fallacious. For Trollope's works have a power and a fascination that is not of the mediocre order and not to be dismissed easily. Indeed, his reputation rose in the 20th century. He was read in times of trouble, chaos and confusion, especially during and after the Second World War. He has been popular ever since. It is said that, in numbers of readers, he is second only to Dickens today. The reason for the resurrection is to be sought first in the basic spirit which his novels reflect. Trollope was sensitive to the *zeitgeist* of his time. He wrote at the time when England enjoyed its phase of stability and prosperity, and he successfully caught the basic feature of life then—order and peace—and brought it out in full for his readers to appreciate. This is what human nature always desires. In addition, his comeback has to do with his creative mind. It is not very fair to dismiss Trollope as purely pecuniary in his literary efforts. To write at 250 words a quarter of an hour is easier said than done. There must have been sufficient time of conception before execution. Trollope's mind must have always been fervent in a boil, busy weaving plausible and intriguing plots and subplots. Although he is essentially not a symbolic writer, his imagination sees pictures and images in places and people and events and tries to piece them together in a realistic way. Trollope claims that he wrote novels through characters, not plots. The readers cannot mistake the fact after reading him that the man knew his business, knew his characters well, knew their locales of life well, and knew their situations and relations well. He did not feel too much need to "make" and plot his stories (although there is subtle, natural plotting and sub-plotting). He did not have to plan ploys (although there is conscious planning and employment of effective ploys). The truth of the matter is that Trollope knew life well. He seemed to have at his fingertips every detail of human existence and a smattering of everything about the life of his age. His mind was adept at digesting reality and representing it in the best possible way. He had also an accurate eye and a keen appreciation for human nature. Put in a nutshell, he possessed the essential qualities that matter most in artistic creation: experience and acumen. Finally, there have been the devoted efforts of modern and contemporary scholars trying to rediscover him. His biography (by Michael Sadleir) came out in the 1920s, and scholars such as Ruth apRoberts, Robert M. Polhemus, and J. R. Kincaid, and the journal, *Trollopian* have all done their best to reconnect him with the readers.

One major feature of Trollope's works is that, unlike most Victorian writers, he was probably the only writer of that period who did not set his stories in the past. He tried to paint a panorama of contemporary life. All his major novels are contemporaneous, almost day to day, from fall to winter to spring and, at most, going five years back in their timeframes. Another fact that sets him apart from his fellow novelists is that he focuses on representing all men and manners of his time, in a way closer to Jane Austen than to Thackeray. Yet another feature of his art is his repeating characters, a trick that he might have picked up from Thackeray. This gives those characters an extra dimension of actuality and vitality, and endows his regional series of novels with a strong sense of continuity and coherence. Furthermore, a typical Trollope story begins with a problem and goes on to fill the book with characters peripheral at first and having at times little or nothing to do with the main plot or character, and then the central event occurs that brings out the major people and puts all, main or minor people and plots in proportion and perspective. He also insists on the use of ordinar, rather than heroic, types as his main characters. Trollope is not quite exactly ironic in sense or tone.

Trollope was a serious literary artist. He was every bit as motivated as were Thackeray and George Eliot. He holds that novelists must teach and spread the truth widely. To him a novelist with any conscience and art at all must preach earnestly as does the clergyman. He admired Thackeray for having kept "barking at the vices and follies of the world around him," and "crying his sermon" as a week-day preacher. Trollope's novels are highly moral.

Now let's take a brief look at some of his major works.

Trollope's best-known novel is the second of his five-book Barset series, *Barchester Towers*. It mainly relates the story of an ecclesiastic struggle between the clergy of the Barchester area. The fight is complicated by the courtship of a rich widow and the people around taking sides. As the story goes, the wardenship of Hiram Hospital is vacant, and two people try to get it. One is the former warden Mr. Harding, and one is Mr. Quiverful, a gentle clergyman. Mrs. Proudie leads one side of the scramble with the help of Mr. Slope, and Archdeacon Grantly champions Harding's cause. In the end Mr. Quiverful gets the post, but Harding is given the Deanship of Barchester Cathedral. His daughter, Eleanor Bold, has two suitors, Mr. Francis Arabin and Mr. Obadiah Slope. Eleanor accepts Mr. Arabin and rejects Mr. Slope. The latter leaves for London in disgrace.

The novel demonstrates Trollope's rich knowledge of the clergy and his deep understanding of human nature. Trollope discovered a mechanism to write about the clergy. Although he admitted that he did not know more about this segment than any ordinary churchgoer, he was good at learning about them as part of his preparation for his creative endeavor. Trollope knew everything about this religious group. The struggle around the wardenship of the Hiram Hospital is fueled actually first by the sectarian differences between the High Church, the more orthodox Catholic sect of the Anglican Church, and the Low Church, the sect that opposes Catholic ritualism and in favor of evangelicalism. Mr. Harding, Archdeacon Grantly, and Mr. Arabin are High Church people who would like to see one of them get the preferment. Bishop Proudie, his overweening wife Mrs. Proudie, and chaplain Slope are all of the Low Church, and would support their candidate by all means. It is worthy of notice that Mr. Slope's first evangelical sermon at Barchester Cathedral alienates him from most of the people in that chapter and paves the way for his eventual humiliation. Seen from a different perspective, the confrontation assumes a new, different stature. Slope is a sleazy city person with his London vanity while the Grantly group are conservative rural folk. City or country, the segment of clergy is portrayed as a group of ordinary humans, which indeed they are, no more and no less. Mrs. Proudie, the self-styled pillar of the Church principles, is the most worldly of all in Barchester. Mr. Slope is an egocentric, opportunist social climber. Harding is serious, Quiverful comic, and Bishop Proudie pathetic. All of them are factional without exception.

Thus the novel fascinates most by the easily identifiable human types it presents. These add considerable color to the social picture. It is important to note that they are not stereotyped. All of flesh and blood, these are dynamic, vibrant with their singularity, and alive with their idiosyncrasies. There are, for instance, Mrs. Proudie who is as usual the manipulator, and Mr. Slope whose divided allegiances decide that he is the eternal loser, to quote just two from a multitude. Mrs. Proudie is an opinionated, power-thirsty, and vainglorious woman. Her basic trait is her desire to dominate and rule. There is nothing she would not do to have things done her way. Overshadowing her weak husband and actually exercising his power, the woman will not settle for anything less than the best, and she emerges a winner in the Barchester ecclesiastic competition. She epitomizes one aspect of human life: self-righteousness and greed for power and control which humans live in perpetual discord. Mr. Slope portrays a different type, selfish, mean, and lacking in integrity. Coming from London as the bishop's chaplain, he becomes the protégé of the bishop's wife, Mrs. Proudie. He keeps two goals afloat before him and determines to achieve them by hook or by crook: winning the hand of the widowed Eleanor Bold, Mr. Harding's daughter, and getting the post of the dean of Barchester. So he first goes along with Mrs. Proudie in her machinations and then turns to support the candidacy of Mr. Harding for warden. In the meantime, he is hopelessly sidetracked by the extraordinary beauty of Madeline Vesey Neroni. In the end he gets nothing. Eleanor rejects him, Neroni exposes him in public, and the deanship falls to Mr. Harding. In addition to these, there are the obvious henpecked Dr. Proudie, the blatant flirt Vesey Neroni, the observant Eleanor Bold, the gentle, obedient, and peace-making Susan Grantly, the partisan Archdeacon, the manipulated Harding, the begging Mrs. Quiverful, and the sophisticated Miss Thorne of Ullathorne. With these characters present and in view of the scramble so serious for them but so petty for the readers, critics tend to detect a mock-heroic dimension to the story.

Barchester Towers, the second book of the series, is a social comedy. There are comic scenes all through the book. Bertie Stanhope's self-induced failure of his proposal to Eleanor, the "seduction" of Slope by Madeline Vesey Neroni's Cleopatra-like witchery, Mr. Harding's antic behavior in moments of factional scheming, and the many scenes in which Mrs. Proudie features are just a few out of many instances. What never ceases to amaze is also the virtuosity with which Trollope reproduces the different registers of the language that characterize the speech of the different people from different social strata, from the learned Archdeacon to the eloquent Mrs. Proudie to the wailing Mrs. Quiverful. Trollope's irony can be sensed, but it is often coupled with wit and wisdom, seldom bitter and trenchant, and never spiteful. His is a very tolerant spirit with abundant sympathies for human failings and foibles. The novel is altogether very pleasant to read.

The Last Chronicle of Barset (1866-1867) is the last of the Barsetshire series. It centers on the rise and fall of the social prestige and position of Rev. Josiah Crawley, a curate. He pays a check of £20.00 for a bill and is accused of having stolen it from Mr. Soames. Crawley gives self-conflicting answers when asked to explain the origin of the check before the magistrates, and is thus committed to trial. Then character judgments and popular reaction begin to go against Crawley, who has to give up his position in the end. Then the truth is brought to light. The check was stolen by a servant, who paid it to Mrs. Arabin to clear her debt to her. Mrs. Arabin put it in the envelope containing her husband—Dean Arabin's gift to Mr. Crawley, but did not tell the Dean. Having thus been rehabilitated, Mr. Crawley is ready for the living of St. Ewold's, now left vacant.

The focus of the novel is the reaction of the people to the problem of the "stolen" check. The plot of the book is rather squeaky, but it works well enough to hook and hold attention. Here Trollope's intimate knowledge and deep understanding of people and life stands him in good stead. Most people come from the middle or upper middle class, and Trollope knows this class well. He brings into the drama quite a few subplots and many social galaxies of people. The subplots are related in story interest and stand as contrasts. These include the Grace Crawley and Major Henry Grantly incident and a host of other people in similar circumstances such as Emily Dunstable and Bernard Dale, Madalina Demolines and John Eames, and Lily Dale and Adolphus Crosbie. The interlocking of the subplots is almost Dickensian. In addition, there are good people like Major Grantly who keeps his commitment to Crawley's daughter in times of adversity and despite family objection; designing and mean-spirited people such as Mrs. Proudie, the Bishop's wife, who takes it upon herself to rescue the "honor" of the Church and engineers the calumny against Crawley; people who have the right limits like the Archdeacon, the social center of life, fantastically wealthy, and the exact antithesis to Crawley; beneficent people such as the Luftons; archetypal kind of wives like Mrs. Grantly, a modest Trollopian woman, quiet, keeping eyes down, and wishing to have a good man; socially acceptable people like Emily Dunstable, Bernard Dale, Madalina Demolines, and John Eames, on whom God smiles; enigmas in human behavior such as that of Lily Dale hot in love with the man who she knows is a louse and treats her badly but rejects a man who loves her with all his heart and soul, and other kinds of people like Adolphus who is a nice problem. Trollope presents a fully developed society here. It is among this God's plenty that Crawley moves and defines himself.

The characterization of Mr. Crawley is a *tour de force* for Trollope. Basically a static character, Crawley shows no change in personality. He is at the center of the plot, unpleasant, abrasive, but Christ-like. He is a touchstone, honest, and pure in an impure world, but he is too admirable for people to emulate. His virtues seem almost flaws. As the central moral character, he provides the frame of reference for this fictional world. He appears to be the wall at which everybody bounces his ball, and the readers tend to decide the goodness of the characters upon the degrees of their sympathy with Crawley. But the curate is obsessed with his honesty, which affects his attitudes toward things and people. Although he is not quite like George Eliot's Silas Marner, a loner cut off from social life, Crawley is nonetheless self-destructive enough. He verges on being anti-social as he refuses to play the game and to belong when the people in this organic society all link and interrelate with each other. The other people feel that they are all a part of the society and should integrate into it, but Crawley seems to go out of his way to fight against this integration. He is doomed to failure. Rather in the fashion of Joseph Conrad's Lord Jim, Crawley's search for good ends in a paradox: he becomes holy but has to face his undoing. He is indeed probably the only true Christian in this lukewarm Christian Trollopian world. But saints cause more trouble, to quote George Bernard Shaw (1856-1950), and Crawley is for sure a saint figure. Crawley is not quite Trollope's cup of tea. Trollope preaches a kind of moral middle ground and advocates participation. The ending of the story is interesting to note. It seems that a person like Crawley is picked up kicking and screaming, and forced back into society. His innocence is cleared, is given a good living, and it is society, not he, who wins out eventually. The happy ending signifies a kind of social integration. The resolution of the plot is truly Trollopian. Trollope is a master at giving his readers a crucial scene when they least expect it. The conclusion of the story tends at first to put off the readers of this 800-page book with a feeling of having been cheated, and then to help them to come to terms with the result that is real, not elaborated as they often discover on second thought. It is one that is for the best of all the people concerned in the context of their lives.

Samuel Butler (1835-1902)

Samuel Butler epitomized the explosive intellectual energy of the Victorian period. He was so learned and was interested in so many things such as religion, evolution, Italian culture, biology, classical studies and biography that he became "a jack of all trades" of an indisputably high order, but remained still a jack of all trades. He was considered a little eccentric and unconventional, did not strive for attention in his lifetime, and did not get very much of it. Although it is not possible for literary history to ignore him, it is not likely, either, that he will take up much space there. The multitude of his writings reveals that he was mostly concerned with the notion of evolution and the Christian faith. He wrote quite a few fictions such as *Erewhon* (1872) and *Erewhon Revisited* (1901). The publication of his famous *The Way of All Flesh* was seen as a major event of his day. Then he sank into a kind of limbo and oblivion from which he has never quite emerged to make a comeback. [6]

Butler is remembered, if he still is, as author of the novel, *The Way of All Flesh* (1903). It is a story of the Pontifex family over a stretch of four generations. Old Mr. Pontifex plans for his son, George, to become a publisher, which the young man does. George, when he becomes the head of the household, would like his son, Theobald, to be a clergyman. The young man resists in vain as the father threatens to disown him, and ends up becoming one. When Theobald receives his own living, he is chosen by Christina, one of the daughters of an old clergyman, and marries her. They have three children, the youngest being Ernest, whose story takes up most of the space of the book. Young Ernest is mistreated both at home by his father and in school by his tyrannical schoolmaster. Physically weak and mentally moody, the lonely boy receives attention from his kind aunt, Althea, who decides to get to know whether the boy deserves her legacy after she leaves the scene. Althea leaves her money secretly with her friend, Edward Overton, who henceforth becomes Ernest's "guarding angel." With Althea around, Ernest begins to develop his own personality. When in college he meets a humbug and is cheated out of his inheritance from his grandfather. It is also there that he gets involved in a charge of assault and serves a prison term. After he gets out, he meets Ellen, the frivolous maid of his father's house, and marries her. But as Ellen is an inveterate drunkard and already married, Ernest is eventually able to get rid of her with the help of Overton. By that time, however, they have already had two children. Afraid that he might mistreat his own kids, Ernest arranges for them to be taken care of in a loving home. He becomes a bachelor, writing well in a London flat. After he dies, Overton, who knows the family history well, writes a family chronicle. Overton is the narrator of the story.

The novel is a typical Victorian book as its values are Victorian. To begin with, the name of the major character, Ernest, represents one important Victorian feature of life: there was a good deal of earnestness then, especially on the part of the thinking segment of the population. Both Dickens and Thackeray worked themselves to an early grave. Darwin devoted all his energy to a cause which brought little or nothing in financial terms. And the rest of the group from Carlyle to Ruskin, Tennyson, Browning, Arnold, and George Eliot—the list is so long—all did their best to be of value to their fellow creatures. Then there is the importance of the family which was considered as another prominent feature of Victorian life: life was so challenging and confusing that the Victorians found the home and the hearth a sanctuary to retreat to after an impossible day. Butler is highly critical of the way the Victorians—the Pontifexes—interact with each other, and he makes it imperative that Ernest has a more human approach to his children.

In addition, the book also reveals the widespread influence of the theory of evolution on people's lives then. Although Butler did not attack the quintessence of Darwinism, i.e. the evolution of the species from lower to higher stages of existence, he was at odds with the theory of natural selection which he considered as "bad human philosophy." Butler stressed the effects of conscious striving and the formation of habits as a process of continuous transmission of memory from generation to generation. This became the core of his "unconscious memory." Butler's ideas on evolution included "habit as inherited memory" and "cunning," or will, or striving in lieu of the blind chance of the Darwinian "natural selection." He could not conceive of a universe where man is passive and has no power to shape his own life. In his opinion, man is creative, learns to be master of his environment, and passes his effort on to the next generation as part of a sustained human striving upward. In *The Way of All Flesh*, there is inherited habit, the effect of the will, and the link between generations through unconscious memory. The older Pontifexes are depicted so as to illustrate the importance of heredity. Ernest grows to be a replica of his great-grandfather, but manages to go beyond that. He goes through phases of growth: as a product of heredity, frustrated with his life, and driven by desire to move forward. But he fails all the way, picks up wisdom through trials and errors, and achieves maturity as a distinct moral, ethical being. He exemplifies Butler's theory that the human will shapes human life, and striving ensures the onward progress of human evolution.

There is another aspect of Victorian life that Butler captures in his works very well: the religious doubt, and the problem involving faith. Ernest, in his painful growing up, shares actually all the doubts of his creator such as his skepticism about resurrection. Yet Butler may also be considered as the first anti-Victorian. *The Way of All Flesh*, along with his other works, constitute a ruthless attack on what has later come under fire—Victorianism—with its hypocrisy, self-righteousness, self-deception, and its moral degeneration.

No one is really interested in Butler's theory now. But thanks to Bernard Shaw, his famous admirer, he has been able to keep a degree of presence in the works of some social thinkers, and has influenced people such as Somerset Maugham (see his *Of Human Bondage*), Thomas Wolfe (see his *Look Homeward, Angel*), and James Joyce, the greatest of Butler's followers (read his *A Portrait of the Artist as a Young Man* and *Ulysses*).

Chapter 15 Hardy • Gissing • Moore • Wilde • Stevenson

Thomas Hardy (1840-1928)

Hardy was born in Dorset, southern England. Son of a builder, he became a builder himself. In his late twenties, he began to write, and became one of the three most preeminent Victorian writers. His writing career went through different phases. In the beginning, Hardy strove hard for recognition as a budding writer. He found Wilke Collins' dictum "Make 'em wait, make 'em laugh, and make 'em cry" fascinating and did his best to create suspense in his works. This was the period when he wrote romances and fantasies like *A Pair of Blue Eyes* (1873) and novels of ingenuity (in his own words) such as *Desperate Remedies* (1871). These were his tentative literary efforts and have been mostly forgotten now. The later phase saw him more reflective and scowling. That had to do with the change that Victorian society had experienced. If there was exuberance and hope in Dickens and still an amount of educated poise and affirmation in George Eliot, life after the 1870s became drastically different with drastic changes in mood and tenor. Science and industrialization went hand in hand in full swing, the nation was heading to the phase of aggressive and barbaric capitalism, and millions of people found themselves struggling for mere existence. Factories straggled across the country; farms went bankrupt; and huge numbers of the poor landed in city slums. The world became increasingly more amoral. Man was no longer a free ethical being in face of the forces out of his control. He was manipulated by fate and destiny and chances, and there was nothing he could do about it. The mood of frustration, despair, and pessimism hanged over the nation, and the age of Emile Zola's naturalism had arrived. Although Hardy did not embrace Zola's naturalistic aesthetic, he was apparently affected: the spirit of determinism characteristic of the naturalistic works of the period permeated his later novels as well. In this aspect and more, Hardy anticipated the coming of the modern novel in his country.

Hardy was a prolific writer, but he has been best remembered and valued for the works he published in this period. These include the six novels—*Under the Greenwood Tree* (1872), *Far from the Madding Crowd* (1874), *The Return of the Native* (1878), *The Mayor of Casterbridge* (1886), *Tess of the D'Urbervilles* (1891), and *Jude the Obscure* (1895). The stories are all set in the fictional southern England region that Hardy named Wessex (actually Dorset), and have become known as the "Wessex novels." As they all relate to the life of this one particular region, Hardy started off the tradition of "regional novels." All of these books, of great quality and high seriousness, pushed him to the forefront of later 19th-century fiction, and placed him among the supreme masters of fiction in world literature. They are all tragedies of a kind, and one of these, *Jude the Obscure*, enraged the squeamish social segment and provoked such a backlash that one Bishop Wakefield was said to throw the book into fire on the grounds of its immorality. The disgusted Hardy vowed to stop writing novels, which he did, and for the last three decades of his life he turned to poetry and became one of the major Victorian poets. His famous verse works include *Poems of Past and Present*, and the epic drama *The Dynasts* (1904-1908). Victorianism killed Hardy the novelist.[1]

Hardy's unique position in Victorian fiction has to do with his stance on the nature of life and the cosmos. Given the problems that challenged traditional faith, different writers in the different periods of the Victorian age have offered different answers. Dickens prescribes benevolence as a cure, Browning effort, Tennyson love, Arnold culture, and George Eliot good choice. Hardy, living as he did in the latter part of the century, came up with an alternative of his own. It is determinist in nature. One may read his poetry, the gist of which is basically the same as that of his "Wessex" novels. The poem that immediately comes to mind is the one entitled "Hap." The world is one of "hap," one in which man is totally helpless. God is vengeful and "powerfuller than I," takes delight in making humans suffer, sees to it that the best hope does not bloom, and obstructs the sun and rain with "crass casualty." With His "purblind doomsters" blighting light out of life, He sees humans as mere stakes in His game of dice. Another of Hardy's poems, "The

Darkling Thrush," depicts a world where things are stark and dying out, "the ancient pulse of germ and birth/ Was shrunken hard and dry," profound gloom overwhelms all, nature is uncaring and even evil, the prospect of the end of things and the helplessness of life conspire to asphyxiate people, and the carol of an aged thrush sounds surprisingly irrelevant against the hopeless backdrop. Another possible footnote to the sad ethos of Hardy's fictional world is his poem, "Ah, Are You Digging on My Grave?" The poem focuses on the insignificance of man in the general scheme of things, and on the fact that happiness, if there is ever anything like this, is only a rare, occasional occurrence in the ambient gloom of the universe. So Hardy's is a world, amoral in nature, where "the President of the Immortals" (in his own words) sits high up on the throne, hostile often or nonchalant at best to the human world.

Hardy's stories are always moving and bewitching. They touch hearts not so much by means of their plots (which are very good) as through the pathos of the emotional tangle, in which his characters get involved invariably and from which they find it impossible to extricate themselves. The pitch of their emotional suffering awakens a warm echo in the human bosom, and jerks out genuine, sincere tears. In this fictional world humans get caught up in the web of Fate, or the malignant universe, or forces, the only job of which is to debilitate and devastate human lives. There is no free will, circumscribed as it is by society. There is no belonging. Hardy's characters travel incessantly and never get anywhere. This is pretty much the essential situation which his novels try to adumbrate. Think of Jude and Sue, restless geographically, emotionally and socially, and of Tess, on the run all the time, and Eustacia, running and getting swallowed into a sad, dark, rainy night. They are tragic probably because they are ahead of their time in thought and action. Twentieth-century people in essence, these characters appear to be outsiders in their own Victorian time. They are all of a "displaced" bunch of individuals not fixed in any economic or social niche and fragile and frail in face of overwhelming odds. Here Hardy deviates consciously from traditional Victorian realism that emphasizes plot more than characterization. For him, characters are distinct entities and form individual motifs and tableaus in the canvas of the novel. They do not blur and merge into a larger narrative landscape. Here, it is definitely to his credit that he manages to bring back to fiction a high sense of tragedy, the Greek sense of fatality. The major characters of the six Wessex novels all assume the stature of the generic heroes and heroines of the Greek tragedies.

Furthermore, Hardy places emphasis on the deeper psychology of his characters. Not only does he take immense delight in dealing with the psychic oddities of his fictional men and women such as Eustacia's inner longing for euphoric oblivion and Sue's predilection to frigidity; he also makes a meticulous effort to trace a real sequence of psychological cause and effect and explore human motives and acts. In his portrayal of the inner world, with its passions and its perversity, Hardy ceases to be a realist both in outlook and technique at times and switches to romantic fictional devices, venturing at times as far as to employ the melodramatic. This is a feat that indicates Hardy's empathy with the modern spirit. For one thing, he was sensitive enough to notice the variety of psychic eccentricities that were to assume the dimension of grotesquery in Sherwood Andrson's *Winesburg, Ohio* and, for another, he was beginning to take a serious look into the interior of man rather than rest content with the tradition of representing the mere externals of life.[2]

Finally, Hardy's language possesses a silent power and charm. It may not be the most exequisite, but it simply touches the mind and the senses. His prose is studded with rhetorical devices, poetic imagery, and metaphors, and is richly connotative. Reading him, one feels the sublimity, the terror, the vastness, the obscurity, and the fascination that can stem only from the panorama of life. He is also famous for his uneven style. Occasionally, his prose shows an uneducated man's appreciation for the long or 12-letter words. He never says anything simply if he can help it. Dreiser and Faulkner can also be guilty in this respect. Some even suggest that Joseph Conrad who wrote in English, his second language, could write better. And Hardy's ideas are not always lucid, and his plots may occasionally jump and dislocate. Despite all these minor flaws, his novels move as no one else's can, and work powerfully on the nerves of the readers. That is the secret of his permanence. Reading him can be a highly enjoyable and soul-cleansing kind of experience. Like Dickens, Goerge Eliot, and Trollpe, Hady is never a bore to his readers.[3]

Let's take a look at some of his major works.

Tess of the D'Urbervilles is the most pastoral of Hardy's novels.[4] Its plot centers on the tragic occurrences of its heroine Tess' life. Tess comes from a farmer's family, the Durbeyfields. "The President of the Immortals" begins to play a cruel joke on the innocent girl when her father learns one day that they are the descendants of the ancient family, the D'Urbervilles. In quest of the family genealogy, the girl comes in contact with Alec D'Urberville, whose claim to the ancient family name is dubious. Before long the rich and guileful Alec manages to seduce the girl and make her pregnant. She gives birth to a child, who dies soon. Out of financial need, Tess goes out to find work on a dairy farm, where she meets Angel Claire. The two fall in love and become engaged. Then comes the wedding night. Too honest to keep any secret, Tess makes a confession about Alec and the child, and Angel leaves her in disgust. In the meantime, Alec takes advantage of the Durbeyfields' poverty and continues to harass Tess so that the shiftless girl gives in and moves in with him. Then the joke goes on with redoubled intensity when the remorseful Angel Claire resurfaces and throws Tess into the abyss of despair. She stabs Alec for hurting her so, and runs away with Angel. They manage to hide for a while in a wood before they come to Stonehenge, where she is arrested. She is hanged later. The turn of events and the moment of catharsis prove that the novel is a classic Aristotlean tragedy.

The king of the world of *Tess of the D'Urbervilles* is, as indicated earlier on, "the President of the Immortals," or maybe variously called "fate," "destiny," or "chance." It represents the forces beyond human control but controlling the lives of the humans. It enforces its shibboleth of predestination, and no amount of human effort can alter its design of darkness. Now Tess is a paragon of innocence. She is pretty, happy by nature, and good-hearted. Like a Greek heroine, she possesses simplicity, nobility, devotion, and sensitivity that make her a towering figure among her kind. What she asks of life is simple enough: to be loved and happy. But she is not to get it because she is at the mercies of the odds against her. Two men must appear in her life to confuse and distract her. One is totally evil; the other apparently good. The two both serve as the instruments of Chance. So many coincidences occur in Tess' life that the hand of Chance is in evidence wherever she goes. If her father had not driven along the road and met with the Parson at the beginning, the great upsetting turmoil that follows would never have happened to her life. The series of accidents that the ominous meeting touches off would not have occurred. If her father was not so obsessed with his "chance" findings and doubtful information, and if the horse had not been killed, Tess would not have been so disposed to her mother's suggestion to go and "look for Alec." The naïve and pubescent girl would not have fallen into Alec's sexual trap, and there would have been no need to "confess" on her wedding night about it. And if the misfortune of the two love-torn farm girls had not occurred, one drunk and one dead, Tess would not have been so ready and eager about "confession," and more accidents would have been averted. But as it is, they go on happening. Angel must not see Tess' letter of confession and appeal, conveniently slipped as it is under the rug rather than above it. She must quarrel with her fellow workers and be left alone on an ominous night for Alec to ride along and give her a lift. Her family must continue to wallow in dire wretchedness so that her loving nature must decide to succumb to Alec's pressure. Angel must wake up from his hypocritical dream of romance and come to his senses and return to look for a Tess now already spoken for. Tess must still love Angel and have no choice but to stab Alec—"the curse of her life"—in the back. Alec is not worthy of Tess' life, but "the President of the Immortals" must have his way with the mortals before he decides that it is high time now she went back to whence she came.

The fate motif is nowhere clearer when she ends up with Angel at the Stonehenge, the monument to the ancient world of myth and mystery. That world is meaningful for her. The present world into which she has stumbled has been too much with her, and she is infinitely too good for it. She must return to where she belongs, and the Stonehenge is the point at which she takes off for it. A pathetic scene occurs toward the end, in which Tess lies on a sacrificial stone in Stonehenge, freed by Time of her geographical limit and ready to be taken to another planet. The novel offers cogent proof that chances play a significant part in Hardy's fictional world. If chances keep occurring as often as they do in *Tess of the D'Urbervilles* and *Jude the Obscure* and indeed Hardy's other works, they stop being chances in the normal sense of the term, and serve to illustrate a pattern of cosmic behavior, i.e. to stand ever opposed to individual endeavors and do all in its power to thwart them. The readers may as well call it "cosmic irony." For Hardy, that decides the fact that there would be only eternal misery in life and no hope for a better eventuality. The spirit of determinist defeatism soaks all the way through the whole of the story.

Seen from a more common, universally applicable perspective, Tess is the stuff of a tragic heroine because of her innate tragic flaw which she can by no means shake off. As such, it must do its work of destruction and encompass her downfall. Tess' personality flaw is this, that she is, very much like Juliet, a one-man's woman. Her life stops at the point with Angel, and loses track of its sense of direction when Angel disappears. Most common people would have forgotten and moved on, but not Tess. Hardy's fictional world operates in such a way that the less sensitive, intelligent and self-conscious ones have better chances of survival, while the clever ones must die out as the universe has no patience with their searching minds. Along with Tess, there is a long gallery of tragic heroes and heroines, such as Eustacia (*The Return of the Native*), Jude and Sue (*Jude the Obscure*), and Mayor Henchard (*The Mayor of Casterbridge*), to quote just a few, who are doomed because they insist on their quest for the true meaning of life. Had Tess been of a less innocent and persistent nature, with a dab of worldliness, and more modern and less classic in behavior, she would have opted to settle for the second best or even less, and would have lived. As it is, she is not amenable to a compromise, which is, in essence, what life is always all about, so she loses touch with life, and must die.

In addition, the novel holds up a mirror for the spirit of the time. *Tess of the D'Urbervilles* is set in an age when the pastoral village life is on its way out and the encroaching feet of modern civilization have moved in. Agriculture and dairy farms are being replaced, and the railway lies a solid menace on the fringe of the village—the backbone of rural life. The spread of literacy (Tess speaks two dialects), the presence of the threshing machine, and the way Londoners handle milk are just some of the indicators of the outside world impinging upon the pastoral scene. The plains are darkening. Nature stops being benevolent and caring, and so does God. Life becomes cold and indifferent, man's ethical being dwindles, and humans are as powerless as are so many flies. In this condition they struggle in vain to survive. As the sword of Fate hangs over the D'Urbervilles from the very outset, Tess' tragedy is a foregone conclusion.

The antithesis between Tess and Alec is worth attention. Tess incarnates the earth; Alec stands as its antagonist. The contact and conflict between the two signifies the tension of the age. Tess is like a pagan goddess, a willow wand symbolic of pre-Christian fertility. She is all pastoral, almost a nature goddess, with her open nature, her impulses, and her sensuality. Spontaneous and romantic, she is the veritable picture of eternal womanhood, femaleness, and tenderness and love. By no means a new woman like Sue Bridehead in *Jude the Obscure*, Tess represents the Arcadian tradition of rural life. Alec, on the other hand, is a product of the industrial age. He makes himself rich through money-lending and usury. Amoral, hard-headed, and sexually aggressive, he has nothing in common with Tess. He is, if anything, whatever she is not in the final analysis. And their contact is tangential, i.e. no more than financial. One needs money and the other has it—it is as simple as that. But Alec sees and seizes his opportunity when the Durbeyfields are in a bad shape. He must spoil the natural beauty, and must break its token and spell—Tess. Thus his move toward Tess assumes the stature of a historical struggle between two ages and two lifestyles. The city must invade the country, and the latter must give in and succumb.

It is necessary to say a few words about Angel Claire. He can be obnoxious to some readers as a sexist rotter. After he admits having an affair with a woman, and hears the naive Tess admitting that she has been raped and has borne a child, he changes instantly into a cold monster and abandons her. Hardy is at pains to tell us in detail that he has mistaken Tess for a pure, unspoiled, innocent young woman. Throughout the whole book, Clare never once sees that his own affair with another woman, both of them responsible adults, is in any way comparable to young Tess' seduction by Alex. Claire's highest concern is whether or not he will "forgive" Tess. He does so because he falls in love with his own romanticized ideal milkmaid, and condemns Tess for not being what he has dreamed. Like most of Hardy's characters, he has no choice; he is acting from his whole background and the character which it has developed. At the end, Claire redeems himself. He repents his abandonment of Tess, and "forgives" her, and he will now, a sadder and a wiser man, make a life with Tess' sister Liza-Lu as Tess has hoped. It is apparent that Hardy tips the scales against him by giving him the sexual misbehavior in the first place when comparing his sexual misbehavior to Tess' seduction. In this connection, the readers need to note the subtitle of the book, "A Pure Woman Faithfully Presented by Thomas Hardy." That Hardy sees

Tess as *pure*, and thus blameless, is a key to the novel, and encourages some readers' scorn of Claire.

Tess of the D'Urbervilles is one of a series of books about women by men, all of which could be called "feminist"—Flaubert's *Madame Bovary,* Tolstoy's *Anna Karenina*, Stephen Crane's *Maggie: A Girl of the Streets*, Theodore Dreiser's *Sister Carrie*, and *Susan Lennox*, by David Graham Philips. Apparently, during the time between the middle of the 19th century and the First World War, some men, at least, were writing about the lot of women in western culture, and *Tess of the D'Urbervilles* is one of the best of their books. It's interesting, too, to learn that Hardy thought of *Tess of the D'Urbervilles* as his best novel.

Three years after *Tess of the D'Urbervilles* came out in print, George Moore (1852-1933) wrote a novel of roughly the same import, *Esther Waters* (1894), to "correct the misimpression" that he was afraid Hardy's Tess may have made. Moore feels that a farm girl does not get pregnant and run about becoming a great heroine to be so involved in such a charming romance. Moore's novel is probably more true to life, but it fails to touch Hardy's book in tragic intensity and power and permanence.

The most urban novel that Hardy could get to write is his famous *Jude the Obscure*.[5] It was his last but has been seen by many as his best novel. It is set in the backwater of Wessex. It is so entitled because it is about the life of a common person who is normally neglected and forgotten. Here is a specimen of Hardy's subtle irony. What he calls "the Obscure" turns out to be a typical Victorian. The story is a frightful piece of incredible horrors, dealing symbolically with a period of serious dislocation at all conceivable levels of English life. Jude Fawley the Wessex villager is a stonemason with aspirations for Christminster (Hardy's coined name for Oxford) religious scholarship. His family has been under a curse that no marriage can end happily. Jude works and reads avidly. He meets Arabella Donn, a sexy country girl, and is tricked into marrying her. Soon Arabella deserts him. Jude finds work in Christminster and meets Sue Bridehead, his cousin. Sue has been a school teacher under principal Phillotson, who is physically repulsive and much older than she is. Sue and Phillotson get married, but the unhappy woman leaves her husband and goes to Christminster, where she finds Jude. A relationship of mutual affection develops between them. Then they get married and have children. The marriage proves repugnant to society, which ostracizes the two from normal social connections. Jude finds it difficult to get a job, and his hope to become a priest is dashed. Arabella resurfaces with their son, Father Time by name, and dumps him to Jude. Life becomes increasingly hard for the family. One night Jude and Sue go out, leaving Father Time to take care of his siblings, and come back only to find that Father Time has killed all the kids and then taken his own life. Sue is inconsolable. Believing that the family curse is at work, she goes back to Phillotson and reunites with him, feeling thoroughly subdued. The desperate Jude never recovers from the family tragedy, and falls seriously sick. He dies in gloom. Arabella alone wins out, triumphant and happy in a different surrounding.

Jude the Obscure is the most contemporaneous of all Hardy's novels. It is an indictment against the class system and Christianity which Oxford represents in particular and probably also the institution of marriage (Hardy suffered in his first marriage). What infuriated the popular taste when the book first came out in print included a number of things such as certain parts of the novel dealing with the relationship of Jude and Sue, the sensual and morally sensitive sections about Jude and the two women in his life, the frank descriptions of sex and sexual desire, the attitude toward marriage, the castigation of social and religious hypocrisy, the sense of hopelessness and determinism—all these outraged and brutalized the established taste then.

The characterization of the three major characters in the novel is worth careful analysis. The two women, Arabella and Sue, can be seen to embody the two aspects of Jude's nature. Arabella, almost a sex animal, is all flesh and desire whereas Sue, at the other end of the spectrum, is all intellect, frigidity, and essentially bodiless. Arabella is sometimes regarded as the true heroine of the book (as D. H. Lawrence views her, for example) as she seems to succeed and have the final word in the end. She reacts to life intuitively. The universe does not concern her; it is with living happily that she is solely preoccupied. Frequently associated with the pig, she represents the highest degree of physicality. All common sense, definitely part of the earth earthy, and sexually ever thirsty, she keeps sidetracking Jude from his quest for goals of a higher order, and inadvertently helps to destroy him. She is the instrument of the vicious universe set on playing a cosmic joke upon the helpless human. It is, in fact, not her destroying Jude; it is the cosmic forces coupled with Jude succumbing to his baser instincts that kill him off. The end when it comes is so sad that people tend to come away with the impression that there is no God, the good ones die out, but those unthinking, simply happy with what life has to offer, prove to be the "fittest to survive." This is a recurrent theme with Hardy.

Sue's inner complexity never fails to offer a riddle for all readers of all generations to unravel. Her problem is both personal and socially induced. There is always room for conjecture as there are half a thousand reasons to speculate about the way she behaves. She is well-educated, intelligent, and independent as she is trained to make a living for herself. She has an autistic, Narcissistic soul which she needs to keep down to be happy with Jude. She is Jude's equal except that the man is too physical for her. Sex is on the whole detestable to her. Hardy portrays Sue as a kind of naked Venus, a specimen of purity and virginity, qualities to which her last name, Bridehead, offers cogent testimony. She is damned as she is unable to come to terms with society. Society, especially Victorian society, pressures women to get married and have children, but she is not the marrying type. Although she is a flirt and is capable of strong passion for the opposite sex, she is not a traditional woman. She is a feminist of a kind. Her image represents the growth of a modern female self-awareness in the last few decades of the 19th century. She is probably the first modern woman to appear in English fiction. So she keeps fighting back and tries to get her revenge. Her weapon is and can only be sexual. She is masochistic to herself and sadistic to men for forcing her to do what she will not. She is restless as she cannot find a place for her to settle down. However, she gradually gives in, not without a sense of revulsion, sets up house with Jude, and has children. But all along in the innermost part of her being, she sees this as society's way of punishing her, and feels guilty and does repentance. Thus between her and Jude an odd situation exists. Together, they feel guilty, but apart, they feel agony. They are so close to one another that separation means death, but staying together, they come to pretty the same ending all the same. But life is such that they have little or no choice but eventually part company and die, one physically and one spiritually. There is of course the non-baptized moody Father Time who cuts in and makes the situation more complicated than it already is. He simply takes matters into his own hands and kills off all the little ones of the family. Sue takes this as a sign of God's wrath and retribution, and feels totally defenseless and crestfallen. Her search together with Jude for meaning and value turns out to be circular: they end up where they first started, in square one. Both can be regarded as the precursors of modern existentialists.

The case of Jude is the most intriguing of all. He is one of the most complex characters in 19th-century English fiction. The most primitive, the lowest socially of all Hardy's characters, and having the least heroic about him, he is nonetheless the stuff of a hero. He has dreams but is never able to fulfill them; he has talents but is never given recognition for them. Jude's failure proves a couple of notions of wide currency at the time: the theory of evolution, and the naturalistic thesis about man and his life. First, social Darwinism stated around the time that man in his recent stage of evolution has developed reason, but is still too emotional to control his will. He is not fit enough to survive the rigors and complexities of modern life, where man is not supposed to expect help from any source, human or divine. Jude reminds the readers, somehow, of his fictional American cousin of roughly the same period, Hurstwood in Theodore Dreiser's *Sister Carrie* (1900). Jude's downfall is inevitable because of his lower instinctive impulses and his inability to strike a balance between reason and emotion. It is the result of the deadly war between the flesh and the spirit that rages in him. He aspires to Sue because she is an intellectual sign and as such represents an attainment of his intellectual desire: being with her can prove to him that he is not base. But he has another side, the animalistic side, that Sue cannot satisfy. No one can be conceivably happy with Sue. For Jude, in addition to her frigidity, his stay with her means sinning as they are breaking a law. Naturally he keeps digressing to Arabella, but he knows that living with Arabella indicates that he is not worthy. Had he kept to Sue and shut Arabella out, or had he stuck with Arabella and forgot about Sue, he would have had a better chance of survival. As it is, he is divided, a truly phrenic nature, and hovering between the two of them and attracted to both at the same time, his doom is sealed. He becomes a lost soul in the cold wide world, with no place to belong, little free will, lonely, weak, incapable of any self-defense, the picture of a rootless traveler through modern life and of a modern existentialist. He is doomed to die out, which he does in the end. In the final analysis Jude has serious flaws in his personality. His judgment is not sound; he fails to understand the nature of the universe and its motives and stumbles along and keeps making the wrong choices. The diagnosis of his tragedy is an interesting psychological study of human nature. His is a case study of Everyman in all time and space. The element of its timelessness comes through well enough to make the novel a solid presence in world literary history.

Then, there is the naturalistic notion about man to consider. Jude's downfall illustrates the new cosmos-individual relationship in the period in which the modern sensibility is dawning on the horizon. The beginning of the novel paints a picture of a boy driving birds against the immensity of the sky and the universe. This sets the tone of the novel, that man is insignificant. Then there is on record Aunt Drusilla's warning that tragedy runs in the genes of the family and that the Fawleys would do better to desist from marriage, which suggests biological determinism. The "oracle" that Jude's misfortune is hereditary in a way, sounds like an ancient Greek curse and forebodes ill for him. It is a spell that he can never break and that will not until it has worked havoc with his life. There is nothing he can do but let the curse run its course. His tragedy indicates the presence of some cosmic forces, hostile to man and set upon frustrating his life. Jude assumes the proportions of some tragic heroic grandeur in his attempt to understand his universe and put up some defenses. Thus the novel is in fact Hardy's version of naturalism, and that explains why morality does not appear as important in Hardy as it is in George Eliot's works. Readers come away with the feeling that there is absolute unfairness towards the end. Hence the immense feeling of pessimism and grimness. This is one of the features of *Jude the Obscure* that tells it apart from the traditional Victorian realist novels. No longer purely Victorian, it shows Hardy in the process of edging toward the modern novel of which Kafka, Conrad, Joyce, and Woolf represent the epitome. *Jude the Obscure* has been called, and rightly, a transitional novel.

George Gissing (1857-1903)

George Gissing was not happy with his world. His mind yielded easily to the stresses of life, and became warped and impulsive. The world was not good enough for him. It was "preposterous" and "sordid," and the common people, for whom his inherited middle class gentility and his classical education made for his inveterate bias and scorn, were to him "base," "mean," and "vulgar." Influenced by the naturalist notion of man and his life, he wrote about poverty, but his works tend to leave the impression that he was fleeing from it rather than fighting and offering a way out. Because there was no easy solution from him and because he was grim all the time, he was not popular in his own day and is not very likely to win very good reception with future readers. [6]

But it is good to note that he was important as a writer in his country's literary history. He was the one who, going against the grain, ruthlessly exposed the corrupton and evil which he thought lay at the core of social life then. To get to know what truly happened then, it is not enough to read Robert Louis Stevenson's romances or Conan Doyle's Shelock Holmes' detective narratives or Rudyard Kipling's exotic scenes of Indian life that smell, occasionally, of the British Empire's imperialistic complacency. Although all three were popular at the time when Gissing was not, the picture of late 19th-century English life would not be complete without his literary efforts.

Gissing has been regarded by some as the least important Victorian novelist and, as such, ignored. But he did a few things for which he is well remembered today. For instance, he created the image of the alienated hero in 19th-century fiction, and was about the only one author of his time writing in the vein of naturalistic, scientific realism. In the latter part of the 19th century, naturalism flourished in America with the influence of Zola's biological and social determinism. But somehow it did not get a foothold in England. There was, strictly, nothing in English fiction like Emile Zola's naturalist works. George Gissing, George Moore, and later Arnold Bennett (1867-1931) may come close to the label, but their tone is muted. What they tried to do what Zola did in France was to open a window in the area of subject matter and show the writers that there existed available for representation a new matter—the lowest of the low in social life. Gissing tried to offer a scientific analysis of life, describing man as trapped in environment and heredity.

Today Gissing is most remembered for his novel, *New Grub Street*.

The story is about the world of literary artists of the time. Two of them, the main characters of the book, whose careers cross, respond to the prevalent social milieu in drastically different ways. Jasper Milvain is more materialistically-minded, and more amenable to the claims that money tends to make on the sensibility of the artist. He is ready to compromise his private vision to cater to philistine needs. Even in matters like love and marriage, Jasper's monetary motives are disconcertingly evident. He has no misgivings whatever about breaking a woman's heart. He proposes to Marian, who cherishes a passion for him, because he knows that she is going to be an heiress of £5,000, but he has no scruples distancing her on learning that she will inherit nothing. Marian in disgust rejects him. He turns his attention to her cousin, Amy, Reardon's young widow, and sees his marriage with her as his gateway to success since she has received a legacy. Amy agrees to marry him because he wrote a good review to honor her late husband, Reardon. This materialist and money-minded opportunist manages to achieve social arrival at the expense of his conscience as an artist.

In contrast with him there is Edwin Reardon, who is more sensitive and loyal to his own voice and less accommodating, and lives a life of dire poverty and struggles in vain for a more comfortable creative milieu. He has to work as a clerk and face the constant hostility and antipathy of his worldly wife. He needs Amy to be his muse, but gets no inspiration from her. Moreover, Amy takes their son, Willie, with her and goes to live with her mother. Then Amy inherits some money and wants to come back and help him. But the proud Reardon declines the offer despite the coersive effort of his friend, Harold Biffen, to persuade him to give Amy a positive response. Biffen's is a rare cultured voice of understanding. But Reardon and Amy achieve final reconciliation because their dying son Willie insists on it and Reardon is so sick that he knows he does not have long to live. A foil to Jasper, Reardon is an idealist to whom artistic integrity means everything. He is self-destructive, and takes delight in self-destruction. Losing contact in his little room, he becomes an alienated urban man, an existentialist. Ultimately he is all alone, and he makes a choice that concerns himself. There is, in his personality, a silhouette of George Gissing himself. The mood of the book is downright gloomy. It is utter despair that Gissing tries to peddle to his readers. Although he wrote about the dilemma of the poor artists, Gissing's topmost concern is here still with the middle class, for the people who suffer most in the novel are those who have known better days.

Thematically, Gissing sees work, not sex, as important, but the work as he portrays it does not succeed. This is anti-Victorian. Success for Gissing means not exactly money and prestige though there is in him veneration for money; he retains his own values and vision as an artist. He does not see society as beneficial as does George Eliot, but feels that it stops the clock and fails to progress. Primarily, *New Grub Street* is not about artists, art, and writing; it is chiefly about money and social poverty, and about the intricate relationship between money and art. Gissing's naturalist novel freezes things, and offers no hope, no solution, but the dead end. In addition, *New Grub Street* simply describes people and events, yet offers little or no psychological depth.

George Moore (1852-1933)

Goerge Moore was an Anglo-Irish writer. He appered to be a singular person on the late Victorian scene. The clumsy young man went to Paris in the 1870s and was influenced by a number of writers he happened to meet there. Balzac, Flaubert, Turgenev, and later Zola all left their imprint on the man. His writing career stretched over half a century, and produced novels, plays, poetry, and a miscellany of other genres. He tried to write in a naturalistic way, and his *A Modern Lover* may be the first conscious English attempt in that direction. He also wrote strictly in the realistic tradition, and helped English fiction move into the new century. All his life he felt he was committed to the quest for beauty in artistic expression. One thing that drew pretty much critical attention was his constant change in subjects and styles, which ended up with nothing unique to him. That might have to do with his impressionable mind and volatile vision. Ultimately, although he kept writing long after the Victorian age ended, he is still seen as part of that age, rather than as a modern writer. [7]

Esther Waters is one of Moore's famous novels. It tells the story of an unmarried mother and her painful life trying to bring up her child. Esther Waters comes from a poor religious family. As her stepfather drives her out to work, she becomes a kitchen-maid at Woodview. The cook, Mrs. Latch, is unkind, neither are her fellow servants there. But her mistress, Mrs. Barfield, likes her pious spirit and invites her to her services on Sundays. In addition, the kind mistress teaches her to read. The one person, who seems to take her side in the servants' bickering, is William Latch, the cook's son, but he is a hopeless gambler on the racing course. One evening, he takes Esther out and seduces her. When Esther comes to her right mind, she repudiates his advances. William then elopes with Mr. Barfield's cousin, Miss Peggy Barfield, and is heard no more for the time. Meanwhile Esther, now pregnant, is dismissed on grounds of morality. She goes and stays with her mother for a while and leaves as she is afraid that her stepfather is exhausting her savings. She works long hours everyday and stays in a workhouse for a time. After his mother dies, her stepfather takes his family to Australia. Esther is left all alone in the world. Then she finds employment with Miss Rice, a writer, who is understanding and nice to her. Then her son Jackie is born and becomes her joy and hope of life. She meets Fred Parsons and is soon betrothed to him. To her surprise William resurfaces, tells her of Miss Barfield's jilting him, and begs to come back to her and their son. Esther agrees despite Fred's repeated warning, and William starts to run a tavern. Life is good for the family for a time. Jackie is placed in a good school and Esther has two maids to wait on her. Then William loses heavily in race gambling and begins to accept bets in his tavern against the law. The police raid the tavern, and William has to pay a heavy fine. He is almost broke. Besides, he contracts tuberculosis, and the doctor advises him to go to Egypt. He and Esther gamble all their money on one race and lose. William dies shortly, and Esther is again homeless and penniless. She goes back to Woodview, only to find that the Barfields are broke. But she stays to work for Mrs. Barfield willingly out of gratitude. Esther feels happy and fulfilled that her son has grown up well and is now enlisted in the army.

Moore did a couple of things that departed from the normal practice of Victorian fiction. One of these was to choose a servant girl's struggle through life as the focus of the novel. Victorian writers had mostly written about middle class women. Even a poor girl like Tess appears to be living a glamorous life. Moore wrote in his circumstantial realistic way about the unmarried mother trying to raise her child against the odds of life, deliberately making it clear that poverty is poverty and no amount of fantasizing and romanticizing can get rid of it. It should be noted on record here that the writing of *Esther Waters* did not mean that George

Moore had more sympathy than did, say, Hardy for the poor and the wretched. Actually he did not, and he did not care about people like Esther. The servants' mundane life simply occurred to him as a subject for his fiction and he took it up in his creative endeavors. But the choice happened to be a good one. Then, the way Moore wrote this novel and other novels pushed realism in English fiction to a new phase, a more modern phase. There was no sentimentalism and no melodrama. Everything was downright true to life: the hardships, the narrowness and hypocrisy of the middle class, the native goodness of Esther, Miss Rice and some other characters, the chicanery, dishonesty and evil of life, the landowner's household, the hospital, the race courses, the streets, the workhouse, a single mother's desperate effort to go through life for her son, and human nature's best manifestation as well as its worst. Moore did not reward the heroic Esther with an inheritance, neither did he punish the villains. It was a common person living her common life, and there was nothing spectacular about it. This lack of glamour has ironically stood out as the novel's strength. The novel and his other works also prove that Moore was highly critical of Victorian culture.

Oscar Wilde (1854-1900)

Wilde was a swashbuckling attention-grabber. He was famous as the leader of the late-Victorian decadent aestheticism. His poetry is commonplace as compared with his fellow writers like Dowson and Johnson. His plays are humorous, clever, but lacking in depth. The one novel he wrote, *The Picture of Dorian Gray* (1991), is a slim volume with a slim plot. But it is worth mentioning because it touches upon a typical Victorian subject, the divided self.[8] The main character of the novel, Dorian Gray, is a handsome young man of means. He visits his artist friend Basil Hallward's studio and is fascinated with the portrait Basil is painting. It is his picture, as young and handsome as he is. Dorian secures the picture and locks it away in a room upstairs. He wishes that the picture could bear all the burden of his sins and his aging instead of himself. He meets Lord Henry Wotton, who proves to be his mentor in depraved life. Sybil Vane, a young actress, adores Dorian as her "Prince Charming," but he treats her cruelly. Then he sees a touch of cruelty in the mouth of the picture, and repents. He goes to look for Sybil to tell her of his make-up plan to marry her, only to learn that she has killed herself with prussic acid. Dorian, filled with remorse, is relieved to hear Lord Wotton dismiss her death as nothing of significance. Dorian continues to indulge in dissipation, and the picture becomes uglier with time. Years pass. On his 38th birthday Dorian shows Basil the changed picture and, in a moment of an angry outburst with himself for having revealed his true nature, he knives Basil. He asks young chemist Alan Campbell to dispose of the body, and Campbell later dies of a mysterious suicide. Sybil's brother, James Vane, comes to seek revenge on Dorian, but is shot accidentally in Dorian's country house, where he has followed Dorian. At last Dorian loses patience with the increasingly withered, wrinkled face on the picture, and decides to destroy it. He stabs it through with a knife, and hears a deathly scream from himself. When his servants come, they find the dead body of their master with a face exactly like that on the picture.

In a balanced historical perspective, the book has its own unique merits. When it first came out, it kicked up a stir and was much talked about in town. Some people accused Wilde of plagiarizing the novel, *A Rebours* (*Against the Grain* in English), of the French novelist J. K. Huysmans (1848-1907). The character of Dorian Gray has been said to be a replica of Huysmans' major character. There is truth in the accusation, but *The Picture of Dorian* Gray has acquired its own entity and has been seen as an authentic narrative on the notion of the double, the split nature of the human soul and human existence that characterizes Victorian life in a sense. Another thing to note about the book is its preface in which Wilde states in his typical aphoristic manner that art is separate from morality and not to be judged in keeping with moral standards and that a book can only be said to be well or badly written. Thus he manages to make the theory of art for art's sake further clear. His assertion of the importance of form that the preface emphasizes has been gradually digested and accepted by later generations. That is one of the reasons why the book, despite its defects in plotting and characterization, has kept its hold upon the imagination of some readers. Another thing to note about the book is its lengthy discussions of many interesting subjects of topical interest with reference to the mindset of the late Victorian aesthetes. These include, among other things, the descriptions of the people of decadence with their tastes, perception of things, and ennui, the aesthetes' criticism of the Victorian age for being dull and morally correct, their views on beauty, marriage and women, their rebellious spirit, their musings on life, art, and artists, their new hedonism, their spiritualization of the senses and search for sensations and beauty and their life of debauchery, their comments on sin and free will and choice and conscience, and a lot more "inside-track" information about this particular coterie of people. Wilde's novel is in fact a good footnote to the mentality of the aesthetes of the time.

The symbolic significance of the story is self-evident. Dorian is an aesthete, and his picture is his soul, conscience, alter-ego, and guide. It has a life of its own. When he first sees himself in the picture in his friend's studio, his self-recognition begins. When he hides the picture, he is trying to hide his soul. Lord Wotton is his temptation, and Basil Hallward his reality check. So he loves the one as intensely as he hates the other. Dorian would like to enjoy life and stay free of social inhibitions and responsibility. But the picture remains as a magic mirror of his whole body and soul, a painful reminder of how far he is gone along the path of decadence and sin. He does not like the idea and makes up his mind to do away with it. He does not know, however, that when he stabs the picture, the time of retribution has come. He has to pay off his hitherto ignored "debts" with his life. In this sense, and in this alone, the novel is moral.

The book has obvious weaknesses. First, the characterization is seriously flawed. There is a lot of telling and description, but not much plot movement. All the three characters are gross portraits, and almost all one-dimensional caricatures. They are puppets taken out and pulled in as the narrator-author pleases and are given no chance to act themselves out. The major figure, Dorian, is a static character himself. He is talked about, but is never given leeway enough to show himself up on stage. Thus all through the narrative, the narrator keeps talking and the characters take backstage most of the time. Then, the little plot that moves in the book does so in an uneven manner. The high-life scenes appear vivid, visible, and much more detailed, and charged with an occasional dreamy atmosphere. It is realistic as if personally experienced, enlivened at times with some touches that smell of melodrama. When it comes to the low-life scenes, they appear non-consecutive and insubstantial, and the narrator or author is somehow out of his element in his narrative. Some scenes like the one in which Dorian kills his friend are not always convincing. Some critics feel that Wilde needed more preparation in the craft of fiction.

Robert Louis Stevenson (1850-1894)

Stevenson suffered from tuberculosis ever since childhood. He traveled to many parts of the world to seek to improve his health. The remarkable thing to note about this eternal invalid is that he never gave up hope and struggled to live longer and do more good for his fellow creatures. He managed to receive a good education and become a very learned person. His imagination was rich and flighty; his pen kept on writing. From these came a torrent of works that offer at once a high moral sense and a gospel of joy and happiness for all. These works have always provided immense entertainment and have never ceased to enrich the human mind and uplift the human morale. In more ways than one, Stevenson went against the Victorian "grain." Whereas most of his fellow writers kept to the moral aesthetic and realism, he veered in a different direction: he wrote romances to season the parochial, down-to-earth lifestyle of his age with a touch of envisaging power to enliven his readers and widen their vistas of life. His principles were lofty and noble. He became immensely popular with his contemporaries who had been through so much change and chaos and had been craving for some freshening means to spirit them away from the humdrum world even for a moment. This they found in grateful Stevenson.

Over the years Stevenson's reputation has gone through phases of rise and fall. After his death he fell into neglect for some time. Some have tended to see him mainly as a writer of children's stories. But the immortal power of his works has managed to assert itself so that he is able to resurrect himself and has remained in evidence in the lives of readers worldwide. Stevenson was not only a novelist, but also a poet, a prose writer, and a playwright. In view of his short career, his literary output is amazingly fabulous. [9]

Of the voluminous amount of his writings, each and every one of which deserves attention, two of his novels stand out for special attention. One of these is his first book, *Treasure Island* (1883), and the other his famous *The Strange Case of Dr. Jekyll and Mr. Hyde* (1886). *Treasure Island* has been a popular novel ever since its publication. The late Victorian period was beset with a multitude of problems, and the common run of mankind suffered poverty and indignity. Stevenson's *Treasure Island* came at a time when the hopeless were daydreaming for comfort and relief of some kind. In addition, from a perspective of universal applicability, the novel satisfies the perennial human desire for unexpected wealth. The story begins with Jim Hawkins finding an oilskin packet in the sea chest of Billy Bones, a dead seaman who stole Captain Flint's treasure map. Jim offers the packet to Trelawney, a squire, and Dr. Livesey. The two men discover the treasure map and decide to ship out to the island where Captain Flint's treasure is buried. The venture is financed by Trelawney and the ship, the *Hispaniola*, has a crew of pirates whom the ship's cook, the one-legged Long John Silver, gathers and controls. Jim, going along with them, detects Long John Silver's mutiny plot, and tells his friends about it. The men desert the ship to the pirates and take over a stockade on the island. Long John Silver and the pirates offer them a safe voyage home in return for the map, and are rejected. Battles between the two sides begin and Jim's friends suffer heavy losses. Jim goes to the ship and fights with the pirate guard Israel Hands, shoots him, and moves the ship to the beach. But he finds his friends gone and Long John Silver and the pirates in control. Long John Silver, who then saves Jim from the angry outburst of the pirates, has the map from the doctor but does not know that the treasure has been discovered and moved away by Ben Gunn, a pirate whom Captain Flint left behind. Jim's friends come back in time to rescue him and Long John Silver from the pirates, and sail off home. Long John Silver jumps ship with his bag of coins, and the rest of the group divide the treasure among them. Jim is the major character of the novel. The boy's courage, wisdom, and sense of integrity touch the readers deeply. Long John Silver is the most glamorous of all the characters. The man is capable of good and evil. He is greedy, murderous, scheming, but can be generous as when he saves Jim. The complexities of his personality add to a simple adventure story a philosophical and psychological depth and an element of timeless universality with which people of all time can identify.

The Strange Case of Dr. Jekyll and Mr. Hyde is interesting not so much because of the idea it embodies as of its way of presenting it. The notion behind the novel is that of the double, i.e. the two aspects of one personality, which runs through many works of both earlier and later times. Its immediate parallel was Oscar Wilde's *The Picture of Dorian Gray* (1891), in which the double takes the form of a portrait. *Dr. Jekyll and Mr. Hyde* tells the story of a well-known London physician Dr. Henry Jekyll, who has been conscious of his double nature since childhood. He does good to increase human knowledge during the day and indulges in shameful behavior at night. He calls himself a double-dealer. With time he discovers a potion that can metamorphose him into a separate person, whom he calls Mr. Edward Hyde. As Mr. Hyde, Jekyll allows his evil side to have its way. Hyde is physically very repulsive and does nothing but evil. On one occasion, for instance, he knocks a child down and tramples her underfoot. His activities draw the attention of Richard Enfield and his distant kinsman Mr. Utterson, a lawyer. The two are surprised to find that their friend Dr. Jekyll has named Hyde as his heir. Jekyll discovers that his potion is losing effect and that he appears more and longer in the image of Hyde and finds it increasingly harder to return to his original form. Then Hyde brutally kills a nobleman and is about to be caught. In the meantime, Jekyll's butler Poole comes to tell Utterson about the odd occurrences in the physician's laboratory. They break into the room and find a dead body. It is Mr. Hyde poisoned to death. They see a note that Dr. Jekyll has written as a confession before he takes his own life.

The novel expresses candidly one fact about human nature that everybody has two sides. Having understood this well, Jekyll proceeds to make the chemical which would separate them so that one side enjoys without restraint and the other works for society without misgivings. He succeeds in his research but finds that, once apart, the evil side becomes dominant and free of the control of the other side. Jekyll represents the Freudian superego, the social self, and Hyde the id, the instinctual human drive. The characterization merits notice as well. Hyde is portrayed as someone hardly human, primitive, and difficult to define. The fifty-year-old Jekyll, large, grave, and serious, has a smooth face with something of a sly cast to it. Utterson is not a mere stock figure either. He is colorful and clearly drawn. The telling is subtle, and the language is refined and condensed.

Chapter 16 Victorian Poetry • Tennyson • Browning • Arnold

Victorian Poetry: An Introduction

Just as the Elizabethan age is predominantly one of poetry and poetic drama, the Victorian age proves to be one for the novel. As to poetry, however, its achievement in this age is not negligible, either. Some labored in the field and successfully made it comparable in popularity to the novel. One thing to notice about the taste of the age is that the Victorians valued mainly "applied" poetry (as against "pure" or "absolute" poetry), applied in the sense of being useful in inculcating moral lessons, or enforcing established values and tastes, or simply as a means of diversion and entertainment. This affected poetic creation, but the poets managed to speak both in a public and a private voice to meet both the need of the audience and that of their own visions. The major figures in the division of poetry include Tennyson, Browning, Arnold, Hopkins, and Clough. Other poets of significance such as Rossetti, Swinburne, and Wilde will be discussed in connection with the poets related to the aesthetic movement of the period, and Thomas Hardy's poetry will be mentioned along with his novels. As to Robert Bridges (1844-1930), it is good to note here that he became poet laureate in 1913, but was little known in his time except for his *The Testament of Beauty* (1929) which enjoyed some critical attention. Bridges was traditional in technique by and large even in the post-*The Waste Land* period of the 1920s.

Alfred Lord Tennyson (1809-1892)

Tennyson was born into a well-to-do clergyman's family in Somersby, Lincolnshire, England. He was educated at Cambridge University where he developed a close friendship with A. H. Hallam. In 1830, when still in college, Tennyson began to publish books of verse, but did not place anything in print for the next ten years because, for one thing, his poetry was harshly criticized and, for another, the death of his best friend Hallam in 1833 caused too much pain for him to handle. The publication of his poems in 1842 received favorable popular attention and established his position as a poet of the first order. In 1847 *The Princess* appeared. He became the poet laureate after the death of Wordsworth in 1850, the year in which his famous *In Memoriam* came out. Other volumes followed which included, among others, *Maud* (1855), *Enoch Arden* (1864), and *The Idylls of the King* (1869-1872).

As tastes and values differ from age to age, only those whose works are capable of universal and eternal application can hope to enjoy universal and eternal appreciation. Tennyson was one of these. Although he spoke mainly to his own age and day, there is something in his poetry that has fascinated today's readers as well. In the Victorian period he was a prophet, communicating the values of the time well and pleasantly to his audience. For instance, his long poem, *The Idylls of the King*, was read and enjoyed with avidity by his contemporaries chiefly for its didactic features. In the 20th century the younger generation was fed up with his moralizing and his technical virtuosity; they looked for something different to help deal with the new and different experience of their own day. Poetry also switched gears and veered in a new direction. Tennyson looked old and out of date and out of place almost overnight. The verse revolution of the first years of the 20th century after his death was spearheaded essentially against traditional poetics, the sum total of which he seemed to represent. Naturally Tennysonianism was under attack. But time and history is always just. Tennyson has survived the storm of change and the temporary declension. Today he is still a welcome presence on the poetic scene though for a different reason. His lyrical genius has proved fascinating and charming. Thus although many have found it possible to discredit him on account of his "weaknesses," no one can disregard him in any way.

Tennyson served his contemporary audience very well. The Victorian period was one of violent uncertainty when history was going through a radical transition and people felt badly lost in a whirlpool of ideas. The Victorians, feeling the acute need for guidance, looked up to their writers for instruction and advice. Their poet laureate became one of their teachers. Tennyson proved to be the true oracular laureate for his time. He was a prophet of many things then, but he offered love first and foremost to his people at a time when the world was becoming amoral and indifferent and alienation was keenly felt all around. In more than one sense Tennyson was a domestic poet, placing abundant emphasis on love, duty and allegiance and on marriage and home and children. Love was to him an ethical force and man's redeeming grace. One of the poet's famous lines, praising love as beautiful and pure and eternal, appears in his *In Memoriam*: "'Tis better to have loved and lost/than never to have loved at all." Love can keep off lust and strengthen man's moral will. King Arthur in *The Idylls of the King* sees love as a force to keep down the base, and teach high thought and all that makes humans human. For Tennyson, marriage and home bring happiness, quiet and comfort, and all that makes life worth living. The young lovers walking in the moonlight may distress the Lady of Shalott, but they are a blissful sight because "lately wed." The "azure pillars of the hearth" in the valley of *The Princess* prove immensely soothing to the maiden who goes there to look for love. The poet always sings praise of the spiritual aspect of love. His *The Vision of Sin*, *Lucretius*, and even *Maud*, among others, illustrate the point most clearly. Tennyson has no patience with any form of social interruption of genuine love. In fact a recurrent theme in his works has been the frustration of a pure love. The poet is furious about the lovers torn apart as, for instance, occurs in *Maud* and "Locksley Hall." To Tennyson love can make or mar a civilization. One way of interpreting *The Idylls of the King* may be to see it as a warning that improper love may lead to the fall of a kingdom. The epic may body forth the poet's sense of frustration with the sensuality and disorientation that Victorian life had already exhibited. Certain observations in the modern novel, *The French Lieutenant's Woman*, could furnish an apt footnote to the central theme of the long poem.

Today, however, Tennyson is appreciated for a radically different reason. Instead of looked up to as a prophet and teacher, he is read and enjoyed for his lyrical genius and for his technical virtuosity. In fact all his life Tennyson worked with the lyric. Although he exhibited other kinds of poetic energies such as the narrative and the didactic in his own time, Tennyson's genius is primarily lyrical, and lyric energy is his primary strength. Tennyson's poetry often reveals two voices, one public and the other private. Generally, his poems composed before 1842 are more private in their thematic focus, but he leaned heavily toward didactic poetry after the 1840s. One feature of his private voice is the poet's love of the lyric form which is noted for its emotional coloring. Tennyson's lyric genius shines through his nature poetry, his incidental and occasional poetry, and his long poetic efforts such as *The Idylls of the King*, *In Memoriam*, *Maud*, and *The Princess*.

First, his nature poetry is a faithful and fascinating description of English country life with its sights, sounds, scents, and habits. It gives the reader moving touches like the soft smell of the earth after rain, the breeze of early dawn caressing fresh flowers in the garden, the falling sound of water in the woods, and the rustle of poplar leaves like the patter of rain. Tennyson's nature poetry is beautiful for a number of reasons: its imitation of the sounds of the English birds which display the poet's delicate sense of sound and power of onomatopoeia—the lark's song, the woodpecker's laughter, the jay's whistle, and the owl's shriek; its representation of nature's infinitude—the sea, the sky, the stars, and space; and its display of the fine and exquisite mind of a poet conscious of the spirituality of nature and sensitive to the juxtaposition and contrast between the ephemeral and the eternal, and the infinitesimal and the infinite, which nature reveals for man.

Then, there is Tennyson's incidental or occasional poetry to consider. These are all full of lyric beauty, too. "Tiresias," "Daisy," "The June Bracken and Heather," and the dedication of *The Idylls of the King* are all graphic illustrations here. The Roman inscriptions aptly condensed, the felicity of Horatian odes, and the unmistakable urbanity in taste—all these qualities and more are simply impressive beyond description. There are also Tennyson's emotionally charged songs that appear in his longer narrative efforts such as *In Memoriam*, with the poet's deep sense of bereavement ("The purple from the distance dies," "The bases of his life are drowned in tears"), the depth of despair that kills all joy in life ("Speakest to me, dearest, lest I should die"), the childhood memories and half-forgotten dreams that keep flooding back to torment the mind, the moan of the sea, the cry of a child lost at midnight—all these and more indicate the lyrical note resounding through Tennyson's poetry. Finally, there are Tennyson's poetic techniques that have been always prized as a rich and original legacy he left to posterity. The music of his language, his exquisite handling of the poetic tricks such as alliteration and anaphora, and his dexterous use of the vowels—all these have been meticulously studied and imitated ever since his time.

Now let's take a look at some of Tennyson's representative works.[2] *The Princess* tells a love story. Its major theme, domestic joy and sorrow, is a modern notion encased in a subject of the past. Princess Ida founds a university for girls to promote her ideals of women's rights. She refuses to marry the prince to whom she was engaged in childhood. The prince enters the university in the disguise of a girl, and is found out. He is in danger. In the meantime the princess' father comes with an army to confront the prince. A fight follows in which the prince and his men are defeated and wounded. The princess, thus moved, turns the university into a hospital to take care of the wounded, and her heart is finally won. The poem is made up of a series of idylls, and some vignettes are inserted here and there to highlight the events such as the prince's seizures, the complex relationships of the prince and the princess with their friends and family, the rearing of Lady Psyche's baby, and the victory of love. The work is not a straightforward narrative; it is a medley of idylls—lyric, descriptive, domestic, and epic. "The Gardener's Daughter" and "Dora" are typical domestic idylls, and there is some hint of the epic idyll in the battle and in the whole epic about the princess.

Another famous work, *In Memoriam*, was written over an extended period of time (1834-1850) when Tennyson was assailed by the uncertainty of faith which the evolutionary science brought about at the time. The poem is, therefore, a record of the poet's spiritual odyssey and recovery of his faith in immortality from his grief over his physical loss. As the poem goes, Hallam dies at the age of 24 when he is just beginning to realize his promise in the prime of his years. His death both enrages and perplexes the poet so that he is beginning to wonder whether God is at strife with nature which is so careless about human life and does not seem to be part of God's creation. For a time he sees God as remote and death as final. He is pained by the irreparable sense of loss and sees no hope of ever uniting with his best friend. He sinks to "wild despair." Then, as the poem continues, he is beginning to feel the strength of man's inward sense of immortality, and indicate his inclination to identify Hallam with Christ in spirit who may save him. He yearns for a mystical contact with the spirit of the lost one and feels the need to revive love as the universal law. He searches for signs of immortality in himself, experiences a swing of moods of content and despair, and suddenly feels a presence when he rereads Hallam's letters: "And all at once it seem'd at last/The living soul was flashed on me." Now aware of the continuity of existence, he experiences a brief communion with the universal spirit, of which Hallam's spirit exists as an indistinguishable part. He feels assured that the world is full of immortal love and becomes affirmative in attitude: "All is well." The thematic importance of this was self-evident in his own time: England was going through a period when people began to feel the increasing impact of the crisis of faith stemming from the theory of evolution. In formal terms *In Memoriam* is an elegy similar to Milton's *Lycidas* or Shelley's *Adonais*. The pattern of the elegiac is visible in the Tennyson poem. There is the progression from the feeling of loss and grief to final triumph of love and affection over sorrow and death. But Tennyson's poem does not follow strictly the traditional elegiac tradition such as taking the impersonal direction of the pastoral elegy as do Milton's or Shelley's. It was his own experience of conversion that supplied the structural pattern of his poem. There is the power of the mystical, the vision of the dead, and the communication between souls. *In Memoriam* is a highly personal elegy.

The work on which Tennyson spent over half century writing on an on-and-off basis, *The Idylls of the King*, was one of the three major epics to come out of the Victorian period, the other two being Robert Browning's *The Ring and the Book* and Gerard Manley Hopkins' *The Wreck of the Deutschland.* [3] *The Idylls of the King* was the poet's effort to awaken responsive echoes in modern bosoms to an ancient tale of heroism and woe, the strengths and weaknesses of which might still be relevant to the life of his age. The evident purpose of the sustained poetic endeavor was to glorify the progress of his age, laud Prince Albert and Queen Victoria as idealized rulers, and commend the major Victorian virtues to cater to the needs of a people clamoring for guidance. In this sense it was the work of a poet laureate serving his monarch and his people.

Now *The Idylls of the King*, containing 12 books based mainly on Thomas Malory's *Morte D'Arthur*, was an adequate documentation and confirmation of the major features of Victorian life. These included, among other things, domestic virtues, the emphasis on the home, family affections and love, hero-worship (hero as the fixed point in the constant flux of history), the identity of the self (indicative of the poet's awareness of the depersonalization process ever intensifying then) and self-realization through duty and service, moral earnestness, and positive achievements. For instance, the *Idylls* stresses the importance of love and conjugal harmony as the basis of sound civilized life. The epic can be seen as a series of love stories—devotion to love ("Lancelot and Elaine"); adulterous passion ("Lancelot and Guinevere"); the lawless passion of Isolt and Tristram, the triangle of Mark, Isolt, and Tristram which mirrors that of Arthur, Guinevere, and Lancelot and which crushes the king's ideal ("The Last Tournament"); the wiles of the flesh ("Merlin and Vivien"); the betrayal of faith ("Pellas and Ettaire"); and marital disharmony ("The Marriage of Geraint" and "Geraint and Enid"). The last book, "The Passing of Arthur," expresses the poet's sense of frustration that his dream of a utopian social order was not happening after all as the life of the senses proved to be so compelling as against the life of the soul. Tennyson wanted to tell his people that illicit love would lead to the downfall of a civilization as that between Lancelot and Guinevere did to Arthur's kingdom.

On the other hand, Tennyson managed to express his private vision in the series of idyllic pictures he put into the epic, as indeed he always did in his other major works. It is important to remember that he was first and foremost an artist and that, although he embraced the prevailing Victorian moral aesthetic well and condemned the voguish decadent aestheticism, he was not in any way indifferent to "the palace of art" he had in mind to construct. In this sense *Idylls of the King* also bodies forth the poet's prophetic vision that the ills of his age, the frenzied getting and spending and the threat of materialism to the life of the soul, the increasingly overwhelming middle-class philistinism in tastes and values, and the weakening or the loss of faith—all these might lead to the decline of the civilization that the Victorians had been busy building. So the epic constitutes an oblique warning to and a criticism of his society as well. Camelot is meant to represent a noble palace of art for him, a symbol of the importance of the life of the mind, and Avilon is portrayed as an emblem of total alienation from the world of the senses. So *The Idylls of the King* reveals the two voices, or the "dissociated sensibility" (as one critic puts it), the public alongside the private, that is in evidence everywhere in Tennyson's works.

Tennyson also draws from the legends for other purposes. For instance, his famous poem, "The Lady of Shalott" (1833), was written in tangential reference to the story of King Arthur, not exactly to talk about the legend but to discuss the poet's aesthetic view of art and artistic creation. "The Lady of Shalott" is, according to the Athurian legend, Elaine, whose father's name, when Anglicized, is Shalott. The story of Elaine and Lancelot is one of love and unrequited love. Elaine loves Lancelot very much but the knight cannot return her affection. Distraught with grief, she dies tragically. Tennyson's poem is actually a play on the death of Elaine. The knight's love is out of her reach because Lancelot is in love with Queen Guinevere. Elaine's love is destined to flourish only in her imagination by envisioning Lancelot as her lover (as in the poem she can only look at the reflection of the knight through her mirror, a distorted image of reality, once removed at least from life itself), but once she is out to get a feel of the reality, she is so sorely disappointed that she can find consolation only in death (as in the poem she dies when she goes out to Camelot, only to find herself face to face with the unadulterated truth of Lancelot's illicit love). The poem is probably Tennyson's way of saying that reality can be so harsh that it can kill if one is not well prepared for it and that love, if not well handled, can be devastating to individuals as well as to the state in the same way illicit love wrecks the legendary kingdom of King Arthur. "The Lady of Shalott" was Tennyson's first work on the subject of the Arthurian legends, and thus proved to be the precursor to his *Idylls of the King*.

Now as the poem goes, it speaks of Camelot and a mysterious woman who resides in a tower on the island of Shalott. It is divided into four parts. Part I (ll. 1-36) introduces Camelot and its people, the island of Shalott and the Lady of Shalott. Part II (ll. 37-72) describes the life of the lady—living all in solitude, her daily work—weaving, and her unspoken curse—not to be drawn to the real world. Part III (ll. 73-117) brings in the sexy male image of Sir Lancelot as an instrument of the curse. And the last part (ll. 118-171) narrates the lady's death and the unraveling of her mystery. What the secluded lady does every day is to look at a mirror and weave a web of life as she sees it reflected from the mirror. The beauties and the lively events of the outside world fascinate the lady so much that she longs to be part of it. Sick of looking at the "shadows" and wishing for a change, she looks down at Camelot, thus inducing the curse to work upon her. Then she sees Sir Lancelot riding by and can no longer refrain herself from making her desired trip to Camelot. There she goes and gets drowned on her way.

The poem, independent of the poet's intentions, can be seen as a highly symbolic work. Everything is nicely loaded. Camelot represents the world of life. The lady is the artist figure, her weaving is her artistic creation, and her mirror the filtering process of reality through her artistic mind. The privacy of the island symbolizes both the isolation of the artist from the world necessary for his creativity and the inescapable condition of the poet's art; it is also an indication of the need to keep intact the private vision of the artist. The curse denotes the attitude—early Tennyson's attitude—toward art and its creation, that an artist is not supposed to be part of the real world, his art is his life and his life is his art, and his private vision is all that matters. The moment the vision vanishes, the artist ceases to have any valid reason to exist. Thus when the lady succumbs to the temptation of the world with Sir Lancelot as its fitting emblem, the curse begins its work on her, and her doom as an artist is sealed. The poem is a clear record of early Tennyson's emphasis on art and the artist's need to keep his privacy and his private voice whole and free from interference. Once it is violated, art is lost. Later Tennyson (post-1842), however, failed to put this in full practice as he became more and more socially engaged.

The poem can also be seen as an exposition on the nature of art. Any work of art is the artist's own creation. The reality that appears in a work of art is not strictly the true reality, but the one that the artist has created in keeping with his vision of life, one that he would like to see in existence. The mirror is his vision, his delusion in a manner of speaking. It is in fact his doorway into another world, very often different from and a distortion of the real world. This is true of the Jewish tale of Lilith, Lewis Carroll's Alice story, or the American poet—John Ashbery's convex mirror, or the modern-day funhouses in amusement parks. As all mirrors reflect a distortion of reality, all art work is by the same token a distortion of life in varying degrees. This is one way to define art, and probably the closest to telling the truth about art.

Robert Browning (1812-1889)

Although late to receive recognition, Browning was considered second only to Tennyson in his own day. He was every bit a representative Victorian as was Tennyson. Browning attended the University of London only for a year and was in a sense home-educated, reading through his father's well-stocked library. This may in a way account for his late start in critical evaluation, but from the 1860s onward he became preeminent and remained very much in evidence all through his life.

As with Tennyson, Browning's reputation rests now on a different basis from that of his own day. In his own time and day he was looked up to as a prophet advocating courage and striving. Today, however, he is remembered for a couple of things he did for modern poetry: His experiment and use of the dramatic monologue and his contribution to the discovery of the mythical method and symbolism in the writing of psychological poetry.

To his own contemporaries, Browning's poetry represents the exuberant and optimistic spirit of his time. His conception of life was basically idealistic and hopeful. His poetry is full of the zeal and gusto that he hopes people should have to brave ever new life. His watchword is "strive." It is the passion and the intensity of feeling alive and active that his poetry celebrates. He was famous then for his concept that the joy of life lies in the living and that it is striving that makes life meaningful. His was a perfect moral world where God is in heaven and all is well here on earth. To him "All the good things /Are ours," which is a poetic statement of the ebullient hopefulness ("Rabbi Ben Ezra"); the world means intensely and good for people, and it is "my meat and drink" to discover its meaning, which is probably Browning's heartiest expression of faith in the joy of living (as is shown in "Fra Lippo Lippi"). Thus as the readers move through his poetry, they will see a gallery of portraits of hard-working and dedicated people: the Grammarian leaves play for work, thirsts for learning, and finds infinite joy in grappling with the world ("Grammarian's Funeral"), and Child Roland keeps pushing on toward a goal which is yet to be defined ("Child Roland to the Dark Tower Came"). Browning's world is full of such prophets, artists, lovers and doers of great deeds for whom exerting one's best offers the greatest gratification for the soul. Life is a kind of struggle through which people prove their worth; it is a struggle toward perfection that probably will never materialize. For Browning's is the philosophy of the imperfect, of "success in failure." In his opinion, man is imperfect, but this the poet chooses to see as an asset rather than anything else: the craving for improvement drives man for ever onward. The motive power for the soul comes from a high ideal ever kept afloat and remote but never achievable as that would mean spiritual death ("Prospice" and "Epilogue to Asolando"). Aspiration is its own reward and is an end in itself; heaven exists, man yearns for it, but finds it ever beyond his reach ("Andrea del Sarto"). Earth's imperfect is eternity's perfect; heaven's purpose is "to perfect the earthen"; "On the earth the broken arcs; in the heaven a perfect round" ("Abt Volger"). So many a Browning hero is what he calls "this high man," with a great thing to pursue; what this "great thing" might be hardly matters; it is the endeavor to achieve it. In keeping with the spirit of his time, Browning offered a kind of philosophy which touched the hearts of the Victorians and excited and inspired them to experience life with courage and hope.

However, Browning is viewed as important today for totally different reasons. First, he made the dramatic monologue a norm as a poetic form for presenting the internal world of the characters. For some ten years from the late 1830s through the 40s, he wrote plays which, although not well received, helped him to discover and perfect the monologue form. His poems, the most famous of which is "My Last Duchess," provide scenarios in which a character is made to speak out his mind and thus reveal his inner psychology. This has a strong modern ring because it often resembles a stream-of-consciousness style in modern writing. It represents a jump in perception on the part of the artist from writing about the externalities of life and people to the scrutiny and exploration of the inner consciousness of the characters. In a sense Browning began the new modern psychological poetry. Take "My Last Duchess" for instance. Here is a veritable psychological enigma for people to unravel. The duke telling his side of the story may not be creditable because he appears to be a psychopath of sorts, high-strung and anxious to rush to self-defense. He may have had the duchess murdered as he boasts of having done, but it may have been all figment of his imagination. The poem says that he is conversing with a visitor, but there is also hint that he may be talking to himself the same way T. S. Eliot's Prufrock may be doing, and the whole thing may have been all pure figment of his imagination. The artistic ambiguity so well embedded in the poem has made it rich and capable of more than one interpretation, and as such has proved immensely fascinating and charming to modern readers and writers.

Browning is valued today very much also because his realism and psychology have made it possible for modern people to discover the use of symbol and myth. Browning embraces realism and opposes the use of myth as overt subject matter. His poetic creation reveals a visible direction that he tries to take toward a psychological use of myth. In "Parleyings with Gerard de Lairesse," he wonders whether he would do better to tell two stories, i.e. to repeat the old myth of Dryope (plucking a bright blossom for her child and getting severe punishment) through the real modern story of an English girl plucking an English homegrown apple. He would take the chances of seeing a double vision here. As an observant critic puts it, it is exactly this double vision that has led to the 20th-century return to myth. A good deal of Browning's poetry such as "Lairesse," "Avison," and the whole "Parleyings" can be best understood only in terms of seeing these as the poet's efforts toward symbolism and the mystical method in poetic creation. For instance, the one thing that seems to lie at the heart of Browning's view of the world is, as critic Langbaum puts it, the recurrent pattern of "impasse and miracle" in his works, or the Andromeda-Perseus pattern, in which somebody like Princess Andromeda is in jeopardy, about to be devoured by the forthcoming sea monster, and some hero like Perseus appears at the critical moment for the rescue. It is suggested that this view of Browning's is traceable to his own rescue of his would-be wife Miss Elizabeth Barrett, an event of unusual significance in his life, from which he derived his enduring faith in the moral goodness of the world for man. Another poem that demonstrates this view at work, "Balaustion's Adventure," features a Greek girl retelling the story of Euripides' *Alcestis*, in which Alcestis the queen, willing to die and go down to Hades in her husband's stead, is snatched back from the clutches of Death by a chivalrous hero—Heracles. Also, underpinning the story of Browning's epic poem, *The Ring and the Book*, is actually the same pattern, whereby the heroine Pompilia is rescued by Caponsacchi on the English patron saint St. George's day from her victimizer Count Guido, and the Pope saves truth by condemning evil. All through the poem the myth—that of a hero suddenly showing up and doing the heroic deed—is present in some form in the minds of almost all the characters, including the debased and the cynical ones. A lot of Browning's other poems such as "Andrea del Sarto" and "Numpholeptos" work in the same vein. Myth in Browning is used to make a statement about the nature of life; it is not to be taken literally.

In addition, Browning is appreciated today for a few more things he did which illustrate the modernity of his thought and his poetry. One of these is his notion of relativism, that truth has more than one facet to show for human understanding at one time and is therefore not absolute. This is a new awareness in the history of human epistemology. *The Ring and the Book* is a good illustration. The story is enveloped in so many layers of falsehoods and obscurities, so many people speak out about the case—the two halves of Rome, the victims (Pompilia and Caponsacchi), the victimizer (Count Guido), the lawyers, the church, and the government, that the truth of the murder case is almost lost in the maze of the views thus presented. Browning is, in a way, ahead of his time here when he suggests through the epic that it is difficult if not altogether impossible to see reality and truth in its totality and finality.

There is also Browning's emphasis on intuition and divided self to consider. Browning believes in human instinct and the power of the unconscious, and sees intuitive experience as the best gateway to knowledge. This has to do with the supreme importance he attaches to the individual soul and to individualism. He stresses the harmony between the senses and the intuitions in an artist and feels that a poet should be a seer speaking intuitively. With tradition as its weapon, intellect is to Browning directly antithetical to human instinct. Most of his major characters perceive the world intuitively and act accordingly. They tend to "go against the flow," and behave like non-conformists and rebels. Fra Lipo Lippi, for instance, paints by instinct and rejects the traditional religious art. Caponsacchi in *The Ring and the Book* flouts social standards and saves Pompilia all through intuition.

As to the subject of the divided self, the Victorian era was one in which man became well aware that life was increasing its encroachment upon his spiritual wholeness, and that his consciousness and his unconscious, his intellect and his imagination, his external world and his inner world were all at work to divide him into two halves. Hence the Victorian representation of the theme of the divided self. Browning proves himself to be one of the most sensitive literary artists of time. There is a visible double awareness in him: he feels pulled in two directions in the tug of war between commitment and private vision. On the whole Browning leans toward commitment and disapproves strongly of the aesthetic movement gathering momentum with time in his day. Advocating the principle that art is founded in reality, Browning sees as doomed to failure anyone who places undue emphasis on self-indulgence and self-expression. It is true that Browning is torn between his divided allegiances, and this is evident in his portrayal of characters such as Aprile, the lyric poet in *Paracelsus*, Abt Volger who plays for his own pleasure, Eglamor, the troubadour in *Sordello*, and Jules the sculptor in *Pippa Passes*—but all these are among his characters whose behavior Browning ultimately disapproves of. His world is peopled with characters whose divided selves keep on interacting with one another and finding a way of addressing their dilemmas. Paracelsus goes on with his endless introspection, and so does Sordello, but all of these try to attain self-integration and integrity through commitment and struggle to achieve a fuller life. Sordello, for instance, comes to realize that the function of a poet is to move people to participation and takes the burden of life and humanity willingly. [4]

Now let's take a brief look at Browning's masterpiece, his epic-length poem, *The Ring and the Book*. Browning did not take much interest in the Greek myths and mythical heroes; he felt drawn to little known people and incidents. There are, in his poetry, no King Arthur and his knights as in Tennyson and no Greek celebrities as in Matthew Arnold. Browning's characters are much less known, and so are his plots. But he took these from the past and did a good job of relating the past to the present and teaching a moral lesson. *The Ring and the Book* offers a good example here. Browning got the subject through reading an old court record which he happened to pick up in a wayside bookstall in a Florentine market. [5]

The story happens in 17th-century Rome. As it goes, the impoverished Count Guido Franceschini marries Pompilia Comparini, believing that she would bring him a fortune. When this does not happen and Pompilia's identity as heir becomes dubious, he wants to get rid of her. He treats her monstrously so that the desperate Pompilia asks Canon Giuseppe Caponsacchi to take her home, which Caponsacchi does, but the Count has the both of them arrested for trial. He accuses Pompilia of committing adultery with Caponsacchi. Pompilia is found guilty and sent to a covenant and Caponsacchi is banished. Then Pompilia goes home to give birth to a son and is murdered one night along with her "foster" parents. Count Guido stabs her to death. He is arrested, tried for murder, and executed on the Pope's order. Pompilia is declared innocent. This is the "Book" in the title. The "Ring" represents the gold of the truth which is so difficult to get at. As the goldsmith, in making a gold ring, moulds the ring with alloy first and then has to get rid of the alloy before he can get the ring out, the poet tries to reach the truth through a process in which he disengages falsehood from fact. The falsehoods come from many perspectives which the poem presents with multiple points of view. The technique employed here will catch on as a technical resource for writers of later generations.

The poem consists of 12 books, beginning with a preface, and moving on to present "Half-Rome"'s opinion on the murder case, that of the "The Other Half-Rome," the impartial stance of "Tertium Quid," Guido's side of the story, Caponsacchi's version, the legal presentations, the Pope's decision, Guido's insolence and collapse, and the execution of the murderer. It is a typical Victorian work because it exemplifies some of the qualities which characterize the era. These include the Victorian emphasis on the family, filial piety, marriage and fidelity, and maternal love. Pompilia is a pattern of virtue. She is a good daughter, a good wife, and a good mother. There is spacious room in her heart and soul for genuine love. She is instinctual, all spiritual innocence and purity, altogether too good for the world in which she lives. As such she lives forever at the tender mercies of the hostile forces of society. Her husband is her antithesis in every possible sense of the term. Just as Pompilia is an etherized spirit, so he is all materialized, self-serving, rational to a fault, always scheming and calculating, and thoroughly adept in exploiting social institutions to his best advantage. There is nothing like love in his person. Marriage is to him just another way of becoming rich quick, and connubial faith means exactly nothing to him. He is altogether the authentic embodiment of conscious intellect at which Browning spearheads his scathing satire. Cruel, violent, and malignant, Count Guido is an archetypal specimen of human evil.

The sharp contrast between the two major characters and the attitudes of society offer ample room for rumination. Although the world of *The Ring and the Book* is by and large a moral one, the impression the reader comes away with after reading the poem is often depressing, not so much because someone good dies a violent underserved death as because of the deep-seated bias that the world holds for so long against the victim. The government, the church (the archbishops to whom Pompilia appeals, the friar), the legal system, and the popular opinion are either too corrupt and too self-centered or too nonchalant and apathetic to care about the fate of an insignificant individual. This represents Browning's social criticism, however oblique it may be. The poem also bodies forth the poet's aesthetic principle, especially in its first and last books where the poet makes it clear that the artist receives his inspiration and sanction for his creation from God, directed by "a Hand/Always above my shoulder," and creates to "[r]epeat God's process in man's due degree." In addition, the artist has a commitment to fulfill to human society: he mediates between the divine and the human and justifies God's ways to man.

Here is a good place to mention Elizabeth Barrett Browning (1806-1861), who was at her death even more famous as a poet than her husband Robert Browning. Her work was emotionally charged, rhetorically exquisite, and morally correct. Her active participation in the cultural and intellectual life of her day endeared her to her people. Her reputation fell in the early part of the 20th century, but in recent decades successful efforts have been made to resurrect her from oblivion. Her well-known *Sonnets from the Portuguese* (1850), 44 in total, records her love with Robert Browning. Her verse-novel, *Aurora Leigh* (1857), addresses the problem of a Victorian woman who wants to be a socially involved poet and yearns for freedom. The poem was warmly received in its day, and is becoming increasingly popular now. Elizabeth Barrett Browning was predominantly a socially engaged realist.

Matthew Arnold (1822-1888)

Arnold lived in an era of change in thought and feeling. Society was becoming increasingly affluent with material progress. The middle class was growing increasingly powerful with the influence of its wealth and its cultural philistinism. The autonomous character of the individual was fast dwindling, and self-serving individualism was becoming the driving force in social life. Values were undergoing a drastic change. The old absolutes seemed to be dying out, but the new ones were having a hard time getting born. With the ideas of evolution up in the air, faith was losing its hold upon popular imagination, and the mythic center that could unify and hold beliefs and values together was fast disappearing. It was, as Arnold calls it, "an age of iron," in which everything appeared to be "sick." The spiritual calm and cheerfulness based on faith disappeared; doubts and feelings of discouragement set in. For intellectually thinking people, life became altogether "excessively modern." There was a visible nostalgia for a lost world of peace and established order.[6]

Arnold was one of those sensitive spirits, almost too sensitive for his time. He keenly felt the sadness of the age, and wrote a poetry that expressed his feeling adequately. His poetry, such as *The Scholar Gypsy*, *Empedocles at Atna*, "Dover Beach," "Lines Written in Kensington Gardens," *Thyrsis*, and *Stanzas from the Grande Chartreuse*, all reveals the intensity of a melancholy that had been widely felt but had awaited apt articulation. Arnold responded to the call of his age and represented "the main movement of mind of the last quarter of a century" (as he put it in 1869). He did it so well that he was and has been known ever since as the Victorian poet of loneliness. This unhappiness had to do with his sense of religious frustration and the highly critical stance he took toward his un-poetical age. His has proved to be one of the best verse products to come out of the Victorian period. Arnold had faith in the permanence of his poetry. He tried to fuse Tennyson's poetical sentiment with Browning's intellectual vigor and abundance, and made the best of his poetic endowment to reflect the Victorian temper. As a result, he received recognition as poet number three of his time immediately after Tennyson and Browning. [7]

Arnold intuited the ills of his society and had a significant message for his people. His poetic characters are all of them his spokesmen. The weary and suicidal Empedocles, the retiring monks in "The Grand Chartreuse," the "I" of "Lines Written in Kensington Gardens" who sees a huge world that roars by and feels so helpless, and the lonely though indomitable Romantic poets in the

"Memorial Verses"—all these are good examples.

On *The Scholar Gypsy*, for instance, Arnold said that he wrote the poem to keep on record his happy days at Oxford. His character—"the scholar gypsy" was, according to available record, from Oxford, and was chosen to voice the poet's own opinion about the life of his day. As the story goes, "The scholar gypsy" is once an Oxford student, but because he is too poor to continue his life there, he joins a group of gypsies and wanders around with them. With time he makes friends with them and manages to learn about their mysteries. He finds that the gypsies' way of life and their art make good sense and decides to leave them and write about his experience when the time comes. Arnold, after reading the 17th-century scholar Joseph Glanville's "The Vanity of Dogmatizing" (1661), which contains a narrative of the scholar gypsy's story, felt that he sensed the spirit of the scholar gypsy still hovering over the beautiful and refreshing landscape of Oxford. He was sure that "the scholar gypsy" could offer a good outlet for venting his depressed feelings and revealing the causes for his dejection. The scholar gypsy serves for him as a counterpoint to modern man. The scholar is all in harmony with life and nature, often as an observant spectator, fond of "retired ground" and always "in a pensive dream." He sits on the bank, dressed in an outlandish manner, watching people busy at work, maidens dancing and children at play, and "waiting for the spark from heaven to fall" to tell his secrets and probably message. He is free from the "sick fatigue," "languid doubt," "disappointments new," and "sad patience, too near neighbor to despair," to which the speaker of the poem finds himself prone. The speaker looks back at the time and life of the scholar nostalgically when the scholar could still wait and hope. What disconcerts the speaker and throws him into the quagmire of despond is "this strange disease of modern life," with its sickening rush and bustle, "its divided aims," its overtaxed heads and palsied hearts. Although the speaker sees a vision of the scholar gypsy somewhere around Oxford (stanza 13) and regards him as immortal (stanza 16), the poem essentially presents an elegy, lamenting over the loss of one who is now long dead and buried somewhere, where tall grass and white flowering nettles cover his grave. The heavenly spark that the scholar gypsy has been waiting for may or may not fall, but it is essential for the individual to keep his integrity in face of the odds of life, since energies, once diffused, will lead to a loss of the sense of direction for the artist.

Needless to say, all these were expressions of Arnold's own feeling about his time, and so the poem has become a statement of its general mood. The verse reads like a pastoral elegy with its rich, picturesque language that reveals the tranquility and beauty of nature around the scholar gypsy. In fact the whole poem is enveloped in a pastoral atmosphere: the shepherd with his sheep, the reaper with his sheaves, the moon blanched–green, the live murmur of a summer's day, the thick corn, the scarlet poppies, the green roots and the yellowing stalks, the pale pink convolvulus in tendrils, the scents and the perfumes, the cool bank in the summer heat, the wide grass meadows in the sunshine, the black-winged swallows, the glittering Thames, maidens dancing in May, and children playing on an April day. The tantalizing colors, sights and sounds indicate the poet's yearning for sinking back into the wholesome milieu of nature, of which the scholar gypsy is part and parcel. The disappearance of the scholar gypsy is emblematic of the vanishing of an ideal past, and the quest that the poet bids the shepherd to undertake to find him represents a search for a lost world of harmony between man and man and between man and nature. Arnold was Romantic in temperament.

"Dover Beach" is almost Arnold's signature poem. Compact and powerful, it is the most effective expression of his temperament as a poet, his hypersensitivity to the subtle change then creeping imperceptibly into Victorian life, and his apocalyptic vision of the future. The whole poem is wrapped up in an atmosphere gloomy, stifling, and essentially melancholy. In the first part of stanza one, the picture is all calm, sweet, and fair: the night, the moon, the land and the bay, and the light that the speaker sees glimmering. Then a note is heard in the second part of the stanza which proves to be the keynote of the work. It is "the grating roar" from the moonlit seashore, contrasting intensely with the bewitching tranquility of the night and indicating the agonizing faithless present. This leads to the second stanza when the speaker recalls Sophocles' writing of the same agony and makes to the painful realization that human misery has been and is still basically the same. In the first part of stanza three, the speaker remembers with tenderness the time when the world was a "sea of faith" with the light of hope; he casts a nostalgic glance back at that golden past to compare it with the drear present. The second part of stanza three pictures a jarringly discordant sea, obviously an apt metaphor for the world he lives in: the incessant turbulence of the sea brings in the eternal sadness. There is cacophony enough, but the sense of harmony and serenity grounded on firm faith is conspicuously absent. Then follows the famous stanza four in which the speaker looks beneath the surface of things and locates the basic ills of modern life. He sees a world of "seems" (or appearances) before him: it looks various, beautiful, and new, all the features which material progress has made Victorian life appear to possess. But stripping its deceptive exterior, he reveals what is "really" true inside. The ever deepening crisis of faith is depriving man of any commendable purpose for which he is born to strive. As a result, the world grows gloomy, and life becomes joyless, loveless, without any sense of certitude, nor peace of mind, nor any help for pain forthcoming from sources either human or divine. The landscape is darkening, the mind is benighted, and there is confusion and chaos among the cohorts of ignorant people who strive or cry amid the city's jarring notes. They squabble over different ideas or for self-interest, all groping in the dark and seeing no light ahead. Hence the dominant mood of agony and despair of the poem and, by extension, the mind of the speaker. The loss of direction is evident, the mind is divided, and the existential nature of life is hinted at, if only obliquely. The very picture of the speaker standing all alone facing Coleridge's "wide, wide sea," with no protection and no support, trying to survive in face of an indifferent universe—this is symbolic and, in a sense, prophetic of a different universe, an amoral one, the naturalistic world that Emile Zola and his fellow writers of a slightly later age were to paint with meticulous care.

Arnold continued his poetic composition in this vein until 1860 when he decided to change gears and veer in a new direction. As poets such as Tennyson and T. S. Eliot regretted, Arnold stopped writing poetry and began his period of prose work. The change had to do with his literary credo. He felt, along with Coleridge before him and Wallace Stevens after, that poetry should bring joy and happiness and love and certitude to an age when these were absent and people were suffering. As a literary critic, Arnold's theory was original in ideas and assured in tone. He has been one of the English critics whose doctrines give people an air of authority and a sense of finality and certitude. Although he could not help giving authentic articulation to the general drift of thought and feeling of his period, he was not satisfied with the dominant sentiment—melancholy—that permeates his poems. So he wrote, instead, for the remainder of his years, a prose scathingly critical but somehow hopeful that he thought would help improve his society more effectively. As a result, works such as *Essays in Criticism* (1865), *Culture and Anarchy* (1869), and *Literature and Dogma* (1873) came out to popular exclaim. Thus he is also well known in literary history as a social critic.

As a social critic Arnold was worried about the direction which England was taking. It was one along which the middle class was trying to push the country forward. The industrial revolution made that class wealthy and powerful, and eminent scholars such as Adam Smith and Thomas Robert Malthus offered justifications for their conduct. In his *The Wealth of Nations*, Smith confirmed their rights to free trade, competition, and laissez-faire, and Malthus, in his "An Essay on the Principle of Population," helped to rid for the rich the horrors of population growth and poverty. The Victorian period was one of triumph for the middle class spirit. With the idea of progress and growth topmost in national consciousness, this class became the shaping influence over the English national way of life and its standards of values and tastes. It produced some of the leaders of all the major fields of activity in the country, had a decisive say in its policy-making, and made the country affluent by means foul or fair.

As Arnold saw it, however, this class was leading the country in a wrong direction. It followed the gospel of getting ahead in the world and wallowed in money and material things. Its tastes were vulgar and low. Showing little or no appreciation for the arts, it impacted all levels of social life vigorously with its tantalizing materialism, and vehemently championed individual license. Arnold felt that this class, strong, dogged, and unenlightened, was harnessing the country in the "bondage to machinery" and increasing popular "proneness to value machinery as the end in itself." As a result, it posed a threat to the best possible human values. It would dominate English society and obscure the national recognition of its real end. This debilitating philistinism stood for Arnold in intolerable contrast with his ideal of "[making] reason and the will of God prevail." This was the reason why Arnold regarded it as the source of "anarchy" for the country. What he meant by "anarchy" was the vanishing of the unifying absolutes and the jeopardizing of social stability. He enunciated his idea eloquently in his works such as *Culture and Anarchy* and *Essays in Criticism*. While giving due recognition to the good side of middle class behavior, Arnold insistently offers, in these writings, his advice as to how to offset or play down its growing philistine influence. He emphasizes the role of culture. He sees culture as "a principle of authority to counteract the tendency to anarchy." It will combat the baneful influence of philistine "machinery," and help society keep its high ideals and live in a way worthy to be called human. Arnoldian "culture" is a social force. It aims at achieving true and full humanity, a balanced and harmonious development of human nature in all its aspects, and a state of mind catholic in taste and striving for its own perfection. His culture prizes the virtues of the impulse toward moral development and self-conquest, and prefers Hellenism to what he calls middle class Hebraism. The former values the spontaneity of consciousness, while the latter stresses strict conscience. Arnold is known as a preacher of Hellenism. He insists that society would have to go through changes in its education, its religion, and its conception of the state. Education should be made to benefit all. Religion should help people learn the will of God and relate their souls to God. The authority of the state should be increased to hold individual freedom in check and keep off centrifugal tendencies. The essence of his culture is a desire after the things of the mind and a striving toward a knowledge of some universal order.

Chapter 17 Clough • Hopkins • Edward Fitzgerald's Rubaiyat • The Aesthetic Movement

Arthur Hugh Clough (1819-1861)

The shepherd poet in Matthew Arnold's elegy, *Thyrsis*, Clough was one of Arnold's closest friends in temperament and sensitivity. The two of them experienced the same dilemma: religious doubt which was actually affecting many similar sensitive spirits of the time such as John Ruskin, Kierkegaard, and Emily Dickinson. Clough's poetry was in fact a footnote to his oscillating mind. There was, however, a noticeable difference between his position and that of Arnold's. Whereas "Dover Beach" reveals a spiritual bleakness and almost despair, Clough's works such as "Easter Day I Naples 1846," "Easter Day II," *Dipsychus* (1850) and "Say Not the Struggle Nought Availeth" (1849), shine forth a glimmer of hope and conviction, however faint and tenuous those might be. Clough was independent in his opinions, and there is a good deal of humor in his works that helps relieve the gloom hanging over his poetic world. And he wrote the best kind of hexameters in English poetry. [1]

All his life Clough was torn between faith and doubt. Throughout his career as a poet, he did not commit himself to a clear position of "yes or no." This hovering between belief and disbelief is well demonstrated in his two "Easter Day" poems. These show him bogged down in the theological dead center of his day. In "Easter Day I" he says, "From the cursed world which is one tomb, Christ is not risen." The people are hopeless and belief-less. There is no heaven or hell. So "Eat, drink, and die." Don't set one's affections on things above because He is dead and there is no life above. But the tone and mood of "Easter Day II" is drastically different. It tells people not to despair and not to feel hopeless. "Though dead, not dead," "Christ is yet risen." In other words, there is life in Heaven after all.

The very title of the long poem *Dipsychus* is sufficient to showcase the poet's apparent dilemma. In fact, Dipsychus is the name of the major character in the poem. He is in Venice, looking around and talking to a companion by the name of Mephisto. The scenario seems to be one similar in nature to Goethe's *Faust* with this difference that Dipsychus is questing for faith and Mephisto is not quite a devil. This young man has, as his name implies, two souls, two selves. His is a veritable divided personality. One part of him is idealistic, gazing upward and anxious to believe, while the other part is worldly, eager to commit himself to the here and now. The two parts of the self keep watching and analyzing one another. Dipsychus has his own standards: he is afraid to sin or commit doctrinal errors. These prove so exacting and make him so scrupulous that he is spiritually sick. For instance, he wants sex and yet his inhibitions hold him back. He makes a move and then draws back. Mephisto says of him: "You're this and that,/ And here and there...." His advice to the young man is to see things as they simply are. In matters of faith Dipsychus wants to believe, yet he knows well that faith does not address all the problems. The dialogues that he carries on with Mephisto are actually his interior monologues that reflect his inner struggle. Thus Mephisto is in fact one part of Dipsychus' self and his adviser in a sense. In the end Dipsychus decides to say goodbye to his "dreams" and embrace the world for what it is. Probably the reading of the poem leaves the impression that the young man's affirmative attitude is not strenuously final, his dilemma is not thoroughly resolved, but he manages to win through to a measure of peace of the mind. Dipsychus is more than one way Clough's self-portrait.

Clough's "Say Not Struggle Nought Availeth" ends with the famous line, "But westward, look, the land is bright," made famous by Winston Churchill who, in the midst of World War II, quoted it to Roosevelt. Clough's "war" in the poem is an inner war, the "enemy" is probably religious skepticism, and the "comrades" are the sources of one's inner spiritual strength to win faith back. So it is like a winning Dipsychus speaking. The poem is a good contrast in tone with "Dover Beach." Clough's other works include such as *Amours de Voyage* and *Bothie of*

Tober-na-Vuolich.

Gerard Manley Hopkins (1844-1889)

Hopkins was educated at Oxford and became a Jesuit after he was converted to Roman Catholicism. He served for a while as a priest in the poor sections of some big cities such as London and Manchester and saw the poverty of the working-class people. The experience proved to be depressing. As his sermons were not always in line with the taste of the church, he was removed to become a professor of Greek at the University of Dublin. He died of typhoid fever at 44. Hopkins wrote a good number of shorter poems and the epic-length *The Wreck of the Deutschland.* He proved himself to be one of the finest Victorian poets both in virtuosity and innovative enthusiasm. However, none of his poems were published until 30 years after his death when his friend Robert Bridges (1844-1930) brought his *Poems* out in print in 1918. Today interest in his poetry and thought is visibly on the increase. [2]

Hopkins was, according to Bridges, odd and obscure, odd in the sense that his mind worked in its peculiar way, and obscure because he was not easily approachable. His epic-length *The Wreck of the Deutschland* is difficult but ranks along with the *Idylls of the King* and *The Ring and the Book* in history. Generally, Hopkins' short nature poems are easier and more pleasant to read, poems that serve basically to reveal the glory of God. His poetry is among the most religious works in English literature. Hopkins was a courageous experimentalist. He wrote in his kind of rhythm which he called the "strung rhythm." This is in fact a variety of accentual meter as has been used in some Old English poetry and Coleridge's "Christabel." Hopkins found this rhythm fascinating because the poet does not have to write in feet but rather emphasizes the number of accents (stresses) in a line. In the contemporary period, American poet Richard Wilbur (1921-) revived this pattern in his poem "Junk." Hopkins is almost excessively pre-occupied with technical devices such as the manipulation of sounds, internal rime, alliteration, and assonance. But he has his own point. His technical concerns are by no means a mere show-off of virtuosity, but all serve to create effect and add intensity.

Let's take a look at some of his works. "The Windhover" (1877) is, as the poet himself said, "the best thing I ever wrote." The octet of the sonnet depicts the beauty and perfection of the windhover's skilled maneuver with the wind. It whirls, soars, circles round, dips, and banks with wind. The poet feels stirred at the sight. It reminds him of Christ upon the cross which the sestet talks about. Through self-sacrifice and his fire of love, Jesus Christ saves humanity and improves human nature. As compared with him, the windhover is only "a minion" in his kingdom. To Hopkins the flight of the windhover is probably not so much a metaphor for the grandeur and perfection of Jesus Christ as a reminder, a manifestation, a eulogy, of it. Thus the poet is successfully justifying the importance of religious life. The poem is a technical wonder in more than one way. Its onomatopeic effect is remarkable, accurately mimicking the sound of the bird's flight. There is also the alliteration, which indicates the poet's love for Old and Middle English. Then there is the skilled manipulation of words like "caught" (catching a glimpse of, instead of actually catching the bird?), "buckle" (bird descending or Christ assuming [buckling on] human nature?), "sheer plod" (Christ improving humanity, i.e. religious life?), and "embers" (moist clods denoting humankind?), thus imbedding nicely an ambiguity for posterity. No wonder that the poem has been profusely commented upon and argued over ever since it came out in print.

Another poem that reveals the poet's tremendous sense of love of God is the sonnet, "Pied Beauty" (1877). "Pied" here means not only variegation, but also contrasts within variety that constitute and sustain what Hopkins terms the *inscape*, or the principle of beauty in things which God makes distinctive as a pattern. Here are this wide range of images—skies, cow, trout, ripe chestnuts, finches wings, landscape, and tradesmen's equipment, all sharing the features of either contrast or variation in color and revealing the inscape of God's creation. The poet, out of love and admiration, calls upon people to praise Him. The well-chosen imagery helps achieve the theme admirably well. Another thing to notice about the poem is its form as a sonnet. Hopkins calls the form the *curtal sonnet*, curtal in the sense of "crop-tailed." The sonnet is cut short in length: instead of an octet (of two quatrains), there are two tercets, and the sestet is replaced by a stanza of four long lines plus one short. Hopkins' other poems like "Peace" are good specimens of such curtal sonnets as well.

The theme of "God's Grandeur" (1877) is self-evident. It is an attack on 19th-century "progress." Industrialization had made the country ugly, people were frenzied with "getting ahead," crazy with "gettings and spendings," and the world became a civilized yet a lost Eden. But all is not lost. God' grandeur will shine forth, the holiness that lives deep down in "things" will revive, and Jesus Christ will rise in the east after a dark night. The poem reveals a huge sense of hope and optimism and faith on the part of the poet.

A much later poem, "Thou Art Indeed Just, Lord, if I Contend" (1889), strikes a radically different note. One of Hopkins' "Terrible Sonnets," the poem has proved to be one of his most enduring works. Its epigram, a Latin quotation from the Vulgate Bible (Jeremiah 12:1), is translated in its first three lines. It is the complaint of the prophet Jeremiah to the Lord about allowing sinners to prosper. Evidently it is also the poet's own complaint. He frets over the fact that, however much he tries, the Lord seems as if He were an enemy, defeating his effort and allowing evil (drinking and lust) to lure him away from his faith (ll.3-9). Spring is in sight; nature flourishes, but not he. He is impotent, producing no work that would serve the Lord's cause and endure (ll. 9-13). The poem ends with a prayer instead of religious conviction. The despair and the doubt that break out of the lines might have to do with the skepticism and the increasing crisis of faith that came in the wake of the spread of the theory of evolution and with the wind of change in social life that began to blow in the aftermath of developing capitalism and commercialism. [3]

Edward Fitzgerald (1809-1883)

Edward Fitzgerald did just about one thing that has proved to be good enough to give him a niche in the literary pantheon of English authors. He translated *The Rubaiyat of Omar Khayyam* into English and then published it in 1859. The slim volume of 75 quatrains caught little attention at first, but then its beauty in thought and form began to work wonders so that its popularity kept gyrating upward in its time and has never lost much of its hold upon the imagination of the readers eve since. Fitzgerald later increased the number of quatrains to slightly over one hundred. Omar Khayyam was an 11th-century Persian astronomer and poet.

Originally independent units, his quatrains express his ideas about the nature of human existence and his *carpe diem* kind of advice to people: "Come, fill the Cup, and in the Fire of Spring/Your Winter-garments of Repentance fling:/ The Bird of Time has but a little way/ To flutter—and the Bird is on the Wing."

What Fitzgerald did was in fact not so much a faithful translation as a limited free rendering of the verse, connecting the isolated quatrains into one whole and endowing them with a tone of melancholy and a mood of longing that reflected the popular spirit of the time. In addition, the Romantic style is embellished with an exquisite structure and accompanied with intoxicating music that reveal the translator-poet's super sensitivity to both rhythm and sound.

The Aesthetic Movement [4]

In the latter part of the Victorian period Britain enjoyed an unprecedented material expansion. The nation became increasingly more affluent. Getting and spending became the predominant pre-occupation of people's endeavors, and insatiable acquisition the driving force of their lives. What Matthew Arnold criticized in his *Culture and Anarchy* became general. National ideals dimmed, the middle class grew, and along with it the influence of its values, its standards of materialism and its cultural philistinism. The way of life, or what people in retrospect have come to call Victorianism, proved inadequate if not thoroughly impossible, to inspire the life of the mind. Tennyson complained in his "Locksley Hall Sixty Years Later" that "half the marvels of my morning" had shrunk into the commonest commonplaces. A visible disparity appeared between the artist's ideal and the unaesthetic taste of the public, and the moral aesthetic of the period became with time too demanding for those intellectually sensitive people. The extreme cultural milieu was bound to provoke a reaction, and eventually it did. The initial signs of a movement away from the dominant stifling constraint began to show up and evolved in time into something known as the Aesthetic Movement, the exact opposite in nature to the heavily didactic tendency of the early and High Victorian period. The movement represents both the perplexed reaction on the part of the thinking minds to the humdrum and dishonest civilization of the Victorian period and an attempt to escape from it.

John Ruskin was among the first to speak out against the prevailing trend. He felt that, as a result of the country's dull modern principles of economy and utility, England was becoming increasingly uglier: there was a disconcerting absence of beauty in person and dress and in the world around in general. Ruskin advised people in his influential writings to stop and admire the graceful past and enjoy the beauty of nature. He wanted to find some kind of mediation between the demands of art and those of a bourgeois society. His *Modern Painters* is actually not about painters; it is about the beauty of nature and the importance of the appreciation of nature. He was telling people to stop in their rush and bustle of getting ahead and see the clouds, the rocks, and the trees. To see clearly was to him poetry, prophecy, and religion all in one. He emphasized the importance of art which he exalted as the highest expression of good life in good society, and he felt that all men should be artists. To him art was life, morality, worship, and the expression of man's totality, and as such was highly necessary for man's moral make-up. It is apparent that Ruskin saw art as closely associated with morality, and would regard the idea of the total autonomy of art cut off from life as unacceptable and heretical. The publication of the three volumes of his *Modern Painters* (1844, 1846, 1860) set the tone and pace for a change which was fast assuming the proportions of a movement with beauty as its watchword. It received the immediate support from preeminent cultural figures such as Wordsworth, Tennyson, the Brownings, Charlotte Bronte, and George Eliot.

A group of young people with poet-painter Dante Gabriel Rossetti (1828-1882) as its chief formed themselves in 1848 into what they called the Pre-Raphaelite Brotherhood and joined the fight for beauty.[5] Raphael (1483-1520) was one of the three greatest painters in the Italian Renaissance, the other two being Da Vinci and Michaelangelo. The so called "Pre-Raphaelite" means "the period before the Renaissance" or the medieval period when pure art was not only tolerated but prized. Rossetti was a typical aesthete. For him the only important thing in life was art; the artist was the ultimate ratio of humanity and was superior to social morality. Art was to him religion; the love of art was his faith; fidelity to inner experience was all that mattered to the artist. The business of the artist was analyzing and painting his own soul. Rossetti introduced in his writings the figure of the conscious aesthete engaged in a single-minded pursuit of beauty. Art and love were the two windows through which beauty shone through. Rossetti's work evoked aesthetic impressions in the minds of the readers. Both his paintings of women and his poetry revealed a physical and sensual attraction, so stunning and alluring that one of the conservative critics of his day termed his verse the fleshly school of poetry and called him the grossest fleshly poet of that school. If people read his poems such as "The Blessed Damozel," "Soul's Beauty," "Body's Beauty," "Nuptial Sleep," "The Kiss," "Sister Helen," and *The House of Life* and look at his paintings of provocative women, they might find the critic's scathing critique justifiable. There is an unmistakable trace of fleshiness and animalism there. However, Rossetti did not like the idea of art for art's sake and the autonomy of art. He was not far gone enough in his aesthetic taste to claim complete independence of art from life and of artists from their social commitments. He believed that art has its moral responsibility and that human passion is more important than pure artistic design. In later years he even regretted having had anything to do with Pre-Raphaelite Brotherhood and hated to be linked with the Aesthetic Movement as represented by Oscar Wilde. His poems like "Jenny," "The Burden of Nineveh," and "On the Refusal of Aid Between Nations" proffer proof enough of the poet's concern with contemporary life. Thus Rossetti was probably only "half-aesthetic."

Here is probably a place as good as any to mention Dante Gabriel Rossetti's sister, Christina Rossetti (1830-1894), who was a poet in her own right and wrote in a different manner from that of her brother. The poem that caught public notice and established her as a poet was "Goblin Market," a fairy tale kind of allegory meant for children. As the story goes, Laura yields to the temptations of the fruits offered by the goblins, asks for more, is refused, and is dying. Her sister Lizze manages to save her. The poem illustrates the conflict that beset the poet all her life. On the one hand her style is very similar with that of the Pre-Raphaelites and, on the other, her theme is very religious, discussing the serious problem of temptation, sin, and redemption. Living as she did in that age of doubts and questions, she kept her private vision intact as an artist: she can be very lyrical and sensuous. But she lived on very high religious principles so that she wrote highly serious devotional verse as well.

Aestheticism as a campaign steadily gathered momentum. With the publication of Ruskin's new books such as *The Seven Lamps of Architecture* (1849) and *Stones of Venice* (1851-1853), it became more visible and audible. An Oxford group of which William Morris was a member stood around Ruskin and made him a hero and a prophet figure. By the end of the 1850s, Algernon Charles Swinburne (1837-1909), Walter Pater (1839-1894), and Arthur Symonds (1865-1945) all took their places in the struggle for beauty. In 1858 William Morris (1834-1896) published his *The Defense of Guinevere and Other Poems* (1858) and added new energy for the movement. *The Defense* was Pre-Raphaelite and medieval in tone and mood. Later Morris took the country by storm with his *The Life and Death of Jason* (1867) and *The Earthly Paradise* (1868-70). In the latter poem, the poet calls himself "an idle singer of an empty day," removed from reality and trying to offer some kind of dream or hope which he is not sure of. There is beauty there, but fragile and impotent and "idle" in face of dull life. Morris also established a factory whose job it was to produce and display beauty in furniture, clothing, colors and shapes for an otherwise philistine world. Later he became a socialist, and was busy with social reform. But he continued to write poetry such as *Sigurd the Volsung* (1876). He also wrote some prose stories like *A Dream of John Ball* (1888) and *News from Nowhere* (1891), stories that offer a vision of a better world. The work of Ruskin and early Morris had an electrifying effect on popular taste. [6]

Young Swinburne brought a sense of change with him when he appeared on the scene. He came out with a strange and excitingly lyrical voice and wrote about some subjects which were to the conservative segment of society unclean, blasphemous, and irreverent. His works proved intensely offensive to established values and taste. He was accused of exhibiting "the foulest beastliness" in his poems with his aggressive sexual images such as biting lips "full of lust and laughter," moist and burning eyelids, and the cry, "O feed me and fill me with pleasure." He was cursed as uttering "a voice from an uncertain, fiery imp from the pit." His volumes of verse such as *Atlanta in Calydon* (a play,1860) and *Poems and Ballads* (1865), singing of "savage desires" like kisses that bruise, incestuous passions, sadism, bisexuality, and lesbianism constituted a downright attack on Victorian respectability. To some conservative minds including T. S. Eliot, Swinburne seemed to derive a good deal of joy from his description of sin and evil. These works fascinated some people, but earned him a notoriety which was to cost him dearly: the coveted job of the poet laureate in the latter part of his career after Tennyson left the scene should have been his as some people have suggested. But he did not and could never have become that anyway: for one thing, he did not think that poetry should be expected to inculcate values; words should be appreciated for their sound rather than their sense, and for another he was in his mind a rebel against the established order of things. Besides, the best of his works was done in his early days, and although he continued to write and his death poems like "The Garden of Proserpine" (1866) are among the very best on the subject, he did not really touch the height of his best performance ever again. It is good to add here that later Swinburne became both "respectable" and "serious." He took no interest in Oscar Wilde's brand of aestheticism, attacked aesthetic painter J. A. M. Whistler's well-known work *Ten O'clock*, and repeatedly claimed that great poetry must have a guiding spirit in it. He turned conservative somehow. Swinburne's other works include such as "Dolores," "Itylus," *Tristram of Lyonesse*, *The Triumph of Time*, *Ave Atque Vale*, and *Songs before Sunrise*.[7]

All through the 1870s the cult of beauty became a fact of life. Then something like a school doctrine began to develop. That had to do with the publication of Walter Pater's *Renaissance* in 1873. [8] For the first time the theory of art for art's sake appeared and art was made out to be the only important thing for people for whom the life of the mind mattered most. The book proved attractive to quite a number of thoughtful and intellectual people, and its ideas were discussed with profuse enthusiasm. It came out at the right moment in history. The aesthetic movement was losing steam in the 1860s as Ruskin's rich *Modern Painters* was not fully understood and the Pre-Raphaelites did not have really definite aims. Pater's book gave a new impetus to the movement. Walter Pater saw beauty in a new, different way. What he advocated in his *Renaissance* was the aesthetic attitude pure and simple. Beauty was to him transient, pure and perfect, and not tainted with anything worldly. The job of the artist was not to improve moral behavior. The artist was supposed to help people live their lives to enjoy as much self-gratification as possible. Human life consisted in a series of impressions or moments of *being* (as against *doing*), each and every one of which was "the sharp apex" between "two hypothetical eternities" in an individual's life. Man's problem was to make the very best of such moments as they passed and make them yield the utmost enjoyment that they were capable of yielding. Life must be lived on a high plane of intellectual effort and must be free of all grossness and mean cares. It is evident that Pater's art was divorced from moral concerns and had no bearing upon human conduct. Art should be loved and appreciated for art's sake. Pater became a new prophet for the ardent young aesthetes. Art was fast becoming a religion for quite a few people, and aestheticism was exercising a measure of impact on the intellectual life of the nation.

For 34 years the "crusade" for beauty went on, and it seemed to be faring well. Then an eccentric young man appeared on the scene and pushed the aesthetic movement in a direction which led to its phase of decadence and eventual doom. Oscar Wilde made his presence felt in 1878, and he changed everything. [9] With him, what W. B. Yeats called "the tragic generation" strode into history. Wilde behaved in a deliberately different way. His velvet coat, knee-breeches, loose shirt with a turned-down collar, long flowing hair, and a lily or sunflower in his hand—all these were designed to catch attention. He appeared often as if he saw a vision or was lost in a kind of meditation of which only the prophetic mind was capable. It was apparent that his was a well-calculated kind of artistic eccentricity. He despised all accepted tastes and values, all the commonplace and "middle-class vulgarities." He saw the love of a pale lily or a bleeding poppy as the symbol of liberation from philistinism. For him art was independent and superior. He wrote in keeping with his literary theory that art was all about self-expression and self-indulgence in aesthetic appetites and had nothing to do with morality. Beauty was his watchword. However, his was a morbid kind of beauty, associated with decay, pale cheeks, sunken eyes, wasted limbs, coffin boards, graves and corpses and skeletons, and sins and diseases. In a word, decadence was its hallmark. There is ample proof of it in Wilde's works. For instance, his *Impressions: I Les Silhouettes* contains such as "the dull dead wind out of tune," "withered leaf [the moon]," and "pallid sand"—all images of lifelessness and tendency to death. In his *Requescat*, there are such as bright golden hair tarnished with rust, and a woman fair and young but dead. His "Apologia" has "the web of pain," "the wasted Day," "the worm that dieth not," and the flower that was trodden upon. His "Harlot's House" houses ghostly dancers, slim silhouetted skeletons, black leaves whirling in the wind, the dead dancing with the dead, the dust whirling with the dust, and dawn, when it comes, creeping in like a frightened girl. And his "The Grave of Keats" offers a picture of weeping violets weaving on the bones of the dead poet. There is no vitality whatever in Wilde's poetic imagery. Wilde was a multi-talented person. He was a poet, a playwright, and a novelist as well. As a poet, he was not great; his plays promised better (if his career was not cut short by his notoriety as a homosexual), and his only novel, *The Picture of Dorian Gray*, though not among the best of Victorian fiction, was unique in its own way. His plays and his novel are discussed separately in the respective chapters of this survey.

A school developed around Wilde. It regarded Ruskin as out of date, invited ridicule and misunderstanding, and made a point of showing off their departures from mainstream behavior on every conceivable occasion. One of the decadence school was Ernest Christopher Dowson (1867-1900). A bohemian poet of the 1890s, he was an example of the "aesthetic Catholic" as shown in his religious poems such as "Nuns of the Perpetual Adoration," "Benedictio Domini," and "Carthusians." He found his age entirely intolerable. His poetry abounds in images of life-weariness and escape, and is immersed in an atmosphere of melancholy. Painting the dark disillusions of the *fin de siecle*, his works serve to reflect in part the mood of the 1890s. He is remembered as the author of the lyric "Cynara," with its melancholy, its weariness, and sadness, all the salient features of his generation. However, Dowson did not possess enough of the decadent spirit to hold his ethical impulse in abeyance; he felt the weakness of the decadents. So in poems like "A Last Word," he called Wilde's group "our perverse and aimless band." His "aimless" may well mean morally "directionless." Dowson was an alcoholic and died early. Then there was Lionel Johnson (1867-1904), a bohemian, whose poetry is about nothing but death and life-weariness. His "By the Statue of King Charles at Charing Cross" is about the dead king, a poem in which he says that life becomes sublime through death. "The Last Music" is about a dead queen: he feels that death has made the queen more beautiful. "The Church of a Dream" talks about dead leaves in an autumnal and pale world, "The Precept of Silence" about desolation, aching, and agony, and "The Red Wind" about weary souls and the red wind of burning death that kills souls. Mention should also be made of A. E. Housman (1859-1936), a professor of Latin, who was not of the group, but composed poetry in a similar vein. He talks about the shortness of life and the transience of love and friendship. His "Loveliest of Trees," "To an Athlete Dying Young," "Bredon Hill," and "With Rue My Heart Is Laden" are all good illustrations. All of this group were concerned with form. Dowson's brevity, Johnson's orderliness, and Housman's deceptive simplicity in diction are their valuable additions to English verse.

Then an opera was staged in the country, which did both a service and a disservice to the movement. *Patience* was a comic burlesque of Oscar Wilde's school. Designed to disgrace it, the opera increased its popularity or notoriety and became a historic monument to its eternal memory. But it did make fun of the movement and caused long and widespread laughter at it, thus helping to kill it for good eventually. It did the job also because it did it at the right moment when the movement was already weakening. The aesthetic movement, after raging across the country for over four decades, began to taper off in the late 1880s and died out altogether in the early 1890s.

The movement has left a permanent imprint upon English life in general and upon artistic creation in particular. The idea of beauty took root in social life. It has been not only tolerated but well prized ever since. Tastes went through some revolutionary change. With regard to art and literature, never again have people emphasized, without second thought, the moral role of the artist at the expense of beauty, form, and craftsmanship. Artists have become a special category of people, and art and form have ceased to be always second to morality. If people were once amazed and scandalized at the "heathenish" statements Oscar Wilde made in his preface to his novel, *The Picture of Dorian Gray*, in which he separates art and morality, then perception and modes of thinking have gone through a drastic change. Individual extravagance and self-indulgence have been taken as part of the norm rather than an exception. Artistic expression has become infinitely richer and more effective as a result and more authentic incidentally. For all these good effects it has had on subsequent developments in life and art, the Victorian aesthetic movement deserves to be remembered.

Chapter 18 Victorian Drama • Shaw • Wilde

Victorian Drama: A Brief Introduction

After Sheridan and Oliver Goldsmith, English drama experienced a general decline. For the first half of the nineteenth century the stage saw no remarkable performance with the one exception of Shelley's *The Cenci* (1819). The causes for the decay are difficult to speculate about. It might have had to do with the middle class want of taste for the dramatic; it might have also to do with the popularity of the novel. The monopoly of serious drama by two major theaters before 1843 might have also contributed to it. In addition, there was the need to cater to the demand for entertainment, which might have also made the milieu less congenial to the dramatic genius. Although many wrote for the theater, including Alfred Tennyson and Matthew Arnold, English drama did not show signs of improvement until after the 1860s when some commendable though modest efforts began to appear. There were T. W. Robertson (1829-1871), trying to bring life and realism to the stage in such works as *Caste* (1867); Henry Arthur Jones (1851-1929) who began to put on the "problem play"; and Arthur Pinero (1855-1934), attempting to delineate real life situations in his works and becoming a bridge between the past and the new age of which George Bernard Shaw was the legitimate representative. Pinero was a popular playwright of manners in his time, and some of his works are still staged occasionally today. He was serious with his business of writing, and often envisioned the whole complexity of his dramatic scenario before he put it down on paper. He said that he always managed to meet his characters and talk with them and get to know them inside out before he began to portray them and assign them the right place in his works. In the area of comedy, the verbal wit experienced a revival in the comedies of W. S. Gilbert (1836-1911) and A. S.

Sullivan (1842-1900). Oscar Wilde made his presence well felt with his comedies around the time. But British drama did not quite regain its value until George Bernard Shaw came on the scene.

George Bernard Shaw (1856-1950)

In the first half of the 19th century, the English stage was still very bleak, with few English plays of magnitude, but strewn with and dominated by importations. The voguish "society drama," patterned on the French "well-made" plays, often focusing attention on the tedious details of the life of a lost woman and on the extravagant lifestyle of the upper classes, exasperated people such as George Bernard Shaw. Not only did he detest the vulgar taste of the "society drama," he was also adamantly negative about the theory of "art for art's sake." Ultimately it was Shaw who gave English drama a new lease of life.

Shaw was a highly prolific writer. In his long career he wrote some 60 plays in addition to a multitude of other forms of writings such as novels, critical essays, and prefaces to some of his plays. In more than one way he exerted a very wholesome influence on the different phases of the development of 20th-century English drama. His most famous plays include *Mrs. Warren's Profession* (1893), *Candida* (1897), *Caesar and Cleopatra* (1898), *Arms and the Man* (1898), *Man and Superman* (1904), *Major Barbara* (1907), *Pygmalion* (1912), *Heartbreak House* (1919), *Back to Methuselah* (1921), and *Saint Joan* (1923). He won the Nobel Prize in 1925.

Shaw had germinal ideas about man and his world. He lived at a time robust with heated discussions and debates. After he came to London in the mid-1870s, Shaw found himself involved in the vortex of different thought systems. He was susceptible to the seminal influence of Henry George's provocative speeches and his book *Progress and Poverty*. He took an immense interest in the exploration of man in relation to his economic status in Karl Marx's *Capital*, which offered him a guideline for understanding and analyzing reality, and from which he derived his lifelong belief that the economic status of a person is a determining factor of his life. In the late 1880s, he joined the socialist Fabian society, and committed himself to helping ameliorate the lot of his fellow creatures. With abundant sympathies for the poor and the downtrodden, he was a ruthless critic of social ills and evils, and made his scathing attacks against corruption and injustices. Shaw was also under the influence of Lester Ward (1841-1913), the American sociologist and his notion of the Life Force, and of Schopenhauer and Nietzsche, the pessimistic German philosophers, and he was a sincere follower of Henrick Ibsen (1828-1906) whose plays dealt with social problems.

Shaw drew the attention of his audience to the serious social questions of the time. He does not move chiefly by plot interest. In his opinion a good play is good not so much because its plot piques the restless curiosity of its audience as because of the conflict of ideas that it presents to provoke thinking. To him no play can be serious without serious discussions of grave problems of life.

Shaw's subjects cover a wide range of social life. These include slum landlordism (*Widower's Houses*, 1892), his views on prostitutes and prostitution (*Mrs. Warren's Profession*, 1893), his attack on Victorian conventions such as home, romantic love, military glory, and idealism (*Arms and the Man*, 1894), and on the movement of Christian socialism (*Candida*, 1895), his views on the Life Force and creative evolution (*Man and Superman*, 1903 and *Back to Methuselah*, 1921), Irish grievances against English rule (*John Bull's Other Island*, 1904), his attack on evangelism (*Major Barbara,* 1907), on inequality between social classes and censure of middle class morality (*Pygmalion*, 1912), on pre-war spiritual poverty in Europe and the shallow Victorian work ethic (*Heartbreak House*, 1917), and the rise of Protestantism in England and nationalism in Europe (*Saint Joan*, 1924) and monarchy and democracy (*The Apple Cart*, 1929).

Shaw's dramatic sense is acute. He has a monstrous comic genius that has endeared him to his audience. His wit diffuses itself into a multitude of jests, quips and quirks throughout his pages. He employs Dickensian caricature types, makes good use of the varieties of the burlesque, such as the mock-heroic parody, historical parody, and mythological burlesque, writes at times in the extravaganza mode, and uses the rich suggestive classic myths as underpinning metaphors. As a satirist, he can be as ruthless as Jonathan Swift. And he despises all conventionalities so that his theories and visions prove to be subversive enough to throw the established tastes and stances off balance. In more than one way, Shaw is a social iconoclast.

Shaw was, and delighted in being, the centre of controversy. He could be cranky, even sarcastic, in his defense of unpopular opinions or practices. He was a non-smoker and a vegetarian long before either of these was widespread, and scornfully belittled anyone who was not. He hated competitive sports—especially "the sport of kings," as the English refer to horse racing. He called the haloed British custom of hunting foxes with hounds and horses "the unspeakable in pursuit of the inedible." He never suffered fools gladly, and must have been a difficult person to live with. He antagonized a lot of people. Serious critics found it hard to reconcile his socialism with his admiration of the superman. But even one of his most adversarial critics (T.R. Barnes) was forced to admit, at the end of his very critical essay on Shaw: "Our best dramatic work is livelier, more serious, more deeply concerned with life than it has been at any time since Fielding. In so far as any one man is responsible for this, that man is Shaw."

Now let's take a look at some of his plays.

Mrs. Warren's Profession is the most remarkable and popular of Shaw's early works. It was included in Shaw's collection, *Plays Unpleasant*. Although first published in 1893, it did not make to the stage until 1902. Censorship prohibited its public performance on grounds of immorality. The play, the first of its kind to present a prostitute as its major character, did not fare any better in New York, where it was performed in 1905 but received immediate interference from the police. The statement that the play makes about the capitalist system and poor people's struggle for survival proved to be too blunt and ruthless for the rich and the ruling class then.

The story is in a nutshell as follows: Mrs. Kitty Warren is an aging but well-off madam who runs a ring of brothels—primly called "private" hotels—in Europe. Her daughter Vivie, a bright young woman of 22, educated at Cambridge, looks forward to a successful career in actuarial accounting. Vivie's mother, Kitty, and Kitty's friends Praed and Sir George Crofts unexpectedly appear.

The conversations that follow are unnerving to Vivie. She learns about her mother's prostitution and her business as a madam. Mrs. Warren tells her that she was so poor when she was young that she had two options before her: either to work as a grossly overworked and criminally under-paid working woman and die a certain death of misery and torment, or to prostitute herself and open a brothel in order to linger longer. Vivie admires her mother's will to life and the courage to fight, but refuses to play the role of a "devoted daughter" when she gets to know from a chance remark from Sir Crofts, her mother's business partner, that the business is still active. Vivie and her mother talk, but at the end of the play Vivie leaves her mother for ever.

The drama is remarkable for a few things. First, its characterization is amazingly rapid and crystalline. The first act introduces virtually everyone. The second act plunges the major characters directly into the whirlpool of intellectual squabbling, and the remaining two acts continue the pitch and push it right up to the resolution. The two major characters tend to perplex people. At the first glance, Mrs. Warren is a rebel, an anti-conventional, choosing "sin" rather than suffering. On second thought, however, she is very traditional at heart as Vivie tells her in the last scene, where they part company for ever. Mrs. Warren worships respectability, and is in fact a believer in the existing system. Vivie, on the other hand, appears at first to accept things as they are, but at heart she is perspicacious about people and life. She proves to be the one who holds a grudge against society and wants to break free of its conventions. She is the true iconoclast.

In the confrontation between mother and daughter. Mrs. Warren tries to hold her daughter with her alternate strategies of brow-beating, sound rationalizing about her life, and retreating and begging, while Vivie undergoes a subtle process of slow but steady recognition of her mother's conventionality, and ends in rejection. The battle of wits between these two minds gives tension to the play. The parting of mother and daughter could be bothersome. Some viewers or readers sympathize with the mother so much that they feel that she deserves better and wish Vivie to relax her stance a little and move closer to her mother.

Arms and the Man: An Anti-Romantic Comedy is famous for its satire of the Victorian conventions. The title is taken from the opening line of Virgil's *Aeneid*. The story is set in a small Bulgarian town during the Balkan War of 1885-1886. The side of Captain Bluntschli, a Swiss mercenary, loses a battle and he is running for life. Passing through a small town, he climbs into the window of a young woman's bedroom and orders her to keep silent about him. The girl, Raina Petkoff, is the daughter of a Bulgarian officer. She has been dreaming of herself falling in love and with her fiancé, Major Sergius Saranoff, living "happily ever after." She is thrilled at the report that her fiancé has won a victory at the front. The fugitive

Swiss startles her because, in his plight of danger and fatigue, the man does not forget to ask for his chocolate cream. But she is also deeply impressed somehow, so that she feeds and hides him and gives him a coat when he leaves and sends a portrait of herself to him. Then Sergius comes back, greets Raina in a moving romantic manner, but flirts with Louka, her maid. Raina's father invites Bluntschli over to talk about the logistics of war which is Bluntschli's forte. Thus he meets Raina, who is changing after she learns about Sergius' silly "glory" and sees him put his arm around Louka. With her romantic exuberance cooled down, she touches ground, and is ready to accept Bluntschli.

The characterization of the play merits some analysis. It is evident that Raina represents the romantic archetype. She is precisely what Bluntschli is not. The Swiss has much common sense and little idealism. He is not a hero, and does not wish to be one. His sense of survival in life is so acute that it antagonizes Raina. The young woman's idealism appears pathetic, but she is not a pathetic person. When she sees the need, she is equal to her quandary and makes the firm correct choice without a murmur. The eventual switch of her romanticism to down-to-earth realism constitutes Shaw's censure of what he sees as the preposterous romantic Victorianism that idealizes both war and love. Bluntschli is a man of reality. His decision to be a solider is his own choice. He is practical, quick, good at paper work, and capable of survival, though he makes a romantic gesture when he comes back to see Raina, and another when he decides to marry her.

Thematically, the play is an exposition of Shaw's notion of the Life Force, an idea that gets fuller treatment in his preface to his *Man and Superman*. Shaw claims that women are always on the offensive in matters of love and procreation. Both Raina and Louka have their fish in their nets. Louka is a sort of superwoman, the prototype of *Man and Superman*'s Ann Whitefield. Although a servant in the Petkoff's household and engaged to Nicola, another servant, she sees life differently from him. She is not happy as a servant, as Nicola is. Louka is forward-looking while Nicola represents 19th-century servility, knowing what he wants and being dreadfully pragmatic. Louka has Sergius in mind and loses no time to get at him. And sure enough he is trapped. Louka will become a lady yet and travel and spend like one. As for Raina, as soon as she stops her romantic nonsense, she begins to see her "victim" and, before long, opts for Bluntschli.

The play is wonderfully symmetrical. It reflects a typical 19th century dramatic pattern, i.e. two sets of lovers changing places in the end. It is immensely entertaining throughout. Shaw's humor here is chiefly verbal with the help of occasional, slight jocular actions. For Shaw was a thoughtful person and as such loved thoughtful laughter and its educational value. To him a comedy should touch as well as amuse, and the best comedy does not serve the senses only. The play's moral sense is self-evident enough for all.

Man and Superman: A Comedy and a Philosophy is probably Shaw's masterwork. The play is an extensive farce that contains an amusing amalgam of diverse doctrines, notions that he gleaned from Bunyan, Goethe, Tolstoy, Wilde, Ibsen, Plato, Shelley, Marx, Nietzsche, and Schopenhauer. The dominant idea of the play is the Life Force. In his 37-page long preface, Shaw claims that it has always been the woman who takes the initiative in the business of love and sex from the beginning of time. The man is to put the food on the table, but the woman is to continue the race. The story, as it goes, pivots on John Tanner, who takes it upon himself to turn all the values upside down. His book, *The Revolutionist's Handbook and Pocket Companion*, holds in contempt all possible established concepts and practices such as honor, marriage, law, democracy, and faith. In addition, it speculates about the features of the Superman. Tanner is appointed along with his antithesis, the conventional Roebuck Ramsden, as Miss Ann Whitefield's guardian. Ann, emblematic of the female vessel for the birth of the Superman and the Life Force, tries to entrap him in marriage, but he is not willing to be her prey. He runs away. Ann, with the Life Force in her, follows close at his heels through the English Channel, the whole of Europe, and catches him in Spain. Reluctantly he submits and admits to her, "The Life Force enchants me: I have the whole world in my arms when I clasp you."

Thematically, the play demonstrates Shaw's optimism about the future that stems from his belief in creative evolution. As he sees it, the only hope is the superman through eugenic breeding (i.e. with mother-woman Ann and artist-man Tanner). This notion bodies forth Shaw's positive morality and his denial of pessimistic Schopenhauer's philosophy. Shaw admires Darwin's theory of evolution and satirizes brutally liberal politics (as those of the bad-tempered socialist Christian Mendoza). There is also an expression of Shavian feminism (which is, taken as a whole, a complicated, obscure sort of feminism). Ann looks like a new woman, assertive, sure of herself, aggressive, and independent in her will and determination. Violet is her opposite. Although Violet has the courage to break the taboo and have pre-marital sex, she takes orders from her man and does not recognize the new moral standard with which Tanner tries to justify her act.

In formal terms the play is exciting to watch. It has an interlude in three scenes with fire and music, the hugely amusing first act in which John Tanner tries to console the ostracized unmarried pregnant Violet but meets her contempt, thus getting the needed deflation, and the famous third act, the Hell scene, in which the captive, dreaming John Tanner meets a mythic version of Ann Whitefield in Dona Ana de Ulloa and the Devil in the person of Mendoza, who declares that Hell is a lot better than Heaven.

Oscar Wilde (1854-1900)

Wilde was first a playwright of comedies. Though he did not live long enough to bring his dramatic powers into full play, his achievement in the field of comedy is by no means negligible. His plays *Lady Windermere's Fan* (1892), *A Woman of No Importance* (1893), *An Ideal Husband* (1895), and *The Importance of Being Earnest* (1895) all enjoyed amazing popularity in his time. In addition to their satirical edge against the polite society of London, the plays are noted for their distinguished stylistic features. Wilde's play *Salome* was published in 1893. It is good to add that Wilde wrote a good number of short stories, one sizeable collection of which is *The Happy Prince and Other Tales*.

Wilde's best comic effort is *The Importance of Being Earnest* although all the four plays mentioned above are commendable works. Wilde, true to form as a sensitive literary artist, managed to catch an essential part of the Victorian temper in this work, i.e. the spirit of being earnest. If Wilde failed to achieve adequate appreciation as a major writer, his earnest literary endeavors should at least entitle him to a place in history. *The Importance of Being Earnest* plays adroitly on the name of "Ernest." The major character, Jack Worthing, is a country dandy who goes to London to have a good time but says he does so to take money to Ernest, his reckless brother. There he takes over the name "Ernest" and meets and falls in love with Gwendolyn, daughter of Lady Bracknell the countess, but is not permitted to marry her as the mother feels uncertain about his identity. Algernon Moncrieff, the countess' nephew, comes to the country in the disguise of Ernest, the reckless brother, to learn about Jack, and there falls in love at first sight with Jack's ward, Cecily Cardew. Gwendolyn also comes to Jack's country estate and finds in her conversation with Cecily that their fiancés have the same name of "Ernest." The misunderstanding between the two young women is resolved when Jack and Algernon both help unravel the mystery. Then Jack gets to know that Algernon is his brother and he was really christened Ernest. The two couples marry and live happily ever after.

Although the plot is slim and the experience of life represented is narrow and far from deep, Wilde left an imprint on his audience with the help of his intimate knowledge of the upper classes and his unique though narrow range of genius in handling language. The play impresses by virtue of its authentic paintings of the overbearing and snobbish nobility. Its portraits of the countess and Gwendolyn generate a genuine sense of verisimilitude to life as if they walked straight out of their West End drawing room onto the stage. Just look at the way the countess orders people to behave to her taste, the way she defines smoking as an "occupation" for the rich, her comments on ignorance and modern education, her notion of decorum and respectability, her inordinate pride in her class and all its values, and also the imposing way Gwendolyn talks to people, and her excessive built-in pride in her family, her folks, and herself, and the audience will make no mistake whatever about the nature of this class of parasites and their personalities.

For Wilde, style matters more than matter, and wit more than character. In formal terms, *The Importance of Being Earnest* falls in the category of high comedy, the success of which depends by and large on wit and wordplay. For instance, Lady Bracknell's questioning John Wrothing shines with the brilliance of verbal wit and its sheer force of comedy. In addition, a normal high comedy entertains by means of such verbal feats as the epigram. *The Importance of Being Earnest* and also his other plays like *Lady Windermere's Fan* all shine with verbal wit and brilliance. "I can resist everything except temptation," "There is only one thing worse than being talked about, and that is not being talked about," or a cynic is "a man who knows the price of everything and the value of nothing"—little gems like these do add to the glitter of the works.

Before leaving him, it is necessary to mention Wilde's last two important works that he wrote while serving term in prison. After he was convicted of homosexuality in May 1895, he was sent to the Reading Goal. There he composed *The Ballad of Reading Goal* (1898) and *De Profundis* (1897). The two works are probably among his best because they represent the true Wilde the man and the artist at his best. *The Ballad of Reading Goal* is probably the best poetry that Wilde ever composed. The poem became instantly popular and ran through a good number of prints in a few weeks. What moves and touches the readers lies in this, that suffering had helped to distill the best out of the man in feeling as well as in poetic craft. The poem, talking about the suffering of a condemned soldier, is actually making a clean breast of the poet's own psychic truth. The soldier is his emotional surrogate. The soldier's prayer that the hangman "[s] trangled into a scream" is in fact his own prayer. Wilde made the point crystal clear when he wrote, "All the woe that moved him so/ That he gave that bitter cry,/ And the wild regrets, and the bloody sweats,/ None knew so well as I:/ For he who lives more lives than one/ More deaths than one must die." In the ballad, Wilde came to see Jesus as the messiah of suffering humankind. Christ came down to save the sinners and gave the blessed Cross to them. He walked through the human bars of the brick prison, and took with his holy hands "The Thief to Paradise." The Lord will not despise "a broken and a contrite heart." Wilde suffered and learned and became a better man and a better poet while in prison. The same vein of thought runs through his last prose work, *De Profundis*.

De Profundis was in fact a long letter Wilde wrote to Alfred Douglass, the man with whom he was accused of carrying on a homosexual relationship. This is Wilde's last prose work, a confession, an apologia, and an explanation of his behavior. A couple of things that merit particular notice here include the level of self-knowledge to which he had managed to attain and his thoughts on Jesus Christ. He learned through his trial and imprisonment that his downfall had all been his own doing. He had been God's favorite, endowed with everything that a human could possibly desire to have—genius, name, position, brilliance, and courage. He knew that he had made some contribution to life: making art a philosophy and philosophy an art; helping alter the minds of men and the color of things; doing and saying things that made people wonder; making drama a personal mode of expression, widening its range, enriching its characterization, and turning everything he touched beautiful; and awaking the imagination of his century so that he became a myth or legend. But he also learned about his misconduct, his enjoying senseless ease, enjoying being a dandy, befriending mean people, wasting his own youth and genius, becoming perverse, contracting the malady or madness of desire, becoming careless of other people, forgetting evil and its punishment, and losing track of his own best judgment and his life in consequence. He came to accept disgrace and humility. This was the howl (or "the scream" or "the cry" in *The Ballad of Reading Goal*) that came right from the depth of his soul. Hence the current title given to the letter—*De Profundis*. In the section on Jesus Christ which makes up a large part of the prose work, he seemed to see clearly the nature of Christianity and the mysteries of life. Jesus Christ was the savior, the one who brought truth and the voice of love, revived human imagination, and made spiritual life accessible to men. Wilde even went so far as to see Jesus as the precursor of the romantic movement in life. He had learned to repent and believe that repentance would lead to absolution. Wilde achieved this heightened awareness only after he had gone through his share of human suffering in life. It is its truthfulness that has made the work great and charming.

Chapter 19 The Early 20th Century • The Edwardians • The Georgians • The War Poets

When Queen Victoria died in 1901, an era was formally over. The new century began with its own particular set of problems, some of which were traceable to the latter part of the previous period. For one thing, the crisis of faith, first clearly felt with the publication of Charles Darwin's *The Origin of Species* (1859), continued into the new century with increased intensity. The German philosopher Nietzsche had declared the death of God in one of his books, and Bertrand Russell had advocated a kind of despairing courage in his famous "A Free Man's Worship" (1918). The former rejected Christian morality, and the latter felt that nothing could save anything beyond the grave. Pessimism was prevalent. Then the British Empire was declining; British imperialism was losing its hold upon the imagination of the people as well as the intellectually thinking segment of the society. In addition, Edwardian England reacted strongly to Victorian moral constraint and reveled in reckless enjoyment, and Europe was heading toward the catastrophe of WWI.

Furthermore, the status of the arts and literature was beginning to undergo a process of redefining. The alienation of the artist, first evident in Victorian aestheticism, now became a widely felt impulse among the artistically minded people. The French symbolists and modernist masters such as James Joyce and Thomas Mann all exhibited their penchant for writing regardless of popular tastes. There was a strong sense of disaffection and a huge drive for change in the literary circles. Important developments in the fields such as psychology, anthropology, and philosophy were exerting a far-reaching influence on literary creation. Sigmund Freud's *Interpretation of Dreams* (1913), James Frazer's multi-volume *The Golden Bough* (1911-1915), and Henry Bergson's new concept of time all contributed in large measure toward the forthcoming artistic and literary experimentation. Although nothing major occurred before the 1920s, a lot was going on in the first years of the 20th century. The Edwardians and the Georgians were not responsive enough to the change in taste and values and continued to write in the transitional period. They did their part for their country's literature. Some such as Joseph Conrad helped to do the spade work for the forthcoming of the new mode of writing—modernism, and the rest of them, Arnold Bennett included, all deserve mention in history. It would be a gross injustice to write them off as of no importannce.

The Edwardians [1]

In her famous essay, "Modern Fiction," Virginia Woolf singled out three novelists of the first years of the 20th century for analysis and branded them as "Edwardians," a nomenclature not favorable in meaning. She was especially relentless when discussing one of these, Arnold Bennett, the other two being H. G. Wells and John Galsworthy. Her major complaint was about their over-emphasis on the description of externalities in their representation of life rather than on the internal world of man which she thought should take precedence over anything else in novel-writing. The authors, who wrote and made their names in this "Edwardian" period when King Edward was on the throne for a decade, also included Joseph Conrad whose novels came close to Mrs. Woolf's definition of the modern novel, Rudyard Kipling, a poet and prose writer, whose writings are brilliant but exhibit in some a degree of imperialistic arrogance and racial bias, and E. M. Forster, probably one of the first writers then sensitive to and aware of the change which materialized into Modernism in the works of Mrs. Woolf, James Joyce, and D. H. Lawrence.

Arnold Bennett (1867-1931)

Bennett came from the pottery region of northern England. Educated at London University, he came under the influence of Zolan naturalism and Russian writer Turgenev's writings. He was H. G. Wells' best friend and made the acquaintance of Turgenev in Paris. He wrote over thirty novels and a miscellany of other writings including a popular play.

Bennett is famous made notorious for his "Five Towns" stories, all of which are based on the pottery towns of northern England. These include *Anna of the Five Towns* (1902), *The Old Wives' Tale* (1908), The Clayhanger Trilogy—*Clayhanger* (1910), *Hilda Lessways* (1911), and *These Twain*, 1915). The descriptions in these novels are true-to-life, naturalistic, reproductions of life there with its filth, stench, poverty, and the overall tedium and gray ugliness that characterized this segment of English society. With the exception of *Anna of the Five Towns*, focusing more on one individual's fortune, all the other tales offer a panoramic view of the life of this wretched part of society.

Bennett is a careful "scientific" observer, an efficient recorder, and a 'good story-teller. Reading him can be a good rewarding experience. In addition to the enjoyment one can never fail to derive from the tales, one can get an authentic version of the reality at the turn of the last century. Indeed, Bennett can serve as a social historian of some kind. One of the things he did not do well, however, was his failure to sense the wind of change already beginning to blow in the new century, and this incurred a very dear price he had to pay in fame and historical placement. The fact of the matter was that he seems to take an immense delight in the minute and accurate portrayal of the exterior details of life, tells his stories with a calm countenance and takes care to avoid comments, and stops right at the point when the interior of the human soul gets involved. This does not mean that the writer has no compassion; Bennett has plenty of it as he says in his journals to the effect that compassion is the hallmark of greatness for a writer. His objective documentation of life was all right as a manner of literary creation—so akin to that of Trollope's—until Mrs. Woolf stood out to say that it was not. Her comments upon his works, which began a new epoch in literary history, sent Bennett all the way down to the nadir of his reputation, from which he has yet to recover.

Rudyard Kipling (1865-1936)

Kipling was born in India, had no college education, and traveled to many parts of the world so that he got to know about the life of all social strata, especially the lower segment, and managed to pick up a good deal of their daily language. All these had some bearing on his writing career. His stories are mostly set in India and cover areas such as India, South Africa, South America, and

London. His subjects are highly inclusive, touching as they do on diverse social manners, the rich and powerful imposing upon the poor and the weak, the superstitions, the supernatural and legendary, adventures, and detective themes. Basically, Kipling is a short-story writer; it is said that the short story as a genre throve after he enriched it with his craft. He also wrote novels and some poetry. But he is best known for his *The Jungle Books* (1894, 1895), a tale of a white child left in an Indian jungle but surviving the inclement environment in the company of his jungle folk—the wolves, bears, tigers, panthers, and elephants. The child, Mowgli, is brought up by Mother Wolf, lives as one of the wolf pack in the brute world for seventeen years before he meets his mother Messua and returns finally to the man pack to which he belongs. The work is a fable in the world tradition of beast fables, with each one of its chapters in obvious contrast to the human world. It has become a classic of its own kind, offering good reading matter for all readers—as a fable for children and as a book of wisdom for adults. It is even good for scholars and philosophers as they can read and meditate upon the nature of the human condition. What detracts from its value as a classic is the fact that Kipling, with his imperialistic and white chauvinistic attitude, reveals a strong racial bias here, that Mowgli may be seen as a white man trying to make out in an inferior milieu in which white virtues cannot take root. Kipling's poem, "The White Man's Burden," is notorious for the author's blatant, repellent show of Anglo superiority. Kipling won the Nobel Prize in 1907.

John Galsworthy (1867-1933)

With 17 novels, over 20 plays, and a dozen volumes of short stories and miscellaneous writings to his credit, Galsworthy was one of the most prolific of the writers of the period and did so well to distinguish himself that he won the Nobel Prize in 1932. He inherited the great tradition of realism in English literature and kept to his traditional way of writing amid the engulfing din of a new way of literary expression— Modernism. Coming as he did from a wealthy Forsyte-like family, he wrote a good deal of his own life into his fictions. His themes focus on the lives and experiences of the rich men of property, their selfishness, their philistinism, their decadence, depravity, and decline, and their fierce conflict with the workers. Galsworthy wrote in such a way that his readers can never feel let down to look for entertainment and moral guidance in reading him. His major works include the three trilogies, *The Forsyte Saga* (1906-1921), *A Modern Comedy* (1924-1928), both consisting of three novels and two interludes, and the last and third—*The End of the Chapter* (1931-1933).

The best known of his works are the Forsyte Saga novels—*The Man of Property* (1906), *In Chancery* (1920), and *To Let* (1921) with the two interludes wedged between them—*The Indian Summer* (1917) and *Awakening* (1920). This is an extended treatment, resumed in *A Modern Comedy*, of the history of one family—of four generations of the Forsytes—from the late Victorian period through the end of WWI. The story covers all the vicissitudes relating and leading up to the final conclusion of the family drama. It narrates in fact the complexities of the experience of one particular social class—the industrialists, parasites, and their like—and the scenes culled from their lives. The major character here is Mr. Soames Forsyte, a man of property, whose relationship with his wife is strained because he sees her as just another piece of his property. He represents the sum total of the vices of the capitalist rich—selfishness, greed, hypocrisy, and tyranny. His beautiful wife, Irene, falls in love with Bosinney, and runs away when Bosinney dies in an accident (*The Man of Property*). In *In Chancery*, the desperate Soames marries a French girl who gives birth to a girl, and Irene, after 12 years of solitude, is married to Julian Forsyte, the prodigal son who ran away from his arranged marriage at the beginning of the saga. She gives birth to a son. Soames still cherishes a passion for Irene. *To Let* tells the story of the next generation: Soames' daughter and Irene's son meet by chance and fall in love at first sight. The union being impossible, the boy, in despair, leaves for America, and the equally sad girl is married off to Michael. The age of the Forsytes is over.

John Galsworthy proves himself to be an impeccable story-teller and a consummate artist in conception and execution.

H. G. Wells (1866-1946)

Wells was a novelist-reformer. He is best remembered for his achievement in science fiction and his prophecies about the outbreak of the two world wars. In actuality, he wrote more than science fiction. His long productive life can be subdivided into three phases—science fiction, social satire, and novels of ideas. He wrote well over 100 volumes, of which over 50 are novels, and a few are collections of short stories and other miscellanies. Wells was once a Fabian, attacked Fascist aggression, and visited the US and the Soviet Union. Writing in the tradition of realism as did Bennett and Galsworthy, he was similarly subject to the negative criticism of the Modernists such as Virginia Woolf and D. H. Lawrence.

Wells has been regarded as one of the founding figures of the genre—science fiction. His science fiction novels reveal his rich imaginative powers. He takes his readers with him in his visionary flights through space and time, and offers them an ample opportunity to observe life from different spatial and temporal perspectives. His stories serve a serious purpose of social satire at the same time they entertain. Wells' prophetic faculty was simply amazing. He visualized man's flight long before the first airplane was born and man's space travel over 60 years prior to the first human landing on the moon. And he foresaw the possibility of a nuclear war. His major science fiction novels include *The Time Machine* (1895), probably his best effort in this field, *The War of the Worlds* (1898), describing as it does the horrors of an Martian invasion of the earth, *The First Men in the Moon* (1901), with its description of life on the moon not substantially different from modern men's actual discoveries on it, and *The Invisible Man* (1897). The titles alone suggest Wells' immense influence on subsequent science fiction novels, some of which are often but dim replicas of the great master's visions.

Joseph Conrad (1857-1924)

To classify Conrad as an Edwardian is to do less justice to him than he really deserves. He was no doubt of that time frame, but he went way beyond it to exhibit a close affinity in temperament with the rising generation of Modernists. His preeminence in English literature relates to the fact that, coming in between the two periods, he acted as a bridge, a liaison, thus helping tide English literature over well from one to the other literary phase. He was an effective transitional figure. [2]

Conrad was a unique, gifted novelist. Born in Ukraine of Polish parentage, he began his 20 years of life on the sea at 17 on a French ship, studied English hard, became a British subject, and retired at 37 to devote his energies to writing. He wrote a good number of novels such as *Almayer's Folly* (1895), *The Outcast of the Islands* (1896), *The Nigger of the Narcissus* (1897), *Lord Jim* (1900), and *Typhoon* (1902), and a good many novellas and short stories, the most famous of which is *The Heart of Darkness* (1902). He also wrote an autobiography, adding to the impressive total of over 30 volumes of writing that he did over a period of some thirty years.

Conrad draws in his literary endeavors mostly from his experience on the sea and in the remote parts of the world. He possesses an unusual power to dramatize such scenes as related to typhoons and such secrets as hidden in the woods. He represents them in an entrancing manner compounded of authentic details and a rich romantic flavor. In theme and form Conrad's works are heavily Modernistic. One of the salient features of his fictions is the strikingly permeating sense of disjunction and fragmentation that characterizes the Modernist works. This feeling of disconnectedness stems from Conrad's adroit weaving into a coherent whole disparate stories that different people tell from different perspectives, so that stories appear within the story dotted with endless discursive digressions. Conrad intends to replicate both the sense of mystery inherent in life and the diverse phases of the mind in a manner very close to being impressionistic. He tries to bring out his theme by means of the momentary impressions it leaves on the mind. This manner of representation enables the writer to approach the various facets of truth at various moments in his various moods. Another feature of his fiction is their psychological explorations and their focus on the interiority of the characters. There is seen in his characters the perpetual feeling of solitude and alienation, the craving for human connection, friendship and compassion which are, however, always conspicuously absent from life. The longing for understanding or luck, if they ever come, seems to come always when it is too late for any good.

Let's take a brief look at some of his major works. Conrad's fictions fall roughly under three categories—the sea novels, the forest novels, and the social novels. A good number of his novels and novellas are set on the sea which is his major source of subjects and inspiration. The two stories, *Lord Jim* and *The Heart of Darkness*, are both among his most fascinating and powerfully influential works. The first of these relates the tragic, highly moral story of a good young man by the name of Jim, the first mate on a ship, who spends his life redeeming a sin he committed at a moment of cowardice and moral defection. The fact was that he left a shipload of helpless Muslim pilgrims to shift for themselves on the sea when his ship knocked on a deserted ship and wrecked and sank. Tormented by his guilty conscience and afraid that people may get to know his story, Jim runs to the Orient where he first works as a clerk at a seaport, and finally lands up on a small island of Malaysians. Here he does his best to help the local people out, fighting against their enemies and winning the appreciative title "Lord Jim." He marries a semi-Malaysian woman and begins to enjoy a hard-won peace of mind. Then in a deal with the treacherous pirates, he fails to protect the safety of the headsman's son and asks to pay for his loss of honor with his own life. He dies willingly to wash clean all his sins.

The interesting thing to note about the narrative method of the novel is that the story is not presented in the chronological order. The story as told looks like a hotchpotch, or a fish cut up into pieces and placed tail over head in a frying pan. The narrative chaos is, however, well deliberated upon and carefully designed. The different parts of the story are nicely tied together with the help of well planted leads and dexterous foreshadowings. This peculiar narrative scheme serves the purpose to help increase the tension and suspense and the sense of mystery with which the story is enveloped. It is also designed to do a much more important job: to examine the different aspects of Jim's complex inner world of guilt and faith in rebirth, and paint a better picture of his soul struggling through self-censure and pain to redemption, regeneration, and spiritual serenity. The disjunctiveness and disorderliness vanish when all the loose ends as part and parcel of a unity are tied up in a knot, tidy and neat enough to knead the readers' bits of impressions into a totality of awareness. Here Conrad took over from George Eliot and Henry James and developed their hitherto not yet well heeded tradition of the psychological novel. Another thing to note is the varying points of view used for the three sections of the book. In the first of these, consisting of the first four chapters, an omniscient narrator helps reveal Jim's interiority for the readers. In the next section, a first-person point of view picks up from chapter five and carries the story through chapter 35. The last section, covering the rest of the novel (chapters 36-45), wraps up the narrative in flashbacks with the help of letters and manuscripts. A book as impressionistic as this tends to inspire different interpretations, as indeed it has done since its inception very much to the author's own expectation.

The novella, *The Heart of Darkness*, has been in a sense more famous, adding as it does the term "the heart of darkness" to the modern literary critical idiom and offering an important theme to literature in general. The novella relates the narrator's voyage to Africa, the continent whose shape resembles that of the human heart, and the heart of which is The Congo. The trip to The Congo as described in the book is not just any trip; it proves to be an attempt on the part of the traveler at self-exploration and self-analysis. As the story goes, the narrator comes to The Belgian Congo and sees the extent of devastation to which the white colonialists have subjected the continent. He learns about Kurtz, the most brutal and atrocious of these colonialists, a dying man who has been there for years, pillaging, cheating and killing large numbers of the local people, and has made himself a veritable satanic demigod figure there. But the man presents a psychological complexity himself. Born of English and French parentage, Kurtz bodies forth the sum total of western education. As a young adventurer, he had his ideal and ambition to come and "civilize" the African "primitives." But the thirst for power and wealth has pushed him into the abyss of crime and punishment. In a very real sense, he has also been a spiritual victim of his own greed, robbery, and eternal loneliness. The narrator sees him dying with screams, "Horror, horror!" condemning probably both himself and the system he represents, the one that has made him suffer inordinately and successfully ruined his life.

Thematically, the man is clearly made out to represent the guilty conscience of the colonialists, in whose heart of hearts lies nothing but darkness. The concluding words, "Horror, horror!" may hint at Kurtz's self-discovery that his life has been a horror to his victims as well as to himself, and that his life as a European colonialist is nothing but horror itself. His tragic death, also a metaphor for all his fellow colonialists, is just as he deserves. The narrator discovers through Kurtz that the heart of the Europeans is all darkness and that the heinous crimes they have committed against humanity prove themselves to be the very savages whom Kurtz once suggested in a report to one international organization that should be exterminated. The book is thus a thorough condemnation of the criminal behavior of the colonialist powers. Profusely commented upon over the years, it has given rise to more than one interpretation. Its rich load of meaning has been well excavated from different perspectives, be it social, historical, mythological, or psychological. The novella is also a formal *tour de force*, effectively employing an amalgam of the symbolic, impressionistic, and fragmentary modes of perception and presentation to dive little by little into the quagmire of guilt and despair of the man's heart and reveal the deep-seated horrors of a soul completely gone evil and unredeemable.

E. M. Forster (1879-1970) [3]

Forster was well aware that, in face of the new reality of the 20th-century world, a change was in order. The writers, he feels sensitively, would have to go down another avenue and the novels would have to be written in a different way if they were true to the new experience of the new age. His literary theories won the approval of the rising generation of the Modernists who, like Virginia Woolf, saw him as a writer up against the Edwardian tradition along with James Joyce and D. H. Lawrence. The idea that Forster expounds well in his collection of speeches, *Aspects of the Novel* (1927), that the novel should not merely follow the common tradition of telling a story but should be written differently, coincides with the stance which Mrs. Woolf holds in her criticism on the Edwardians. In actual writing, however, Forster was in essence a transitional figure in between literary periods. His subjects touch upon such themes as the inner world of man, the sense of estrangement and alienation, and the relationship between man and nature, all themes that smell strongly of Modernism.

Forster's famous novel, *Passage to India* (1924), written in the traditional manner, tries to represent and explore the psychological facet of man. Forster claims in the novel that hope stems from the human connection or "communion" by means of which man can vanquish hopelessness. On the other hand, he seems to be saying that it is impossible for the East and the West to connect with one another as there is no road leading from Britain to India and there exists in fact a vast void of nothingness beneath the deceptive surface of the rush and bustle of life. This suggests Forster's awareness of the nihilist spirit engulfing the first years of the 20th century. One striking feature to note about the novel is its symbolism. Its three sections—the mosque, the cave, and the temple—constitute an adequate expression of its plot priorities—the possibility, the barrier, and the opposition—all pertinent to the connection of the two hemispheres; they manage to leave a faint ray of hope for the readers. In addition, Forster hooks and holds attention often by means of his spectacular plot interest. His authorial comments and advices often smack strongly of Fielding and Thackeray.

Katherine Mansfield (1888-1923)

It is difficult to pigeonhole Katherine Mansfield. She is placed here merely because this is her time frame. Mansfield's achievement in the area of the short story has been such that she represents a milestone in the history of the genre. She was born into a household of a rich merchant and banker in Wellington, New Zealand and was educated in London. Well read and sensitive to French influence and Checkov's short story tradition, Mansfield began writing at the age of 20. As she was gaining recognition, she contracted tuberclulosis and had to move constantly in Europe in search of warmth and the sun. Her literary career was abruptly cut short by her untimely death.

Mansfield draws profusely from her recollections of her childhood, her family, and her native city. Her best work, "Prelude" (1918), is a good example. Other stories of this nature include, among others, "At Bay," "The Garden Party," and "Her First Ball." Mansfield's subjects are more about individuals than direct social concerns. She finds value in personal responses and impressions and tries to derive "the real thing" from these reflections. In formal aspects, Mansfield places more focus on the excavation of the psychology of her characters rather than on the detailed decription of the exteriors. Sensitive to the change in values and tastes of the time, she employs the impressionist mode of representation at times. There is not much of a plot, or coherent narrative in her stories. Her handling of space and time, as she did with her "The Daughters of the Late Colonel" (1920), indicates that she was not indifferent to the rising modernist mode of writing. Her collections of short stories include *Bliss and Other Stories* (1920), *The Garden Party and Other Stories* (1922), *The Dove's Nest and Other Stories* (1923), *Something Childish and Other Stories* (1924). Her critical writings, over 100 in number, are collected in her *Novels and Novelists* (1930).

Let's take a look at one of her oft-anthologized short stories, "Miss Brill." This is about an old spinster in her fifties, who lives in a small French seaside town. Apparently far from well-to-do, she tries to eke out her simple and frugal livelihood by teaching English and reading newspapers to an old gentleman four afternoons a week. Her old fur delights her enormously, and an almond cake is her weekend treat. Her one luxury in life seems to be her regular Sunday visit to a little park where people gather to enjoy company as well as the Sunday band concert. She would go and sit, watch people move and eavesdrop their conversations, and feel happy and well rested. On this particular autumn Sunday she goes, sees people of different ages and characters, communicates internally with them, and feels an empathy with them all. She seems to be having an experience of a mystical kind that she is an integral part of the play that is being staged in the park and that she is and has actually been an actress all along! Whatever happiness this epiphany of hers has generated is soon neatly dashed when she hears the cruel young couple ridiculing her, within her earshot, as a stupid old thing and her fur "like a fried whiting." She has received a hurt from which it will take time to recover. As she gets back to the little cupboard of her home, she hears "something crying."

The theme of the story is self-evident. The thing that can make people feel happy is, as it shows, the sweet feeling of being a link in the chain of humanity. The magnetism that draws the solitary woman to the park Sunday after Sunday is exactly this revitalizing sense of human connection. Miss Brill manages to make to the realization that the world is a stage and life a play. For her it seems that, if there is no fellowship, there is nothing. That is the reason why she feels so sad when she gets home on that devastating day that her soul starts weeping. In addition, the way Mansfield portrays the character is interesting to note. She takes care to choose not only the length of every sentence, but even the sound of every sentence. She chooses the rise and fall of every paragraph to fit her character's mood on that day at that moment. After she wrote it, Mansfield tells us, she read it aloud numbers of times until her sketch got nearer to a musical composition. She made sure that there must not be one single word out of place, or a word that could be taken out. That was the way she generally did with all her writings as a serious literary artist. There is also the narrative point of view that she employs in the writing of the story for people to consider. Although the story is narrated in the third-person point of view, the readers tend to feel, after they read and reflect upon it, that it is a first-person narrative, as if it was Miss Brill telling her own story. The method used here is Henry James' selective omniscience. Mansfield uses Miss Brill as the center of consciousness in the telling so that the readers readily identify with the major character, thinking through her mind, seeing through her eyes, and embracing her stance on people and things. That is precisely what James did with his *Portrait of a Lady*.

The Georgians [4]

The Georgians were a group of lyrical poets whose works were included in Sir Edward Marsh's *Georgian Anthologies* (1916-1917). They wrote and published mainly between 1910 and 1920. These included, among others, John Drinkwater, D. H. Davies (1871-1940), Walter de la Mare (1873-1956), W. W. Gibbon, Edward Thomas, Rupert Brooke, Robert Graves, and Edmund Blunden. Some of D. H. Lawrence's lyrics were also included in the Georgian anthologies, though these were different and superior. The Georgians rejected the avant-garde aesthetic kind of poetry of the last decade of the 19th century and turned back to tradition. They observed poetically nature, love, and rural traditional English life and wrote about these in a style gentle, less self-conscious, and more easily approachable. They sang sweet pastoral songs in praise of the temporal serenity and stability that England had enjoyed before WWI and offered an avenue of escape for the people in the period of chaos after it. These poets were capable of sentimental lapses and skilled in traditional metrics. Receiving warm welcome from the general readers, they sold enviously well. But they were harshly criticized later for their want of depth in thought and feeling. The Georgians lost their vogue in the 1920s when a wind of change started blowing and swept them aside. The pastoral mode of writing was out of place on the post-WWI scene, and a verse revolution was visibly under way. The Imagist movement had already started, and Modernism was fast burgeoning into shape. From then on Yeats and Eliot began their domination, and the Georgians were ignored for some three decades. Then the poets of the 1950s veered away from high modernism and Dylan Thomas and turned to tradition, dredging in their literary endeavors these Georgians from the deeps of oblivion. It is good to know that the famous American Robert Frost was in England around this time and became a Georgian as well: he was probably the best of the group. The discussion here will focus on some of these English poets and leave Lawrence and Frost for some other occasions.

Rupert Brooke (1887-1915)

The typical Georgian in feeling and style was probably Rupert Brooke who fought and died during WWI. His two volumes of verse, *Poems* and *1914 and Other Poems*, came out in print in 1911 and 1915 respectively. The latter book was especially popular in the next decade. Brooke became famous for "the very few incomparable war sonnets" that he wrote in 1914. His vision of war was clearly Romantic. In contrast to the modern view that debunks and de-romanticizes war and heroism, Brooke feels that war purifies, and death is heroic. There is a good deal of ebullience and naïve appreciativeness in his poetry. "The Soldier" (1914) is a good illustration. Here the poet-soldier faces death with joy. There is no fear, no regret, and no hesitation. He has nothing but his country in mind, with her flowers, her love, her air, rivers and suns, thoughts, sights and sounds, happy dreams, laughter, "and gentleness,/ In hearts at peace, under an English heaven." He is part and parcel of his native England for which he dies willingly. His country purifies, so do war and death: his heart will shed away all evil, and become "[a] pulse in the Eternal mind [.]" There is no thought of self but a lot of gratitude and appreciation for what his country has done for him. The poet-soldier believes that his death will add credit to his beloved motherland. Brooke would make Stephen Crane and his successors like Ernest Hemingway and Joseph Heller turn in their graves with his war poems.

However, the heroic spirit that his sonnets manage to exalt and beautify has been prized greatly by his countrymen in times of crisis like wars, and he has been regarded as a token of the continuity of the nation's patriotic tradition. His poetry is somehow crude in diction but rich and touching in the sentiments that the poet feels genuinely from the bottom of his soul.

Edward Thomas (1876-1917)

The most appreciated Georgian poet is perhaps Edward Thomas, whose lucid nature poems impressed W. H. Auden and other poets of a later generation. Thomas was born in London and was educated at Oxford. During most of his life, he made his living by writing book reviews and editing and writing books. His life was a struggle to support his family and stay alive. In 1915 he enlisted in the army and went to the war, and was killed in 1917. His poetic career began in 1914 when he experienced a creative outburst. His theme is the natural world that mediates for human suffering. He also wrote a number of "war poems" that portray, among other things, his love for his country. His mood is basically melancholy.

"Adlestrop" (1915) is a good Thomas poem to begin with in the discussion here. Here the poet sits in late June at a station, the train draws up, but no one stirs. It leaves the platform bare and the rest of the world—the station, the willows, willow-herb, grass, the meadowsweet, haycocks, cloudlets, and him—"still and lonely." Then he hears the sweet soothing voice of a blackbird and becomes aware of the faint but sure chorus of all the birds in Oxfordshire and Gloucestershire. He feels that he is not still and lonely after all with this musical backdrop for his existence. Another poem, "The Owl" (1915), sketches the poet's fear of loss and death and suffering that the war and poverty may bring to his fellow creatures. Here the poet turns in after a tiring night trip in the cold North wind, and enjoys now the comforts of life—food, warmth, and the rest, but the plaintive strains of the owl, shaken out "long and clear" out there, keep reminding him of the hardships of the night that he has been through, but "all who lay under the stars,/ Soldiers and poor..." have still to face. The same dominant ideas of solitude and warm humanity mingle with a touch of despair and noble heroism in his poem "Rain" (1916). The first few lines portray a poet of mixed feelings toward the wild midnight rain: he feels both bleak in his solitude on this dark night in face of impending death, and blessed to die since life has been "this solitude" to him. But he does not want his fellowmen to die like him; for him the wild rain—a metaphor for the war or his disappointing life—has left nothing worth dying for except to die for something perfect and not disappointing. This can be love for his country or anything like a noble undertaking.

Thomas' war poems reveal his tragic awareness of the devastating and debilitating effects of wars. He is different from Rupert Brooke in his representation of the war because he lived a couple of years longer to witness its disastrous impact on human life. "As the Team's Head Brass" (1917) is a good illustration. The poem is set in the fields where the ploughman is working with his team of horses. The poet-narrator sits by and talks with him. The farmer complains about the war killing his fellow farmers and his working mates and leaving farm work undone and making life impossible. There is mention of casualties and injuries. The ploughman sounds like a philosopher when he says, "If we could see all might seem good" (l. 32), revealing the unpredictability of life and the helplessness of the humans. The poem is also interesting for its symbolism. The blizzard that fells the tree and the lovers who disappear and resurface can both be symbolic in a way. The former can be seen as a symbol of the war, while the lovers, leaving the scene at the beginning when the subject of the war is about to be brought up and returning in the end when the subject is closed with the ambiguous vision of a better world, could signify the life force that may be eclipsed for a while but always manages to endure.

Robert Graves (1895-1985)

Graves had a long and complex career. He began as a Georgian, embraced Metaphysical values in midstream, but turned back to his earlier forms of writing in the latter part of his career. Graves' early work shared the Georgian rural serenity and simplicity though he took inspiration from Celtic legends and models like John Skelton (ca. 1460-1529), and wrote in a romantic vein. Some of his early poems were included in the Georgian anthologies. He went to the war and came back alive, only to write about it to escape from the traumatizing war experience. This went on until he met the American poet Laura Riding in the mid-1920s and got in touch with the Fugitives like John Crowe Ransom. Then sensitive to the change in the 1920s, he and Laura Riding published *A Survey of Modernist Poetry* (1927), contributed to the Metaphysical revival, and wrote the poems that were to make his fame. He was influenced by John Crowe Ransom and E. E. Cummings. One thing to note about Graves was his successful attempt to stay away from the Modernist or avant-garde rhetoric so much up in the air at his time. Imagism, Eliot and Pound, and even the New Criticism all failed to impress him. His style continued to be elegant, coherent, and discursive despite Eliot's paramount influence of impersonality and parataxis. Love was his major theme until the late 1940s when his book *The White Goddess* (1948) appeared in print. Through this synthesis of his myth, he hoped to achieve a primordial kind of unity as a stay against modern chaos. In the mid-20th-century endeavor of the Movement poets, Graves' reputation grew as he became one of the poets the younger generation admired. In his long life Graves published some seventeen volumes of poetry and many volumes of historical novels. He proved himself to be one of the notable poets of the 20th century.

"Down, Wanton, Down!" (1933) is a typical Graves poem both in theme and form. The theme is about lust and love; the form is traditional with its graceful regularity, but full of Metaphysical wit and conceits. The work is a knotted puzzle that takes a good deal of intellectual energy to unravel. A closer look at it would reveal that the "wanton" in the title is in fact lust which, as the poem moves, takes the form of the phallus. Then it is interesting or even scary to find that stanzas I and II refer actually to acts of sexual intercourse while the remaining three read the phallus a lecture on how lust repels love and beauty. The implication seems to be that love may not be able to endure as it is nearly always associated with lust.

Graves' "The White Goddess" (1953) merits mention here chiefly because it embodies Graves' faith in the Great Mother, the female principle she represents, and his view that poetry needs her help to recover its lost vitality. The poem alludes to the poet's book by the same title.

War Poetry

WWI was one of the most devastating experiences that humankind had to go through. Of all of its catastrophic effects, one has stood out for ever engraved on human memory: it killed so many people and so many promising young men. For the discussion here, people tend to think, among others, of T. E. Hulme (1881-1917), Rupert Brooke, Charles Sorley (1895-1915), Edward Thomas, Wilfred Owen, and Isaac Rosenberg (1890-1918). Most of these people wrote about the war that killed them. Thus the poetry that gets written in this period acquires an exceptional quality of poignant immediacy. Most of the poems are short but vital and intense. As the war's dehumanizing technology deprived man of his history-making role, man lost his control of the war and his self and was no longer heroic. As a result there was no epic to come out of it. But as the poets fought and died in the trenches, their responses to the reality of war were vigorous and emotionally loaded. There were different modes of writing about the war. As mentioned earlier, Rupert Brooke's approach was traditional and romantic. There was also Charles Hamilton Sorley who tries to transcend the military aspect of the war and exhibit an ironic kind of resignation and Christian stoic spirit. This is evident in his poems like "Such, Such Is Death," "Return," and "All the Hills and Vales Along."

David Jones (1895-1974) was probably the only soldier-poet who wrote about the war in an epic manner. His well-known *In Parenthesis*, a Modernist work by all standards (and Jones was a Modernist), was begun in 1929 over ten years after the war, and was published in 1937. It is a long poem-prose—as there is both prose and poetry in it—with some plot interest. The "writing" (as Jones himself calls it) describes an experience equally powerful as poets Wilfred Owen and Siegfried Sassoon experienced it but well mediated and mellowed by space and time. Jones was able to see the war from an epic perspective, encase it in the mythic milieu of Welsh-Arthurian mythology, and endow it with some universal and historical dimension of significance. But he also felt the want of the epic nature of the war: He was conscious that man was controlled rather controlling in the game, and it was difficult to paint him in a heroic color the way Homer does Odysseus in his *Odyssey*. Jones' soldiers do not know where to go and what to do except as told, they are moved around and struggle but are unaware that they have already been wrapped up in death's embrace. There is not much debunking of the war in the way Jones wrote about it. It is an experience removed from its immediate milieu and replayed in the mind over and over so that it has lost its sting. The retrospective poet was able to see and tell about it in a detached, distant, manner.

But Wilfred Owen, Siegfried Sassoon (1886-1967) and Isaac Rosenberg were not. Face to face with it, they saw the war in a different light. To them, war is pointlessly destructive, and should be written about so as to enhance human awareness of its senseless nature. Their poetry, as expressions of the immediate impact of the war upon sensitive minds, offers a new mode of looking at the war and writing about it. Siegfried Sassoon's "war poems" corroborated his attitude of protest to the war. One of the things particularly notable about this poet was that he wrote to his commanding officer a public statement, protesting the authorities to change the defensive nature of the war for aggressive purposes. Himself in the trenches, Sassoon saw at close quarters how the war and those prolonging it made the young soldiers suffer and die and described the nightmarish experience of the soldiers there in a meticulously detailed, concrete, realistic manner. Reading Sassoon, one visualizes oneself actually in the trenches and going through it all. There is a good deal of bitterness in his poetry.

One gets the same kind of impression reading Isaac Rosenberg. To him the soldiers are doomed. His "Break of Day in the Trenches" (1916) tends to send chills down the spine. What touches the readers to the quick is the pathetic tone in which the poet-soldier talks to a rat when he is in the trenches at break of dawn. Instead of being joyous and hopeful, the dawn here in the torn fields of France appears as disgusting and hateful because it drives the protective darkness away and exposes the fine young men, "sprawled in the bowels of the earth" there, to "the shrieking iron and flame" hurling over them and thus to "the whims of murder." The biting irony comes through when the readers realize, as indeed did the soldier, that the rat has much better chances to survive.

Wilfred Owen (1893-1918)

Wilfred Owen was probably the finest war poet to come out of WWI. He enlisted in 1917, was wounded and hospitalized, returned to combat duty after recovery, and was killed one week before the war ended. His poetry is noted for its abundance of compassion and its technical achievements, one of which is the para-rhyme or off-rhyme he pioneered. His *Collected Poems* appeared in 1920. Owen's war poems were composed between January 1917 when he was first sent to the Western Front and his death in November 1918. The best of his work was written during a period of intense creativity from August 1917 to September 1918. For Owen there was no time for gradual growth; his was a forced maturity. His sensitive mind faced a sudden and drastic combination of stimulus and challenge and met it with an admirable creative outburst. The spark of originality illumines all his poetry so that it will ever shine among the greatest of war poems.

Owen's major theme is war and "the pity of war." He calls his poems elegies which he feels may be consolatory to posterity though not to his generation. His writing calls attention to the overall reality of civilized life, one grim aspect of which is hidden and should be revealed in full. That aspect for Owen is war. He condemns it and refuses to pacify and be pacified. So there is an arid irony in Owen's work. His sonnet—"Anthem for Doomed Youth" (1917)—is a good example of his way of writing an elegy for the war dead. Instead of the consolation that an elegy normally offers, Owen's sonnet is informed with incontrollable anger and accusation throughout. The title itself is anger poeticized. There is boundless compassion in the "anthem" and equally boundless wrath at the fact that the war dooms youth to premature death. The octave raises a question the answer of which is condemnation of war. The war scenes are vivid to the senses and increase the awareness of war as evil as the lines keep piling up on top of each other. The sestet is about a memorial but Owen represents it in his unique way. For he feels that the grief caused by such an atrocity is not to be palliated by anything conventional. The war is not just and justifiable, death is not to be glossed over, and both should be remembered. For youths killed on the battlefield there is no need for a conventional memorial service, because it tends to put the dead in requiem and the living in forgetfulness. There is no need for bells, candles, flowers, and the pall. Instead, Owen urges remembrance and compassion as reflected in such actions as the shining of the boys' eyes, the paling of the girls' cheeks, the tenderness of patient minds, and the slow drawing-down of blinds (which probably signals the fact that sadness must end as well). The sonnet's note of warning is evident. Owen's originality here as indeed in most of his works lies in this, that he projects himself into the facts, and conveys his sentiment effectively with images and symbols of his own, drawn from his own experience of actual war life rather than resorting to readily available traditional stereotyped ones.

The theme of "the pity of war" is announced explicitly in his famous poem, "Strange Meeting" (1918). The meeting is strange because it occurs in Hell between the ghosts of two dead soldiers. The two fought on opposing sides and one of them, the speaker, killed the other. Now that they end up where they are in the same plight, the speaker says that there is no cause to mourn now. But the other seems to disagree. For him there is, in fact, though it is pointless to him now. The cause to mourn for him is the life, his life, cut short and wasted, and the hopelessness to get it back (ll. 15-16). His life was good once: he made the best of it—the joy and the sorrow of it all (ll. 16-21). People might laugh at his joy, but his sorrow must die with him now. It is the sorrow that he keenly feels as he died without telling the truth about the "pity of war, the pity war distilled." As a result, nations progress but continue to war with one another; people both wise and courageous continue to march into Hell (ll.26-33). He would rather enlighten and save them from bloodshed with his own death in the way—he hints—Jesus did for mankind (ll. 35-40). The implication is that the war is senseless, causing senseless deaths, and people fail to see this and continue the senseless mutual slaughter. Here lies the pity of war. This is an elegy not just for one person but for all, not just for one period but for all time.

"Strange Meeting" is also noted for the innovative rhyme pattern it introduces for the first time in English literary history. It is known as para-rhyme or "the half rhyme" or "off-rhyme," or two words with the same consonants but different vowels that match with one another at the end of the lines. Thus in the poem the end words of every two lines rhyme with one another in this "half" way: "escaped" with "scooped," "groined" with "groaned," "bestirred" with "stared," "eyes" with "bless," "hall" with "hell" and so on right up to the end of the work with fair regularity. The immediate effect of this scheme is the feeling of something left imperfect, shortchanged, or to be desired, and of there being room for setting things to rights. This form matches the theme perfectly well: war cuts short lives that have yet to be fully lived, and people do not seem to be aware of it, which is "the pity of war." Owen's off-rhyme has influenced later writers such as those of the 1930s.

Chapter 20 The 1920s • Woolf • Joyce

The 1920s: An Introduction

The turn of the 20th century witnessed tremendous changes in English social and spiritual life. The British Empire was undergoing a grave crisis. Internally it was sinking into an abyss of mounting problems. Extremes of wealth and poverty became intolerably acute. Slums increased incredibly where the city poor wallowed in the slough of wretchedness and struggled in vain for a light at the end of their tunnel. Mortality rate skyrocketed among the working class and their families; strikes occurred that helped paralyze national economy, and national morality plummeted along with productivity. Abroad the country was feeling the increasing impact of the economic depression then enveloping the whole of Europe in its clutches. The tension between the imperialist powers was fast approaching its breaking point. In addition, as a consequence of its ruthless robbery and plunger of its colonies, Britain began to face the alarming enormity of the threat of the national independence struggles of those oppressed peoples. Then WWI broke out, and ended up devastating all around, with Britain bearing its brunt first and foremost. The Empire lost its world power supremacy as well as its economic dominance in Europe. The war became a watershed for it. Nothing in the country after the event could ever be the same again.

The changes chiefly occurred also in the wake of the advances in science and technology and the growing crisis of faith, which these managed to intensify. The skepticism and questioning of faith, which had begun in the latter half of the Victorian period, continued into the new century with redoubled intensity, and gradually deprived the world of man of its underpinning mythic center as the notion of God was losing its credence. The point was made dismally clear to all by the famous English philosopher, Bertrand Russell (1872-1970), whose analysis of the spiritual state of the West proved to be the most thorough-going in nature and the most seminal in influence. Russell stated to the effect in his "A Free Man's Worship" (1918) that science has made the world devoid of meaning, that man must recognize his insignificance in the universe, and that his life is short and powerless, and doom awaits him, ruthless and dark. This was an authentic reflection of the mood of depression, despair, and emotional turmoil that followed the crisis of faith in the West. Roundabout the time, other events of comparable significance had occurred to impress the vulnerably impressionable minds of the people. These included, among others, James Frazer's monumental 12-volume *The Golden Bough* that came out in print during the years 1911-1915, and Sigmund Freud's (1856-1939) *The Interpretations of Dreams*, which was published in 1913. In addition, there was the new concept of time that first emerged in the works of Henri Bergson (1859-1941), the French philosopher. All these did a good deal toward altering the mode of thinking and perception of the people in a significant way.

By far the most important developments in the field of philosophy and psychology during this period that impacted literary creativity and criticism should be Bergson's notion of time and Freud's theory of psychoanalysis. First, there was Bergson's philosophical theory concerning time, memory, and consciousness. To Bergson time is not to be merely measured in clock time, or the traditional representations of hours, days, months, and years. Instead of being mere extended images of space, time as Bergson sees it is continuous, an indivisible continuity, a succession of qualitative changes which melt into and permeate one another, without precise outlines, and without any tendency to externalize themselves in relation to one another. This is time in the mind, subjective in nature, or psychological time, indicating the incessant flow of the consciousness. In keeping with this new concept, true reality—the self—exists in psychological time; selfhood continues its existence in memory; typical memory is unconscious memory, which is the most perfect union of past and present and reflects the true nature of the soul. In order to achieve self-recognition, man must peek through the thick curtain of the "superficial self," and remove the many tiers of barriers between reality and consciousness so as to reveal the ever fluid nascent consciousness, thought, and feeling, along with the intrinsic internal relations. Bergson finds the conventional novel wanting in this, that, instead of seeing a character as a process of ceaseless becoming, it fails to get at the true nature of things and represent true reality, as it treats time as mere space and renders "a slice of life" in a superficial, chronological or sequential order. Thus the "stream of consciousness" method soon appeared as a new mode of representing human experience, and Bergson's philosophy of time helped pave the way for the rise of modernism or "stream of consciousness" literature.

Then, there was Freud's theory of "the subconscious" which, explaining as it does man's irrational behavior, added impetus to the emergence of the new form of literary expression. According to Freud, the human psyche consists of two parts—the "ego" and the "id" or the instinctual impulses. The "ego" is both consciousness and sub-consciousness while the id, the storehouse of all basic human instincts, is the most nebulous, unapproachable part of the human body. The id, as part of the subconscious, is repressed by the consciousness and the ego, both of which keep to logic and order. As repressed desires are often sexual by nature, the growth of sexual consciousness constitutes, as Freud sees it, one important aspect of human development. Freud's interpretation of dreams fascinated many writers. A dream, Freud finds, is the process in which the human subconscious becomes active, and the "psychological self" tries to assert itself by getting rid of external inhibitions. Though still repressed to some extent, this assertion serves as some form of satisfaction to the subconscious. Dreams have their own language and syntax as a result of the compromise between the conscious and the subconscious. This theory of psychoanalysis offered the latitude for writers to explore and describe the new area of experience—the human subconscious, and led straight to the advent of the "stream of consciousness" literature of the 1920s. Freudian influence on the field of literature was not just limited to creative literary endeavors of the time; it impacted literary criticism in no small way. Beginning with Virginia Woolf's criticism of the Edwardians, new critical standards were to be set, whereby a new system of critical values was to evolve and get enforced and a clear line of demarcation was to be drawn between traditional and modern novels. The new critical system would depreciate and disparage the conventional novels for placing focus solely on the externalities of life; it would also help promote the modern way of expression and its emphasis on the excavation of the inner world of man. Now the stage was set for the forthcoming of modernism. [1]

Sure enough, the years 1912-1914 saw the appearance of all kinds of innovations. Writers and sensitive minds began to take a fresh look at man and his life, and discovered substantive changes in the relationship between man and man, between man and nature, and between man and self. The various levels of tension that these caused, the absurdity of life, the growing sense of alienation, the evil side of nature, and the existentialist crisis of man—all these came to the surface crying for attention, and gave rise inevitably to the diverse attitudes of negativity such as pessimism, nihilism, and existentialism (that came later in time). These feelings permeated the literary works of the period.

Among those wide awake and aware of these occurrences was the perspicacious Virginia Woolf (1882-1941), the famous English modern novelist, who made the historic observation, that around December 1910, human nature changed. This was a precise summary of what was happening in the field of art and literature then. Around this time something unusual occurred in music, ballet, drama, and the fine arts, which shocked the audience into a pained recognition of the fact that old artistic standards were beside the point in face of modern experience and that something different would have to be found for a more faithful representation of life and reality. There was the post-Impressionist art exhibition in London, introducing such modern painters as Van Gogh of Holland, Paul Cezanne and Paul Gauguin of France, and Pablo Picasso of Spain. Along with that, translations of the works of the Russian writers Anton Chekhov and Feodor Dostoevsky appeared in English in 1909 and 1912 respectively, which helped shake people out of their old ways of perception and thinking.

It was obvious that the new, varied experience of the period demanded a new, varied mode of expression. Europe was simmering with the innovative zeal. Paris emerged as the center of experimental art and literature to which ambitious, struggling artists and writers flocked. Impressionism appeared along with Dadaism and Expressionism. Symbolism and surrealism became stylish and popular. The younger generation felt a heightened sense of urgency and showed an unprecedented amount of enthusiasm for experimentations of various kinds. A revolution was in the offing. The new writers wrote in a manner that defied most of the accepted rules, and dealt with subjects that, by and large, had not been dealt with before, thus pushing the boundaries of literature further back. A multitude of new ways and techniques were employed in novel writing, and a new style was being created along with a very large reading audience. This audience was in large measure a very fragmented one, as modern life was fragmented and dislocated. The West of the time was, philosophically and religiously, a fragmented civilization without any unified set of beliefs any longer which once characterized the world of Dante's *Divine Comedy*, Chaucer's *The Canterbury Tales*, or Shakespeare's plays.

While older writers such as William Butler Yeats, Edwin Arlington Robinson and Theodore Dreiser were still writing to keep step with the changing times, High Modernism cut in and began to dominate the world of literature and art. Modernist masters were busy at work, and the works of permanent power and appeal came out in print in quick succession. In the field of the novel, James Joyce's *Ulysses*, Virginia Woolf's *Mrs. Dalloway* and *To the Lighthouse*, Thomas Mann's *The Magic Mountain*, and Marcel Proust's *Remembrance of Things Past* were out there, and in the field of poetry T. S. Eliot and William Butler Yeats were the most prominent of all to make their voices heard. All these combined well with other efforts such as the works of Ernest Hemingway (1899-1961) and William Faulkner (1896-1962) to shine forth the splendor of the new era, that of Modernism. [2]

Modernism represents a new mode of perception, a major feature of which is disjunctive irony. In the Christian West, God is the unifying mythic center, the provider of values for all, and the source of the original sense of wholeness. As long as He is or is believed to be on the scene, all is whole and well. Now in the new century, as noted earlier on, God seemed to be gone, and life appeared to be fragmentary and chaotic. This immensely affected the concepts of selfhood and the world. This fact of life and the mode of thinking that stemmed from it were both to be far-reacting in consequences and have a definitive influence on a good number of important issues. One of these concerned the question of truth and reality and involved the whole system of human epistemology. Another issue related to the breakdown of communication, and the resulting sense of alienation between the self and the world. When the self was cut off from others, acute self-consciousness would follow, from which would come an overwhelming subjectivity and immense stress on the self as the sole agent constituting reality. The burden on the self and the sense of disaffection with it was fraught with consequences. That would and did lead to the desire to discover more authentic levels of selfhood, and to the concern with depth and interiority, the urge to explain the inner life, and the attempt to retrieve a lost self. All these accounted more or less for the extraordinary amount of experimentation of the period: the new formal means to better express the new sense of reality, the reformulation of the notion of time, the new methods of character portrayal, the experiments with points of view, structure and style, and the use of such as the technique of the stream of consciousness and symbolism.

Some critics have even suggested that the concern with technique in this period became an end in itself, which was a faint indication of art for art's sake, and literature turned on itself, becoming self-referential and self-reflective. The attempt to cope with chaos and fragmentation led to inward transcendence, to the construction of a more perfect world, a literary cosmos, a self-imposed and self-contained sense of wholeness and harmony in art (though not in life). It also led to art as a refuge, an ideal, a moral force, a counterpoint against the disorderliness of life, and offering relief from the disjunctiveness in its complete attempt to forgo the actual world. There was a search all through for unity and fusion, and there was always the thorny problem that the physical world existed to which it was impossible not to adhere for value and meaning. The modernist endeavor was not an easy escape, but a move of desperation, and a struggle between acknowledging and subverting the phenomenal world. Modernism, which first originated from the struggle against the meaninglessness of life, managed ultimately to achieve a degree of success in its attempt, in its epistemology to redefine reality, to discover or create new meanings, in its turning to art, irony, experimentalism, and formalism, and its depiction of the crisis of consciousness. Now in retrospect, people have come to see that the value of Modernism inheres not so much in the answers it has furnished, as in its presenting to the world the awareness of crisis in every aspect of life. Eventually, Modernism would come around to rejoicing in the actual world because it would bump into its wall and reach the end of its blind alley. When that happened, Postmodernism would take over.

Modernism as a movement was international in scope and served well to reflect and record the temper of the times. The impact it has had on literary history as a whole cannot be underrated. The major authors and their masterpieces that came out of it were all among the greatest ever produced in history, and some of these such as *Ulysses* and *The Waste Land* have become milestones in world literature, comparable in power and permanence to Homer's *Odyssey* or Dante's *The Divine Comedy*, or Shakespeare's *Hamlet*. The Modernist momentum began to taper off after raging for over a decade, and the early years of the 1930s saw a new scenario of life, a new awareness and a new vision burgeoning into shape—Postmodernism. The Modern masters like Virginia Woolf and T. S. Eliot were sensitive enough to the impact of the wind of change, and quick enough to change gears and veer in a new direction. The major cause was the change of the social and cultural climate in the new decade of the 1930s; the esthetic crisis intrinsic in the body of Modernism—the excessive emphasis on the psychological but undue neglect of the external part of life—also helped lead finally to the impasse impossible for it to avoid, i.e. the sense of inspiration began to drain away in face of the new reality. This occurred in the first years of the 1930s when a new page was turning over in literary history.

Virginia Woolf (1882-1941)

Born into a distinguished cultured family, Virginia Woolf lost her mother when small and lived with an overbearing father. One fact of her life that did her irrevocable hurt was her sexual harassment by her stepbrother. All her life she had to grapple with the subsequent emotional disturbance, and became sexually repressed and even rigid. It was said that her marriage with the best of men for her, Leonard Woolf, was not actually consummated. But the Woolfs lived happily together and Leonard did a lot that contributed toward her mental recovery. They established their own press—the Hogarth Press—to help struggling Modern writers. The years of her marriage proved to be the most productive of her life. Her residence at Bloomsbury, London became the center of what came to be known as the Bloomsbury Group, whose members comprised the most distinguished writers of the literary world of the day. Ultimately it declined but not before it had left its imprint on the art and literature of the time. Virginia Woolf maintained her sanity up to 1941 when the despair in the deeps of her soul proved to be too much for her so she drowned herself eventually. Some critics have described her as a suffering genius. [3]

No one has been showered, in recent years, with such critical attention and recognition as has Virginia Woolf. That has to do with her true greatness, originality, and uniqueness. She discovered art as her mission and learned about reality and the expression of disillusion. Devoting all her body and soul to her literary creation, she became a prolific writer, with a good number of novels and short stories as well as hundreds of essays of critical acumen under her belt. In addition, there is the rich legacy of the volumes of her diary and letters. Her major novels include *Jacob's Room*, *Mrs. Dalloway* (1925), *To the Lighthouse* (1927), *The Years*, and *Between the Acts*, and her famous literary commentaries such as "Modern Fiction" served as solid spade work for the rise and dissemination of the Modernist spirit in her time. She wrote along with Joyce and Proust and was said to be reading *Ulysses* and *Remembrance of Things Past* while writing *Mrs. Dalloway*, though it was a matter of competition rather than influence here between the masters. As compared with Joyce and Proust, she is more influential, championing a worthy cause as best as she could, though she was somehow restricted in her subjects and her scope of experience and representation.

Mrs. Woolf was probably the person who announced the coming of the new age with her clear voice and vision. She began by attacking the traditional manner of novel-writing. In her essay, "Modern Fiction" (1924), she locates the major weakness of the traditional novel in its focus on depicting exterior details but ignoring any dip into the inner world of man. She feels that traditional novelists try to meet the tyrannical need for plot interest, creating probable, impeccable tragedies, comedies, and love stories with characters well dressed like real people, while life can be very different and can be represented radically differently. To her, the human mind receives every day "a myriad of impressions" which do not always provide the right stuff for any plot interest in a tragedy or comedy or a love story, nor lead to any logical traditional endings. Life appears to her like "a luminous halo" that envelopes people all the time in their waking consciousness.

In her incisive criticism, she singles out for her point of analysis Arnold Bennett (1867-1931), who she says does the best job as expected of the best craftsman in painting externalities, but makes no effort to touch the human consciousness. Branding him and Galsworthy and Wells as Edwardians and materialists, she compares them to the "spiritual" James Joyce whose focus is the exact opposite of theirs—the flow of the mind.

Woolf thus called for a new kind of novel, like *Ulysses*, and asked writers to explore and portray the inner life. As a result, modern writers all did their best to bring to attention the workings of the mind, which is often irrational, mysterious, subconscious, fluid, operating through free associations, disjunctive, and lacking in causality and sequential order. The stream-of-consciousness method of writing thus became the vogue. Although the copyright for this method was not theirs, it was these people who made it more perfect and better as a medium of narration. The "streaming" is by no means a giving free rein to the flow of the consciousness; there is conscious selection and artistic manipulation on the part of the authors. The Modernists were very serious with their literary art.

If the novel is to reveal the hidden and interior life of the people, the only world of any truth is the internal world. It is in fact a heterocosm of its own kind (or another world from the one with which the readers have been hitherto acquainted). Then the definition of reality would have to change totally as well. And sure enough, the change became immediately manifest in Woolf's works as well as those of other Modernist masters. To Woolf, the world in which we live is disjunctive, fragmentary, and disorderly. Chaos is so ubiquitous that an ordered world as imposed from outside like a mythic center is nothing but an illusion. The purpose of the Modernist writings is to reveal the true nature of the modern human condition and its disconcerting absence of meaning, purpose, and order. Characterization rather than plot thus becomes the topmost concern for writers, and sequential time gives way to psychological time, as the age of Modernism is one of psychological depths, and not so much one of actions as of opinions of actions. Woolf, along with her fellow Modernists, made for the triumph of internalization, and showed new maps of the mind with their vivid pictures of self-consciousness. They made it their job as Modernists to seek order and form in a world in which neither seemed clearly present. In a sense, the works of Woolf represent the sum total of the Modernist art of novel-writing. They reveal the author's compulsion to recreate the human spiritual experience through art, to increase the popular recognition of the subconscious and the irrational behavior of man at the mercy of the irrational emotions and impulses, and to generate a psychological shock effect on the readers at large. They offer a new vision of character.

Mrs. Woolf's notion of art merits special attention. The one thing that Woolf tried to do in her writing career was to discover the significance of art through her own writing endeavors. To her, art is important because it gives meaning to life, helps conquer the inevitable disillusionments of life, and provides the fulfillment of happiness that nothing else can offer. In other words, art time conquers real time. She believes that art can create a man-made paradise. The way to do it is through catching the ideal moments of an otherwise disappointing life, and making them enjoyable with the medium of language. Those moments, "moments of epiphany" in Joyce's description, or "moments of being" in Woolf's, when the mind lives life to the fullest, can bring people happiness and pleasure and help them peek at the "order" absent from real life, and get through the surface to the very nature of things. These moments, measured personally and freed of linearity, are the telescoping of the past, the present and the future in one. They represent stasis in flux, time out of time, spatialized, and involving the transfiguration of the ordinary world. These are the times when one experiences release and unity. Woolf's works are a record of those moments in the lives of her characters.

Take *To the Lighthouse* for example. Here one evening Mrs. Ramsay is thinking. Sitting by the window at nightfall, she sees the waves splashing at the shoreline, and her mind suddenly spirits itself, over and beyond the cares and worries of her real world, away to another, the one in the distance where the lighthouse stands, and where she finds everything pure, transparent, and full of celestial happiness. In that brief moment, or a "moment of her being," Mrs. Ramsay experiences the very taste of bliss and the true union of the self with the world. Her soul relishes the moment of serenity in a transcendental fashion and feels the utmost gratification. Now she is renewed and reenergized enough to face life again with confidence and hope. As it is evident that these moments are not always enough to sustain human morale in face of adversity, the fate of a number of Woolf's characters such as Septimus (*Mrs. Dalloway*) and Roda (*The Waves*) is inevitably tragic in the end.

For over ten years Mrs. Woolf advocated the new mode of writing strenuously in her works. She wrote a number of novels on the strength of her conviction about the nature of life and the way literature should be written. There is not much of a plot in most of her major works; the reflection of the mind's responses becomes her major feature of characterization. Both Mrs. Dalloway and Mrs. Ramsay, the major figures in her two famous works, are overly reflective. Their lives appear to be the flow of endless impressions. With *The Waves*, people stop thinking and begin dreaming, and the novel is an uninterrupted process of six people coming in and out of their dreams in roughly the same way the people in Joyce's *Finnegans Wake* behave. Woolf's characters tend to be transcendental. Suffering a growing sense of one's self being cut off, they move away from a dissatisfying outer world to discover some ultimate reality beyond oneself. As their interiority grows and the self keeps receding, they lose their link with external reality, which is, in effect, a significant part of the basis and reason for their being. The fact of the matter was, and will always be, that a moment cannot by definition last long, and the ordinary world cannot be wished away despite any amount of the sincerest wishful thinking on the part of the author. Here was, from the very outset, embedded and hidden the crisis point for the Modernist kind of writing.

So when she had taken the portrayal of interior life in the method of stream of consciousness to its farthest possible point, Mrs. Woolf found herself face to face with what would inevitably occur—the disintegration and the loss of the self for her characters. Since obsessive concern with depth is validated by the belief and assumption that character is intact, depth and surface begin to clash. This was in fact where the Modernist effort as a whole met its esthetic crisis. Life and art are inter-dependable. Mrs. Ramsay's ideal world would have been impossible for her mind (art) to conjure up had the lighthouse (life), "stark and straight" as it is, not stood there for it to weave a web on. Modernism that began with a negative vision of life could not hope to get far in its undertaking, and would have in time to give way to something new in the next phase of literary evolution.

For Woolf the crisis point came in the 1930s when she began to see her limitations. As she was not quite willing to give the devil its due and recognize the value of life and its role in literature (as was the case with other Modernists), she found it difficult to see deeper into life and felt her source of inspiration beginning to dwindle and show signs of exhaustion. She felt it increasingly difficult, if not totally impossible, to continue with her description of inner life. Drowned in the depth of things, she no longer perceived the things in life well as a whole. At the same time new, younger people appeared in the new decade with a new attitude toward their new reality. Rejecting psychology and transcendence and favoring causality and plot, these writers of the new generation saw chaos and fragmentation and absurdity as an inherent part of life and embraced reality for what it was. They happily faced and described life as it was and found it the right and rewarding kind of experience in writing. This was the beginnings of what was to be known as Postmodernism. This offered a bridge between the self and the world.

The older generation of writers such as Mrs. Woolf and T. S. Eliot were sensitive to the change in values and tastes. Eliot's *Four Quartets* is in tone and mood already partly postmodernist at least. Woolf was probably the first to change in a new direction. This occurred in such works as *The Years* and *Between the Acts*. The change of tenor in these works can be traced further back to *The Waves*, in which positive language about life being "happy, tolerable, and good" has appeared. This indicates the realization on the part of the author that harmony and order inhere in the very disorder of life just as the incessant rise and fall of the billowy waves represent the normal rhythm of the sea. In *The Years* Woolf touched earth from her "ivory tower" and, instead of focusing on interiority, she made a conscientious effort to describe the external world in detail. Her diary entries of the time noted that she became aware of the many valuable things that existed in the outer world and that she decided to resist the temptation from the "inner" one. This novel, one of thoroughly the 1930s, reveals Woolf's fascination with the plentitude of the real world—the dull booming of London, the court, the theater, the young girl with her naked arms, the old man chewing his sandwich on a bus—in a word, life with all its beautiful and ugly facets portrayed at its fullest. No one here lives ever in illusion, on the horizon or at the bottom of the sea like Mrs. Dalloway or Mrs. Ramsay or Roda. They are all solidly in touch with reality.

This represents the beginning of the end of the internalization of the idealizing, subjective novel. [4]

Now let's take a look at Mrs. Woolf's most famous works—*Mrs. Dalloway* and *To the Lighthouse.* [5] The first of these tells mainly about one day in the life of the middle-aged Mrs. Clarissa Dalloway in relation to those connected with her. It is narrated in the stream-of-consciousness method, pure and simple, and there is not much of a plot interest. Mrs. Dalloway is the upper class housewife of a British Member of Parliament. On this fine June day she is out shopping to get ready for her evening party. She feels happy to be out in the fresh air, seeing people, and hearing the boisterous bustle of London. There she meets an old acquaintance and thinks for a while of his ever sick wife. She sees a limousine and speculates about the passenger inside. The things around activate her memory and send her back to her youth, her husband, and her lesbian-oriented daughter whose tutor-friend is a religious fanatic. She thinks of love, her uncertainty of love for her husband and daughter and theirs for her, her old-time crush on the two men—her future husband Richard, and Peter Walsh who left for India after her marriage, and her own unnatural love for Sally, a girl friend. The point that keeps recurring in her mind is, What would have happened had she not married Richard for the security and social position that she thought he would give her as a hopeful cabinet minister or a prime minister? She feels trapped.

At the same time Mrs. Dalloway is down town, Septimus Smith is sitting in a park with his wife Lucrezia. His odd behavior and talk of suicide frighten her. Septimus, a war hero, has just about everything to make him and his wife happy—a good job and the promise his employer keeps talking about that he has, but he feels sad as he sees nothing but horror and hypocrisy in the world he lives in. He has visions from a dead war comrade, and detests the doctor who comes to help him. Lucrezia takes him to a distinguished psychiatrist, Sir. Bradshaw by name, who advises to move him away to "a quiet rural area."

In the meantime, Mrs. Dalloway is home, her husband is away to lunch with a woman she never likes, and presently Peter arrives for a call. Peter asks her if she is happy, and is surprised to see her so engrossed with her party. He has led a more tangled life, having divorced, returned to London, and fallen in love with another woman. Now Mrs. Dalloway's party is in progress, and turns out to be a complete success with both the incumbent prime minister and her former lover Peter Walsh present for her. Then she hears of Septimus' suicide and feels deeply affected: she feels "like him." Looking back at her own life, she realizes that she has been existing for others, snobbish, trivial, and neurotic, no longer the "Clarissa" that she was, having sacrificed her ties with Peter and Sally. She is getting old. Peter feels still drawn to Clarissa Dalloway.

The important thing to notice about the novel is the intertwining of its two narrative threads relating to Clarissa and Septimus. Woolf exhibits her consummate craftsmanship in forestalling any possible impression of structural dislocation. The unity of the novel is first ensured by the similarity in character between the two major figures. Although they do not meet, they are roughly of the same mindset and reinforce one another mutually. Both are Modernist by temperament, moody and unhappy with their lot; both feel guilty, Clarissa for her rejecting Peter, and Septimus for his inability to feel a comrade's death; both are thinking and sensitive and easily hurt; both are mentally unstable (Clarissa also contemplated suicide, intensely unhappy with her marriage and her distance from her daughter); both arrive at the tragic awareness of the world and their selfhood; both are intensely individualistic and try to counterpoint and impose order on the disorder of their lives, but neither succeeds, one ending in physical death to stop time, and the other in a symbolic one. Between them they stand for the Modern Everyman with his complex psychological make-up of the male and the female fibers.

Furthermore, some other tricks are at work to connect the two worlds. One of these is using something the people from the different spheres share somehow as a common experience—a car, a plane, a child, a singer, or chiming clocks. Then there is the author's deft choice of a thing or a word or a movement that serves well as a reminder of the linkage between the streams of consciousness of different people. The jumps from person to person and from one thing to another are well smoothed out enough to avoid possible bumping ruggedness in the narrative terrain. For instance, Septimus' death trickles through to Clarissa's ears at the party via her psychiatrist friend—Bradshaw (who happens to be Septimus' psychiatrist), and Septimus' throwing himself out of the window before he is moved to the country sends Clarissa through the time channel back to a time she recalls when she never threw anything more than a shilling into the Serpentine of Hyde Park. That brings her to a fountain where Peter once asked about her intention to marry Richard Dalloway, and Richard, now in her mind's eye, reminds her of his promise as a possible prime minister which did not materialize (but she does have a prime minister as her guest at her party today). She feels suddenly old and insignificant and a sense of failure in her effort for success. Thus one thing leads naturally to the next and the narrative flows smoothly on and on. In *Mrs. Dalloway*, memory plays a big role in the author's manipulation of the stream of consciousness. In addition, the party serves well as an effective wire-puller, tying up all the loose threads in a closely knit knot. The major characters all appear, either physically or in the conversations, giving the story a wonderful sense of inclusiveness and finality. Also deserving attention is the ever present narrator, whose voice directs and screens the thoughts of the characters for the readers.

This voice becomes even more clearly defined in *To the Lighthouse* (1927), which is also a stream of consciousness narrative. Here in this novel, there is Mrs. Ramsay, over fifty years old, with her husband, a philosophy professor, and their eight children to take care of. A party is going on at the Ramsays' summer cottage house on the Isle of Skye in the Hebrides Islands. There are a poet, Mr. Carmichael, and a young woman artist, Lily Briscoe. Lily finds it difficult to paint a picture of the cottage and goes to the beach for a walk. She needs assurance and the living of life for her creative effort. She enjoys her stay with the Ramsays most. Mrs. Ramsay is planning to visit the nearby lighthouse in a sailboat. She is also thinking of the money (fifty pounds) for the repair of their house. After dinner, the children are put to bed and the guests are gone, and Mrs. Ramsay joins her husband in the library, knitting while he reads. They agree not to go to the lighthouse as the weather is turning stormy. They never get to do it the whole summer. For many years after they come back from the summer, they never return to their summer cottage. A lot occurs in the time that intervenes. Mrs. Ramsay dies, so do some of her children in childbirth or the war. The summer house stands in sore neglect—the wallpaper peeling down, with rust, mildew, spider webs, and dust everywhere. Then with the war over, the Ramsays come back with some friends like the poet Carmichael and the painter Lily Briscoe. One morning Mr. Ramsay and his children get ready for the visit to the lighthouse. The son is put in charge of the preparations, and Lily tries to paint the cottage once more. The family trip is successful and ends with the happy Mr. Ramsay praising his son for a job well done.

To the Lighthouse is noted for its thematic and structural unity. In thematic terms the novel advocates the author's unique vision of art and literature. This has been defined as the androgynous vision, or one that combines both the female and the male principles in artistic creation. Neither principle alone will produce the best work of art. The opposition of the two genders is illustrated in the antithetical character traits of Mrs. Ramsay versus Mr. Ramsay. The latter is all logic and reason while the former is all imagination. The man is scientific and metaphysical while the woman is intuitive, mystical, and metaphoric. The contrast between the two is obvious. The first of the three sections of the novel, "The Window," depicts Mrs. Ramsay sitting there watching the lighthouse and lost in thought. She is the feminine all through. As the center of attention in this part of the book, she organizes everything and takes care of meticulous details. But as her vision is limited and dependent on male intelligence, she fails in many things: The dinner is tedious; her effort to bring pairs together ends in no marriage; and her plan to visit the lighthouse never materializes. Lily the painter in part one is probably too heavily influenced by Mrs. Ramsay to complete her painting. But she feels the two principles at once in her viewpoint, which makes her the stuff for an ideal artist in the final section of the book, "The Lighthouse." Her androgynous vision matures in the final stroke, i.e. the line she draws in the middle of the picture, which appears final and symmetrical.

Section two, "Time Passes," is important as a testing of the book's ideals. It is an observation of what happens to the question of the androgynous vision first raised in section one. Here is a stepping back, an observation from an esthetic distance, with the real focus not so much on inter-personal relationships as on a look at the human and non-human world. "Nothing" seems to be the key word here. The total fracture and horror and the insensibility of death and nature, the fall of the wallpaper, the mildewed books, the separation, the ending of human assumptions, nature's indifference—all these denote a tension between the aesthetic as fixity and the existential as process and the connection between them. One of these two is to win out in the third section of the book. The section as a whole reads like a poetic interlude with important family events inserted in square brackets. In section three Lily Briscoe experiences a moment of ecstasy, a sense of a vision fulfilled. She feels at one with all time and is filled with sympathy for the human condition. Thus she is able to finish her painting, which embodies a perfect aesthetic view, acts as a mediating medium between real life and the human ideal, and indicates the successes of art patterning or subordinating the world. It means that Woolf had not by this point of her career accepted the world yet.

James Joyce (1882-1941)

Joyce was born into a declining Irish middle class family. He received a good Jesuit education, but the rigidity of the religion and its repressive effect turned him away from the church to literature. His literary passions included such world masters as Dante, Flaubert, Ibsen, and Tolstoy, and his first essay on Ibsen, published when he was a student at the University of Dublin, won the admiration of the aging Norwegian playwright himself. After college, he went to Europe and stayed there for the rest of his life (1902-1941), going back to Ireland only a few times for a brief stay mostly. His longest sojourn there occurred during 1903-1904 when he went back to see his dying mother and met his future wife. He was financially never comfortable all his life. He tried to make ends meet by doing odd jobs such as teaching English and lecturing on Ireland and literature.

But Joyce never lost sight of his priority—the ambition to write the greatest literature of his time. He was such a conscious literary artist that he spent years on the writing of one book. His *The Portrait of the Artist as a Young Man* (1916) took ten years and three thorough revisions to finish, *Ulysses* (1922) 10 years for conception and 8 years for execution, and *Finnegans Wake* (1939) a whole of 16 years. His first important work, *Dubliners*, came out in 1907. Seldom if ever did he try to cater to the need of publication and revise his work against his best judgment. Although he believed that a true artist had to go into self-exile, Joyce wrote about his native Dublin all his life. He felt adamant that universality inheres in particularity, and Dublin is the gateway to the heart of all the cities in the world. Joyce was serious with both his thematic and technical concerns. In thematic terms, one important thing to note about him is that he never forgot to promote the spiritual freedom of his native country with his writings. Irish nationalism features prominently in his works. Although overshadowed sometimes with minute depiction of life in its variegated forms, the theme of Irish discontentment and struggle for freedom always appears as a clear narrative thread. In *Ulysses* as well as other works, Joyce has in mind to authentically reflect the mood of his country and his people. Steven's complaints and Bloom's wrestling him away from British violence are good illustrations out of *Ulysses* alone. Furthermore, Joyce loves the common people. He finds great value in love and compassion. He loves life itself and believes that love makes life worth living and makes man invincible. Finally—and this is probably the most important, there is his preoccupation with art and its mission in life. It is true that Joyce takes nothing short of the whole of life as the province of his fictional representation—history, philosophy, art and literature, man, his nature, and his cosmos, human epistemology and ontology, psychology, the psychic fabric of man, and the list can go on and on for ever. But it is conspicuous that one thing always stands out in bold relief on his fictional canvas, that is, art and its relation to life. Scan his *Dubliners*, *The Portrait of an Artist as a Young Man*, *Ulysses*, and *Finnegans Wake*, and the readers will find that the man is exclusively obsessed with the exploration of art and its various dimensions of meaning. All of his major works relate to art and artist and their bearing on life. It is important to keep this in mind while reading Joyce; otherwise one would find oneself at a great disadvantage as a reader.

With regard to his formal features, Joyce is noted for his frank representation of reality. He embraces realism against romanticism. He is outspoken on important social issues, and insists on portraying all the aspects of man—the good as well as the evil side. For him characterization matters more than does plot. His descriptions of the sex encounters, the details of the human body, and the impure thoughts that flit through the minds of his characters proved to be repulsive and infuriating to the conservative taste at the time, but he did not care much about following the tyranny of opinion. Joyce is also well renowned for his adroit use of the stream-of-consciousness technique and his contribution to its subsequent popularity as an effective stylistic medium. In addition, Joycean language has always been a topic of immense interest to people. It is poetic, accurate, forceful, connotative, rhythmic, musical, picturesque, aptly polyglottic, and humorous beyond description. Thus by pushing both thematic and formal boundaries infinitely further back, he has become "the writers' writer" in literary history. Joyce's influence over the other writers both of his own and later generations can never be overrated. [6]

Before discussing *Ulysses* in some detail, a few words about his other works are in order. Joyce's first published book, *Dubliners*, is a collection of 15 stories, the most famous of which are "The Dead" and "Araby" (as critical consensus seems to suggest). Although the narrators of the stories are different, they are all in essence the fictional externalizations of the author's inner world and the process of his emotional and psychic growth. The setting is more or less the same for these stories: dismal, dreary and dull, and the major characters are basically out of the same mold—they aspire for something infinitely better than their lot has offered them. For instance, the narrator "I" in the oft-anthologized story "Araby" is probably a replica of the childhood Joyce. Imaginative, sensitive, and romantic by nature, the boy feels dissatisfied with his gloomy and humdrum environment and wishes to spirit himself away to a place where the life of his mind could enjoy a more congenial kind of atmosphere. Very soon, sure enough, he spots the object for his imagination to weave a romantic web about—Mangan's older sister, and his mind begins to run wild around her. He falls in love, feels entranced with her, and plans to buy a present for her from the market-place, "Araby." There he goes, sees the least romantic place (most incompatible with the romantic connotation of its name), and meets a young saleswoman, probably similar in age and silhouette to Mangan's sister. As she takes little or no interest in him and hurries away to resume her flirting with some young men there, the boy feels disgusted and suddenly makes to the realization that Mangan's sister may not have taken any notice of him at all, either. He ends up with strong self-censure, a heightened awareness of himself, and a step closer to manhood. The readers of the story have good reason to presume that Joyce as a boy might have behaved in a similar or symbolically similar way toward his own native land, which accounted for his ultimate self-exile in the end. But he left his country, it should be noted, only to write about it well, which is a point all his works have offered adequate proof of.

The Portrait of an Artist as a Young Man tells in fact Joyce's own story: Joyce lived through all that the major character of the book Stephen Dedalus goes through. It is not, however, an autobiography *per se*, as Stephen comes out of the book a totally independent person. The novel takes a close look at the author's surrogate—Stephen's striving for and attainment to psychological maturity from childhood through young manhood, and examines the development of the author's own artistic sensibility. The book ends with Stephen locating his ideal in artistic creation and asserting his belief that self-exile offers the way for him to realize it. So he leaves for Europe. The novel consists of five chapters, each of which covers one phase of the major character's growth. The first chapter records the occurrences of Stephen's childhood, the second his sexual awakening, the third his penitence and forgiveness, the fourth the discovery of his artistic bent, his epiphany on the nature of life, and his decision to reject the holy vocation and embrace art, and the fifth, the last chapter, his initial artistic experiences with art, the lengthy discussions on aesthetics, his experience of writing a poem, some fragments from his diary, and his determination to break with his family, his religion, and his country to devote all to art. *The Portrait* is well noted for its varied styles and its experiment with the stream-of-consciousness technique.

Finnegans Wake represents a radical departure from the novelic tradition and has been seen as an extreme illustration of the Modernist stance that the modern novel no longer places its emphasis on story-telling. Joyce said on one occasion himself that the book is meant for the ideal insomniacs. The novel, circular in structure, with no beginning or end, adumbrates a dream world, one in which a Dublin family all dream in their sleep. The first reading may be confusing as the readers find it difficult to decide on the identity of the major dreamer: a character in the book or the author himself. There are 17 chapters in the book, each of which depicts one of the 17 phases of a dream. Each phase varies with its twists and turns, the substance of the dream keeps changing every moment, and no dream occurrence receives long coverage. The book is thematically all-inclusive: the past, present, and future, all essential human relationships such as those between man and woman, age and youth, life and death, and love and hate. The description of the dream state reaches perfection and reveals a profundity, the depth of which is simply unfathomable. Comprehension is made incredibly harder to achieve with the author's use of other languages than English, and his endless puns and wordplay and coined words with which the book is strewn. There are some who speculate that a college of literary critics need to scour the whole of the novel, scrutinize its every word and sentence, and compile a book of the length of the *Encyclopedia of Britannica* to explicate and make full sense of it. And someone has actually tried to do some pilot work of this nature, writing over 50 pages to footnote just one page of the novel. It is interesting to note that this novel writes about a Dublin night which begins at dusk and ends at daybreak whereas *Ulysses* paints its daytime cityscape. [7]

Now let's take a close look at his masterwork *Ulysses*.

Ulysses describes the experiences of a few people during the day of Thursday, June 16, 1904 and the few hours early the next morning. The day was chosen because, as some people speculate, it was the one on which the author met his future wife, but as others say, it was the day on which she became unfaithful to him for the first time. The novel is made up of 18 chapters in three parts with a varying number of chapters in each. Part 1 comprises the first three chapters, focusing on one of the major characters—Steven Dedalus; part 2, the next twelve chapters, devoted mainly to another major figure—Leopold Bloom; and part 3 the last three chapters, telling about the meeting of the three characters as well as Molly's inner thoughts. The novel consists in the scenes in which the three major characters appear alone or with others, and records, among other things, their inner world and their sensual impressions. [8]

Bloom is the dominant figure in the novel, taking up most of the space in the 12 chapters of part 2 of the novel. He is a middle-aged Jew, an ordinary person, an advertising businessman, without special job skills. Married now for 16 years, he has had two children with his wife, Molly—a daughter, and a son whose death as a 10-day-old infant has left an indelible imprint of gloom upon the both of them. The couple has not had sex for some ten years, and Bloom has been suspicious of Molly carrying on an affair with somebody. On the day of June 16, 1904 Bloom feels exceptionally bad as he knows Molly is to meet her lover Boylan, and even sees a vision of adultery between them on one occasion. After breakfast he goes out. He visits the church, takes a bath, attends a funeral, does his usual advertising business, rents a love story for Molly, goes to a restaurant to write a love letter over lunch, goes to a bar and gets involved in a debate on social and national issues, sits for a while on the beach, thinks impossible thoughts about a girl lost in thought there, visits a hospital to see a woman in labor, and meets Steven at ten p.m. He helps him out of trouble, invites him home to stay for the night, goes to bed after the young man leaves, finds traces of Boylan's stay but decides to let it go and make up with Molly. He comes to see his own share of the fault for his family discord during his long, ruminating day and decides to make his wife happy.

Steven appears as the focus of the first three chapters of the novel and shows up only briefly in the rest of the book (in chapters 7 and 9 of part 2) until chapter 14. A struggling poet fresh from college, the young man feels lost and depressed in face of the repressive rule of the British and the Roman Catholic Church and the general conservative milieu of Irish life. He has just lost his mother, has few or no friends in life and in literary career, and feels at odds with life itself. His father is worried and furious over his indiscreet social contacts. Bloom, who happens to know the old man, feels a fatherly feeling for young Steven when, in his visit to the hospital, he sees him already drunk but still going to a bar with his friends. He decides to follow him. The young drunkard goes and raises hell within a brothel and hallucinates profusely. He runs raving into the streets and gets beaten up by two English soldiers. Bloom makes peace with the brothel and manages to rescue him from the soldiers. He takes him to a café for a rest before bringing him home. The two of them feel an affinity between them, converse on a number of topics, and agree to disagree on some others. Steven declines Bloom's offer to stay for the night but promises to come often for a visit and do mutual teaching with Molly.

Molly does not appear until chapter 4 in which she makes a brief appearance. Then except in chapter 10 in which she is seen raising her white arm to throw money to a sailor, she is present in visions only, either in Bloom's deliberations or in the conversations of other people. The last chapter of the novel, however, is her chapter, which offers a panoramic view of her fluid mind in operation. Here she lies in bed in a semi-conscious reverie, and her consciousness seems to be streaming out of focus. It recollects many people and incidents that constitute virtually her whole life, but it always roams back to one point of reference—her husband. She makes to the realization that he is the best of all men for her—dependable, frugal, and considerate, and decides to give him another chance. The novel ends with her exuberant affirmation of life and hints at a happy future with Bloom.

Ulysses is a veiled autobiography. Joyce wrote a good deal of his life into it. He appears as Steven most of the time and as Bloom some of the time, while Molly offers a faint, leery image of his wife. Many descriptions of Steven and his life have a solid basis in Joyce's actual life experiences. Steven's alcoholic and improvident father, his childhood experience of poverty, his Jesuit education, his dubious response to it, i.e. with both a sense of alienation from it and some belief in it, St. Thomas Aquinas's overwhelming influence with which the novel is infused, the day June 16, 1904 on which Joyce did meet his future spouse, his rescue on a June, 1904 day from his fierce street fight by a middle-aged Jew who had an adulterous wife, his love for Dublin with its specific street names, its sights and sounds, its political and religious shows, its extremes of wealth and poverty, its races, sects, and currents of thoughts—all these and more are in fact direct quotations from the author's own life. In addition, *Ulysses* can be seen as a blue book to Dublin, Joyce's beloved city. It is a Dublin from past to present, from cradle to grave, a Dublin that could be replicated, as some people say, with the help of the descriptions of it in *Ulysses* if ever by any chance it should vanish from sight.

Ulysses is a highly symbolic book. It is so especially in view of its structural features. Its structure bears such a striking resemblance to Homer's *Odyssey* that the novel is a perfect book of the classic's echoes and parallels. The classic story is a three-sectional narrative, with part 1 relating the story of Telemachus (Odysseus' son) venturing out to look for his father, part 2 the wanderings of Odysseus on the sea in his attempt to get back home, and part 3 the final happy family reunion. Although Joyce's *Ulysses* is anything but a story about Ulysses—there is no mention of the name or Ithaca or Penelope or the man's adventures on the sea, the modern novel does approximate the classic's structure admirably well. As noted earlier on, it begins with Steven going out, continues with Bloom roaming around but always with his mind riveting on his wife Molly, and concludes with the two men meeting the woman in a resemblance of a family reunion. The author deliberately builds in some hints in the title and the wanderings of the major figures, and adroitly imbeds some allusions to the Homeric classic. If the readers take the novel's different chapters into account, they will easily find that Joyce's chapter plots coincide with those of Homer's book very well. The first chapter of Joyce's novel resembles the classic *Odyssey*'s Telemachus getting fed up with his mother's suitors and getting ready to go and look for his father, its second chapter similar to the classic's Telemachus asking advice from old councilor Nestor about his father's whereabouts, its third describing Steven's fluid thought changing very much like the shape of Proteus, the plot of its fourth chapter similar to the classic's Calypso detaining Odysseus, and that of the fifth chapter reminding people of Homer's island of Lotus-Eaters. Moving on, the readers will find further that Joyce's chapter six approximates Homer's narrative of the hades, his chapter seven Homer's narrative of Aeolus (god of winds), his eight that of the classic's narrative of the cannibalistic Lestryonians, his nine that of the classic's Scylla and Charybdis incident, his ten the classic's Wandering Rocks, his eleven the classic's encounter with the Sirens, his twelve the classic's Cyclopes incident, his thirteen the classic's Nausicaa's kindness, his fourteenth the classic's disaster at Trinacria, the island of the sun, his fifteenth the classic's sojourn with Circe, his sixteenth the classic's Eumaeus (the shepherd), his seventeenth the classic's return to Ithaca, and his eighteenth the classic's union with Penelope.

As a result of the novel's title and these textual insinuations, it has been a critical commonplace to see its description of Bloom's listless wandering around and his petty adventures on that summer day in Dublin as a parody of the Homeric *Odyssey*, and compare Bloom, the simple advertising businessman, to the resourceful Ulysses, the adulterous Molly to the faithful Penelope, and Steven to Ulysses' son, Telemachus. Although people differ on the validity and value of the comparison—some feel that the Homeric work gives Joyce just a structural skeleton, and some even call the comparison a stereotyped critical trick, it remains a fact, nonetheless, that the similarity between the two great books cannot be mistaken, and it may be worthwhile spending time just on hunting for the sources. But the readers should note and bear in mind that the metaphor has a very grand purpose to accomplish. The ironic twist that Joyce's story gives to the classic one is meant to reveal the vast difference between the great and the petty, the heroic and the ordinary, and the noble and the degraded. The meaningful Homeric heroic life is held up in effective contrast to its spiritually poor modern counterpart, to form the backdrop against which modern existence with its absurdity is enacted and found wanting. This is probably what *Ulysses* sets out to do for modern people: to throw their weaknesses in relief by means of a mirror of the grandeur of the past. This is a supreme illustration of the symbolic significance of the novel.

By the sheer force of its thematic and formal distinction, the novel stands out now as a classic rarity in literary history. Thematically, the novel mainly discusses Bloom in relation to fate. The man is going through a slough of despond but sees no rescue from either angel or man. His despair is traceable to the death of his son that still rankles in his memory. Neither is his present life anything but happy. He still loves his wife Molly dearly, but knows that she is not happy, and is just about to meet with her lover, Boylan, a slick, vulgar philistine of a concert manager, but he does not want to do anything to stop the tryst from happening. It is a sad and absurd kind of life to which Bloom has to pluck up his courage to face up squarely. In addition, there does not seem much for him to look forward to in the future. He is driven to think of Steven as a better lover for Molly. His mood of gloom and loneliness is pathetic enough to body forth the temper of modern times. But the good part of the story is that all is not lost. He is not giving up on his marriage. Generous and good-hearted, he opts to ignore bad luck, be self-critical, and try to make a success of life. This positive gesture (possibly the result of his day-long deliberations) echoes Molly's conscious response and provides a ray of hope in the end for them both. There is reason to believe that the man and his wife will surmount the barrier of alienation and come together to live happily again. Here Joyce wishes to affirm the indomitable human spirit, indeed as one character—Steven—states in chapter 17 when he talks about the value of literature. To Joyce selfless love is the best of virtues of the common people.

In formal terms, the novel is unique in characterization and in style. The portrayal of the major figures is impressive in at least two striking aspects. First, the three major characters represent three different human archetypes in education, taste, and attitude toward life, with Steven the most cultured, Bloom in the middle of the social and educational ladder, and Molly settling comfortably at the bottom. Bloom is an outsider in life, a "Joyce" in expatriation. He is portrayed as one representing the sum total of the salient features of his race. He seems to be the archetypal everyman, but he is in fact more than that. His over-preoccupation with meticulous thoughts of sexual and physiological matters sets him off instantly from the common crowd. Steven is weak, learned, always complaining, and capable of coming out with statements of proverbial proportions. Elegant in artistic taste and careful with speech, he is a difficult person to fathom: Having lost his faith but still keeping some of its tenets intact, and a free thinker with a self-imposed bondage of dogmas and metaphysics, he embodies the veritable specimen of the effete modern intelligentsia. Some critics see in him a Joyce the young artist; he is possibly a vague assertion and an externalization of the author's spirit. Molly Bloom is a singer, vulgar, kind, and thirsty for love. Commonplace and traditional in her mode of thinking, she is about the only one of the three who loves life and enjoys living, capable of offering a ready, rich emotional response to the lovely trifles of daily existence. So Steven and Bloom are the thinking types among the people and as such tend to find it hard to say "yes" to life and feel ill at ease in their milieu, while Molly is positive about life, craves for it, and makes the best of the moments of her being. Together the three represent the modern humankind and the strands of modern sensibility. The book thus offers both a reflection of human nature and its universal application and makes an acrid comment upon modern life.

Another thing to notice about the novel's characterization is that the book manages to flesh out Bloom with the help of the other characters such as Steven and Molly. Bloom is a person of an exceptionally complex texture. There exist in him the two polar extremes of intellectual and worldly character traits. He is knowledgeable and learned in his own way, a thinking kind of person whose excessive thinking weakens and turns him into a morose person. This facet of his personality is basically represented by Steven. On the other hand, he is unwilling to give up on life. He hates Molly for her infidelity, but loves her and cares about his life with her. There is still such physicality in him that he is not indifferent to love and sex. In this sense Molly represents a fraction of this side of his personality.

The novel's style is peerless in its surprising variety. Chapters differ in their dominant stylistic features: some employ direct narration (as, for instance, in chapter 1 of part 1 and chapters 1 and 3 of part 2), others use stream of consciousness (as occurs in many chapters especially in relation to the major characters), and still others indulge in the parody of many nonfiction forms such as newspaper headlines (chapter 4 of part 2), music (chapter 8 of part 2), mystery plays and slapsticks (chapter 12 of part 2), pedagogic questions and answers (chapter 2 of part 3). There is also the parody of literary styles and authors such as the funny narrator in chapter 9 of part 2, the writer for a women magazine in chapter 10 of part 2, the series of authors and weeklies in chapter 11 of part 2, and the elegant journalistic style in chapter 2 of part 3. The multiple narrative points of view and the constant change of styles meet the need for conveying a variety of information and depicting fresh details from different sources. The change marks Joyce's deliberate innovative effort with a new literary technique.

Another feature to note here is the way the characters converge and diverge. These happen at times in a haphazard manner as if by the dark design of fate. In connection with this is the recurrence of certain leitmotifs for cumulative symbolic effect. Joyce's is the voice of the book, detached, God-like, non-judgmental. He accepts everything as natural, and completely ignores abnormality. The absence of judgment is characteristic of Joyce's life values.

Furthermore, Joyce has diverse literary devices and tricks up his sleeves to promote effect. He can be poetic as when he deals with Steven, yet lyrical and harmonious as with Bloom with the use of alliteration and a lively, rhythmic mode of expression to adumbrate various kinds of depression and anxiety. Joyce's diction varies well and consistently with different characters. For Steven who tends to meditate on subjects of a metaphysical and spiritual nature, Joyce uses polysyllabic words of classic origins, abstractions, and words best suited for philosophical discourses; Bloom speaks the language of the man in the street; while for Molly, the language is vivacious, animated, and sexually provocative, just to indicate that she is an emblem of fertility and a positive life force. There are, among other things, linguistic games like puns, changes of word order, repetitions, abuses of verbs, and imitations of sounds which, along with references to places known only to the author probably and the use of foreign words, have made for the good number of textual obscurities for the readers.

Ulysses is the first stream of consciousness novel to appear in English literary history. Although there is lucid direct telling in some portions of the book, most of the story is narrated in the stream of consciousness manner. The most famous illustration of this narrative method occurs in the last chapter, the one wholly devoted to an extended, almost uninterrupted monologue. One glaring linguistic feature of the chapter is its conspicuous absence of punctuations. The chapter is not punctuated actually except for the presence of the two periods in the whole of it. As to other "oddities" that characterize the famous chapter, it suffices to list such as absence of paragraphing, capitalization, and the occasional obscure identity of the pronoun "he." The chapter records one famous scene in literature: a woman lying in bed thinking (which is a reminder of the beginning chapter of the French Modernist Marcel Proust's *Remembrance of Things Past*, where one spoiled brat lies in bed, turning from side to side, thinking and thinking). Joyce's character here is thinking her lewd and confused thoughts.

As the last chapter goes, Molly is now in bed, lying awake for over 40 pages. Her consciousness streams through her mind in a seemingly haphazard manner. Although the chapter is strewn with insignificant details, some leitmotifs keep recurring. These include, among other things, her strong desire for sex (which indicates her love of life), her unswerving love for Bloom, her capacity for compassion, and her sense of spiritual certitude. It is true that she enjoys sex with Boylan, who is physical enough for her animalistic desires, yet she loves Bloom more for his respect and courtesy to old women and beggars, his higher level of education, and his understanding of her as a woman. The chapter ends with her passion for the man which reaches its warmest and happiest pitch in the last couple of pages. The last few words, "yes I will Yes," reasserts the recovery and affirmation of the human spirit that seems lost in the midst of a confusing multitude of sidetracking trifles of life. As Bloom asks her to serve him breakfast at the beginning of the chapter, there is reason to believe that he is going to have it and that in bed, too.

Now let's take a closer look at the woman's monologue. Her thoughts generally (though not always) find expression in her continual associations with people and occurrences that have appealed to her sexual urges. The following thoughts, for instance, flash through her mind's screen in quick succession: Bloom's request for being served breakfast in bed, his politeness to miserly, gabby old women like Mrs. Riordan and also to waiters and beggars, his contacts with other women, suspecting that he is writing a love letter, her love of a soul-paralyzing kiss,

Boylan's big genitalia and her sex with him, her row with Bloom over Josie and making up with him, remembering Bloom's handsome youth when they first fell in love, thinking of Josie's lousy life with her dotty husband and of Mrs. Maybrick poisoning her husband, feeling that she and Bloom are perhaps mutually lucky, thinking of her lovers—Boylan who likes her feet and Bartell dArcy kissing her in church, Bloom begging her for her underwear, her extramarital liaison and trysts with Boylan, liking Boylan's way of making love, eagerly expecting him at 4, thinking of her upcoming trip to Belfast with him, visualizing her love-making with him at Belfast, recollecting his pigheadedness at the Mallow Concert at Maryborough, hoping to make love with him on the train to Belfast, recollecting her singing at Howth, reminiscing about her lover Lt. Gardner and his death of enteric fever in war, thinking of a regiment passing in review, of Boylan's father making money by selling horses to the cavalry, of Boylan giving her presents with his father's money, of going around town shopping with him, and of Boylan being rich and single, thinking of getting money out of him, wondering if Boylan likes her, thinking of love-making with him, of his anger about creepy Lenehan, anxious about looking well and dressing more in style for Boylan, feeling that Bloom should work in an office to make more money, recalling her pleading with Mr. Cuffe who looked at her bosom and still fired Bloom, recalling Boylan's sucking her beautiful breasts, thinking of the male sex organ covered with a cabbage leaf, of Bloom's one-time suggestion, when he lost his job, that she pose naked for a photographer to make money, feeling disgusted with aggressive male vulgarity, thinking of her great breast of milk when she nursed Milly, of Bloom sucking her breasts and wanting to milk her into tea, thinking of writing a book, entitled "Master Poldy," to record Bloom's odd ideas, her orgasm with Boylan that afternoon, a train whistle and the rain reminding her of Gibraltar and its heat, thinking of her faded frock, her friendship with Mrs. Stanhope and her husband "Wogger," and the bullfight at La Linea, and wishing to return to Gibraltar, thinking of Mrs. Stanhope and her husband's departure, her boredom without a visitor or a letter, of Milly writing a letter to Bloom but sending only a card to her, wishing to receive a love letter from Boylan, worrying about being thrown out when old, thinking of her first love letter from Lt. Mulvey, of their lying together in a wild cove, of the fun she had with him, wondering what has become of him now after 20 years, thinking of men running around the world, of Lt. Gardner dead of fever in the Boer War in South Africa, another train whistle reminding her of Love's Old Sweet Song and her upcoming performance., thinking snobbishly of the Irish girl singers, of Lt. Gardner, of making love with Boylan, of her becoming a prima donna if she had not married Bloom, uneasy with Bloom sleeping at her side, thinking of the winter at Gibraltar when she was ten, thinking fondly of Bloom coming back drunk at 4 in the morning, of playing with the cat, of meals for tomorrow and of a picnic, mentioning Boylan, thinking of boating with Bloom, feeling lonely at night, recollecting Bloom's promise for their honeymoon, feeling scared alone at night, uneasy about Bloom sending Milly away on account of her closeness with Boylan, thinking of her relationship with Milly and worrying about her, thinking of her irritating theater experience, of Boylan failing to make her pregnant, of their love making that afternoon, afraid of suffering from some women's disease and commenting on her doctor, fondly recollecting her first meetings with Bloom, amused at the way he sleeps at the foot of the bed, thinking of their frequent moves in their 16 years' married life, suspicious that Bloom is a liar about his love affairs, worried that he has spent money on a woman today and at the Dignam's funeral, commenting negatively on men's behavior and determined to protect her husband from mockery, remembering singer Simon Dedalus and his son Stephen Dedalus, fondly recollecting of Stephen as a boy, imagining him as a young poet, romanticizing her relationship with him, thinking of Boylan as rough and crude, resenting men's freedom in sex and wanting it for herself, unhappy about Bloom never embracing her but kissing her bottom weirdly, her strong desire for sex, wishing for the world to be governed by women, sadly thinking of the death of their son that alienated her and Bloom, of women as a dreadful lot of bitches, of preparing breakfast for Bloom, of Stephen and Gibraltar, of Bloom's request for breakfast again, hoping that Stephen would come and stay with them, thinking of getting up early the next morning and going to the markets, planning to clean and do up the house for the coming of Stephen, her love of nature and God, her comments on atheism, reminiscing about Bloom's marriage proposal to her 16 years ago on Howth head, remembering him calling her a flower of the mountain that the sun shone upon, still loving him because he understands women, thinking lovingly of the beauties of nature and life, and of the day she spent with Bloom on Howth head, happily accepting his proposal.

Chapter 21 Lawrence • Yeats • Imagism • T. S. Eliot

D. H. Lawrence (1885-1830)

Lawrence came from a working class family. His father was a coal miner, inarticulate but warm and intimate, while his mother was a school teacher, different in temper and behavior. Lawrence was sensitive to the influence of both parents, pulled as he was at the same time in the two directions of intellectual aspirations and warm human contact. His close attachment to his mother led him to the complexities of human love, and his paternal background set the realistic tone in his representation of life. Thus reading Lawrence can be a very intriguing experience: often it is a painting of one or more aspects of love set against a gray backdrop of real life. His stories are all well set in their locales and reflect the life of his time well. Lawrence was a versatile genius. In addition to the novels for which he is mainly renowned, he also excelled in the short story and poetry. His major short stories include “"Odour of Chrysanthemum,” “Daughters of the Vicar,” “The Ladybird,” and “The Rocking-Horse Winner.” Lawrence was also a poet. His poetry is thematically similar to his novels, dwelling on love, maternal love (“End of Another Home Holiday” among others), and on nature as a counterpoint to the human loss of innocence and instinctive response (*Birds, Beasts, and Flowers*). In poetry, he wrote rhymeless, stanzaless free verse, and gave priority to the representation of human feelings rather than to poetic form and structure. His poetry, often rough with signs of hasty composition, offers an index to his own experiences, feelings, and responses to life in general. Lawrence was one of the great modern masters to come out of the period. His influence is still on the increase today. In 1985, fifty-five years after his death, a monument was erected to his memory in the Westminster Abbey, London, where he enjoys fame in the hall of fame along with Byron and Lewis Carroll.

Lawrence was heavily influenced by Freudianism. He placed emphasis on the depiction of the inner world and the irrational and called for the emancipation of the id. However, he also quarreled with Freud in his essays, "Psychoanalysis and the Unconscious" and "Fantasia of the Unconscious," in which he made clear his stance on psychoanalysis as a theory. Lawrence hated the tyranny of reason and the rational in life. To him the great and the beautiful come from within the inner soul, not from the progress of society and science. The evil of modern mechanical civilization lies in its ruthless violation of the human soul, harnessing it to social, economic, and political commitments, and depriving it of its original, pious ability—the instinct to love in a pure and sincere way, thus totally dehumanizing man. To Lawrence, what was detestable in Freudianism was its clinical quality, and its rationalization of love, which disappeared from life because of Freud's loquacious theorizing about it. This was an intolerable sacrilege that Lawrence felt that modern science had committed against life. Because of the pressure and the corrupting effect of modern civilization, man began to love rationality, human relationship became alienated and cold, and the process of depersonalization intensified. What essentially set Lawrence off from Freud was the novelist's faith in will as against Freud's belief in reason, which is a moot point traceable further back in western cultural history. Although they differed in approach, they agreed upon the principle—the significance of the subconscious and the irrational, and so in the final analyis there was no essential discrepancy in their positions.

Lawrence calls for the restoration of man's true selfhood to its pristine purity. He feels that the most sacred thing is love, and the sacred can be realized only in the love between a man and a woman. Only in love can man restore his true emotional self. Sex is the highest expression of individuality, and modern man's tragedy lies in seeing sex as the fulfillment of an animal desire and in repressing love's irrationality. Lawrence regards sex as his religion, sees the essence of religious experience as one's own experience, and feels that the emotion that makes humans human should exist independent of traditional and social conscience and commitment. All his life Lawrence wrote to censure modern western society and communicate his prophetic—though a little desperate and decadent—vision that the end of western civilization is in sight, man should live in the primitive way, and his new life should begin with the freedom of sex.

Lawrence's major theme is love. His *Sons and Lovers* (1913) treats of a mother's dominant and debilitating love over the sons, his *The Rainbow* (1815) and *Women in Love* (1920) deal with the possible unconscious influences on human relationships, marriage, and personal fulfillment, and his *Lady Chatterley's Lover* praises genuine unfettered love between a man and a woman. Lawrence's other works include *Aaron's Rod* (1922), *Kangaroo* (1923), and *The Man Who Died* (1927). *The Man Who Died* is an interesting novel in more than one way. It gives the biblical story of resurrection an unusual yet charming twist. After Jesus' death, as the story goes, the crucified person dies and is interred as Christ, but Jesus the man does not die. This man, now nameless, admitting the mistake that he has made acting as Christ, comes to the shrine of the Egyptian fertility goddess, learns the secret of sex from a fair-haired priestess of the goddess, and discovers his own love as a human being. He is thus restored to the innocence of his consciousness, and gets to know his mistake in having led humankind astray. He learns that the salvation of the soul lies in intimate living, and becomes Jesus after Christ's resurrection. [1]

Let's take a look at his major novels, *Sons and Lovers*, and *Lady Chatterley's Lover* (1928). The first of these is autobiographical. Here the author quotes his own experience of the first twenty five years of his life authentically. His protagonist's parents and his loves are all based on the real people and real incidents from his own life. The story is set in a northern mining town. The major character is Paul Morel. His father, Walter Morel, is a collier, the bread-earner of the family. Because the man is crude in taste and drinks heavily, he is not on good terms with his snobbish, intellectually aggressive wife—Gertrude Morel. The mother makes up her mind to bring up her children, William and Paul especially, so that they will stop being miners in the footsteps of their father. William does well, gets to London, but dies young in disappointment there. Paul, now the sole object of his mother's attention and care, loves her and hates his father who he thinks makes life impossible for her. The father, thus pushed out of family warmth, finds solace more in his cups. Now Paul meets Miriam, falls in love with the coy girl, but his mother comes in between as a barrier. Later Paul feels drawn to Clara, a married woman, mainly in a physical way, but Clara wants to get back to her husband. Paul goes to Miriam and is intimate with her but knows that she is not for him. Later his mother is terminally ill with cancer and suffers so much that Paul gives her an overdose of morphine to end her pain. Now free from her mother's control, he returns to Miriam and finally decides that they are not meant for one another. He wants to die but thinks the better of it. With his endearing memory of his mother in mind, he parts with his father and begins a new life.

The novel's major theme is its exposition of the "Oedipus complex" and its negative impact upon human growth. The story is visibly Oedipal in the son's hate for the father and his over-dependence on his mother. The father's being driven out of the family's emotional life and the fact that Paul has to live separately from his father after his mother's death—these are somewhat parallel to the ancient Oedipus' behavior. Paul's psychically erratic love for his over-assertive and possessive mother is another, more significant, indication of the Oedipus complex at work. The son is all the time aware of the presence of her mother as a shaping factor in his life, yet there is nothing he can or indeed would be willing to do about it. He allows his whole emotional being to be dominated by his mother's love, and leaves little or no room in his heart for any other involvement. Despair sets in as a matter of course when he finds himself facing the spiritual vacuum that his bereavement generates for him. So the novel ends on a tragic note. Its description of the mother-son relationship is an eye-opener and a reminder of the complexities of the human psyche. Despite the author's disclaimer, *Sons and Lovers* is a post-Freudian book. [2]

The other characters are all well knit into the overall picture. William's death foretells the fate awaiting Paul, who does not, however, decipher its message right until the time of despair after his mother's death when he thinks of death as an easy way out. Miriam is also well portrayed as part of the Oedipus drama. Coy and passive as she is, the girl is essentially a copy of Paul's mother in intensity of love, possessive appeal, and the desire to make Paul part of her emotional being. Although she is sincere in her offering herself to Paul, the young man feels the tension fast tearing him to pieces in the fierce tug of war that rages within him. Paul somehow sensitively feels that Miriam represents another loving trap for him and, since it is a trap, he does not want it. Clara kicks in mainly to stop the gap in Paul's sexual life, but she serves a more important function. Her encounter with him is educational as it takes him into an area of experience hitherto unknown to him, i.e. the first taste of life as an adult living and acting his self out on his own. Clara finds Paul wanting in this aspect and inadvertently helps him to see his weakness later in time. Paul's effort to bring the divorced Clara back to her husband might be a sign of his recognition that the man deserves the love he as an outsider has violated, and this might be a gesture of reconciliation with his own father, whose love life he as son has helped to destroy.

As to the father, he appears degraded and despised most of the time as unworthy of his more refined family. He serves as the "murdered" father figure in the Oedipal replay. It was true that Lawrence the author did not feel the urge to do right by the father at the time of writing this novel, but later in his career he came to see his injustice in his portrayal of his father in the image of Mr. Morel. As it is, nonetheless, the novel is not totally lacking in passages of affirmative descriptions of this rugged, rude, but really loving father and husband. He is seen at times very alive, caring, and in touch with normal life. This has to do probably with two facts lingering in Lawrence's subconscious mind: his—or human—recognition of the father's influence in life and an unconscious praise of the working class virtues which Lawrence knew too well to ignore.

The novel that helped mar and make his reputation is the highly controversial *Lady Chatterley's Lover*.[3] It is a story about natural and spontaneous love and warm, personal contact. Lady Connie Chatterley is sexually thirsty. She has not had good sex for ten years as her husband Sir Clifford Chatterley is paralyzed from waist down due to a war wound. She has had some sterile contact with playwright Michaelis, a family friend, and adoration from artist Duncan, another family connection, but neither can give her what she desperately needs—genuine love and a true marriage. Her chance meeting with Oliver Mellors, the gamekeeper on her family forest grounds offers her a gleam in an otherwise totally dreary milieu of gloom. The two find irresistible mutual attraction in one another and have many sexually exhilarating trysts and intimate sexual encounters in the natural setting of the woods. Eventually they decide to stop the hide and seek and get married regardless of everything.

What Lawrence had in mind to do was clear and simple. He would like to draw attention to the established inhibitions—tradition, class, family, morals and ethics—that all conspire to kill the natural and spontaneous quality of life for which alone love is worth having. He further traced the constraints and limitations back to the modern mechanical civilization and pointed at the pernicious intellectuation like Freud's clinical analysis. To him any sweet spontaneity and genuineness will dwindle and vanish under the microscope of an analytical mind such as Freud's. The story proved to be scandalous and brutalizing to genteel taste, so that it was banned for a long time after it was out in print, and its author had to suffer the harassment of the jarring din of protest. It was not until 1960, over thirty years after his death, that the ban was lifted and Lawrence received some degree of rehabilitation.

The two major characters—Connie and Oliver—are the archetypal images of the primitive human being. Although both are of the upper class in education and taste, they are bias-free in regard to class and sympathies and stay close to nature. In other words, both manage to retain their primordial innocence that alone makes an individual a natural man, in tune with nature and appreciating its ennobling virtues intuitively. They are truly whole and human, free from the taint of civilization and reason. Connie seeks genuine love, which is available only in a genuine human being. A lady with all that would make her picky and snobbish, she does not condescend to start contact with Oliver, a mere handyman of the family, and does not even bother to know about his background. She appreciates his love for its own sake, and decides to throw her financial security away and marry him for the man that he is. Oliver is an interesting specimen of the humankind. A miner's son, well educated and equipped for a job a lot better than a gamekeeper's, he chooses to be close to the source of vital life. He detests the upper class values, and despises modern ways of life and business transaction. He loves Connie for her true and pristine humanity that is very rare in the modern world. Thus the two of them live in the bliss of the Garden of Eden and between them body forth the very antithesis to the rest of the fallen world, i.e. Clifford with his rationalizations, Michaelis and Duncan with their emptiness, and Connie's sister Hilda with her built-in class prejudice. The forest functions as the symbol of a paradise where man can hope to relive their simple, innocent, and happy lives. As such it acts as a foil to the civilized world of Sir Chatterley's and his company and points at modern civilization as the root cause for the failure of human existence.

In formal terms, the novel is as uninhibited as its theme. For instance, its representation of sex was too open and forthright for the taste of his time. The way it replays the conversations between Connie and Oliver, with the use of the forbidden four-letter word and the way it describes their exuberant sex—all these proved to be, then, too detailed and physical for the imagination. In historical perspective, Lawrence did a tremendous lot toward pushing the boundaries of literary expression infinitely further back for modern and contemporary writers; the evolution of literature in the last seventy years would have been drastically different without the interference of Lawrence. But as is almost always the case with prophets of various kinds, he suffered enormously and inevitably for being one. D. H. Lawrence did not think much of the way Joyce wrote about love. He thought of himself as treating love with reverence while Joyce did not. Incidentally he considered himself a clean writer and saw Joyce as dirty. *Lady Chatterley's Lover* may have been his own evidence of support.

Yeats and Anglo-Irish Literature and the Irish Revival

It is a good place here to talk about Anglo-Irish literature briefly. Anglo-Irish literature covers the works of the writers who are Irish either by birth or by residence. Irish traditions in literature reach far back in time. The Irish have had a long history of literary expression. Ancient Irish singers managed to keep their Celtic myths and legends alive so well as to define and affect the modes of perception and writing of the later generations. [4]

After the first known modern Irish writer Geoffrey Keating (1570?-1644), there were all through the 18th century Jonathan Swift (who had little Irish about him), Richard Brinsley Sheridan with his well-known plays, and Oliver Goldsmith, whose *She Stoops to Conquer* has proved to be one of the three eminent 18th-century plays still in evidence in world theater today (the other two being Sheridan's *Rivals* and *The School for Scandal*); and all through the 19th century there were famous writers such as poet Caesar Otway (1980-1842), novelists Charles Lever (1806-1872), William Carleton (1794-1860), Patrick Kennedy (1801-1873), and Gerald Griffin (1803-1840), playwright George Bernard Shaw who in a very real sense reinvented the English drama, poet-novelist-playwright Oscar Wilde who was the leading figure of the 1880s Victorian aesthetic movement, and women writers like Jane Francisca Wilde (1826-1896, mother of Oscar Wilde). Centuries of concerted effort toward a distinct literary expression did the spadework for the Irish literary revival in the latter part of the 19th century.

The Irish literary revival was in fact an offshoot of a larger national movement for independence. The Irish people had for long fought against the British dominion. One major event in recent memory was the Irish Uprising of the early twentieth century which was ruthlessly repressed. Writers like William Butler Yeats were actively involved in their nation's struggle for freedom. When the Irish Free State was established in 1922, Yeats became one of its first senators. Thus the nationalist spirit fueled the literary movement for a clear voice of the nation's own.

The immediate contributors to this revival included poets such as Thomas Osborne Davis (1814-1845), Thomas D'Arcy McGee (1825-1868), Charles Gavan Duffy (1816-1903), James Mangan (1803-1849), Samuel Ferguson (1810-1886), Timothy Daniel Sullivan (1827-1914), and William Allingham (1824-1889). There were also Standish O'Grady (1846-1928), whose *The History of Ireland: The Heroic Period* (1878) influenced the direction of modern Irish literature, and Douglass Hyde (1860-1949) whose book of folktales in Gaelic impacted Irish literary development.

In the Irish literary revival William Butler Yeats played a major role. Along with him there were George William Russell (also known as A. E., 1867-1935), James Stephens, Katherine Tynan, F. R. Higgins, and Padriac Colum. These poets received more critical attention after the death of Yeats. In addition, there were William Kirkpatrick Magee (also known as John Eglinton), Augusta Persse, Lady Gregory (1859-1932) who encouraged Yeats' interest in drama, John Millington Synge (1871-1909), the famous playwright, and a good many other lesser talents whose names are not listed here merely because of space constraint.

From later 19th century through the present, quite a few Anglo-Irish writers have featured prominently in modern and contemporary literary history. The names that come immediately to mind include William Butler Yeats, James Joyce, George Moore, Samuel Beckett, and Seamus Heaney. English literature would have been totally different without the contribution of the successive generations of Anglo-Irish writers.

William Butler Yeats (1865-1939)

Yeats was born in Dublin but spent much of his childhood in London, where his father moved to become a member of the Pre-Raphaelite Brotherhood. Yeats was well educated and well read and had a capacity for a wide range of interest in a great variety of subjects. A number of things happened to him that impacted his major interest—poetry. These included his childhood experience of the Irish country life which helped develop his enormous interest in Ireland and Irish folklore; his involvement in the nation's independence struggle against England and becoming one of the first senators of the Irish Free State; his lifelong fascination with mysticism and the occult; and his long and unrequited love for Maud Gonne, an Irish revolutionist. There was in addition his acquaintance with Lady Augusta Gregory, an Irish nationalist playwright, with whom he established the Irish National Theater, where he worked as a director and a playwright for the most part of his adult life. The theater later became the famous Abbey Theater, a center of the Irish Literary Revival and one of Yeats' great contributions to Ireland. He was also influenced by a number of factors such as Blake, Shelley, the Celtic folklore, and the French symbolists.

Yeats lived and wrote in a period of transition. He came on the scene in between Swinburne and T. S. Eliot, and made himself a name comparable to, if not greater than, theirs. In a sense, modern English poetry began with W. B. Yeats as much as it did with Eliot and Pound. Yeats and Eliot dominated the first half of the 20th century. Yeats was a playwright, a prose writer and a poet with volumes of writing in all three genres, but his reputation has been built mainly on his poetry.

Yeats wrote with extraordinary facility. By the early 20th century, he had written and edited nearly one hundred volumes including his 8-volume complete works, of which such early writings as *The Wanderings of Oisin* (1889) and *The Countess Kathleen and Various Legends and Lyrics* (1892) are peerless portraits of the Romantic and dreamy Celtic twilight. This was done during the first or the "nineties" (1890s) phase of his career, one in which his contact with the

Pre-Raphaelites such as Lionel Johnson and Ernest Dowson, his visit to the county of Sligo, his mother's home place in the west of Ireland, and his reading of Standish O'Grady's *History of Ireland: Heroic Period* and some translations of Gaelic poetry all featured prominent in the love poems of his early fuzzy Romanticism. Poems like "The Stolen Child," "The Rose of the World," and "The Lake Isle of Innisfree" are among the finest of all time. He would have gone down in history as a significant late Victorian poet had he not written anything else.

But Yeats' was a dynamic personality. His sensibility never stopped self-refining and redefining. His career can be divided roughly into four broad phases. The first of these was the one in which he was interested in Irish folklore and wrote his early Romantic dreamy poems. The second stretched from the late 1880s through the first decade of the 20th century when he was involved in Irish nationalism and discovered Ireland as a literary subject and composed works to express support for Irish nationalism and the Irish struggle for national indepencdence. Then the third phase followed in the 1920s. He was quick enough to sense the change of values at the turn of the 20th century and made himself readily amenable to its ethos. T. S. Eliot's rediscovery of the Metaphysical poets and Ezra Pound's Imagist endeavor, now underway as the first chapter of modern poetry, both impacted the older poet. His friendship with Pound twenty years his junior has proved to be one of the most meaningful relationships in modern poetry. In fact, Yeats was malleable enough to Pound's energetic influence and re-oriented his own poetic composition in step with the temper of the time. As a result, Yeats' career entered a new phase, and his style became more distinctive. *The Green Helmet* (1912) and *Responsibilities* (1914) reveal clearly that he had left the 19th century behind and that for him the phase of "Romantic Ireland" was over as he declared in his "September 1913." From then onward volumes poured out that were to establish him as a major poet of the 20th century. These include, among others, *The Wild Swans at Coole* (1917), *Michael Robartes and the Dancer* (1920), *The Tower* (1928), and *The Winding Stair* (1933), the last two representing Yeats at his best. From 1928 through his death, which can be seen as the last phase of his career, Yeats' style underwent another substantive change. Imitating folk ballads, he wrote some simple, pleasant, unornamented poems such as *Crazy Jane*, *Lapiz Lazuli,* and *Long-Legged Fly*. All of these are affirmative in attitude and ebullient with a sense of pride which endows tragedy with meaning and chaos with order.

Yeats had a huge sense of mission. He knew that he was faced with a world in decay and disintegration and that his time was to witness some apocalypse of a terrible kind. As he was not a believer of the Christian faith, he felt he needed a thought "system" in his world of "a bundle of fragments" that would explain the truth about the world and the soul in a coherent way. That system constituted, naturally, what any great author must possess: a consistent vision with which to hold all of his creations together. Yeats felt that the vision was crucial to his career because it was to him "a last defense against the chaos of the world." He hoped that the system would link his individual poems up into one integral whole. It is good to note here that Yeats' spiritual outlook had a tremendous impact upon his work. His interest in things esoteric—mysticism, occult, spiritualism, magic, astrology, reincarnation and the supernatural, telepathy, clairvoyance, theosophical beliefs, spiritual ecstasy and intuition, the Hermetic Order of Golden Dawn (a European ritual magic), and many complex historical and spiritual concepts—all these influenced the way he composed his poetry. He believed that it was essential for him to develop his own concepts of life's cycle.

Years of painstaking quest followed, in which he found value in many things such as the "great memory," Indian reincarnation, the Cabbalist doctrine, the Great Wheel, the spirit world, and finally his "lunar parable." The new symbolic system, or his personal mythology, as explained in his book, *A Vision* (1925), includes the 28 phases of the moon and sees everything, such as personalities and phases of civilized history, as all interrelated. There is in it astrology as well as traces of thought from the influential *The Decline of the West* by Oswald Spengler (1880-1936). Yeats' vision gave a sense of direction to his writing, and its cohesive power made it possible for his individual works to footnote one another and become part and parcel of a unity of thought. Yeats' mythology, like Blake's, was one of a personal kind. The readers do not necessarily have to know about its elaborate content; it is too complex and time-consuming to do that. But it is importat to know that it exists, as the awareness can be of help in understanding his poetry better. What he discovered, in fact, may not be as important as the processes of discovery in which the poet kept remaking himself and achieved maturity. Yeats is a recognized world poet and one of the two or three greatest poets of the 20th century. He has received abundant critical attention as such. He was awarded the Nobel Prize in 1923. [5]

Let's take a look at some of his individual poems.

Yeats' early poems, though not his best efforts, are nonetheless intriguing to read—all dreamy lyrics, evocative, and nostalgic. One of these is his "The Lake Isle of Innisfree." In his childhood, Yeats visited his maternal grandparents' home in the beautiful County Sligo in west Ireland, and his experience there colored much of his early poetry. He learned about the folklore and Irish myth and felt committed to writing a poetry Irish in subject matter and tone. "The Lake Isle of Innisfree" is typical in describing his beloved Sligo in its slow pace and natural imagery. The Lake Isle of Innisfree is located in the county. It impressed the mind of the boy so much that years later he was to say that he had the ambition then to live some day in a cottage on a little island called Innisfree. The ambition takes material shape in the poem in lines such as these: "I will arise and go now, and go to Innisfree,/ And a small cabin build there, of clay and wattles made." In a way his love for Sligo became the basis for his ceaseless life-long effort to promote the spirit of Ireland's native heritage. He strove to revive in his people a sense of glory that Ireland's past possessed. Thus there is a good deal of Irish myth and Irish landscape description in such poems as "The Rose of the World" and "The Man Who Dreamed of Faeryland." The poem "Who Goes with Fergus?" derives its subject from the Irish heroic legend of King Fergus, a romantic who gave up his throne to live in the woods as a philosopher. The question, who goes with Fergus now, is answered well in the poem and suggests that love goes with Fergus, because the king rules over nature, and all nature is love and is everywhere: "For Fergus rules the brazen cars,/ And rules the shadows of the wood,/ And the white breast of the dim sea/ And all disheveled wandering stars." The first phase of Yeats' career was one in which the poet contributed immensely to the rediscovery and revival of the Irish heritage and identity and the Irish traditional culture. [6]

The next phase came when Yeats was involved with Irish nationalism. It was romantic by and large, but colored now with a heavy touch of realism. Around the mid 1880s, Yeats got in touch with John O'Leary, the staunch Irish nationalist, a man of great courage and integrity, a token of all that was true to Irsih culture and identity. O'Leary died later a martyr to his country's indepencdence. Yeats also got to know other Irish patriots, and began to write to help promote the Irish independent spirit among his people and develop Irish national feelings. His early dreaminess began to weaken and fade to make way for his new-found masculine style in his poems, the focus of which now switched from the traditional past to the burning present issues of independence from England. His famous poem "September 1913" turned out to be a watershed in his poetic composition. It was a bitter satire on the mood of his people. Although devoted to his country's struggle for independence, Yeats felt somehow disillusioned by the apathy of his countrymen. His contempt was obvious for the frenzy of the popular—especially the middle class'—getting and spending, which he saw as a life devoid of dignity or nobility of spirit. He sighed heavily at the fact that Ireland had lost its ideal and its tradition. "Romantic Ireland is gone,/ It's with O'Leary in the grave." Other works that came out of the period such as "Easter 1916" also echoed his strong nationalist feelings. One thing to note about Yeats' zeal about Irish nationalism was the fact that he received immense encouragement from Maud Gonne, the intense revolutionary, the woman he loved long and hard. Maud never returned his love but his passion for her inspired him to write quite a number of beautiful romantic lyrics. "Adam's Curse" expresses his deep grief over unrequited love; and "When You Are Old" declares his unconditional commitment to his love. The latter immortalizes his love when he says that, even when she is old, he will still love her and love her for her soul:"…one man loved the pilgrim soul in you,/ And loved the sorrows of your changing face." Despite the fact that Yeats was later married and had a happy family, Maud remained the major figure in his life and the indispensable impulse for the finest love poetry he ever wrote. Yeats' romantic phase lasted up to the first years of the 20th century.

A substantive change came about in the nature of his poetry in the 1920s when he embraced the new values of the new verse and became a major voice along with T. S. Eliot and Ezra Pound in representing the spirit of the time. "Leda and the Swan," "The Second Coming," and "Byzantium" that came out of the period are all among the greatest poems of the 20th century. They constitute part of Yeats' system. "Leda and the Swan," essentially a Miltonic sonnet, tells the Greek myth of the seduction of Leda, the Spartan queen, by the God of gods, Zeus, who takes on the form of a swan. The ravishing is both done with and leads to violence. The swan is all power and does not bother about how its victim reacts. It simply swoops down, grabs her up, and rapes her. The ravished girl is portrayed as completely overwhelmed: staggering, caught, helpless, and terrified. Violence begets violence. The ghastly act sows the seeds for more ghastly ones in the future: Leda gives birth to two children, Clytemnestra who is to help murder her husband Agamemnon, and Helen who is to cause the fall of Troy (as referred to in ll. 10-11). Had Leda known what Zeus had known about these terrible events and had his power, she would have done something to forestall bloodshed. But as it is, there is nothing a mortal like her could do to change anything. The tone of the poem illustrates the poet's attitude of disapproval, even antagonism, to the divine act. The rime scheme is regular until the sestet, where the half rime occurs in *up/drop* (ll. 11, 14), allowing the reader to hear the heavy fall of the body of the girl suddenly carelessly released. It is interesting to note that "Leda and Swan" fits in Yeats' new system, according to which every new age in the history of the West, be it classical or Christian, was heralded by a bird (the divine in disguise), and a new phase began always in violence.

"The Second Coming" (1921) can be read on different levels of significance. One interpretation, purely based on textual evidence and the overall impression the poem tends to make, can be summed up as follows: The world is chaotic, violent, faithless, and evil; it needs saving, and an apocalypse is imminent; but what is coming is a terrible beast, a horror to birds and, by extension, to all living species. If we approach the poem from a socio-historical perspective, we may know that the poem was composed in 1919, a time when the poet's homeland was in the grips of violence and death (two years before the Irish Free State was born) and Europe had been sorely devastated by WWI. On top of this the crisis of faith continued with redoubled intensity in face of fragmentation of life, the best portrait of which was Eliot's *The Waste Land* (1922). A deeper layer of meaning can be found when we take Yeats' personal mythology into account. Yeats' sees the world as governed by a Great Wheel which turns round once every "twenty centuries," when one age ends and a new one begins. The second coming that the poem talks about clearly proclaims the end of the Christian era and the beginning of another, which is evil in nature and destroys the life of the present rather than bring hope for a better one.

"Sailing to Byzantium" (1927) is a four-stanza poem about the agony of old age and the wish for immortality, achievable by way of art and poetry. In the first stanza the speaker, or persona—an old man, an ageing poet, finds himself in a country, physical in its details, but really metaphorical as it is one of death, where all live and die without any concern for "unaging intellect." In the 2nd stanza the old man, disgusted with his own ephemeral dying body, becomes aware of his soul's eternal vitality and decides to sail to Byzantium and study the "[m]onuments of its magnificence," which is another way of saying that he is leaving the physical world behind for paradise. In the last two stanzas he is in Byzantium face to face with hallmarks of immortality—the mosaic images of the saints laid on the background of gold adorning the Byzantine cathedral of St. Sophia (l. 18), and the clockwork golden bird singing on the golden bough in the emperor's palace (l. 30). He is burned with the desperate desire to die out of his physical form and prays for the sages to transfigure him into an eternal art form (ll. 21-24). Byzantium becomes a symbol of paradise, of his vision of immortality. The poem suggests that an artifice, like Keats' Grecian urn (hinted at in l. 27), or singing, or a great poem, is an eternal monument. Yeats' aspiration as a poet was to write such poems.

The "Crazy Jane" group of poems, eight in all, are among the most memorable and probably the greatest of Yeats' poems. Here Yeats seems to put his "system" aside and faces life on its at once physical and philosophical levels of meaning. The gist of Jane's story—if such can be pieced up—is that, when young, the girl overflows with passion and ignores the advances of a divinity student in favor of Jack the journeyman, the person who is full of animal spirits. They enjoy love to the fullest extent. As soon as the student becomes a holy cleric (and finally a bishop), he has Jack banished, but Jane's fidelity remains. Time flies, Jane becomes old, ugly and poor, and the Bishop is now interested in her soul. Jane does not believe in his nonsense, and holds to her view of life as before. There is a touching existential ring about Jane's craziness about life: joy exists beyond tragedy. The style is in the form of a ballad, all simple, limpid, and intense "words for music." Now the first of these eight peoms, "Crazy Jane and the Bishop," tells Jane's feeling of disgust about the Bishop's vicious remark about her and Jack living like beasts together. In the second poem, "Crazy Jane Reproved," Crazy

Jane ignores what people say about her and goes on loving the roaring, ranting journeyman. The third, "Crazy Jane on the Day of Judgment," in the form of a conversation between Jane and a "he" (the bishop, or God, or the conventional lot all taken together), recounts two views on love with Jane reaffirming her thirst for passionate love and living regardless of all consequences. The fourth, "Crazy Jane and Jack the Journeyman," reiterates Jane's stance on passion and love. The fifth, "Crazy Jane on God," is about Jane's love of joy in passional experience without moral considerations. In the sixth, "Crazy Jane Talks with the Bishop," she tells the man now concerned with her soul that, though she lives in a sty, her soul is clean and safe. The seventh, "Crazy Grown Old Looks at the Dancers," presenting Jane as a spectator-commentator, restates that passion may be destructive like "the lion's tooth," but it is the only thing that makes life worth living. The last of these, "Crazy Jane on the Mountain," continues Jane's role as an observer, jealous, reminiscent, grieving for the loss of youth, but still aching for passional experience. The overall impression that the "Crazy Jane" series makes is that the devil-may-care style of hard living is its own reward, and its own justification if needed, which is a concept of life essentially secular in nature.

Imagism

The poetic scene in the 1920s was dominated by T. S. Eliot and William Butler Yeats. Though born and educated first in America, and basically an American author, T. S. Eliot has been, like Henry James, claimed as an English poet as he was a naturalized British subject. He is included here as a major part of the singing strength of England at the time. As to the sketchy introduction of the Imagist movement here, it is deemed necessary since the movement originated in England and was first masterminded by T. E. Hulme, a brilliant young English poet-critic of the time, whose potential growth was cut short by his untimely death in WWI. [7]

The new age demanded proper literary expression. Between 1912 and 1922 there came a great poetry boom in England and America. To express the modern spirit, the sense of fragmentization and dislocation was in large measure the aim of quite a few modern literary movements, of which Imagism was one. It came, it is true, as a reaction to the traditional English poetics with its iambic pentameter, its verbosity, and extra-poetic padding; but it served, first and foremost, to meet the need of expressing the temper of the age. Nobody propounded the point more convincingly than the first Imagist theorist, the English writer T. E. Hulme. Hulme suggests that modern art deals with expression and communication of momentary phases in the poet's mind. Poetic techniques, he goes on to state, should become subtle enough to record exactly the momentary impressions. The key word here is "momentary." The most effective means to express these momentary impressions is through the use of one dominant image. "Each word must be an image seen." The image is a representation of a physical object, and the reader is made to react to it as such. "Each sentence should be a lump; a piece of clay, a vision seen." Hulme advises the poet to seek the hard, personal word for expression. These became the basic principles on which the movement was launched.

The Imagist poem was the invention of a small group of English and American poets who came together in the first years of the 20th century to work out some new way of writing poetry. The movement underwent three phases in its brief and yet immensely important history. It first began in London in the years 1908-1909. A young Englishman, T. E. Hulme, founded in 1908 a Poets' Club which met in Soho every Wednesday to dine and discuss poetry. The presiding spirit of the period was Hulme who theorized a lot on poetic technique, insisting on "absolutely accurate presentation and no verbiage." Ezra Pound was present at some of the meetings, though, according to the first historian of the movement, F. S. Flint, he did not contribute much except by talking about some Provencal poets. It seems that there was a lot of talking but not as much writing. Hulme died in the First World War.

The second phase of the movement was the period of some three years (1912-1914) when Ezra Pound took over and championed the new poetry. Something like an Imagist manifesto came out in 1912 in which Pound and Flint laid down three Imagist poetic principles: (1) Direct treatment of the "thing," whether subjective or objective; (2) To use absolutely no word that does not contribute to the presentation; and (3) As regarding rhythm, to compose in the sequence of the musical phrase, not in the sequence of a metronome. The first principle, with its emphasis on direct treatment, indicates a desire to make the expression resemble the "object" as closely as art can make it. By "direct," Pound means no fuss, frill, or ornament. The second stresses economy of expression, a reaction to the nineteenth-century tendency of philosophical "padding" of extra-poetic matter, or "emotional slither." To Ezra Pound any unnecessary word represents a loss of precision and a moral and artistic defection. The third concerns a breaking away from conventional prosody and the use of free verse, and the interrelationship between music and verse. Pound did not mean to sponsor "free verse" as the only verse form to use: he advocated freedom in verse. "Free Verse" means form, not formlessness. It is not "free"; as T. S. Eliot once said, "No 'vers' is 'libre' for the man who wants to do a good job." Neither was it new with the Imagists. Free verse went as far back as Milton. But it was with the Imagists that it became a legitimate poetic form. Free verse is a poetic mode closely allied to music; hence the third principle relates to verse form and music at the same time. In 1914, Pound edited the first anthology of Imagist poems, entitled *Des Imagistes*, which included poets such as Hilda Doolittle, Richard Aldington, F. S. Flint, and some prominent American poets. The third phase of Imagism (1914-1917) was one in which Amy Lowell took over from Pound, and the movement gradually lost its momentum. The most concise of the Imagists, H. D. (Hilda Doolittle), became wordier, and the six principles that Amy Lowell and other Imagists worked out were in essence an expansion and an adulteration of the first Imagist manifesto of 1912. In this period three anthologies came out respectively in 1915, 1916, and 1917, edited by Amy Lowell, all entitled *Some Imagist Poets*. After 1917 Imagism ceased to be a movement.

Images exist in all poetry, but the image of the imagists has something new to offer. T. E. Hulme said that the image must enable one "to dwell and linger upon a point of excitement, to achieve the impossible and convert a point into a line." Pound defined an image as that which presents an intellectual and emotional complex in an instant of time, and later he extended this definition when he stated that an image was "a vortex or cluster of fused ideas" "endowed with energy." An Imagistic presentation is hard, clear, un-blurred, done by means of the chosen "exact word." And the exact word, according to Richard Aldington, another of the first Imagists, must bring the effect of the object before the reader as it had presented itself to the poet's mind at the time of writing. An Imagist poem enables the reader to see the physical thing rather than put him through an abstract process. Lucid logical exposition is no good poetry. The best poetic effect is visual and concrete. Thus an Imagist's image represents a moment of revealed truth, truth revealed by a physical object presented and seen as such. An Imagist poem, therefore, often contains a single dominant image, or a quick succession of related images. Its effect is meant to be instantaneous.

In the history of English and American poetry, Imagism was only a transient phase of no longer than a decade. In 1908 it began. During 1912-1914 it gathered momentum and put out a manifesto with immense activity around Ezra Pound, and it continued, under Amy Lowell, to grow for a while until it tapered off after 1917. Its limitations are apparent. A single dominant image can supply energy for a two-line poem of Pound's ("In a Station of the Metro") or a 16-word one of Williams' ("The Redwheel Barrow"), but it is hardly capable of sustaining a longer poetic effort. Thus no great poetry came out of the movement. Its own aesthetics stunted its growth into something more ambitious and eternal. But the movement was important in a number of ways in the development of modern poetry. It was a rebellion against the traditional poetics which failed to reflect the new life of the new century. It offered a new way of writing which was valid not only for the Imagist poets but for modern poetry as a whole. In fact, it is no exaggeration to state that the movement was a training school in which many great poets learned their first lessons in the poetic art. Almost all major modern poets were in one way or another associated with it and benefited from it in a significant way. Its literary theories and poetic forms have continued to exercise their influence on modern and contemporary poetry. It is this movement that helped to open the first pages of modern English and American poetry.

T. S. Eliot (1888-1965)

T. S. Eliot was born in St. Louis, Missouri and was educated at Harvard and later at Oxford. He read Dante, who was to become his most admired poet, and Jules Laforgue, the French poet brilliant in portraying modern cityscape with his unusual wit and visual imagery, who endowed Eliot with a unique, fresh, and original tone. Eliot explored the Metaphysical poetry of the seventeenth century and contributed to its modern and contemporary revival. He settled down in 1915 in England, teaching, working as a bank clerk, writing book reviews for publishers, suffering intensely from an unhappy marriage, and all the while composing poetry. Eliot's poetry was becoming noted for its fresh visual imagery, its flexible tone, and highly expressive rhythm. "The Love Song of J. Alfred Prufrock" was printed in 1911. "Gerontion" came out in 1920, to be followed two years later by the epochal epic, *The Waste Land*. "Hollow Man" appeared in print in 1925, exhibiting a pessimism no less depressing than *The Waste Land*. The publication of *Ash Wednesday* (1930) and *Four Quartets* (1943) indicated that the poet had turned conservative. Eliot was also a playwright. He excelled in the dramatic monologue and studied the Senecan tradition seriously. His dramatic works include *Sweeney Agonistes*, *Murder in the Cathedral*, *The Cocktail Party*, and *The Confidential Clerk*. [8]

Eliot was also a distinguished literary critic. Although his criticism was in large measure an elaboration of and a guide to his own literary practice, he became "a giver of laws and the arbiter of taste" in the new poetry and criticism. With a sound training in philosophy and classic literature, his criticism possessed an air of authority and offered a measure of reassurance. The basic themes of his criticism concerned the relationship between tradition and individual talent, and between the past, the present, and the future. His famous doctrine on poets and poetry is known as the "impersonal theory," or the theory of impersonality and objectivity. Eliot claims that "[t]he progress of an artist is a continual self-sacrifice, a continual extinction of personality." He employs the term "depersonalization" for this critical notion. One of the things that this theory emphasizes is the relation of a poem to the poems by other authors and suggests "the conception of poetry as a living whole of all the poetry that has ever been written." It explains the importance of tradition, the past. To T. S. Eliot the past is of great significance to writers. In his famous "Tradition and the Individual Talent," he states that a writer should have the historical sense which is a perception of both the pastness of the past and its presence, and should write with the feeling that the whole literature of the past has a simultaneous existence and composes a simultaneous order. The past should be altered by the present as much as the present is directed by the past. "What is to be insisted upon is that the poet must develop or procure the consciousness of the past and that he should continue to develop this consciousness throughout his career." T. S. Eliot himself was well acquainted with the whole of the literature of Europe from Homer and the whole of the literature of his own country. He wrote with an acute consciousness of the past.

Another thing that this theory tries to focus on is the relation of the poem to its author. To T. S. Eliot, what the poet has to express, is not a "personality," but a particular medium in which impressions and experiences combine in peculiar and unexpected ways. Impressions and experiences that are important for the man (the poet) may take no place in poetry, and those which become important in the poetry may be not so to the man, the personality. Thus poetry is not a turning loose of emotion, but an escape from it; it is not an expression of personality, but an escape from it. In this way universal applicability can be achieved. Incidentally, it is the poetry, not the poet, that should be the focus of critical attention, and a work of art is an independent entity. All these ideas of Eliot's would necessarily lead to the emergence of the New Criticism in later years and influence a whole generation of poets. Eliot himself practiced the theory in his own writing. The "impersonal" feature of his poetry continued in his creative endeavor until his composition of *Four Quartets* in the mid 1930s when he felt the temptation of the self-reflective mood and tone and began to sound in certain sections of the long poem like a Postmodernist. Eliot's theory became something like a law for English and American poets for over two decades from the mid 1920s through the 1950s. Collections of his critical essays include *The Sacred Wood*, *Essays on Style and Order*, *Elizabethan Essays*, *Essays Ancient and Modern*, *The Use of Poetry and the Use of Criticism* and *After Strange Gods*.

Eliot's was a highly refined sensibility. He was one of the first if not the first to sense the futility and fragmentization of modern life and see modern society at its most disgusting. As Archibald MacLeish, one of his followers, noted eloquently, Eliot's poetry said more about the modern chaos in fifty or sixty lines than all the social critics and their volumes put together. But his search for order, form, and discipline led him toward conservatism and to religion for salvation. In 1927 he announced that he was a royalist in polities, a classicist in literature, and an Anglo-Catholic in religion, a declaration which, though it shocked few, angered and hurt a good many followers. To people like Hemingway, he was very much what Wordsworth had been to Robert Browning: a lost leader. Ultimately as a poet, Eliot was to transcend his politics and religion and even his literary principles and remain a monument in modern poetry. He won the Nobel Prize for Literature in 1948.

Eliot's poetry is difficult to read, and more so for us Chinese. To appreciate his poetry, it is good to understand that the essence of his thought lies in the interaction between the past, the present, and the future. "In some minds," Eliot stated in a lecture on *Ulysses*, "certain memories, both from reading and from life, become charged with emotional significance. All these are used, so that intensity is gained at the expense of clarity." Later Eliot developed this notion into his famous principle of "objective correlative": In his opinion, "The only way of expressing emotion in the form of art is by finding an 'objective correlative'; in other words, a set of objects, a situation, a chain of events which shall be the formula of that particular emotion; such that when the external facts, which must terminate in sensory experience, are given, the emotion is immediately evoked." Poetry that expresses emotion in this method tends naturally to be impersonal, in keeping with the "impersonal theory." In poems where this principle is applied, authorial presence tends to be effaced as much as possible. It is difficult for such poetry to be meditative in tone and autobiographical in subject. The poet frequently has to have a surrogate, a persona, to speak for him. A distance exists between the text of the work and the response of its readers. The sense of immediacy in appreciation would be somewhat diminished. These are some of the points regarding the theory to which the Postmodernist poets of the 1950s and 1960s would object, but not before Eliot had enjoyed ascendancy for over a quarter of a century.

Now let us take a look at *The Love Song of J. Alfred Prufrock* and *The Waste Land*, for a further experience of Eliot's poetry. *The Love Song of J. Alfred Prufrock* depicts a timid middle-aged man going (or thinking of going) to propose marriage to a lady but hesitating all the way there. It takes the form of a soliloquy, an interior monologue like that of Browning's "My Last Duchess." Whether the man actually leaves his spot at all remains a question. Most probably he stays where he is all the while, allowing his imagination to run wild. Prufrock is the image of an ineffectual, sorrowful, tragic twentieth-century Western man, possibly the modern intellectual who is divided between passion and timidity, between desire and impotence. His tragic flaw is timidity; his "curse" is his idealism. Knowing everything, but able to do nothing, he lives in an area of life and death; and caught between the two worlds, he belongs to neither. He craves love but has no courage to declare himself. He despairs of life. He discovers its emptiness and yet has found nothing to replace it. Thus the poem develops a theme of frustration and emotional conflict. It has a very distinct modern coloring.

Prufrock is a middle-aged dandy, well dressed, and self-conscious to a fault. He lives in an urban world, a world with no social unity, but with elegance and beauty of a kind such as divorced from force and vitality. It is a trivial world of total emptiness ("I have measured out my life with coffee spoons"). Here walks (or he imagines himself walking) this man with an obsession he cannot handle in the natural way, afraid of rejection, of being misinterpreted, of speaking out his mind and proposing to a lady ("[forcing] the moment to its crisis"). Here is an extreme example of the Hamlet problem: a man harassed with self-doubt, never reaching that "Readiness is all" state with his inability to act and be alive at the moment. Neurotically desperate, Prufrock can conceive a heroic action which he is incapable of fulfilling; he can see his actions on the grandest level but do not a thing. He sees himself as Lazarus coming back from the dead, but can not break through his deadness. He sees himself as John the Baptist, that vigorous, dynamic, committed human being that he is by all standards not. He is most probably sexually inadequate. At the end of the poem he fancies himself "in the chambers of the sea / By seagirls wreathed with seaweed red and brown," but the "human voices" wake him up from his reverie. Unable to bring himself and his world together and build a base for meaningful action, Prufrock, with his physical impotence, represents the spiritual impotence of archetypal modern man. What is redeeming is probably his self-perception: he sees his own absurdity.

The poem is interesting also for its method of presentation. The readers do not move in a sequential fashion. Apart from the surreal vividness which characterizes certain parts of the poem, there are elliptical structures, strange juxtapositions, an absence of bridges, so that the whole seems broken; nothing is explained in a logical manner. The readers have to make leaps in their reading and appreciation, as the poet seems to jump from one scene to another and from one idea to another without warning. It is important to note here, however, that the association of images establishes the general feeling. Nothing is discordant, irrelevant, or abrupt any more, and everything is falling in place when the overall mood of the poem is perceived.

Commenting on James Joyce, T. S. Eliot remarked once that the only way the modern writer has of "giving shape and significance to the immense panorama of futility and anarchy which is contemporaneous history" is by indicating or "manipulating a continuous parallel between contemporaneity and antiquity." Now out of this famous statement three things come immediately that merit careful analysis. The first is the feeling that the modern world presents an "immense panorama of futility and anarchy." Indeed, no one, in the first decades of this century, sensed the confusion and fragmentization of modern life more keenly than did T. S. Eliot. No one was more aware of the horrid and sordid aspect of the modern experience. "The contemplation of the horrid or sordid or disgusting, by an artist, is the necessary and negative aspect of the impulse toward the pursuit of beauty," he states in *The Sacred Wood.* "The negative is the more importunate." Secondly, there is the keenly felt need to "[give] shape and significance" to the meaningless, futile, and chaotic experience of modern man. To T. S. Eliot modern human experience is chaotic, irregular, and fragmentary, and it is the poet's job to form new wholes out of disparate experiences. This fusion of disparate elements into an artistic form and order is the very poetic process for the modern poet. The fragmentary nature of life is projected rather than analyzed. The best way to do this is through finding an "objective correlative." Then comes the third point, the poet's use of "antiquity," the past, the tradition, from which a poet can perfectly legitimately draw. A poet should have his unified sensibility, and "one of the surest tests for this sensibility is," as T. S. Eliot states in *The Sacred Wood,* "the way in which a poet borrows.... A good poet will usually borrow from authors remote in time, or alien in language, or diverse in interest." The "welding process" that follows, transmuting borrowed materials into something better or different, characterizes Eliot's own literary creative endeavors. His method is, in part, to rely on past literatures and cultures which fuse in his mind with his own personal and private agonies into something rich and strange, something universal and impersonal. Eliot holds that the negative qualities of the modern world can be sensed only through contrast with the positive qualities of an older world. To appreciate all this, it is good to take a look at *The Waste Land*.

T. S. Eliot composed *The Waste Land* in the autumn of 1921, while taking a vacation at Lausanne, western Switzerland. Before returning to London, he visited Pound at Paris and left the draft with him. Pound blue-penciled it and reduced its length which was nearly twice as long as its present form. Impressed by this editorial feat, T. S. Eliot dedicated the poem to him. The epigraph of the poem represents the motif, the somber mood, of *The Waste Land,* emblematic of life in death, of a desperate struggle to attain salvation. The title of the poem draws its significance from the Fisher King story, which is a part of the Grail legend. As the story goes, the Fisher King sins against God, who then punishes him by making him sexually impotent. The disability of the King is reflected on his land, so that his kingdom becomes a waste land. Hence the title. To restore the King to virility and his land to fertility, a quest is undertaken to search for the Holy Grail, the cup which is said to have been used by Jesus Christ at the Last Supper and later brought to Britain by Joseph of Arimathea. Thus the story of the Fisher King and the quest of the Holy Grail serve as the governing myth of *The Waste Land.* One of the major features of the poem is incidentally that sexual failure connotes spiritual debilitation.

As modern poets experience chaos and dislocation, a driving intellectual ambition is seen present in all their poems to "shore fragments together" for order and meaning. Their poems are a mélange of fragmentary experiences, incidents and episodes, shifting without much notice from one to the other, rather than in a traditional narrative manner. These poems can be subdivided into different sections, not formally connected, but all subsumed into a thematic whole. *The Waste Land* is a good illustration. Here we see an ideal parataxis which is the stylistic norm of the poem, as paratactic structures usually indicate a sense of discontinuity and unrelatedness. The five parts of the poem, "The Burial of the Dead," "A Game of Chess," "The Fire Sermon," "Death by Water," and "What the Thunder Said" do not have sufficient formal connection between them. Things stop and begin without explicable shift: the transition from the unreal city of London to a Cleopatra sitting in splendor, from the scene in a pub to "Sweet Thames [running] softly," from Saint Augustus coming to Carthage to "Phlebas the Phoenician, a fortnight dead," to the nightmarish imagery, the reminders, of the waste land—the change is abrupt and jerky, with no hint of logical order and causal relationship. This radical disconnectedness is true even of the transitions between the different sections within any one part of the poem, and between the different ideas within any one section. Through gaps, absence of connective tissues, and discordant juxtapositions, the poet intends the reader to see and feel the fragmentary nature of life.

The Waste Land reveals its author's strong historical sense. It uses the past as a yardstick to measure the present and underscore what is missing from the present. For example, he juxtaposes the passionate love of Tristram and Iseult with the passionless hyacinth girl who faces a bare and cold sea, the perfunctoriness of the typist with the sensitivity of Oliver Goldsmith's lovely woman, Cleopatra with the wealthy lady who cries out, "What shall I do now? What shall I do?" and waits "for a knock upon the door," Elizabeth and Leicester with the girl who murmurs helplessly "what should I resent?" —in a word, Eliot is trying to throw into relief the negative qualities of the present by contrasting them with the positive ones of the past, and shock the reader into a recognition of the dismal truth about modern life. The long poem is certainly eloquent social criticism. It is true that, when the poem first came out, its effect was overwhelming to an audience used to reading comfortable nineteenth-century authors like Dickens. It was the poem of despair for the 1920s and 1930s. However, the readers will find as they read along that the poem moves, through recurrent reminders of the modern waste land, toward a hope of regeneration and builds toward the possibility of restoring order and life. There is an underlying desire on the part of the poet to help create order and sense out of a disorderly and senseless existence. T. S. Eliot is able, through his discovery of the myth of desolation and rebirth, to find sanction for his doctrine which the thunder states as "Give, Sympathize, Control," or self-surrender, immersion in the problems of others, and submission to God's control. He would like to help to rehabilitate those beliefs which people know but shrink from and discredit.

Eliot's search for salvation for the West continued in his *Ash Wednesday* and *Four Quartets*; he hoped to find it in religious belief and self repentance. The *Four Quartets* is the best work of the later phase of his career, and some critics claim that it is one of the best long poems (if not the best) to come out of the twentieth century. The four quartets are "Burnt Norton," "East Coker," "The Dry Salvages," and "Little Gidding." The first of these was written as a separate work in the mid 1930s, and the rest were composed between 1940 and 1942. Later Eliot put these together as *Four Quartets*. The poem is quite different from *The Waste Land* in many aspects such as speech, mood, and tone, so much so that it sounds like a Postmodernist poem in some of its passages. In certain parts of the long poem, the speech is personal, the mood is reflective, the presentation is continuous and discursive and less allusive, and the emphasis on the significance of the past is toned down so much that there is little social critique in evidence in the poem. Eliot must have felt the inevitable Postmodernist impulse, which was forthcoming in a decade. The *Four Quartets* is easier to read, and the personal and autobiographical nature of some of its passages and their meditative style have endeared the author to his readers. But Eliot did not become a prophet figure for the new—the postwar—period; his influence declined along with that of the New Criticism. All this is seen in retrospect, and all is now history. The mist of time has cleared up, and Eliot has remained probably the best poet of his generation and his century.

Chapter 22 Poetry of the 1930s • Auden • The Audenic Group • Thomas • Empson

The decade of the 1930s was one of "crisis and dismay" (to quote W. H. Auden). The effect of the Great Depression in the United States spread soon to this side of the Atlantic. With the serious social and economic dislocations that followed, the existing English system seemed to be "an organism ... dying," as one critic of the time put it. England and Europe both experienced turmoil and chaos. Fascism appeared. Nazi Germany grew aggressive and sinister. Spain was in the throes of the civil war from which Franco was emerging a dictator. In the meantime, new ideas about possible changes were up in the air. Marxism and the Soviet Union became a fashion, so did Freudianism, both appealing to the literary circles as well as the people in general. Literary expression underwent a significant change. It acquired a clearer social function. As Modernist writing reached only a small readership, the style of the new decade was oriented to communicate with a larger audience.

The poets of the 1930s were conditioned by the literary milieu peculiar to them only. The *fin de siecle* aestheticism was recent history. Avant-garde experimentation had lost its vogue. As early as the 1930s, High Modernism had begun to give way to something new. It had made its enormous impact, but its mode of writing had proved to be too difficult even for the masters of the style to continue without change. These poeple had found it fascinating to write differently. So by the 1930s Virginia Woolf had written her more plot-intense *The Years*, quite a departure from her other works like *The Waves*, and T. S. Eliot had begun composing his more personal and more reflective *Four Quartets*, different and more endearing to the readers than his previous works. Change had become inevitable and gradually visible. The impersonal and disjunctive style was giving way, along with the vision it had embodied, to something different.

In addition, High Modernism was difficult not merely for the readers at large;

it was more so for later writers to surpass it. A new way of writing would have to be found. Modernism, though still lingering and haunting, was no longer binding. Yeats and Eliot proved to be both repellent and attractive. The new generation of poets did not approve of the prevailing pessimistic view of life and man. They believed in the ameliorating capacity of art. For them the Modernist demand on art and artists was too rigorous, and they had a strong desire to blaze a trail of their own. As a result, they rebelled against the older tradition. Some of them, like the Auden group, tried to write a more approachable poetry of ordinary life and speech so as to reach out to a more politically minded audience. These poets did not care much if they were perfect in form. They agreed that art and poetry should be distinct from the previous mode of creation.

It is good to note that the decade of the 1930s was also a period of diverse, prolific writing. Yeats and Eliot were still writing. So were the Georgians. There were, among others, Edith Sitwell, Edwin Muir, Rudyard Kipling, John Betjeman, and Stevie Smith. Alongside the Auden group, there was William Empson who persevered in his New Critical or Metaphysical mode of writing regardless of the dominant temper of the time. In the mid-1930s, a new force became visible on the scene. Young Dylan Thomas and George Barker and the Surrealists reacted vehemently to the Modernist and Audenian ways of writing and started what has come to be known as the Romantic revival. The movement continued to gather momentum in the next decade until the 1950s when its excesses enraged the still younger generation, essentially the Movement poets such as Philip Larkin and Donald Davie, and gave way to the postwar new wave of writing. This will be taken up in more detail in the chapters that follow. For the discussion here, the focus will be on Auden and the Auden Group as Auden was the leading poet of the decade, touching on other significant figures such as Dylan Thomas and William Empson along the way.

During the war years that followed, no important poetry was written. There were some expressions of religious despair, a movement called the "New Apocalypse" movement dealing with the subconscious elements of human nature, some poetry urging people to accept the irrational and myth as the basis of life, and poetry expressing the sense of forthcoming crisis, human vulnerability, and compassion for human suffering. But basically no great work came out of the war period. [1]

W. H. Auden (1907-1973)

English poetry of the 1930s was associated with W. H. Auden. Auden was born in York, England and was educated at Oxford. He was the most important poet of the post-T. S. Eliot generation, or the 2nd-generation modernists, and its acknowledged leader and spokesman. Auden was a learned man. When still a student at Oxford, he was widely read in ancient Greek literature, Old English poetry (with its prominent features of alliteration and kennings), and the myths and legends of Iceland. He was indebted to Hopkins, Hardy, and T. S. Eliot. Later on he took an enormous interest in the theories of Sigmund Freud and Karl Marx. He was well acquainted with geology, biology, psychology, anthropology, and sociology, which explains, among other things, his scientific, clinical approach to poetry and his concept of man evolving and struggling in a—say—sometimes geological cosmos. Auden went through a variety of experiences. He was in pre-Nazi Germany, taught school, and had the first-hand experience of the Depression. His sympathies were mainly with the Left in the early 1930s. He went to Spain in the Spanish civil war, where he felt disgusted with the communist intrigues, and rejected Marxism later to become a Christian. He witnessed the actual "Waste Land" of England and the West of his time and Europe at war. He toured Belgium and Iceland, visited Japan-invaded China, co-authored books with his friends Stephen Spender and Christopher Isherwood, and emigrated in 1939 to the US, where he became a citizen and taught at a few universities including Harvard. He was an influence over American poetry of the 1940s and 1950s.

Auden's poetry was the record of his thoughts and experiences in the different phases of his life. His early poetry was political in theme. Vibrant and powerful partly because shocking and violent, it tried to analyze the ills of his time from a Freudian and Marxist perspective. From the late 1930s he changed to a more religious view of life and the world, focusing more on personal responsibility and traditional values. Later in his career, he came to realize that evil will be here to stay and that times may change but not the brutal nature of existence (as is evidenced in his "The Shield of Achilles" [1955]). Suspicious of all attempts to reform life, he sought solace in love and friendship and religious feeling. In formal terms Auden was always a consummate artist, gleaning from all possible traditions, and coalescing them well in his versification. His facile combination of high art with popular and colloquial elements constitutes a special fascination. Auden's poetry is noted for its variety of styles and forms, its musical aspect, and its comic element and light touch. Thoughtful, playful, and deep, it can awaken echoes when read at different times and by different people. There is a lot of power and permanence in the man. Reading him is similar to reading T. S. Eliot: the readers enjoy both what he says and how he says it and feel instantly that they are in contact with genius. This is particularly true of early Auden.

The tone of Auden's early poetry was that of a young prophet's. As one of the disaffected young men, he saw an England where "nobody is well," and demanded action and attention to meet the exigencies of his time. He felt that English energy was decaying. It might take a revolution (probably one from top down by small groups of disenchanted middle-class liberals like him) to renew that energy and save English values and standards. Writers should criticize the old and envision a new life. Young Auden described himself as a "pink liberal." His politics seemed to be Marxist, though in retrospect it was more accurately that of a radical liberal. His *The Orators*, while attacking the injustices of the 1930s, clearly projects the daydreams of urgent social change and suggests the cures for the ills. The most belligerent of all Auden's work in the period was perhaps his "A Communist to Others" (1933). Here the poet sees a world floundering. He calls for alliance with the workers, satirizes the stance of liberal intellectuals as false and harmful, and feels the future belongs to the working class. His poems written in this period, such as "1929," "Spain 1937," and "September 1, 1939," and his drama, *The Dance of Death* (1933) in which Karl Marx appears toward the end, all illustrate the sincere social concern on the part of the author.

The change that Auden underwent in his attitude toward Marxism became obvious at the end of the decade. Whereas there is an obvious trace of Marxist influence in the second part of his "1929," disillusionment sets in his "September 1, 1939," a poem that he wrote to sum up his experiences in the 1930s. He was then in New York, and a new phase was beginning. It was natural that "September 1, 1939" concludes on a religious note, which pointed to the later development of his career. Auden was never a communist. His interest in Marx and Freud stemmed from his desire to learn how to help analyze and redress the problems of his time. He was never committed to any political platform. "I hate pompositas and all authority," as he says in his *Letters from Iceland* (1936).

Auden had always a religious view of man and life. His lasting values were in essence moral and religious. As a moralist, he was fundamentally committed to Christianity. Even in the 1930s when he was at his most purposive, his concern was human rather than political. The notion of love, for instance, sustains throughout his poetry. Ultimately, his was essentially Christian love, but the idea of love had been evolving in his poetry. In the beginning it seemed to be the only human motive to him in the first section of his *The Orators*, where he introduces Dante's ideas on love as a remedy to current problems. Then the notion became larger than self-love, i.e. one of a social nature that bordered on human fellowship and compassion. Eventually, when he became a professed Christian, it became Christian love.

1940 could be a watershed in Auden's career. He had gone to the US a couple of years earlier and decided to stay. A change had come over him gradually. The fight in him seemed to be tapering off to a calmer observation, then to some philosophical rumination. The later phase of Auden's career thus began. Some claim that, with the outbreak of WWII, Auden lost his cutting-edge thematic and formal thrust. This is not exactly the case as a careful reading of his post-1940 works will reveal a different facet, maybe a deeper layer, of the poet's mind at work. It is true that later in life Auden became conservative, wrote religious poetry, and was regarded by some as a Lost Leader. It is also true that the later Auden was not as well charged and pregnant with a sweeping power as he was in his early career. But people need to note well the soft human touch in between his lines that was no less moving. Neither was his religious earnestness. He merely switched his focus to analysis of human foibles, but still managed to retain his quest for ideal life in his poetry.

Another thing to note about the poet's later phase is that, from the 1940s through his death, he took interest in the ideas of Soren Kierkegaard, the existentialist Danish philosopher (1813-1855) and his contemporary, Reinhold Niebuhr (1892-1971), the American theologian. There is in his later poetry frequent allusion to Kierkegaard's notion of man concerned with his nature and salvation and Niebuhr's concept of man's moral dilemma. To Auden the humans have their problems; they struggle through them; they may fail or succeed; and all the time they listen to no other warnings but the choice of their own will. All this is because they are human. They are not perfect, neither is their world. They try to build the Just City though they know the job can never be done. Here Auden dissects man's weaknesses and expresses his quest for an ideal existence that is morally higher and nobler. The best of Auden is impersonal, viewing the human condition at a distance.

After he settled down in the US, he wrote four long poems and some shorter ones. The long works include *New Year Letter* (1941), *The Sea and the Mirror* (1944), *For the Time Being* (1944), and *The Age of Anxiety* (1947). In these works he did not sound as resolute as he had used to be. It might have to do with the emigration. The last phase of his career, with volumes of verse such as *About the House* (1967) and *City without Walls* (1970), reveals a consummate style of personal tone and easy informality. Later in life Auden seemed to think that poetry was ineffectual to make things happen.[2] Basically a poet, Auden was a multi-talented writer. Other areas of his interest included plays, social criticism, travelogues, and war reportage. His major books of verse include, among others, *Poems* (1930), *Orators* (1932), *On this Island* (1937), *Another Time* (1940), *Nones* (1951), *About the House* (1967), and *City without Walls* (1971). The best of his criticism was collected in *The Dryer's Hand* (1962). Auden was always prolific, especially so in the decade of the 1930s when he published the majority of his most exciting works in nine volumes.

Let's take a look at a couple of his poems. A good point to begin would be the poem, "Spain 1937," written during the Spanish civil war. It is a work which showcases Auden at his most radical and revolutionary. The 92-line poem can be divided roughly into three parts. The first part of the first 24 lines relates both the good and evil aspects of the past and puts today's struggle in proper historical prospective: the past achievements in trade, scientific and technological inventions, and ancient enginerring feats, religions, prophecies, and fanatic bigotry, myths and superstitions, adventures and explorations, the theory of evolution, and the beginnings of the modern age, yet "[y]esterday all the past," "[b]ut today the struggle." The second part (ll. 25-68) deals with the sense of confusion and loss of orientation on the part of modern people who find themselves, all of a sudden, completely thrown upon their own to shift for survival. It begins with the question of vision and direction as to where to go next: "O my vision, O send me the luck of the sailor" (ll. 28), probably envious of the ancient Odysseus who had the guide of the helping gods and Teresias the prophet; "O show us/ History the operator..." (ll. 34-36); or beseeching earnestly for the coming of the messiah whatever form it may take—dove, papa or engineer (ll. 43-44). But life refuses to comply, humbly reducing itself to a nonentity (ll. 45-52), willing to go with the choice of the people, be it a Republican victory ("To build the Just City), or its defeat which would mean "the Romantic Death" and gravely affect the future. People flock over from everywhere to Spain, the hot spot of the time, and try to help address the issue there (ll. 57-68). The third section envisions tomorrow and its glory. Tomorrow is the future with advances in sciences, medicine, life in general, love and romance, "but today the struggle" (l. 80). Today people face increasing casualties, political debates, the expedient means of relief, a dying and desperate reality, and a history not to be able to help or pardon our inadequacies to deal with our problems. There is a keen sense of frustration and disillusionment. Basically the tone is pessimistic, hopeless, but with an acute awareness of one's historic responsibility and implied intention to try to do one's best. The poem is basically a call to action.

Radically different is the tone of a later work, the well-known short poem "Muse des Beaux Arts" (1940), which is mainly about the painting, *The Fall of Icarus*, by Flemish painter Pierter Breughel (1520-1569). The painting is based on Ovid's *Metamorphoses*, in which one of the mythological stories describes the fall of Icarus from the sky. Ovid's original portrays the amazement of the plowman, the shepherd, and the fisherman who stand by and look on the macabre scene with compassion for the downfall of their fellow human being. But Breughel's painting represents them as being apathetic: the plowman may have heard the splash of the fall but it does not concern him as an important failure, for he turns away and goes on with his plowing. Neither does the death bother the ship as it sails on calmly. Auden does not spare Nature either: the sun shines as Emily Dickinson's sun does in her poem, "Apparently without surprise." Auden here satirizes "the human position" to human suffering as represented in the painting by Breughel and his father, Breughel the Elder (to whose *The Census*, also called *The Numbering at Bethlehem*, and *The Massacre of the Innocents* the poem alludes to in ll. 5-8 and ll.9-13 respectively), or by "The Old Masters": the position from which mutual love and compassion are conspicuously absent. This Auden sees as an essential weakness of human nature that needs addressing. The idea of love here is social by nature. One more thing about the poem is that it is written in the conversational style for which Auden is noted.

"As I Walked Out One Evening" could be another example of the later Auden who, while still skeptical and satirical, became semi-religious in tone and color as well as lyrical. The poem is his "pastiche of a folk-song." It is the poet's comment on the inevitable process of nature in relation to the fate of man and to human nature. As it goes, the poet walks outdoors one evening and hears two songs. One of these is that of a young lover, making gigantic promises the way the romantic lover of Robert Burns' "Oh My Love Is Like a Red, Red Rose" makes. The hyperboles he uses are no less hyperbolic as Burns' lover's: Auden's parody of the older poet is obvious. Then Auden hears a different note from the song of the clocks, which reminds people of the presence of Time the Grim Reaper. No matter what humans say and do, they will be to Time "fields of harvest wheat." The time of harvesting will come, the cupboard will become "glacier," the bed the desert, and the crack in the long-used teacup the lane to death. Although the end is inevitable, life is still a blessing. When all is over with the lovers, life goes on. It is not pessimism about life; it is about nature taking its course, and the fact that there is nothing that could be done about it. So there is a sense of helplessness and determinism not quite counter-pointed and dispelled by the brief line, "Life remains a blessing." Lines 55-56 add more than one dimension of meaning to the poem. These could be read as a passing religious observation on human nature. The human heart is crooked, the human neighbor is crooked, and by inference all humans are crooked. Human nature being what it is, the best that people can do is to love your neighbor. Romantic love could only end in doom should it fail to become part of a larger love. The intertwining of the Christian with the political and the social elements is so subtle, so imperceptible, and so typical of the best of Auden.

The Audenic Group

For English poetry, the 1930s was a predominantly Marxist decade. The Audenic group—Stephen Spender, Day-Lewis, Louis MacNeice and their associates—felt inspired, embraced the Leftist stance, and expressed tremendous hope in face of the adversity of life. In the late thirties, however, a lot occurred to dampen and dash this enthusiasm. The Soviet-German Pact, the triumph of the Fascists in the Spanish war, the atrocities of Hitler's Nazi regime—all these and more disgusted Auden and his group and led them to part company with the Leftist camp. They became aware that they had been "an odd lot" earlier in the decade. They veered in a new direction, wrote differently, and became famous for it.

The Audenic group was not a group or a movement in the sense of being organized as such. In fact the members did not meet in one room until 1947, long after the label was placed on them. These were brilliant and anxious young men with a huge sense of mission to help change their society, being all of them acutely self-conscious that they had insights to offer. The group became first known through an anthology entitled *New Signatures* (1932) and another entitled *New Country: Prose and Poetry by the Authors of New Signatures* (1933), both being edited by Michael Roberts (1902-1948). The emphasis was on the newness of the writers included in these collections. Although working on their own, the group shared the notion of writing poetry about different subjects and in different ways from the first-generation modernists. They would like to take poetry out of the hands of an elite readership to the masses and move it out of the obscurity into which the modernist artifice of ellipsis, paratactic syntax, and learned allusions had thrown it. They used ordinary speech to write a poetry that verged on propaganda and placed their art at the service of a new life. Their separate efforts were concerted by the cementing influence of W. H. Auden, from whom all the rest of the group received inspiration and learned to write. They read him carefully, "shuddered" at his haunting powers, smelt "a change of air," and saw the "beginning of good." Auden caught the sensibility of his age.

The poets of the group and—by extension—of the period shared basically the same kind of experience and went through roughly the same process of growth.

They began with the Modernists, some Romantics and probably D. H. Lawrence very much in their minds, moved to embrace the socially and politically engaged verse that was largely written for the consumption of the working class, then felt disappointed and disillusioned, and moved on to a new phase at the end of the decade. It was a generation of divided allegiances and consciences, sore in the midst of a tug of war between the forces pulling them in two directions of writing in the service of society vs. writing in the private mode. All these phases are adequately reflected in the works of such poets as Spender, Lewis, MacNeice, John Lehmann, Glyn Jones, and Geoffrey Grigson (1905-1985) who was to be one of the most severe critics of Dylan Thomas.

Now Stephen Spender (1909-) was born in London and educated in Oxford. His was archetypal of the experience of the generation in the 1930s. He began as a liberal, witnessed the social change in Europe from democracy to Nazism, fought in the Spanish war, joined the Communist party and left it, wrote to help with the working class, and later turned to writing to project his private vision. Spender was editor of two important journals of the time, *Horizon* and *Encounter*. He wrote a lot of poetry in the 1930s, including some Marxist poems and patriotic sonnets, which emphasized social over individual priorities. His social concern was deep and genuine, and his poetry could be topical and doctrinaire. One of his early works, entitled "The Pylons," using images like the pylons and aircraft as symbols of hope, was the reason why the Audenic group became also known as "the Pylon Poets." Spender's verse is testimony to his spiritual odyssey in that decade. For instance, his "I Think Continually of Those Who Were Truly Great" (1933) brims over with idealism and hope, and his "Not palaces, an era's crown" calls for the establishment of a world without hunger and inequalilty, one that is almost communist in design. However, his "Ultima Ratio Regum" (1939) is radically different in tone and tenor. Telling coolly about the death of an idealistic innocent youth in the Spanish civil war, the poem reveals a mind already divested of its blind zest, and lucid enough now for a rational evaluation of ideas, actions, and consequences.

Louis MacNeice (1907-1963) has been regarded as second only to Auden in achievement in his generation of poets. He was born in Belfast and educated in Oxford. Like his contemporaries, he wrote some didactic lyrics in keeping with the period spirit, but he was not extreme in terms of social engagement. He was never Leftist in his belief and felt no need to change it as did his other Oxford friends. His association with them was actually a careless affair: His poems appeared in *Oxford Poetry: 1929* along with those of Auden, Spender and Day-Lewis. MacNeice was always a good craftsman. He wrote about his world to reveal its ills and problems, and also to appreciate and celebrate life. His "Sunday Morning" (1933) exhibits an awareness of transience and mortality as well as the advice to enjoy the moment as much as possible. So does his "The Sunlight on the Garden" (1937) which, in addition to the *carpe diem* spirit, adds a graver concern typical of the 1930s: the allusion to Mark Anthony's speech in Shakespeare's *Anthony and Cleopatra* in line 19 of the poem is well loaded; it seems to be foretelling about the forthcoming tragedy of not only an individual but of the empire as well.

The same vein of writing is continued in his famous poem "Bagpipe Music" (1937). Bagpipe music represents a tradition in Scotland. Everything, as listed in the poem, such as the Yogi-Man and Blavatsky's theosophy, is traditional, representing a temporary alleviation rather than a revolutionary solution of the situation of the 1930s in general and the state of the Scottish economy in particular. Society is confused and has no purpose with its petty desires and cares. It needs direction, deep thinking, and a vision of the future. The last stanza invokes a sense of sadness as it raises a question not for the thirties only, but for all time: nothing stays and Time will have its way in the end anyway. There is plenty of humor and satire in it, and the off-rhymes of the poem add an impressive effect to the half-measures it satirizes. Louis MacNeice was a many-talented writer. He also wrote radio drama, translated some Aeschylus and Goethe, and produced an amount of literary criticism as well.

Cecil Day-Lewis (1904-1972) was a distinguished poet of his time. He met Auden at Oxford and came under his influence. His *The Magic Mountain* (1933) was a Leftist piece by virtue of its fighting rhetoric, its prophesy of ruin, and its call for "the entrance" of a new order. He joined the Communist party in 1935 and did some agitating work. But toward the end of the decade, he quit mainly because he felt that social engagement compromised his art. All his life he looked up to Thomas Hardy as his model. From the late 1930s onward, he composed mostly in the nineteenth-century modes.

Dylan Thomas (1914-1953)

The emergence of Dylan Thomas and the Romantic revival he brought into English poetry in the 1930s were the natural corollary of the evolution of English poetry from Auden and Empson. Although Auden rebelled against High Modernism, he has been seen as representing the 2nd generation of the New Criticism. The concepts of the new school of criticism and the dominance it exercized over poetry writing and critism had contributed to the constraining milieu of the 1930s along with the demanding left-oriented aesthetics, its exhortations, and its images of revolution, war, and politics. A reaction was already simmering in the literary world of Britain and the United States. Something different was about to erupt and impact the literary scene. Sure enough, the fresh voice of Dylan Thomas burst out in the mid-1930s to the surprise—and the joy—of the readers as well as critics. This has come to be known as the Romantic revival of the 1930s. The revival became a trend partly because people still loved the Romantic mode and feeling. These poets, Dylan Thomas and his associates, were brought up in Romantic traditions. These included the concept of nature as sacred and mystical, pastoral lyricism, emotional outburst, meditation, the self, the subconscious and the irrational, the intuitive and visionary powers of the mind, and the power of the imagination. The people called themselves Romantics, had little sympathy for Auden and Empson's Metaphysical kind of poetry, and tended to use a florid and melodious diction. These Neo-Romantics included other poets such as George Barker, Ruth Pitter, Kathleen Raine, Lawrence Durrell, Vernon Watkins, and Sidney Keyes. It is good to note that, whereas these reacted against Yeats, Eliot, Auden, and Empson, they were not indifferent to their influence. At the same time, they were also sensitive to that of Blake, Wordsworth, and Whitman. The Romantic revival gathered momentum in the 1940s until it became too dominant for the next generation, that of the 1950s, to tolerate. Then a reaction set in, and the phase of Movement poetry began. For our discussion here we will dwell on Dylan Thomas in some detail.

Dylan Thomas was a famous Welsh poet. He was born in Swansea, Wales and was educated in the grammar school there, where his father was a teacher of

English. As a boy, Thomas was fragile in health but rich and wild in imagination. Impractical to a fault, he was fascinated with the power of words and their sensory appeal. His great literary passions included James Joyce, Gerard Manley Hopkins, and D. H. Lawrence. Although he rebelled against T. S. Eliot and Auden, these Modernist masters left their imprint on him as well. He admired John Donne for his clever conceits. He was sensitive to the influences of Freud and modern psychology. From Surrealism he learned but he was not part of that movement. Thomas was precocious. He became known with the publication of his *Eighteen Poems* (1934) and *Twenty-Five Poems* (1936). Some of his early poems were published in T. S. Eliot's *Criterion*. *The Map of Love* came out in 1939, *Deaths and Entrances* in 1946, and his final *Collected Poems* in1952. Dylan Thomas also wrote a mock-Joycean autobiography, *Portrait of the Artist as a Young Dog* (1940) and a popular play, *Under Milk Wood: A Play for Voices* (1954). He was never financially comfortable, always struggling to support his family, but lived a boisterous, turbulent, bohemian life with a reputation for gustatorial lovemaking. In addition, Thomas felt, with time, his creative power dwindling. The one weakness that killed him was his excessive drinking. He died after drinking a procession of straight whiskeys in New York in 1953.

Dylan Thomas was a poet of unequivocal power. He has appeal to all who read him. He may not be understood; he may be misunderstood; but his impact is irresistible. His flowing Romantic rhetoric and apocalyptic vision, his non-conformism, and his magnificent readings of his own and others' poetry in his impressive sonorous voice over the BBC and on his three lecture tours in the US (1950, 1952, 1953)—all these increased his popularity and made him into a legend. He enjoyed both admiration and severe criticism. He was an influence over his contemporaries. There were imitators like the "New Apocalyptic" movement of the 1940s as anthologized in such as *The New Apocalypse* (1939), and there were staunch defenders in face of negative criticism against him. He was one of the most controversial poets in recent memory. He has been accused of being excessively obscure and wanting in imaginative coherence. A reaction set in after his death. The argument was whether Thomas had been overrated as a poet. Now with the publication of his *Letters* (1957) and further detailed research, Dylan Thomas has shaken off a lot of the shadow of negativity about his work.

Thomas' themes are large. They cover such as birth, life, love, sex, and death. Childhood is one of his favorite subjects. He wrote quite a bit about the unborn child in its ovular, embryonic and fetal stages. He loves describing the beauty of the natural landscape. And there are of course love and sex. His other subjects include human relationships (such as friendships and tyranny), poetry as a craft and the poetic process, war and man's inhumanity, and God (faith and reason and free thought). Basically, Thomas focuses on the unity of life, the continuous process of life, death, and new birth. To him man gets born from the mother's womb and begins dying at that very moment. So he derives consolation from the unity of man with nature, present with past, and life with death, and refuses to mourn the death of a child as he puts it in a poem. Thomas's poetry possesses a strong pristine quality, singing without reserve of primitive desires, and pushing these forcefully into the human consciousness. There is also a kind of despair and determinism that reminds one of the religious nature of his philosophy (amateurish as it may be). Many of Thomas' famous poems exhibit his awareness of life's mutability and his sadness about it. Altogether he was a Neo-Romantic poet capable of wild flights of imagination and meaningful recollections.

One thematic concern with Thomas was the representation of the chaotic world in which he and his fellow men have to face the destructive powers trying to control them. This view of his may have to do with his experience in life. His life was not a happy one, suffering from alcoholism and promiscuity, and being high-strung all the time. His works, especially his early poems, seem to portray a "womb and tomb" situation of his—and, by extension, human—existence. There are dreams and madness, ghosts and vampires and witches. The forces in control of man are associated often with sex and occasionally with the atrocity of war. It is a world of terror, a nightmarish one, because not supported by faith. Thomas does not hide the facts of life, however painful; he accepts them. At the bottom of his soul lies his yearning for affirmation. He made it clear that his poetry is "the record of my individual struggle from darkness toward some measure of light." Death, he believes, can be transcended. His rhetoric is bardic and rapt, and in his message shines forth the persevering human spirit in face of encroaching darkness. Some of his oft-anthologized poems include "Poem in October," "A Refusal to Mourn the Death by Fire, of a Child in London," "Fern Hill," and "Do Not Go

Gentle into That Good Night."

Thomas was very concerned with poetic forms. His poetry abounds in complex, unexpected images. He was good at weaving threads of different colors skillfully into the tapestry of his poetry, be they from the *Bible*, Welsh legends, Freudianism, Metaphysical wit, modernism, symbolism, and surrealism. He was meticulously careful with his sound effect, syntactical effectiveness, and the moving power of his images. His language is emotionally loaded and pregnant with meaning. One major feature of his poetry is its unconventionality, its rebelliousness against accepted usages, which accounts for his obscurity.[3]

Let's take a look at some of his more approachable poems. "Over Sir John's Hill" is as good as any to begin with.[4] It starts off with the description of a scene that the poet observes from his window overlooking the estuary of the Taf and Towy rivers somewhere in South Wales. There the hawk in the fiery light of the setting sun is catching and eating little birds like sparrows, and a heron stalking around fishing and eating his dinner of fish. The poet understands the import immediately: "I ... /read... /Death clear as a buoy's bell:/ All praise of the hawk on fire in hawk-eyed dusk be sung." Here lies the theme of the poem. It is a poem about death, inevitable death, death that cannot be avoided and is therefore not hateful. There is a hint that death is not the end but a part of the natural process. Some have claimed that the poem is about justice in keeping with the law of nature. The hawk killing the birds and the birds flying up to him to be killed and the heron eating his fish dinner quietly when the birds' feathers are scattered—all these are unavoidable as a matter of natural fact. And so is the hawk with a noose on his neck and the heron carrying his own headstone with him; the heron seems holy because it is a symbol of the workings of nature. There is no criminal; there is no crime and punishment. No one is guilty and no one has any choice. The poet may pray that God have mercy on the birds and save them, but God does not seem to do anything about the situation. The poem reveals Thomas' skepticism as well. He said on one occasion of his poems as "poems in praise of God's world by a man who doesn't believe in God."

"Fern Hill" is another of Thomas' lucid poems. Fern Hill was the farm of the poet's aunt where the poet spent his childhood on holidays. So the poem is on the whole a recapture of the poet's childhood experience. It is the adult looking back, but the backward glance is not much removed from a child's perspective. This kind of double focus endows the poem with a sense of poignancy. The poem begins with the boy playing on a farm with the apple boughs, the lilting house, green grass, trees, leaves, barley, and the rivers of light. He was as happy as a prince, noticing the presence of time, but unaware of its encroachment as suggested by "night" and "windfall." The happy prince becomes the happy shepherd, green, carefree, singing with calves singing and foxes barking, and notices that the day will end with the setting sun. Stanzas 3 and 4 portray Fern Hill as Eden where the happy child plays and melts himself into nature. However, there is still a different, subtly imbedded note as, for instance, the second half of the 3rd stanza suggests. The stanza rings differently with the child lying down to sleep and the rest of the world rushing into night. The last two stanzas sum up the carefree childhood with a heightened awareness of Time as the villain, who turns the farm into "a childless land," and puts the child in the chains of adulthood and death. The boy speaker takes up all the happy part; the adult glancing back notices the shadow of Time moving. There is little meditation and less moralizing. It is a straightforward account of the inevitable loss of innocence and of Death as an unavoidable part of the human scenario. Here in a kind of nostalgic rant, Thomas' inward gaze is face to face with the mystery of his own growing up.

Dylan Thomas' most widely known poem is perhaps his "Do Not Go Gentle into That Good Night." This is a villanelle, a fixed poetic form with its hard and fast rules that originated from medieval French courtly poetry. Thomas' use of this form in this poem is an ample indication of his technical virtuosity. The theme of the poem is self-evident: to encourage people to strive and persevere in face of adversity and death. The last stanza of the poem makes it clear that the poem is addressed to the poet's father, a former schoolmaster, now a semi-invalid, going blind. Now the father was suffering from tongue cancer and had lost his previous glitter, and the distressed poet wrote to help the old man pluck up his courage and challenge death itself. The five stanzas of the poem describe the heroic responses of the five specimens of humanity in face of inevitable death: they all rage against the approach of the last moment and refuse to submit to the leisure and the effortless existence that "that good night" promises to provide. These include the wise men, the good men, the wild men, the grave men, and his father who had already been pushed onto "the sad height." As these categories cover practically all sane and wide-awake humanity, the poem sounds like a battle cry for all mankind to rise and fight back the encroachment of death. An interesting interpretation of the poem seems to suggest that Dylan Thomas himself, not afraid of death, put his own advice to practice in his own life and challenged Death with his own life when he drank excessively in New York and tested the limits of death's menace and power. He died young and fighting.

Thomas can be difficult and obscure. For years he appeared to be incomprehensible to some very insightful critics of his time. His subjects are not really new. As to his vocabulary, the number of his frequently used words amounts to some thirty-six hundred as commonly used by a seaside village boy like him. There is really nothing very new in what he says. The fact is that his newness lies in how he says it; and how he says it has to do with how he observes. First of all, it should be noted that his is a very peculiar mode of perception of the world around him. For example, he imagines how babies speak in the womb, or how the dead is not dead, or what goes on in God's mind before Creation. Then there is his language to consider. The resources of language are common to all people as a convention on which they depend for meaning. People use them in their commonly accepted—orthodox or conventional—ways for communication, and expect others, the authors included, to do the same. If anyone violates the established way of saying things, people will be bewildered. This was what happened in the case of Dylan Thomas. He could be very unconventional in expression. Generally words and images are associative; they interrelate and interact with one another to make sense; and their mutual referentiality creates a context which encases and ensures clear meaning. The context is to a particular word or image what water is to fish. Once "displaced," words and images cease to evoke coherent connections just as fish dies, and this is when difficulty or obscurity occurs. Now Thomas' poetic imagination is highly idiosyncratic. It deploys words and images often in a manner way out of the expectation of the readers. He may impose impossible demands on words or images, using them in different ways and assigning different, unconventional meanings to them, so that they lose their customary associations in their contexts, and the readers often find it just impossible to guess at what they mean.

What people need then when they read authors like Thomas is, first, patience with unconventionality (which is often a hallmark of genius) and, second, a careful, careful perusal of their texts. And sure enough some years after Thomas' death, some patient and careful scholars have combed through Thomas' poetry and its related sources and have found coherence and meaning where to his severe critics there was none at the time when he was alive and immediately after his death. Notable examples include H. H. Kleinman's *The Religious Sonnets of Dylan Thomas* (1963) and William York Tindall's *A Reader's Guide to Dylan Thomas* (1962). They have found that, although Thomas was concerned with melody, he was not "drunk with melody" as one of his most severe critics, Robert Graves, put it on one occasion. Thomas knew the meanings of the words he used and worked hard to make them fit into his rhythmical framework. He was not ranting; he was singing; and he was always inspired. Although scholarship has not addressed all the difficulties, a new image of Thomas has appeared. The message seems to be that Thomas is great, although his kind of greatness may take time and effort to appreciate.

William Empson (1906-1984)

Mention has to be made of William Empson as he represented a distinct vein of critical thinking and poetry writing which enriched the poetic output of his country in this period. Empson may not be a great poet, nor has he ever been seen as a top-notch critic, but his poetry and criticism have both been very influential in their way. He wrote mainly a New Critical kind of poetry, exemplifying the major features of the New Critical poem. This kind of poetry kept the basic Modernist values such as economy, wit, irony, impersonality, and meticulous care with form, but it abandoned or toned down other High Modernist features such as extreme fragmentation, paratactic syntax, ellipsis, symbolism and myth, cross-culturalism, and allusions. As a result it became cautious and traditional, and less revolutionary and disorienting, and was more amenable to all tastes and more popular with the rising younger generation of the 1940s. Empson paid a good deal of attention to the poem as a well-wrought urn, with its coherent form, coherent images and figures, rhymes and stanzas, and integrated attitude and vision. His works were basically rational, witty, rigorous in meters and stanzas, and were strewn with metaphors often very difficult to understand. He was particularly good at using puns and paradoxes and concepts or terms from modern physics and mathematics. All these have made for his obscurity. There were traces of Metaphysical influence in his poetry. Empson's poetry is included in his *Poems* (1935) and *The Gathering Storm* (1940). By the time he was thirty, he had written most of his poems. He also taught in Japan in the 1930s and later in China.

Empson was a New Critic. As a student of I. A. Richards who contributed a good deal to the rise and growth of the New Criticism, Empson developed Richards' critical thought in his famous critical work *Seven Types of Ambiguity* (1930), a trail blazer in itself both in subject and exposition, which impacted poetry writing and criticism in some way. His other critical works include such as *The Structure of Complex Words* (1951) and *Milton's God* (1961), which are not quite comparable in conception and execution to his *Seven Types of Ambiguity*.

Chapter 23 Fiction of the 1930s • Huxley • Orwell • Waugh • Greene • Isherwood

It is a critical commonplace to state that, in the 1930s and ever since, English fiction has not been as good as it used to be. No one has written to display the kind of spiritual exigency as did Joseph Conrad, or touch James Joyce in the use of language, or approach D. H. Lawrence in terms of vibrant energy and destructive obsession. Some critics even claim that modern fiction has stopped writing about moral and ethical values, and its decline is inevitable. Whereas there is truth in all these, it is evidently not the whole truth, and it certainly does not mean that people can ignore the distinguished literary performance of such writers as Graham Greene, George Orwell, Samuel Beckett, Henry Green, Ivy Compton-Burnett, Elizabeth Bowen, Evelyn Waugh, J. B. Priestley and Christopher Isherwood in the 1930s and that of the whole host of postwar writers.

One thing to note about the fiction of this period was its refusal to deal with serious international crises. The attitude of engagement of the previous years and its emotional excitement seemed to have impacted the poets of the period since the 1930s, but not the fiction that appeared to be atavistic in the works of such writers as C. P. Snow, Joyce Cary, and George Orwell. In other words, these writers reverted back to the traditional plot and characterization which modernist masters had despised and almost discarded. Although they still inherited certain formal features of the previous generation, the writers of the 1930s were no longer "Modernist." This going beyond the modernist endeavor and back to the traditions of the Victorian and still earlier periods was an obvious reaction to the modernist innovations. Thus people have noticed that C. P. Snow comes closer to George Eliot, John Galsworthy and Arnold Bennett in style; Joyce Cary seems to be imitating Laurence Sterne, Henry Fielding and Charles Dickens; and Graham Greene appears to be kith and kin of Wilkie Collins, Louis Stevenson, and early Joseph Conrad. As to Ivy Compton-Burnett, she does not go even one step beyond

1910, and George Orwell seeks help and finds value in the naturalistic styles of George Gissing and Emile Zola. The writers of this period seemed to agree that the experimentation of the 1920s was over and outdated and that the best course of action for them was to retreat from its adventurous endeavoor. Such rhetoric as technique, experiment, and form almost vanished. The modern artistic novel seemed to have few or no worshippers in this period.

There are many complex reasons for such changes in mood and style. First, Britain was no longer the dominating world power it used to be after the damaging experience of WWI and the subsequent worldwide depression. It gradually lost out to the United States. This development impacted the growth of English fiction in no small way. The world that the writers of this period had to face was a totally different one from the one in which the Modernist masters pushed the novel to the acme of its growth. British writers focused now more on Britain and felt less concerned with "international" or European literary creativity. If Joyce, Woolf, Lawrence, and Conrad thought not only of Britain, and if their novels tended to be "international" both in theme and form, the writers such as Graham Greene and Evelyn Waugh were preoccupied more with native, local, parochial matters. The common feature that their works share is their limited scope in subject matter and length. Graham Greene, the most successful of modern and contemporary English novelists, seldom if ever wrote a book of over eighty thousand words. His novels are simple in plot and direct in expression with no more than a few characters fleshing out his fictional scenarios. Thus, all the accepted values were subject to doubt in the new era, and the writers found it hard to write a serious comedy and the more so to produce a tragedy. But they all managed to bring their best side out in their creative endeavors.

Another thing to notice about this period is that the huge external changes and the increasing pressure that these brought to bear upon the writers tend to orient them so that they became more "introverted." They seemed to feel that engagement with life and its major problems leads to a dead end, whereas detachment offers a refuge and an avenue to safety. No one believes with D. H. Lawrence any more in rebirth that follows the phoenix burning itself to death, or accepts along with Conrad the transitory salutary effect of the soul's salvation, or declares with Forster's assurance that human connection ensures the hope for survival. Thus people have noticed that the writers tried to avoid handling subjects like world wars with their sound and fury and the disaffection and despair that stemmed from the big changes. They found, instead, the areas of personal interest fascinating. There is, incidentally, little mention of contemporary occurrences in the works of writers such as Bowen, Compton-Burnett, Henry Green, and Evelyn Waugh. Samuel Beckett and Graham Greene were among the few who dealt with subjects both of a personal and social nature.[1]

There were quite a few names out of the period that demand attention. These include, among so many others, Aldous Huxley (1894-1963), George Orwell (1903-1950), Evelyn Waugh (1903-1966), Graham Greene (1904-1991), Christopher Isherwood (1904-1986), Joyce Cary (1888-1957), and Compton-Burnett (1884-1967). There was also the famous Samuel Beckett (1906-1989) whom we'll pass on here for a later discussion as his major works appeared in the contemporary period.

Aldous Huxley (1894-1963)

Aldous Huxley was grandson of the famous Thomas Huxley (1825-1895), the strenuous and discreet defender of Charles Darwin's theory of evolution. He was educated at Oxford University and started writing soon after college. Versatile and prolific, he wrote copiously on a variety of topics and in a variety of literary genres, and achieved an international renown for himself. Although he is seen as a minor major novelist, he did help reflect, in his moderate, sometimes distorting fashion, the spirit of his century. His well-known novels include *Crome Yellow* (1921), *Point Counter Point* (1928), and *Brave New World* (1932).[2]

Brave New World has been seen as Huxley's best literary effort. The novel, a dystopia, basically tells the story of a Savage in confrontation with a well-developed civilized society. The Savage is brought to London and feels intrigued in a world so new to him. Here he sees a scientifically planned social order in which people live in content with their assigned places in society. He learns that the people are all born from incubators, brought up in nurseries, classified from birth in keeping with their prenatal manipulated levels of intelligence, and conditioned through education so that they are happy with their social placement. This is what, as he comes to see it, generates an ideal social stability so absent from human life everywhere else. Then the Savage discovers to his great dismay that something absolutely essential to meaningful life is missing from the new world, i.e. individual identity and freedom, love, and independent thinking. He decides to denounce the scientifically imposed order of peace and harmony. He feels so frustrated and incapable of handling the stress that he finds his easy exit out of it in suicide. The novel paints a picture of horror of a future that Huxley envisages will be forthcoming with science and civilization fast advancing, totalitarianism steadily taking over, and natural human life and human nature itself ever on the defensive retreat in face of fatal threat. Huxley apparently deems it impossible to shake off the shadow of his prophetic vision, and so he paints an even more dreadful picture about the future human condition in his *Brave New World Revisited* (1958). Here the author makes his final plunge in the abyss of pessimism, decadence, and despair, from which he never recovers. *Brave New World* is in essence an acrid satire in which the author manages to bring his full mature powers into play for the best effect possible for his art. Though it deserves a commendable mention, as a creative endeavor, its vision is flawed. The author's view of life and its prospect is somewhat morbid and as such lacking in creditability.

George Orwell (1903-1950)

Orwell started off with his leftist sympathies in the 1930s, came well under the influence of the socialist ideas afloat then, took an active part in the Spanish Civil War, but ended up sorely frustrated with Stalinism. He seemed to feel that the system of socialism and communism he had embraced could pose a serious threat to the principle of individual freedom, of which he had been a staunch exponent. He was adamant in his critical stance that art is closely intertwined with politics, and made a point of choosing the subjects of a more ponderous political significance. His famous works, *Animal Farm* (1945) and *Nineteen Eighty-Four* (1949), both well illustrate his preoccupation with political considerations and his disappointment with communism as he saw it practiced in the Soviet Union then. The former of these two novels, in fact a political fable in which human society is likened to the animal world, is probably pointing fingers at the Soviet society, the silhouette of which is easily perceivable in the occurrences on the animal farm. The plot is well designed to approximate and satirize Stalin and his system. The novel begins with the Old Major, an old boar, relating his ideal of an animal society in which human rule is done away with and all animals live in equality and happiness. This inspires the Animalist Revolution that drives out all the humans from the farm, so that all the animals, boar, horse, donkey, mare, monkey, and raven, can live in equality and bliss. Then a rift occurs between the two leading boars, Snowball and Napoleon, and Napoleon drives Snowball away to establish himself as the absolute ruler. He betrays Old Major's ideal and even signs a business contract with his human neighbors. All the animals are thus placed back in square one and suffer enslavement as before. The hint at Stalin as Napoleon is obvious. The ideal may be the initial communist ideal, the two boars and their quarrel may be intended to replicate the historical scenario between Trotsky and Stalin, and the contract may refer to the Soviet-German pact that was signed before the outbreak of WWII. It is no wonder that *Animal Farm* played an important part in the post-WWII anti-Soviet campaign. [3]

Orwell's anti-tyranny stance is best illustrated in his *Nineteen Eighty-Four*. Here is a fictional country, Oceania, a world where everything is regulated from above—love, marriage, speech and language, thinking, and history. Independent thinkers are burned to ashes; human movement is closely monitored by the thought police; and social life is all gloom and terror. The tyrant here is known as "Big Brother," and the common man is Winston Smith, a member of the Outer Ring of the party. Winston cherishes an ideal of his own, keeps a secret journal, falls in love with Julia and makes her his mistress, and so breaks all the taboos. He is arrested by the secret police, made to suffer incredibly, and has to submit to the authority of the ruler to save his neck. The spearhead of the novel is once again pointed directly at the Soviet Union.

Orwell was one of the disillusioned Western intellectuals first enamored with and then alienated from the Soviet Union and its ideal. He was probably the most vehement and aggressive of the turncoats.

Evelyn Waugh (1903-1966)

Waugh inherited the English literary satirical tradition and wrote caustic satires all his life. Most of his novels are modeled on one constant thematic and structural pattern, that an innocent young man experiences his rise and fall in a world of evil and treachery. Simple, honest, and naïve, the young man, still emotionally growing, easily becomes a tragic plaything in the hands of the evil powers he comes in contact with. Waugh derives his satiric power from a number of exquisite devices that he employs at will. One of these is his use of his protagonist as a means to reveal the direct contrast between the alarming social corruption on the one hand and the total helplessness of the good and innocent folks on the other. Such a youth appears always in his major works: as Paul in his *Decline and Fall* (1928), Adam in *Vile Bodies* (1930), and Tony in *A Handful of Dust* (1934). The bitter experience of his protagonists offers a good opportunity for him to lash out at society relentlessly. In addition, Waugh is noted for his other satiric features as well. One of these is his skillful use of the pastoral and the lyric touches in the portrayal of evil characters, which brings out the contrast between good and evil in bold relief. Another feature is the use of a factual and indifferent tone in mentioning serious matters such as a death. Here the author backs out of the scene in detachment to allow the characters to mention a grave subject in a very brief manner; in this way, the nonchalance of a cold universe is effectively revealed. Other notable features include verbal irony as a way of self-exposure and self-censure, which is especially powerful in handling the silly and evil characters. Capable of blending the comic within the tragic and remorseless in his attacks upon the evil and the absurd in life, Waugh has won himself a place in the literature of his century.[4]

In a sense any of Waugh's novels is good enough for a thematic and formal analysis. Let's take a look at his *Decline and Fall*, his first work of importance, which smacks strongly of black humor. It tells the sad story of a young man, a divinity student, Paul Pennyfeather by name. Paul lives through an eventful phase of his life—wrongly expelled from Oxford University, becoming a school teacher in Wales, falling in love by accident with Margot Beste-Chetwiynde, a rich woman, who happens to be a criminal running a "white-slave" trade (making her fortune by selling the virginity of poor girls), serving prison time as her scapegoat, and escaping from prison with the help of Sir Humphrey Maltravers, Minister of Transport, whom Margot now marries. Then Paul "dies" on the operation table, grows a mustache to look different, changes his name, and returns to continue his study for the Church at Oxford. The novel seems to be saying that in a world which is by and large amoral, Paul as an insignificant common person lives at the tender mercies of the people who have the power and privilege to do as they please. He is, as his last name suggests, mere feathers and worth no more than a penny. Margot and her minister-husband can "kill" and "resurrect" a human life the way jugglers and God figures do, whereas the common run of mankind is supposed to run their show like funny, wretched puppets. One important stylistic feature to note here is the matter-of-fact tone in which the good number of references are made to the variety and the severity of the vices that exist in the different government agencies and the rich segments of society. The plainness of the narrative style contrasts beautifully well with the force of satire that it generates.

Graham Greene (1904-1991)

Greene's literary career spanned over half a century. Although his reputation was at its highest in the contemporary period and has been seen as one major postwar novelist, he was closely associated with the 1930s in which some of his major works were written. That warrants his inclusion in the discussion here. One thing to note about Greene is the fact that his thematic focus has remained constant all through his long and productive life: He is probably one of the best, if not the best, of his generation to depict the dilemma in which modern man has managed to land himself up. Greene's subjects may appear to be wide-ranging—strikes, political assassinations, world finance, the Spanish Civil War, the Vietnam-French conflicts, pre-Castro Cuba, the pre-Independence Congo, faith and religion, socialism, and Marxism. But no matter what he writes about, be it different people, places, and events, careful perusal will reveal his all-time concern with man, his condition, his fallen state, his moral quandary, his social and ethical problems, his psychic conflicts, the temptation of evil, and the sordidness and meaninglessness of his life as a whole. Generally Greene's early novels are more religious-oriented while his contemporary works cover a variety of subjects of political interest. His mode of representation is peculiar, rendering the whole and the general truth through the portrayal of a part and the specific. Often set in an exotic milieu, where violence and crimes are the order of the day, his stories mostly center on a petty common person lost in an odd labyrinth of an environment and shifting the best he can for himself. Very prolific and popular and aspiring for the Nobel Prize, Greene kept writing right up to the end of his life. He has won for himself a prominent place in history, but not the prize he coveted. His major works include *The Power and the Glory* (1940), *The Heart of the Matter* (1948), and *The Human Factor* (1978).[5]

The Power and the Glory has been seen as Greene's most successful work. It tells a story of three men, utterly different in identity, job description, and temperament. One of these is a priest who is the only one of his holy orders left in the whole of Mexico after the country shuts down all the churches and banishes all the holy clerics. The fact is that he was about to escape when he was called upon to do a holy duty for a dying woman. He is not the best of his kind, drinking (so nicknamed "the Whisky priest"), choosing to be a priest because he is good at nothing else, and having fathered a daughter, whose mother saves his neck when he comes to their village for refuge. Thus he appears to be an evil person to all people including himself. Now frightened and desperate on the run from the police pursuit, he spends his time dodging the arrest the best he can and seeking consolation in his cups. He meets a poor mulatto—one of the three major characters—and is betrayed and thrown in prison. There he meets the lieutenant who has been in hot pursuit of him, but failing to recognize him, sets him free out of sympathy. The priest meets the mulatto again and knowingly falls into the villain's new trap out of his sense of duty to God. He is arrested once more and is sentenced to death. On the night of his execution, however, another priest appears.

Greene was basically a religious writer. *The Power and the Glory* is a good illustration of his religious concern. The structure of the story approximates very much that of the biblical story of the Passion: Jesus (the priest) is betrayed by Judas (the mulatto), and is sentenced reluctantly by the Roman general Pilate (the policeman). The priest is human rather than a paragon of virtue, but he is not totally without any redeeming quality. He keeps his unswerving faith in God, stays awake and aware of his religious duties, and is equal to the occasion, at the critical moments of his life, when he feels called upon to behave the way a hero and a martyr is supposed to do. He knows, for instance, that he will miss his boat and end up in danger when a boy comes along to beseech him to administer the last rites for his mother, and he is certain that the mulatto will tell him off, but he feels bound by his sense of duty and cannot bring himself to do otherwise. He dies, but reappears in the end as Jesus is resurrected in the *Bible*. The other man in the novel, the policeman, possesses a uniqueness of his own: He is persistent and earnest to a fault, but not entirely without a sense of justice and compassion. The common denominator between him and the priest is the love that fills both hearts and their sensitivity to love. Their encounter in prison, though brief, exemplifies the spiritual communion possible to achieve between human beings. When the priest says to the police officer, "You are a good man," and the officer replies, "You are not a bad person either," the understanding and friendship that they manage to achieve exhibit the best effect of human connection in life. As to the mulatto, he is to the priest more or less what the biblical Judas is to Jesus Christ. He promises to be good and faithful as Judas does, and betrays the holy man all the same in the end.

Women Writers Ivy Compton-Burnett (1884-1967)—Elizabeth Bowen (1899-1973)— Rebecca West (1892-1985)

The 1930s saw the rise of some women writers after Virginia Woolf and Katherine Mansfield (1888-1923). Although different in theme and form, these writers shared one common thematic focus—women and their lives and their inner world. Among these stood out a few whose works have made an impression upon the readers. These include Ivy Compton-Burnett, Elizabeth Bowen, Jeans Rhys, Mary Webb, Flora Thomson, Rose Macaulay, and Rebecca West. Our discussion here will touch upon some of them.

Compton-Burnett began to publish in the 1920s, but came to prominence in the next decade. She was preoccupied with the depiction of English life in the period stretching from the latter part of the 19th century through the early years of the 20th century. This she managed to do well by focusing upon the life of the country gentility with which she was fully acquainted. Going through the period of both financial and moral decline, this class experienced a grotesque and absurd phase of life of tyranny, guilt, violence, and incest that occurred in their closed and narrow circle. Compton-Burnett's characters often appear larger than life, behaving in ways exaggerated, boldly envisioned, yet humanly conceivable. Compton-Burnett is noted for her careful handling of language, her exquisite choice of words, and her adept manipulation of dialogues so as to help push the story steadily to its climax and achieve the best possible narrative effect in plot structuring and portrayal of characters. In theme Compton-Burnett did not go beyond the early 20th century. She was a prolific author, writing a total of twenty novels in her long career. Her major works include *Men and Wives* (1931), *A Family and a Fortune* (1939), and *Two Worlds and Their Ways* (1949). [6]

Another woman writer who became famous at the time was Elizabeth Bowen (1899-1973). In terms of subject matter, Bowen's range is wide and varied, but in theme she keeps one thing always topmost in her mind—the adumbration of young women's life and their emotional world. Although she wrote basically in the traditional manner, she was hypersensitive to the pervasive influence of the Modernist innovation in the craft of fiction and tried to delineate the inner world in a fresh and minute way. Her critical observations on the craft of the novel have been of value to later literary criticism. Her major novels are *The Death of the Heart* (1938), and *The Heat of the Day* (1949). Her work on literary criticism, "The Novelist's Craft" (1956), is an important work on novel-writing.

Rebecca West (1892-1985) merits mention here for a good reason. She enjoyed high esteem in her time as one of the best journalists, and one of the most sensitive and observant literary critics. She was one of the earliest writers who became aware of the power and permanence of the rising generation of writers still struggling then such as James Joyce. Her systematic comments upon Henry James, James Joyce, and D. H. Lawrence reveal her acute critical acumen rare for her time. In her protracted career West also wrote quite a few novels, some of which, such as *The Fountain Overflows* (1956), have won critical acclaim.

The Leftist-Oriented Writers J. B. Priestley (1894-1984) Christopher Isherwood (1904-1986)

The 1930s was a decade in which leftist-oriented writings bloomed in Europe as well as in England. The severity of the crisis and the extent of suffering of the people and the subsequent spread of the influence of the Soviet Union and Marxism colored literary creativity so much that social concern became the major thematic focus for a good number of leftist and proletarian writers in their creative endeavors. These include, among others, Sean O'Casey (1880-1964), Lewis G. Gibbon (1901-1935), and Walter Greenwood (1903-1974). These writers and quite a number of others appeared on the scene and made the working class' voice of protest well heard. Their works were basically "period" pieces, reflecting and catering to the needs and the mood of their time. They did a lot to help boost the morale of the working class and keep it on its alert in its fight for survival. The weakness that detracted from their permanence was probably their over-emphasis on the effect of propaganda at the expense of the quality of their works as art. Their contemporary descendant, Alan Sillitoe for one, detects the problem and has been trying to elevate propaganda stuff to the level of matter fit for more conscientious artistic treatment.

In addition to the growth of proletarian literature, other forms of leftist-oriented writings appeared also to make an impression on their time and on posterity. Such writers as J. B. Priestley (1894-1984) and Christopher Isherwood (1904-1986) all tried to respond in their unique way to the new *zeitgeist* of the new decade. Priestley came from a working-class family, received his education at Cambridge, and started writing after college. His was a long, productive life. His multi-volume output includes novels, plays, and critical commentaries. Priestley was a realist. He was concerned with the human condition in the years of the Depression and wrote about the worries and fears of the lower strata of society in face of joblessness and bankruptcy. His works of the period spearheaded their critical edge against the ills of society. Basically a novelist, Priestley also wrote a good number of plays, the most famous of which include *Dangerous Corner* (1932) and *An Inspector Calls* (1945). He was popular as a playwright for over 20 years in the West End of London theaters.

Priestley's most popular and successful literary effort was his novel, *The Good Companions* (1929), which has been long on the top of the best-sellers' list. It is a tragi-comic story of success and pain. The major characters are three homeless people—Elizabeth Trant, an old spinster at 35, who inherits some money and is now out to enjoy her new-found freedom, Jess Oakroyd on the run because fed up with his nagging wife and his rebellious and spiteful son, and Inigo Jollifant, a former teacher, now workless as he offended his principal. They meet by accident and become friends as they share a sense of frustration with reality and the spirit of escape. Elizabeth meets and takes over a traveling vaudeville company, Jess becomes the company's handyman, and Inigo joins it as its song writer. They pool their resources together—Elizabeth with her money, Jess his skills, and Inigo his gift of composing popular songs—to resuscitate the bankrupt musical group. The troupe, now the Good Companions, tours the rural and mining areas around, encounters hard times, but eventually achieves some success. It experiences both joys and worries, and ends up well and happy for all. Elizabeth tastes life for the first time and eventually marries a doctor, her long-time suitor. Jess is happy now that his thirst for adventures is quenched. Inigo falls in love with Susie Dean, the comedian of the group.

The story appeals to popular taste as a moving success story, with its emphasis on the human spirit and ingenuity in face of adversity and the group effort to tide over difficult times. The optimism never fails to awaken warm echoes from the readers. Another feature to note about the book is its vivid, authentic portrayal of all walks of life in the country and towns, their miseries and misfortunes, their pathos and their idiosyncracies, and the general wretchedness of life for people on the lower rung of the social ladder in those years. Essentially a good mix of happiness and pain, the novel ends on a note of helplessness at the fickleness and futility of life itself.

Christopher Isherwood (1904-1986)

Isherwood was a left-oriented realist in the 1930s, and wrote his best works in the decade. He focused his creative energies on the depiction of the social and political problems of his day and supported all the causes of a leftist orientation. He became an active member of the Audenic group and wrote political plays in collaboration with Auden. Later he came to China and reported well on the anti-Japanese war efforts of the Chinese people. In the later 1940s he immigrated to America and became a US citizen in 1946. Still later he embraced Indian religious philosophy.

The 1930s was Isherwood's "European" period in which he wrote his famous works such as those relating the Berlin stories. After his immigration to the United States, his "American" period began. All his works share one feature: they are all in a way tied up with an individual's quest for truth about life and about self. Isherwood was essentially autobiographical. Some of his characters and some of the narrators of his stories are clearly his own representations. Isherwood is a highly readable writer.[7]

Isherwood's most famous works are his Berlin stories that appear in his novels *Mr. Norris Changes Trains* (1935), *Goodbye to Berlin* (1937), and *The Berlin Stories* (1946). Having lived in pre-Hitler Berlin for over three years (1929-1933), he learned about the city and its psychology from inside. *Goodbye to Berlin*, probably the most renowned of all his works, is a coherent amalgam of several "loosely connected" diaries and sketches, and a short novel, with an overlapping cast of characters. There are altogether six parts in the book—"A Berlin Diary (Autumn 1930)," *Sally Bowels*, a short novel, "On Ruegen Island (Summer 1931)," "The Nowaks," "The Landauers," and "A Berlin Diary (Winter 1932-3)." The book touches upon the various aspects of Berlin life—social, political, economic, and cultural, and paints a full gallery of humanity—the rich and the poor, the people with different sexual orientations, the people with different faiths such as Christians and Jews, the Weimar Republic struggling in the throes of death, the rise of the brooding Nazis, and the looming menace of a monster steadily climbing to power. Society is beset with ills of all kinds, and Berlin is disintegrating. The book seems to suggest that the spiritual dearth among the people, their morbidity, nonchanlance, acquiescence, and lack of fellowship connection—all these might be, by and large, responsible for Hitler's rise to power.

One notable feature of the book is its interesting "dynamic portraits." The characters are basically a group of people living on the fringes of conventional life. Mr. Norris is a flagellant, Sally an eccentric bohemian singer, Otto Nowak a gay, and Fraulein Schroeder a sort of snob. The name of the narrator is Isherwood. Living in this dying city, the young man suffers detachment, disenchantment, and despair in the shadow of the past and the fear and uncertainty for the future. He is groping in the dark, observing, non-judgmental, but trying to make sense of what defies comprehension. The ultimate historical value of *Goodbye to Berlin* lies in the fact that it records facts of history. It functions, as the book claims it does, as "a camera with its shutter open," and offers an intimate portrait of Berlin and its popular mindset which made Hitler's advent a fact of history. Isherwood as an author observes and presents, and is seldom convincingly analytical, but he can be very emotional at times.

Chapter 24 Postwar Poetry

It is difficult to pigeonhole contemporary English authors neatly, and this is the case especially with contemporary English poets. The postwar scene of English poetry was a colorful one. On the one hand, the Modernist poets and works were still highly visible. T. S. Eliot enjoyed enormous fame in the afterglow of the Nobel Prize he won in 1948. Robert Graves and William Empson were popular and attractive. The Metaphysical style, which T. S. Eliot did very much to resurrect and revive, was still in vogue. The Romantics of the previous decades like Dylan Thomas, Edwin Muir, Edith Sitwell, and also many younger poets continued to write in the same vein. On the other hand, a new generation was emerging. Literary historians have tended to label the new poets of the 1950s all as part of what has come to be known as "Movement" poetry, while in actuality different groups existed and tried to exhibit their own identities. Thus alongside the Movement poets, there were poets like Roy Fuller, C. H. Sisson, and R. S. Thomas, and poets who were part of The Group such as Alan Brownjohn, George Macbeth, and Peter Redgrove. Whereas some mention will be made of these in passing, the following discussion will focus more on the Movement poets.

The "Movement" poets included, among others, Philip Larkin, Donald Davie, D. J. Enright, Thom Gunn, Robert Conquest, John Wain, Elizabeth Jennings, Kingsley Amis, and John Holloway. These people wrote in a drastically different way from the poets of the war years. Fed up with the experimental Romantic efforts of Dylan Thomas and his contemporaries to shape life and the world, they reacted strongly by veering in a new direction, and came to grips downright with their new, different reality. They were concerned with the social changes that postwar Laborite Britain was going through, and tried to examine life in an honest, realistic manner. In addition, they felt the acute need to cater to a broader readership than the Modernist endeavor had served, and they could be anti-intellectual and anti-cultural in their stance. With these new people on the scene and their new ideas up in the air, the phase of "Movement" poetry in English literary history had begun. Most of the younger poets of the 1950s were either part of the Movement or shared its values.

The Movement poets became famous partly as a result of the critical attempts to introduce them. Some of these critical efforts were accidental; some others were deliberate and serious. The term, "the Movement," first appeared in 1954 in an article by J. D. Scott, the literary editor of the *Spectator*, who was discussing the features of the new poetry of postwar Britain. Although it was used there in a jocular manner, the label sank deep in memory and gained wide currency. The "Movement" poets were first made known as a group in an anthology entitled, *Poets of the 1950s* (1955), edited by D. J. Enright, and then again in another, better known, anthology, *New Lines* (1956), by Robert Conquest. Then the rest of the world as well as Britain became alert that a new frame of reference had appeared for gauging the mood of postwar Britain. It is necessary to add that the Movement poets wrote also novels and literary criticism in addition to poetry and that the group was heterogeneous in ideas and practices rather than monolithic in any sense of the term.

What the Movement poets reacted particularly against was Dylan Thomas' kind of "arrangement of images of sex and violence tapped straight from the unconscious... or evok[ing] without comment naivetes and nostalgias of childhood" (as Robert Conquest put it), or his abandoning orthodox forms of articulation or letting the objects "[tumble] pell-mell, together" (to quote Donald Davie). They chose, instead, the traditional rational forms of communication as exemplified by the minor Augustans of the 18th century. The rebellion against Dylan Thomas and his generation of poets was actually part of the larger postwar reaction to the dominance of T. S. Eliot and the Metaphysical mode of writing as shown in the works of William Empson.

The Movement poets shared some essential literary features and qualities in their works. They were, for instance, self-expressive, intuitive, obscure, experimental, realistic, and concerned with formal control. Their style is generally plain, direct, deflated, personal, and formal. Their diction is lean and spare. There is not much room for Dylan Thomas' Romantic rhetoric or his mysticism or

Empson's elaborate punning. The Movement poets regarded T. S. Eliot and Ezra Pound as continental influences, and appreciated much better A. E. Housman (1859-1936), Thomas Hardy, the Georgians, and the 18th- and 19th-century poets such as Thomas Gray, William Cowper, and William Wordsworth.

Movement poetry tended to be depressing in mood and tone. This was in part traceable to the quandary in which they found themselves in postwar Britain. What happened then was that the Labor Party was putting their "socialist" policies in practice. The unions waxed stronger. More housing estates were erected. TV and automobiles became part of daily life. There was the welfare state with National Health and other benefits. But life was also showing its downside: it was tawdry and spiritless. The writers of the period were caught in a dilemma: they liked the Socialist ideals all right, but lacked a strong faith in them. There is a good deal of hurt and pain and fear in their works. The Movement took English poetry along a road that Dylan Thomas and his followers had never thought of traversing.[1]

Philip Larkin (1922-1985)

The dominant figure of the Movement was Philip Larkin. He was born in Coventry, England and educated at Oxford. For many years he worked as the head librarian at Hull University. He was under the influence of both Yeats (as is evident in his first volume of verse *The North Ship* [1945]) and Hardy (as revealed in his *The Less Deceived* [1955] and *The Whitsun Weddings* [1964]) before he found his mature style. Larkin produced a fairly small output. His fourth and last volume of verse, *High Windows* came out in 1974. In the last eight years of his life he wrote little or nothing that was significant. Early in his career, he also wrote some novels, *Jill* (1946) and *A Girl in Winter* (1947). Larkin was a landmark in the literary history of his country. Together with his contemporaries such as Kingsley Amis, Donald Davie, and Thom Gunn, he wrote a new kind of poetry in order to be true to the spirit of his age. He did his best to help revive the 18th- and 19th-century literary tradition of his country and oppose what the Movement termed foreign influences such as that of the High Modernists—Eliot's or Pound's.

Larkin's poetry is plain in style, almost free from metaphors and melodious rhetoric. It rejects Dylan Thomas' kind of Romantic vision of things. Larkin's subject is daily life as being lived by the common people. He seldom if ever goes beyond his range, which is not a wide one, but which he manages to make the best of with his poetic gift. He generally paints life in drab and gloomy colors. There is a good deal of disillusionment, skepticism, and hopelessness in his work. The way he writes is interesting to note. His poems normally begin with the poet-speaker observing some object or person or place or anything from the external world and then move on with his inspired deliberations. Larkin is mostly personal and even Confessional in tone, with the "I" frequently featuring as the speaker and clinging to his own voice and view obdurately. His power lies in the fact that his personal truth often coincides with public truth and becomes identical with it.

Let's take a look at some of his poems. "Poetry of Departures" (1955) is probably a good place to begin with as it offers the readers something like a statement of purpose for his poetic career. Basically the poem talks about two possible courses of action for human beings to take in life. One of these is the Romantic one: "He chucked up everything/ And just cleared off [,]" or in other words, just "walked out on the whole crowd [,]" with no worries and cares, simply leaving the earth earthy behind. The other is the realistic one: "[to] swagger the nut-strewn roads/ Crouch in the fo'c'sle [.]" Here is a plodding through, with promises to keep, and responsibilities to discharge. The first one thrills as it is everybody's dream, audacious, purifying, and elemental. It is "artificial," however, not practical enough, not quite in keeping with common sense. Ultimately life is not always swashbuckling, not always heroic. Very often it is humdrum, drab, and dreary with everything, bed, books, china, "in perfect order." It is, in a word, not exciting, but we have got to live with that. The title of the poem, which has little physical connection with its content, metaphorically sums it up well: The poet would "depart" from the road taken, take the realistic course of action, and write realistically about life here and now.

Generally, Larkin's work is short and lyrical. As is noted earlier on, he sees something, describes it, and reflects on it. For instance, when he sees a couple of young people together somewhere, he would guess that they are making out, the girl is wearing some protection, and they are feeling the bliss of hot and wet love and sex. Then reflection cuts in. That kind of bliss, he would tell us, is the paradise that old people always dream of, the kind of bliss he had when he was young forty years ago. There is living, sweating in the dark, totally forgetting God or any inhibition, just plain freedom and happiness. Then in the midst of the thought of joy and abandonment, the poet, now no longer young, thinks of the high church windows, its glass, the blue sky beyond, and the nothingness that stretches endless still beyond that. Thus beginning with a sort of nostalgia, a sense of loss, the poet turns back on himself, now over sixty years old, for whom, he thinks, nothing is going to happen ever again except, probably, for death. The sense of bliss leads suddenly, abruptly, to a sense of horror of having to face eternity. This would be possibly the experience that people have reading his famous poem—"High Windows."

So Larkin sounds, and is, generally sad, but is not without any saving grace. "Home Is So Sad" is a good example. It conveys an acute sense of being deserted, lonely, disillusioned, and nostalgic for the good old days gone by never to return. The "home" of the poem used to be a joyous and hopeful place that strove upward. There were pictures, cutlery, music in the piano, and of course, people there. Now though the things are still there, the home withers and stops trying to be a better place. The ending is full of longing for the lost past, and of a desperate clinging to and reluctance to part with it. All this is amply delineated with that terse yet fully loaded "That vase." The tone verges almost on being sentimental. But a different interpretation could be that such warmth of feeling could indicate the resilience of a mind against overwhelming odds.

One of the reasons for this built-in sadness can be probably found in Larkin's most oft-anthologized poem, "Church Going" (1955). Its structuring pattern is still descriptive-meditative. It begins with a jocular, almost irreverent tone, "Once I am sure there's nothing going on/ I step inside [the church]...." Then it goes on with a basically matter-of-fact, but occasionally mildly judgmental description of the interior of the church: matting, seats, stone, books, flowers, "some brass and stuff/ Up at the holy end," the organ, the silence, the font, the new roof, the lectern, the verses, and the donation box. Then with the third stanza, the rumination begins. What is the use of the churches? What would we do when they fall out of use? Are they unlucky places? What remains when superstition, belief, and even disbelief die? As he sees the church fast becoming increasingly less recognizable and purposeless, he starts wondering whether anyone except some grotesque will ever visit "this accoutred frowsty barn" again, now a mere symbol of marriage, birth and death. But he feels good to stand in silence there and feels sure that the place is a serious house on serious earth for serious people, a place where "all our compulsions meet,/ Are recognized, and robed as destinies." Serious people will feel some spiritual need to "gravitate" toward it. Then the poet becomes aware that this is also a place where "so many dead lie around."

The poem portrays a mind confused, skeptical, and vacillating because it is in the process of losing its faith. The poet has been told all along that the church is a good place to "grow wise in," but seeing it deserted, begins to feel uncertain about it. This is the basic reason for so much negativity in the tone and mood of the whole work and so little affirmation, and the basic reason for the feeling of desolation that permeates it all. A mind that hovers between belief and disbelief inevitably suffers agony. Though there is a feeble affirmation that does help a little toward dispelling the sense of gloom, the poem still ends on a note of helplessness if not exactly despair, as it associates the church with the painful consciousness of death.

The fear of death is another probable cause for Larkin's sadness. For Larkin, death is inevitable, life is empty, and fear of death shortchanges living. This is the point that keeps undercutting any sense of happiness that his observation may initially bring to his work. For him—and for his age and generation, death is forever a heavy load on the mind, especially when the mind is losing or has lost its underpinning faith. "Aubade" (1977) is a graphic illustration. This poem was possibly Larkin's last work of any weight before "[poetry] abandoned me" as he put it. It is an honest confession about his (man's, for that matter) fear of death and old age along with it. As true to form with Larkin, the poem begins with a description of the external world and then turns inward in a painfully meditative manner. "I" drinks all night and falls asleep, but wakes up at four a.m., stares at the curtain edges that "will grow light" with dawn, and sees "what's really always there." It is death, always wide awake, never resting, waiting to bring people forever a day nearer to its clutches. "I" begins to worry about when "I" will die, and feels overwhelmed by the dread and the horror of inevitable death. His mind turns blank, not because he has not lived as he should, but because of the fear of the emptiness that total annihilation will bring. The awareness of it is the most terrible of truths. Then the poet turns on the uselessness of religion the way no devout Christian would, and talks about the omnipresent invisibility of death, in a tone parodying Matthew Arnold's "Dover Beach," "That this is what we fear—no sight, no sound,/ No touch or taste or smell, nothing to think with,/ Nothing to love or link with,/ The anaesthetic from which none come round." The sense of despair stems from the knowledge that there is NOTHING we could do in face of the last onslaught of the Grim Reaper. It will happen if nothing else happens and nothing, even being brave, can pull us back to this side of the grave. This is very much Bertrand Russell speaking in the early years of the 20th century in his famous "A Free Man's Worship." Then the poem comes to its end: daylight breaks in, life resumes its daily routine, and it moves on despite his wavering, suffering mind. The impression the readers tend to come away with is that, although he cowers and suffers, he refuses to accept the inevitable and tries to live as if it was "business usual." This is a show of a moral victory as there is implied a kind of toughness and perseverance, a kind of indomitable spirit, not very far from Russell's "despairing courage." Thus the poem is still an aubade, a morning song to love and life, all right, though with an undertone of pain and fear tucked away beneath the surface there.

Donald Davie (1922-1995)

Donald Davie was an influential figure in the Movement years of the 1950s. As one of the first dissenters vehemently opposing the vogue of W. H. Auden, the Romantic Dylan Thomas, and the Empsonian or Metaphysical kind of poetry, Davie "rediscovered" the values of the minor 18th-century poets such as Cowper, Goldsmith, Crabbe, and Isaac Watts, and made these predominant for Movement poetry. He became a neo-Augustan. What impressed him about Augustan poetry was the intrinsic connection between its moral and formal concerns. Davie did not like the Modernist-Symbolist ideas about poetry; he showed his firm opposition to the Confessional poets like Robert Lowell, Sylvia Plath and Theodore Roethke and to the great masters such as W. B. Yeats and T. S. Eliot. However, he was very sympathetic to Pound's poetry, which he thought had been unfairly misunderstood, and he also wrote some poems akin to Confessional poetry in tone. His great influences were F. R. Leavis and Yvor Winters. His major works have been included in such volumes as *Brides of Reason* (1955), *Selected Poems 1950-1970* (1972), *Three for Water Music and the Shires* (1981), *Collected Poems 1970-1983* (1983), *To Scorch or Freeze* (1988), and *Collected Poems* (1990). Donald Davie taught in many countries like Ireland, Russia, and USA (At Stanford and Vanderbilt).

Donald Davie was conservative and traditional. To him the present—post-imperial Britain—is vulgar, confused, and devoid of virtue, and hope is "a sickly dream." Modern life is cramped with its "small and mean utilities." England needs to affirm the values of the past as it is now experiencing a serious moral decay. Davie also frequently discusses poetry, poets, and poetic forms. He believes that, in face of the philistine modern world, the poet has a clear social purpose to accomplish as a moralist (see for example his "Hypochondriac logic" in *Brides of Reason* [1955]). It is the job of the poet to write in a form that will help people get to know their place in the world and the general scheme of things better. Poetry is also a means of discovering universal truths and offering a space in the vast unknowable to accommodate "the man going mad inside...." He was a moralist all his life. Donald Davie was capable of self-criticism. While raving against the decadent London which he sees as a symbol of the depravity of the present, he is sober enough to know that depravity exists not just in the external world but also inside his head and heart. The readers of his "Revulsion" and "St. Paul's Revisited" (the 2nd part of "Depravity: Two Sermons") will readily see the point clearly.

Donald Davie's subjects mostly relate to England. He wrote to grapple with the reality of his time. Although he offers a variety of images in his works—elegant angels caught in song, the clink of coins in his father's pocket, or the jingle of harness when a horse moves, his poetry is often concerned with geography and history and as such is analytical, dry, and knotty. He is not easy to read as he can be obscure and baffling. Davie takes a huge interest in American culture as well. His works from his "Sequence to Francis Parkman" (1961) through the series "Goodbye to the USA," and also poems on English sailors like James Trevenen (on whom he wrote a 500-line poem) in America all reveal his sustained obsession with North America.

Davie insists that style should be connected with morality. The formal control of rhyme, meter, and syntax should help affirm moral values. His devotion to traditional forms was life-long and unflinching. His syntax is impeccable, and his diction chaste by and large though, with time, some relaxation has been observed. Davie's attitude toward language is clear. The key word he used in his first book of criticism about poetry is "chastity." He feels that language and syntax need purifying. The perfection of the word serves to strengthen social and moral law and helps man to come to terms with himself.

Donald Davie was a well-known critic. His critical works such as *Purity of Diction in English Verse* (1953) and *Articulate Energy: An Inquiry into the Syntax of English Poetry* (1958) did a lot toward helping establish the poetic values of the Movement poets. He was a passionate and truly caring critic of his time. Donald Davie as a poet and critic of importance of his time has not always been fully appreciated. He expressed his frustration at what he called "the inattentive world" when he said later in life that he wrote to the Glory of God which was the one and only justification for him. Faith became more and more important as he grew older. He was an example of intellectual courage and integrity of his age.

Thom Gunn (1929- 2004)

Thom Gunn is about the youngest of the Movement poets. He began his career as such, but has changed significantly both in theme and style over the years ever since. Gunn was educated at Cambridge and came under the influence of William Empson, R. F. Leavis, and the Metaphysical school of poetry. The Augustan virtues of moral responsibility and formal virtuosity, so pervasive in England in the 1950s, left its permanent imprint on his work, too. When he moved over to Stanford, California in the mid-1950s, he studied under Yvor Winters who drew his attention to the poetry of William Carlos Williams. In addition, there was the distinct American lifestyle, its unique cultural and social milieu with its sex, outdoor nakedness, and of course the LSD experiment that he did in the purely American atmosphere. All these were factors that conspired to work on his poetic sensibility. A change soon became visible. Although he has kept his traditional meters and rhymes, his subjects, his diction, and his vision of life and man have revealed clear Williamsian features. Thom Gunn has kept writing and publishing all these years. The volumes of verse include *Fighting Terms* (1954), *The Sense of Movement* (1957), *My Sad Captains* (1961), *Touch* (1967), *Moly* (1971), and *The Man with Night Sweats* (1992), to name just a few. Gunn's poetry in its development defies neat classification on the whole. He is one of those on the contemporary scene who touch people with the beauty of their art and the impact of their power. Gunn is one of the finest poets of his time.

Thom Gunn's is a very exquisite sensibility. He is not unlike Philip Larkin in his mode of poetic creation. Generally he observes life, and then contemplates and draws out the hidden moral that he feels exists in life and experiences. The sense of immediacy of the experience is often undercut by the sudden distancing that comes with the deliberation, but the poetic effort manages to exert a subtle impact on the readers' mind. Here we see the influence of the Metaphysical and the Augustan art at work.

Let's take a look at his "Considering the Snail" (1956) just for an illustration. The poet-speaker sees a snail trying to worm through a tunnel of wet grass blades all night. Drenched all over but moved by some desire and purpose, it has kept crawling and groping in the dark. The poet begins to wonder what power is propelling it forward as he thinks with admiration of "the slow passion/ to that deliberate progress" that the snail makes. Now the world of the snail looks like one devoid of compassion and camaraderie. Dark and rainy and full of unknowns like in "a wood," its world offers obstacles to progress. The snail is solitary; its survival and progress depend solely on its own effort and determination, but it struggles onward. The poem seems to point to two features of human existence, especially in modern life: aloneness, and the human resilience. It is hard to define which one of these is a more positive postulate for life. Aloneness, which constitutes a major condition of modern life, may be construed as negative in terms of human and social interrelatedness, but it could also be seen as an index to the human insistence on individuality and self-assertion.

The same tone is heard in a good number of the poet's early works, for instance, his works of the 1950s and early 1960s. "My Sad Captains" (1956) and "On the Move" (1961) stand close scrutiny as well as any other. The captains of the first poem here are warriors of a distant past. They do not appear to the mind of the poet until late at night when they begin to shine as stars. Their force may have been "wasteful," and their efforts may have been repeated, impetuous, and sad "failures." But these people have tried and lived and left a scratch on the stone of eternity. They still live "perfectly embodied" in the minds of people like the stars revolving "with disinterested/ hard energy." This is a paean to human striving. Failure or otherwise is neither here nor there in evaluating human lives. What matters most is the fact that living consists in striving. Like the snail braving the unknown before it, the captains of the past may not have gotten anywhere in their world of "chaos," but they had that desire, that passion, that drive, which alone defines the worth of human existence. The title denotes the warmth that the poet feels toward their memory and the sympathy with which he identifies himself with them.

"On the Move" (1957) is one of Gunn's most famous poems. Its colloquial American epitaph, "Man, you gotta Go [,]" bespeaks its theme well. Here we see a band of motorcyclists, in goggles and gleaming black jackets, keep on moving through town after town, detached from all around and completely on their own, belonging nowhere and reaching no destination. Unlike the blue jay that follows a hidden purpose, or the swallows that have a "home" in the trees and the undergrowth, these "[b]oys" have neither a clear purpose nor a place to rest. They are baffled, inarticulate, seemingly insignificant on the scene. In a world that is devoid of values, they hide their personality, keep their skepticism in check, and yield to their will to find the absolutes and define themselves. They seek their instincts and traverse a different route from those taken. If nothing is in sight, they believe they are getting nearer "by not keeping still." The young motorcyclists are restless because they are confused, disenchanted, and in discord with both nature and man. But they do not easily give up; they keep on searching. It may be a futile quest, but the effort helps assert their selfhood. For them moving is a positive course of action as it reveals determination, overrides doubt, and asserts man's sense of self-worth and dignity in face of chaos and negativity.

From the 1970s onward, some change has been observable in the poet's vision if not exactly in his style. His poem, "From the Wave," is a good example. Here the poet sees the surfers (or probably himself as one of them) riding on the wave and moving with it, and achieving triumph and possession. They curl their feet, balance their weights by imitating the wave, turning half wave and half men and turning into seals, and come back in success. The essential difference in vision between this poem and the ones discussed earlier on lies in this, that here exists the oneness of the human with the natural world, and the surfers have the support of the wave in their striving. They have to lose their identity a little, integrating and becoming one with the wave, but they manage to keep their minds as against "the mindless heave" of the wave and keep their distinctness when the wave loses its. This observation of Gunn's about human existence is significant because it deals with the paradox of the vexed relationship between the self and the world, and by extension between the self and the community. Self-assertion is essential, but is meaningful only against the backdrop of contact and fellowship, which signifies, sadly but unavoidably, the surrender of a portion of one's self.

English Poetry since the 1960s and 1970s

English poetry of the 1960s and 1970s was on the whole a reaction to the Movement poetry of the previous decade. It was a revival of a kind, an enthusiasm for Augustan poets. The poets of these two decades exhibited something in common such as attacking Movement poetry and being open to influences abroad like Robert Lowell, John Berryman, Ezra Pound, William Carlos Williams, and Wallace Stevens. The tension, that coheres in their works, between the strong influences of the native English styles (such as the elegiac and the Baroque) and those from outside, American as well as European (Modern and Postmodernist), proves to be a source of fascination to the readers. The major poets of the period are C. H. Sisson, Geoffrey Hill, Ted Hughes, and Charles Tomlinson. While the following discussion focuses on their works, mention should also be made of some younger poets who belong properly to a later period. We mean Tony Harrison (1937-) who writes about his own life and family experiences, James Fenton (1949-) who draws often from his war experience in Cambodia, Craig Raine (1944-), good with his unexpected metaphors, and John Stallworthy (1935-), noted for his themes of love and family with its joys and sorrows. The poetry of these poets is often humorous, satiric, and quasi-popular as they are anxious to reach a wide audience.

Charles Tomlinson (1927-)

Now we begin with Charles Tomlinson, one of the best poets of the period under discussion. Although not always comparable to poets such as Thom Gunn and Geoffrey Hill, Tomlinson has written impressive works. He has been sensitive to the influences of various poetic traditions and styles. These include, among others, Augustan poetry, Ezra Pound, Wallace Stevens, Hart Crane, and William Carlos Williams. Tomlinson is noted for his sensory observations, suggestive imagery, and moral insistence. He has published books of verse such as *Relations and Comforts* (1951), *The Necklace* (1955) and *Seeing Is Believing* (1958). A good Tomlinson poem would be "The Atlantic," a poem describing the motions of a wave. Here the poet begins with the onrush of the wave from the ocean toward the shore, its foam and its billowing, and its reaching the shore where "Unravelled now/ And the shore, under its lucid pane,/ Clear to the sight, it is spent." Then the poet relates how the wave interacts with the sunlight, "dyeing the uncovering beach/ With sunglaze," before it is pulled back to where it comes. The interesting thing to note about the poem is its ending. Having depicted the movement of the wave in minute detail and successfully drawing the attention of the readers to it, the poem seems to conclude on a meditative note, with a moral for the readers: "That which we were,/ Confronted by all that we are not,/ Grasps in subservience its replenishment." It sounds a little reproachful and somewhat edifying, reproachful almost in a Thoreauvian sense that people define themselves by external measures rather than internal, and edifying that they should locate resources for growth within themselves. Tomlinson talks about his growth as a poet in his *Some Americans* (1981).

Ted Hughes (1930-1998)

Ted Hughes was a prominent poet of the period. He was born in Yorkshire, and his father was a veteran from World War I. These facts became two important factors in his poetic career. Yorkshire with its crude and cruel natural landscape and the war with its atrocities and casualties both impressed Hughes' poetic imagination and decided in large measure his thematic concerns. Hughes' work deals in the main with existence. He focuses on the struggle for survival and the pain and suffering that come along with it. His world, especially in his early poetry, is one "red with tooth and claw," and there is not much of a hope there. [2]

"Pike" (1959) and "Relic" (1960) are good examples here. The first of these describes a world of horror. The pike are killers from birth with their "malevolent aged grin," stalking the marine world and terrorizing it. The poet kept three of these at one time behind glass and found, very soon, two of these swallowed by the other. And he found, on another occasion, two fish trying to swallow each other, "Two, six pounds each, over two feet long,/ High and dry and dead in the willow-herb—" because they spared nobody including their own kind: "One jammed past its gills down the other's gullet [.]" This resembles the world of "Relic," which is a fully drawn naturalistic one, where "The deeps are cold:/ In that darkness camaraderie does not hold:/ Nothing touches but clutching, devours." This is a world where jaws "go down jaws": there is no choice—either you eat or get eaten. The poet, having sighted a jawbone at the shore, contemplates over it and comes to realize a grim truth: "Time in the sea eats its tail, thrives, casts/ These Indigestibles, the spars of purposes/ That failed far from the surface. None grow rich/ In the sea. This curved jawbone did not laugh/ But gripped, gripped and is now a cenotaph." The jawbone had gripped and eaten others, but was gripped and eaten in the end, and became a monument of its own life and death. The connotation that we derive from many of Hughes' works like this tends to be that the world of nature is similar to and suggestive of human nature.

Ted Hughes' thematic focus is reinforced by his other volumes like *Crow* (1970) and *Moortown* (1979). *Crow* is a sequence Hughes started writing in 1966. The idea came from his acquaintance with an American painter who wanted Hughes to write about his drawings of the crow. Hughes made good use of the opportunity to illustrate his own ideas about the world and life in general. He weaves a story into his writings about the pictures: Nightmare is skeptical about God's wisdom of creating the world, and is challenged to do better. So Nightmare brings Crow into being to play with God. God and Crow then engage one another in different difficult situations from which Crow emerges more intelligent. The world of Crow is full of pain and anguish, and the occurrences here are often grotesque and brutal. Crow is an unpleasant creature, mean, aggressive, and violent, but he manages to survive the worst of any existential experiences. The readers tend to have mixed feelings toward Crow, feelings of both dislike and affection. Hughes probably suggests that there is something of the creature in all of us. The poems in *Moortown* do no less to body forth the poet's vision of existence. For example, the poem "Birth of Rainbow" portrays a world so harsh and cruel that survival would be a miracle. Rainbow is the name of a calf. It is so called because its mother happens to stand at the end of the rainbow at its birth. The place of birth is a snow-covered ridge. The time is when a hailstorm is coming. The calf gets born, the cow eats up the blood, and both are left to shift for themselves when the people run for shelter in face of a forthcoming storm. If rainbow signifies God's presence and His protection as it normally does to people, then the birth of the calf Rainbow occurs in the absence of both.

Geoffrey Hill (1932-)

Geoffrey Hill writes to reveal the extent of human suffering and the evil of the human heart. To him evil comes from the human heart. It is the heart that betrays and persecutes, and causes pain. Although he is capable of compassion, Hill's tone is generally harsh and condemnatory. He does not spare himself in his censure of human behavior.

Hill's poems are impersonal, objective, well-made artifacts. His syntax can be disjunctive. Some of his works reveal the imprint of American poets such as Allen Tate and Robert Lowell (especially in the latter's early works). The influence of the Metaphysical poets is clearly visible. One other important influence on him is William Butler Yeats.

Hill has a strong sense of history. He tries to establish a connection between the present and the legendary and mythic past. The past serves to illustrate how the present has come to be what it is, and how human nature and human behavior never seem to change for the better. Such works include, among others, "Of Commerce and Society," "Funeral Music," *Mercian Hymns*, "An Apology for the Revival of Christian Architecture in England," and *The Mystery of the Charity of Charles Peguy*. Hill's important poems in the 1960s are the eight sonnets in the sequence *Funeral Music*. Recording the statements of the people executed in medieval England, the poems harp on themes such as pain and despair, self-sacrifice, and belief in God. His *Mercian Hymns* (1971) possesses a mythical dimension that mirrors modern life.

Hill's concern can be religious as is shown in his sequences such as "The Pentecost Castle" and "Lachrimae." Take the first of the "Lachrimae" poems for instance. It is entitled "Lachrimae Verae." Here the speaker sees the image of the crucified Jesus and acknowledges him as the Savior of mankind. The fact that the image is holy yet man-made connotes an unwilling kind of skepticism that affects him. As a result, no matter how much he tries to be pious and devoted to His faith, he feels that Jesus cannot change and save him. Jesus or His image has no connection with his—human—soul. The man's dilemma here lies in this, that, along with his desire for faith, there is also his sober self-recognition that he is not changing for the better. Hence the emotional agony and a sense of helplessness that is built in the texture of the poem. As is usual with Hill, the style here is formal and ambiguously connotative.

Hill's "September Song *born 19.6.32—deported 24.9.42*" (1968) is a poem fully loaded both in meaning and tone. It is about the gassing of the Jews in the Nazi concentration camps. The fury is toned down so that what is left is simply a flat, almost matter-of-fact, narrative. As the poem says, one of the victims was a child who was born on June 19, 1932. The idea of the cruel existence for the child hovers silently over every line and every word. The poet's voice is muffled because he feels so overwhelmed and so aghast at man's inhumanity to man. The child's misfortune was all caused from the outset by its fellow creatures: he was first "undesirable" to his parents (probably) and then to his persecutors, the Nazis, definitely who, not forgetting and passing him over in their criminal plan, "touched" and "deported" him from this life. The usually joyous season (September) becomes murderous and the beautiful roses turn ruthless. There is no longer God's plenty; there is only more evil and pain than people can handle. The poet feels so much about the child's death that he thinks he has died: "(I have made/ an elegy for myself it/ is true) [.]" The fact is that the poet was born on June 18, 1932. In making an elegy for himself, he has made one for all of his own kind.

Tony Harrison (1937-)

Tony Harrison stands apart from his contemporaries in theme and style. His uniqueness has to do with his humble origins and his education in classics. He was born into a working class family in Leeds, yet received a good conservative education in classics at the university there that molded his stylistic taste. Both facts of his life sank deep in his consciousness and produced a tension that gave his poetry its distinctive identity. In subject and attitude, he is a working class poet, demotic and subversive; in style, he is classic with his iambs, couplets, his 16-line sonnets, which contrasts with and is often ridiculed (or seemingly so) by his subject. His most famous work is a continuous long sequence of poems entitled *The School of Eloquence* (1976, 1978, 1981, 1987).

Harrison is proud of his working class background. "Heredity" (1978) is a graphic illustration. It is a poem of two couplets. The first of these is apparently a reproduction of someone's question about the origin of his poetic talent. The query—"How you became a poet's a mystery!/ Wherever did you get your talent from?"—this itself is a composite of admiration and disbelief. It is direct and blunt, but not without a note of flattery, probably asked by a condescending middle class sycophant and snob. The second couplet is an answer caustic and poignant with a huge sense of pride: "I say: I had two uncles, Joe and Harry—/ one was a stammerer, the other dumb." The vehemence of the reply may suggest a mild degree of self-consciousness and self-defensiveness, which reinforces the note of pride.

And he is class-conscious. He knows that the working class has been "flayed, grey, mad, dumb," that "not one gentleman [who has made them suffer]'s been brought to book," and that "the tongueless man gets his land took" ("National Trust" [1978]). He knows that his father's class has been like "book ends" that "say nothing," and "worn out on poor pay," its life has been "shattered to smithereens." Though "a clumsy talker" who can only scrawl on an envelope, his father loves more deeply ("Book Ends"). The readers come away with the same impression after reading many a poem like this and like the one entitled "Marked with D." Harrison's love of his class is nowhere more evident than here in these

The School of Eloquence poems. So in his poetry, instead of "opening my trap/ to busk the class that broke him for the pence/ that splash like brackish tears into our cap" ("Turns"), he "the scholar" tries to be their tongue, their voice, "to bridge that gap" that books have created between them.

The most moving of his works deals with his relationship with his parents. He portrays the bond that existed between him and his parents in a heartwarming tone. The way he talks about his father in "Long Distance" (1981)—the old man's bereavement, his genuine love for his dead wife, his longing to join her in the other world, and his "dumb" way of handling his emotion—probably his incommunicativeness—reveals the intense love that the son feels for both his parents and his pride of having had them as parents. One thing to notice about the poem is its introduction, into poetry, of the colloquial speech, his father's working class speech. In his effort to speak for his father's class, Harrison often goes an extra mile to court the possible danger of formal awkwardness that the incongruity between subject and style may generate. The classy classic iambs contrast nicely with the uneducated speech they encase.

Seamus Heaney (1939-)

Seamus Heaney is, as some critics claim, "the best Irish poet since W. B. Yeats," and one of the greatest contemporary English poets. His work has been among the most profusely commented upon of his contemporaries. Heaney was born into a Roman Catholic family in Ulster, Northern Ireland and was educated at Queen's University at Belfast. He taught English at the University of California at Berkeley in 1970-1971 and read William Carlos Williams and Robert Creeley. In 1972 he moved to the Republic of Ireland where he stayed for a few years before he began teaching in various universities in England and the US. Now he is a professor at Harvard (since 1984) and also a professor at Oxford (since 1989). His volumes of verse include *Death of a Naturalist* (1966), *Door into the Dark* (1969), *Sweeney Praises the Trees* (1981), *The Haw Lantern* (1987), *Sweeney's Flights* (1992), *The Spirit Level* (1999), and a translation of the Anglo-Saxon epic *Beowulf* (2000). Heaney's thematic concerns cover such as his celebration of the rural people with their crafts and skills and their contribution to communal life, his native land's long history of invasion and violence from which he draws, and his search for salvation for his country as well as for himself as an artist.

Heaney writes a lot about the common people of his land. From the outset of his career he was determined to speak for the voiceless and the oppressed very much like Tony Harrison. The meticulous care with which he depicts their daily life and routine activity shows the deep love he feels for them. For instance, a blacksmith, working away at his forge, attracts the poet's attention. His observation of the forge is all inclusive, the old axels, the iron hoops, the hammer and the anvil's short-pitched ring, the sparks spreading out like a fantail, the hissing sound of the new shoe toughening in water, and the blacksmith diffusing himself into the different shapes of his products amid the dint which is music to the poet's ear. The blacksmith is gratified to hear the clatter of hoofs and know that he has done his bit to keep the "traffic flashing in rows" ("The Forge" [1969]). To the poet the forge possesses a metaphysical dimension of significance: it is a holy place with its anvil immovably set in the center as an alter; it is "a door into the dark," through which people explore the origin and mystery of human life. Another poem of his, "Digging" (1964), is vastly suggestive; it has been read as Heaney's statement of purpose for his career or his intention to excavate the past and history. But it could be understood on a mere physical level. It is a paean of the hardworking older generations. It was digging that they did, but they did it happily to perfection. And perfection in anything is not easy to come by. The middle bulk of seven stanzas out of the nine of the poem, all devoted to the minute description of the father and grandfather's labors, reveals the deep admiration and love Heaney has for his at once extraordinary and ordinary ancestors.

Heaney's "Mother of the Groom" (1972) is another poem showing his love and admiration for the common people. He observes them carefully and tries to bring the best virtues out of them. This work is simple but rich in meaning. At the wedding of her son, the mother naturally takes back stage. But the poet zooms in on her and envisions what goes through her mind. Amid the solemnity and the excitement of the occasion, the mother's mind is seen to switch back to the time when the groom was her little boy, bathing, kicking, and "[s]lipping her soapy hold." Now he is getting married, her lap is "voided," and she needs time to get ready and welcome her daughter-in-law. The poem ends praising her happy and permanent marriage and, by extension, her son's as well. The short poem brims over with so much love (motherly and conjugal), so much fidelity and warmth of human feeling, and so much of a sense of optimism about life past, present, and future, that hardly anyone could ever forget it once they have read it.

At one point in the earlier phase of his career, Heaney was a kind of political poet (although he has seldom treated the factional feuds of Northern Ireland directly). He came under a great influence in 1967 when he read the book, *The Bog People*, by P. V. Glob, a Danish archaeologist. The bog poems in his verse volumes—*North* (1975) and *Bog Poems* (1975)—reveal Heaney's deep concern with the suffering of the people of Northern Ireland. Glob's book, describing as it does how the bog people of Jutland were ruthlessly sacrificed to the Mother Goddess in the early Iron Age, offers a parallel which Heaney sees between the ancient rites and the human and material sacrifices that the "bog" of Northern Ireland has been making to "Mother Ireland." The fraternal war atrocities of the region have made the life of the people a veritable nightmare. One of his powerful poems denouncing such savageries is his "Casualty" (1979). A poor, honest, skilled fisherman is killed by the British Army's Parachute Regiment because he inadvertently breaks the curfew that the warring factions have imposed on the people: "He was blown to bits/ Out drinking in a curfew/ Others obeyed, three nights/ After they shot dead/ The thirteen men in Derry." The poem shows graphically how terrorized the fisherman and the people in general feel in face of death: "I see him as he turned/ In that bombed offending place,/ Remorse fused with terror/ In his still knowable face,/ His cornered outfaced stare/ Blinding in the flash." The poet feels despair and finds "a door into the dark" only in the self-exile on the vast expanse of the sea. But if he succeeds in escape out of the prison of his external world, he fails to get away from the internal prison of his self and his memory. He is more faithful than he imagines himself to be, for the dead fisherman lives in his mind, keeps asking why he is killed, and the poet is apparently at a loss as to what to say in reply.

A dominant thematic concern for Heaney is to find "a door into the dark" which is good enough for the redemption of all humans as well as himself. He seems to have found it in what he calls "displacement." One may have to be displaced the way Wordsworth was from one's good place of nurture and move to live somewhere else in order to retain sanity and help achieve salvation. Self-exile is a form of displacement whereby to find freedom. James Joyce and some of the other "familiar ghosts" from Heaney's own past or Irish literary history in *Station Island* (1984) offer him good advices in this regard. Joyce went away but returned a faithful émigré to his native land in his literary creations. This is "epiphany" for Heaney. Heaney does not seek escape in space. He banishes himself into time and imagination. Thus he writes about his land's history of violence and hopes to make the past usable as a foil and a mirror to the present. In poem after poem, such as "Shoreline," "Ocean's Love to Ireland," "Bog Oak," "For the Commander of the 'Eliza,'" and "At a Potato Digging," Heaney has been revealing the persistent horror of the human condition. In poems like "Punishment," "The Tollund Man," and "Bog Queen," the connection and comparison between the past and the present illustrate Heaney's overriding concern with the perennial tragic nature of human life. Heaney's flight into the past is also footnoted in his fascination with the legendary Irish king Sweeney.

In addition, poetry and imagination also offer the poet a place where to displace and relocate himself; and language can also be an avenue of self-exile. This is evident in the volumes of verse such as *Wintering Out* (1973), *North* (1975), and *Field Work* (1979). The image of self-exile on the sea in "Casualty" appears once again when the readers hear Joyce speak in the last section of *Station Island*: "... Keep at a tangent./ When they make the circle wide, it's time to swim// out on your own and fill the element/ with signatures on your own frequency,/ echo soundings, searches, probes, allurements,// elver-gleam in the dark of the whole sea." Heaney has been searching, probing, engraving his own signatures, and speaking on his own frequencies. Writing has become his way of coping and helping to cope. When read this way, Heaney assumes an immensely new magnitude as an Anglo-Irish poet.

Craig Raine (1944-)

Craig Raine is a highly imaginative and inventive poet. He is considered to be the leading figure in a group that has come to be known as the Martians, after the title of his second volume of verse, *A Martian Sends a Postcard Home* (1979).

Poet James Fenton (1949-) named them as "the Martians." The other famous name in the group is Christopher Reid. The Martians are ingenious in their poetic expression. They say things in ways totally odd to the readers. It is true that they set out to describe this ordinary world, but they end up making it out as if it were a strange and alien one. Reading Raine can be quite a demanding but delightful mental exercise. The effect is often funny and even ridiculous, but it is rewarding. Raine is fascinated with John Donne's work and is very much influenced by the latter's Metaphysical wit. His major influence is James Joyce whose "descriptive lust" holds a special appeal to his imagination. Raine's poems on his childhood and family bespeak the impact of Robert Lowell's *Life Studies* as well.

Craig Raine once wrote in his long poem "The Prophetic Book" about the acquisition of one's language: "I was lost in the labyrinth./ Language waited to speak/ and then I was home in my head,/ hearing the sound of Javanese, /catching the cadence/ of everyinthay ackwardsbay." As Craig Raine states, the word "Javanese" is part of a secret language invented and spoken by certain prostitutes, and this language of dislocated English serves at once to communicate and conceal when the prostitutes speak before their clients. The double nature of language has become one of the notable aspects of contemporary British poetry. As Raine sees it, every good writer invents the language for himself in order "to revitalize the outworn."

Raine is certainly inventive, experimental, and even idiosyncratic in his "descriptive lust." He suggests rather than tells in a blunt way. His poetry exhibits a tremendous amount of wit and ingenuity in the use of his singular metaphors. He seems to play with his readers with his magic wand of poetry that changes the familiar into the unfamiliar, deals out riddles, and demands their imagination to figure out the answers to these problems. In this way he manages to make a much deeper impression upon the readers' minds than by merely using the language and rhetoric already well known to them. "The Onion, Memory" (1978) is a good example. It is full of descriptions that border on elaborate riddles. The scenario here is that of a man revisiting his ex-wife. The couple walk the "old ground" together, which is another way of saying "recollecting life." The recollection is suggested rather than directly presented, embodied as it is in an odd but interesting formula of "objective correlative." They go through the old places where they used to go when still married: the road with its tractor ruts, the green commons, the village bakery, a hotel dining room, then going back home, with wind howling outside and jelly stored away in the fridge, doing what they used to do at home, one slicing onions and one sewing up dresses, recalling the past that makes the speaker feel sad, thinking how time steals by and life is unfulfilled. The poem ends up with the speaker stumbing into the washing on the line and imagining that he sees ghosts and death there. The mood is touching as it involves human softness in feeling and a pathetic desire that life cannot fulfill. It is in fact a tragic theme in the disguise of a grotesque, playful exterior form.

What merits attention is the imagery used in the poem. Here mud ridges are "tiny dinosaurs/ prehistoric, crenallated, cast/ between the tractor ruts in mud." The image of "the dinosaur" may connote the duration of their divorce or some degree of nostalgic backward glance. A boy swinging on a tree is "a junior Douglas Fairbanks [a famous actor noted for his daredevil feats in the 1920s]/ swinging on the chestnut's unlit chandelier [.]" Here the idea of abandon and joy without anxiety seems to be embedded. The spiked fence put up around the tree by the town corporation to forbid people to swing on it becomes "corporation spears." The grass on the green is "[g]reen, tacky phalluses [,]" the erotic image being probably a reminder of their first kiss there or doing something else intimate as lovers or indicating what they feel about one another at the moment. The dough going through the baking process is seen as a shortened human life journey from crib to coffin, suggesting the sense of transience, helplessness and regret that they have not done better in life. The flowers—the arum lilies and the gladioli—are all the beautiful images of the hotel maids waiting at the dinner table, where the uncooked herrings blink a tearful eye, the candles palpitate, and Russian violinists "bow and scrape" on the tape. The dining scene is a medley of joy and grief. The trees, sword grass, white thorns, all bow to force (of the wind) and control, and the jelly in the fridge seems to suggest order and self-control that bring a sense of balance. Now back home the couple make love, and grief and regret fill their hearts. The memory of the past reveals the humanity in both man and woman. The onion symbolizes memory probably because of its multiple layers and its lasting poignant smell. The ending of the poem is significant where the speaker sees the washing on the line as "headless torsos, faceless lovers, friends of mine." The image here is spooky and hellish, indicating that his day or probably his life would end in such a gloom. What is moving about "The Onion, Memory" is the tension between the funny art form and the serious subject that it tries to address. As the readers work through the knotted "metaphors" and feel constantly amused, they become slowly and steadily aware that beneath the jocular surface lies an emotional tangle: a painful nostalgia, a backward glance of yearning, a deep sigh of remorse, and a tragic sense of the irretrievability of the past and the emotional hell of the present.

The title poem of his second book, "A Martian Sends a Postcard Home," is Raine's signature work. It describes an alien's perception of the people and things in the world of earth. It is distorted and bizarre, but tremendously intriguing. This Martian sees everything familiar to the earthlings and describes it in a way that often requires an effort for humans to understand. So books are "Caxtons": the Martian is learned enough about the cultural history of England to know the name of the first English printer of books—William Caxton (1422-1491). The alien calls books "mechanical birds with many wings": "wings" is perhaps his way of saying "pages." The printed words and lines are the bird's "markings." As the Martian apparently does not know the words for *cry* or *laugh*, he says "they [books] cause the eyes to melt/ or the body to shriek without pain" when he should have said "they make people cry or laugh." The birds do not fly, however; they perch on the hand (or "held by the hand" as we may put it). This is followed by his descriptions of mist, rain, the automobile, and the watch and the clock, all immensely clever and bewitching puzzles to unravel. Then there is the telephone which is "a haunted apparatus" or "a ghost" in the home; answering the phone is "[carrying] it/ to their lips and soothe it to sleep/ with sounds." Nightfall is when "all colours die"; making love is "they hide in pairs// and read about themselves—/ in colour, with their eyelids shut." It is often a feat to decipher the Martian language which, capable of more than one interpretation, can jostle the readers out of their normal mode of seeing the world and reminds them of the benefits of diverse perspectives.

James Fenton (1949-)

James Fenton's is "a parsimonious brilliance" as some critics have put it. His output is small, but it is unique and powerful. His poetry is often "narrative," telling a story in a compressed way. It presents facts but refuses to moralize; Fenton would like the readers to digest those facts alone. This objectivity has to do with Fenton's interest in the world around him. The fact that he went as a journalist to Vietnam, Cambodia, and Germany in the 1970s and to the Far East in the 1980s has proved significant to his poetic creation. He has learned from those areas of intense human conflict and suffering about the negative side of the world and felt the horror of its darkness. Fenton is a consummate artist, his styles ranging all the way from open form to regular meters and rhymes. He can be obscure sometimes.

One of Fenton's most famous poems is perhaps his "A German Requiem" (1981). Although there is no direct reference to the Jews killed during WWII except for the names of the dead (ll. 49-50) and the oblique mention of "so many died" (l. 43) and Jewish Passover (ll. 63-64), it is meant to be an elegy to those innocent victims of the Nazi holocaust. The poem can also be seen as an indication of the poet's awareness of the transitorines of life (2nd stanza: ll. 12-24) and the inevitable, enduring menace of mortality. The sense of helplessness is so acute that people have to forget the shadow in order to enjoy the sun. In other words, there is so much pain for the living to face the dead that they "must forget" in order to move on. A requiem is a ritual, a special mass, to pacify the spirits of the dead. "A German Requiem" describes a ritual of this kind that helps people remember to forget so as to assign the souls of the victimized Jews to oblivion and eternal rest, and at the same time make it more possible to live their own lives. The poignancy of the poem stems not so much from the depiction of the details of the holocaust as from the agonized effort to desist from recollection.

The first three lines of the poem begin with a reference to the workmen leveling off the old "houses" and "streets" of the graveyard (an act made more obvious in the middle of the poem [ll.40-41]). The dismantling is an attempt to forget. The speaker is tongue-tied: "Oh, if I were to begin, if I were to begin to tell you/ The half, the quarter, a smattering of what we went through!" But he did not even try to begin to tell. The people find peace not so much for the dead as for themselves when they annually meet once or twice to remember in order to forget for the rest of the year ("How comforting it is, once or twice a year,/ To get together and forget the old times" [ll. 25-26]). They find it easier and better for the living to let go of the memory of the past (ll. 34-41). There is a touch of pathos both in the imagined reproach on the part of the dead for forgetting them, and in the sense of helplessness on the part of the living for having to come to terms with the fact in this way that their loved ones are dead ("It is not what he wants to know./ It is what he wants not to know./ It is not what they say./ It is what they do not say" [ll. 76-80]).

Another famous Fenton poem is "Wind" (1983), one that consists of four quatrains. The first stanza is well loaded. The opening line, "This is the wind, the wind in a field of corn," is physical enough, but what follows immediately gives the wind and the field of corn a metaphorical significance: the crowds fleeing from a major disaster down valleys and dry riverbeds (probably real-life scenes that Fenton saw with his naked eyes in his career as a journalist) appear to be the "corn" in the field subject to the threat of a ruthless coercive power of which "the wind" stands as a symbol. The nature of the disaster is anybody's guess. A nuclear holocaust has been suggested as apt enough to fit the category of "major." In fact, it could be anything that would present a "major" threat to human existence (such as biochemical weaponry). The second stanza further defines the wind as a rumor of "something" that threatens to bring "fire and sword" to the world and so horrifies its inhabitants. The next stanza is also rich enough to warrant more than one interpretation. For one thing, it seems to relate one of the speaker's own experiences: it could be a war scene that he witnessed. It could also be his vision of the primordial, probably biblical past when human discord first began. In both cases the notion is firmly embedded that human nature is not capable of change for the better. A thousand years is as meaningful and meaningless as two seconds in terms of human change as it never occurs. The last stanza touches further on human nature and the nature of human life. It raises a question that the humankind might become self-knowing enough to ask; the implication is that most probably they will not ask, as the very fact of asking indicates that they can become better. If they ever ask, the question is self-reflexive and self-critical; it is about the nature of the "smithy" of "the hilt of the sword": the evil sword was manufactured by the human mind and heart and was then out of control. As to the common run of mankind, they are the powerless "corn" at the tender mercies of the wind. The poem is a powerful indictment against human nature as the source of pain and suffering.

Chapter 25 Postwar Fiction

Postwar Fiction: A Brief Introduction

The war made everything different. Postwar Britain experienced immense changes. Democratization and socialization occurred, values were shifting, and class differences became less acute. Relative affluence was returning, and a "welfare" state was in the works. People tended to value the day-to-day experience and take it easy. It became apparent that the new period called for its own literary expression. The writers who had emerged in the prewar decades found the postwar mood no longer congenial to their imaginative endeavors. Some of them were losing critical favor; and some literary periodicals were shutting down. Literary tastes underwent some drastic change. High modernism with its formal innovations was felt to be out of date, and people began to look backward beyond Joyce and Eliot to a time, the 18th and the 19th centuries, when there was a good story telling in fiction. There was little demand for adventure but a strong desire for the traditional and the familiar forms.

The younger writers responded well to the daunting challenges of the time. The young intellectuals of the 1950s, very often coming from the bottom rung of the middle class, very often "scholarship boys," were the rising members of the lower middle class. They were normally iconoclastic and anti-established standards. Ambitious and disillusioned, they lashed out against contemporary society. In formal terms they were in revolt against the high literary ideals of modernism and wrote in a deliberately vulgar, comic, and satirical vein. They created characters that represented their radical, parochial attitudes and became known as "the Angry Young Men." The epithet, "the Angry Young Men," was originally a journalistic term used to describe a group of playwrights and novelists of the mid-1950s, but it has also come to refer loosely to the major characters that these authors have created. For instance, Kingsley Amis' Jim Dixon in his *Lucky Jim* (1954), William Cooper's Joe Lunn in his *Scenes from Provincial Life* (1950), and John Gerald Braine's Joe Lampton in his *Room at the Top* (1957)—all these, authors and characters alike, come under the label of "the Angry Young Men." John Wain and Angus Wilson were also connected with this group. John Osborne's Jimmy Porter in his play *Look Back in Anger* (1956), Alan Sillitoe's Arthur Seaton in his novel *Saturday Night and Sunday Morning* (1958) and Philip Larkin's John Kemp in his *Jill* (1946), all from the working class, fit well in here, too. Special mention should be made here of John Osborne's play, *Look Back in Anger*, which, giving manifest expression to the disaffection of the postwar generation, gave it the name of "the Angry Young Man."

In addition to these writers, there were quite a number of others working diligently on the postwar literary scene. These include, among others, Lawrence Durrell, William Golding, Doris Lessing, Iris Murdoch, C. P. Snow, and Muriel Spark. Mention should also be made of those writers who, although they made their presence felt in the 1930s, became really established in the post-WWII years. The names that immediately come to mind include Antony Powell, Joyce Cary, and Henry Green. In age they were of the 1930s generation, but they did their most important work in the 1940s and 1950s. Although few of the writers of the recent period have come up with masterworks comparable in stature to those of the 1920s, they have done their best to add to the success of English fiction. Some of the writers may not be included in the following discussion on account of the limited space, but it does not mean that they have achieved less in their careers. For instance, Joyce Cary (1888-1957), whose *The Horse's Mouth* has become one of the popular postwar novels, shows genuine concern with the creation of a work of art rather than with his personal views; Muriel Spark, "the Surrealist Jane Austen," is so called by some for her finest books—*Memento Mori* and *The Prime of Miss Jean Brodie*; and Angus Wilson (1913-1991) was not indifferent to the Modernist experimentation though basically not an innovator, his best work being *Anglo-Saxon Attitudes* (1956). For the discussion here we will choose a few of these for analysis and leave the rest to the readers' own discretion.[1]

Kingsley Amis (1922-1995)

Amis was an important literary figure of his time. As a novelist, he became a leading figure of the "Angry Young Man" group, and as a poet, he was considered to be one important member of the Movement poetry coterie. Kingsley Amis tried to explore the social problems of his age and developed his personal signature with time. Both funny and serious, presenting serious problems in a funny way, Amis became about the finest comic novelist to come out of the period. His kind of comedy leans toward black humor, and he has this knack of making his readers first laugh but then experience the pathos of the situation or the person that they laugh at. Amis is both good at choosing his comic subject and at its effective portrayal. His common practice is to draw caricatures by means of exaggeration, so that his characters often appear at once real and improbable. His plots are fascinating though often slim. When the decade of the 1950s was left behind, Amis had already made himself famous and rich, and as such he lost his aggressive satirical edge and stopped being neither young nor angry. His humor dimmed as well in time. Amis is a prolific writer. His major works include such novels as *Lucky Jim* (1953), *That Uncertain Feeling* (1955), *I Like It Here* (1958), *The Anti-Death League* (1966), *The Green Man* (1970), and *The Old Devils* (1986).

Lucky Jim is a satiric comedy. It spearheads its satiric edge against a world of fakes in which Jim Dixon lives. Jim is a new lecturer of medieval history in a provincial college. Coming as he does from a lower middle class background, he feels anxious to get on in life. He takes little interest in his area of focus, but loves to have a good time with pretty women and a few drinks. In his effort to move ahead, he has to put up with people whom he hates to have to deal with because they are all fakes. These include, among others, Professor Welch, a well-to-do, malicious, scheming academic, whose word can make or mar Jim's career at the college; Margaret Peel, a neurotic and self-serving lecturer, whose attachment makes Jim miserable beyond words; and Bertrand Welch, Professor Welch's son, a fake bohemian, a calculating lover, an aggressive social climber, competing with Jim both in love and job hunting. Jim is anti-intellectual, but he is intellectually thinking. The phoneyness around him drives Jim crazy. He is an angry young man. His disaffection leads to self-revelation.

But Jim seeks social arriving himself. In his eagerness to keep his job, he does things of which he may not feel proud in his moment of truth and awareness. These include such as writing an absurd article on medieval shipbuilding, trying to worm into the graces of Professor Welch by agreeing to extol the senior professor's views in his "Merrie England" lecture, and attending a cultural evening at the Welch's. There he meets Christine Callaghan, a spontaneous girl, whose uncle Julius Gore-Urquhart, a devotee of the arts, is looking for a private secretary. Bertrand pretends to be in love with Christine, but really uses her to help get Gore-Urquhart's job. Jim feels Christine's charisma and values her as a person more when she helps him to cover up the mess he causes in the house of the Welch's. They get close to one another, but have to part company under the pressure of Margaret and Bertrand. The college festival night arrives. Jim comes to lecture, half drunk, and makes a funny, irreverent speech that jabs at, instead of lauding, Professor Welch. Jim loses his job, but gets the position that Gore-Urquhart offers. As Christine has broken up with Bertrand, she is attractively available. Jim Dixon, the guy whose behavior borders on the ridiculous, looks forward to a gratifying romance. He is lucky indeed.

The characterization of Jim Dixon is a *tour de force* of Amis'. Jim is not really a much better person in behavior than the bunch of fakes around him. In fact he is a fake himself, capable of compromising his integrity. He does not want Margaret, but he could, even willingly, walk into her trap. He hates Professor Welch's guts, but he accepts his manipulation. He does not seem to deserve the luck that comes his way. What is saving in him, however, is his better nature, from which comes his self-knowledge. He knows that he is a sham himself, and feels bad about it. He has an inner world where he lives a self-critical life. He is slightly better because he is less false and more capable of self-mockery. Whereas the world around is all pretences, Jim manages to retain an ounce of spontaneous and authentic humanity, which tells him apart from those about him. In addition, Jim Dixon is brilliant in terms of intellection. His speech at the college festival shines with the refulgence of his intellectually thinking mind. Although he makes no big effort toward his success, he is thinking. So he knows about his world, and knows how to hit the nail on the head. He knows what to do and how to do it. He is half drunk, but it is exactly at such moments that he becomes strangely lucid, loosens up from traditional inhibitions, and intuits the verities of life in general and college life in particular. He is no fool as he appears to be. Incidentally, that scene has become Kingsley Amis' best creative effort, and one of the most unforgettably comic in recent literary history. *Lucky Jim*, with its farcc, acutc social observation, and linguistic subtlety all in one, has proved to be one of the great books to come out of the 1950s.

Amis is a pace setter for the fiction of his age. His Jim Dixon in *Lucky Jim* is an archetypal creation, a new hero for fiction. Graceless, yet sensitive and tough in contact with the phony, this character is a specimen of an angry young man, representing the whole group of fictional protagonists that were to people the novels of the time. In a very real sense, the fictional Jim Dixon also bodies forth the temper of the young generation of intellectuals of the 1950s, educated in grammar schools, struggling and disaffected, and angry in a world into which they had a hard time fitting. But as was the case with his creator, Jim Dixon is going through a phase of his life; people can predict with a degree of safety that with time he will get established and stop being young and angry. [2]

Lawrence Durrell (1912-1990)[3]

Lawrence Durrell was a novelist and a poet. As he lived mostly in the eastern Mediterrannean, his works are set basically there. His most famous work is his *Alexandria Quartet*, a work of magnitude to come out of the contemporary period. Critical opinions differ as to its value and permanence. Some see it as an ambitious work that fails to touch world masterpieces. Others regard it as one of the few creations of the period under discussion that come closest to being a major work. Whatever the case may be, it is apparent that it is not to be easily ignored. It carries weight in recent fiction.

The *Quartet* consists of four novels: *Justine* (1957), *Balthazar* (1958), *Mountolive* (1958), and *Clea* (1960). Overall, it is a bewitching story with its maze of interrelationships, its mystery of a political conspiracy unraveled in a slow, agonizing suspense, its plain and bold sexuality and voluptuousness, and all this happening against the backdrop of the beautiful, exciting, and decadent city—Alexandria. Its scope and its fast-moving pace hook and hold the readers at its tender mercies.

The four-volume novel tells a story of love and political intrigue. The time frame is about the 1930s and 1940s, some time before, during, and after the end of WWII. The major character, L. G. Darley, is an Anglo-Irish school teacher and a budding writer. Living in Alexandria, Egypt, he picks up wisdom in love and life and learns about the art of writing. His love life constitutes in a way his odyssey to self-realization and recognition of the need for art. This aspect of his experience is intricate and intriguing. Altogether he has three love affairs (the Greek Melissa, the Jewish Justine, and the French Clea), that is, not including one secret love with Amaril, a romantic gynecologist. The political side of the story relates to the espionage and counter-espionage between the Copts and the Muslims. The Copts plot to protect their interests against their enemies by providing aid to the establishment of Israel in Palestine. Darley is in fact a British agent as Justine is a Coptic one. At the beginning of the story, he prepares himself to become a novelist and write a "Once upon a time" kind of story. He meets Percy Pursewarden, a cynical English writer, who eventually becomes a mentor figure in his career. Darley takes an interest in Justine Hosnani, the Jewish wife of a Coptic banker and conspirator, and tries to get to know her through reading and writing about her and through physical contact with her. He has an affair with her and, when that fails, he withdraws to an island to meditate and sort out his experiences and thoughts. Justine both hurts and teaches him so that he gets ready to embrace art as a liberating force. He falls in love with Clea, a fellow artist, who leads him to selfless love. With Pursewarden and Clea helping, Darley matures as a writer.

One of the novel's major themes relates to love, sexual love to be more exact. Durrell himself leaves no doubt when he says of his work that it is an investigation of modern love. The *Quartet* is true to form full of sexual encounters. It is an exploration of sex in all its aspects. The presentation of its variety is such that people tend to get the impression that the world of Durrell's Alexandria is one of total depravity and decadence. There are, for instance, Darley sleeping with both a mother and her daughter; Justine being promiscuous beyond description; husbands permitting wives to have affairs; a brother committing incest with his sister, and so much more of other kinds of perversity. In addition, there are cross-dressing homosexuality and lesbianism, both behaviors being frowned upon as aberrant at that time. Alexandria, a beautiful fairyland as it is portrayed, looks to a detached reader-observer like the biblical God-condemned Gomorrah or Sodom.

Durrell's characters are almost all of them steeped in this debased and debasing milieu, and almost all of them are hopelessly egocentric. They love themselves more than anything else. Their sexual love seems to be a kind of quest for the salvation of their selfhood, rather than as a means to connect with their fellow creatures and the world in general so as to endow their lives with meaning. Such a kind of love fails because it never goes beyond the physical to reach the spiritual plane, and it limits more than liberates the humanity of the "lovers." No love in the whole of the *Quartet* has produced any positive effect on anyone's life. A good example is Justine. She is cursed as it were with "the Check," which is a helpless inability to feel. This may have been caused by her harassed childhood when she was poor and raped, and by her debilitating experience as a child prostitute and the loss of her child. As a result she seeks cure through sexual encounters with men and does not succeed because she is motivated by self salvation. Durrell seems to suggest that physical sex does not help toward ameliorating the human condition. Some other avenue will have to be sought and found.

This leads to the second, perhaps the more important theme of the *Quartet*: art as a way leading to salvation. Indeed, Durrell makes the point very clear through his artist characters. There are quite a few of them, trying to solve the mystery of life and find the truth about it. There is Justine's first husband, Jacob Arnauti, who tries to probe into Justine's psychic world through writing about her. His book, *Moeurs*, fails in its purpose because his perception is marred: he overlooks Justine's wound left by the death of her child. There is then Darley, the young writer, who does not always comprehend what he observes. Pursewarden's notebooks indicate that Pursewarden, the novelist, suffers from and becomes well aware of the pain of physical self-love. So he is able to "tell [his] ego to go to hell" and sees truth through art. As he writes, his personality grows and ultimately transcends his art. His is to Durrell the vision of the artist as seer. Clea, relating herself to Justine (love) and Pursewarden (art), locates herself in between and beyond, manages to achieve the unity of love and art and live beyond both, and thus best exemplifies Durrell's theme, that art purifies; it manures the psyche; and it is the only way to fulfillment.

William Golding (1911-1993) [4]

William Golding was born in Cornwall. When still young, he took an enormous interest in literature and read a good many works. He went to Oxford, where he received his BA in English literature, and later taught literature at a Salisbury school. After the war, he began writing, and his first book, *Lord of the Flies*, established him as a rising star on the scene and paved the way for him to win the Nobel Prize in 1983. Instead of talking about the war, Golding's novel describes a group of boys working out their lives on an isolated island. In later years Golding wrote quite a few stories along roughly the same line. One thing interesting to note about these is their settings. The stories are set usually in a place far from "the old world": either on a wild island (like *Lord of the Flies* [1954]), or on a rock in the Atlantic (as is *Pincher Martin* [1956]), or in a primitive world (as is *The Inheritors* [1955]), or a medieval town (as is *The Spire* [1964]). Golding's vision is consistent. He would like to examine man's weakness in anatomic precision. His insights have been eye-opening enough to warrant the awarding the Nobel Prize on literature to him.

William Golding's theme is the dark side—or evil—of human nature. *Lord of the Flies* is the most adequate illustration of the point. The story is simple in plotline. A group of boys ages 6 to 12 are left on a desert island as a result of a plane crash. Completely on their own in a world where there is no adult guidance and supervision, the children begin to take life into their own hands. As they differ on the issue of how to live as a group, they take different courses of action. Ralph, the leader figure, would like to establish law and order, but Jack Merridew wants to go hunting and killing. He forms his own separate group and leads some boys away. Soon the two distinct notions of life and modes of behavior come to clash with one another, and things begin to happen at an amazing rapidity. First Piggy gets killed by Roger, Jack's "executioner." Then Simon is murdered. Jack gets the upper hand, and Ralph has to hide himself to run from his hot pursuit. The twins,

Sam and Eric (known as Samneric) are threatened with torture if they refuse to tell on his whereabouts. Jack's gang sets the island on fire in order to drive Ralph out in the open. The fire catches the attention of a passing ship, which then comes over to stop their barbarism and take them back to their country.

William Golding prefers his story to be called "a fable," which it certainly is. A fable is a veiled story about the truth of human existence. It is generally, as is the case with *Aesop's Fables*, timeless and placeless because of the universally applicable nature of the verities revealed. Goling's fable here is one about the nature of man. Instead of recreating and replicating their civilized way of life in a new, bleak environment as Robinson Crusoe does, the boys of the *Lord of the Flies* simply return to the primitive, pristine state of human existence and mentality, and repeats the dark, tragic side of human history of tyranny, violence, fanaticism, intolerance, and confrontation. Thirsty for power and blood, and resorting to barbaric rituals and superstitions, they fight and kill each other, thus revealing the naked heart of darkness that exists at the center of their beings. This may be called in Christian terms "Original Sin" or simply evil, which resides as part of the human consciousness and breaks out loose to do irreparable damages whenever and wherever possible. This is probably what the title of the book means. Whatever forms it takes in the novel—"the Lord of the Flies" may allude to the biblical Beelzebub or the Greek mythic Zeus or the tattoo that Jack and his group have come to worship, it is the devil figure, the souce of evil, and the story of the *Lord of the Flies* is just about this devil that lives in all humans.

The technical aspect of the book is also interesting to talk about. One conspicuous feature is its symbolism, which is multiple and complex and capable of more than one interpretation. In addition to the title, there are the boys to consider. Though naive because not fully initiated into the adult world yet, the children are not innocent in the Adamic sense: Adam and Eve do not have any knowledge, but the boys do. They represent clear categories of human attributes. Ralph is clear reason incarnate, Jack primitive passion, Piggy moral awareness, and Simon conscience and thinking. In these terms their interaction assumes the immediate significance of a society in operation, or a miniature of it. As their behavior becomes atavistic and their passion overwhelms their reason, human degeneration and dehumanization occur. Piggy's death signals the boys' loss of control over their lives and returning to barbarism, and Simon's murder, or the death of conscience, marks the beginning of the reign of darkness. Individual events are symbolic as well. Ralph's obsession of keeping a fire going is, for example, highly meaningful: it can be a sign of hope of rescue and eventual survival. Then there are Piggy's glasses. That he loses them one at a time indicates the boys' gradual loss of values and sense of direction.

The basic tone of *Lord of the Flies* can be different to different readers. One interpretation may see it as not totally pessimistic. The story tells a truth, one that keeps haunting the readers, but it does so to warn and alert them to a brutal fact about man and his life that humans tend to ignore and forget. It does not mean to denigrate the human race; as a matter of fact, the end of the story connotes some hope of surviving well and good. The boys fail to behave better, as the captain of the rescuing ship says, but there is room for improvement as they are allowed to live and learn. There is reason to imagine that, once they merge back into the civilization from which they were wrenched off for a while, the boys may become more responsible and conscionable. On the other hand, however, a different perspective would be to see it embody a different kind of outlook on man and his world: If one sees the boys' desert island as a microcosm for the human world, of which the rescuing adults are a part, then the next question, rhetorical by and large, would be, who is going to stop the adults grabbing at each other's throats if evil continues to grow in their hearts? Golding tries to tell the dismal truth about this side of the human situation in the form of a fable, which renders it timeless and placeless for the readers.

Doris Lessing (1919-) [5]

Doris Lessing is one of the most successful prolific British novelists of the recent decades. She was born in Persia of British parents and lived in Rhodesia (now Zimbabwe) until she settled down in England in 1949. Basically a realist, she took interest in writing in the mythic mode in the 1970s. In the 1980s she reverted back to the realistic mode, though still exhibiting some traces of fantasy at times. Since the 1990s she has been writing a good number of short stories. Doris Lessing's themes are wide and varied: social problems, political concerns, racial questions, and feminist views on life and love relationships, but she focuses mostly on black-white relations and on the life of the woman in a male-oriented world. Her commitment to life and society is evident in all her fiction. Her major works include the five novels of her Children of Violence series (1952-1969), *The Golden Notebook* (1962), *Briefing for a Descent into Hell* (1971), *Canopus in Argos: Archives* (1979-1983), *The Diaries of Jane Somers* (1983-1984), *The Fifth Child* (1988), and many volumes of short stories such as *A Man and Two Women*.

Doris Lessing's best known work is her novel, *The Golden Notebook*. It is about a middle-aged woman's experience in a man's world. Anna Freeman Wulf is an expatriate single parent with a 13-year-old daughter, Jane, to support and depend on emotionally. A writer of a commercially successful book on the royalties of which she lives, she keeps four notebooks, one an account of her life in Africa, one a record of her days as a communist, one in which she creates a female character, Ella, as her alter ego, and one that covers her present life experiences and thoughts. Anna's best friend is Molly Jacobs, a Jewish actress, also a single parent, whose adult son is blind from his suicide attempt and tries to make everyone miserable. Molly was once involved in communist cultural activities. Anna and Molly are close and try to work it out in a world in which life for women is a struggle. Anna's American boy-friend, Saul Green, can be a difficult person, but he proves to be a source of support for Anna. Both Anna and Molly try desperately to find meaning in relationships as well as in social work.

The characterization of Anna is a feat in fiction, beautifully done through the medium of the four notebooks and the supportive portrait of Molly. First, the notebooks help reveal Anna's personality graphically. One of these tells about her political experience: she has been a liberal, a communist, and a disillusioned idealist. One other portrays her as an individual: independent, free, and wishing to attain the freedom that the male gender enjoys in life. One third shows her engaged in self-scrutiny: placing herself as Ella in an imagined scenario, and examining the Anna-Ella parallel for self-searching. Ella is Anna in disguise. She looks like her creator, living through similar experiences— a writer, divorced, depressed, and on the brink of collapse because of a failed relationship. Ella suffers disorientation and is saved by a new attachment to an American. Anna's imaginative effort offers a chance of distancing herself from the confused mess of her real life and seeing things from a different approach. Then, there is Molly, her duplicate of sorts in actual life, warm, vibrant, sharing the same convictions and struggling for self-realization. The two women lean on each other. Anna ends up achieving salvation both in life and in writing. In a way the portrayal of Anna represents Doris Lessing's independent-minded response to women's life in the modern world.

The novel is structurally intriguing. It reads like a novelist writing about a novelist, with stories within the story and novels within the novel. Each of the notebooks is divided into four sections, the last of which forms part of the major portion of the book, and the major portion is prefaced with a "Free Woman" section. There is another section in the book, also called "The Golden Notebook," which attempts to weave the disparate narrative threads about the different Annas in the four notebooks into a recognizable web. The novel ends with a "Free Woman" section. It sounds complicated, but it works well for structuring the development of the story.

Iris Murdoch (1919-)

Iris Murdoch was born in Dublin, Ireland and grew up in the suburbs of London. While still at Oxford, she began to help edit periodicals. She was a radical and joined the communist party at one time. Later she worked in the United Nations and traveled to Europe, where she met Satre, the French existentialist author-philosopher and came under his influence. She devoted herself wholly to writing in 1963, and has been very prolific. So far she has written over twenty novels such as *Under the Net* (1954), *The Sandcastle* (1957), *The Bell* (1958), *A Severed Head* (1961), *The Black Prince* (1973), and *The Sea, the Sea* (1978). Murdoch is a philosopher-writer.

The Bell (1958) is Murdoch's fourth and finest novel. It is an artistic rendering of myth and reality well intertwined. As the story goes, middle-aged Michael Meade establishes a lay religious community at his ancestral estate, Imber Court, close to the Imber Abbey of which Mother Clare is the abbess. It is by and large a community of misfits, social or spiritual or both, soul-sick and at odds with the world. These include Nick and Catherine Fawley, twin brother and sister in their late twenties, Toby Gashe, a boy of eighteen about to go to Oxford, Paul and Dora Greenfield, the unhappily married couple, and James Tayper Pace, an energetic settlement worker (the only exception here as he is a man of faith). Meade was once a schoolmaster and had a homosexual relationship with his pupil Nick Fawley. When he sees Toby in the group, he fails to resist the temptation to kiss him. This infuriates and saddens Nick. Young Catherine, a neurotic, about to become a nun, loves Meade in secret. Young Dora, who has been away because unhappy with her marriage, comes to join her middle-aged husband, and learns about an ancient legend. As the legend goes, a 14th-century Imber nun took a lover, the Imber Abbey was thus placed under a curse, and the bell of the Abbey fell into the lake. Meade's community, believing a new bell would do it good, plans to install one. Then Toby discovers the old bell by accident and schemes with Dora to replace the new bell with the old one. They inadvertently sound the old bell and foil their own design. The bell installation ceremony is not to come off anyway because Nick plots for the new bell to fall again into the lake. The community disintegrates. Catherine survives her suicide attempt but becomes mentally weak. Nick commits suicide. Toby is sent home. Mother Clare and Pace dissolve the Imber Court. Meade leaves for London, and so does Dora for a new chapter in her life.

The major theme of the novel is love, or failure of love. The major characters are Michael Meade and Dora Greenfield, the one representing the failure of love and the other the saving grace of love. Both survive the dissolution of the Imber Court community as they are awake to the importance of love in life. Meade is a good man. He had studied for a religious call, but when he was schoolmaster he was led into a homosexual relationship by his pupil, Nick Fawley, and lost his chance to become a priest. Now Meade establishes Imber Court and sees it as a fulfillment of his religious aspiration. As he is afraid of his sexual orientation, he fails to offer love for Nick Fawley, now a 28-year-old drunkard. Nick is the evil figure in the group. When still a boy, he cost Meade his vocation. Now at Imber Court he takes Toby to task for attracting Meade's attention and for planning with Dora to reinstall the old bell. He attempts to frighten his sister from entering the nunnery and thwarts the community's effort to dedicate the new bell. Rejected and rejecting, he commits suicide eventually. Meade feels infinite remorse for his death. Another person around Meade is Nick's sister Catherine, whose girlish love for Meade is doomed. She tries to drown herself and becomes mentally unstable. Meade accepts all the responsibility for her. He is harshly censured by Pace and learns a moral lesson from the end of his community. Now as to Dora, she is a loving person and enjoys being loved. She represents the life impulse in the novel along with Mother Clare. As her husband mistreats her, she leaves him, has an affair with a reporter, and then comes to Imber Court. There she is not appreciated for her views and her physical aliveness, and she is critical of others and the nuns in the Abbey nearby. She tries to help install the old bell and saves Catherine from her suicide attempt. Ultimately she learns from her experience at Imber Court, stops running from her failed marriage, and starts a new life as an art teacher.

The thematic focus of the novel is probably the idea, that love saves. Its fitting symbol is the bell, with the inscription on its rim—"*Vox ego sum Amoris. Gabriel vocor* [I am the voice of love. I am called Gabriel]." The bell embodies a curse—suppression of love—which only love can remove. As it is "the voice of love," its burial at the bottom of the lake suggests the absence of love in the community, which may be the root cause for the spiritual sickness affecting the members there. Its projected reinstallation indicates the members' growing awaremess of the importance of love and their dire need for it. They would like to become normal and merge back into the life of general humanity. The ancient story of the bell, which has survived the obliteration of time, may connote the fact that love is highly necessary for the spiritual wellness of all people of all time and that the community needs nothing else as the effective cure for its disease. By the same token, the failure of the reinstallation is pregnant with meaning, too. On the one hand, it means that love is not easy to come by and that regeneration is a difficult undertaking, while on the other, it is also educational to those anxious about renewal and eager to turn over a new page in life. One of these people is Meade, who becomes a better person. The other is Dora, who has now a new life to look forward to. The tragedy of the twin brother and sister is a moral story about love and life as well.

The novel is unique in terms of characterization. One question to ask is, whose novel is it? Is it Dora's or Nick's or what? It is about both, but ultimately it is really more about Michael Meade. Meade is a good person suffering from spiritual and physical self-denial. He needs to pick up some essential qualities in order to heal himself and become whole. Mother Clare acts as a spiritual guide. She is the affirmer of faith and selfhood on the basis of her love of God, who inspires Meade to establish the Imber Court, and whose nunnery in its close vicinity forms a foil to Meade's court in self-fulfillment. Dora is a mentor figure for Meade as well. Full of enthusiasm about life, she offers an example of living in a vital and vibrant manner, independent in opinion, free of inhibitions, and believing in staying truly alive. Nick is Meade's warner, his negative mirror image, who teaches him to act differently. As he is basically a man of faith and an eager and perceptive learner, Meade is able to grow in self-knowledge and moral strength and survive the traumatic experience of his life.

John Wain (1925-)

Wain is one of those postwar novelists who turned away from the prewar craze for experimentation and went back to the 18th-century tradition of a good story-telling. His concern is with the life of the present, where he tends to find man wanting in dignity and moral worth in face of adversity. His vision of life is basically tragic, that life is suffering and survival is difficult. His plot is solid and peopled with well delineated characters. Very often his hero is a modern man, a sensitive rebel, yet an effete person not dynamic enough to chart out the course of his own life. Such is the case with Charles Lumpley in his first work, *Hurry on Down* (1953). Charles is very much like Kingsley Amis' Jim, not happy with his life, hating his lot, and resenting all that is middle class and commonplace. He drifts through life, changing jobs as his survival requires, and getting what he needs by means fair or foul. He is, in a word, a picaresque hero, basically kind and malleable enough to cope with the "slings and arrows" of the world. The novel borrows from the 18th century two important narrative tricks: the structural device of chainning events together and the authorial intrusion. A similar rebellion against established values occurs in *Strike the Father Dead* (1962). Here the father, who is a professor of classics and a token of pre-war values, represents tradition, and the son, Jeremy Coleman, is not happy under his thumb. The young man wants to be a jazz pianist and live a life of his own. He struggles, succeeds in life, and learns about it.

Wain's most tragic novel is probably his *The Pardoner's Tale* (1979). The book entwines two stories well in one artistic framework: the first-person narrative of Gus Howkins, an elderly man estranged from his wife, and a third person story about the major character, Giles Hermitage, a writer working on the Howkins story. A sensitive, lonely individual, depressed and spiritually poor, and assailed by a deathwish, Giles Hermitage tries to survive through art. As a novelist, he endeavors to make sense of his life and the world through his creations. He gets in contact with a woman, Mrs. Chichester-Redfern, whose experience in life is similar in nature to his and who would like to get some answers to her questions about her life through art as well. She would like the novelist to write a story in which her husband, who had deserted her, would feature as a suffering individual. She is clearly the emblem of the death force. Her daughter, Diana, is her opposite. She accepts life and is lively, jumping from one man's bed to another, and feeling fulfilled. At the bottom of Diana's life, however, something vital is missing, too, as her life is pure existence, with no intimacy, not much of an attachment, but a good deal of alienation and the feeling of being all bottled up in her own cosmos. The whole novel is set in a gloomy milieu of sterility and meaninglessness. Wain is very postmodern in spirit.

John Fowles (1926-)

Fowles is at once a popular and a serious novelist. He never fails to fascinate his readers; reading him can always be an enjoyable experience. His stories are basically traditional in nature, or love stories in its various forms, that present little or no obscurity in comprehension. However, the way he writes his novels merits particular attention. There seems to be some kind of pattern that underpins his stories: the hero undertakes a quest, with the guidance of some wise man, and finds the woman he loves and becomes spiritually whole. Fowles' major novels include *The Collector* (1963), *The Magus* (1965), *The French Lieutenant's Woman* (1969), *The Ebony Tower* (1974), *Daniel Martin* (1977), and *Mantissa* (1982). Fowles has also written a miscellany of other things such as poetry, short fiction, essays, and philosophy.

Although critics have seen his formal experiments in different ways, Fowles has been, in a very serious sense, regarded as a postmodernist novelist. He enjoys experimenting with a number of important things relating to fiction such as points of view, the notion of time, metafiction, parody, the ways a story ends, and emphasis on his characters' efforts to internalize their harrowing experiences.

Let's take a close look at his most famous novel, *The French Lieutenant's Woman*. The story is set in Victorian England. Charles Smithson, the protagonist, is a true-to-form Victorian gentleman, expecting to inherit a title and wealth from his uncle and get married to a rich young lady—Ernestina Freeman. Then he meets Sara Woodruff, a woman of disrepute, who is said to have been a mistress for a French lieutenant. Hence her nickname, the French lieutenant's woman. She is unusually pretty and her gloom adds remarkably well to her attraction. Charles seeks the advice of a doctor—Dr. Grogan, the prototype of a modern psychologist, and learns more about her. He feels so irresistibly drawn to her with time that his passion soon amounts to obsession. He has an affair with her in a hotel and becomes the object of the vicious scandal that his servant spreads about him. The event discredits him thoroughly in the eyes of his leisured class, so that he is ruined and ostracized. When he packs up and goes to the hotel for Sara, however, he is dismayed to find her already gone. Then he spends a long time and does everything humanly possible to search for her and finds her eventually. The story ends, as the book suggests, in more ways than one: one of these, happily, as the two reunite and live happily ever after, and one other, in separation, when Sara rejects him, not even telling him that she has borne him a daughter. Other suggestions for possible endings include Charles' vision of his marrying Ernestina and the author's narrative scheme to have him die in the course of his quest.

The characterization is unique. Charles, not happy with his life, good and well provided as he is, embodies the nascent self-awareness of the modern man. He may not know what he wants exactly, but he is searching. The fact that he feels the monotony of his humdrum existence is an evident signal that he is thirsting for change. At first he may just experience this feeling at the subconscious level of his being, but he becomes increasingly aware of his emotional quandary when he comes in contact with Sara Woodruff, who proves to be an odd fascination that he finds impossible to shake off. Then when he meets her again at the mysterious

Undercliff, he is hopelessly carried away. He feels the magnetism of her tug so much that he forgets everything—his proper behavior, his commitments, and his future—just so as to enjoy the self-gratification that the moment can offer. Thus torn between his love for the rich yet conventional Ernestina and the mysterious, irrational, but erotically captivating Sara Woodruff, he experiences a fall and a rise, a fall from his present secure status and a rise to the attainment of his full self-knowledge and psychic maturity. Although he suffers total disgrace and isolation, he feels good and happy and would have lived for the rest of his life in perfect contentment had Sara not deserted him. Charles is a bundle of contradictions. On the one hand, he is rational enough to know that he should marry Ernestina and keep his position, while on the other, he is emotionally drawn to the unknown course of life to which Sara is pulling him. He has his internal fight and decides to take the road not taken and brave the dangers of a new world ahead. His quest for Sara is actually a quest for self identity.

Sara attracts a good deal of attention. She is a sensitive woman, with an independent spirit. She may even be seen as the prototype of the emerging modern woman, or a precursor to feminism. She chafes in her social bracket, and struggles to assert her presence. Sara does not care about what society thinks of her, but enjoys the licence that the stigmacious title "the French lieutenant's woman" gives her. She is, in the opinion of her society, already a whore, the lowest of the low among women so that society cannot be just and good to her anyway. Whatever she may do would not help with her life in it because she is already "formulated" like a helpless insect "sprawling on a pin." That is at least one of the reasons why she lets the slander about her being a prostitute spread and refuses to do a single thing about it. She behaves in her unique way, be it with the sanction or censure from society. It is not that she envies anyone; that would have placed her in a very conventional pigeonhole. She is contented with her obscurity and feels even superior to the privileged women like her employer, the pretentious Mrs. Poulteney, or the spoiled brat of a wealthy heiress, Ernestina Freeman. To some of her contemporaries like Dr. Grogan, she is a psychological enigma, or mentally unstable. Her sexual encounter with Charles may be motivated more out of self-assertion and self-satisfication than out of anything like love. In view of her social position or her attitude toward life which is largely negative because life is cruel to her, she may not be ready or able to love Charles as a spouse figure in her life. Her melancholia indicates her hostility toward the class-oriented, male-Chauvinist society of her time and her incompatibility with it. It is impossible for her to feel good and at ease there unless there is a change in its nature. Sara would like to demonstrate to the leisured class that she is not only a human being but a better one than the whole bunch of them put together. Her disappearance can be a declaration of her female independence from the patriarchial social order and her overall victory over all the parasites that she has left behind.

The novel is metafictional in more than one way. Metafiction, a postmodernist form of writing about fiction in the form of fiction, is a style of fictive narrative that tries to tell the readers that fiction is fiction and is not an illusion of reality as the realists have tried to "deceive" the readers into believing. All through *The French Lieutenant's Woman*, the author keeps telling the readers (and throwing in all sorts of reminders such as Hitler, radar, and TV) that, although the story is about Victorian England, his is a fictional story, not a reality. Furthermore, contrary to traditional realists who try to make their fiction look like reality, metafiction writers feel skeptical about the idea of authentic representation of reality and write novels not so much to tell a story as to shock the readers' expectations. In this connection, they tend to use burlesque and parody as a means of subverting the readers' sense of complacency. Burlesque or parody is a manner of writing in which an effort is made to imitate an original in order to poke fun at it or to reveal the discrepancy between the imitation and the original. The story of *The French Lieutenant's Woman* is an obvious parody of the Victorian, traditional realistic, narrative method; it is good story telling until the author feels the urge to jog his readers out of their comfortable mode of reception and their anxious search for the real story. He does this by alerting them to the fact that their search will end in failure as there is nothing like the real story. Thus, as noted earlier on, the novel offers a number of endings instead of only one, just to make it difficult, if not entirely impossible, for the readers to locate and pin down the real story.

Now the ending of the story of *The French Lieutenant's Woman* is interesting because confusing to some readers. Out of the few options that the author has provided, there are two notable endings that we may examine in more detail. The happy conclusion of the story occurs when Charles, after a persisitent painstaking search, finally finds Sara and their daughter Lalage. They unite and live happily together ever after. This should have satisfied the taste of the Victorian readers, who attached importance to wholesome social functioning and family values. But Fowles' are contemporary readers, who are well aquainted with the modern philosophies such as nihilism and existentialism and have been through the baptism of modern life. The tragic ending may be provided to cater to their relish. It is interesting to note that the story itself has already prepared the readers for a tragic resolution. First, the woman Sara is not portrayed as a Victorian woman pure and simple. She is endowed with the qualities of the new, modern age, which is just around the corner in the new century. She does not like the idea of marriage and rejects Charles' offer. Then the man Charles, seasoned as he is with all life's experiences, is no longer a Victorian gentleman pure and simple, either. He has become an independent individual standing right at the threshold of the modern time. In face of Sara's rebuttal, he makes his own choice, accepts the situation and leaves graciously, and turns over a new page in his life.

Alan Sillitoe (1928-)

Among the writers of "the Angry Young Man," Alan Sillitoe stands out as particularly unique in his thematic focus. He writes exclusively about the life of his class, the working class. He seems to have inherited the tradition of the proletarian writers of the 1930s and embraced the contemporary "new left" current of thinking that seeks to keep the working class aware of its own identity in face of modern temptations and distractions. But he has written differently. He manages to turn the proletarian type of propagandist discourse into an engaging fictional narrative.

Alan Sillitoe's protagonists are mostly angry young men, coming from working family backgrounds and working mostly in factories. They are sorely frustrated and furious with their lot. However, they are not molded on the same fictional pattern as are some other "angry young man" type of characters. They are, in a word, not angry in the same way Osborne's Jimmy Porter or Amis' Jim Dixon is. Sillitoe's young men are always part of their class. They do not move upward out of their social stratum; they are temporarily lost, feel extrememly unhappy, and behave in an odd or even grotesque manner, but whatever extravagance they exhibit, the bottom line is that they do not leave their class. Their spiritual odyssey generally begins with their loss of direction, sliding downhill and wallowing in meaninglessness, and groping in alienation and woe until they see the glimmer of light at the end of their long tunnel. Then they manage to overcome their egocentricism, place themselves back in their social group, and experience salvation through positive and balanced self-realization. They always find rebirth of a kind in affiliation. Alan Sillitoe's fiction covers basically the growth of their class consciousness and the journey that they traverse from benighted aloneness to solid belonging. Sillitoe extols the working class and its virtues such as mutual love, solidarity, and hard work

Sillitoe's best fiction is probably his first novel, *Saturday Night and Sunday Morning* (1958). As the title clearly indicates, the book consists of two parts, "Saturday Night" and "Sunday Morning." The protagonist is Arthur Seaton, a factory lathe worker. When he appears in "Saturday Night," Arthur is twenty-one years old, physically strong and full of ideas about life. It is apparent that he feels that he is the victim of a gross injustice, the nature of which, however, he cannot define. To him, society, employer, and tradition and all the rest of whatever he vaguely lumps together as life—all these seem to form a conspiracy against him. He rebels against all indiscriminately and indiscreetly. Nothing is sacred to him; no one deserves his love; and all wrongs him one way or another. He becomes self-indulgent and cares only about his petty interests. He goes to pubs, drinks profusely, goes fishing, and moves in and out of relationships. There is a girl, Doreen Greatton by name, who is devoted to him, but he finds her distasteful and does nothing to return her warm love. At the same time he takes an immense delight in perversity, keeping tryst with married young women (in fact two sisters), and successfully courting disaster itself. So, on one of the Saturday nights, he is soundly beaten up by one of the husbands and ends up his weekend in wounds and agony. He touches hell in his life. This proves to be a blessing in disguise, however, as it makes him think good and deep. Now back to square one in life, he is awake enough to size up his situation. His "Sunday Morning" begins in self-censure and self-loathing. He hurls at himself all the negativity that he has done at life and is bent on self-improvement. He recalls his life at the village where his grandfather lived and worked as the village blacksmith. He sinks himself back into the wholesome milieu of nature, fishing and meditating. And he finally patches up with Doreen and confirms his love for her. Then comes the point at which he experiences a kind of regeneration when he goes and visits his aunt Ada, whose large-hearted love is the fitting symbol of a class family. Arthur is no longer alone. Accepting life, he is accepted back in his class and his community. The end of the novel finds him well reoriented and poised at the threshold of his new life.

Among the clusters of contemporary literary constellations, Sillitoe seems to be solitary in his creative endeavors. He leans toward neo-Marxism in his stance. Running counter to the vogue of the neo-picaresque and other contemporaneous traditions, he perseveres in his effort to affirm the value of belonging to one's class, in his case, the working class. He deals with themes that the proletarian writers of the 1930s generally did, but he writes as a novelist does, not as a propagandist. Thus where his predecessors of the decade of the Depression failed to make an enduring imprint, he has succeeded: he has upgraded their stuff to the level of art. This reveals the impact of the new left on Sillitoe.

Anthony Powell (1905-2000)

Powell was educated at Oxford and first began to publish in the early 1930s. His 1930s novels such as *Afternoon Man* (1931), *Venusberg* (1932), and *From a View to a Death* (1933) are all good social satires. But his reputation rests mainly on his ambitious 12-volume work, *A Dance to the Music of Time* (1951-1975). This consists of four trilogies that cover the 30-odd years of experience of the protagonist's life. Likening life to a dance in which both meaningful rhythm and fickle whirling around occur at intervals, the series is essentially comic-tragic, indicating as it does that tragedy inheres in comedy, and genuine anxiety and sorrow lie beneath a graceful surface of humor and even playfulness. The first trilogy (1951-1955) covers the protagonist—Nicholas Jenkins' life from 1921 through the early 1930s. He is in school, goes through college, makes friends, falls in love, and gets close to the leftist forces at the beginning of the 1930s. The second trilogy (1957-1962) tells about Jenkins' experiences in the rest of the decade of the 1930s: emerging as a straggling novelist, getting married to a girl of noble parentage, and his young adulthood being brought to conclusion by a combination of events such as the rise of Fascism, the Spanish Civil War, the abdication of King Edward VIII, and the outbreak of WWII. The third trilogy (1964-1968) relates the story of his six years' military service, and the last trilogy (1971-1975) records his life after the war when he resumes his work as a novelist and meets his surviving friends. The war leaves behind a war-torn London and a Britain both happy and sad, more on the sad side perhaps in its elegiac mood.

The multi-volume fiction is noted for its rich gallery of people, over 200 in number, its bewitching plot interest, and its fascinating language with its numerous allusions and metaphors. No less impressive is its subtle balance between immediate involvement and attachment in judgment, and its biting social censure and satire. The books serve well as country's social-historical record or a fictional approximation of that exceptional phase of history. Though not strictly autobiographical, the work is heavily personal in nature as the author obviously wrote a good deal of himself into the story.

Chapter 26 Postwar Drama

Postwar Drama: A Brief Sketch

The decades of the 1930s and 1940s were a dull and uninspired period for English drama. Its progress slowed down somehow after the success of Shaw's brilliant plays. The theater was either flooded with stereotyped social plays, or with some left-oriented and political dramas that were not well balanced in their thematic and artistic concerns: they reflected the wretched existence of the lower classes well enough, but somehow neglected the formal aspect of the dramatic art. Although there were some experimental efforts in some small theaters, and some occasions to offer opportunities for new works to appear on stage, these did not get far in their endeavors. Thus the department of drama seemed again to lag a few steps behind the other divisions of poetry and fiction when the postwar era set in. But it did not stay that way for long. Some figure of magnitude was soon to appear and tower way above his contemporaries, and some other important, younger playwrights were to follow in his footsteps and push the theater further forward. The man was Samuel Beckett, who was to help revive English drama after Shaw with his amazing successes on the postwar stage. Then there were John Osborne, a chanticleer of some kind to his generation of writers, and Harold Pinter and Tom Stoppard, who were to pick up where the older dramatists left off and make headway in their unique fashion.

Beckett was a monumental figure in postwar English theater. He was instrumental in revitalizing the fine dramatic traditions by bringing in an existentialist and absurdist element, and ushering in the era of the drama of the absurd in recent literary history. Absurdist plays explore the absurd nature of the human condition. The world that the drama of the absurd tries to delineate seems to be one in which God no longer smiles upon the humankind, and man is thrown back upon himself for survival. As a result, modern man feels an acute sense of futility and meaninglessness, and sees no light at the end of the tunnel. This was the basic factor that helped decide the tragic theme of the drama of the absurd. However, the absurd dramatists chose to present the sorry plight of man in a humorous vein, in the form of black comedy, so that people watch and laugh, then feel the pain, and achieve a heightened awareness of the nature of their lives. Such plays are therefore often tragi-comedies. The 1950s and the first part of the 1960s was the period in which the drama of the absurd prospered as a fashion. It tapered off then and melted into the genre as an intrinsic part of its warp and woof. Late-comers such as Tom Stoppard have tried to reinvent it, but then decided to change gears after a moderate degree of success in their absurdist endeavors. The following discussion of some important plays in this tradition also includes John Osborne's works as they share a lot with the absurdist works out there around the time. It is good to note, however, that John Osborne is slightly different, representing as he does another major element of the postwar mood.

Samuel Beckett (1906-1989)

Beckett was one of the most significant Anglo-Irish writers whose writings have inconceivably enriched English literature. Sensitive and well educated, he came heavily under the influence of James Joyce's Modernist experimentation and the French existentialist philosophy. Beckett is well known as an absurd dramatist as well as a novelist of no negligible standing. Within his long and productive career overarching half a century from the 1930s through the postwar period, he wrote works that are strongly suggestive of the two prominent literary phases—Modernism and postmodernism, and this feature has helped make him a truly seminal figure in the literature of his century. The novels that he wrote in the 1930s, comic, mature, and philosophical satires on social life, constitute part and parcel of the literary milieu of that age. As a playwright, he helped bring the drama of the absurd into existence in the 1950s and1960s, and has been regarded as the most important post-Shaw playwright in recent literary history. Beckett is also well renowned for his daring formal experimentation. His major works include such novels as *Murphy* (1938), and the trilogy *Molly* (1951), *Malone Dies* (1951), and *The Unnamable* (1953), and his plays like *Waiting for Godot* (1953), *Endgame* (1958), and *Embers* (1959). He won the Nobel Prize in 1969. [1]

Beckett's major concern is with the human condition. Through his experience in life and especially during WWII as a French freedom fighter, he learned about the nature of modern life and man's lot in the universe so that he felt the need to increase the awareness of his fellow creatures and keep them wide awake about their plight. He came to sense acutely the absurdity of human life and its purposelessness, and understand well the human dilemma of having to make out in a basically Godless world. The frustration, the agony, the spiritual dearth that people experience—all these generate a sense of urgency in him the artist to bring the problem out into the open in a form, every bit absurd as life itself, just so that people will see the true nature of their condition better and do something about it. This was also probably the reason for the advent of the absurd drama as well as the absurd novel in the West of the 1960s. Beckett stood in the forefront of that Absurd tradition.

Beckett's stance of rebellion is cosmic in nature. The basic tenor of his tone falls in step with the modern human experience that man's life seems to be all a cosmic joke. His basic thematic focus is to throw in relief modern man's rootlessness, want of identity, and hopelessness. His protagonists are made out to be shiftless and effete creatures (such a character appears, for instance, in his "The End," in which the man finds it difficult either to live or die and so wait for death all day). They are clownish, often ridiculous in action and speech, pathetically obdurate in temperament, but they do not strike people as totally worthless and despicable. In this sense they reveal the basic plight of modern man's condition, of which many are unaware though already suffering in it. In a word, they are all existentialists of a kind trying to make sense of their senseless lives. They may embody the inquisitive, questing spirit of the intellectually thinking section of the humankind, never ready to settle for anything short of the absolute truth and certitude. As these are absent from their universe, they feel homeless, insecure, and indecisive as to whether "to be or not to be." But they do not die; they just manage to hang on there with their incessant questioning. Their physical and spiritual bleakness is often indicated in a Beckett play by means of a bleak setting with little in the background except for a tree, or a road, and there is little or no room for maneuver or any initiative for change. The plot is slim and its events are wanting in coherent or causal relationship. There is little activity of significance, yet often a good deal of talking that leads nowhere, and a good deal of questioning that gets no definitive answers. Yet the talking goes on, so does the questioning. Thus Beckett's dramas exhibit a kind of symbolism too deep sometimes to fathom easily. They are often capable of more than one interpretation. Beckett helped break the back of the realistic tradition.

Let's take a look at the most famous of all his plays, *Waiting for Godot* (1952). The work is thematically concerned with man's salvation through God's grace. The plot is slim enough. Two tramps, Estragon and Vladimir, come together and wait for Godot, though neither is sure whether they are doing the right thing. On one occasion they want to hang themselves, but decide to wait for Godot first. Then Pozzo comes up driving Lucky his servant, the tramps wrangle with Pozzo about his treatment of Lucky, but the subject gets nowhere eventually. Pozzo would sell Lucky. Lucky weeps but kicks Estragon when the latter helps wipe his tears. Estragon weeps. Pozzo complains about Lucky making life intolerable for him, and the tramps abuse Lucky for doing that. Pozzo philosophizes on the haphazard nature of life, is praised by the tramps, and orders Lucky to dance for them for their appreciation. Estragon mocks at Lucky's dance but fails to imitate it. Pozzo orders Lucky to think for the group, and Lucky comes up with incoherent words on God, Hell, sport and the suburbs and is silenced by the others who seize his hat. Pozzo and Lucky leave. Then a boy comes to say that Godot will come next morning and leaves with the tramps' message that he has seen them. Estragon decides to go barefoot, and the two separate for the night. When they meet again it is the following evening. The boots are still there. They talk of the day before, but cannot recall much. Then they think they hear voices of the dead around them and try to outspeak them. They remember talking nonsense yesterday and doing that for the past fifty years. They find the boots and Lucky's derby hat, and play exchanging hats for a while. Then Pozzo and Lucky appear again, with Pozzo blind, now dragged by a mute Lucky. The tramps want to help as members of the human race, but fall down while trying to raise Pozzo. They call Pozzo "all humanity," and suddenly get up without difficulty. Pozzo says that life is momentary and time does not matter, and then leaves with Lucky. Days and nights pass, the boy comes and goes with messages, Godot does not appear, and the tramps decide to hang themselves again if Godot does not come the next night. They end up staying where they are. [2]

The theme of the play seems to be self-evident. The drama depicts a world that goes through a phase of crisis of faith. Godot, the miniature of God in point of fact, never appears despite the long anxious waiting on the part of the vagabonds. No one is sure any more whether God still exists, and all are worried that He does not care any more about his creatures, even though He may still be around somewhere. He has already shown his indifference to man's lot, feeling no love and compassion for humanity, or the need to communicate with it. He may have condemned the human species without good reason, and have pushed it over to the abyss of agony and suffering. The play has been seen as the most effective of its kind as a drama of the absurd.

Waiting for Godot is unique in its peculiar want of either sense or action in the traditional sense of the terms. The play seems to be a monstrous pile of nonsense, filled with a whole lot of "sound and fury," but "signifying nothing." The tramps engage in no meaningful activities. They talk nonsense and so do Pozzo and Lucky. There is no meaningful relationship between these people, either in pairs or as a group except they stay together to keep company. A striking sense of absurdity and sterility keeps assailing the readers as well as the audience. Yet the nonsense that people read or hear is not entirely without its redeeming virtue: It amuses and, more important, forces people to think good and deep about the questions that keep popping up: why do these people behave the way they do? Don't they inhabit the same universe as we do? Then the sense of absurdity begins to break through, and the readers and the audience begin to relate to the absurdity of the existence of the characters. They begin to sense it existing in their own lives and realize the absurd nature of the human condition in general.

In terms of action, although there is a lot of movement, there is little activity that makes sense or leads to any visible result. Estragon trying in vain to take off his boot, but getting it done with Vladimir's help; the vagabonds quarrelling a bit and managing to patch up in the end; Vladimir giving his friend a carrot to nimble at; Vladimir trying to smile yet failing to do it well as he is also in pain; Lucky's incoherence and Puzzo's long-windedness, the tramps playing their silly games for want of something better to do, and on top of these all, the conspicuous absence of any sequential or causal plot interest—all these indicate clearly the lack of sense and purpose in human existence. "Nothing happens," as one character puts it in the play. The two tramps, Vladimir ("Didi") and Estragon ("Gogo"), are waiting for God's grace, which is nonetheless not forthcoming. They have at times lost hope and thought seriously of suicide, but their vague faith somehow gets the upper hand and keeps them waiting. They wait and do nothing else that may endow their lives with purpose and meaning, except that they keep talking about their piteous want of salvation. As to Godot, he is a nebulous entity. He may be a landowner, but may also serve as a token of God or God's grace to the poor wretches. But he never appears in person except in the form of his messenger, a boy, who tells to the tramps that Godot is not coming. In addition to the main plot, there is a subsidiary plot of a kind in which Puzzo and his servant Lucky make their appearance with little action but long speeches (Lucky is made to speak as the group thinker). The question then would be, how has the play managed to sustain the audiences' interest through its numerous performances across the world over the years?

The secret may lie in the dramatic question that the play evokes but never, even to the end, adequately answers, "What happens in the end?" Did the poor guys see Godot and receive what they have been hoping for? The end of the play, with the two still waiting, offers at best only a half-answer. The answer, possibly various with different people, lies ultimately with the audiences themselves. It is a demanding question, a challenge to both their intellect and their imagination, but rewarding for their thinking minds. For it touches upon the very nature of life as it is lived. The time was after WWII, the intellectual milieu was existentialist by and large, and the people felt the truth of the Existentialist tenets—alienation, gloom, and helplessness in face of an utterly humdrum, static environment. The tramps body forth the common humanity in their homelessness, want of physical and spiritual belonging, their purposelessness resulting from their loss of orientation, and their despair when confronting a void of hopelessness. The redeeming quality these people possess, which delights the common run of mankind and hold and hook the audience, is their wish to live on and their hope that comes from their wish. The fact that the two are still waiting may indicate the strength of the human spirit—its tenacity and perseverance and its never giving up on life and man. This spirit is in itself a counterpoint to any debilitating factors, be it science and technology or the crisis of faith or the sense of meaninglessness that it generates. This spirit can help modern man to transcend his own spatial and temporal—Existentialist—limits and invigorate his life with significance. Thus, when properly understood, the drama can be infinitely uplifting and inspiring to the audience. This, then, may account for the permanent fascination that the play holds for people even today.

John Osborne (1929-)

John Osborne is a preeminent English playwright. Coming as he is from a poor and obscure background, he suffered poverty in his boyhood and kicked about at different odd jobs before he became an actor. He was never able to receive a college education. All these helped decide his thematic and formal concerns as a playwright. He has written over twenty plays. His famous play, *Look Back in Anger*, caught and expressed the mood of his time so well, as J. D. Salinger's *The Catcher in the Rye* and William Golding's *Lord of the Flies* do respectively for their time, that it has become a landmark of a kind in recent history. It gave rise to the epithet "The Angry Young Man" that has since labeled under its umbrella a number of young struggling writers of the 1950s. It has also served to categorize the group of characters in their works. *Look Back in Anger* was an immediate commercial success. It has long been in evidence in London, Paris, and New York. It is a work of some power and permanence despite its clear social and political coloring. [3]

Let's take a close look at the play. It tells a simple but fascinating story. Jimmy Porter, a young thinking person, feels unjustly placed in society because he is from a working class background. He has intellectual energy, lots of wit and fire, and an eloquent tongue. Jimmy is angry. He is angry because his father, a man committed to a righteous cause, is left to die in misery. He is angry because he is placed at a disadvantage in his quest for a true and good life. And he is angry with the middle class from which his wife comes. He is up in protest. He lashes out at all that he thinks keeps putting him and people like him down. These include the old social order at large and his upper-middle-class wife, Alison, at home, and they bear the brunt of his cruel attacks. His friend, Cliff Lewis, who stays with the Porters, is milder, more tolerant, and a lot less vehement though he is also from similar humble origins. Alison is miserable, Cliff defends her, but Jimmy remains angry and restless. Alison's friend, Helena Charles, steps in to cash on the situation. She moves in, Cliff resents her maneuvering and moves out, and Helena advises Alison to stand up to Jimmy and leave him. Alison, now pregnant, walks out, loses her baby, and in utter misery, comes back to ask Jimmy for forgiveness. Alison's father, Colonel Redfern, comes for Alison after he learns of the Porters' discord from Helena's telegraph, and finds that he likes his son-in-law. The Porters reconcile with one another, and Helena leaves in disappointment.

The characterization of Jimmy Porter is John Osborne's great achievement. Jimmy is a vibrant person, masculine, dynamic, caring, but capable of cruel verbal violence at people and things that he considers less than genuine. He yearns and strives for an authentic existence, dislikes sham morality intensely, and loves to grapple with the quintessence of life. He is ever ready to help get rid of injustice and suffering for others as well as for himself. He is adamant as far as his stance on life goes. A graphic illustration is his relationship with Alison. He cannot accept her wholly until she changes her person. Coming as she does from an affluent background, Alison has suffered little and cares less about other people. She is self-centered and lives on her inherited principles. Jimmy helps, if only too cruelly, to shape her into a new woman. She loses her baby and learns the meaning of Jimmy's idea of suffering. She acquires a new vision and becomes compassionate for others. Jimmy is in a slightly altered sense Professor Higgins in George Bernard Shaw's play, *Pygmalion*.

The symbolism of the play is obvious and effective. To begin with, there is the flat of the Porters, a prison cell of a space, confining and constraining, with little hope for an exit or a peek at the world outside. The room defines Jimmy's view of his wretched existence. The church bells that keep ringing when Jimmy is fuming at his injustice are a mild but insistent reminder that faith is more rewarding. There is also the reference to T. S. Eliot, the bad guy, the symbol of conservative values in religion, politics, and literary creative endeavor, and to

George Orwell, the good guy, emblematic of fellowship and community spirit. These embody the aspects of the values of Jimmy's generation.

Harold Pinter (1930-)

Pinter was one of the most gifted playwrights to come out of the 1950s and 1960s. For over 40 years now he has written prolifically on various subjects. His major plays such as *Birthday Party* (1958), *The Caretaker* (1960), *The Homecoming* (1965) have all become classics.

Pinter's major thematic concern is with people's internal fabric of fears, desires, guilt, and sexual drives that debilitate and jeopardize their chances of survival. His plots follow a general pattern: people live a well-ordered life, often within an enclosed space like a room, where they live as if they played games, then some outsider kicks in to break their external peace, and offers a backdrop upon which they splatter the complexities of their true inner landscape of negativity. Then some violent mental battle ensues, truth is let out, and a psychic breakdown is experienced. This happens over and over in his works such as *The Room* (1957), *The Birthday Party* (1958), *The Homecoming* (1965), and *The Caretaker* (1960). Pinter has written some screenplays as well. Since the 1980s, he has switched gears and veered radically toward the political arena.

Let's take a look at a couple of his major plays. One of these is his *The Birthday Party*. As the story goes, Stanley, a former pianist in his late thirties, now a boarder, has settled and eased himself comfortably into the company of his landlady—Meg—as her surrogate son. He is feeling fine with his routine manner of behavior, indulging in his fantasies, exchanging trivialities with his hosts, and flirting a little with Meg. Now two men, Goldberg and McCann by name, suddenly appear at this rundown seaside home, and pose a threat to Stanley's well established way of life. The outsiders seem to have been looking for Stanley. But Stanley feels that they have come to cart Meg off in a wheelbarrow. Then a young woman in her twenties, Lu Lu by name, comes into the midst of this group and flirts with the men (Act I). Meg holds a birthday party for Stanley, at which the two strangers try between them to torment Stanley mentally. Stanley behaves in an odd way, first beating a drum at a wild tempo and marching around the room, and then appearing in a game of the blindman's bluff. When the lights come back on, he appears, with his glasses broken, all over Lu Lu, who lies on a table (Act II). The next morning he comes out neatly dressed and expressionless. Then he is taken downstairs by the two visitors and put in a waiting car. Before they leave for a healer, Meg's husband calls out to Stanley to stand up to them and not let them do with him as they please (Act III).

The play is capable of more than one interpretation. Some see the drama as symbolic of human growth; others explain it away with the idea of art being encroached upon by worldliness; still others regard the intrusion of Goldberg and McCann as a bodying forth of the shaping influence in the modern west—the Judaic-Christian faith, destroying Stanley's—modern man's—self-constructed life of complacency. In addition, there is also the notion that Stanley may have been suffering from the agony of some childhood guilt and needs an outlet for his strenuous Oedipus impulse. The play leaves its audience often with a number of queries that need to be worked out after the curtain falls.

Another provocative and challenging Pinter play is his *The Homecoming*, which is probably Pinter's masterwork. Here the peace and stability of a home of men is jeopardized by a visiting woman. The play is set in a shabby North London house in which Max lives together with his brother Sam and his two sons—Lenny and Joey. Ruth comes with her husband Teddy (another son of Max's) to visit her father-in-law's house and begins to interact with the males under the same roof. She is such a life force, with such a robust sexual and emotional energy, and proves herself to be such an enigma to them all that this thirty-year-old woman successfully jogs them all out of their set ways and brings them inside out. Her dominance is multiple. She exercises her emotional control over her father-in-law, her psychological power over her homosexually-oriented brother-in-law Lenny, and her irresistible sexual appeal over the boxer Joey, the most physical of the three brothers. Max, the seventy-year-old, is shaken out of his patriarchal authority and his happy illusion about his happy past and is reduced to an absolutely abject condition when he crawls over to Ruth for a kiss in the end. Even Uncle Sam feels impelled to come out with the truth about Max's wife—her promiscuity. Teddy, Ruth's intellectual husband, stands aloof and looks on when all the men seem to pay their advances to her. He even helps his brother Lenny arrange for her prostitution. Thus Ruth the outsider eventually comes out as the person in control and the hitherto "happy" household disappears. She does not go with her husband Teddy when he departs for the United States. She stays to be a prostitute for the family.

Pinter is noted for his superb stagecraft. He has many dramatic tricks up his sleeves to keep his audience riveted on his dramas. One of these is the suspense he manages to generate such as in *The Birthday Party*. People are mystified and piqued as to the identities of Stanley and the two visitors—Goldberg and McCann, or in *The Homecoming*, where Max presents an exciting psychic enigma. One other major formal feature in Pinter's works is the effective use of irony. People say one thing and mean another. Their communication is in fact a miscommunication as the readers need to detect the truth between the lines and beneath the surface. The irony of his characters' lives lies in this, that they all seem contented and all right whereas the truth is just the opposite. Hence the need for a medium, in the form of an outsider, to externalize their inner texture. There is, in addition, Pinter's language to consider. Pinter is exceptionally good at using tricks such as pauses, silences, and double *entendres* to convey the ironic aspect of people and life. His observation on language explains the way he handles his dramatic language to help achieve his themes. He feels that the speech people hear indicates what is not heard and that it is a cover-up of some kind for the true meaning, or in his words, "a constant stratagem to cover nakedness." For Pinter, needless to say, the biggest game in drama is to uncover the naked truth about life and people.

Tom Stoppard (1937-)

Stoppard was born in Czechoslovakia and came to England in 1946. He was sensitive to the profound influence of the tradition of the absurd dramas of the older generation such as Samuel Beckett and Eugene Ionesco (1912-1994), and wrote to continue it in his own manner in the English theater. The play that made his name as an absurd dramatist was his comedy, *Rosencrantz and Guildenstern Are Dead* (1967). It was the point at which he steadily climbed to the peak of his absurd dramatist career in the 1970s. His other major works include *Arcadia*

(1993), acclaimed as his masterpiece, *Indian Ink* (1993), and *The Invention of Love* (1997). Stoppard has also written for radio and television. One of the screenplays is the Oscar winning *Shakespeare in Love* (1998).

Stoppard is an iconoclast of his own kind. Coming as he did on the scene at a time when the absurdist drama had had its heyday, Stoppard was not merely to inherit and follow a great tradition. He set out to reinvent it so as to give it a new lease of life. Basically absurdist, he differs from Beckett or Eugene Ionesco in his characterization and use of language. Stoppard re-creates characters. He borrows characters and plotlines from other writers like Shakespeare, Oscar Wilde, and Beckett in a manner known as "travesty" and remakes his borrowings into distinct entities. His characters suffer from despair, but they do not always live on in total gloom. In formal terms, Stoppard deviates from the absurdist tendency to emphasize the deficiency of the communicative power of language in modern life. He stresses its importance to eloquence and cogent reasoning. He loves "language juggling."

Let's take a look at his most popular play, *Rosencrantz and Guildenstern Are Dead*. The story is simple in plot. It is a three-act play in which two minor characters borrowed from Shakespeare's *Hamlet*, Rosencrantz and Guildenstern, act as its protagonists. These Elizabethan courtiers are both fitted out with cloak, hat and stick, and a huge leather moneybag. Rosencrantz looks more or less like his comrade, Guildenstern, so that it is difficult to distinguish him from the other, but he introduces himself as Guildenstern. They are, however, different in temperament: Rosencrantz is dull, and Guildenstern philosophical. Guildenstern thinks about their destiny, and together they think why they have come there. Then they remember that they have been asked to go to the King's palace for reasons they do not know. They are waiting for somebody to come and tell them about it. While waiting the two of them play word games, or guessing the sides of a coin and gambling a little. But they do not seem to be playing simply to kill time; they were doing so with a sense of urgency that indicates they are using the games as a way of avoiding something. Then the Tragedians come. These are a troupe of six traveling actors—Alfred, a boy, the Player, a horn player, a flutist, and a man who moves the cart of props. The Player is the spokesperson for the Tragedians; he is a man of few principles. "A comic pornographer and a rabble of prostitutes," as

Guildenstern calls him. They are on their way to court where they are commissioned by Hamlet to play a drama of his design. On seeing the two people, they perform for them just to make some money on the side (end of act one). In acts two and three Rosencrantz and Guildenstern go to court to play their parts there in the play. Both serve as Claudius' spies to find out why Hamlet behaves oddly. One of them pretends to be Hamlet so that the other can test him out for an answer to the king's query. Eventually they fall into Hamlet's trap and are condemned to die. At the end of the play, the Tragedians become the pirates, Hamlet escapes amidst the pirates' attack, but the two "spies" disappear, possibly for good.

The play is an apt illustration of Stoppard's powers as a dramatist. It reveals his consummate skill with which he presents a question of a profound metaphysical nature within the subtle framework of a comedy. Stoppard's ambition is to achieve what he calls "the perfect marriage between the play of ideas and farce or perhaps even high tragedy." In thematic terms, the play adumbrates an existentialist and absurdist world in which people seem to suffer from a severe debilitation in action and communication. The two characters—Rosencrantz and Guildenstern, totally innocent, live in a world so sophisticated for them that they die without even knowing for what they die. As George Bernard Shaw says in one of his plays, "Yours is not to ask why, but to do and die," the piteous plight of these two people lies in the fact that they die without even thinking of asking, because they do not think much and they are overwhelmed by fear and anxiety, living at the mercies of the forces that they have no means of understanding or controlling.

In the original—Shakespeare's—*Hamlet* both Rosencrantz and Guildenstern are Hamlet's school friends. They are enlisted in King Claudius' service as spies without knowing what they are really doing. Stoppard apparently uses their innocence to approximate modern man's rudderlessness in life. The two innocents play games to pass time, which is clearly inspired by Beckett's *Waiting for Godot*. Stoppard's innocents play meaningless games not so much for fun to kill time as for fending off their inner feelings of despair and doom. They act out their parts or their lives against the backdrop of a desert, or wilderness, painted in bleak expressionistic shapes, where there is no light, hope, nor anything close to salvation. They get involved in Hamlet's confrontation with Claudius, yet they do not know why they are, or what parts are assigned to them. They think they should be informed, but they are so "abandoned" (probably by God in the Godless world) that they get surprisingly little explanation at the end of the play (and for that matter, of their lives).

Stoppard makes a dexterous use of this dislocation to achieve the play's superb comic effect. From his point of view, this sense of disjunction, between hope and fulfillment and the intensity of the anxiety that it generates, constitutes the basic causes for the innocents' pain, their absurd behavior, and the laughter their absurdity evokes among the audience. It is a kind of laughter very much in the nature of the black comedy, which produces an inevitable feeling of sadness at the characters' rootlessness, their having nowhere to belong, their falling into the quagmire of despond, or ending up in a no man's land between faith and despair. Helpless and desperate in face of malicious odds, these abandoned individuals survive or die all depending on how they shift for themselves, with whatever resources at their disposal. These may include their companionship, mutual compassion, and the amount of sense of humor that they still have for self-mockery in order to keep their sanity.

Although not Stoppard's very best dramatic effort, *Rosencrantz and Guildenstern Are Dead* has been so popular over the time that it has become almost its author's signature play. It is now a prescribed text in many British schools.

It is good to note here that Stoppard has his moral concerns for man. He does not like to leave man hanging over there in the absurdist void of modern existence. As he has faith in the human potential, man's perseverance and courage to face up to life's challenges, there is always room in his plays for vivacity and a good laugh even in the depths of despair. In his later works he would demonstrate the need for action rather than surrender to absurdity; he would help locate the medium as a foil against absurdity. Stoppard's weaknesses, as some critics say, are that sometimes he plays games for no conceivable reasons and that some of his plays can be too intellectual and demanding for audiences and readers alike. With all said and done, there is no doubt that he is one of the most impressive playwrights on the contemporary scene.

A Tentative Conclusion

Generally, contemporary English writers tend to back out of the boisterous chaos of the larger world into their smaller, insular serenity. Feeling, as they do, unable to offer visions of a prophetic nature to save the world from its inevitable fall into disorder and discord, they let nature take over and walk down the world stage to settle for a safer, more defensive placement in history. It is true that they focus more on the less significant, even trivial and parochial, themes, and produce few major works as did Shakespeare, Dickens, or Tolstoy, but they have offered their redeeming best to their readers. In fact there is a good deal of exquisiteness and grace and even grandeur in contemporary literature. Tiny in conception and finely wrought in execution, a good many contemporary works of genuine art have made their power keenly felt. This mode of composition may become a trend that will catch on in future development. The macroscopic works such as Dante's *Divine Comedy* or Milton's *Paradise Lost*, taking as they do the whole panorama of human existence as their legitimate province, or Tolstoy's *War and Peace*, aiming at the world at large as its game—all these stupendous literary endeavors may have just vanished as a tradition into history, and the dexterously wrought microscopic kinds of art, dealing with the parts rather than the whole of human experience, may be just taking over as the dominant fashion of literary creations. There is, however, also a strong likelihood that the present period lies wedged just like a valley in between two towering peaks and that the future has in store a new height for people to scale and conquer. If this is the case, it would be mere meaningless conjecture as to when the new peak will begin to loom, but literature will move and improve along with the ever forward-moving life. The readers can rest assured of this at least to stay ever awake and alert and feel good and at ease.

Notes and References

Chapter 1 The Old English (Anglo-Saxon) Period • *Beowulf* • The Middle English Period

1. See also Greenfield, Stanley B. *A New Critical History of Old English Literature*. New York: New York University Press, 1986; *The Oxford Companion to English Literature*. New York: 2000; Sampson, George, and R. C. Churchill. *The Concise Cambridge History of English Literature*. England: Cambridge Univ. Press, 1972; and Cosbey, Robert. Lectures. Nankai Univrsity, China, 1979.

2. See Brooke, Stopford Augustus. *The History of Early English Literature; Being the History of English Poetry from Its Beginnings to the Accession of King Alfred*. Freeport, NY: Books for Libraries Press, 1970. *The Earliest English Poems: A Bilingual Edition*. Trans. Michael Alexander. Berkeley: Univ. of California Press, 1966.

3. For the discussion of *Beowulf*, refer also, among others, to Chambers, R. W. *Beowulf: An Introduction to the Study of the Poem with a Discussion of the Stories of Offa and Finn*. Cambridge, England: Cambridge University Press, 1959; and Irving, E. B. *A Reading of Beowulf*. New Haven: Yale Univ. Press, 1968, and *Introduction to Beowulf*. New Jersey: Prentice Hall, 1969; and *An Anthology of Beowulf Criticism*. Indiana: University of Notre Dame Press, 1963.

4. Hoyt, Robert S. *Life and Thought in the Early Middle Ages*. Minneapolis: University of Minnesota Press, 1967; *Critical Approaches to Medieval Literature*. New York: Columbia University Press, 1965. *Medieval Epics*. New York: Modern Library, 1963; Barber, Richard W. *King Arthur: Hero and Legend*. New York: St. Martin's Press, 1986. *Twentieth-Century Interpretations of Sir Gawain and the Green Knight: A Collection of Critical Essays*. NJ: Prentice Hall, 1968. Jones,

George Fenwick. *The Ethos of the Song of Roland*. Baltimore: Johns Hopkins Press,1963; and *Philological Essays: Studies in Old and Middle English Language and Literature, in Honour of Herbert Dean Meritt*. The Hague: Mouton, 1970.

Chapter 2 Chaucer • The Pre-Elizabethan Period • More

1. See Loomis, Roger Sherman. *A Mirror of Chaucer's World*. New Haven: Princeton University Press, 1965, and Howard Donald Roy. *Chaucer: His Life, His Works, His World*. New York: Dutton, 1987. Brown, Peter, ed. *A Companion to Chaucer*. Malden, MA: Blackwell, 2000. *The Poetry of Chaucer: A Guide to Its Study and Appreciation*. Gloucester, MA: Smith, 1957. Winny, James. *Chaucer's Dream-Poems*. New York: Barnes and Noble, 1973. Hill, John M. *Chaucerian Beliefs: The Poetics of Reverence and Delight*. New Haven: Yale Univ. Press, 1991.

2. For the discussion of *The Canterbury Tales*, refer also, among others, *Sources and Analogues of Chaucer's Canterbury Tales*. New York: Humanities Press,1958. Root, Robert, K. *Discussions of the Canterbury Tales*. Boston: Heath, 1961. Whittock, Trevor. *A Reading of the Canterbury Tales*. Cambridge, England: Cambridge Univ. Press, 1968. *Critics on Chaucer*. Miami: University of Miami Press, 1970.

3. See, among others, Eisner, Sigmund. *A Tale of Wonder: A Source Study of The Wife of Bath's Tale*. New York: B. Franklin, 1969.

4. Faulkner, Dewey, ed. *Twentieth-Century Interpretations of The Pardoner's Tale*. New Jersey: Prentice, 1973.

5. French, Robert Dudley. *A Chaucer Handbook*. New York: F. S. Crofts & Co., 1947.

6. See, among others, Thompson, Karl F. *Middle Ages, Renaissance, and Reformation*. New York: Harcourt, Brace & World, 1964, and also Daiches, David. *A Critical History of English Literature*. New York: Ronald Press Co., 1960.

7. *St. Thomas More: Utopia*. Ed. Edward Surtz, S. J. London: Yale Univ. Press, 1964. All references here are to Edward Surtz's edited verson of the book. See also *Twentieth-Century Interpretations of Utopia: A Collection of Critical Essays*. New Jersey: Prentice Hall, 1968.

Chapter 3 The Elizabethan Age • Spenser • Sidney • Marlowe

1. See Rowse, A. L. *The England of Elizabeth: The Structure of Society.* New York: Collier Books, 1966. *Elizabethan Theatre*. New York: St. Martin's Press, 1967. Nicholl, Charles. *Elizabethan Writers*. London: NPG, 1997. Berry, Philippa. *Of Chastity and Power: Elizabethan Literature and the Unmarried Queen*. London: Routledge, 1994. Saintsbury, George. *A History of Elizabethan Literature.* New York: Russell & Russell, rpt. 1970. Muir, Kenneth. *Introduction to Elizabethan Literature*. New York: Random House, 1967. *Elizabethan Plays: Written by Shakespeare's Friends, Colleagues, Rivals and Successors; To Wit: Christopher Marlowe, John Lyly, Robert Greene ... [and others]*. Boston: Little, Brown, and Company, 1933.

2. *Spenser: A Collection of Critical Essays.* NJ: Prentice Hall, 1968. *Essential Articles for the Study of Edmund Spenser.* Hamden, CT: Archon Books, 1972.

3. See, among others, Hales, John W. *The Faerie Queene*. Mallette, Richard. *Spenser and the Discourses of Reformation England.* Lincoln, NE: Univ. of Nebraska Press, 1997. Roger, Sale. *Reading Spenser: An Introduction to The Faerie Queene*. New York: Random House, 1968.

4. *The Prince of Poets: Essays on Edmund Spenser.* New York: New York University Press, 1968.

5. On Philip Sidney, see Klein, Lisa M. *The Exemplary Sidney and the Elizabethan Sonneteer*. Newwark, NJ: The Univ. of Delaware Press, 1998. Rose, Mark. *Heroic Love: Studies in Sidney and Spenser*. MA: Harvard Univ. Press, 1968, and Worden, Blair. *The Sound of Virtue: Philip Sidney's Arcadia Elizabethan Politics*. New Haven: Yale Univ. Press, 1996.

6. *A New History of Early English Drama*. New York: Columbia University Press, 1997.

7. On Christopher Marlowe, see Redner, Harry. *In the Beginning Was the Deed: Reflections on the Passage of Faust*. CA: University of California Press, 1982. *Twentieth-Century Interpretations of Doctor Faustus: A Collections of Critical Essays*. New Jersey: Prentice Hall, 1969. *The Herculean Hero in Marlowe,*

Chapman, Shakespeare, and Dryden. New York: Columbia Univ. Press, 1962. Also *Critics on Marlowe*. Miami: University of Miami Press, 1970; Rowse, A. L. *Christopher Marlowe, His Life and Work*. New York: Harper & Row, 1965.

Chapter 4 Shakespeare • Bacon • Jonson • *King James' Bible*

1. Holden, Anthony. *William Shakespeare: The Man behind the Genius: A Biography*. MA: Little, Brown, and Co., 1999; Kott, Jan. *Shakespeare Our Contemporary*. New York: Norton, 1946; Montrose, Louis Adrian. *The Purpose of Playing: Shakespeare and the Cultural Politics of the Elizabethan Theatre*. Chicago: Univ. of Chicago Press, 1996; and Bloom, Harold. *Shakespeare: The Invention of the Human*. New York: River Head Books, 1998.

2. Alexander, Peter. *The Poems of William Shakespeare*. New York: The Heritage Press, 1985; Hotson, Leslie. "More Light on Shakespeare's Sonnets." *Shakespeare Quarterly* 2.2 (1951); Hubler, *Shakespeare's Sonnets*. New York: Basic Books, 1962; Parker, David. "Verbal Moods in Shakespeare's Sonnets." *Modern Language Quarterly* 30.3 (1969); and Stephen, Booth. "Shakespeare's Sonnets: Self, Love, and Art." *Modern Language Quarterly* 35.1 (1974).

3. *Shakespeare Reread: The Texts in New Contexts*. Ed. Russ McDonald. Gelven, Michael. *Truth and the Comedic Art*. Albany, NY: The State University of New York Press, 2000. Bradley, A. C. *Shakespearean Tragedy*. 1904. New York: Penguin, 1991 (The best and bewitching commentary on the tragedies). Bevington, David, ed. *Twentieth-Century Interpretations of Hamlet*. Englewood Cliffs, NJ: Prentice Hall, 1968. Cantor, Paul. *Shakespeare: Hamlet*. England: Cambridge Univ. Press, 1989. Greenblatt, Steven. *Hamlet in Purgatory*. Princeton, NJ: Princeton Univ. Press, 2001.

4. On *Macbeth* see, among others, Coles, Blanche. *Shakespeare Studies: Macbeth*. New York: AMS Press, 1969.

5. Zagorin, Perez. *Francis Bacon*. Princeton: Princeton University Press, 1998; *The Legacy of Francis Bacon*. Georgia: Georgia State University, 1971; Wallace, Karl Richards. *Francis Bacon on the Nature of Man: The Faculties of Man's Soul: Understanding, Reason, Imagination, Memory, Will, and Appetite*.

Illinois: University of Illinois Press, 1967.

6. Summers, Claude J. *Ben Jonson Revised.* New York: Twayne Publishers, 1999; *Ben Jonson: A Collection of Critical Essays*. NJ: Prentice Hall, 1963; Dunn, Esther Cloudman. *Ben Jonson's Art*: *Elizabethan Life and Literature as Reflected Therein*. New York: Russell & Russell, 1963; and Knoll, Robert E. *Ben Jonson's Plays: An Introduction*. Nebraska: University of Nebraska Press, 1964.

Chapter 5 The 17th Century • Donne • Milton • Dryden • Bunyan • The Restoration Theater

1. Bennett, Joan. *Five Metaphysical Poets: Donne, Herbert,. Vaughan, Crashaw, Marvel*. Cambridge, England: Cambridge Univ. Press, 1964.

2. Carey, John. *John Donne, Life, Mind, and Art*. New York: Oxford Univ. Press, 1981; *John Donne: A Collection of Critical Essays*. New Jersey: Prentice Hall, 1962; Louthan, Doniphen. *The Poetry of John Donne: A Study in Explication*. New York: Bookman Associates, 1951; and Stampfer, Judah. *John Donne and the Metaphysical Gesture*. New York: Funk and Wagnalls, 1970.

3. Lewalski, B. K. *The Life of John Milton: A Critical Biography*. Malden, MA: Blackwell, 2000; Rogers, John. *The Matter of Revolution: Science, Poetry, and Politics in Age of Milton*. Ithaca, NY: Cornell Univ. Press, 1998; Fish, S. E. *How Milton Works*. Cambridge, MA: Harvard Univ. Press, 2001; Porter, Louis. *Preface to Milton*. New York: Scribner's, 1971; Tricomi, Albert H. *Reading Tudor-Stuart Texts through Cultural Historicism*. Florida: University Press of Florida, 1996; and Anselment, Raymond A. *The Realms of Apollo: Literature and Healing in Seventeenth-Century England*. Delaware: University of Delaware Press, 1995.

4. Fixler, Michael. *Milton and the Kingdoms of God*. Evanston: Northwest Univ. Press, 1964; Baker, Arthur E., ed. *Milton: Modern Essays in Criticism*. Oxford: Oxford Univ. Press, 1965; Evans, J. M. *The Miltonic Moment*. Kensington, KY: Univ. of Kentucky Press, 1998; Kranidas, Thomas, ed. *New Essays on Paradise Lost*. Berkeley, CA: California Univ. Press, 1969.

5. *Twentieth-Century Interpretations of Samson Agonistes: A Collection of Critical Essays*. Ed. G. B. Crump. New Jersey: Prentice Hall, 1968.

6. Ricks, C. B. *Milton's Grand Style*. Oxford: Clarendon, 1963.

7. *Critical Essays on John Dryden*. Ed. J. A. Winn. New York: Pretice Hall International, 1997.

8. Hume, R. D. *Dryden's Criticism*. Ithaca, NY: Cornell, 1970.

9. On Bunyan see, among others, Spargo, Tamsin. *The Writings of John Bunyan*. VT, USA: Ashgate, 1997. Mullett, Michael A. *John Bunyan in context*. Pittsburg: Duquesne University Press, 1997.

10. Hotson, Leslie. *The Commonwealth and Restoration Stage*. New York: Russell & Russell, 1962; Wilson, John Harold. *A Preface to Restoration Drama*. Boston: Houghton Mifflin, 1965; *Restoration Dramatists*. NJ: Prentice Hall, 1966; Peters, Julie Stone. *Congreve, the Drama, and the Printed Word*. Stanford: Stanford University Press, 1990. Sieber, Anita. *Character Portrayal in Congreve's Comedies The Old Batchelour, Love for Love, and The Way of the World*. Lewiston: E. Mellen Press, 1996; Perry, Henry Ten Eyck. *The Comic Spirit in Restoration Drama: Studies in the Comedy of Etherege, Wycherley, Congreve, Vanbrugh, and Farquhar*. New York: Russell & Russell, 1962; Canfield, J. Douglas. *Tricksters & Estates: On the Ideology of Restoration Comedy*. Kentucky: University Press of Kentucky, 1997; and Connely, Willard. *Brawny Wycherley: First Master in English Modern Comedy*. Port Washington, New York: Kennikat Press, 1969.

Chapter 6 The Classic Age • Pope • Johnson • Gray • Goldsmith • Sheridan

1. Miller, Samuel. *A Brief Retrospect of the Eighteenth Century: Part First in Two Volumes, Containing a Sketch of the Revolutions and Improvements in Science, Arts, and Literature during That Period*. New York: B. Franklin, 1970; and Chapin, Chester Fisher. *Personification in Eighteenth-Century English Poetry*. New York: Octagon Books, 1968.

2. Edwards, Thomas R. *This Dark Estate: A Reading of Pope*. CA: University of California Press, 1963; Jones, John A. *Pope's Couplet Art*. Ohio: Ohio University Press, 1969; and *Twentieth-Century Interpretations of The Rape of the Lock: A Collection of Critical Essays*. NJ: Prentice Hall, 1969; Williams, Aubrey L. *Pope's Dunciad: A Study of Its Meaning*. Hamden, CT: Archon Books, 1968;

Russo, John Paul. *Alexander Pope: Tradition and Identity*. MA: Harvard University Press, 1972; and *Critics on Pope*. Miami: University of Miami Press, 1968.

3. White, Douglas H. *Pope and the Context of Controversy: The Manipulation of Ideas in An Essay on Man*. Chicago: University of Chicago Press, 1970.

4. *Johnson's England: An Account of the Life & Manners of His Age*. Oxford: Clarendon Press, 1965; Bate, Walter Jackson. *Samuel Johnson*. New York: Harcourt Brace Jovanovich, 1977; Piozzi, Hester Lynch. *Anecdotes of Samuel Johnson*. Freeport, NY: Books for Libraries Press, 1969; *Samuel Johnson as Book Reviewer: A Duty to Examine the Labors of the Learned*. Delaware: University of Delaware Press, 2001; and *Samuel Johnson: A Collection of Critical Essays*. NJ: Prentice Hall, 1965.

5. *Twentieth-Century Interpretations of Boswell's Life of Johnson: A Collection of Critical Essays*. NJ: Prentice Hall, 1970; and Halliday, F. E. *Doctor Johnson and His World*. New York: 1968.

6. McCarthy, B. Eugene. *Thomas Gray: The Progress of a Poet*. Madison, NJ: Fairleigh Dickinson University Press, 1997; and Kaul, Suvir. *Thomas Gray and Literary Authority: A Study in Ideology and Poetics*. Stanford, CA: Stanford University Press, 1992

7. Reed, Amy Louise. *The Background of Gray's Elegy: A Study in the Taste for Melancholy Poetry, 1700-1751*. New York: Russell & Russell, 1962; Sickels, Eleanor Maria. *The Gloomy Egoist: Moods and Themes of Melancholy from Gray to Keats*. New York: Octagon Books, 1969; and *Twentieth-Century Interpretations of Gray's Elegy: A Collection of Critical Essays*. NJ: Prentice Hall, 1968.

8. Kirk, Clara Marburg. *Oliver Goldsmith*. New York: Twayne Publishers, 1967.

9. *Sheridan Studies*. England: Cambridge University Press, 1995; and Cove, Joseph Walter. *Sheridan*. Port Washington, New York: Kennikat Press, 1970.

Chapter 7 Movement toward Romanticism • Thomson • Young • Cowper • Crabbe • Blake • Burns

1. *Eighteenth-Century English Literature*. New York: Harcourt, Brace & World, 1969; Goodridge, John. *Rural Life in Eighteenth-Century English Poetry*.

Cambridge University Press, 1995; and Deane, Cecil Victor. *Aspects of Eighteenth-Century Nature Poetry*. New York: Barnes & Noble, 1968.

2. Paolucci, Henry. *James Thomson's The City of Dreadful Night: A Study of the Cultural Resources of Its Author and a Reappraisal of the Poem*. Wilmington, DE: Griffon House Publications, 2000; Walker, Imogene B. *James Thomson (B.V.), A Critical Study*. Westport, CT: Greenwood Press, 1973.

3. Free, William N. *William Cowper*. New York: Twayne Publishers, 1970; and Quinlan, Maurice James. *William Cowper: A Critical Life*. Westport, CT: Greenwood Press, 1970.

4. Haddakin, Lilian. *The Poetry of Crabbe*. London: Chatto & Windus, 1955.

5. On William Blake see, among others, Bentley, G. E. *A Stranger from Paradise, A Biography of William Blake*. New Haven, CT: Yale Univ. Press, 2001; Berger, P. *William Blake: Poet and Mystic*. New York: Haskell House, 1968; *Blake: A Collection of Critical Essays*. NJ: Prentice Hall, 1966.

6. For Robert Burns, see also Craigie, W. A. *A Primer of Burns*. Port Washington, New York: Kennikat Press, 1970; Keith, C. *The Russet Coat: A Critical Study of Burns' Poetry and Its Background*. New York: Haskell House, 1971; Low, Donald A., ed. *Robert Burns: A Critical Heritage*. Boston: 1974; and Crawford, R., ed. *Robert Burns and Cultural Authority*. Iowa City: Univ. of Iowa Press, 1997.

Chapter 8 18th-Century Fiction • Swift • Defoe • Richardson • Fielding • Sterne • Smollett

1. See, among others, Yin, Qiping, et al. *A History of Criticism of English Fiction*. Shanghai, China: 2001; Fulford, Tim. *Landscape, Liberty, and Authority: Poetry, Criticism, and Politics from Thomson to Wordsworth*. England: Cambridge University Press, 1996; Ellis, Markman. *The Politics of Sensibility: Race, Gender, and Commerce in the Sentimental Novel*. Engalnd: Cambridge University Press,1996; Rawson, C. J. *Order from Confusion Sprung: Studies in Eighteenth-Century Literature from Swift to Cowper*. London: Allen and Unwin, 1985; Watt, I. P. *The Rise of the Novel: Studies in Defoe, Richardson, and Fielding*. CA: Univ. of California Press, 1957.

2. On Jonathan Swift, see, among others, Nokes, D. *Jonathan Swift: A Critical Biography*, New York: Oxford Univ. Press, 1985; *Swift: A Collection of Critical Essays*. NJ: Prentice Hall, 1964; Forster, M. P. *A Casebook on Gulliver among the Houyhnhnms*. New York: Crowell, 1961.

3. For Daniel Defoe, see *Critical Essays on Daniel Defoe*. London: G. K. Hall, 1997; *Twentieth-Century Interpretations of Robinson Crusoe: A Collection of Critical Essays*. NJ: 1969; Vickers, I. *Defoe and the New Sciences*. England: Cambridge Univ. Press, 1996.

4. Rivero, A. J. *New Essays on Samuel Richardson*. New York: St. Martin's Press, 1996; Gwilliam, T. *Samuel Richardson's Fictions of Gender*. CA: Stanford Univ. Press, 1993; Konigsbery, I. *Samuel Richardson and the Dramatic Novel*. Lexington: Univ. of Kentucky Press, 1968; Gopnik, I. *A Theory of Style and Richardson's Clarissa*. The Hague: Mouton, 1970; *Twentieth-Century Interpretations of Pamela: A Collection of Critical Essays*. NJ: Prentice Hall, 1969.

5. *Henry Fielding: The Critical Heritage*. London: Routledge, 1969; *Fielding: A Collection of Critical Essays*. NJ: Prentice Hall, 1962; Goldberg, H. *The Art of Joseph Andrews*. Chicago: Chicago Univ. Press, 1969; Dudden, F. H. *Henry Fielding: His Life, Works, and Times*. Hamden, CT: Archon Books, 1966; *Henry Fielding: The Tentative Realist*. Oxford: Clarendon Press, 1967; Digeon, A. *The Novels of Fielding*. New York: Russell & Russell, 1962.

6. Cross, W. L. *The Life and Times of Laurence Sterne*. New York: Russell & Russell, 1967; Kraft, Elizabeth. *Laurence Sterne Revisited*. New York: Twayne, 1996; *Laurence Sterne: A Collection of Critical Essays*. NJ: Prentice Hall, 1968.

7. Douglas, A. *Uneasy Sensations and the Body*. Chicago: Chicago Univ. Press, 1995; Kahrl, G. M. *Tobias Smollett: Traveler-Novelist*. New York: Octagon Books, 1968; Skinner, John. *Constructions of Smollett: A Study of Genre and Gender*. London: Associated University Press, 1996; Beasley, J. C. *Tobias Smollett: Novelist*. Athens: University of Georgia Press, 1998.

Chapter 9 The Romantic Period • Wordsworth • Coleridge • Scott • Austen

1. Prickett, Stephen. *The Romantics*. London: Methuen, 1981; Elwin, Malcolm. *The First Romantics*. New York: Russell & Russell, 1967; and Cosbey, Robert. Lectures. Nankai University, China, 1979; Dowden, Edward. *The French Revolution and English Literature*. Port Washington, New York: Kennikat Press, 1967; Egendorf, Laura K., ed. *English Romanticism*. CA: Greenhaven Press, 2001; Frye, Northrop. *A Study of English Romanticism*. New York: Random House, 1968.

2. Pinion, F. B. *A Wordsworth Companion: Survey and Assessment*. London: Macmillan, 1984.

3. Moorman, Mary Trevelyan. *William Wordsworth: A Biography*. Oxford: Clarendon Press, 1957-65; Thompson, Thomas William. *Wordsworth's Hawkshead*. Oxford: Oxford Univ., 1970; Elwin, Malcolm. *The First Romantics*. New York: Russell & Russell, 1967.

4. On Wordsworth's literary theory, see Murray, R. N. *Wordsworth's Style: Figures and Themes in the Lyrical Ballads of 1800*. Nebraska: University of Nebraska Press, 1967; and Sneath, E. Hershey. *Wordsworth, Poet of Nature and Poet of Man*. Port Washington, New York: Kennikat Press, 1967.

5. Baker, Carlos, ed. *William Wordsworth's The Prelude, Selected Poems and Sonnets*. New York: Holt, Rinehart and Winston, Inc., 1966. Gilpin, George H. *Critical Essays on William Wordsworth*. London: G. K. Hall: 1990. Hartman, Geoffrey H. *Wordsworth's Poetry 1787-1814*. New Haven: Yale Univ. Press, 1964 (A seminal, exhaustive study of Wordsworth's poetry. A very valuable resource for reading Wordsworth).

6. Chambers, E. K. *Samuel Taylor Coleridge: A Biographical Study*. Oxford: Clarendon Press, 1963; Fogle, Richard Harter. *The Idea of Coleridge's Criticism*. CA: University of California Press, 1962; Lowes, John Livingston. *The Road to Xanadu: A Study in the Ways of the Imagination*. Boston: Houghton Mifflin, 1964; Jackson, J. R. de J. *Coleridge: The Critical Heritage*. New York: Barnes & Noble, 1970; Worthen, John. *The Gang: Coleridge, the Hutchinsons & the Wordsworths*

in 1802. New Haven: Yale University Press, 2001; Baker, James Volant. *The Sacred River: Coleridge's Theory of the Imagination*. Westport, CT: Greenwood Press, 1969; Richards, Ivor Armstrong. *Coleridge on Imagination*. London: Routledge & Paul, 1962.

7. Adair, Patricia M. *The Waking Dream: A Study of Coleridge's Poetry*. New York: Barnes and Noble Inc., 1968 (A detailed holistic analysis of the texts of Coleridge's poetry with cogent supportive evidence from the poet's notebooks and other external sources. A very valuable resource for the study of Coleridge); Beer, John B. *Coleridge the Visionary*. New York: Collier Books, 1962; *Coleridge: A Collection of Critical Essays*. NJ: Prentice Hall, 1967; and *Twentieth-Century Interpretations of The Rime of the Ancient Mariner: A Collection of Critical Essays*. NJ: Prentice Hall, 1969. Barth, J. Robert. *Coleridge and Christian Doctrine*. MA: Harvard University Press, 1970.

8. See Cockshut, A. O. J. *The Achievement of Walter Scott*. 1969; Devlin, D. D. *The Author of Waverley: A Critical Study of Walter Scott*. New York: 1971; Johnson, Edgar. *Sir Walter Scott: The Great Unknown*. 1970; Lauber, John. *Sir Walter Scott*. 1966; and Welsh, Alexander. *The Hero of the Waverley Novels*. New York: 1963.

9. Collins, Irene. *Jane Austen and the Clergy*. Ohio: Hambledon Press, 1994; *Critics on Jane Austen*. Miami: University of Miami Press, 1970; Handley, Graham. *Jane Austen*. New York: St. Martin's Press, 1992; O'Farrell, Mary Ann. *Telling Complexions: The Nineteenth-Century English Novel and the Blush*. Texas: Duke University Press, 1997; *Readings on Pride and Prejudice*. CA: Greenhaven Press, 1999; and *Twentieth-Century Interpretations of Pride and Prejudice: A Collection of Critical Essays*. NJ: Prentice Hall, 1969.

Chapter 10 Byron • Shelley • Keats

1. *The Young Romantics and Critical Opinion, 1807-1824: Poetry of Byron, Shelley, and Keats as Seen by Their Contemporary Critics*. New York: St. Martin's Press, 1973.

2. Franklin, Caroline. *Byron: A Literary Life*. New York: Palgrave, 2000; Graham, Peter W. *Lord Byron*. New York: Twayne, 1998; Grosskurth, Phyllis.

Byron: The Flawed Angel. Boston: Houghton Mifflin, 1997; Longford, Elizabeth H. P. *The Life of Byron*. Boston: Little, Brown, 1976; and *Lord Byron the European: Essays from the International Byron Society*. Lewiston: E. Mellen Press, 1997.

3. *Byron: A Collection of Critical Essays*. NJ: Prentice Hall, 1963; *Byron: The Critical Heritage*. New York: Barnes and Noble, 1970; Marchand, Leslie Alexis. *Byron's Poetry: A Critical Introduction*. Boston: Houghton Mifflin, 1965.

4. *Twentieth-Century Interpretations of Don Juan: A Collection of Critical Essays*. NJ: Prentice Hall, 1969; and Soderholm, James. *Fantasy, Forgery, and the Byron Legend*. Kentucky: University Press of Kentucky, 1996.

5. Dowden, Edward. *The Life of Percy Bysshe Shelley*. New York: Barnes and Noble, 1966.

6. Reiter, Seymour. *A Study of Shelley's Poetry*. New Mexico: University of New Mexico Press, 1967; and *Shelley: A Collection of Critical Essays*. NJ: Prentice Hall, 1965.

7. Grabo, Carl Henry. *Prometheus Unbound: An Interpretation*. New York: Gordian Press, 1968.

8. Hewlett, Dorothy. *A Life of John Keats*. New York: Barnes & Noble, 1970; and *The Last Journey of John Keats*. Films for the Humanities and Sciences, 1998.

9. Crawford, Alexander Wellington. *The Genius of Keats: An Interpretation*. New York: Russell & Russell, 1967; *Keats: A Collection of Critical Essays*. NJ: Prentice Hall, 1964; Matthews, G. M. *Keats: The Critical Heritage*. New York: Barnes & Noble, 1971;

10. *Twentieth-Century Interpretations of Keats' Odes: A Collection of Critical Essays*. NJ: Prentice Hall, 1968; Patterson, Annabel M. "'How to Load... and Bend': Syntax and Interpretation in Keats' 'To Autumn.'" *PMLA* 94(1979): 449-58. Trilling, Lionel. *The Moral Obligation to Be Intelligent: Selected Essays*. New York: Farrar, Straus, Giroux, 2000.

Chapter 11 The Victorian Period • Victorian Prose • Carlyle • Mill • Newman

1. Altic, Richard D. *The English Common Reader*; Buckley, Jerome. *The Victorian Temper: A Study in Literary Culture*. New York: Vintage Books, 1951;

Clark, G. Kitson. *The Making of Victorian England*; Houghton, Walter E. *The Victorian Frame of Mind*; Young. *Portrait of an Age*; R. C. Cosbey. Lectures. Nankai University, China, 1979; and O'Farrell, Mary Ann. *Telling complexions: The Nineteenth-Century English Novel and the Blush.* Texas: Duke University Press, 1997; Cruse, Amy. *The Victorians and Their Reading*. Boston, Houghton Mifflin, 1935; Holloway, John. *The Victorian Sage*. New York: Norton, 1965.

2. Masson, David. (on Carlyle) Neff, Ernest. *Carlyle and Mill: An Introduction to Victorian Thought* (1964).

3. Albee, Ernest. *A History of English Utilitarianism*. Plamenatz. *The English Utilitarians*. Somervell, D. C. *English Thought in the Nineteenth Century.*

Chapter 12 Victorian Fiction • Dickens • Thackeray

1. Miller, Joseph Hillis. *The Form of Victorian Fiction* (1968); Swisher, Clarice. *Victorian Literature*. CA: Greenhaven Press, 2000;

2. Forster, John. *The Life of Charles Dickens* (1872-74/ standard and still irreplaceable); Kaplan, Fred. *Dickens: A Biography*. New York: Avon Books, 1988; and Johnson, Edgar. *His Tragedy and Triumph*. New York. Viking, 1977; Bowen, John. *Other Dickens: Pickwick to Chuzzlewit.* New York: Oxford Univ. Press, 2000.

3. *Dickens the Craftsman: Strategies of Presentation*. Carbondale: Southern Illinois Univ. Press, 1970; House, Humphry. *The Dickens World*. New York: Oxford University Press,1960; Priestley, J. B. *Charles Dickens and His World.* New York: Viking Press, 1969; Newlin, George. *Everyone in Dickens*. Westport, CT: Greenwood Press, 1995; and Bowen, John. *Other Dickens: Pickwick to Chuzzlewit*. New York: Oxford University Press, 2000; and Davis, Paul B. *Charles Dickens A to Z: The Essential Reference to His Life and Work*. New York: Facts On File, 1998.

4. Manning, Sylvia Bank. *Dickens as Satirist*. New Haven: Yale University Press, 1971; *Twentieth-Century Interpretations of Hard Times: A Collection of Critical Essays*. NJ: Prentice Hall, 1969.

5. *Dickens: A Collection of Critical Essays*. NJ: Prentice Hall, 1967; Lucas, John. *The Melancholy Man. A Study of Dickens' Novels*. London, Methuen, 1970;

Stang, G. Robert. *Expectations Well Lost: Dickens' Fable for His Time.*

6. *Twentieth-Century Interpretations of Bleak House: A Collection of Critical Essays*. NJ: Prentice Hall, 1968.

7. Monsarrat, Ann. *An Uneasy Victorian: Thackeray the Man, 1811-1863.* New York: Dodd, Mead, 1980; Williams, Ioan M. *Thackeray*. New York: Arco, 1969; *Thackeray: A Collection of Critical Essays*. NJ: Prentice Hall, 1968; Tillotson, Geoffrey. *Thackeray: The Critical Heritage*. New York: Barnes and Noble, 1968.

Chapter 13 Charlotte and Emily Bronte • Meredith

1. Shorter, Clement King. *The Brontes and Their Circle*. New York: Dutton, Kraus Reprint, 1970; Gaskell, Elizabeth Cleghorn. *The Life of Charlotte Bronte*. New York: Penguin Books, rpt. 1997; Miller, Lucasta. *The Bronte Myth*. New York: Knopf, 2004; Stebbins, Lucy Poate. *A Victorian Album: Some Lady Novelists of the Period*. New York: AMS Press, 1966.

2. Laar, Elisabeth Th. M. van de. *The Inner Structure of Wuthering Heights: A Study of an Imaginative Field*. The Hague: Mouton, 1969; *Twentieth-Century Interpretations of Wuthering Heights: A Collection of Critical Essays*. NJ: Prentice Hall, 1968; Gerin, Winifred. *Emily Bronte: A Biography*. Oxford: Clarendon, 1971; and Crandall, Norma. *Emily Bronte, a Psychological Portrait*. New York: R. R. Smith Publisher, Kraus Reprint Co., 1970.

3. Curle, Richard. *Aspects of George Meredith*. New York: Phaeton Press, 1970; Swanson, Donald Roland. *Three Conquerors: Character and Method in the Mature Works of George Meredith*. The Hague: Mouton, 1969; Stevenson, Lionel. *The Ordeal of George Meredith: A Biography*. New York: Russell & Russell, 1967.

Chapter 14 George Eliot • Trollope • Butler

1. Leavis, F. R. *The Great Tradition: George Eliot, Henry James, Joseph Conrad*. New York: New York University Press, 1969; Carlisle, Janice. *The Sense of an Audience: Dickens, Thackeray, and George Eliot at Mid-Century*. Athens:

University of Georgia Press, 1981; Holloway, J. *The Victorian Sage*. New York: Norton, 1965; and Stump, Reva. *Movement and Vision*. Seattle: 1959.

2. Sprague, Rosemary. *George Eliot: A Biography*. Philadelphia: Chilton Book Co., 1968; Gerald Bullet. *George Eliot: Her Life and Books*. New Haven: Yale Univ. Press, 1978.

3. *Critical Essays on George Eliot*. New York: Barnes & Noble, 1970; Parrish, Morris Longstreth. *Victorian Lady Novelists: George Eliot, Mrs. Gaskell, The Bronte sisters*. New York: Franklin, 1969.

4. Hardy, Barbara Nathan. *Middlemarch: Critical Approaches to the Novel*. New York: Oxford University Press, 1967. Gerould, Winifred. *A Guide to Trollope*. Westport, CT: Greenwood Press,1970; Helling, Rafael. *A Century of Trollope Criticism*. Port Washington, New York: Kennikat Press, 1967; and Kincaid, James R. *The Novels of Anthony Trollope*. Oxford: Clarendon Press, 1977.

5. Joad, C. E. M. *Samuel Butler, 1835-1902*. Freeport, New York: Books for Libraries Press, 1969.

Chapter 15 Hardy •Gissing •Moore •Wilde •Stevenson

1. Hardy, Evelyn. *Thomas Hardy: A Critical Biography*. New York: Russell & Russell, 1970; Weber, Carl Jefferson. *Hardy of Wessex, His Life and Literary Career*. New York: Columbia University Press, 1965; *Thomas Hardy: The Critical Heritage*. New York: Barnes & Noble, 1970.

2. Southerington, Frank Rodney. *Hardy's Vision of Man*. New York: Barnes & Noble, 1971; Bailey, James Osler. *The Poetry of Thomas Hardy: A Handbook and Commentary*. NC: University of North Carolina Press, 1970; Marsden, Kenneth. *The Poems of Thomas Hardy: A Critical Introduction*. New York: Oxford University Press, 1969.

3. *Thomas Hardy after Fifty Years*. Totowa, NJ: Rowman And Littlefield, 1977.

4. *Hardy: A Collection of Critical Essays*. NJ: Prentice Hall, 1963; Holloway, John. Lawrence, D. H. *On Tess and Her Two Men; Jude and His Two Women* (away from the provincial, a point stressed by John Holloway).

5. Clifford, Emma. "The Child, The Circus, and *Jude the Obscure*" (one of

the best studies on *Jude*); Alvarez, A. "Jude the Obscure: Afterword." *Jude the Obscure*. Thomas Hardy. New York: New American Library, 1961.

6. Korg, Jacob. *George Gissing: A Critical Biography*. Seattle: University of Washington Press, 1963; Brandes, G. M. C. *Naturalism in Nineteenth-Century English Literature*. New York: Russell & Russell, 1957.

7. *George Moore's Mind and Art*. New York: Barnes & Noble, 1970.

8. Kenilworth, Walter Winston. *A Study of Oscar Wilde*. New York: Haskell House Publishers, R. F. Fenno, 1972; Rudnicki, Stefan. *Wilde: A Novel*. LA: Dove Books, 1998; and Small, Ian. *Oscar Wilde: Recent Research: A Supplement to "Oscar Wilde Revalued."* Greenshore, NC: ELT Press, 2000.

9. Calder, Jenni. *Robert Louis Stevenson: A Life Study*. New York: Oxford Univ. Press, 1980; Masson, R. O. *Robert Louis Stevenson*. Port Washington, NY: Kennikat Press, 1970; Smith, Vanessa. *Literary Culture and the Pacific: Nineteenth-Century Textual Encounters*. New York: Cambridge Univ. Press, 1998.

Chapter 16 Victorian Poetry • Tennyson • Browning • Arnold

1. *Tennyson: The Critical Heritage*. London: Routledge and K. Paul; Barnes and Noble, 1967; Fausset, Hugh I'Anson. *Tennyson: A Modern Portrait*. New York: Russell & Russell, 1968; Culler, A. Dwight. *The Poetry of Tennyson*. New Haven: Yale University Press, 1977; Walker, Hugh. *The Age of Tennyson*. Port Washington, New York: Kennikat Press, 1972.

2. Marshall, George O. *A Tennyson Handbook*. New York: Twayne Publishers, 1963; *Critical Essays on the Poetry of Tennyson*. New York: Barnes and Noble, 1960; Marshall, G. O. *A Tennyson Handbook*. New York: Twayne, 1963.

3. Ryals, Clyde de L. *From the Great Deep: Essays on Idylls of the King*. Ohio: Ohio University Press, 1967.

4. Drew, Philip. *The Poetry of Browning: A Critical Introduction*. London: Methuen, 1970; *Browning: The Critical Heritage*. New York: Barnes and Noble, 1970; and Brockington, Alfred Allen. *Browning and the Twentieth Century: A Study of Robert Browning's Influence and Reputation*. New York: Russell & Russell, 1963; Flew, Josiah. *Studies in Browning*. New York: Haskell House, 1970;

Johnson, E. D. H. *The Alien Vision of Victorian Poetry*. Hamden, CT: Archon Books, 1963.

5. Altick, Richard Daniel. *Browning's Roman Murder Story: A Reading of The Ring and the Book*. Chicago: University of Chicago Press, 1968. *The Old Yellow Book: Source of Browning's The Ring and the Book*. New York: Haskell House, 1970.

6. Honan, Park. *Matthew Arnold, a Life*. MA: Harvard University Press, 1983; Super, R. H. *The Time-Spirit of Matthew Arnold*. Michigan: University of Michigan Press, 1970.

7. *Matthew Arnold: A Collection of Critical Essays*. NJ: Prentice Hall, 1973; Tinker, Chauncey Brewster. *The Poetry of Matthew Arnold: A Commentary*. New York: Russell & Russell, 1970; Cruse, Amy. *The Victorians and Their Reading*. Boston: Hooghton Mifflin, 1935.

Chapter 17 Clough • Hopkins • Edward Fitzgerald's *Rubaiyat* • The Aesthetic Movement

1. Chorley, Katharine Campbel. *Arthur Hugh Clough: The Uncommitted Mind: A Study of His Life and Poetry*. Oxford: Clarendon Press, 1962; *Arthur Hugh Clough: The Critical Heritage*. London: Routledge, 1972; Harris, Wendell V. *Arthur Hugh Clough*. New York: Twayne Publishers, 1970.

2. Hutchinson, Gloria. *A Retreat with Gerard Manley Hopkins and Hildegard of Bingen: Turning Pain into Power*. Cincinnati, Ohio: St. Anthony Messenger Press, 1995; Clotter, James Finn. *Inscape: The Christology and Poetry of Gerard Manley Hopkins*. Pittsburgh: Univ. of Pittsburgh Press, 1972; Miller, J. Hillis. *The Disappearance of God*. Cambridge, MA: Harvard Univ. Press, 1963; Lawler, Justus George. *Hopkins Reconstructed: Life, Poetry, and the Tradition*. New York: Continuum Publishing Co., 1998;

3. Pick, John. *Gerard Manley Hopkins, Priest and Poet*. Oxford: Oxford Univ. Press, 1966 (Unsurpassed on its analyses of Hopkins' notions of *instress* and *inscape*); MacKenzie, Norman H. *A Reader's Guide to Gerard Manley Hopkins*. Ithaca: Cornell Univ. Press, 1981 (A valuable source book); *Gerard Manley Hopkins: The Critical Heritage*. London: Routledge, 1987; Downes, David

Anthony. *Hopkins' Achieved Self*. Lanham, MD: University Press of America, 1996; Hartman, Geoffrey H. *Hopkins: A Collection of Critical Essays*. NJ: Prentice Hall, 1966; McChesney, Donald. *A Hopkins Commentary: An Explanatory Commentary on the Main Poems, 1876-89*. New York: New York University Press, 1968; Mariani, Paul L. *Commentary on the Complete Poems of Gerard Manley Hopkins*. Ithaca: Cornell Univ. Press, 1970.

4. Hough, Graham Goulden. *The Last Romantics*. New York: Barnes & Noble, 1961.

5. Faxon, A. C. *Dante Gabriel Rossetti*. New York: Abbeville Press, 1989; Sonstroem, David. *Rossetti and the Fair Lady*. Middletown, CT: Wesleyan Univ. Press, 1970; Johnston, R. D. *Dante Gabriel Rossetti*. New York: Twayne, 1969.

6. Mackail, J. W. *The Life of William Morris*. New York: Haskell House, 1970; Thompson, Paul Richard. *The Work of William Morris*. New York: Viking Press, 1967; Grennan, Margaret Rose. *William Morris, Medievalist and Revolutionary*. New York: Russell & Russell, 1970.

7. Fuller, Jean O. *Swinburne: A Biography*. New York: Schocken Books, 1971; Hyder, Clyde Kenneth. *Swinburne's Literary Career and Fame*. New York: Russell & Russell, 1963; Drinkwater, John. *Swinburne: An Estimate*. Hamden, CT: Archon Books, 1969; and *Algernon Swinburne: The Critical Heritage*. London: Routledge, 1970.

8. On Pater see Benson Arthur C. *Walter Pater*. London: Macmillan, 1968.

9. Knox, Melissa. *Oscar Wilde & the Critics*. Canadian House, 1999; Mahaffey, Vicki. *States of Desire: Wilde, Yeats, Joyce, and the Irish Experiment*. New York: Oxford University Press, 1998;

Chapter 18 Victorian Drama • Shaw • Wilde

1. Henderson, Archibald. *George Bernard Shaw: Man of the Century*. New York: Da Capo Press, 1972; Pearson, Hesketh. *George Bernard Shaw: His Life and Personality*. New York: Atheneum, 1963.

2. Brown, Julia Prewitt. *Cosmopolitan Criticism: Oscar Wilde's Philosophy of Art*. Virginia: University Press of Virginia, 1997; Gelven, Michael. *Truth and the Comedic Art*. New York: State University of New York Press, 2000; Holland,

Vyvyan. *Oscar Wilde with 146 Illustrations*. London: Thames and Hudson, 1960.

Chapter 19 The Early 20th Century • The Edwardians • The Georgians • The War Poets

1. For the Edwardians, see Hepburn, James G. *The Art of Arnold Bennett*. Indiana: Indiana University Press, 1963; Barker, D. *Writer by Trade: A Portrait of Arnold Bennett*. New York: Atheneum, 1966; Barker, Dudley. *The Man of Principle: A Biography of John Galsworthy*. New York: Stein and Day, 1969; *Kipling and the Critics*. New York: New York University Press, 1965; and Ellmann, Richard. *Edwardians and Late Victorians*. New York: Columbia Univ. Press, 1960.

2. On Conrad, see *Conrad: A Collection of Critical Essays*. NJ: Prentice Hall, 1966; Bendz, Ernst Paulus. *Joseph Conrad: An Appreciation*. Folcroft, PA: Folcroft Library Editions, 1973; Griffith, John W. *Joseph Conrad and the Anthropological Dilemma: "Bewildered Traveller."* New York: Oxford University Press, 1995; Karl, Frederick Robert. *A Reader's Guide to Joseph Conrad*. New York: Farrar, Straus and Giroux, 1969; Meyer, Bernard C. *Joseph Conrad: A Psychoanalytic Biography*. New Haven: Princeton University Press, 1967; Najder, Zdzislaw. *Joseph Conrad, A Chronicle*. New Brunswick, NJ: Rutgers University Press, 1983; O'Flaherty, Liam. *Joseph Conrad: An Appreciation*. New York: Haskell House, 1973; and *The Oxford Reader's Companion to Conrad*. New York: Oxford University Press, 2000.

3. On Forster, see Kelvin, Norman. *E. M. Forster*. Illinois: Southern Illinois University Press, 1967; *Perspectives on E. M. Forster's A Passage to India: A Collection of Critical Essays*. New York: Barnes and Noble, 1968; Thomson, George H. *The Fiction of E. M. Forster*. Michigan: Wayne State University Press, 1967.

4. For early 20th-century poetry, see *British Poetry 1880-1920: Edwardian Voices*. New York: Appleton-Century-Crofts, 1969; Blunden, Edmund. *War Poets, 1914-1918*. England: Longman, 1969; Moore, Thomas Sturge. *Some Soldier Poets*. Freeport, NY: Books for Libraries, 1968.

Chapter 20 The 1920s • Woolf • Joyce

1. On the 1920s, see Everdell, W. R. *The First Moderns: Profiles in the Origins of Twentieth-Century Thought*. Chicago: Chicago University Press, 1997; Kumar, Shiv Kumar. *Bergson and the Stream of Consciousness Novel*. New York: New York Univ. Press, 1963;

2. On Modernism, see Wilde, Alan. Lectures. Temple University, Philadelphia, 1982.

3. See Gordon, Lyndall. *Virginia Woolf, A Writer's Life*. New York: Norton, 1984; Lee, Hermione. *Virginia Woolf*. New York: A. A. Knopf, 1997; and Todd, Pamela. *Bloomsbury at Home*. New York: H. N. Abrams, 1999;

4. *Critics on Virginia Woolf*. Miami: University of Miami Press, 1970; *New Essays on Virginia Woolf*. Dallas, TX: Contemporary Research Press, 1995; and *Virginia Woolf: A Collection of Critical Essays*. NJ: Prentice Hall, 1971.

5. Bazin, Nancy Topping. *Virginia Woolf and the Androgynous Vision*. New Brunswick, NJ: Rutgers University Press, 1973; *Twentieth-Century Interpretations of To the Lighthouse: A Collection of Critical Essays*. NJ: Prentice Hall, 1970.

6. On Joyce, see Hodgart, Matthew John Caldwell. *James Joyce: A Student's Guide*. London: Routledge & K. Paul, 1978; Kelly, Joseph. *Our Joyce: From Outcast to Icon*. Texas: University of Texas Press, 1998; Heller, Vivian. *Joyce, Decadence, and Emancipation*. Illinois: University of Illinois Press, 1995; Jin, Di. *Ahamrock and Chopsticks: James Joyce in China: A Tale of Two Encounters*. Hong Kong: City Univ. of Hong Kong Press, 2001; and Jin, Di. "Foreword." *Ulysses*. Trans. Jin, Di. Tianjin, China: 1987.

7. Cheng, Vincent John. *Joyce, Race, and Empire*. Cambridge, England: Cambridge University Press, 1995; *Portraits of an Artist: A Casebook on James Joyce's A Portrait of the Artist as a Young Man*. New Hampshire: Odyssey Press, 1962; Begnal, Michael H. *A Conceptual Guide to Finnegans Wake*. PA: Pennsylvania State University Press, 1974; and Tindall, William York. *A Reader's Guide to Finnegans Wake*. London: Thames and Hudson, 1969.

8. Smith, Paul Jordan. *A Key to the Ulysses of James Joyce*. New York: Haskell House Publishers, 1969; Gillespie, Michael Patrick. *Recent Criticism of*

James Joyce's Ulysses: An Analytical Review. Rochester, NY: Camden House, 2000; Knowles, Sebastian D. G. *The Dublin Helix: The Life of Language in Joyce's Ulysses*. FL: University Press of Florida, 2001; Hayman, David. *Ulysses: The Mechanics of Meaning*. NJ: Prentice Hall, 1970; Thornton, Weldon. *Voices and Values in Joyce's Ulysses*. FL: University Press of Florida, 2000.

Chapter 21 Lawrence • Yeats • Imagism • T. S. Eliot

1. On Lawrence, see Meyers, Jeffrey. *D. H. Lawrence: A Biography*. New York: Knopf, 1990; Weiss, Daniel. *Oedipus in Nottingham: D. H. Lawrence*. Seattle: University of Washington, 1962.

2. *D. H. Lawrence: A Collection of Critical Essays*. NJ: Prentice Hall, 1963. Sanders, Scott R. *D. H. Lawrence: The World of the Five Major Novels*. New York: Viking Press, 1974; *D. H. Lawrence and Sons and Lovers: Sources and Criticism*. New York: New York University Press, 1965; Goodheart, Eugene. *The Utopian Vision of D. H. Lawrence*. Chicago: University of Chicago Press, 1963.

3. Spilka, Mark. *The Love Ethic of D. H. Lawrence*. Indiana: Indiana University Press, 1955; Tedlock, E. W. *D. H. Lawrence, Artist & Rebel: A Study of Lawrence's Fiction*. New Mexico: University of New Mexico Press, 1963.

4. *A Century of Irish Drama: Widening the Stage*. Indiana: Indiana University Press, 2000; Ellmann, Richard. *Four Dubliners—Wilde, Yeats, Joyce, and Beckett*. Washington, DC: Library of Congress, 1986; Magee, William Kirkpatrick. *Irish Literary Portraits*. Freeport, NY: Books for Libraries Press, 1967; Mahaffey, Vicki. *States of Desire: Wilde, Yeats, Joyce, and the Irish Experiment*. New York: Oxford University Press, 1998; and Mahony, Christina Hunt. *Contemporary Irish Literature: Transforming Tradition*. New York: St. Martin's Press, 1998.

5. See Forster, R. F. *W. B. Yeats: A life*. Oxford: Oxford Univ. Press, 1997; Beum, Robert Lawrence. *The Poetic Art of William Butler Yeats*. New York: F. Ungar Pub. Co., 1969; Seiden, Morton Irving. *William Butler Yeats: The Poet as a Mythmaker, 1865-1939*. Michigan: Michigan: State University Press, 1962.

6. On his works, see Koch, Vivienne. *W. B. Yeats: The Tragic Phase: A Study of the Last Poems*. CT: Crchon Books, 1969; Stallworthy, John. *Between the Lines: Yeats' Poetry in the Making*. Oxford: Clarendon Press, 1963; Stock, A. G. *W. B.*

Yeats: His Poetry and Thought. England: Cambridge Univ. Press, 1961.

7. For an exhaustive treatment of the subject see Stanley Coffman, *Imagism, A Chapter, or the History of Modern Poetry*. Norman: Univ. of Oklahoma Press, 1951 (Still the best and the most seminal of its kind so far); and also Pratt, William. *The Imagist Poem, Modern Poetry in Miniature*. New York: 1963.

8. Pinion, F. *A T. S. Eliot Companion* (1988); Sharpe, T. *T. S. Eliot, A Literary Life* (1992); Moody, Anthony David. *Tracing T. S. Eliot's Spirit: Essays on His Poetry and Thought* (1996); and Reeves, Gareth. *T. S. Eliot's The Waste Land* (1994). Also O'Connor, William Van. *Sense and Sensibility in Modern Poetry.* Chicago: 1948; Perkins, David. *A History of Modern Poetry*. Oxford:1987; Gardener, H. *The Composition of "Four Quartets"* (1977).

Chapter 22 Poetry of the 1930s • Auden • The Audenic Group • Thomas • Empson

1. On the 1930s see Maxwell, D. E. S. *Poets of the Thirties*. New York: Barnes & Noble, 1969.

2. Greenberg, Herbert J. *Quest for the Necessary: W. H. Auden and the Dilemma of Divided Consciousness*. Cambridge, MA: Harvard University Press, 1968; Hoggart, Richard. *Auden: An Introductory Essay*. London: Chatto & Windus, 1965; Monroe K. Spears, ed. *Auden: A Collection of Critical Essays*. Englewood Cliffs, NJ: Prentice Hall, 1964, and *The Poetry of W. H. Auden: The Disenchanted Island*. London: Oxford Univ. Press, 1968.

3. Fitz Gibbon, Constantine. *The Life of Dylan Thomas*. Boston: Little, Brown, 1965; Cox, C. B., ed. *Dylan Thomas: A Collection of Critical Essays*. Englecliffs, NJ: Prentice Hall, 1968; Emery, Clark. *The World of Dylan Thomas*. Coral Gables, FL: Univ. of Miami Press, 1962; Moynihan, William T. *The Craft and Art of Dylan Thomas*. Ithaca, NY: Cornell Univ. Press, 1966; Thomas, Dylan. *The Notebooks of Dylan Thomas*. CT: New Directions, 1967.

4. Brinnin, John Malcolm, ed. *A Casebook on Dylan Thomas*. New York: Thomas Y. Crowell Company, 1960; Maud, Ralph. *Entrances to Dylan Thomas' Poetry*. Pittsburgh: University of Pittsburgh Press, 1963; Reddington, Alphonsus M. *Dylan Thomas: A Journey from Darkness to Light*. New York: Paulist Press, 1968.

Chapter 23 Fiction of the 1930s • Huxley • Orwell • Waugh • Greene • Isherwood

1. On the fiction of the 1930s, see Allen, Walter E. *The Modern Novel in Britain and the United States*. New York: Dutton, 1964;

2. *Aldous Huxley: A Biography.* New York: Knopf, 1974; *Aldous Huxley Recollected: An Oral History*. Walnut Creek, CA: Altamira Press, 1999; Firchow, P. E. *Aldous Huxley: Satirist and Novelist*. Minneapolis: Univ. of Minnesota Univ. Press, 1972.

3. On Orwell, see Hitchens, Christopher. *Why Orwell Matters*. New York: Basic Books, 2002; Lief, Ruth Ann. *Homage to Oceania: The Prophetic Vision of George Orwell*. Ohio: Ohio State University Press, 1969; Voorhees, Richard J. *The Paradox of George Orwell*. Indiana: Purdue University, 1961.

4. On Waugh see Beaty, Frederick L. *The Ironic World of Evelyn Waugh: A Study of Eight Novels*. Illinois: Northern Illinois University Press, 1992. Patey, Douglas Lane. *The Life of Evelyn Waugh: A Critical Biography*. Boston: Blackwell Publishers, 1998.

5. *Graham Greene: A Collection of Critical Essays*. NJ: Prentice Hall, 1973. *Graham Greene: Some Critical Considerations*. Kentucky: University of Kentucky Press, 1963.

6. On Compton-Burnett, see Sprigge, Elizabeth. *The Life of Ivy Compton-Burnett*. New York: G. Braziller, 1973.

7. On Isherwood, Wilde, Alan. *Christopher Isherwood*. New York: Twayne Publishers, 1971; *Christopher Isherwood: Myth and Anti-Myth*. New York: Columbia University, 1978.

Chapter 24 Postwar Poetry

1. See *Contemporary Poets*. New York: St. Martin's Press, 1980; Perkins, David. *A History of Modern Poetry: Modernism and After*. MA: Harvard Univ. Press, 1987; Rosenthal, M. L. *The New Poets: American and British Poetry Since World War II*. New York: Oxford Univ. Press, 1967; Spears, M. K. *Dionysus and*

the City: Modernism in Twentieth-Century Poetry, New York: Oxford Univ. Press, 1970; Jarniewicz, Jerry. "After Babel: Translation and Mistranslation in Contemporary British Poetry." *European Journal of English* 6.1 (2002): pp. 87–104.

2. Feinstein, Elaine. *Ted Hughes: The Life of a Poet*. Boston: W. W. Norton, 2001; Middlebrook, D. W. *Her Husband: Hughes and Plath—A Marriage*. New York: Viking, 2003.

Chapter 25 Postwar Fiction

1. On recent Fiction, see *Modern British Literature*. Detroit: St. James Press, 2000; Rabinovitz, Rubin. *The Reaction Against Experiment in the English Novel, 1950-1960*. New York: Columbia Univ. Press, 1977; Hansen, Elaine Tuttle. *Mother Without Child: Contemporary Fiction and the Crisis of Motherhood*. CA: University of California Press, 1997.

2. Whitbread, Thomas, et al., eds. *Six Contemporary Novels*. Texas: Univ. of Texas Press, 1962.

3. On Durrell, see Fraser, G. S. *Lawrence Durrell: A Critical Study*. New York: Dutton, 1968; Friedman, A. W. *Lawrence Durrell and the Alexandria Quartet: Art for Love's Sake*. Norman: Univ. of Oklahoma Press, 1970.

4. Dick, Bernard F. *William Golding*. New York: Twayne Publishers, 1967.

5. Showalter, Elaine. *A Literature of Their Own: British Women Novelists from Bronte to Lessing*. Princeton, NJ: Princeton Univ. Press, 1999; Burkom, Selma Ruth. *A Reconciliation of Opposites: A Study of the Works of Doris Lessing. Doris Lessing: A Life Considered*. Ann Arbor, Mich: Films for the Humanities and Sciences, 2000.

Chapter 26 Postwar Drama

1. On Beckett, see Ben-Zvi, Linda. *Samuel Beckett*. New York: Twayne Publishers, 1986; Blau, Herbert. *Sails of the Herring Fleet: Essays on Beckett*.

Michigan: University of Michigan Press, 2000; *Engagement and Indifference: Beckett and the Political*. New York: State University of New York Press, 2001.

2. Kenner, Hugh. *A Reader's Guide to Samuel Beckett*. New York: Farrar, Straus and Giroux, 1973, and *Samuel Beckett, a Critical Study*. CA: University of California Press, 1968 (both Kenner books offer backgrounds and detailed analyses of Beckett's works); *A Casebook on Waiting for Godot*. New York: Grove Press, 1967; *Twentieth-Century Interpretations of Endgame: A Collection of Critical Essays*. NJ: Prentice Hall, 1969.

3. Carter, Alan. *John Osborne*. Edinburgh: Oliver and Boyd, 1969.

Index